THE
PHYSICIAN

by Noah Gordon

SIMON AND SCHUSTER

NEW YORK

Copyright © 1986 by Noah Gordon
All rights reserved
including the right of reproduction
in whole or in part in any form
Published by Simon and Schuster
A Division of Simon & Schuster, Inc.
Simon & Schuster Building
Rockefeller Center
1230 Avenue of the Americas
New York, New York 10020
SIMON AND SCHUSTER and colophon are registered trademarks of
Simon & Schuster, Inc.
Designed by Eve Kirch
Manufactured in the United States of America

1 3 5 7 9 10 8 6 4 2

Library of Congress Cataloging in Publication Data
Gordon, Noah.
The physician.
I. Title.
PS3557.068P49 1986   813'.54   86–3834
ISBN: 0-671-47748-X

*With my love
for Nina,
who gave me Lorraine*

Fear God and keep his commandments;
  for this is the whole duty of man.
                                  —Ecclesiastes 12:13

I will give thanks unto Thee,
  for I am fearfully and wonderfully made.
                                  —Psalms 139:14

As to the dead, God will raise them up.
                                  —Qu'ran, S. 6:36

They that be whole need not a physician,
  But they that are sick.
                                  —Matthew 9:12

PART ONE

Barber's Boy

Chapter 1

THE DEVIL IN LONDON

These were Rob J.'s last safe and secure moments of blessed innocence, but in his ignorance he considered it hardship to be forced to remain near his father's house with his brothers and his sister. This early in the spring, the sun rode low enough to send warm licks under the eaves of the thatched roof, and he sprawled on the rough stone stoop outside the front door, enjoying the coziness. A woman was picking her way over the broken surface of Carpenter's Street. The street needed repair, as did most of the small frame workingmen's houses thrown up carelessly by skilled artisans who earned their living erecting solid homes for those richer and more fortunate.

He was shelling a basket of early peas and trying to keep his eyes on the younger children, his responsibility when Mam was away. William Stewart, six, and Anne Mary, four, were grubbing in the dirt at the side of the house and playing secret giggly games. Jonathan Carter, eighteen months old, lay on a lambskin, papped, burped, and gurgling with content. Samuel Edward, who was seven, had given Rob J. the slip. Somehow crafty Samuel always managed to melt away instead of sharing work, and Rob was keeping an eye out for him, feeling wrathful. He split the green pods one after another and scraped the peas from the waxy seedcase with his thumb the way Mam did, not pausing as he noted the woman coming directly to him.

Stays in her stained bodice raised her bosom so that sometimes when she moved there was a glimpse of rouged nipple, and her fleshy face was garish with cosmetics. Rob J. was only nine years old but a child of London knew a trollop.

"Here now. This Nathanael Cole's house?"

He studied her resentfully, for it wasn't the first time tarts had come to their door seeking his father. "Who wants to learn?" he said roughly, glad his Da was out seeking work and she had missed him, glad his Mam was out delivering embroidery and was spared embarrassment.

"His wife needs him. She sent me."

"What do you mean, *needs* him?" The competent young hands stopped shelling peas.

The whore regarded him coolly, having caught his opinion of her in his tone and manner. "She your mother?"

He nodded.

"She's taken labor bad. She's in Egglestan's stables close by Puddle Dock. You'd best find your father and tell him," the woman said, and went away.

The boy looked about desperately. "Samuel!" he shouted, but bloody Samuel was off who-knows-where, as usual, and Rob fetched William and Anne Mary from their play. "Take care of the small ones, Willum," he said. Then he left the house and started to run.

Those who may be depended upon to prattle said Anno Domini 1021, the year of Agnes Cole's eighth pregnancy, belonged to Satan. It had been marked by calamities to people and monstrosities of nature. The previous autumn the harvest in the fields had been blighted by hard frosts that froze rivers. There were rains such as never before, and with the rapid thaw a high tide ran up the Thames and tore away bridges and homes. Stars fell, streaming light down windy winter skies, and a comet was seen. In February the earth distinctly quaked. Lightning struck the head off a crucifix and men muttered that Christ and his saints slept. It was rumored that for three days a spring had flowed with blood, and travelers reported the Devil appearing in woods and secret places.

Agnes had told her eldest son not to pay heed to the talk. But she had added uneasily that if Rob J. saw or heard anything unusual, he must make the sign of the Cross.

People were placing a heavy burden on God that year, for the crop failure had brought hard times. Nathanael had earned no pay for more than four months and was kept by his wife's ability to create fine embroideries.

When they were newly wed, she and Nathanael had been sick with love and very confident of their future; it had been his plan to become wealthy as a contractor-builder. But promotion was slow within the carpenters' guild, at the hands of examination committees who scrutinized test projects as if each piece of work were meant for the King. He had spent six years as Apprentice Carpenter and twice that long as Companion Joiner. By now he should have been an aspirant for Master Carpenter, the professional classification needed to become a contractor. But the process of becoming a Master took energy and prosperous times, and he was too dispirited to try.

Their lives continued to revolve around the trade guild, but now even the London Corporation of Carpenters failed them, for each morning Nathanael reported to the guild house only to learn there were no jobs. With other hopeless men he sought escape in a brew they called pigment: one of the carpenters would produce honey, someone else brought out a few spices, and the Corporation always had a jug of wine at hand.

Carpenters' wives told Agnes that often one of the men would go out and bring back a woman on whom their unemployed husbands took drunken turns.

Despite his failings she couldn't shun Nathanael, she was too fond of fleshly delight. He kept her belly large, pumping her full of child as soon as she was emptied, and whenever she was nearing term he avoided their home. Their life conformed almost exactly to the dire predictions made by her father when, with Rob J. already in her, she had married the young carpenter who had come to Watford to help build their neighbor's barn. Her father had blamed her schooling, saying that education filled a woman with lascivious folly.

Her father had owned his small farm, which had been given him by Aethelred of Wessex in lieu of pay for military service. He was the first of the Kemp family to become a yeoman. Walter Kemp had sent his daughter for schooling in the hope that it would gain her a landowner's marriage, for proprietors of great estates found it handy to have a trusted person who was able to read and do sums, and why should it not be a wife? He had been embittered to see her make a low and sluttish match. He had not even been able to disinherit her, poor man. His tiny holding had gone to the Crown for back taxes when he died.

But his ambition had shaped her life. The five happiest years of her memory had been as a child in the nunnery school. The nuns had worn scarlet shoes, white and violet tunics, and veils delicate as cloud. They had taught her to read and to write, to recognize a smattering of Latin as it was used in the catechism, to cut clothing and sew an invisible seam, and to produce orphrey, embroidery so elegant it was sought after in France, where it was known as English Work.

The "foolishness" she had learned from the nuns now kept her family in food.

This morning she had debated about whether to go to deliver her orphrey. It was close to her time and she felt huge and clumsy, but there was little left in the larder. It was necessary to go to Billingsgate Market to buy flour and meal, and for that she needed the money that would be paid by the embroidery exporter who lived in Southwark on the other side of the river. Carrying her small bundle, she made her way slowly down Thames Street toward London Bridge.

As usual, Thames Street was crowded with pack animals and stevedores moving merchandise between the cavernous warehouses and the forest of ships' masts on the quays. The noise fell on her like rain on a drought. Despite their troubles, she was grateful to Nathanael for taking her away from Watford and the farm.

She loved this city so!

"Whoreson! You come back here and give me my money. Give it on back," a furious woman screeched at someone Agnes couldn't see.

Skeins of laughter were tangled with ribbons of words in foreign languages. Curses were hurled like affectionate blessings.

She walked past ragged slaves lugging pigs of iron to waiting ships. Dogs barked at the wretched men who struggled under their brutal loads, pearls of sweat gleaming on their shaven heads. She breathed the garlic odor of their unwashed bodies and the metallic stink of the pig iron and then a more welcome smell from a cart where a man was hawking meat pasties. Her mouth watered but she had a single coin in her pocket and hungry children at home. "Pies like sweet sin," the man called. "Hot and good!"

The docks gave off an aroma of sun-warmed pine pitch and tarred rope. She held a hand to her stomach as she walked and felt her baby move, floating in the ocean contained between her hips. On the corner a rabble of sailors with flowers in their caps sang lustily while three musicians played on a fife, a drum, and a harp. As she moved past them she noted a man leaning against a strange-looking wagon marked with the signs of the zodiac. He was perhaps forty years old. He was beginning to lose his hair, which like his beard was strong brown in color. His features were comely; he would have been more handsome than Nathanael save for the fact that he was fat. His face was ruddy and his stomach bloomed before him as fully as her own. His corpulence didn't repel; on the contrary, it disarmed and charmed and told the viewer that here was a friendly and convivial spirit too fond of the best things in life. His blue eyes had a glint and sparkle that matched the smile on his lips. "Pretty mistress. Be my dolly?" he said. Startled, she looked about to see to whom he might be speaking, but there was no one else.

"Hah!" Ordinarily she would have frozen trash with a glance and put him out of mind, but she had a sense of humor and enjoyed a man with one, and this was too rich.

"We are made for one another. I would die for you, my lady," he called after her ardently.

"No need. Christ already has, sirrah," she said.

She lifted her head, squared her shoulders, and walked away with a seductive twitch, preceded by the almost unbelievable enormity of her child-laden stomach and joining in his laughter.

It had been a long time since a man had complimented her femaleness, even in jest, and the absurd exchange lifted her spirits as she navigated Thames Street. Still smiling, she was approaching Puddle Dock when the pain came.

"Merciful mother," she whispered.

It struck again, beginning in her abdomen but taking over her mind and entire body so that she was unable to stand. As she sank to the cobbles of the public way the bag of waters burst.

"Help me!" she cried. "Somebody!"

A London crowd gathered at once, eager to see, and she was hemmed in by legs. Through a mist of pain she perceived a circle of faces looking down at her.

Agnes groaned.

"Here now, you bastards," a drayman growled. "Give her room to breathe. And let us earn our daily bread. Get her off the street so our wagons can pass."

They carried her into a place that was dark and cool and smelled strongly of manure. In the course of the move someone made off with her bundle of orphrey. Deeper within the gloom, great forms shifted and swayed. A hoof kicked a board with a sharp report, and there was a loud whickering.

"What's all this? Now, you cannot bring her in here," a querulous voice said. He was a fussy little man, potbellied and gap-toothed, and when she saw his hostler's boots and cap she recognized him for Geoff Egglestan and knew she was in his stables. More than a year ago Nathanael had rebuilt some stalls here, and she grasped at the fact.

"Master Egglestan," she said faintly. "I am Agnes Cole, wife of the carpenter, with whom you are well acquainted."

She thought she saw unwilling recognition on his face, and the surly knowledge that he couldn't turn her away.

The people crowded in behind him, bright-eyed with curiosity.

Agnes gasped. "Please, will somebody be kind enough to fetch my husband?" she asked.

"I can't leave my business," Egglestan muttered. "Somebody else must go."

No one moved or spoke.

Her hand went to her pocket and found the coin. "Please," she said again, and held it up.

"I'll do my Christian duty," a woman, obviously a streetwalker, said at once. Her fingers closed over the coin like a claw.

The pain was unbearable, a new and different pain. She was accustomed to close contractions; her labors had been mildly difficult after the first two pregnancies but in the process she had stretched. There had been miscarriages before and following the birth of Anne Mary, but both Jonathan and the girl child had left her body easily after the breaking of the waters, like slick little seeds squirted between two fingers. In five birthings she had never experienced anything like this.

Sweet Agnes, she said in numb silence. Sweet Agnes who succors the lambs, succor me.

Always during labor she prayed to her name saint and Saint Agnes helped, but this time the whole world was unremitting pain and the child was in her like a great plug.

Eventually her ragged screams attracted the attention of a passing midwife, a crone who was more than slightly drunk, and she drove the spectators from the stables with curses. When she turned back, she studied Agnes with disgust. "Bloody men set you down in the shit," she muttered. There was no better place to move her. She lifted Agnes' skirts above her waist and cut away the undergarments; then on the floor in front of the gaping pudenda she brushed away the strawy manure with her hands, which she wiped on a filthy apron.

From her pocket she took a vial of lard already darkened with the blood and juices of other women. Scooping out some of the rancid grease, she made washing movements until her hands were lubricated, then she eased first two fingers, then three, then her entire hand into the dilated orifice of the straining woman who was now howling like an animal.

"You'll hurt twice as much, mistress," the midwife said in a few moments, lubricating her arms up to the elbows. "The little beggar could bite its own toes, had it a mind to. It's coming out arse first."

Chapter 2

A FAMILY OF THE GUILD

Rob J. had started to run toward Puddle Dock. Then he realized that he had to find his father and he turned toward the carpenters' guild, as every member's child knew to do in time of trouble.

The London Corporation of Carpenters was housed at the end of Carpenter's Street in an old structure of wattle-and-daub, a framework of poles interwoven with withes and branches thickly overlaid with mortar that had to be renewed every few years. Inside the roomy guild house a dozen men in the leather doublets and tool belts of their trade were seated at the rough chairs and tables made by the house committee; he recognized neighbors and members of his father's Ten but didn't see Nathanael.

The guild was everything to the London woodworkers—employment office, dispensary, burial society, social center, relief organization during periods of unemployment, arbiter, placement service and hiring hall, political influence and moral force. It was a tightly organized society composed of four divisions of carpenters called Hundreds. Each Hundred was made up of ten Tens that met separately and more intimately, and it wasn't until a member was lost to a Ten by death, extended illness, or relocation that a new member was taken into the guild as Apprentice Carpenter, usually from a waiting list that contained the names of sons of members. The word of its Chief Carpenter was as final as that of any royalty, and it was to this personage, Richard Bukerel, that Rob now hurried.

Bukerel had stooped shoulders, as if bowed by responsibility. Everything about him seemed dark. His hair was black; his eyes were the shade of mature oak bark; his tight trousers, tunic, and doublet were coarse woollen stuff dyed by boiling with walnut hulls; and his skin was the color of cured leather, tanned by the suns of a thousand house-raisings. He moved, thought, and spoke with deliberation, and he listened to Rob intently.

"Nathanael isn't here, my boy."

"Do you know where he can be found, Master Bukerel?"

Bukerel hesitated. "Pardon me, please," he said finally, and went to where several men were seated nearby.

Rob could hear only an occasional word or a whispered phrase.

"He's with *that* bitch?" Bukerel muttered.

In a moment the Chief Carpenter returned. "We know where to find your father," he said. "You hasten to your mother, my boy. We'll fetch Nathanael and follow close behind you."

Rob blurted his gratitude and ran on his way.

He never stopped for a breath. Dodging freight wagons, avoiding drunkards, careening through crowds, he made for Puddle Dock. Halfway there he saw his enemy, Anthony Tite, with whom he had had three fierce fights in the past year. With a pair of his wharf-rat friends Anthony was ragging some of the stevedore slaves.

Don't delay me now, you little cod, Rob thought coldly.

Try, Pissant-Tony, and I'll really do you.

The way someday he was going to do his rotten Da.

He saw one of the wharf rats point him out to Anthony, but he was already past them and well on his way.

He was breathless and with a stitch in his side when he arrived at Egglestan's stables in time to see an unfamiliar old woman swaddling a newborn child.

The stable was heavy with the odor of horse droppings and his mother's blood. Mam lay on the floor. Her eyes were closed and her face was pale. He was surprised by her smallness.

"Mam?"

"You the son?"

He nodded, thin chest heaving.

The old woman hawked and spat on the floor. "Let her rest," she said.

When his Da came he scarcely gave Rob J. a glance. In a straw-filled wagon Bukerel had borrowed from a builder they took Mam home along with the newborn, a male who would be christened Roger Kemp Cole.

After bringing forth a new baby Mam had always shown the infant to her other children with teasing pride. Now she simply lay and stared at the thatched ceiling.

Finally Nathanael called in the Widow Hargreaves from the nearest house. "She can't even suckle the child," he told her.

"Perhaps it will pass," Della Hargreaves said. She knew of a wet nurse and took the baby away, to Rob J.'s great relief. He had all he could do to care for the other four children. Jonathan Carter had been trained to the pot but, missing the attention of his mother, seemed to have forgotten the fact.

His Da stayed home. Rob J. said little to him and maneuvered out of his way.

He missed the lessons they had had each morning, for Mam had made them seem like a merry game. He knew no one so full of warmth and loving mischief, so patient with slowness of memory.

Rob charged Samuel with keeping Willum and Anne Mary out of the house. That evening Anne Mary wept for a lullaby. Rob held her close and called her his Maid Anne Mary, her favorite form of address. Finally he sang of soft sweet coneys and downy birds in the nest, tra-la, grateful that Anthony Tite was not a witness. His sister was more round-cheeked and tender-fleshed than their mother, although Mam had always said Anne Mary had the Kemp side's features and traits, down to the way her mouth relaxed in sleep.

Mam looked better the second day, but his father said the color in her cheeks was fever. She shivered, and they piled extra covers on her.

On the third morning, when Rob gave her a drink of water he was shocked by the heat he felt in her face. She patted his hand. "My Rob J.," she whispered. "So manly." Her breath stank and she was breathing fast.

When he took her hand something passed from her body into his mind. It was an awareness: he knew with absolute certainty what would happen to her. He couldn't weep. He couldn't cry out. The hair rose on the back of his neck. He felt pure terror. He could not have dealt with it had he been an adult, and he was a child.

In his horror he squeezed Mam's hand and caused her pain. His father saw and cuffed him on the head.

Next morning when he got out of bed, his mother was dead.

Nathanael Cole sat and wept, which frightened his children, who had not absorbed the reality that Mam was gone for good. They had never before seen their father cry, and they huddled together white-faced and watchful.

The guild took care of everything.

The wives came. None had been Agnes' intimate, for her schooling had made her a suspect creature. But now the women forgave her former literacy and laid her out. Ever after, Rob hated the smell of rosemary. If times had been better the men would have come in the evening after their work, but many were unemployed and people showed up early. Hugh Tite, who was Anthony's father and looked like him, came representing the coffin-knockers, a standing committee that met to make caskets for members' funerals.

He patted Nathanael's shoulder. "I've enough pieces of hard pine tucked away. Left over from the Bardwell Tavern job last year, you recall that nice wood? We shall do right by her."

Hugh was a semiskilled journeyman and Rob had heard his father speak scornfully of him for not knowing how to care for tools, but now Nathanael only nodded dully and turned toward the drink.

The guild had provided plenty, for a funeral was the only occasion where drunkenness and gluttony were sanctioned. In addition to apple cider and barley ale there was sweet beer and a mixture called slip, made by mixing honey and water and allowing the solution to ferment for six weeks. They had the carpenter's friend and solace, pigment; mulberry-flavored wine called morat; and a spiced mead known as metheglin. They came laden with braces of roasted quail and partridge, numerous baked and fried dishes of hare and venison, smoked herring, fresh-caught trout and plaice, and loaves of barley bread.

The guild declared a contribution of tuppence for almsgiving in the name of Agnes Cole of blessed memory and provided pallholders who led the procession to the church, and diggers who prepared the grave. Inside St. Botolph's a priest named Kempton absentmindedly intoned the Mass and consigned Mam to the arms of Jesus, and the guildsmen recited two psalters for her soul. She was buried in the churchyard in front of a little yew tree.

When they returned to the house the funeral feast had been made hot and ready by the women, and people ate and drank for hours, released from poverty fare by the death of a neighbor. The Widow Hargreaves sat with the children and fed them tidbits, making a fuss. She clasped them into her deep, scented breasts where they wriggled and suffered. But when William became sick it was Rob who took him out behind the house and held his head while he strained and retched. Afterward, Della Hargreaves patted Willum's head and said it was grief; but Rob knew she had fed the child richly of her own cooking and for the rest of the feasting he steered the children clear of her potted eel.

Rob understood about death but nevertheless found himself waiting for Mam to come home. Something within him would not have been terribly surprised if she had opened the door and walked into the house, bearing provisions from the market or money from the embroidery exporter in Southwark.

History lesson, Rob.

What three Germanic tribes invaded Britain during the A.D. *400s and 500s?*
The Angles, the Jutes, and the Saxons, Mam.
Where did they come from, my darling?
Germania and Denmark. They conquered the Britons along the east coast
and founded the kingdoms of Northumbria, Mercia, and East Anglia.
What makes my son so clever?
A clever mother?
Ah! Here is a kiss from your clever mother. And another kiss because you have
a clever father. You must never forget your clever father . . .

To his great surprise, his father stayed. Nathanael seemed to want to talk to the children, but he could not. He spent most of his time repairing the thatch in the roof. A few weeks after the funeral, while the numbness was still wearing off and Rob was just beginning to understand how different his life was going to be, his father finally got a job.

London riverbank clay is brown and deep, a soft, tenacious muck that is home to shipworms called teredines. The worms had created havoc with timber, boring in over the centuries and riddling wharves, so some had to be replaced. The work was brutal and a far cry from building fine homes, but in his trouble Nathanael welcomed it.

To Rob J. fell the responsibility for the house, although he was a poor cook. Often Della Hargreaves brought food or prepared a meal, usually while Nathanael was home, when she took pains to be scented and good-natured and attentive to the children. She was stout but not unattractive, with a florid complexion, high cheekbones, pointed chin, and small plump hands that she used as little as possible in work. Rob had always tended his brothers and sister, but now he had become their sole source of care and neither he nor they liked it. Jonathan Carter and Anne Mary cried constantly. William Stewart had lost his appetite and was becoming pinch-faced and large-eyed, and Samuel Edward was cheekier than ever, bringing home swear words that he threw at Rob J. with such glee that the older boy knew no solution but to clout him.

He tried to do whatever he thought *she* would have done.

In the mornings, after the baby had been given pap and the rest had received barley bread and drink, he cleaned the hearth under the round smoke hole, through which drops fell hissing into the fire when it rained. He took the ashes behind the house and got rid of them and then swept the floors. He dusted the sparse furnishings in all three rooms. Three times a week he shopped at Billingsgate to buy the things Mam had managed to bring home in a single weekly trip. Many of the stall owners knew him; some made the Cole family a small gift with their condolences the first time he came alone—a few apples, a piece of cheese, half a small salt cod. But within a few weeks he and they were used to one another and he haggled with them more fiercely than Mam had done, lest they think to take advantage of a child. His feet always dragged on the way home from market, for he was unwilling to take back from Willum the burden of the children.

Mam had wanted Samuel to begin school this year. She had stood up to Nathanael and persuaded him to allow Rob to study with the monks at St. Botolph's, and he had walked to the church school daily for two years before it became necessary for him to stay home so she would be free to work at embroidery. Now none of them would go to school, for his father couldn't read or write and thought schooling a waste. He missed the school. He walked through the noisome neighborhoods of cheap, close-set houses, scarcely remembering how once his principal concern had been childish games and the specter of Pissant-Tony Tite. Anthony and his cohorts watched him pass without giving chase, as if losing his mother gave him immunity.

One night his father told him he did good work. "You have always been older than your years," Nathanael said, almost with disapproval. They looked at one another uneasily, having little else to say. If Nathanael was spending his free time with tarts, Rob J. didn't know it. He still hated his father when he thought of how Mam had fared, but he knew that Nathanael was struggling in a way she would have admired.

He might readily have turned over his brothers and sister to the Widow, and he watched Della Hargreave's comings and goings expectantly, for the jests and sniggers of neighbors had informed him that she was the candidate to become his stepmother. She was childless; her husband, Lanning Hargreaves, had been a carpenter killed fifteen months before by a falling beam. It was customary that when a woman died leaving young children the new widower would remarry quickly, and it caused little wonder when Nathanael began to spend time alone with Della in her house. But such interludes were limited, because usually Nathanael was too tired. The great piles and bulwarks used in constructing the wharves had to be hewn square out of black oak logs and then set deep into the river bottom during low tide. Nathanael worked wet and cold. Along with the rest of his crew he developed a hacking, hollow cough and he always came home bone-weary. From the depths of the clammy Thames mud they ripped bits of history: a leather Roman sandal with long ankle straps, a broken spear, shards of pottery. He brought home a worked flint flake for Rob J.; sharp as a knife, the arrowhead had been found twenty feet down.

"Is it Roman?" Rob asked eagerly.

His father shrugged. "Perhaps Saxon."

But there was no question about the origin of the coin found a few days later. When Rob moistened ashes from the fire and rubbed and rubbed, on one side of the blackened disk appeared the words *Prima Cohors Britanniae Londonii.* His church Latin proved barely equal. "Perhaps it marks the first cohort to be in London," he said. On the other side was a Roman on horseback, and three letters, IOX.

"What does IOX mean?" his father asked.

He didn't know. Mam would have, but he had no one else to ask, and he put the coin away.

They were so accustomed to Nathanael's cough it was no longer heard. But one morning when Rob was cleaning the hearth, there was a minor commotion out front. When he opened the door he saw Harmon White-lock, a member of his father's crew, and two slaves he had impressed from the stevedores to carry Nathanael home.

Slaves terrified Rob J. There were various ways for a man to lose his freedom. A war prisoner became the *servi* of a warrior who might have taken his life but spared it. Free men could be sentenced into slavery for serious crimes, as could debtors or those unable to pay a severe wite or fine. A man's wife and children went into slavery with him, and so did future generations of his family.

These slaves were great, muscular men with shaven heads to denote their bondage and tattered clothes that stank abominably. Rob J. couldn't tell if they were captured foreigners or Englishmen, for they didn't speak but stared at him stolidly. Nathanael wasn't small but they carried him as if he were weightless. The slaves frightened Rob J. even more than the sight of the sallow bloodlessness of his father's face or the way Nathanael's head lolled as they set him down.

"What happened?"

Whitelock shrugged. "It's a misery. Half of us are down with it, cough-ing and spitting all the time. Today he was so weak he was overcome as soon as we got into heavy work. I expect a few days of rest will see him back on the wharves."

Next morning Nathanael was unable to leave the bed, his voice a rasping. Mistress Hargreaves brought hot tea laced with honey and hovered about. They spoke in low, intimate voices and once or twice the woman laughed. But when she came the following morning, Nathanael had a high fever and was in no mood for badinage or niceties, and she left quickly.

His tongue and throat turned bright red and he kept asking for water.

During the night he dreamed, once shouting that the stinking Danes were coming up the Thames in their high-prowed ships. His chest filled with a stringy phlegm that he couldn't rid himself of, and he breathed with increasing difficulty. When morning arrived Rob hastened next door to fetch the Widow, but Della Hargreaves declined to come. "It appeared to me to be thrush. Thrush is highly impartible," she said, and closed the door.

Having nowhere else to turn, Rob went again to the guild. Richard Bukerel listened to him gravely and then followed him home and sat by the foot of Nathanael's bed for a time, noting his flushed face and hearing the rattling when he breathed.

The easy solution would have been to summon a priest; the cleric would do little but light tapers and pray, and Bukerel could turn his back without fear of criticism. For some years he had been a successful builder, but he was beyond his depth as leader of the London Corporation of Carpenters, trying to use a meager treasury to accomplish far more than could be achieved.

But he knew what would happen to this family unless one parent survived, and he hurried away and used guild funds to hire Thomas Ferraton, a physician.

Bukerel's wife gave him the sharp edge of her tongue that night. "A physician? Is Nathanael Cole suddenly gentry or nobility, then? When an ordinary surgeon is good enough to take care of any other poor person in London, why does Nathanael Cole need a physician to charge us dear?"

Bukerel could only mumble an excuse, for she was right. Only nobles and wealthy merchants bought the expensive services of physicians. Ordinary folk used surgeons, and sometimes a laboring man paid a ha'penny to a barber-surgeon for bloodletting or questionable treatment. So far as Bukerel was concerned, all healers were damned leeches, doing more harm than good. But he had wanted to give Cole every chance, and in a weak moment he had summoned the physician, spending the hard-earned dues of honest carpenters.

When Ferraton came to the Cole house he had been sanguine and confident, the reassuring picture of prosperity. His tight trousers were beautifully cut and the cuffs of his shirt were adorned with embroidery that immediately gave Rob a pang, reminding him of Mam. Ferraton's quilted tunic, of the finest wool available, was encrusted with dried blood and vomitus, which he pridefully believed was an honorable advertisement of his profession.

Born to wealth—his father had been John Ferraton, wool merchant—Ferraton had apprenticed with a physician named Paul Willibald, whose prosperous family made and sold fine blades. Willibald had treated wealthy people, and after his apprenticeship Ferraton had drifted into that kind of practice himself. Noble patients were out of reach for the son of a trades-man, but he felt at home with the well-to-do; they shared a commonality of attitudes and interests. He never knowingly accepted a patient from the laboring class, but he had assumed Bukerel was the messenger for someone much grander. He immediately recognized Nathanael Cole as an unworthy patient but, not wishing to make a scene, resolved to finish the disagreeable task as quickly as possible.

He touched Nathanael's forehead delicately, looked into his eyes, sniffed his breath.

"Well," he said. "It shall pass."

"What is it?" Bukerel asked, but Ferraton didn't reply.

Rob felt instinctively that the doctor didn't know.

"It is the quinsy," Ferraton said at last, pointing out white sores in his father's crimson throat. "A suppurative inflammation of a temporary na-ture. Nothing more." He tied a tourniquet on Nathanael's arm, lanced him deftly, and let a copious amount of blood.

"If he doesn't improve?" Bukerel asked.

The physician frowned. He would not revisit this lower-class house. "I had best bleed him again to make certain," he said, and did the other arm. He left a small flask of liquid calomel mixed with charcoaled reed, charging Bukerel separately for the visit, the bleedings, and the medicine.

"Man-wasting leech! Ball-butchering gentleman prick," Bukerel mut-tered, gazing after him. The Chief Carpenter promised Rob he would send a woman to care for his father.

Blanched and drained, Nathanael lay without moving. Several times he thought the boy was Agnes and tried to take his hand. But Rob remembered what had happened during his mother's illness and pulled away.

Later, ashamed, he returned to his father's bedside. He took Nathanael's work-hardened hand, noting the horny broken nails, the ingrained grime and crisp black hairs.

It happened just as it had before. He was aware of a diminishing, like the flame of a candle flickering down. He was somehow conscious that his father was dying and that it would happen very soon, and was taken by a mute terror identical to the one that had gripped him when Mam lay dying.

Beyond the bed were his brothers and sister. He was a young boy but very intelligent, and an immediate practical urgency overrode his sorrow and the agony of his fear.

He shook his father's arm. "Now what will become of *us?*" he asked loudly, but no one answered.

Chapter 3

THE PARCELING

This time, because it was a guildsman who had died and not merely a dependent, the Corporation of Carpenters paid for the singing of fifty psalms. Two days after the funeral, Della Hargreaves went to Ramsey, to make her home with her brother. Richard Bukerel took Rob aside for a talk.

"When there are no relatives, the children and the possessions must be parceled," the Chief Carpenter said briskly. "The Corporation will take care of everything."

Rob felt numb.

That evening he tried to explain to his brothers and his sister. Only Samuel knew what he was talking about.

"We're to be separated, then?"

"Yes."

"Each of us will live with another family?"

"Yes."

That night someone crept into bed beside him. He would have expected Willum or Anne Mary, but it was Samuel who threw his arms around him and held on as if to keep from falling. "I want them back, Rob J."

"So do I." He patted the bony shoulder he had often whacked.

For a time they cried together.

"Will we never see one another again, then?"

He felt a coldness. "Oh, Samuel. Don't go daft on me now. Doubtless we'll both live in the neighborhood and see each other all the time. We'll forever be brothers."

It comforted Samuel and he slept some, but before dawn he wet the bed as if he were younger than Jonathan. In the morning he was ashamed and could not meet Rob's eyes. His fears were not unfounded, for he was the first of them to go. Most of the members of their father's Ten were still out of work. Of the nine woodworkers only one man was able and willing to

26

take a child into his family. Along with Samuel, Nathanael's hammers and saws went to Turner Horne, a Master Carpenter who lived only six houses away.

Two days later a priest named Ranald Lovell came with Father Kempton, the man who had sung the Masses for both Mam and Da. Father Lovell said he was being transferred to the north of England and wanted a child. He examined them all and took a fancy to Willum. He was a big, hearty man with pale yellow hair and gray eyes that Rob tried to tell himself were kind.

White and tremulous, his brother could only nod as he followed the two priests out of the house.

"Goodbye, then, William," Rob said.

He wondered wildly if perhaps he couldn't keep the two small ones. But he was already doling out the last of the food from his father's funeral, and he was a realistic boy. Jonathan and his father's leather doublet and tool belt were given to a Companion Joiner named Aylwyn who belonged to Nathanael's Hundred. When Mistress Aylwyn came, Rob explained that Jonathan was trained to pot but needed napkins when afraid, and she accepted the wash-thinned cloths and the child with a grin and a nod.

The wet nurse kept the infant Roger and received Mam's embroidery materials. Richard Bukerel informed Rob, who had never seen the woman.

Anne Mary's hair needed washing. He did it carefully, as he had been taught, but still some soap got into her eyes and it was harsh and burning. He wiped her dry and held her as she wept, smelling her clean seal-brown hair that gave off a scent like Mam's.

Next day the sounder pieces of furniture were taken by the baker and his wife, name of Haverhill, and Anne Mary went to live above their pastry shop. Clutching her hand, Rob brought her to them: Goodbye, then, little girl. "I love you, my Maid Anne Mary," he whispered, holding her close. But she seemed to blame him for all that had happened and wouldn't bid him farewell.

Only Rob J. was left, and no possessions. That evening Bukerel came to see him. The Chief Carpenter had been drinking, but his mind was clear. "It may take long to find you a place. It's the times, no one has food for an adult appetite in a boy who cannot do a man's work." After a brooding silence he spoke again. "When I was younger everyone said if we could only have a real peace and get rid of King Aethelred, the worst king who ever ruined his generation, then times would be good. We had invasion after invasion, Saxons, Danes, every bloody kind of pirate. Now finally we've a strong peacekeeping monarch in King Canute, but it's as if nature conspires to hold us down. Great summer and winter storms do us in. Three years in a row crops have failed. Millers don't grind grain, sailors stay in port. No one builds, and craftsmen are idle. It's hard times, my boy. But I'll find you a place, I promise."

"Thank you, Chief Carpenter."

Bukerel's dark eyes were troubled. "I've watched you, Robert Cole. I've seen a boy care for his family like a worthy man. I'd take you into my own home if my wife were a different kind of woman." He blinked, embarrassed by the realization that drink had loosened his tongue more than he liked, and got heavily to his feet. "A restful night to you, Rob J."

"A restful night, Chief Carpenter."

He became a hermit. The near-empty rooms were his cave. No one asked him to table. His neighbors were unable to ignore his existence but sustained him grudgingly; Mistress Haverhill came in the morning and left yesterday's unsold loaf from the bakery and Mistress Bukerel came in the evening and left cheese in tiny portion, noting his reddened eyes and lecturing that weeping was a womanly privilege. He drew water from the public well as he had before, and he tended house but there was nobody to put the quiet and plundered place into disorder and he had little to do but worry and pretend.

Sometimes he became a Roman scout, lying by the open window behind Mam's curtain and listening to the secrets of the enemy world. He heard drawn carts go by, barking dogs, playing children, the sounds of birds.

Once he overheard the voices of a knot of men from the guild. "Rob Cole is a bargain. Somebody should grab him," Bukerel said.

He lay there guilty and covert, listening to others talk about him as if he were someone else.

"Aye, look at his size. He'll be a great workhorse when he gets his full growth," Hugh Tite said grudgingly.

What if Tite took him? Rob considered in dismay the prospect of living with Anthony Tite. He wasn't displeased when Hugh snorted in disgust. "He won't be old enough for Apprentice Carpenter until another three years and he eats like a great horse right now, when London is full of strong backs and empty bellies." The men moved away.

Two mornings later, behind the same window curtain, he paid dearly for the sin of eavesdropping when he overheard Mistress Bukerel discussing her husband's guild office with Mistress Haverhill.

"Everyone speaks of the honor of being Chief Carpenter. It places no bread upon my table. Quite the reverse, it presents tiresome obligations. I am weary of having to share my provision with the likes of that great lazy boy in there."

"Whatever will become of him?" Mistress Haverhill said, sighing.

"I have advised Master Bukerel that he should be sold as an indigent. Even in bad times a young slave will fetch a price to repay the guild and all of us for whatever has been spent on the Cole family."

He was unable to breathe.

Mistress Bukerel sniffed. "The Chief Carpenter will not hear of it," she said sourly. "I trust I'll convince him in the end. But by the time he comes around, we shall no longer be able to recover costs."

When the two women moved away, Rob lay behind the window curtain as though in fever, alternately sweating and chilled.

All his life he had seen slaves, taking it for granted that their condition had little to do with him, for he had been born a free Englishman.

He was too young by far to be a stevedore on the docks. But he knew that boy slaves were used in the mines, where they worked in tunnels too narrow to admit the bodies of men. He also knew that slaves were wretchedly clothed and fed and often were brutally whipped for small infractions. And that once enslaved, they were owned for life.

He lay and wept. Eventually he was able to gather his courage and tell himself that Dick Bukerel would never sell him for a slave, but he worried that Mistress Bukerel would send others to do it without informing her husband. She was fully capable of such an act, he told himself. Waiting in the silent and abandoned house, he came to start and tremble at every sound.

Five frozen days after his father's funeral, a stranger came to the door.

"You are young Cole?"

He nodded warily, heart pounding.

"My name is Croft. I am directed to you by a man named Richard Bukerel, whom I've met while drinking at the Bardwell Tavern."

Rob saw a man neither young nor old with a huge fat body and a weather-beaten face set between a freeman's long hair and a rounded, frizzled beard of the same gingery color.

"What's your full name?"

"Robert Jeremy Cole, sir."

"Age?"

"Nine years."

"I'm a barber-surgeon and I seek a prentice. Do you know what a barber-surgeon does, young Cole?"

"Are you some kind of physician?"

The fat man smiled. "For the time being, that's close enough. Bukerel informed me of your circumstances. Does my trade appeal to you?"

It didn't; he had no wish to become like the leech who'd bled his father to death. But even less did he wish to be sold as a slave, and he answered affirmatively without hesitation.

"Not afraid of work?"

"Oh, no, sir!"

"That's good, for I would work your arse off. Bukerel said you read and write and have Latin?"

He hesitated. "Very little Latin, in truth."

The man smiled. "I shall try you for a time, chappy. You have things?"

His little bundle had been ready for days. *Am I saved?* he wondered. Outside, they clambered into the strangest wagon he had ever seen. On either side of the front seat was a white pole with a thick stripe wrapped around it like a crimson snake. It was a covered cart daubed bright red and decorated with sun-yellow pictures of a ram, a lion, scales, a goat, fishes, an archer, a crab . . .

The dappled gray horse pulled them away and they rolled down Carpenter's Street and past the guild house. He sat frozen as they threaded through the tumult of Thames Street, managing to cast quick glances at the man and now noting a handsome face despite the fat, a prominent and reddened nose, a wen on the left eyelid, and a network of fine lines radiating from the corners of piercing blue eyes.

The cart crossed the little bridge over the Walbrook and passed Egglestan's stables and the place where Mam had fallen. Then they turned right and rattled over London Bridge to the southern side of the Thames. Moored beside the bridge was the London ferry and, just beyond, the great Southwark Market where imports entered England. They passed warehouses burned and wasted by the Danes and recently rebuilt. On the embankment was a single line of wattle-and-daub cottages, the mean homes of fishermen, lightermen, and wharf workers. There were two shabby inns for merchants attending market. And then, bordering the wide causeway, a double line of grand houses, the manors of the rich merchants of London, all of them with impressive gardens and a few built on piles driven into the marsh. He recognized the home of the embroidery importer with whom Mam had dealt. He had never traveled beyond this point.

"Master Croft?"

The man scowled. "No, no. I'm never to be called Croft. I'm always called Barber, because of my profession."

"Yes, Barber," he said. In moments all of Southwark was behind them, and with rising panic Rob J. recognized that he had entered the strange and unfamiliar outside world.

"Barber, where are we going?" he couldn't refrain from crying.

The man smiled and flicked the reins, causing the dappled horse to trot.

"Everywhere," he said.

Chapter 4

THE BARBER-SURGEON

Before dusk they made camp on a hill by a stream. The man said the gray plodder of a horse was Tatus. "Short for Incitatus, after the steed the emperor Caligula loved so much he made the beast a priest and a consul. Our Incitatus is a passing fair animal for a poor beggar with his balls cut off," Barber said, and showed him how to care for the gelding, rubbing the horse with handfuls of soft dry grass and then allowing him to drink and go to grazing before they tended to their own needs. They were in the open, a distance from the forest, but Barber sent him to gather dry wood for the fire and he had to make repeated trips to accumulate a pile. Soon the fire was snapping, and cooking had begun to produce odors that weakened his legs. Into an iron pot Barber had placed a generous amount of thick-sliced smoked pork. Now he poured out most of the rendered fat and into the sputtering grease cut a large turnip and several leeks, adding a handful of dried mulberries and a sprinkling of herbs. By the time the pungent mixture had cooked, Rob had never smelled anything better. Barber ate stolidly, watching him wolf down a large portion and in silence giving him another. They mopped their wooden bowls with chunks of barley bread. Without being told, Rob took the pot and bowls to the stream and scrubbed them with sand.

When he had returned the utensils he went to a nearby bush and passed water.

"My blessed Lord and Lady, but that is a remarkable-looking peter," Barber said, coming up on him suddenly.

He finished before his need and hid the member. "When I was an infant," he said stiffly, "I had a mortification . . . there. I'm told a surgeon removed the little hood of flesh at the end."

Barber gazed at him in astonishment. "Took off the prepuce. You were circumcised, like a bleeding heathen."

32

The boy moved away, very disturbed. He was watchful and expectant. A dankness rolled toward them from the forest and he opened his small bundle and took out his other shirt, putting it on over the one he wore.

Barber removed two furred pelts from the wagon and flung them toward him. "We bed outside, for the cart is full of all manner of things."

In the open bundle Barber saw the glint of the coin and picked it up. He didn't ask where it had been gotten, nor did Rob tell him. "There's an inscription," Rob said. "My father and I . . . We believed it identifies the first cohort of Romans to come to London."

Barber examined it. "Yes."

Obviously he knew a lot about the Romans and valued them, judging from the name he'd given his horse. Rob was seized with a sick certainty that the man would keep his possession. "On the other side are letters," he said hoarsely.

Barber took the coin to the fire to read in the growing dark. "IOX. *Io* means 'shout.' *X* is ten. It's a Roman cheer for victory: 'Shout ten times!' "

Rob accepted the coin's return with relief and made his bed near the fire. The pelts were a sheepskin, which he placed on the ground fleece up, and a bearskin, which he used as a topping. They were old and smelled strong but would keep him warm.

Barber made his own bed on the other side of the fire, placing his sword and knife where they could be used to repel attackers or, Rob thought fearfully, to slay a fleeing boy. Barber had removed a Saxon horn which he wore on a thong around his neck. Closing the bottom with a bone plug, he filled it with a dark liquid from a flask and held it toward Rob. "My own spirits. Drink deep."

He didn't want it but feared to refuse. A child of working-class London was threatened with no soft and easy version of the boogerman but instead was taught early that there were sailors and stevedores anxious to lure a boy behind deserted warehouses. He knew of children who had accepted sweetmeats and coins from men like these, and he knew what they had to do in return. He was aware that drunkenness was a common prelude.

He tried to refuse more of the liquor but Barber frowned. "Drink," he commanded. "It will set you at ease."

Not until he had taken two more full swallows and was set to violent coughing was Barber satisfied. He took the horn back to his own side of the fire and finished the flask and another, finally loosing a prodigious fart and settling into his bed. He looked over at Rob only once more. "Rest easy, chappy," he said. "Sleep well. You have nothing to fear from me."

Rob was certain it was a trick. He lay under the rank bearskin and waited with tightened haunches. In his right hand he clutched his coin. In his left hand, although he knew that even if he had Barber's weapons he would be no match for the man and was at his mercy, he gripped a heavy rock.

But eventually there was ample evidence that Barber slept. The man was an ugly snorer.

The medicinal taste of the liquor filled Rob's mouth. The alcohol coursed through his body as he snuggled deep in the furs and allowed the rock to roll from his hand. He clutched the coin and imagined the Romans, rank upon rank, shouting ten times for heroes who wouldn't allow themselves to be beaten by the world. Overhead, the stars were large and white and wheeled all over the sky, so low he wanted to reach up and pluck them to make a necklace for Mam. He thought of each member of his family, one by one. Of the living he missed Samuel the most, which was peculiar because Samuel had resented him as eldest and had defied him with foul words and a loud mouth. He worried whether Jonathan was wetting his napkins and prayed Mistress Aylwyn would show the little boy patience. He hoped Barber would return to London very soon, for he longed to see the other children again.

Barber knew what his new boy was feeling. He had been exactly this one's age when he found himself alone after berserkers had struck Clacton, the fishing village where he was born. It was burned into his memory.

Aethelred was the king of his childhood. As early as he could remember, his father had cursed Aethelred, saying the people had never been so poor under any other king. Aethelred squeezed and taxed, providing a lavish life for Emma, the strong-willed and beautiful woman he had imported from Normandy to be his queen. He also built an army with the taxes but used it more to protect himself than his people, and he was so cruel and blood-thirsty that some men spat when they heard his name.

In the spring of Anno Domini 991, Aethelred shamed his subjects by bribing Danish attackers with gold to turn them away. The following spring the Danish fleet returned to London as it had done for a hundred years. This time Aethelred had no choice; he gathered his fighters and warships, and the Danes were defeated on the Thames with great slaughter. But two years later there was a more serious invasion, when Olaf, King of the Norwegians, and Swegen, King of the Danes, sailed up the Thames with ninety-four ships. Again Aethelred gathered his army around London and managed to hold the Norsemen off, but this time the invaders saw that the cowardly king had left his country vulnerable in order to protect himself. Splitting up their fleet, the Norsemen beached their ships along the English coast and laid waste to the small seaside towns.

That week, Henry Croft's father had taken him on his first long trip after herring. The morning they returned with a good catch he had run ahead, eager to be first in his mother's arms and hear her words of praise. Hidden out of sight in a cove nearby were half a dozen Norwegian long-boats. When he reached his cottage he saw a strange man dressed in animal skins staring out at him through the open shutters of the window hole.

He had no idea who the man was, but instinct caused him to turn and run for his life, straight to his father.

His mother lay on the floor already used and dead, but his father didn't know that. Luke Croft pulled his knife as he made for the house, but the three men who met him outside the front door were carrying swords. From afar, Henry Croft saw his father overpowered and taken. One of the men held his father's hands behind his back. Another pulled his hair with both hands, forcing him to kneel and extend his neck. The third man cut off his head with a sword. In Barber's nineteenth year he had witnessed a murderer executed in Wolverhampton; the sheriff's axman had cleaved off the criminal's head as if killing a rooster. In contrast, his father's beheading had been clumsily done, for the Viking had required a flurry of strokes, as if he were hacking a piece of firewood.

Hysterical with grief and fear, Henry Croft had run into the woods and hidden himself like a hunted animal. When he wandered out, dazed and starving, the Norwegians were gone but they had left death and ashes. Henry had been collected with other orphan boys and sent to Crowland Abbey in Lincolnshire.

Decades of similar raids by heathen Norsemen had left the monasteries with too few monks and too many orphans, so the Benedictines solved two problems by ordaining many of the parentless boys. At nine years of age Henry was administered vows and instructed to promise God that he would live in poverty and chastity forever, obeying the precepts established by the blessed St. Benedict of Nursia.

It gained him an education. Four hours a day he studied, six hours a day he performed damp, dirty labor. Crowland owned vast tracts, mostly fens, and each day Henry and the other monks turned the muddy earth, pulling plows like staggering beasts in order to convert bogs into fields. It was expected that the rest of his time would be spent in contemplation or prayer. There were morning services, afternoon services, evening services, perpetual services. Every prayer was considered a single step up an interminable stairway that would take his soul to heaven. There was no recreation or athletics, but he was allowed to pace the cloister, a covered walk in the shape of a rectangle. To the north side of the cloister was the sacristy, the buildings in which the sacred utensils were kept. To the east was the church; to the west, the chapter house; to the south, a cheerless refectory consisting of a dining room, kitchen, and pantry on the ground floor and a dormitory above.

Within the rectangle were graves, the ultimate proof that life at Crowland Abbey was predictable: tomorrow would be identical to yesterday and eventually every monk would lie inside the cloister. Because some mistook this for peace, Crowland had attracted several noblemen who had fled the politics of Court and Aethelred's cruelty and saved their lives by taking the cowl. These influential elite lived in individual cells, as did the true mystics who sought God through agony of spirit and pain of body brought on by hair shirts, inspired pinching, and self-flagellation. For the other sixty-seven males who wore the tonsure despite the fact that they were uncalled and unholy, home was a single large chamber containing sixty-seven sleeping pallets. If Henry Croft awoke at any moment of any night he might hear coughing and sneezing, assorted snores, sounds of masturbation, the wounded cries of dreamers, the breaking of wind, and the shattering of the silence rule through unecclesiastic cursing and clandestine conversations which almost always were about food. Meals at Crowland were very sparse.

The town of Peterborough was only eight miles away, but he never saw it. One day when he was fourteen years old he asked his confessor, Father Dunstan, for permission to sing hymns and recite prayers at the riverside between Vespers and Night Song. This was granted. As he walked the river meadow, Father Dunstan followed at a discreet distance. Henry paced slowly and deliberately, his hands behind his back and his head bowed as though in worship worthy of a bishop. It was a beautiful and warm summer's evening with a fresh breeze off the water. He had been taught about this river by Brother Matthew, a geographer. It was the River Welland. It rose in the Midlands near Corby and easily slipped and wriggled to Crowland like a snake, thence flowing northeast between rolling hills and fertile valleys before rushing through coastal swamps to empty into the great bay of the North Sea called The Wash.

Surrounding the river was God's bounty of forest and field. Crickets shrilled. Birds twittered in the trees and cows looked at him with dumb respect as they grazed. There was a little cockleboat pulled up on the bank.

The following week he asked to be allowed to recite solitary prayer by the river after Lauds, the dawn service. Permission was granted and this time Father Dunstan didn't come. When Henry got to the riverbank he put the little boat into the water, clambered in, and pushed off.

He used the oars only to get into the current, then he sat very still in the center of the flimsy boat and watched the brown water, letting the river take him like a fallen leaf. After a time, when he knew he was away, he began to laugh. He whooped and shouted boyish things. *"That* for you!" he cried, not knowing whether he was defying the sixty-six monks who would be sleeping without him, or Father Dunstan or the God who was seen at Crowland as such a cruel being.

He stayed on the river all day, until the water that rushed toward the sea was too deep and dangerous for his liking. Then he beached the boat and began a time when he learned the price of freedom.

He wandered the coastal villages, sleeping wherever, living on what he could beg or steal. Having nothing to eat was far worse than having little to eat. A farmer's wife gave him a sack of food and an old tunic and ragged trousers in exchange for the Benedictine habit that would make woolen shirts for her sons. In the port of Grimsby a fisherman finally took him on as helper and worked him brutally for more than two years in return for scant fare and bare shelter. When the fisherman died, his wife sold the boat to people who wanted no boys. Henry spent hungry months until he found a troupe of entertainers and traveled with them, lugging baggage and helping with the necessities of their craft in return for scraps of food and their protection. Even in his eyes their arts were clumsy but they knew how to bang a drum and draw a crowd, and when a cap was passed surprising numbers in their audiences dropped a coin. He watched them hungrily. He was too old to be a tumbler, since acrobats must have their joints broken while they are still children. But the jugglers taught him their trade. He mimicked the magician and learned the simpler feats of deception; the magician taught him that he must never give the impression of necromancy, for all over England the Church and the Crown were hanging witches. He listened carefully to the storyteller, whose young sister was the first to allow him inside her body. He felt a kinship with the entertainers, but the troupe dissolved in Derbyshire after a year and everyone went separate ways without him.

A few weeks later in the town of Matlock, his luck took a turn when a barber-surgeon named James Farrow indentured him for six years. Later he would learn that none of the local youths would serve Farrow as prentice because there were stories linking him to witchcraft. By the time Henry heard the rumors he had been with Farrow two years and knew the man was no witch. Though the barber-surgeon was a cold man and bastardly strict, to Henry Croft he represented genuine opportunity.

Matlock Township was rural and thinly populated, without upper-class patients or prosperous merchants to support a physician, or the large population of poorer folk to attract a surgeon. In a far-flung farm area surrounding Matlock, James Farrow, country barber-surgeon, was all there was, and in addition to administering cleansing clysters and cutting and shaving hair, he performed surgery and prescribed remedies. Henry did his bidding for more than five years. Farrow was a stern taskmaster; he beat Henry when the apprentice made mistakes, but he taught him everything he knew, and meticulously.

During Henry's fourth year in Matlock—it was the year 1002—King Aethelred committed an act that would have far-reaching and terrible consequences. In his difficulties the king had allowed certain Danes to settle in southern England and had given them land, on condition that they would fight for him against his enemies. He had thus bought the services of a Danish noble named Pallig, who was husband to Gunnhilda, the sister of Swegen, King of Denmark. That year the Vikings invaded England and followed their usual tactics, slaying and burning. When they reached Southampton, the king decided to pay tribute again, and he gave the invaders twenty-four thousand pounds to go away.

When their ships had carried the Norsemen off, Aethelred was shamed and fell into a frustrated fury. He ordered that all Danish people who were in England should be slain on St. Brice's Day, November 13. The treacherous mass murder was carried out as the king ordered, and it seemed to unlock an evil that had been festering in the English people.

The world had always been brutal, but after the murders of the Danes life became even more cruel. All over England violent crimes took place, witches were hunted out and put to death by hanging or burning, and a blood lust seemed to take the land.

Henry Croft's apprenticeship was almost completed when an elderly man named Bailey Aelerton succumbed while under Farrow's care. There was nothing remarkable about the death, but word quickly spread that the man had died because Farrow had stuck him with needles and bewitched him.

The previous Sunday, in the small church in Matlock the priest had disclosed that evil spirits had been heard carousing at midnight about the graves in the churchyard, engaged in carnal copulation with Satan. "It is abominable to our Saviour that the dead should rise through devil-skill. They who exercise such crafts are God's enemies," he thundered. The Devil was among them, the priest warned, served by an army of witches disguised as human creatures and practicing black magic and secret killing.

He armed the awestruck and terrified worshipers with a counterspell to be used against anyone suspected of witchcraft: "Arch sorcerer who attacks my soul, your spell shall be reversed, your curse returned to you a thousandfold. In the name of the Holy Trinity restore me to health and strength again. In the name of God the Father, God the Son, and God the Holy Ghost. Amen."

And he reminded them of the biblical injunction, *Thou shalt not suffer a witch to live.* "They must be sought out and eradicated if each of you does not wish to burn in the terrible flames of Purgatory," he exhorted them.

Bailey Aelerton died on Tuesday, his heart stopping as he hoed in the field. His daughter claimed she had seen needle holes on his skin. No one else had seen them for certain, but Thursday morning a mob came into Farrow's barnyard just after the barber-surgeon had mounted his horse, preparing to visit patients. He was still looking down at Henry and giving him instructions for the day when they pulled him from the saddle.

They were led by Simon Beck, whose land abutted Farrow's. "Strip him," Beck said.

Farrow was trembling as they ripped off his clothing. "You are an arse, Beck!" he shouted. "An arse!" He looked older unclothed, his abdominal skin loose and folded, rounded shoulders narrow, muscles soft and wasted, penis shriveled small above a huge purple sac.

"Here it is!" Beck cried. "Satan's mark!"

On the right side of Farrow's groin, plainly seen, were two small dark specks, like the bite of a serpent. Beck nicked one with the point of his knife.

"*Moles!*" Farrow shrieked.

Blood welled, which wasn't supposed to happen with a witch.

"They are smart as smart," Beck said, "able to bleed at will."

"I am a barber and not a witch," Farrow told them contemptuously, but when they tied him to a wooden cross and carried him to his own stock pond, he began to scream for mercy.

The cross was flung into the shallow pond with a great splash and held beneath the surface. The crowd quieted, watching the bubbles. Presently they pulled it up and gave Farrow a chance to confess. He was still breathing, and sputtered weakly.

"Do you own, neighbor Farrow, that you have worked with the Devil?" Beck asked him kindly.

But the bound man could only cough and gasp for air.

So they immersed him again. This time the cross was held under until the bubbles stopped coming. And still they didn't raise it.

Henry could only watch and weep, as if seeing them kill his father again. He was man-grown, no longer a boy, yet he was powerless against the witch-hunters, terrified they would take the notion that the barber-surgeon's prentice was the sorcerer's assistant.

Finally they released the submerged cross and recited the counterspell and went away, leaving it to float in the pond.

When all were gone, Henry waded through the ooze to pull the cross ashore. A pink froth showed between his master's lips. He closed the eyes that accused sightlessly in the white face and picked duckweed from Farrow's shoulders before cutting him free.

The barber-surgeon had been a widower with no family and therefore the responsibility fell upon his servant. He buried Farrow as quickly as possible.

When he went through the house he discovered they had been there before him. No doubt they were seeking evidence of Satan's work when they took Farrow's money and liquor. The place had been picked clean, but there was a suit of clothes in better condition than those he had on, and some food, which he put into a sack. He also took a bag of surgical instruments and captured Farrow's horse, which he rode out of Matlock before they should recollect him and come back.

He became a wanderer once again, but this time he had a craft and it made all the difference. Everywhere there were ailing people who would pay a penny or two for treatment. Eventually he learned the profit that could be found in the sale of medications, and to gather crowds he used some of the ways he had learned while traveling with the entertainers.

Believing he might be sought, he never stayed long in one place and avoided use of his full name, becoming Barber. Before long these things were woven into the fabric of an existence that suited him; he dressed warmly and well, had women in variety, drank when he pleased and ate prodigiously at every meal, vowing never to hunger again. His weight quickly increased. By the time he met the woman he married, he weighed more than eighteen stone. Lucinda Eames was a widow with a nice farm in Canterbury, and for half a year he tended her animals and fields, playing husbandman. He relished her small white bottom, a pale inverted heart. When they made love she poked the pink tip of her tongue out of the left corner of her mouth, like a child doing hard lessons. She blamed him for not giving her a child. Perhaps she was right, but she had not conceived with her first husband either. Her voice became shrill, her tone bitter, and her cooking careless, and long before the year with her was over he was remembering warmer women and pleasurable meals, and yearning for surcease from her tongue.

* * *

That was 1012, the year Swegen, King of the Danes, gained control of England. For ten years Swegen had harried Aethelred, eager to shame the man who had murdered his kinsmen. Finally Aethelred fled to the Isle of Wight with his ships, and Queen Emma took refuge in Normandy with her sons Edward and Alfred.

Soon afterward Swegen died a natural death. He left two sons, Harold, who succeeded him to the Danish kingdom, and Canute, a youth of nineteen who was proclaimed King of England by Danish force of arms.

Aethelred had one attack left in him and he drove the Danes off, but almost immediately Canute was back, and this time he took everything except London. He was on his way to conquer London when he heard that Aethelred had died. Boldly, he called a meeting of the Witan, the council of wise men of England, and bishops, abbots, earls, and thanes went to Southampton and chose Canute to be the lawful king.

Canute showed his genius for healing the nation by sending envoys to Normandy to convince Queen Emma to marry her late husband's successor to the throne, and she agreed almost at once. She was years older than he but still a desirable and sensuous woman, and sniggering jokes were told about the amount of time she and Canute spent in chambers.

Even as the new king was hastening toward marriage, Barber was fleeing it. He simply walked away from Lucinda Eames' shrewishness and bad cooking one day, and resumed traveling. He bought his first wagon in Bath, and in Northumberland he took his first boy in indenture. The advantages were apparent at once. Since then, over the years he had trained a number of chaps. The few who had been capable had earned him money, and the others had taught him what he required in a prentice.

He knew what happened to a boy who failed and was sent away. Most met with disaster: the lucky ones became sexual playthings or slaves, the unfortunate starved to death or were killed. It bothered him more than he cared to admit, but he couldn't afford to keep an unlikely boy; he himself was a survivor, able to harden his heart when it came to his own welfare.

The latest, the boy he had found in London, seemed eager to please but Barber knew that appearances could mislead where apprentices were concerned. It was of no value to worry the issue like a dog with a bone. Only time would tell, and he would learn soon enough whether young Cole was fit to survive.

Chapter 5

THE BEAST IN CHELMSFORD

Rob woke with the first milky light to find his new master already about, and impatient. He saw at once that Barber didn't begin the day in high spirits, and it was in this sober morning mood that the man took the lance from the wagon and showed him how it should be used. "It's not too heavy for you if you use both hands. It doesn't require skill. Thrust as hard as you are able. If you aim for the middle of an attacker's body you're liable to stick him someplace. If you slow him with a wound, chances are good that I can kill him. Do you comprehend?"

He nodded, awkward with a stranger.

"Well, chappy, we must be vigilant and keep weapons at hand, for that is how we stay alive. These Roman roads remain the best in England, but they aren't maintained. It is the Crown's responsibility to keep them open on both sides to make it hard for highwaymen to ambush travelers, but on most of our routes the brush is never cut back."

He demonstrated how to hitch the horse. When they resumed traveling, Rob sat next to him on the driver's seat in the hot sun, still plagued by all manner of fears. Soon Barber directed Incitatus off the Roman road, turning onto a barely usable track through the deep shadow of virgin forest. Hanging from a sinew around his shoulders was the brown Saxon horn that once had graced a great ox. He placed it to his mouth and pushed from it a loud, mellow noise, half blast, half moan. "It signals everyone within hearing that we aren't creeping up to cut throats and steal. In some remote places, to meet a stranger is to try to kill him. The horn says we are worthy and confident, able to protect outselves."

At Barber's suggestion Rob tried to take a turn at signaling, but though he puffed his cheeks and blew mightily, no sound emerged.

"It needs older wind and a knack. You'll learn it, never fear. And more difficult things than blowing a horn."

The track was muddy. Brush had been laid over the worst places but it demanded tricky driving. At a turn in the road they went directly into a slick and the wagon's wheels sank to the hubs. Barber sighed.

They got out and took a spade to the mud in front of the wheels and then collected fallen branches in the woods. Barber carefully placed pieces of wood in front of each wheel and climbed back up to take the reins.

"You must shove brush under the wheels as they start to move," he said, and Rob J. nodded.

"Hi–TATUS!" Barber urged. Shafts and leather creaked. "Now!" he shouted.

Rob deftly placed the branches, darting from wheel to wheel as the horse strained steadily. The wheels hesitated. There was slippage, but they found purchase. The wagon lurched forward. When it was on dry road Barber hauled back on the reins and waited for Rob to catch up and climb onto the seat.

They were spattered with mud, and Barber stopped Tatus at a brook. "Let us catch some breakfast," he said as they washed the dirt from their faces and hands. He cut two willow poles and got hooks and line from the wagon. From the shaded place behind the seat he pulled out a box. "This is our grasshopper box," he said. "It is one of your duties to keep it filled." He lifted the lid only far enough to allow Rob to stick his hand inside.

Living things rustled away from Rob's fingers, frantic and spiky, and he pulled one gently into his palm. When he withdrew his hand, keeping the wings folded between his thumb and forefinger, the insect's legs scrabbled frantically. The four front legs were thin as hairs and the hind two were powerful and large-thighed, enabling it to be a hopper.

Barber showed him how to slip the point of the hook just beneath the short section of tough, ridged shell behind the head. "Not too deep or he'll bleed molasses and die. Where have you fished?"

"The Thames." He prided himself on his ability as a fisher, for he and his father often had dangled worms in the broad river, depending on the fish to help feed the family during the unemployment.

Barber grunted. "This is a different kind of fishing," he said. "Leave the poles for a moment and get on your hands and knees."

They crawled cautiously to a place overlooking the nearest pool and lay on their bellies. Rob thought the fat man daft.

Four fish hung suspended in glass.

"Small," Rob whispered.

"Best eating, that size," Barber said as they crept away from the bank. "Your big river trouts are tough and oily. Did you note how these drifted near the head of the pool? They feed facing upstream, waiting for a juicy meal to fall in and come floating down. They're wild and wary. If you stand next to the stream, they see you. If you tread strongly on the bank, they feel your step and they scatter. That's why you use the long pole. Stand well back and lightly drop the hopper just above the pool, letting the flow carry it to the fish."

He watched critically as Rob swung the grasshopper where he had directed.

With a shock that traveled along the pole and sent excitement up into Rob's arms, the unseen fish struck like a dragon. After that it was like fishing in the Thames. He waited patiently, giving the trout time to doom itself, and then raised the tip of the pole and set the hook as his father had taught him. When he pulled in the first flopping prize they admired its bloom, the gleaming background like oiled walnut wood, the sleek sides splattered with rainbowy reds, the black fins marked with warm orange.

"Get five more," Barber said, and disappeared into the woods.

Rob caught two and then lost another and cautiously moved to a different pool. The trouts hungered after grasshoppers. He was cleaning the last of the half dozen when Barber came back with a capful of morels and wild onions.

"We eat twice a day," Barber said, "mid-morning and early evening, same as all civilized folk.

> *To rise at six, dine at ten,*
> *Sup at five, to bed at ten,*
> *Makes man live ten times ten.*"

He had bacon, and cut it thick. When the meat was done in the blackened pan he dredged the trouts in flour and did them crisp and brown in the fat, adding the onions and mushrooms at the last.

The spines of the trouts lifted cleanly from the steaming flesh, freeing most of the bones. While they enjoyed the fish and the meat, Barber fried barley bread in the flavored fat that remained, covering the toast with husky slices of cheese he allowed to melt bubbly in the pan. To finish, they drank the cold sweet water of the brook that had given them the fish.

Barber was in better cheer. A fat man had to be fed to be at his best, Rob perceived. He also realized that Barber was a rare cook, and he found himself looking toward each meal as an event of the day. He sighed, knowing he wouldn't have been fed like this in the mines. And the work, he told himself contentedly, wasn't at all beyond him, for he was perfectly able to keep the grasshopper box filled and catch trouts and place brush beneath the wheels whenever the wagon became stuck in the mud.

The village was Farnham. There were farms; a small, shabby inn; a public house that emitted a faint smell of spilled ale as they passed; a smithy with long wood piles near the forge; a tanner's that exuded a stink; a sawyer's yard with cut lumber; and a reeve's hall facing a square that wasn't really a square so much as a widening in the midsection of the street, like a snake that had swallowed an egg.

Barber stopped at the outskirts. From the wagon he took a small drum and a stick and handed them to Rob. "Bang it."

Incitatus knew what they were about; he lifted his head and neighed, raising his hooves as he pranced. Rob pounded the drum proudly, infected by the excitement they were causing on both sides of the street.

"Entertainment this afternoon," Barber called. "Followed by treatment of human ills and medical problems, great or small!"

The blacksmith, his knotted muscles outlined by grime, stared after them and stopped pulling his bellows rope. Two boys in the sawyer's yard left the lumber they had been stacking and came running toward the sound of the drum. One of them turned and hurried away. "Where are you bound, Giles?" the other shouted.

"Home to fetch Stephen and the others."

"Stop and tell my brother's lot!"

Barber nodded in approval. "Spread the word," he called.

Women emerged from the houses and called to one another as their children merged in the street, jabbering and joining the barking dogs that followed after the red wagon.

Barber drove slowly down the street from one end to the other and then turned around and came back.

An old man who sat in the sun near the inn opened his eyes and smiled toothlessly at the commotion. Some of the drinkers came out of the public house, carrying their glasses and followed by the barmaid wiping wet hands on her apron, her eyes shining.

Barber stopped in the little square. From the wagon he took four folding benches and set them up joined together. "This is called the bank," he said to Rob of the small stage thus formed. "You'll erect it at once whenever we come to a new place."

On the bank they placed two baskets full of little stoppered flasks that Barber said contained medicine. Then he disappeared into the wagon and pulled the curtain.

* * *

Rob sat on the bank and watched people hasten into the main street. The miller came, his clothing white with flour, and Rob could tell two carpenters by the familiar wood dust and chips on their tunics and hair. Families settled to the ground, willing to wait in order to obtain a place close to the bank. Women worked at tatting and knitting while they tarried, and children chattered and squabbled. A group of village boys stared at Rob. Aware of the awe and envy in their eyes, he struck poses and swaggered. But in a little while all such foolishness was driven from his head, because like them he had become part of the audience. Barber ran onto the bank with a flourish.

"Good day and good morrow," he said. "I'm comforted to be in Farnham." And he began to juggle.

He juggled a red ball and a yellow ball. His hands seemed scarcely to move. It was the prettiest thing to see!

His fat fingers sent the balls flying in a continual circle, at first slowly and then with blurring speed. When he was applauded, he reached into his tunic and added a green ball. And then a blue. And, oh—a brown!

How wonderful, Rob thought, to be able to do that.

He held his breath, waiting for Barber to drop a ball, but he controlled all five easily, talking all the while. He made people laugh. He told stories, sang little songs.

Next, he juggled rope rings and wooden plates and after the juggling performed feats of magic. He caused an egg to disappear, found a coin in a child's hair, made a handkerchief change color.

"Would you be beguiled to see me cause a mug of ale to vanish?"

There was general applause. The barmaid hurried inside the public house and appeared with a foaming mug. Placing it to his lips, Barber downed its contents in a single long swallow. He bowed to good-natured laughter and applause, and then asked the women in the audience if anyone desired a ribbon.

"Oh, indeed!" exclaimed the barmaid. She was young and full-bodied, and her response, so spontaneous and artless, drew a titter from the crowd.

Barber's eyes met the girl's and he smiled. "What is your name?"

"Oh, sir. It is Amelia Simpson."

"Mistress Simpson?"

"I am unmarried."

Barber closed his eyes. "A waste," he said gallantly. "What color ribbon would you like, Miss Amelia?"

"Red."

"And the length?"

"Two yards should do me perfectly."

"One would hope so," he murmured, raising his eyebrows.

There was ribald laughter, but he appeared to forget her. He cut a piece of rope into four parts and then caused it to be rejoined and whole, using only gestures. He placed a kerchief over a ring and changed it into a walnut. And then, almost in surprise, he brought his fingers to his mouth and pulled something from between his lips, pausing to show the audience that it was the end of a red ribbon.

As they watched he pulled it out of his mouth, bit by bit, his body drooping and his eyes crossing as it continued to emerge. Finally, holding the end taut, he reached down for his dagger, placed the blade close to his lips, and cut the ribbon free. He handed it to the barmaid with a bow.

Next to her was the village sawyer, who stretched the ribbon on his measuring stick. "Two yards, exact!" he pronounced, and there was great applause.

Barber waited for the noise to die and then held up a flask of his bottled medicinal. "Masters, mistresses, and maidens!

"*Only* my Universal Specific Physick . . .

"Lengthens your allotted span, regenerates the worn-out tissues of the body. Makes stiff joints supple and limp joints stiff. Restores a roguish sparkle to jaded eyes. Transmutes illness to health, stops hair from falling and resprouts shiny pates. Clarifies dimmed vision and sharpens dulled intellects.

"A most excellent cordial more stimulating than the finest tonic, a purgative gentler than a cream clyster. The Universal Specific fights bloating and the bloody flux, eases the rigors of the childbed and the agony of the female curse, and eradicates the scorbutic disorders brought back to shore by seafaring folk. It is good for brute or human, a bane to deafness, sore eyes, coughs, consumptions, stomach pains, jaundice, fever, and agues. Cures any illness! Banishes care!"

Barber sold a good deal of it from the bank. Then he and Rob set up a screen, behind which the barber-surgeon examined patients. The ill and the afflicted waited in a long line to pay a penny or two for his treatment.

That night they ate roast goose at the public house, the only time Rob had ever eaten a purchased meal. He thought it especially fine, though Barber pronounced the meat overdone and grumbled at lumps in the mashed turnip. Afterward Barber brought onto the table a chart of the

British island. It was the first map Rob had seen and he watched in fascination as Barber's finger traced a squiggly line, the route they would follow over the coming months.

Eventually, eyes closing, he stumbled sleepily back to their campsite through bright moonlight and made his bed. But so much had happened in the past few days that his dazzled mind fought sleep.

He was half awake and star-searching when Barber returned, and somebody was with him.

"Pretty Amelia," Barber said. "Pretty dolly. A single look at that wanting mouth, I knew I would die for you."

"Mind the roots or you'll fall," she said.

Rob lay and listened to the wet sounds of kissing, the rasp of clothing being removed, laughter and gasping. Then the slithering of the furs being spread.

"I had best go under, because of my stomach," he heard Barber say.

"A most prodigious stomach," the girl said in a low, wicked voice. "It will be like bouncing on a great comforter."

"Nay, maid, here is my great comforter."

Rob wanted to see her naked, but by the time he dared to move his head the tiny bit necessary, she was no longer standing, and all he could see was the pale glimmer of buttocks.

His breathing was loud but he could have shouted for all they cared. Soon he watched Barber's large plump hands reach around to clutch the rotating white orbs.

"Ah, Dolly!"

The girl groaned.

They slept before he did. Rob fell asleep finally and dreamed of Barber, still juggling.

The woman was gone when he was awakened in the chill dawning. They broke camp and rode from Farnham while most of its people were still in bed.

Shortly after sunrise they passed a blackberry bramble and stopped to fill a basket. At the next farm Barber took on provender. When they camped for breakfast, while Rob made the fire and cooked the bacon and cheese toast, Barber broke nine eggs into a bowl and added a generous amount of clotted cream, beating it to a froth and then cooking without stirring until it set into a soft cake, which he covered with dead-ripe blackberries. He appeared pleased at the eagerness with which Rob downed his share.

That afternoon they passed a great keep surrounded by farms. Rob could see people on the grounds and earthen battlements. Barber urged the horse into a trot, seeking to pass it quickly.

But three riders came after them from the place and shouted them to a stop.

Stern and fearsome armed men, they examined the decorated wagon curiously. "What is your trade?" asked one who wore the light mail of a person of rank.

"Barber-surgeon, lord," Barber said.

The man nodded in satisfaction and wheeled his horse. "Follow."

Surrounded by their guard, they clattered through a heavy gate set into the earthworks, through a second gate in a palisade of sharpened logs, then across a drawbridge above a moat. Rob had never been so close to a stately fastness. The enormous keep house had a foundation and half-wall of stone, with timbered upper stories, intricate carvings on porch and gables, and a gilded rooftree that blazed in the sun.

"Leave your wagon in the courtyard. Bring your surgeon's tools."

"What is the problem, lord?"

"Bitch hurt her hand."

Laden with instruments and flasks of medicinal, they followed him into the cavernous hall. The floor was flagged with stone and spread with rushes that needed changing. The furniture seemed ample for small giants. Three walls were arrayed with swords, shields, and lances, while the north wall was hung with tapestries of rich but faded color, against which stood a throne of carved dark wood.

The central fireplace was cold but the place was redolent of last winter's smoke and a less attractive stench, strongest when their escort stopped before the hound lying by the hearth.

"Lost two toes in a snare, a fortnight ago. At first they healed nicely, then they festered."

Barber nodded. He shook meat from a silver bowl by the hound's head and poured in the contents of two of his flasks. The dog watched with rheumy eyes and growled when he set down the bowl, but in a moment she started to lap up the specific.

Barber took no chances; when the hound was listless, he tied her muzzle and lashed her feet so she couldn't use her paws.

The dog trembled and yipped when Barber cut. It smelled abominably, and there were maggots.

"She will lose another toe."

"She mustn't be crippled. Do it well," the man said coldly.

When it was done, Barber washed the blood from the paw with the rest of the medicinal, then bound it in a rag.

"Payment, lord?" he suggested delicately.

"You must wait for the Earl to return from his hunting, and ask him," the knight said, and went away.

They untied the dog gingerly, then took the instruments and returned to the wagon. Barber drove them away slowly, like a man with permission to leave.

But when they were out of sight of the keep, he hawked and spat. "Perhaps the Earl would not return for days. By then, if the dog were well, perhaps he would pay, this saintly Earl. If the dog were dead or the Earl out of sorts with constipation, he might have us flayed. I shun lords and take my chances in small villages," he said, and urged the horse away.

Next morning, he was in better mood when they came to Chelmsford. But there already was an unguent seller set up to entertain there, a sleek man dressed in a gaudy orange tunic and with a mane of white hair.

"Well met, Barber," the man said easily.

"Hullo, Wat. You still have the beast?"

"No, he turned sickly and became too mean. I used him in a baiting."

"Pity you didn't give him my Specific. It would have made him well."

They laughed together.

"I have a new beast. Do you care to witness?"

"Why not?" Barber said. He pulled the wagon up under a tree and allowed the horse to graze while the crowd gathered. Chelmsford was a large village and the audience was good. "Have you wrestled?" Barber asked Rob.

He nodded. He loved to wrestle; wrestling was the everyday sport of working-class boys in London.

Wat began his entertainment in the same manner as Barber, with juggling. His juggling was skillful, Rob thought. His storytelling couldn't measure up to Barber's and people laughed less frequently. But they loved the bear.

The cage was in the shade, covered by a cloth. The crowd murmured when Wat removed the cover. Rob had seen an entertaining bear before. When he was six years old his father had taken him to see such a creature performing outside Swann's Inn, and it had appeared enormous to him. When Wat led this muzzled bear onto the bank on a long chain, it seemed smaller. It was scarcely larger than a great dog, but it was very smart.

"Bartram the Bear!" Wat announced.

The bear lay down and pretended to be dead on command, he rolled a ball and fetched it, he climbed up and down a ladder, and while Wat played a flute he danced the popular clog step called the Carol, turning clumsily instead of twirling but so delighting the onlookers that they applauded the animal's every move.

"And now," Wat said, "Bartram will wrestle all challengers. Anyone to throw him will be given a free pot of Wat's Unguent, that most miraculous agent for the relief of human ills."

There was an amused stir but no one came forward.

"Come, wrestlers," Wat chided.

Barber's eyes twinkled. "Here is a lad who is not fear-struck," he said loudly.

To Rob's amazement and great concern, he found himself propelled forward. Willing hands aided him onto the bank.

"My boy against your beast, friend Wat," Barber called.

Wat nodded and they both laughed.

Oh, Mam! Rob thought numbly.

It was truly a bear. It swayed on its hind legs and cocked its large, furry head at him. This was no hound, no Carpenter's Street playmate. He saw massive shoulders and thick limbs, and his instinct was to leap from the bank and flee. But to do so would defy Barber and everything the barber-surgeon represented to his existence. He made the less courageous choice and faced the animal.

His heart pounding, he circled, weaving his open hands in front of him as he had often seen older wrestlers do. Perhaps he didn't have it quite right; someone tittered, and the bear looked toward the sound. Trying to forget that his adversary wasn't human, Rob acted as he would have toward another boy: he darted in and tried to unbalance Bartram, but it was like trying to uproot a great tree.

Bartram lifted one paw and struck him lazily. The bear had been declawed but the cuff knocked him down and halfway across the stage. Now he was more than terrified; he knew he could do nothing and would have fled, but Bartram shambled with deceptive swiftness and was waiting. When he got to his feet he was wrapped by the forelimbs. His face was pulled into the bear, which filled his nose and mouth. He was strangling in scruffy black fur that smelled exactly like the pelt he slept on at night. The bear was not fully grown, but neither was he. Struggling, he found himself looking up into small and desperate red eyes. The bear was as afraid as he, Rob realized, but the animal was in full control and had something to harry. Bartram couldn't bite but it was obvious he would have; he ground the leather muzzle into Rob's shoulder and his breath was strong and stinking.

Wat reached his hand toward the little handle on the animal's collar. He didn't touch it, but the bear whimpered and cringed; he dropped Rob and fell onto his back.

"Pin him, you dolt!" Wat whispered.

He flung himself down and touched the black fur near the shoulders. No one was fooled and a few people jeered, but the crowd had been entertained and was in good humor. Wat caged Bartram and returned to reward Rob with a tiny clay pot of unguent, as promised. Soon the entertainer was declaiming the salve's ingredients and uses to the crowd.

Rob walked to the wagon on rubbery legs.

"You did handsomely," Barber said. "Dove right into him. Bit of a nosebleed?"

He snuffled, knowing he was fortunate. "The beast was about to do me harm," he said glumly.

Barber grinned and shook his head. "Did you note the little handle on its neckband? It's a choke collar. The handle allows the band to be twisted, cutting off the creature's breathing if it disobeys. It is the way bears are trained." He gave Rob a hand up to the wagon seat and then took a dab of salve from the pot and rubbed it between thumb and forefinger. "Tallow and lard and a touch of scent. And, oh, but he sells a good deal of it," he mused, watching customers line up to hand Wat their pennies. "An animal guarantees prosperity. There are entertainments built around marmots, goats, crows, badgers, and dogs. Even lizards, and generally they take in more money than I do when I work alone."

The horse responded to the reins and started down the track into the coolness of the woods, leaving Chelmsford and the wrestling bear behind them. The shakiness was still in Rob. He sat motionless, thinking. "Then why do *you* not entertain with an animal?" he said slowly.

Barber half-turned in the seat. His friendly blue eyes found Rob's and seemed to say more than his smiling mouth.

"I have you," he said.

Chapter 6

THE COLORED BALLS

They began with juggling, and from the start Rob knew he would never be able to perform that kind of miracle.

"Stand erect but relaxed, hands at your sides. Bring your forearms up until they're level with the ground. Turn your palms up." Barber surveyed him critically and then nodded. "You must pretend that on your palms I have placed a tray of eggs. The tray can't be allowed to tilt for even a moment or the eggs will slide off. It's the same with juggling. If your arms don't remain level, the balls will be all over the ground. Is this understood?"

"Yes, Barber." He had a sick feeling in his stomach.

"Cup your hands as though you're to drink water from each of them." He took two wooden balls. He placed the red ball in Rob's cupped right hand and the blue ball in his left. "Now toss them up the way a juggler does, but at the same time."

The balls went over his head and fell to the ground.

"Observe. The red ball rose higher, because you have more strength in your right arm than in your left. Therefore you must learn to compensate, to use less effort from your right hand and more from your left, for the throws must be equal. Also, the balls went too high. A juggler has enough to do without having to pull back his head and peer up into the sun to see where the balls have gone. The balls should come no higher than here." He tapped Rob's forehead. "That way you see them without moving your head."

He frowned. "Another thing. Jugglers never *throw* a ball. The balls are *popped.* The center of your hand must pop up for a moment so that the cup disappears and your hand is flat. The center of your hand drives the ball straight up, while at the same time the wrist gives a quick little snap and the forearm makes the smallest of motions upward. From the elbows to the shoulders, your arms shouldn't move."

53

He retrieved the balls and handed them to Rob.

When they reached Hertford, Rob set up the bank and carried out the flasks of Barber's elixir and then took the two wooden balls off by himself and practiced popping. It hadn't sounded hard but he found that half the time he placed a spin on the ball when he threw it up, causing it to veer. If he hooked the ball by hanging on to it too long it fell back toward his face or went over his shoulder. If he allowed a hand to go slack, the ball traveled away from him. But he kept at it, and soon he grasped the knack of popping. Barber seemed pleased when he showed his new skill that evening before supper.

The next day Barber stopped the wagon outside the village of Luton and showed Rob how to pop two balls so their paths crossed. "You can avoid collisions in midair if one ball has a head start or is popped higher than the other," he said.

As soon as the show had begun in Luton, Rob stole away with the two balls and practiced in a small clearing in the woods. More often than not, the blue ball met the red ball with a small clunking sound that seemed to mock him. The balls fell and rolled and had to be retrieved, and he felt stupid and out of sorts. But nobody watched except a woods mouse and an occasional bird, and he continued to try. Eventually he was able to see that he could pop both balls successfully if the first one came down wide of his left hand and the second one went lower and traveled a shorter distance. It took him two days of trial and error and constant repetition before he was sufficiently satisfied to demonstrate it to Barber.

Barber showed him how to move both balls in a circle. "It looks more difficult than it is. You pop the first ball. While it is in the air, you shift the second ball into the right hand. The left hand catches the first ball, the right hand pops the second ball, and so on, hop, hop, hop! The balls are sent into the air quickly by your pops, but they come down much slower. That's the juggler's secret, that's what saves jugglers. You have plenty of time."

By the end of a week Barber was teaching him how to juggle both the red and the blue from the same hand. He had to hold one ball in his palm and the other farther forward, on his fingers. He was glad he had large hands. He dropped the balls a lot but finally he caught on: first red was tossed up, and before it could drop back into his hand, up went blue. They danced up and down from the same hand, hop, hop, hop! He practiced every moment that he could, now—two balls in a circle, two balls crossing over, two balls with the right hand only, two balls one-handed with the left. He found that by juggling with very low pops he could increase his speed.

They held over outside a town called Bletchly because Barber bought a swan from a farmer. It was scarcely more than a cygnet but nevertheless larger than any fowl Rob had ever seen prepared for table. The farmer sold it dressed but Barber fussed over the bird, washing it painstakingly in a running stream and then dangling it by the legs over a small fire to singe off the pinfeathers.

He stuffed it with chestnuts, onions, fat, and herbs as befit a bird that had cost him dear. "A swan's flesh is stronger than a goose's but drier than a duck's and so must be barded," he instructed Rob happily. They barded the bird by wrapping it completely in thin sheets of salt pork, overlapped and molded snugly. Barber tied the package with flaxen cord and then hung it over the fire on a spit.

Rob practiced his juggling near enough to the fire so that the smells were a sweet torment. The heat of the flames drew the grease from the pork, basting the lean meat while the fat in the stuffing melted slowly and anointed the bird from within. As Barber turned the swan on the green branch that served as a spit, the thin skin of pork gradually dried and seared; when finally the bird was done and he removed it, the salt pork crackled and broke away. Inside, the swan was moist and delicate, slightly stringy but nicely larded and seasoned. They ate some of the flesh with the hot chestnut stuffing and boiled new squash. Rob had a great pink thigh.

Next morning they rose early and pushed hard, buoyed by the day of rest. They stopped for breakfast by the side of the track and enjoyed some of the swan's breast cold with their toasted bread and cheese. When they had finished eating, Barber belched and gave Rob a third wooden ball, painted green.

They moved like ants across the lowlands. The Cotswold Hills were gentle and rolling, beautiful in their summer softness. The villages nestled in the valleys, with more stone houses than Rob had been accustomed to seeing in London. Three days after St. Swithin's Day he was ten years old. He made no mention of it to Barber.

He was growing; the sleeves of the shirt Mam had sewn purposely long now ended well above his knobby wrists. Barber worked him hard. He performed most of the chores, loading and unloading the wagon at every town and village, hauling firewood and fetching water. His body was making bone and muscle of the fine rich food that kept Barber massively round. He had become quickly accustomed to wonderful food.

Rob and Barber were getting used to each other's ways. Now when the fat man brought a woman to the campfire it was no novelty; sometimes Rob listened to the sounds of humping and tried to see, but usually he turned over and went to sleep. If the circumstances were right, on occasion Barber spent the night in a woman's house, but he was always at the wagon when morning came and it was time to leave a place.

Gradually there grew in Rob an understanding that Barber tried to cosset every woman he saw and did the same to the people who watched his entertainments. The barber-surgeon told them the Universal Specific was an Eastern physick, made by infusing the ground dried flower of a plant called Vitalia which was found only in the deserts of far-off Assyria. Yet when they ran low on the Specific, Rob helped Barber to mix up a new batch and he saw that the physick was mostly everyday liquor.

They didn't have to inquire more than half a dozen times before finding a farmer with a keg of metheglin he was happy to sell. Any variety would have served, but Barber said he always tried to find metheglin, a mixture of fermented honey and water. "It's a Welsh invention, chappy, one of the few things they've given us. Named from *meddyg*, their word for physician, and *llyn*, meaning strong liquor. It is their way of taking medicine and it is a good one, for metheglin numbs the tongue and warms the soul."

Vitalia, the Herb of Life from far-off Assyria, turned out to be a pinch of niter, stirred well into each gallon of metheglin by Rob. It gave the strong spirits a medicinal bite, softened by the sweetness of the fermented honey that was its base.

The flasks were small. "Buy a keg cheap, sell a flask dear," Barber said. "Our place is with the lower classes and the poor. Above us are the surgeons, who charge fatter fees and sometimes will throw the likes of us a dirty job they don't wish to soil their own hands on, like tossing a bit of rotten meat to a cur! Above *that* sorry lot are the ruddy physicians, who are full of importance and cater to gentlefolk because they charge most of all.

"Do you ever wonder why this Barber doesn't trim beards or cut hair? It's because I can afford to choose my tasks. For here's a lesson, and learn it well, apprentice: By mixing a proper physick and selling it diligently, a barber-surgeon can make as much money as a physician. Should all else fail, that is all you would have to know."

When they were through mixing the physick for sale, Barber got out a smaller pot and made some more. Then he fumbled with his clothing. Rob stood transfixed and watched the stream tinkle into the Universal Specific.

"My Special Batch," Barber said silkily, milking himself.

"Day after tomorrow we'll be in Oxford. The reeve there, name of Sir John Fitts, charges me dear in order not to run me out of the county. In a fortnight we'll be in Bristol, where a tavern-keeper named Potter always utters loud insults during my entertainments. I try to have suitable small gifts ready for men such as these."

When they reached Oxford, Rob didn't disappear to practice with his colored balls. He waited and watched until the reeve appeared in his filthy satin tunic, a long, thin man with sunken cheeks and a perpetual cold smile that seemed prompted by some private amusement. Rob saw Barber pay the bribe and then, in reluctant afterthought, offer the bottle of metheglin.

The reeve opened the flask and drank its contents down. Rob waited for him to gag and spit and shout for their immediate arrest, but Lord Fitts finished the final drop and smacked his lips.

"Adequate tipple."

"Thank you, Sir John."

"Give me several flasks to carry home."

Barber sighed, as if put upon. "Of course, my lord."

The pissy bottles were scratched to mark them as different from the undiluted metheglin, and kept separate in a corner of the wagon; but Rob didn't dare to drink any honey liquor for fear of making a mistake. The existence of the Special Batch made all metheglin nauseating, perhaps saving him from becoming a drunkard at an early age.

Juggling three balls was wickedly hard. He worked at it for weeks without great success. He started by holding two balls in his right hand and one in his left. Barber told him to begin by juggling two balls in one hand, as he had already learned. When the moment seemed right, he popped the third ball in the same rhythm. Two balls would go up together, then one, then two, then one . . . The lone ball bobbing between the other two made a pretty picture, but it wasn't real juggling. Whenever he tried a crossover toss with the three balls he met with disaster.

He practiced every possible moment. At night in his sleep he saw colored balls dancing through the air, light as birds. When he was awake he tried to pop them like that but he quickly ran into trouble.

They were in Stratford when he got the knack. He could see nothing different in the way that he popped or caught. He had simply found the rhythm; the three balls seemed to rise naturally from his hands and return as if part of him.

Barber was pleased. "It's my natal day, and you have given me a fine gift," he said. To celebrate both events they went to market and bought a joint of young venison, which Barber boiled, larded, seasoned with mint and sorrel, and then roasted in beer with small carrots and sugar pears. "When is your birth day?" he asked as they ate.

"Three days after Swithin's."

"But it is past! And you made no mention of it."

He didn't answer.

Barber looked at him and nodded. Then he sliced more meat and heaped it on Rob's plate.

That evening Barber took him to the public house in Stratford. Rob drank sweet cider but Barber downed new ale and sang a song celebrating it. He had no great voice but he could carry a tune. When he was finished there was applause and the thumping of mugs on tables. Two women sat alone in a corner, the only women there. One was young and stout and blond. The other was thin and older, with gray in her brown hair. "More!" the older one cried boldly.

"Mistress, you are insatiable," Barber called. He threw back his head and sang:

> *"Here's a merry new song of a ripe widow's wooing,*
> *She bedded a scoundrel to her sad undoing.*
> *The man he did joss her and bounce her and toss her*
> *And stole all her gold for a general screwing!"*

The women shrieked and screamed with laughter and hid their eyes behind their hands.

Barber sent them ale and sang:

> *"Your eyes caressed me once,*
> *Your arms embrace me now . . .*
> *We'll roll together by and by*
> *So make no fruitless vow."*

Surprisingly agile for one so large, Barber danced a frenzied clog with each of the women in turn, while the men in the public house clapped their hands and shouted. He tossed and whirled the delighted women easily, for under the lard were the muscles of a dray horse. Rob fell asleep soon after Barber brought them to his table. He was dimly aware of being awakened and of the women's support as they helped Barber to lead him, stumbling, back to the camp.

When he awoke next morning the three lay beneath the wagon, tangled like great dead snakes.

He was becoming intensely interested in breasts and he stood close and studied the women. The younger had a pendulous bosom with heavy nipples set in large brown circles in which there were hairs. The older was nearly flat with little bluish dugs like a bitch's or sow's.

Barber opened one eye and watched him memorizing the women. Presently he extricated himself and patted the cross and sleepy females, waking them so he could rescue the bedding and return it to the wagon while Rob hitched the animal. He left them each the gift of a coin and a bottle of Universal Specific. Scorned by a flapping heron, he and Rob drove out of Stratford just as the sun was pinking the river.

Chapter 7

THE HOUSE ON LYME BAY

One morning when he tried to blow the Saxon horn, instead of merely a
hiss of air the full sound emerged. Soon he proudly marked their daily way
with the lonely, echoing call. As summer ended and the days grew increasingly shorter, they began to travel southwest. "I have a little house in
Exmouth," Barber told him. "I try to spend each winter on the mild coast,
for I dislike the cold."

He gave Rob a brown ball.

Juggling with four balls was not to be feared, for he already knew how
to juggle two balls in one hand, and now he juggled two balls in each. He
practiced constantly but was forbidden from juggling while traveling in the
seat of the wagon, for he often erred and Barber wearied of reining the
horse and waiting for him to clamber down and collect the balls.

Sometimes they came to a place where boys of his age splashed in a river
or laughed and frolicked, and he felt a yearning for childhood. But he was
already different from them. Had they wrestled a bear? Could they juggle
four balls? Could they blow the Saxon horn?

In Glastonbury he played the fool by juggling before an awestruck
gaggle of boys in the village churchyard while Barber performed in the
square nearby and could hear their laughter and applause. Barber was
cutting in his condemnation. "You shall not perform unless or until you
become a genuine juggler, which may or may not occur. Is this understood?"

"Yes, Barber," he said.

They finally reached Exmouth on an evening in late October. The
house was forlorn and desolate, a few minutes' walk from the sea.

"It had been a working farm, but I bought it without land and thereby
cheaply," Barber said. "The horse is stalled in the former hay barn and the
wagon goes into that shed meant for the storing of corn." A lean-to which

60

had sheltered the farmer's cow kept firewood from the elements. The dwelling was scarcely larger than the house on Carpenter's Street in London and had a thatched roof too, but instead of a smoke hole there was a large stone chimney. In the fireplace Barber had set an iron pot hanger, a tripod, a shovel, large fire irons, a cauldron, and a meat hook. Next to the fireplace was an oven, and in close proximity was an enormous bedstead. Barber had made things comfortable during past winters. There was a kneading trough, a table, a bench, a cheese cupboard, several jugs, and a few baskets.

When a fire was on the hearth, they rewarmed the remains of a ham that already had fed them all week. The ripening meat tasted strong and there was mold in the bread. It was not the master's sort of meal. "Tomorrow we must lay in provision," Barber said moodily.

Rob got the wooden balls and practiced cross-throws in the flickering light. He did well but eventually the balls ended on the floor.

Barber took a yellow ball from his bag and tossed it on the floor, where it rolled to nestle with the others.

Red, blue, brown, and green. And now yellow.

Rob thought of all the colors of the rainbow and felt himself sinking into the deepest of despairs. He stood and looked at Barber. He was aware the man could see a resistance in his eyes that had never been there before but couldn't help himself.

"How many more?"

Barber understood the question and the despair. "None. That is the last of them," he said quietly.

They worked to prepare for winter. There was enough wood but some of it needed splitting; and kindling had to be gathered, broken, and piled near the fireplace. There were two rooms in the house, one for living and one for foodstuffs. Barber knew exactly where to go to obtain the best provision. They got turnips, onions, a basket of squash. At an orchard in Exeter they picked a barrel of apples with golden skins and white flesh and carried it home in the wagon. They put up a keg of pork in brine. A neighboring farm had a smokehouse and they bought hams and mackerel and had them smoked for a fee, and then hung them with a bought quarter of mutton, high and dry against the time they would be needed. The farmer, accustomed to people who poached or produced what they ate, said wonderingly that he never had heard of a common man purchasing so much meat.

Rob hated the yellow ball. The yellow ball was his undoing.

From the start, juggling five balls felt wrong. He had to hold three balls in his right hand. In his left hand, the lower ball was pressed against his palm by his ring finger and little finger, while the top ball was cradled by his thumb, forefinger, and middle finger. In his right hand, the lower ball was held the same way, but the top ball was imprisoned between his thumb and forefinger and the middle ball was wedged between his forefinger and middle finger. He could scarcely hold them, much less juggle.

Barber tried to help. "When you juggle five, many of the rules you have learned no longer apply," he said. "Now the ball can't be popped, it must be thrown up by your fingertips. And to give you enough time to juggle all five, you must throw them very high. First you toss a ball from your right hand. Immediately a ball must leave your left hand, then your right again, then your left again and then your right, THROW–THROW–THROW– THROW–THROW! You must toss very quickly!"

When Rob tried, he found himself beneath a shower of tumbling balls. His hands stabbed at them but they fell all about him and rolled to the corners of the room.

Barber smiled. "So here is your winter's work," he said.

Their water tasted bitter because the spring behind the house was choked by a thick layer of decaying oak leaves. Rob found a wooden rake in the horse's barn and pulled out great heaps of black, sodden leaves. He dug sand from a nearby bank and spread a thick layer in the spring. When the roiled water settled, it was sweet.

Winter came fast, a strange season. Rob liked an honest winter with snow on the ground. In Exmouth that year it rained half the time, and whenever it snowed the flakes melted on the wet earth. There was no ice save for tiny needles in the water when he drew it from the spring. The wind always blew chill and dank from the sea and the little house was part of the general dampness. At night he slept in the great bed with Barber. Barber lay closer to the fire but his great bulk shed a considerable warmth.

He had come to hate juggling. He tried desperately to manage five balls but was able to catch no more than two or three. When he was holding two balls and trying to catch a third, the falling ball usually struck one of those in his hand and bounced away.

He began to undertake any activity that would keep him from practicing juggling. He took out the night soil without being told, and scrubbed the stone pot each time. He split more wood than was necessary and constantly replenished the water jug. He brushed Incitatus until the horse's gray pelt shone, and braided the beast's mane. He went through the barrel of apples one by one to cull out rotten fruit. He kept an even neater place than his mother had kept in London.

At the edge of Lyme Bay he watched the white waves batter the beach. The wind drove straight out of the churning gray sea, so raw it made his eyes water. Barber noted his shivering and hired a widowed seamstress named Editha Lipton to cut down an old tunic of his own into a warm kirtle and tight trousers for Rob.

Editha's husband and two sons had been drowned at sea in a storm that had caught them fishing. She was a full-bodied matron with a kind face and sad eyes. She quickly became Barber's woman. When he stayed with her in the town, Rob lay alone in the large bed by the fire and pretended the house was his own. Once, in a sleety gale when cold wind found its way through the cracks, Editha came to spend the night. She displaced Rob to the floor, where he clutched a wrapped hot stone, his feet bound with pieces of the seamstress's buckram. He heard her low, gentle voice. "Should not the boy come in with us, where he can be warm?"

"No," Barber said.

A short while later, as the grunting man labored on her, her hand drifted down through the darkness and rested on Rob's head as lightly as a blessing.

He lay still. By the time Barber was finished with her, her hand had been withdrawn. After that, whenever she slept in Barber's house Rob waited in the dark on the floor next to the bed, but she never touched him again.

"You don't progress," Barber said. "Pay heed. The value of my prentice is to entertain a crowd. My boy must be a juggler."

"Can I not juggle four balls?"

"An outstanding juggler can keep seven balls in the air. I know several who can handle six. I need only an ordinary juggler. But if you can't manage five balls, I'm soon to be done with you." Barber sighed. "I've had boys in number, and of all of them only three were fit to be kept. The first was Evan Carey, who learned to juggle five balls very well but had a weakness for drink. He was with me four prosperous years past apprenticeship, until he was stabbed to death in a drunken brawl in Leicester, a fool's end.

"The second was Jason Earle. He was clever, the best juggler of all. He learned my barber's trade but married the daughter of the reeve in Portsmouth and allowed his father-in-law to turn him into a proper thief and bribe collector.

"Boy before last was marvelous. Name of Gibby Nelson. He was my bloody food and drink until he caught a fever in York and died." He frowned. "The damned *last* boy was a twit. He did same as you, he could juggle four balls but couldn't get the hang of managing the fifth, and I rid myself of him in London just before I found you."

They regarded one another unhappily.

"You, now, are no twit. You're a likely chap, easy to live with, quick to do your work. But I didn't get the horse and rig, or this house or the meat hanging from its rafters, by teaching my trade to boys I can't use. You will be a juggler by springtime or I must leave you somewhere. Do you see?"

"Yes, Barber."

Some things Barber could show him. He had him juggle three apples, and the spiky stems hurt his hands. He caught them softly, yielding his hand a bit at each catch.

"Observe?" Barber said. "Because of the slight deference, an apple already held in your hand doesn't cause a second caught apple to bounce out of your grasp." He found that it worked with balls as well as apples. "You make progress," Barber said hopefully.

Christmastide crept up on them while their attention was elsewhere. Editha invited them to accompany her to church and Barber snorted. "Are we a bloody household, then?" But he made no objection when she asked if she could take just the boy.

The little wattle-and-daub country church was crowded and therefore warmer than the rest of bleak Exmouth. Rob hadn't been in a church since leaving London and nostalgically breathed the incense-and-people stink and gave himself up to the Mass, a familiar haven. Afterward the priest, who was difficult to understand because of his Dartmoor accent, told of the birth of the Saviour and of the blessed human life that ended when He was slain by the Jews, and he spoke at great length of the fallen angel Lucifer with whom Jesus eternally grapples in defense of all. Rob tried to choose a saint for special prayer but ended up addressing the purest soul his mind could conceive. *Watch over the others, please, Mam. I am fine, but help your younger children.* Yet he couldn't forbear to ask a personal request: *Please, Mam, help me to juggle five balls.*

They went directly from the church to a roast goose turning on Barber's spit, and a plum-and-onion stuffing. "If a man has goose on Christmas he'll receive money all through the year," Barber said.

Editha smiled. "I've always heard that to receive money you must eat goose on Michaelmas," she said, but didn't argue when Barber insisted it was on Christmas. He was generous with spirits and they had a jolly meal.

She wouldn't stay the night, perhaps because at Christ's birth her thoughts were with her dead husband and sons, as Rob's were elsewhere.

When she had gone home, Barber watched him clean up after their meal. "I shouldn't grow too fond of Editha," Barber said finally. "She's only a woman and we shall soon abandon her."

The sun never shone. Three weeks into the new year the unchanging grayness of the skies worked its way into their spirits. Now Barber began to drive him, insisting that he stay at his practice no matter how miserable his repeated failure. "Don't you recall how it was when you tried to juggle three balls? One moment you couldn't, and then you were able. And the same thing happened with the blowing of the Saxon horn. You must give yourself every chance to juggle five."

But no matter how many hours he kept at it, the result was the same. He came to approach the task dully, understanding even before he began that he must fail.

He knew spring would come and he wouldn't be a juggler.

He dreamed one night that Editha touched his head again and opened great thighs and showed him her cunt. When he awoke he couldn't remember what it had looked like but a strange and terrifying thing had occurred during the dream. He wiped the mess from the fur bedcover when Barber was out of the house and scrubbed it clean with wet ashes.

He was not so foolish as to suppose that Editha might wait for him to become a man and then marry him, but he thought it would improve her condition if she should gain a son. "Barber will leave," he told her one morning as she helped him carry in the wood. "Could I not stay in Exmouth and live with you?"

Something hard came into her fine eyes but she didn't look away. "I can't maintain you. To keep only myself alive, I must be half seamstress and half whore. If I had you too, I should be any man's." A stick of wood fell from the pile in her arms. She waited until he had replaced it, then she turned and went into the house.

After that she came less often and gave him only a scarce word. Finally she didn't come at all. Perhaps Barber was less interested in his pleasure, for he grew more fretful.

"Dolt!" he shouted as Rob J. dropped the balls still another time. "Use only three balls this time but throw them high, as you would in juggling all five. When the third ball is in the air, clap your hands."

Rob did so, and there was time after the handclap to catch the three balls.

"You see?" Barber said, pleased. "In the time spent clapping, you would have been able to toss up the other two balls."

But when he tried, all five collided in the air and once again there was chaos, the man cursing and balls rolling everywhere.

Suddenly, spring was short weeks away.

One night when he thought Rob was asleep, Barber came and adjusted the bearskin so it lay warm and snug under his chin. He stood over the bed and looked down at Rob for a long time. Then he sighed and moved away.

In the morning Barber took a whip from the cart. "You don't think on what you are doing," he said. Rob never had seen him whip the horse, but when he dropped the balls the lash whistled and cut his legs.

It hurt terribly; he cried out and then he began to sob.

"Pick up the balls."

He collected them and threw again with the same sorry result, and the leather slashed across his legs.

He had been beaten by his father on numerous occasions, but never with a whip.

Again and again he retrieved the five balls and tried to juggle them but couldn't. Each time he failed, the whip cut across his legs, causing him to scream.

"Pick up the balls."

"Please, Barber!"

The man's face was grim. "It's for your good. Use your head. Think on it." Although it was a cold day, Barber was sweating.

The pain did impel him to think on what he did, but he was shuddering with frantic sobbing and his muscles seemed to belong to someone else. He was worse off than ever. He stood and trembled, tears wetting his face and snot running into his mouth, as Barber lashed him. I am a Roman, he told himself. When I'm grown I'll find this man and kill him.

Barber struck him until blood showed through the legs of the new trousers Editha had sewn. Then he dropped the whip and strode from the house.

The barber-surgeon returned late that night and fell drunkenly into bed.

In the morning when he awoke his eyes were calm but he pursed his lips when he looked at Rob's legs. He heated water and used a rag to soak them free of dried blood, then he fetched a pot of bear fat. "Rub it in well," he said.

The knowledge that he'd lost his chance hurt Rob more than the cuts and the welts.

Barber consulted his charts. "I set out on Maundy Thursday and will take you as far as Bristol. It's a flourishing port and perhaps you may find a place there."

"Yes, Barber," he said in a low voice.

Barber spent a long time readying breakfast and when it was ready he lavishly dealt gruel, cheese toast, eggs and bacon. "Eat, eat," he said gruffly.

He sat and watched while Rob forced down the food.

"I'm sorry," he said. "I was a runagate boy myself and know life can be hard."

Barber spoke to him only once all the rest of the morning. "You may keep the suit of clothes," he said.

The colored balls were put away and Rob practiced no more. But Maundy Thursday was almost a fortnight away and Barber continued to work him hard, setting him to the scrubbing of the splintery floors in both rooms. Each spring at home Mam had also washed down her walls and he did that now. There was less smoke in this house than there had been in Mam's but these walls appeared never to have been washed, and there was a marked difference when he was done.

On a midafternoon the sun magically reappeared, turning the sea blue and glittery and gentling the salty air. For the first time Rob could understand why some folks chose to live in Exmouth. In the woods behind the house small green things began to finger through the wet leaf mold; he picked a potful of fern shoots and they boiled the first greens with bacon. The fishing men had ventured into the calming seas and Barber met a returning boat and bought a fearsome cod and half a dozen fish heads. He set Rob to cubing salt pork and tried the fat meat slowly in the fry pan until it was crisp. Then he brewed a soup, merging meat and fish, sliced turnip, rendered fat, rich milk, and a bit of thyme. They enjoyed it silently with a crusty warm bread, each aware that very soon Rob wouldn't be eating fare such as this.

Some of the hung mutton had turned green and Barber cut away the spoiled part and carried it into the woods. There was a fierce stench from the apple barrel, in which only a fraction of the original fruit survived. Rob tipped the barrel and emptied it, checking each pippin and setting aside the sound ones.

They felt solid and round in his hands.

Recalling how Barber had helped him to learn a soft catch by giving him apples to juggle, he popped three of them, *hup-hup-hup*.

He caught them. Then he popped them again, sending them high, and clapped his hands before they fell.

He picked up two more apples and sent all five up, but—surprise!—they collided and landed on the floor somewhat squashily. He froze, not knowing Barber's whereabouts; he was certain to be beaten again if Barber discovered him wasting food.

But there was no protest from the other room.

He began putting the sound apples back into the barrel. It had not been a bad effort, he told himself; his timing appeared to be better.

He chose five more apples of the proper size and sent them up.

This time it came very close to working, but what failed was his nerve and the fruit came crashing down as if dispersed from its tree by an autumn gale.

He retrieved the apples and sent them up again. He was all over the place and it was herky-jerky instead of smooth and lovely, but this time the five objects went up and came down into his hands and were sent up again as though they were only three.

Up and down and up and down. Over and over again.

"Oh, Mam," he said shakily, although years later he would debate with himself over whether she had anything to do with it.

Hup-hup-hup-hup-hup!

"Barber," he said loudly, afraid to shout.

The door opened. A moment later he lost the whole thing and there were falling apples everywhere.

When he looked up he cringed, for Barber was rushing at him with his hand raised.

"I saw it!" Barber cried, and Rob found himself in a joyous hug that compared favorably to the best efforts of Bartram the bear.

Chapter 8

THE ENTERTAINER

Maundy Thursday came and went and they remained in Exmouth, for Rob had to be trained in all aspects of the entertainment. They worked on team juggling, which he enjoyed from the start and quickly came to perform exceedingly well. Then they moved to legerdemain, magic equal in difficulty to four-ball juggling.

"The Devil doesn't license magicians," Barber said. "Magic is a human art, to be mastered the way you conquered juggling. But it is much easier," he added hastily, seeing Rob's face.

Barber gave him the simple secrets of white magic. "You must have a bold and audacious spirit and put a confident face on anything you do. You require nimble fingers and a clean manner of work, and must hide behind a patter, using exotic words to adorn your actions.

"The final rule is by far the most important. You must have devices, gestures of the body, and other diversions that will cause the spectators to *look anywhere but at what you are truly doing.*"

The finest diversion they had was one another, Barber said, and used the ribbon trick to demonstrate. "For this I need ribbons of blue, red, black, yellow, green, and brown. At the end of every yard I tie a slip knot, and then I roll the knotted ribbon tightly, making small coils that are distributed throughout my clothing. The same color is always kept in the same pocket.

" 'Who would like a ribbon?' I ask.

" 'Oh, I, sirrah! A blue ribbon, two yards in length.' They seldom ask for longer. They do not use ribbon to tether the cow.

"I appear to forget the request, going on to other matters. Then *you* create a bit of flash, perhaps by juggling. While you have their eyes I go to this left tunic pocket, where blue is always kept. I appear to cover a cough with my hand, and the coil of ribbon is in my mouth. In a moment, when their attention again is on me, I discover the ribbon's end between my lips

69

and pull it, bit by bit. When the first knot reaches my teeth, it slips. When the second knot arrives I know I am at two yards, and I cut the ribbon and present it."

Rob was delighted to learn the trick yet let down by the unlovely manipulation, feeling cheated of the magic.

Barber continued to disillusion him. Soon, if he wasn't yet passing fine as a magician, he did yeoman's work as a magician's helper. He learned little dances, hymns and songs, jokes and stories he didn't understand. Finally, he magpied the speeches that went with the selling of the Universal Specific. Barber declared him a swift learner. Well before his boy thought it possible, the barber-surgeon declared that he was ready.

They left on a foggy April morning and made their way through the Blackdown Hills for two days in a light spring rain. On the third afternoon, under a sky turned clear and new, they reached the village of Bridgeton. Barber halted the horse by the bridge that gave the place its name and appraised him. "Are you all set, then?"

He wasn't certain, but nodded.

"There's a good chap. It's not much of a town. Whoremongers and trulls, a busy public house, and a good many customers who come from far and wide to get at both. So anything's allowed, eh?"

Rob had no idea what that meant, but he nodded again. Incitatus responded to the reins and pulled them across the bridge at a promenade trot. At first it was as it had been before. The horse pranced and Rob pounded the drum as they paraded the main street. He set up the bank on the village square and carried three oak-splint baskets of the Specific onto it.

But this time, when the entertainment began he bounded onto the bank with Barber.

"Good day and good morrow," Barber said. They both began to juggle two balls. "We're comforted to be in Bridgeton."

Simultaneously each took a third ball from his pocket, then a fourth and a fifth. Rob's were red, Barber's blue; they flowed up from their hands in the center and cascaded down on the outside like water in two fountains. Their hands moving only inches, they made the wooden balls dance.

Eventually they turned and faced each other on opposite sides of the bank as they juggled. Without missing a beat, Rob sent a ball to Barber and caught a blue one that had been thrown to him. First he sent every third ball to Barber and received every third ball in return. Then every other ball, a steady two-way stream of red and blue missiles. After an almost imperceptible nod from Barber, every time a ball reached Rob's right hand he sent it hard and fast, retrieving as deftly as he threw.

The applause was the loudest and best sound he'd ever heard.

Following the finish he took ten of the twelve balls and left the stage, seeking refuge behind the curtain in the wagon. He was gulping for air, his heart pounding. He could hear Barber, who was not perceptively short of breath, speaking of the joys of juggling as he popped two balls. "Do you know what you have when you hold objects such as these in your hand, Mistress?"

"What is that, sirrah?" asked a trull.

"His complete and perfect attention," Barber said.

The reveling crowd hooted and yelped.

In the wagon Rob prepared the trappings for several pieces of magic and then rejoined Barber, who consequently caused an empty basket to blossom with paper roses, changed a somber kerchief into an array of colored flags, snatched coins out of thin air, and made first a flagon of ale and then a hen's egg to disappear.

Rob sang "The Rich Widow's Wooing" to delighted catcalls, and then Barber quickly sold out his Universal Specific, emptying the three baskets and sending Rob into the wagon for more. Thereupon a long line of patients waited to be treated for numerous ailments, for although the loose crowd was quick to jape and laugh, Rob noted they were extremely serious when it came to seeking cures for the illnesses of their bodies.

As soon as the doctoring was done, they made their way out of Bridgeton, for Barber said it was a sink where throats would be slit after dark. The master was obviously satisfied with their receipts, and Rob settled into sleep that night cherishing the knowledge that he had secured a place in the world.

Next day in Yeoville, to his mortification he dropped three balls during the performance, but Barber was comforting. "It's bound to happen on occasion in the beginning," he said. "It will occur less and less frequently and finally not at all."

Later that week in Taunton, a town of hardworking tradesmen, and in Bridgwater, where there were conservative farmers, they presented their entertainment without bawdiness. Glastonbury was their next stop, a place of pious folk who had built their homes around the large and beautiful Church of St. Michael.

"We must be discreet," Barber said. "Glastonbury is controlled by priests, and priests look with loathing upon all manner of medical practice, for they believe God has given them sacred charge of men's bodies as well as their souls."

They arrived the morning after Whit Sunday, the day that marked the

end of the joyous Easter season and commemorated the descent of the Holy
Ghost upon the apostles, strengthening them after their nine days of prayer
following the ascension of Jesus into Heaven.

Rob noted no fewer than five unjoyous priests among the spectators.

He and Barber juggled red balls, which Barber, in solemn tones, likened
to the tongues of fire representing the Holy Spirit in Acts 2:3. The spectators were delighted with the juggling and applauded lustily, but they fell
silent as Rob sang "All Glory, Laud and Honor." He had always liked to
sing; his voice cracked at the part about the children making "sweet hosan-
nas ring" and it quavered on the very high notes, but he did fine once his
legs stopped jiggling.

Barber brought out holy relics in a battered ash-wood chest. "Pay
attention, dear friends," he said in what he later told Rob was his monk's
voice. He showed them earth and sand carried to England from Mounts
Sinai and Olivet; held up a sliver of the Holy Rood and a piece of the beam
that had supported the holy manger; displayed water from the Jordan, a
clod from Gethsemane, and bits of bone belonging to saints without number.

Then Rob replaced him on the bank and stood alone. Lifting his eyes
heavenward, as Barber had instructed, he sang another hymn.

> *"Creator of the Stars of Night,*
> *Thy people's everlasting light,*
> *Jesu, Redeemer, save us all,*
> *And hear thy servants when they call.*
>
> *Thou, grieving that the ancient curse*
> *Should doom to death a universe,*
> *Hast found the medicine, full of grace,*
> *To save and heal a ruined race."*

The spectators were moved. While they were still sighing, Barber was
holding out a flask of the Universal Specific. "Friends," he said. "Just as the
Lord has found the medicine for your spirit, I have found the medicine for
your body."

He told them the story about Vitalia the Herb of Life, which obviously
worked equally well with the pious as with sinners, for they bought the
Specific greedily and then lined up by the barber-surgeon's screen for
consultations and treatment. The watching priests glowered but had been
sweetened with gifts and soothed by the religious display, and only one old
cleric made objection. "You shall do no bleeding," he commanded sternly.

"For Archbishop Theodore has written that it is dangerous to bleed at a time when the light of the moon and the pull of the tides is increasing." Barber was quick to agree.

They camped in jubilation that afternoon. Barber boiled bite-sized pieces of beef in wine until tender and added onion, an old turnip that was wrinkled but sound, and new peas and beans, flavoring all with thyme and a bit of mint. There was still a wedge of an exceptional light-colored cheese bought in Bridgwater, and afterward he sat by the fire and with obvious gratification counted the contents of his cash box.

It was perhaps the moment to broach a subject that lay heavy and constant on Rob's spirit.

"Barber," he said.

"Hmmm?"

"Barber, when shall we go to London?"

Intent on stacking the coins, Barber waved his hand, not wishing to lose count. "By and by," he murmured. "In the by-and-by."

Chapter 9

THE GIFT

Rob mishandled four balls in Kingswood. He dropped another ball in Mangotsfield but that was the last time, and after they offered diversion and treatment to the villagers of Redditch in mid-June he no longer spent hours every day practicing his juggling, for the frequent entertainments kept his fingers supple and his sense of rhythm alive. He quickly became an assured juggler. He suspected that eventually he could have learned to manage six balls but Barber would have none of that, preferring that he use his time assisting in the barber-surgeon's trade.

They traveled north like migrating birds, but instead of flying they wended their way slowly through the mountains between England and Wales. They were in the town of Abergavenny, a row of rickety houses leaning against the side of a sullen shale ridge, when for the first time he aided Barber in the examinations and treatment.

Rob J. was afraid. He had more fear in him than the wooden balls had inspired.

The reasons people ailed were such a mystery. It seemed impossible for a mere man to understand and offer helpful miracles. He knew Barber was smarter than any man he had ever known, to be able to do that.

The people lined up in front of the screen, and he fetched them one by one as soon as Barber had finished with the preceding person, and led them to the partial privacy afforded by the flimsy barrier. The first man Rob took back to his master was large and stooped, with traces of black on his neck and ingrained in his knuckles and under his fingernails.

"You could do with a wash," Barber suggested, not unkindly.

"It's the coal, you see," the man said. "The dust sticks when it is dug."

"You dig coal?" Barber said. "I've heard it's poison to burn. I've seen at first hand that it produces a stink and heavy smoke that doesn't readily rise through the smoke hole of a house. Is there a living in such poor stuff?"

"It is there, sir, and we are poor. But lately there are aches and swellings in my joints, and it pains me to dig."

Barber touched the grimy wrists and fingers, poked a pudgy fingertip into the swelling at the man's elbow. "It comes from inhaling humors from the earth. You must sit in the sun when you can. Bathe frequently in warm water but not hot, for hot baths lead to a weakness of the heart and limbs. Rub your swollen and painful joints with my Universal Specific, which you may take internally with profit as well."

He charged the man sixpence for three small flagons and another tuppence for the consultation, and didn't look at Rob.

A stout, tight-lipped woman came with her thirteen-year-old daughter who was betrothed to wed. "Her monthly blood is stopped up within her body and never flows," the mother said.

Barber asked if she had ever had a blood period. "For more than a year they came every month," the mother said. "But for five months now, nothing."

"Have you lain with a man?" Barber asked the girl gently.

"No," the mother said.

Barber looked at the girl. She was slim and comely, with long blond hair and watchful eyes. "Do you vomit?"

"No," she whispered.

He studied her, and then his hand went out and tightened her gown. He took her mother's palm and pressed it against the small round belly.

"No," the girl said again. She shook her head. Her cheeks became bright and she began to weep.

Her mother's hand left her stomach and smashed across her face. The woman led her daughter away without paying, but Barber let them go.

In rapid succession he treated a man whose leg had been ill-set eight years before and who dragged his left foot when he walked; a woman plagued by headache; a man with scabies of the scalp; and a stupid, smiling girl with a terrible sore on her breast who told them she had been praying to God for a barber-surgeon to come through their town.

He sold the Universal Specific to everyone except the man with scabies, who didn't buy though it was strongly recommended to him; perhaps he didn't have the tuppence.

They moved into the softer hills of the West Midlands. Outside the village of Hereford, Incitatus had to wait by the River Wye while sheep poured through the ford, a seemingly endless stream of bleating fleece that thoroughly intimidated Rob. He would have liked to be more at ease with animals, but though his Mam had come from a farm, he was a city boy. Tatus was the only horse he had handled. A distant neighbor on Carpenter's Street had kept a milch cow, but none of the Coles had spent much time near sheep.

Hereford was a prosperous community. Each farm they passed had a hog wallow and green rolling meadows flecked with sheep and cattle. The stone houses and barns were large and solid and the people generally more cheerful than the poverty-burdened Welsh hillsmen only a few days' distance. On the village green their entertainment drew a good crowd and sales were brisk.

Barber's first patient behind the screen was about Rob's own age, although much smaller in build. "Fell from the roof not six days past, and look at him," said the boy's father, a cooper. A splintered barrel stave on the ground had pierced the palm of his left hand and now the flesh was angry as a puffed-up blowfish.

Barber showed Rob how to grasp the boy's hands and the father how to grip his legs and then he took a short, sharp knife from his kit.

"Hold him fast," he said.

Rob could feel the hands trembling. The boy screamed as his flesh parted under the blade. A greenish-yellow pus spurted, followed by a stink and a red welling.

Barber swabbed the wound free of corruption and proceeded to probe into it with delicate efficiency, using an iron tweezers to pull out tiny slivers. "It's bits from the piece that damaged him, you see?" he said to the parent, showing him.

The boy groaned. Rob felt queasy but held on while Barber proceeded with slow care. "We must get them all," he said, "for they contain peccant humors that will mortify the hand again."

When he was satisfied the wound was free of wood, he poured some Specific into it and bound it in a cloth, then drank the rest of the flask himself. The sobbing patient slipped away, happy to leave them while his father paid.

Waiting next was a bent old man with a hollow cough. Rob ushered him behind the screen.

"Morning phlegm. Oh, a great deal, sir!" He gasped when he talked.

Barber ran his hand thoughtfully over the skinny chest. "Well. I shall cup you." He looked at Rob. "Help him to disrobe partially, so his chest may be cupped."

Rob removed the old man's shirtwaist gingerly, for he appeared fragile. To turn the patient back toward the barber-surgeon, he took both of the man's hands.

It was like grasping a pair of quivering birds. The sticklike fingers sat in his own, and from them he received a message.

Glancing at them, Barber saw the boy stiffen. "Come," he said impatiently. "We mustn't take all day." Rob didn't seem to hear.

Twice before Rob had felt this strange and unwelcome awareness slip into his very being from someone else's body. Now, as on each of the previous occasions, he was overwhelmed by an absolute terror, and he dropped the patient's hands and fled.

Barber searched, cursing, until he found his apprentice cowering behind a tree.

"I want the meaning. And *now!*"

"He . . . The old man is going to die."

Barber stared. "What kind of poor shit is this?"

His apprentice had begun to cry.

"Stop that," Barber said. "How do you know?"

Rob tried to speak but couldn't. Barber slapped his face and he gasped. When he began to talk the words poured, for they had been roiling over and around in his mind since before they had left London.

He had felt his mother's impending death and it had happened, he explained. And then he had known his father was going, and his father had died.

"Oh, dear Jesus," Barber said in disgust.

But he listened carefully, watching Rob. "You tell me you actually felt death in that old man?"

"Yes." He had no expectation of being believed.

"When?"

He shrugged.

"Soon?"

He nodded. He could only, hopelessly, tell the truth.

He saw in Barber's eyes that the man recognized this.

Barber hesitated and then made up his mind. "While I rid us of the people, pack the cart," he said.

They left the village slowly but once out of sight drove as fast as they dared over the rough track. Incitatus pounded through the river ford with a great noisy splashing and, just beyond, scattered sheep, whose frightened bleating almost drowned out the roar of the outraged shepherd.

For the first time Rob saw Barber use the whip on the horse. "Why are we running?" he called, holding on.

"Do you know what they do to witches?" Barber had to shout above the drumming of the hooves and the clattering of the things inside the wagon.

Rob shook his head.

"They hang them from a tree or from a cross. Sometimes they submerge suspects in your fucking Thames and if they drown they are declared innocent. If the old man dies, they'll say it is because we are witches," he bawled, bringing the whip down again and again on the back of the terrified horse.

They didn't stop to eat or relieve themselves. By the time they allowed Tatus to slow, Hereford was far behind, but they pushed the poor beast until daylight was gone. Exhausted, they made their camp and ate a poor meal in silence.

"Tell it again," Barber said at last. "Leaving nothing out."

He listened intently, interrupting only once to ask Rob to speak louder. When he had gotten the boy's story he nodded. "In my own apprenticeship, I witnessed my barber-surgeon master wrongfully slain for a witch," he said.

Rob stared at him, too frightened to ask questions.

"Several times during my lifetime, patients have died while I treated them. Once in Durham an old woman passed away and I was certain a priestly court would order trial by immersion or by the holding of a white-hot iron bar. I was allowed to leave only after the most suspicious interrogation, fasting, and almsgiving. Another time in Eddisbury a man died while behind my screen. He was young and apparently had been in health. Troublemakers would have had fertile ground but I was fortunate and no one barred my way when I took to the road."

Rob found his voice. "Do you think I've been . . . touched by the Devil?" It was a question that had plagued him all through the day.

Barber snorted. "If you believe so, you're foolish and a twit. And I know you to be neither." He went to the wagon and filled his horn with metheglin, drinking it all before speaking again.

"Mothers and fathers die. And old people die. That's the nature of it. You're certain you felt something?"

"Yes, Barber."

"Can't be mistook or fancying, a young chap like you?"

Rob shook his head stubbornly.

"And I say it was all a notion," Barber said. "So we've had enough of fleeing and talking and must gain our rest."

They made their beds on either side of the fire. But they lay for hours without sleeping. Barber tossed and turned and presently got up and opened another flask of liquor. He brought it around to Rob's side of the fire and squatted on his heels.

"Supposing," he said, and took a drink. "Just *suppose* everyone else in the world had been born without eyes. And you were born with eyes?"

"Then I would see what no one else could see."

Barber drank and nodded. "Yes. Or imagine that we had no ears and you had ears? Or suppose we didn't have some other sense? And somehow, from God or nature or what you will, you've been given a . . . special gift. Just *suppose* that you can tell when someone is going to die?"

Rob was silent, terribly frightened again.

"It's bullshit, we both comprehend that," Barber said. "It was all your fancy, we agree. But just *supposing* . . . " He sucked thoughtfully from the flask, his Adam's apple working, the dying firelight glinting warmly in his hopeful eyes as he regarded Rob J. "It would be a sin not to exercise such a gift," he said.

In Chipping Norton they bought metheglin and mixed another batch of Specific, replenishing the lucrative supply.

"When I die and stand in line before the gate," Barber said, "St. Peter shall ask, 'How did you earn your bread?' 'I was a farmer,' one man may say, or 'I fashioned boots from skins.' But I shall answer, *'Fumum vendidi,'*" the former monk said gaily, and Rob's Latin was equal to the task: *I sold smoke.*

Yet the fat man was far more than a peddler of questionable physick. When he treated behind the screen he was skillful and often tender. What Barber knew to do, he knew and did perfectly, and he taught Rob a sure touch and gentle hand.

In Buckingham, Barber showed him how to pull teeth, having the good fortune to come upon a drover with a rotting mouth. The patient was as fat as Barber, a pop-eyed groaner and womanly screamer. Midway, he changed his mind. "Stop, stop, stop! Set me free!" he lisped bloodily, but there was no question that the teeth needed pulling, and they persevered; it was an excellent lesson.

In Clavering, Barber rented the blacksmith's shop for a day and Rob learned how to fashion the lancing irons and points. It was a task he would have to repeat in half a dozen smithies all over England during the next several years before he satisfied his master he could do it correctly. Most of his work in Clavering was rejected, but Barber grudgingly allowed him to keep a small two-edged lancet as the first instrument in his own kit of surgical tools, an important beginning. As they made their way out of the Midlands and into the Fens, Barber taught him which veins were opened for bleeding, bringing him unpleasant memories of his father's last days.

His father sometimes crept into his mind, for his own voice was beginning to sound like his father's; its timbre deepened, and he was growing body hair. The patches weren't as thick as they would become, he knew, for through helping Barber he was quite familiar with the unclothed male. Women remained more of a mystery, since Barber employed an enigmatically smiling, voluptuous doll they called Thelma, on whose naked plaster form females modestly indicated the area of their own affliction, making examination unnecessary. It still made Rob uneasy to intrude into the privacy of strangers, but he became accustomed to casual inquiry about bodily function:

"When were you last at stool, master?"

"Mistress, when shall you have your monthly flow?"

At Barber's suggestion Rob took each patient's hands into his own when the patient came behind the screen.

"What do you feel when you grasp their fingers?" Barber asked him one day in Tisbury as he dismantled the bank.

"Sometimes I don't feel anything."

Barber nodded. He took one of the sections from Rob and stowed it in the wagon and came back, frowning. "But sometimes . . . there is *something?*"

Rob nodded.

"Well, what?" Barber said testily. "*What* is it you feel, boy?"

But he couldn't define it or describe it in words. It was an intuition about the person's vitality, like peering into dark wells and sensing how much life each contained.

Barber took Rob's silence as proof that the feeling was imagined. "I think we'll return to Hereford and see whether the old man has not continued to exist in health," he said slyly.

He was annoyed when Rob agreed. "We can't go back, you dolt!" he said. "For if he's indeed dead, shouldn't we be putting our heads into the noose?"

He continued to scoff at "the gift," often and loud.

Yet when Rob began neglecting to take the patients' hands, he ordered him to resume. "Why not? Am I not a cautious man of business? And does it cost us to indulge this fancy?"

In Peterborough, only a few miles and a lifetime away from the abbey from which he had fled as a boy, Barber sat alone in the public house throughout a long and showery August evening, drinking slowly and steadily.

By midnight, his apprentice came looking for him. Rob met him reeling along the way and supported him back to their fire. "Please," Barber whispered fearfully.

He was amazed to see the drunken man lift both hands and hold them out.

"Ah, in the name of Christ, please," Barber said again.

Finally Rob understood. He took Barber's hands and looked into his eyes.

In a moment Rob nodded.

Barber sank into his bed. He belched and turned on his side, then fell into untroubled sleep.

Chapter 10

THE NORTH

That year Barber didn't make it to Exmouth in time for winter, for they had started out late and the falling leaves of autumn found them in the village of Gate Fulford, in the York Wolds. The moors were lavish with plants that made the cool air exciting with their spice. Rob and Barber followed the North Star, stopping at villages along the way to very good business, and drove the wagon through the endless carpet of purple heather until they reached the town of Carlisle.

"This is as far north as I ever travel," Barber told him. "A few hours from here Northumbria ends and the frontier begins. Beyond is Scotland, which everyone knows to be a land of sheep-buggers, and perilous to honest Englishmen."

For a week they camped in Carlisle and went every evening to the tavern, where judiciously bought drinks soon resulted in Barber's learning about available shelter. He rented a house on the moor with three small rooms. It was not unlike the little house he owned on the southern coast but lacked a fireplace and a stone chimney, to his displeasure. They spread their beds on either side of the hearth as if it were a campfire, and they found a nearby stable willing to board Incitatus. Once again Barber bought winter's provision lavishly, in the easy manner with money that never failed to give Rob a wondering sense of well-being.

Barber laid in beef and pork. He had thought to buy a haunch of venison, but three market hunters had been hanged in Carlisle during the summer for killing the king's deer, which were reserved for nobles' sport. So they bought fifteen fat hens instead, and a sack of feed.

"The chickens are your domain," Barber told Rob. "They are yours to feed, to slaughter upon my request, to dress and pluck and ready for my pot."

He thought the hens were impressive creatures, large and buff-colored, with unfeathered shanks and red combs, wattles, and earlobes. They made no objection when he robbed their nests of four or five white eggs every morning. "They think you're a big bloody rooster," Barber said.

"Why don't we buy them a chanticleer?"

Barber, who liked sleeping late on cold winter mornings and therefore hated crowing, merely grunted.

Rob had brown hairs on his face, not exactly a beard. Barber said only Danes shaved but he knew it wasn't true, for his father had kept his face hairless. In Barber's surgical kit was a razor and the fat man nodded grumpily when Rob asked to use it. He nicked his face, but shaving made him feel older.

The first time Barber ordered him to kill a chicken made him feel very young. Each bird stared at him out of little black beads that told him they might have grown to be friends. Finally he forced his strong fingers to clench around the nearest warm neck and, shuddering, closed his eyes. A strong, convulsive twist and it was done. But the bird punished him in death, for it didn't easily relinquish its feathers. Plucking took hours, and the grizzled corpse was viewed with disdain when he handed it to Barber.

Next time a chicken was called for, Barber showed him genuine magic. He held the hen's beak open and slid a thin knife through the roof of the mouth and into the brain. The hen relaxed at once into death, releasing the feathers; they came away in great clumps at the slightest pull.

"Here is the lesson," Barber said. "It is just as easy to bring death to man, and I've done so. It's harder to keep hold of life, harder still to maintain a grasp on health. Those are the tasks to which we must keep our minds."

The late fall weather was perfect for the picking of herbs, and they scoured the woods and moors. Barber especially wanted purslane; steeped in the Specific, it produced an agent that would cause fevers to break and dissipate. To his disappointment, they found none. Some things were more easily gathered, such as red rose petals for poultices, and thyme and acorns to be powdered and mixed with fat and spread on neck pustules. Others required hard work, like the digging of yew root that would help a pregnant woman to hold back her fetus. They collected lemon grass and dill for urinary problems, marshy sweet flag to fight deterioration of memory because of moist and cold humors, juniper berries to be boiled for opening blocked nasal passages, lupine for hot packs to draw abscesses, and myrtle and mallow to soothe itchy rashes.

"You've grown faster than these weeds," Barber observed wryly, and it was true; already he stood almost as tall as Barber and he had long since outstripped the clothing Editha Lipton had made for him in Exmouth. But when Barber took him to a Carlisle tailor and ordered "new winter clothes that will fit for a while," the tailor shook his head.

"The boy still grows, does he not? Fifteen, sixteen years? Such a lad outgrows clothing quickly."

"Sixteen! He's not yet eleven!"

The man looked at Rob with respect-tinged amusement. "He'll be a *large* man! And he's certain to make my raiment appear to shrink. May I suggest that we make over an old garment?"

So another suit of Barber's, this one of mostly-good gray stuff, was recut and sewn. To their general hilarity it was far too wide when first Rob put it on, yet much too short in the arms and the legs. The tailor took some of the material left over from the width and extended the pants and the sleeves, hiding the joined seams with rakish bands of blue cloth. Rob had gone without shoes most of the summer but soon the snows were due, and he was grateful when Barber bought him boots made of cowhide.

He walked in them across Carlisle's square to the Church of St. Mark and sounded the knocker on its great wooden doors, which were opened at length by an elderly curate with rheumy eyes.

"If you please, Father, I seek a priest name of Ranald Lovell."

The curate blinked. "I knew a priest so named, served the Mass under Lyfing, in the time when Lyfing was Bishop of Wells. He is dead these ten years come Easter."

Rob shook his head. "It's not the same priest. I saw Father Ranald Lovell with my own eyes but several years ago."

"Perhaps the man I knew was Hugh Lovell and not Ranald."

"Ranald Lovell was transferred from London to a church in the north. He has my brother, William Stewart Cole. Three years younger than I."

"Your brother by now may have a different name in Christ, my son. Priests sometimes bring their boys to an abbey, to become acolytes. You must ask others everywhere. For Holy Mother Church is a great and boundless sea and I am but a single tiny fish." The old priest nodded kindly and Rob helped him to close the doors.

A skin of crystals dulled the surface of the small pond behind the town tavern. Barber pointed out a pair of ice gliders tied to a rafter of their little house. "Pity they aren't larger. They won't fit, for you have an uncommonly great foot."

The ice thickened daily, until one morning it gave back a solid thunk when he walked out to the middle and stamped. Rob took down the too-small gliders. They were carved from stag antler and were almost identical to a pair his father had made for him when he was six years old. He had quickly outgrown those but had used them for three winters anyway, and now he took these to the pond and tied them onto his feet. At first he used them with pleasure, but their edges were nicked and dull and their size and condition did him in during his first attempt to turn. His arms flailing, he fell heavily and slid a good distance.

He became aware of someone's amusement.

The girl was perhaps fifteen years old. She was laughing with great enjoyment.

"Can you do better?" he said hotly, at the same time acknowledging to himself that she was a pretty dolly, too thin and top-heavy but with black hair like Editha's.

"I?" she said. "Why, I cannot, and would never have the courage."

At once his temper disappeared. "They were meant more for your feet than mine," he said. He stripped them off and carried them to where she stood on the bank. "It's not at all difficult. Let me show you," he said.

He quickly overcame her objections and soon was fastening the runners to her feet. She couldn't stand on the unaccustomed slickness of the ice and clutched at him, alarm widening her brown eyes and causing her thin nostrils to flare. "Don't fear, I have you," he said. He supported her weight and propelled her along the ice from behind, conscious of her warm haunches.

Now she was laughing and squealing as he pushed her around and around the pond. She was Garwine Talbott, she said. Her father, Aelfric Talbott, had a farm outside the town. "What is your name?"

"Rob J."

She chattered, revealing a store of information about him, for it was a small town; she already knew when he and Barber had come to Carlisle, their profession, the provision they had bought, and whose house they had taken.

She soon liked being on the ice. Her eyes gleamed with pleasure and the cold turned her cheeks ruddy. Her hair flew back, revealing a small pink earlobe. She had a thin upper lip but her lower lip was so ripe it appeared almost swollen. There was a faded bruise high on her cheek. When she smiled, he saw that one of her lower teeth was crooked. "You examine people, then?"

"Yes, of course."

"Women as well?"

"We have a doll. Women point out areas of their ailment."

"What a pity," she said, "to use a doll." He was dazzled by her sidelong glance. "Does she have a fine appearance?"

Not so fine as yours, he wished to say but lacked the courage. He shrugged. "She is called Thelma."

"Thelma!" She had a breathless, ragged laugh that made him grin. "Eh," she cried, glancing up to see where the sun stood. "I must get back there for late milking," and her soft fullness leaned into his arm.

He knelt before her on the bank and removed the gliders. "They are not mine. They were in the house," he said. "But you may keep them for a while and use them."

She shook her head quickly. "If I bring them home he would near kill me, wanting to learn what things I did to get them."

He felt a rush of blood to his face. To escape his embarrassment he picked up three pine cones and began juggling for her.

She laughed and clapped her hands, and then in a breathless rush of words told him how to find her father's farm. Leaving, she hesitated and turned back for a moment.

"Thursday mornings," she said. "He doesn't encourage visitors, but Thursday mornings he brings cheeses to the market."

When Thursday came he didn't seek out the farm of Aelfric Talbott. Instead he loitered fearfully in his bed, afraid not of Garwine or her father but of things that were happening within him that he couldn't comprehend, mysteries he had neither the courage nor the wisdom to confront.

He had dreamed of Garwine Talbott. In the dream they had lain in a hayloft, perhaps in her father's barn. It was the kind of dream he had had several times about Editha, and he tried to wipe his bedding without catching Barber's attention.

The snow began. It dropped like heavy goose down, and Barber lashed hides over the window holes. Inside the house the air became foul, and even by day it was impossible to see anything except right next to the fire.

It snowed four days, with only brief interruptions. Searching for things to do, Rob sat next to the hearth and fashioned pictures of their various herbs. Using charcoal sticks rescued from the fire, on bark ripped from firewood, he sketched curly mint, the limp blossoms of drying flowers, the veined leaves of the wild bean trefoil. In the afternoon he melted snow over the fire and watered and fed the chickens, being careful to swiftly open and close the door to the hens' room, for despite his cleaning the stink was becoming impressive.

Barber kept to his bed, nipping metheglin. On the second night of the snowfall he floundered his way to the public house and brought back a quiet blond trull named Helen. Rob tried to watch them from his bed on the other side of the hearth, for although he had seen the act many times he was puzzled by certain details which lately had made their way into his thoughts and dreams. But he was unable to penetrate the thick darkness and studied only their heads illuminated in the firelight. Barber was rapt and intent but the woman appeared drawn and melancholy, someone engaged in joyless work.

After she had left, Rob picked up a piece of bark and a stick of charcoal. Instead of sketching the plants he tried to shape the features of a woman.

Heading for the pot, Barber stopped to study the sketch and frowned. "I appear to know that face," he said.

A short time later, back in his bed, he lifted his head from the fur. "Why, it is Helen!"

Rob was very pleased. He tried to make a likeness of the unguent seller named Wat, but Barber could identify it only after he added the small figure of Bartram the bear. "You must continue your attempts to re-create faces, for I believe it is something that can be useful to us," Barber said. But he soon grew tired of watching Rob and went back to drinking until he slept.

On Tuesday the snow finally stopped falling. Rob wrapped his hands and head in rags and found a wooden shovel. He cleared a path from their door and went to the stables to exercise Incitatus, who was growing fat on no work and a daily ration of hay and sweet grain.

On Wednesday he helped some boys of the town shovel the snow from the surface of the pond. Barber removed the hides that covered the window holes and let cold sweet air into the house. He celebrated by roasting a joint of lamb, which he served with mint jelly and apple cakes.

Thursday morning Rob took down the ice gliders and hung them around his neck by their leather thongs. He went to the stables and put only the bridle and halter on Incitatus, then he mounted the horse and rode out of the town. The air crackled, the sun was bright and the snow pure.

He transformed himself into a Roman. It was no good pretending to be Caligula astride the original Incitatus because he was aware that Caligula had been crazy and had met an unhappy end. He decided to be Caesar Augustus, and he led the Praetorian Guard down the Via Appia all the way to Brundisium.

He had no difficulty in finding the Talbott farm. It was exactly where she had said it would be. The house was tilted and mean-looking, with a sagging roof, but the barn was large and fine. The door was open and he could hear someone moving about inside, among the animals.

He sat on the horse uncertainly, but Incitatus whinnied and he had no choice but to announce himself.

"Garwine?" he called.

A man appeared in the doorway of the barn and walked slowly toward him. He was holding a wooden fork laden with manure that steamed in the cold air. He walked very carefully and Rob could see he was drunk. He was a sallow, stooped man with an untrimmed black beard the color of Garwine's hair, who could only be Aelfric Talbott.

"Who are you?" he said.

Rob told him.

The man swayed. "Well, Rob J. Cole, you do not have luck. She isn't here. She's run off, the dirty little whore."

The shovel of dung moved slightly and Rob was certain he and the horse were about to be showered with smoking-fresh cow shit.

"Go away from my holding," Talbott said. He was crying.

Rob rode Incitatus slowly back toward Carlisle. He wondered where she had gone and if she would survive.

He was no longer Caesar Augustus leading the Praetorian Guard. He was just a boy trapped in his doubts and fears.

When he got back to the house he hung the ice gliders up on the rafter and didn't take them down again.

Chapter 11

THE JEW OF TETTENHALL

There was nothing left to do but wait for spring. New batches of the Universal Specific had been brewed and bottled. Every herb Barber had sought, except for purslane to fight fevers, had been dried and powdered or steeped in physick. They were tired of practicing juggling, weary of rehearsing magic, and Barber was sick of the north and jaded with drinking and sleeping. "I am too impatient to linger while winter peters out," he said one morning in March, and they abandoned Carlisle too early, making slow progress southward because the roads were still poor.

They met the springtime in Beverley. The air softened, the sun emerged and so did a crowd of pilgrims who had been visiting the town's great stone church dedicated to St. John the Evangelist. He and Barber threw themselves into the entertainment, and their first large audience of the new season responded with enthusiasm. All went well during the treatments until, ushering the sixth patient behind Barber's privacy screen, Rob took the soft hands of a handsome woman.

His pulse hammered. "Come, mistress," he said faintly. His skin prickled with dread where their hands were glued together. He turned and met Barber's gaze.

Barber whitened. Almost savagely, he pulled Rob away from listening ears. "Are you without doubt? You must be certain."

"She will die very soon," Rob said.

Barber returned to the woman, who wasn't old and appeared to be in good estate. She made no complaint of her health but had come behind the screen to buy a philter. "My husband is a man of increasing years. His ardor flags, yet he admires me." She spoke calmly, and her refinement and lack of false modesty gave her dignity. She wore traveling clothes sewn of fine stuff. Clearly, she was a woman of wealth.

"I don't sell philters. That is magic and not medicine, my lady."

She murmured regret. Barber was terrified when she didn't correct his form of address; to be accused of witchcraft in the death of a noblewoman was certain destruction.

"A draught of liquor often gives the desired effect. Strong, and swallowed hot before retiring." Barber would accept no payment. As soon as she was gone, he made his excuses to the patients he hadn't yet seen. Rob was already packing the wagon.

And so they fled again.

This time they barely spoke throughout the flight. When they were far enough away and safely camped for the night, Barber broke the silence.

"When someone dies in an instant, a vacantness creeps into the eyes," he said quietly. "The face loses expression, or sometimes purples. A corner of the mouth sags, an eyelid droops, limbs turn to stone." He sighed. "It isn't unmerciful."

Rob didn't answer.

They made their beds and tried to sleep. Barber rose and drank for a while but this time didn't give the apprentice his hands to hold.

Rob knew in his heart that he wasn't a witch. Yet there could be only one other explanation, and he didn't understand it. He lay and prayed. *Please. Will you not remove this filthy gift from me and return it whence it came?* Furious and dispirited, he couldn't refrain from scolding, for meekness hadn't gained him much. *It is such a thing as might be inspired by Satan and I want no further part of it,* he told God.

It seemed his prayer was granted. That spring there were no more incidents. The weather held and then improved, with sunny days that were warmer and drier than usual, and good for business. "Fine weather on St. Swithin's," Barber said one morning in triumph. "Anyone will tell you it means we'll have fine weather forty more days." Gradually their fears subsided and their spirits rose.

His master remembered his birth day! On the third morning after St. Swithin's Day, Barber made him a handsome gift of three goose quills, ink powder, and a pumice stone. "Now you may scribble faces with something other than a charcoal stick," he said.

Rob had no money to buy Barber a natal gift in return. But late one afternoon his eyes recognized a plant as they passed through a field. Next morning he stole out of their camp and walked half an hour to the field, where he picked a quantity of the greens. On Barber's birth day Rob presented him with purslane, the fever herb, which he received with obvious pleasure.

It showed in their entertainment that they got on. They anticipated each other, and their performance took on gloss and a keen edge, bringing splendid applause. Rob had daydreams in which he saw his brothers and sister among the spectators; he imagined the pride and amazement of Anne Mary and Samuel Edward when they saw their elder brother perform magic and pop five balls.

They will have grown, he told himself. Would Anne Mary recall him? Was Samuel Edward still wild? By now Jonathan Carter must be walking and talking, a proper little man.

It was impossible for an apprentice to advise his master where to direct their horse, but when they were in Nottingham he found opportunity to consult Barber's map and saw they were near the very heart of the English island. To reach London they would have to continue south but also veer to the east. He memorized the town names and locations, so he could tell if they were traveling where he so desperately wanted to go.

In Leicester a farmer digging a rock from his field had unearthed a sarcophagus. He had dug around it but it was too heavy for him to raise and its bottom remained gripped by the earth like a boulder.

"The Duke is sending men and animals to free it and will take it into his castle," the yeoman told them proudly.

There was an inscription in the coarse white-grained marble: DIIS MANI-BUS. VIVIO MARCIANO MILITI LEGIONIS SECUNDAE AUGUSTAE. IANUARIA MA-RINA CONJUNX PIENTISSIMA POSUIT MEMORIAM. " 'To the gods of the under-world,' " Barber translated. " 'To Vivius Marcianus, a soldier of the Second Legion of Augustus. In the month of January his devoted wife, Marina, established this tomb.' "

They looked at one another. "I wonder what happened to the dolly, Marina, after she buried him, for she was a long way from her home," Barber said soberly.

So are we all, Rob thought.

Leicester was a populous town. Their entertainment was well attended, and when the sale of the physick was finished they found themselves in a flurry of activity. In quick succession he helped Barber to lance a young man's carbuncle, splint a youth's rudely broken finger, and dose a feverish matron with purslane and a colicky child with chamomile. Next he led behind the screen a stocky, balding man with milky eyes.

"How long have you been blind?" Barber asked.

"These two years. It began as a dimness and gradually deepened until now I scarce detect light. I am a clerk but cannot work."

Barber shook his head, forgetting the gesture wasn't visible. "I am able to give back sight no more than I can give back youth."

The clerk allowed himself to be led away. "It's a hard piece of news," he said to Rob. "Never to see again!"

A man standing nearby, thin and hawk-faced and with a Roman nose, overheard and peered at them. His hair and beard were white but he was still young, no more than twice Rob's age.

He stepped forward and put his hand on the patient's arm. "What is your name?" He spoke with a French accent; Rob had heard it many times from Normans on the London waterfront.

"I am Edgar Thorpe," the clerk said.

"I am Benjamin Merlin, physician of nearby Tettenhall. May I look at your eyes, Edgar Thorpe?"

The clerk nodded and stood, blinking. The man lifted his eyelids with his thumbs and studied the white opacity.

"I can couch your eyes and cut away the clouded lens," he said finally. "I've done it before, but you must be strong enough to endure the pain."

"I care nothing for pain," the clerk whispered.

"Then you must have someone deliver you to my house in Tettenhall, early in the morning on Tuesday next," the man said, and turned away.

Rob stood as if stricken. It hadn't occurred to him that anyone might attempt something that was beyond Barber.

"Master physician!" He ran after the man. "Where have you learned to do this . . . couching of the eyes?"

"At an academy. A school for physicians."

"Where is this physicians' school?"

Merlin saw before him a large youth in ill-cut clothing that was too small. His glance took in the garish wagon and the bank on which lay juggling balls and flagons of physick whose quality he could readily guess.

"Half the world away," he said gently. He went to a tethered black mare and mounted her, and rode away from the barber-surgeons without looking back.

Rob told Barber of Benjamin Merlin later that day, as Incitatus pulled their wagon slowly out of Leicester.

Barber nodded. "I've heard of him. Physician of Tettenhall."

"Yes. He spoke like a Frenchy."

"He's a Jew of Normandy."

"What's a Jew?"

"It's another name for Hebrew, the Bible folk who slew Jesus and were driven from the Holy Land by the Romans."

"He spoke of a school for physicians."

"Sometimes they hold such a course at the college in Westminster. It's widely said to be a piss-poor course that makes piss-poor physicians. Most of them just clerk for a physician in return for training, as you are apprenticing to learn the barber-surgeon trade."

"I don't think he meant Westminster. He said the school was far away."

Barber shrugged. "Perhaps it's in Normandy or Brittany. Jews are thick as thick in France, and some have made their way here, including physicians."

"I've read of Hebrews in the Bible, but I had never seen one."

"There's another Jew physician in Malmesbury, Isaac Adolescentoli by name. A famous doctor. Perhaps you may glimpse him when we go to Salisbury," Barber said.

Malmesbury and Salisbury were in the west of England.

"We don't go to London, then?"

"No." Barber had caught something in his apprentice's voice and had long known that the youth pined for his kinsmen. "We go straight on to Salisbury," he said sternly, "to reap the benefits of the crowds at the Salisbury Fair. From there we'll go to Exmouth, for by then autumn will be on us. You understand?"

Rob nodded.

"But in the spring, when we set out again we'll travel east and go by way of London."

"Thank you, Barber," he said in quiet exultation.

His spirits soared. What did delay matter, when finally he knew they would go to London!

He daydreamed about the children.

Eventually his thoughts returned to other things. "Do you think he'll give the clerk back his eyes?"

Barber shrugged. "I've heard of the operation. Few are able to perform it and I doubt the Jew can. But people who would kill Christ will have no difficulty in lying to a blind man," Barber said, and urged the horse to go a bit faster, for it was nearing the dinner hour.

Chapter 12

THE FITTING

When they reached Exmouth it wasn't like coming home but Rob felt far less lonely than he had two years before, when he had first seen the place. The little house by the sea was familiar and welcoming. Barber ran his hand over the great fireplace, with its cooking devices, and sighed.

They planned a splendid winter's provision, as usual, but this time would bring no live hens into the house out of deference to the fierce stink chickens imparted.

Once again Rob had outgrown his clothing. "Your expanding bones lead me straight into penury," Barber complained, but he gave Rob a bolt of brown-dyed woollen stuff he had bought at the Salisbury Fair. "I'll take the wagon and Tatus and go to Athelny to select cheeses and hams, stopping overnight at the inn there. While I'm away you must clean the spring of leaves and begin to work up the season's firewood. But take the time to bring this woven wool to Editha Lipton and ask her to sew for you. You recall the way to her house?"

Rob took the cloth and thanked him. "I can find her."

"The new clothing must be expandable," Barber said as a grumbled afterthought. "Tell her to leave generous hems which can be let out."

He carried the fabric wrapped in a sheepskin against the chill rain that appeared to be Exmouth's prevailing weather. He knew the way. Two years before, he had sometimes walked past her house, hoping for a glimpse.

She answered his knock on her door promptly. He nearly dropped his bundle as she took his hands, drawing him in from the wet.

"Rob J.! Let me study you. I've never seen such alterations as two years have made!"

He wanted to tell her she had scarcely changed at all, and was struck dumb. But she noted his glance and her eyes warmed. "While I have become old and gray," she said lightly.

94

He shook his head. Her hair was still black and in every respect she was exactly as he had remembered, especially the fine and luminous eyes.

She brewed peppermint tea and he found his voice, telling her eagerly and at length where they had been and some of the things he had seen.

"As for me," she said, "I'm better off than I had been. Times have become easier, and now people are again able to order garments."

It reminded him why he had come. He unwrapped the sheepskin and showed the material, which she pronounced to be sound woollen cloth. "I hope there is sufficient quantity," she said worriedly, "for you've grown taller than Barber." She fetched her measuring strings and marked off the width of his shoulders, the girth of his waist, the length of his arms and legs. "I'll make tight trousers, a loose kirtle, and an outer cloak, and you'll be grandly clothed."

He nodded and rose, reluctant to leave.

"Is Barber waiting for you, then?"

He explained Barber's errand and she motioned him back. "It's time to eat. I can't offer what *he* does, being fresh out of aged royal beef and larks' tongues and rich puddings. But you'll join me in my country woman's supper."

She took a loaf from the cupboard and sent him into the rain to her small springhouse to fetch a piece of cheese and a jug of new cider. In the gathering dark he broke off two willow withes; back in the house, he sliced the cheese and the barley bread and impaled them on the wands to make cheese toast over the fire.

She smiled at that. "Ah, that man has left his mark on you for all time."

Rob grinned back at her. "It's sensible to heat food on such a night."

They ate and drank and then sat and talked companionably. He added wood to the fire, which had begun to hiss and steam under the rain that came in through the smoke hole.

"It grows worse outside," she said.

"Yes."

"Folly to walk home in darkness through such a storm."

He'd walked through blacker nights and a thousand worse rains. "It feels snow," he said.

"Then I have company."

"I'm grateful."

He went numbly out to the spring with the cheese and the cider, not daring to think. When he came back into the house she was in the process of removing her gown. "Best peel the wet things off," she said, and got calmly into the bed in her shift.

He removed the damp trousers and tunic and spread them on one side of the round hearth. Naked, he hastened to the bed and lay down next to her between the pelts, shivering. "Cold!"

She smiled. "You've been colder. When I took your place in Barber's bed."

"And I was sent to sleep on the floor, on a bitter night. Yes, that was cold."

She turned to him. " 'Poor motherless child,' I kept thinking. I so wished to let you into the bed."

"You reached down and touched my head."

She touched his head now, smoothing his hair and pressing his face into her softness. "I have held my own sons in this bed." She closed her eyes. Presently she eased the loose top of her shift and gave him a pendulous breast.

The living flesh in his mouth made him seem to remember a long-forgotten infant warmth. He felt a prickling behind his eyelids.

Her hand took his on an exploration. "This is what you must do." She kept her eyes closed.

A stick snapped in the hearth but went unheard. The damp fire was smoking badly.

"Lightly and with patience. In circles as you're doing," she said dreamily.

He threw back the cover and her shift, despite the cold. He saw with surprise that she had thick legs. His eyes studied what his fingers had learned; her femaleness was like his dream, but now the firelight allowed him the details.

"Faster." She would have said more but he found her lips. It was not a mother's mouth, and he noted she did something interesting with her hungry tongue.

A series of whispers guided him over her and between heavy thighs. There was no need for further instruction; instinctively he bucked and thrust.

God was a qualified carpenter, he realized, for she was a warm and slippery moving mortise and he was a fitted tenon.

Her eyes snapped open and looked straight up at him. Her lips curled back from her teeth in a strange grin and she uttered a harsh rattling from the back of her throat that would have made him think she lay dying if he hadn't heard such sounds before.

For years he had watched and heard other people making love—his father and his mother in their small and crowded house, and Barber with a long parade of doxies. He had become convinced that there had to be magic within a cunt for men to want it so. In the dark mystery of her bed, sneezing like a horse from the imperfect fire, he felt all anguish and heaviness pumping from him. Transported by the most frightening kind of joy, he discovered the vast difference between observation and participation.

Awakened next morning by a knocking, Editha padded on bare feet to open the door.

"He's gone?" Barber whispered.

"Long since," she said, letting him in. "He went to sleep a man and awoke a boy. He muttered something about needing to clean out the spring, and hurried away."

Barber smiled. "All went well?"

She nodded with surprising shyness, yawning.

"Good, for he was more than ready. Far better for him to find kindness with you than a cruel introduction from the wrong female."

She watched him take coins from his purse and set them on her table. "For this time only," he cautioned practically. "If he should visit you again . . ."

She shook her head. "These days I'm much in the company of a wainwright. A good man, with a house in the town of Exeter and three sons. I believe he will marry me."

He nodded. "And did you warn Rob not to follow my pattern?"

"I said that when you drink, very often it makes you brutish and less than a man."

"I don't recall telling you to say that."

"I offered it out of my own observation," she said. She met his gaze steadily. "I also used your very words, as you instructed. I said his master had wasted himself on drink and worthless women. I advised him to be particular, and to ignore your example."

He listened gravely.

"He wouldn't suffer me to criticize you," she said drily. "He said you were a sound man when sober, an excellent master who shows him kindness."

"Did he really," Barber said.

She was familiar with the emotions in a man's face and saw that this one was suffused with pleasure.

He seated his hat and went out the door. As she put the money away and returned to bed, she could hear him whistling.

Men were sometimes comforters and often brutes but they were always puzzles, Editha told herself as she turned onto her side and went back to sleep.

Chapter 13

LONDON

Charles Bostock looked more like a dandy than a merchant, his long yellow hair held back with bows and ribbons. He was dressed all in red velvet, obviously costly stuff despite its layer of soil from travel, and wore high-pointed shoes of soft leather meant more for display than rough service. But there was a bargainer's cold light in his eyes and he sat a great white horse surrounded by a troop of servants all heavily armed for defense against robbers. He amused himself by chatting with the barber-surgeon whose wagon he allowed to travel with his caravan of horses laden with salt from the brine works at Arundel.

"I own three warehouses along the river and rent others. We chapmen are making a new London and therefore are useful to the king and to all English people."

Barber nodded politely, bored by this braggart but happy for the opportunity to travel to London under protection of his arms, for there was much crime on the road as one drew nearer to the city. "What do you deal in?" he asked.

"Within our island nation I mostly purchase and sell iron objects and salt. But I also buy precious things which are not produced in this land and bring them here from over the sea. Skins, silks, costly gems and gold, curious garments, pigments, wine, oil, ivory and brass, copper and tin, silver, glass, and such like."

"Then you're much traveled in foreign places?"

The merchant smiled. "No, though I plan to be. I've made one trip to Genoa and brought back hangings I thought would be bought by the richer of my fellow merchants. But before merchants could buy them for their manor houses, they were eagerly acquired for the castles of several earls who help our King Canute to govern the land.

"I'll make at least two voyages more, for King Canute promises that any merchant who sails to foreign parts three times in the interests of English commerce will be made a thane. At present I pay others to travel abroad, while I tend to business in London."

"Please tell us the news of the city," Barber said, and Bostock agreed loftily. King Canute had built a large monarch's house hard by the eastern side of the abbey at Westminster, he disclosed. The Danish-born king was enjoying great popularity because he had declared a new law that allowed any free Englishman the right to hunt on his own property—a right that previously had been reserved for the king and his nobles. "Now any land-owner can kill himself a roebuck as if he were monarch of his own land."

Canute had succeeded his brother Harold as King of Denmark and ruled that country as well as England, Bostock said. "It gives him domi-nance over the North Sea, and he's built a navy of black ships that sweep the ocean of pirates and give England security and her first real peace in a hundred years."

Rob scarcely heard the conversation. While they stopped for the dinner meal at Alton he put on an entertainment with Barber, paying the rent for their place in the merchant's entourage. Bostock guffawed and wildly applauded their juggling. He presented Rob with tuppence. "It will come in handy in the metropolis, where fluff is dear as dear," he said, winking.

Rob thanked him but his thoughts were elsewhere. The closer they drew to London, the more exquisite was his sense of anticipation.

They camped in a farmer's field in Reading, scarcely a day's journey from the city of his birth. That night he didn't sleep, trying to decide which child to attempt to see first.

Next day he began to see landmarks he remembered—a stand of distinc-tive oaks, a great rock, a crossroads close by the hill on which he and Barber had first camped—and each made his heart leap and his blood sing. They parted with the caravan in the afternoon at Southwark, where the merchant had business. Southwark had more of everything than when last he had seen it. From the causeway they observed that new warehouses were being raised on the marshy Bank Side near the ancient ferry slip, and in the river foreign ships were crowded at their moorings.

Barber guided Incitatus across the London Bridge in a line of traffic. On the other side was a press of people and animals, so congested that he couldn't turn the wagon onto Thames Street but was forced to proceed straight ahead to drive left at Fenchurch Street, crossing the Walbrook and then bumping over cobbles to Cheapside. Rob could scarcely sit still, for the old neighborhoods of small and weather-silvered wooden houses ap-peared not to have changed at all.

Barber turned the horse right at Aldersgate and then left onto Newgate

Street, and Rob's problem about which of the children to see first was solved, for the bakery was on Newgate Street and so he would visit Anne Mary.

He remembered the narrow house with the pastry shop on the ground floor and watched anxiously until he spotted it. "Here, stop!" he cried to Barber, and slid off the seat before Incitatus could come to a halt.

But when he ran across the street, he saw that the shop was a ship chandler's. Puzzled, he opened the door and went inside. A red-haired man behind the counter looked up at the sound of the little bell on the door and nodded.

"What's happened to the bakery?"

The proprietor shrugged, behind a pile of neatly coiled rope.

"Do the Haverhills still live upstairs?"

"No, it's where I live. I heard there had formerly been bakers." But the shop had been empty when he bought the place two years before, he said; from Durman Monk, who lived right down the street.

Rob left Barber waiting in the wagon and sought out Durman Monk, who proved to be lonesome and delighted at a chance to talk, an old man in a house full of cats.

"So you are brother to little Anne Mary. I recall her, a sweet and polite kitten of a girl. I knew the Haverhills well and thought them excellent neighbors. They have moved to Salisbury," the old man said, stroking a tabby with savage eyes.

It made his stomach tighten to enter the guild house, which was the same as his memory in every detail, down to the chunk of mortar missing from the wattle-and-daub wall above the door. There were a few carpenters sitting about and drinking, but there were no faces Rob knew.

"Is Bukerel here?"

A carpenter set down his mug. "Who? Richard Bukerel?"

"Yes, Richard Bukerel."

"Passed on, these two years."

Rob felt more than a twinge, for Bukerel had shown him kindness. "Who is now Chief Carpenter?"

"Luard," the man said laconically. "You!" he shouted to an apprentice. "Fetch Luard, there's a lad."

Luard came from the back of the hall, a chunky man with a seamed face, young to be Chief Carpenter. He nodded without surprise when Rob asked him to supply the whereabouts of a member of the Corporation.

It took a few minutes of turning the parchment pages of a great ledger. "Here it is," he said finally, and shook his head. "I've an expired listing for a Companion Joiner named Aylwyn, but there's been no entry for several years."

Nobody in the hall knew Aylwyn or why he was no longer on the rolls.

"Members move away, often to join a guild elsewhere," Luard said.

"What of Turner Horne?" Rob asked quietly.

"The Master Carpenter? He's still there, at the house he's always had."

Rob sighed in relief; he would at any rate see Samuel.

One of the men who had been listening rose and drew Luard aside, and they whispered.

Luard cleared his throat. "Master Cole," he said. "Turner Horne is foreman of a crew that's raising a house on Edred's Hithe. May I suggest that you go there directly and speak with him?"

Rob looked from one face to another. "I don't know Edred's Hithe."

"A new section. Do you know Queen's Hithe, the old Roman port by the river wall?"

Rob nodded.

"Go to Queen's Hithe. Anyone will direct you to Edred's Hithe from there," Luard said.

Hard by the river wall were the inevitable warehouses, and beyond them the streets of houses in which lived the common people of the port, makers of sails and ships' gear and cordage, watermen, stevedores, lightermen, and boat builders. Queen's Hithe was thickly populated and had its share of taverns. In a foul-smelling eating house Rob received directions to Edred's Hithe. It was a new neighborhood that began just at the edge of the old, and he found Turner Horne raising a house on a piece of marshy meadow.

Horne came down from the roof when he was hailed, looking displeased that his work was interrupted. Rob remembered him when he saw his face. The man had run to florid flesh and his hair had turned.

"It's Samuel's brother, Master Horne," he said. "Rob J. Cole."

"So it is. But how you have grown!"

Rob saw pain flood into his decent eyes.

"He had been with us less than a year," Horne said simply. "He was a likely boy. Mistress Horne was fairly smitten with him. We had told them again and again, 'Don't play on the wharves.' It is worth a grown man's life to get behind freight wagons when a driver is backing four horses, never mind a nine-year-old's."

"Eight."

Horne looked inquiringly.

"If it happened one year after you took him in, he was eight," Rob said.

His lips were stiff and didn't seem to want to move, making talk difficult. "Two years younger than I, you see."

"You would know best," Horne said gently. "He's buried in St. Botolph's, on the right rear side of the churchyard. We were told it's the section where your father was laid to rest." He paused. "About your father's tools," he said awkwardly. "One of the saws has snapped but the hammers are quite sound. You may have them back."

Rob shook his head. "Keep them, please. To remember Samuel," he said.

They were camped in a meadow near Bishopsgate, close to the wetlands in the northeast corner of the city. Next day he fled the grazing sheep and Barber's sympathy and went in the early morning to stand in their old street and recall the children, until a strange woman came out of Mam's house and threw wash water next to the door.

He wandered the morning away and found himself in Westminster, where the houses along the river dwindled and then the fields and meadows of the great monastery became a new estate that could only be King's House, surrounded by barracks for troops and outbuildings in which Rob supposed all manner of national business was conducted. He saw the fearsome housecarls, who were spoken of with awe in every public house. They were huge Danish soldiers, handpicked for their size and fighting ability to serve as King Canute's protection. Rob thought there were too many armed guards for a monarch beloved of his people. He turned back toward the city and, without knowing how he reached it, eventually was close to St. Paul's when a hand was laid on his arm.

"I know you. You're Cole."

Rob peered at the youth and for a moment was nine years old once more and unable to make up his mind whether to fight or take to his heels, for it was unmistakably Anthony Tite.

But there was a smile on Tite's face and no henchmen were visible. Besides, Rob observed, he was now three heads taller and a good deal heavier than his old foe; he slapped Pissant-Tony on the shoulder, suddenly as glad to see him as if they had been best friends as small boys.

"Come into a tavern and talk of yourself," Anthony said, but Rob hesitated, for he had only the tuppence given to him by the merchant Bostock for juggling.

Anthony Tite understood. "I buy the drink. I've had wages for the past year."

He was an Apprentice Carpenter, he told Rob when they had settled into a corner of a nearby public house and were sipping ale. "In the sawpit," he said, and Rob noted his voice was husky and his complexion sallow.

He knew the work. An apprentice stood in a deep ditch, across the top of which a log was laid. The apprentice pulled one end of a long saw and all day breathed the sawdust that showered him, while a Companion Joiner stood on a lip of the pit and managed the saw from above.

"Hard times appear to be at an end for carpenters," Rob said. "I visited the guild house and saw few men lolling about."

Tite nodded. "London grows. The city already has one hundred thousand souls, one-eighth of all Englishmen. There is building everywhere. It's a good time to apply to prentice the guild, for it's rumored that soon another Hundred will be established. And since you were son to a carpenter . . ."

Rob shook his head. "I already have a prenticeship." He told of his travels with Barber and was gratified at the envy in Anthony's eyes.

Tite spoke of Samuel's death. "I've lost my mother and two brothers in recent years, all to the pox, and my father to a fever."

Rob nodded somberly. "I must find those who are alive. Any London house I pass may contain the last child born to my mother before she died, and given away by Richard Bukerel."

"Perhaps Bukerel's widow would know something."

Rob sat straighter.

"She has remarried, to a greengrocer named Buffington. Her new home is not far from here. Just past Ludgate," Anthony said.

The Buffington house was in a setting not unlike the solitude in which the king had built his new residence, but it was hard by the dankness of the Fleet River marshes and was a patched shelter instead of a palace. Behind the shabby house were neat fields of cabbages and lettuces, and surrounding them was an undrained moor. He stood for a moment and watched four sulky children; carrying sacks of stones, they circled the mosquito-loud fields in a silent, deadly patrol against marsh hares.

He found Mistress Buffington in the house and she greeted him. She was sorting produce into baskets. The animals ate their profits, she explained, grumbling.

"I remember you and your family," she said, examining him as if he were a select vegetable.

But when he asked, she couldn't recollect her first husband ever mentioning the name or whereabouts of the wet nurse who had taken the infant christened Roger Cole.

"Did no one write down the name?"

Perhaps something showed in his eyes, for she bridled. "I cannot write.

Why did *you* not obtain the name and write it, sirrah? Is he not your brother?"

He asked himself how such responsibility could have been expected of a young boy who had been in his circumstances; but he knew she was more right than wrong.

She smiled at him. "Let's not be uncivil toward one another, for we have shared hard earlier days as neighbors."

To his surprise she was studying him as a woman looks at a man, her eyes warm. Her body was slimmed by labor and he saw that at one time she had been beautiful. She was no older than Editha.

But he thought wistfully of Bukerel and remembered the terrible righteousness of her niggardly charity, reminding himself that this woman would have sold him for a slave.

He gave her a cool stare and muttered his thanks, and then he went away.

At St. Botolph's Church the sacristan, an old pockmarked man with uncut hair of dirty gray, answered his knock. Rob asked for the priest who had buried his parents.

"Father Kempton is transferred to Scotland, these ten months now."

The old man took him into the church graveyard. "Oh, we are become powerfully crowded," he said. "You was not here two years past, for the scourge of pox?"

Rob shook his head.

"Lucky! So many died, we buried straight through every day. Now we are pressed for space. People flock to London from every place, and a man quickly reaches the two score of years for which he may reasonably pray."

"Yet you are older than forty years," Rob observed.

"I? I'm protected by the churchly nature of my work and have in all ways led a pure and innocent life." He flashed a smile and Rob smelled liquor on his breath.

He waited outside the burial house while the sacristan consulted the Interment Book; the best the fuddled old man could do was lead him through a maze of leaning memorials to a general area in the eastern portion of the churchyard, close by the mossy rear wall, and declare that both his father and his brother Samuel had been buried "near to here." He tried to recall his father's funeral and thus remember the site of the grave, but couldn't.

His mother was easier to find; the yew tree over her grave had grown in three years but still was familiar.

Suddenly purposeful, he hurried back to their camp. Barber went with him to a rocky section below the bank of the Thames, where they chose a small gray boulder with a surface flattened and smoothed by long years of tidal flow. Incitatus helped them drag it from the river.

He had planned to chisel the inscriptions himself, but was dissuaded. "We're here overlong," Barber said. "Let a stonecutter do it quickly and well. I'll provide for his labor, and when you complete apprenticeship and work for wages you'll repay me."

They stayed in London only long enough to see the stone inscribed with all three names and dates and set in place in the churchyard beneath the yew.

Barber clapped a beefy hand on his shoulder and gave him a level glance. "We are travelers. We're able at length to reach every place where you must inquire after the other three children."

He spread out his map of England and showed Rob that six great roads left London: northeast to Colchester; north to Lincoln and York; northwest to Shrewsbury and Wales; west to Silchester, Winchester, and Salisbury; southeast to Richborough, Dover, and Lyme; and south to Chichester.

"Here in Ramsey," he said, stabbing a finger at central England, "is where your widow neighbor, Della Hargreaves, went to live with her brother. She'll be able to tell you the name of the wet nurse to whom she gave the infant Roger, and you will seek him when next we return to London. And down here is Salisbury, where, you are told, your sister Anne Mary has been taken by her family the Haverhills." He frowned. "Pity we didn't have that news when we were lately in Salisbury during the fair," he said, and Rob felt a chill with the realization that he and the little girl may well have passed by one another in the crowds.

"No matter," Barber said. "We'll return to Salisbury on the way back to Exmouth, in the fall."

Rob took heart. "And everywhere we go in the north," he said, "I'll ask priests and monks if they know of Father Lovell and his young charge, William Cole."

Early next morning they abandoned London and took to the wide Lincoln Road leading to the north of England. When they left behind all houses and the stink of too many people and stopped for an especially lavish breakfast cooked by the side of a noisy stream, each agreed that a city was not the finest place to breathe God's air and enjoy the sun's warmth.

Chapter 14

LESSONS

On a day in early June the two of them lay on their backs by a brook near Chipping Norton, observing clouds through leafy branches and waiting for trouts to bite.

Propped onto two Y-shaped branches stuck into the ground, their willow poles were unmoving.

"Late in the season for trouts to be hungry for hackles," Barber murmured contentedly. "In a fortnight, when hoppers are in the fields, fish will be caught faster."

"How do male worms tell the difference?" Rob wondered.

Nearly dozing, Barber smiled. "Doubtless hackles are alike in the dark, like women."

"Women aren't alike, day or night," Rob protested. "They appear similar, yet each is separate in scent, taste, touch, and feel."

Barber sighed. "That's the true wonder that lures man on."

Rob got up and went to the wagon. When he came back he held a square of smooth pine on which he had drawn the face of a girl in ink. He squatted by Barber and held out the board. "Do you make her out?"

Barber peered at the drawing. "It's the girl from last week, the little dolly in St. Ives."

Rob took back the sketch and studied it, pleased.

"Why have you placed the ugly mark on her cheek?"

"The mark was there."

Barber nodded. "I recall it. But with your quill and ink, you're able to make her prettier than reality. Why not allow her to view herself more favorably than she's seen by the world?"

Rob frowned, troubled without understanding why. He studied the likeness. "At any rate, she hasn't seen this, since it was drawn after I left her."

"But you could have drawn it in her presence."

Rob shrugged and smiled.

Barber sat up, fully awake. "The time has come for us to make practical use of your capability," he said.

Next morning they stopped at a woodcutter's and asked him to saw thin rounds from the trunk of a pine. The slices of wood were a disappointment, being too grainy for easy drawing with quill and ink. But rounds from a young beech tree proved to be smooth and hard, and the woodcutter willingly sliced a medium-sized beech in exchange for a coin.

Following the entertainment that afternoon, Barber announced that his associate would draw free likenesses of half a dozen residents of Chipping Norton.

There was a rush and a flurry. A crowd gathered around Rob, watching curiously as he mixed his ink. But he was long since schooled as a performer and inured to scrutiny.

He drew a face on each of six wooden discs, in turn: an old woman, two youths, a pair of dairy maids who smelled of cows, and a man with a wen on his nose.

The woman had deepset eyes and a toothless mouth with wrinkled lips. One of the youths was plump and round-faced, so it was like drawing features on a gourd. The other boy was thin and dark, with baleful eyes. The girls were sisters and looked so much alike that the challenge was in trying to capture their subtle difference; he failed, for they could have exchanged their sketches without noticing. Of the six, he was satisfied only with the last drawing. The man was almost old, and his eyes and every line of his face contained melancholy. Without knowing how, Rob captured the sadness.

With no hesitation, he drew the wen on the nose. Barber didn't complain, since all the subjects were visibly pleased and there was sustained applause from the onlookers.

"Buy six bottles and you may have—free, my friends!—a similar likeness," Barber bawled, holding the Universal Specific aloft and launching into his familiar discourse.

Soon there was a line in front of Rob, who was drawing intently, and a longer line before the bank, on which Barber stood and sold his medicine.

Since King Canute had liberalized the hunting laws, venison began to appear in butchers' stalls. In the market square of Aldreth town, Barber bought a great saddle of meat. He rubbed it with wild garlic and covered it with deep slashes that he filled with tiny squares of pork fat and onion, larding the outside richly with sweet butter and basting continually while it roasted with a mixture of honey, mustard, and brown ale.

Rob ate heartily, but Barber finished most of it himself along with a prodigious amount of mashed turnip and a loaf of fresh bread. "Perhaps just a bit more. To keep up my strength," he said, grinning. In the time Rob had known him he had increased remarkably—perhaps, Rob thought, as much as six stone. Flesh ridged his neck, his forearms had become hams, and his stomach sailed before him like a loose sail in a stiff wind. His thirst was as prodigious as his appetite.

Two days after leaving Aldreth they arrived in the village of Ramsey, where in the public house Barber gained the proprietor's attention by wordlessly swallowing two pitchers of ale before imitating thunder with a belch and turning to the business at hand.

"We're looking for a woman, name of Della Hargreaves."

The proprietor shrugged and shook his head.

"Hargreaves, her husband's name. She's a widow. Came four years ago to be with her brother. His name I don't know, but I ask you to ponder, for this is a small place." Barber ordered more ale, to encourage him.

The proprietor looked blank.

"Oswald Sweeter," his wife whispered, serving the drink.

"Ah. Just so, Sweeter's sister," the man said, accepting Barber's money.

Oswald Sweeter was Ramsey's blacksmith, as large as Barber but all muscle. He listened to them with a slight frown and then spoke as though unwilling.

"Della? I took her in," he said. "My own flesh." With pincers he pushed a cherry-red bar deeper into glowing coals. "My wife showed her kindness, but Della has a talent for doing no work. The two women didn't get on. Within half a year, Della left us."

"To go where?" Rob asked.

"Bath."

"What does she do in Bath?"

"Same as here before we threw her away," Sweeter said quietly. "She left with a man like a rat."

"She was our neighbor for years in London, where she was deemed respectable," Rob was obligated to say, though he had never liked her.

"Well, young sir, today my sister is a drab who would sooner swive than labor for her bread. You may find her where there are whores." Pulling a flaming white bar from the coals Sweeter ended the conversation with his hammer, so that a savage shower of sparks followed them through his door.

* * *

It rained for a solid week as they made their way up the coast. Then one morning they crawled from their damp beds beneath the wagon to find a day so soft and glorious that all was forgotten save their good fortune in being footloose and blessed. "Let us take a promenade through the innocent world!" Barber cried, and Rob knew exactly what he meant, for despite the dark urgency of his need to find the children he was young and healthy and alive on such a day.

Between blasts of the Saxon horn they sang exuberantly, hymns and raunchiness, a louder signal of their presence than any other. They drove slowly through a forested track that alternately gave them warm sunlight and fresh green shade. "What more could you ask," Barber said.

"Arms," he said at once.

Barber's grin faded. "I'll not buy you arms," he said shortly.

"No need for a sword. But a dagger would seem sensible, for we could be set upon."

"Any highwayman will think twice on it," Barber said drily, "since we are two large folk."

"It's because of my size. I walk into a public house and smaller men look at me and think, 'He's big but one thrust can stop him,' and their hands drift to their hilts."

"And then they notice that you wear no arms and they realize you're a puppy and not yet a mastiff despite your size. Feeling like fools, they leave you alone. With a blade on your belt you should be dead in a fortnight."

They rode in silence.

Centuries of violent invasions had made every Englishman think like a soldier. Slaves weren't allowed by law to bear arms and apprentices couldn't afford them; but any other male who wore his hair long also signified his free birth by the weapons he displayed.

It was true enough that a small man with a knife could easily kill a large youth without one, Barber told himself wearily.

"You must know how to handle weapons when the time comes for you to own them," he decided. "It's a portion of your instruction that has been neglected. Therefore, I'll begin to tutor you in the use of the sword and the dagger."

Rob beamed. "Thank you, Barber," he said.

In a clearing, they faced one another and Barber slipped his dagger from his belt.

"You mustn't hold it like a child stabbing at ants. Balance the knife in your upturned palm as if you intended to juggle it. The four fingers close about the handle. The thumb can go flat along the handle or can cover the fingers, depending on the thrust. The hardest thrust to guard against is one that is made from below and moving upward.

"The knife fighter bends his knees and moves lightly on his feet, ready to spring forward or back. Ready to weave in order to avoid an assailant's thrust. Ready to kill, for this instrument is for close and dirty work. It's made of the same good metal as a scalpel. Once having committed yourself to either, you must cut as though life depends on it, for often it does."

He returned the dagger to its scabbard and handed over his sword. Rob hefted it, holding it before him.

"*Romanus sum,*" he said softly.

Barber smiled. "No, you are not a bleeding Roman. Not with this English sword. The Roman sword was short and pointed, with two sharp steel edges. They liked to fight close and at times used it like a dagger. This is an English broadsword, Rob J., longer and heavier. The ultimate weapon, that keeps our enemies at a distance. It is a cleaver, an ax that cuts down human creatures instead of trees."

He took back the sword and stepped away from Rob. Holding it in both hands he whirled, the broadsword flashing and glittering in wide and deadly circles as he severed the sunlight.

Presently he stopped and leaned on the sword, out of wind. "You try," he told Rob, and handed him the weapon.

It gave Barber scant comfort to see how easily his apprentice held the heavy broadsword in one hand. It was a strong man's weapon, he thought enviously, more effective when used with the agility of youth.

Wielding it in imitation of Barber, Rob whirled across the little clearing. The broadsword blade hissed through the air and a hoarse cry rose from his throat without volition. Barber watched, more than vaguely disturbed, as he swept through an invisible host, cutting a terrible swath.

The next lesson occurred several nights later at a crowded and noisy public house in Fulford. English drovers from a horse caravan moving north were there along with Danish drovers from a caravan traveling south. Both groups were overnighting in the town, drinking heavily and eyeing one another like packs of fighting dogs.

Rob sat with Barber and drank cider, not uncomfortably. It was a situation they had met before, and they knew enough not to be drawn into the competitiveness.

One of the Danes had gone outside to relieve his bladder. When he returned he carried a squealing shoat under his arm, and a length of rope. He tied one end of the rope to the pig's neck and the other end to a pole in the center of the tavern. Then he hammered on a table with a mug.

"Who is man enough to meet me in a pig-sticking?" he shouted over to the English drovers.

"Ah, Vitus!" one of his mates called encouragingly, and began to hammer on his table, quickly joined by all his friends.

The English drovers listened sullenly to the hammering and the shouted taunts, then one of them walked to the pole and nodded.

Half a dozen of the more prudent patrons of the public house gulped their drinks and slipped outside.

Rob had started to rise, following Barber's custom of leaving before trouble could begin, but to his surprise his master placed a staying hand on his arm.

"Tuppence here on Dustin!" an English drover called. Soon the two groups were busily placing bets.

The men were not unevenly matched. Both looked to be in their twenties; the Dane was heavier and slightly shorter, while the Englishman had the longer reach.

Cloths were bound across their eyes and then each was tethered to an opposite side of the pole by a ten-foot length of rope bound to his ankle.

"Wait," the man named Dustin called. "One more drink!"

Hooting, their friends brought them each a cup of metheglin, which was quickly drained.

The blindfolded men drew their daggers.

The pig, which had been held at right angles to both of them, was now released to the floor. Immediately it tried to flee but, tethered as it was, it could only run in a circle.

"The little bastard comes, Dustin!" somebody shouted. The Englishman set himself and waited, but the sound of the animal's scurrying was drowned out by the shouts of the men, and the pig was past him before he knew it.

"*Now*, Vitus!" a Dane called.

In its terror the shoat ran straight into the Danish drover. The man stabbed at it three times without coming close, and it fled the way it had come, squealing.

Dustin could home in on the sound, and he came toward the shoat from one direction while Vitus closed in from the other.

The Dane took a swipe at the pig and Dustin drew a sobbing breath as the sharp blade sliced into his arm.

"You Northern fuck." He slashed out in a savage arc that didn't come near to either the squealing pig or the other man.

Now the pig darted across Vitus' feet. The Danish drover grasped the animal's rope and was able to pull the pig toward his waiting knife. His first stab caught it on the right front hoof, and the pig screamed.

"Now you have him, Vitus!"

"Finish him off, we eat him tomorrow!"

The screaming pig had become an excellent target and Dustin lunged toward the sound. His striking hand skittered off the shoat's smooth side and with a thud his blade was buried to his fist in Vitus' belly.

The Dane merely grunted softly but sprang back, ripping himself open on the dagger.

The only sound in the public house was the crying of the pig.

"Put the knife down, Dustin, you've done him," one of the Englishmen commanded. They surrounded the drover; his blindfold was ripped off and his tether was cut.

Wordlessly, the Danish drovers hurried their friend away before the Saxons could react or the reeve's men could be summoned.

Barber sighed. "Let us through to him, for we're barber-surgeons and may give him succor," he said.

But it was clear that there was little they could do for him. Vitus lay on his back as if broken, his eyes large and his face gray. In the gaping wound of his open stomach they saw that his bowel had been cut almost in half.

Barber took Rob's arm and drew him down to squat alongside. "Look on it," he said firmly.

There were layers: tanned skin, pale meat, a rather slimy light lining. The bowel was the pink of a dyed Easter egg, the blood was very red.

"It is curious how an opened-up man stinks far worse than any opened-up animal," Barber said.

Blood welled from the abdominal wall and with a gush the severed bowel emptied itself of fecal matter. The man was speaking weakly in Danish, perhaps praying.

Rob retched but Barber held him close to the fallen man, like a man rubbing a young dog's nose in its own waste.

Rob took the drover's hand. The man was like a bag of sand with a hole in the bottom; he could feel the life running out. He squatted next to the drover and held his hand tightly until there was no sand left in the bag and the soul of Vitus made a dry rustling sound like an old leaf and simply blew away.

* * *

They continued to practice with arms, but now Rob was more thought-ful and not quite so eager.

He spent more time thinking about the gift, and he watched Barber and listened to him, learning whatever he knew. As he became familiar with ailments and their symptoms he began to play a secret game, trying to determine from outward appearances what bothered each patient.

In the Northumbrian village of Richmond they saw waiting in their line a wan man with rheumy eyes and a painful cough.

"What ails that one?" Barber asked.

"Most likely consumption?"

Barber smiled in approval.

But when it was the coughing patient's turn to see the barber-surgeon, Rob took his hands to lead him behind the screen. It wasn't the grasp of a dying person; Rob's senses told him that this man was too strong to have consumption. He sensed that the man had taken a chill and soon would be rid of what was merely passing discomfort.

He saw no reason to contradict Barber; but thus, gradually, he became aware that the gift was not only for predicting death but could be useful in considering illness and perhaps in helping the living.

Incitatus pulled the red cart slowly northward across the face of England, village by village, some too small to have a name. Whenever they came to a monastery or church Barber waited patiently in the cart while Rob inquired after Father Ranald Lovell and the boy named William Cole, but nobody had ever heard of them.

Somewhere between Carlisle and Newcastle-upon-Tyne, Rob climbed onto a stone wall built nine hundred years before by Hadrian's cohorts to protect England from Scottish marauders. Sitting in England and gazing out at Scotland, he told himself that his most likely chance of seeing some-one of his own blood lay in Salisbury, where the Haverhills had taken his sister Anne Mary.

When finally they reached Salisbury, he received short shrift from the Corporation of Bakers.

The Chief Baker was a man named Cummings. He was squat and froglike, not so heavy as Barber but fleshy enough to advertise his trade. "I know no Haverhills."

"Will you not seek them out in your records?"

"See here. It is fair time! Much of my membership is involved in Salisbury Fair and we are harried and distraught. You must see us after the fair."

All through the fair, only part of him juggled and drew and helped to treat patients, while he kept watch constantly for a familiar face, a glimpse of the girl he imagined she had grown to be.

He didn't see her.

The day after the fair he returned to the building of the Salisbury Corporation of Bakers. It was a neat and attractive place, and despite his nervousness he wondered why the houses of other guilds were always built more soundly than those of the Corporations of Carpenters.

"Ah, the young barber-surgeon." Cummings was kinder in his greeting and more composed, now. He searched thoroughly through two great ledgers and then shook his head. "We've never had a baker name of Haverhill."

"A man and his wife," Rob said. "They sold their pastry shop in London and declared they were coming here. They have a little girl, sister to me. Name of Anne Mary."

"It's obvious what has happened, young surgeon. After selling their shop and before coming here, they found better opportunity elsewhere, heard of a place more in need of bakers."

"Yes. That's likely." He thanked the man and returned to the wagon.

Barber was visibly troubled but advised courage. "You mustn't give up hope. Someday you'll find them again, you will see."

But it was as if the earth had opened and swallowed the living as well as the dead. The small hope he had kept alive for them now seemed too innocent. He felt the days of his family were truly over, and with a chill he forced himself to recognize that whatever lay ahead for him, most likely he would face it alone.

Chapter 15

THE JOURNEYMAN

A few months before the end of Rob's apprenticeship they sat over pitchers of brown ale in the public room of the inn at Exeter and warily discussed terms of employment.

Barber drank in silence, as if lost in thought, and eventually offered a small salary. "Plus a new set of clothing," he said, as if overcome by a burst of generosity.

Rob hadn't been with him six years for nothing. He shrugged doubtfully. "I feel drawn to go back to London," he said, and refilled their cups.

Barber nodded. "A set of clothing every two years whether needed or not," he added after studying Rob's face.

They ordered a supper of rabbit pie, which Rob ate with gusto. Barber tore into the publican instead of the food. "What meat I find is overly tough and stupidly seasoned," he grumbled. "We might make the salary higher. *Slightly* higher," he said.

"It *is* poorly seasoned," Rob said. "That's something you never do. I've always been taken by your way with game."

"How much salary do you hold to be fair? For a chap of sixteen years?"

"I wouldn't want a salary."

"Not have a salary?" Barber eyed him with suspicion.

"No. Income is gotten from sale of the Specific and treatment of patients. Therefore, I want the income from every twelfth bottle sold and every twelfth patient treated."

"Every *twentieth* bottle and every twentieth patient."

He hesitated only a moment before nodding. "These terms to run one year, when they may be renewed upon mutual agreement."

"Done!"

"Done," Rob said calmly.

Each of them lifted his mug and grinned.

"Hah!" said Barber.

"Hah!" said Rob.

Barber took his new expenses seriously. One day when they were in Northampton, where there were skilled craftsmen, he hired a joiner to make a second screen, and when they reached the next place, which was Huntington, he set it up not far from his own.

"Time you stood on your own limbs," he said.

After the entertainment and the portraits, Rob sat himself behind the screen and waited.

Would they look at him and laugh? Or, he wondered, would they turn away and go back to stand in Barber's line?

His first patient winced when Rob took his hands, for his old cow had trod upon his wrist. "Kicked over the pail, the bitchy thing. Then, as I was reaching to set it right, the cursed animal stepped on me, you see?"

Rob held the joint tenderly and at once forgot about anything else. There was a painful bruise. There was also a bone broken, the one that ran down from the thumb. An important bone. It took him a little time to bind the wrist right and fix a sling.

The next patient was the personification of his fears, a slim and angular woman with stern eyes. "I have lost my hearing," she declared.

Upon examination, her ears did not seem to be plugged with wax. He knew nothing that could be done for her. "I cannot help you," he said regretfully.

She shook her head.

"I CANNOT HELP YOU!" he shouted.

"THEN ASK TH'OTHER BARBER."

"HE CANNOT HELP YOU EITHER."

The woman's face had grown choleric. "BE DAMNED TO HELL. I SHALL ASK HIM MYSELF."

He was aware both of Barber's laughter and the amusement of other patients as she stomped away.

He was waiting behind the screen, red-faced, when he was joined by a young man perhaps a year or two older than he. Rob restrained an impulse to sigh as he looked at a left forefinger in an advanced stage of mortification.

"Not a beautiful sight."

The young man was whitish in the corners of his mouth but managed a smile nevertheless. "I mashed it chopping wood for the fire all of a fortnight ago. It hurt, of course, but appeared to be mending nicely. And then . . ."

The first joint was black, running into an area of angry discoloration that became blistered flesh. The large blisters gave off a bloody flux and a gaseous stink.

"How was it treated?"

"A neighbor man cautioned me to pack it with moist ashes mixed with goose shit, to draw the pain."

He nodded, for it was a common remedy. "Well. It's now a consuming sickness that, if allowed, will eat into the hand and then the arm. Long before it gets into the body, you will die. The finger must come off."

The young man nodded gamely.

Rob allowed the sigh to escape. He had to be doubly certain; to take an appendage was a serious step, and this one would miss the finger for the rest of his life as he tried to earn his living.

He walked to Barber's screen.

"Something?" Barber's eyes twinkled.

"Something I need to show you," Rob said, and led the way back to his patient, the fat man following at a more labored pace.

"I've told him it must come off."

"Yes," Barber said, and the smile was gone. "That was correct. You wish assistance, chappy?"

Rob shook his head. He gave the patient three bottles of the Specific to drink and then carefully collected everything he would need, so he wouldn't have to go searching in the middle of the procedure or shout for Barber's help.

He took two sharp knives, a needle and waxed thread, a short piece of board, rag strips for binding, and a little fine-toothed saw.

The youth's arm was lashed to the board so that his hand was palm up. "Make a fist without the mortified finger," Rob said, and wrapped the hand with bandages and tied it off so the sound digits were out of the way.

He enlisted three strong men from the nearby loungers, two to hold the youth and one to grasp the board.

A dozen times he had witnessed Barber doing this and twice had done it himself under Barber's supervision, but never before had he attempted it alone. The trick was to cut far enough away from the mortification to stop its progress, while at the same time leaving as much of a stub as possible.

He picked up a knife and sliced into sound flesh. The patient screamed and tried to rise out of his chair.

"Hold him."

He sliced a circle all around the finger and paused for a moment to soak up the bleeding with a rag before slitting the healthy section of finger on both sides and carefully flaying the skin toward the knuckle, making two flaps.

The man holding the board let go and began to vomit.

"Take the board," Rob told the one who had been holding the shoulders. There was no trouble with the transfer, for the patient had fainted.

Bone was an easy substance to cut, and the saw made a reassuring rasping as he took off the finger.

He trimmed the flaps carefully and made a neat stump as he had been taught, neither so tight as to give pain nor so loose as to give trouble, then took up the needle and thread and made a good job of it with small, thrifty stitches. There was a bloody ooze that he washed away by pouring the Universal Specific over the stump. Rob helped carry the groaning youth to where he could recover in the shade under a tree.

After that in quick succession he bound a sprained ankle, dressed a deep sickle cut in a child's arm, sold three bottles of the physick to a widow cursed with the headache and another half dozen bottles to a man with the gout. He was beginning to feel cocky when a woman came behind the screen with the wasting sickness.

There was no mistaking it; she was gaunt and her skin was waxy, with a sheen of perspiration on her cheeks. He had to force himself to look at her, having sensed her fate through his hands.

" . . . do not desire to eat," she was saying, "nor can I keep anything I eat, for what is not spewed forth rushes through me in the form of bloody stools."

He placed his hand on her poor abdomen and felt the bumpy rigidity, to which he guided her palm.

"Bubo."

"What is bubo, sirrah?"

"A lump that grows by feeding on healthy flesh. You feel a number of buboes beneath your hand."

"There is terrible pain. Is there no medicine?" she said calmly.

He loved her for her courage and was not tempted to lie for mercy's sake. He shook his head, for Barber had told him that many persons suffered from bubo of the stomach and each died of the sickness.

When she had left him wishing he had become a carpenter, he saw the severed finger on the ground. Picking it up and wrapping it in a rag, he carried it to where the recovering youth lay under the tree and placed it in his good hand.

Puzzled, he looked at Rob. "What shall I do with it?"

"The priests say you must bury lost parts to await you in a churchyard, so you may rise whole again on Judgment Day."

The young man thought on it and then nodded. "Thank you, barber-surgeon," he said.

When they reached Rockingham the first thing they saw was the white hair of the unguent seller named Wat. Next to Rob on the wagon seat, Barber grunted in disappointment, assuming that the other mountebank had preempted their right to put on an entertainment there. But after they had exchanged greetings, Wat put their minds to rest.

"I give no performance here. Instead, let me invite you both to a baiting."

He took them to see his bear, a large scarred beast with an iron ring through its black nose. "It is sickly and would soon die of natural causes, so bruin shall make me a final profit tonight."

"Is this Bartram, whom I wrestled?" Rob asked, in a voice that sounded strange in his ears.

"No, Bartram is long gone, baited four years past. This is a sow, name of Godiva," Wat said, and replaced the cloth over the cage.

That afternoon Wat observed their entertainment and the subsequent sale of physick; with Barber's permission, the unguent peddler climbed onto their bank and announced the bear-baiting that would take place that evening in the pit behind the tannery, admission half a penny.

By the time he and Barber arrived, dusk had fallen and the meadow surrounding the pit was illumined by the leaping flames of a dozen pitch torches. The field was loud with profanity and male laughter. Trainers held back three muzzled dogs that strained against their short leashes: a raw-boned brindle mastiff, a red dog that looked like the mastiff's smaller cousin, and a large Danish elkhound.

Godiva was led in by Wat and a pair of handlers. The shambling bear was hooded, but she smelled the dogs and instinctively turned to face them.

The men led her to a thick post in the center of the pit. Stout leather fastenings were attached to the top and the bottom of the pole, and the pitmaster used the lower set to tether the bear by her right hind.

Immediately there were cries of protest. "The upper strap, the upper strap!"

"Tether the beast's neck!"

"Fasten her by the nose ring, you bloody fool!"

The pitmaster was unmoved by calls or insults, for he was experienced. "The bear is declawed. Therefore it would be a dull show indeed if her head were tied. I allow her the use of her fangs," he said.

Wat untied the hood from Godiva's head and sprang back.

The bear looked about in the flickering light, staring with small puzzled eyes at the men and the dogs.

She was obviously an old beast and far from her prime, and the men shouting the wagering odds received few bets until they offered three to one on the dogs, which looked savage and fit as they were led to the lip of the pit. Their trainers scratched their heads and massaged their necks, then slipped off the muzzles and leashes and stepped away.

At once the mastiff and the smaller red dog went low on their bellies, their eyes fixed on Godiva. Growling, they darted in to snap at air and then retreated, for they were not yet aware that the bear's claws were gone and they feared and respected them.

The elkhound loped around the perimeter of the pit, and the bear cast nervous glances at him over her shoulder.

"You must watch the small red dog," Wat shouted in Rob's ear.

"He would seem the least fearsome."

"He is from a remarkable line, bred down from the mastiff to kill bulls in the pit."

Blinking, the bear stood erect on her hind paws with her back against the pole. Godiva appeared confused; she saw the real threat of the dogs but she was a performing animal and accustomed to tethers and the screams of human beings, and she wasn't angry enough to suit the pitmaster. The man picked up a long lance and jabbed one of her wrinkled dugs, slicing off a dark nipple.

The bear howled in pain.

Encouraged, the mastiff flew in. What he wanted to tear was soft underbelly, but the bear turned and the dog's terrible teeth ripped into her left haunch. Godiva bellowed and swiped. If her claws had not been cruelly removed when she was a cub, the mastiff would have been disemboweled, but the paw brushed harmlessly. The dog sensed it was not the danger he had expected and spat out hide and meat and bore in for more, maddened now by the taste of blood.

The small red dog had launched himself through the air at Godiva's throat. His teeth were as awful as the mastiff's; his long underjaw locked into the upper jaw and the dog hung beneath the bear's muzzle like a great ripe fruit from a tree.

At last the elkhound saw it was time, and he leaped at Godiva from the left, climbing over the mastiff in his eagerness to get at her. Godiva's left ear and left eye were taken out in the same slashing bite, and crimson gobbets flew as the beast shook her ruined head.

The bull dog had locked into a great fold of thick fur and loose skin; its gripping jaws placed enough relentless pressure on the bear's windpipe so that she began to suck for air. And now the mastiff had found her stomach and was tearing at it.

"A poor fight," Wat shouted, disappointed. "They already have the bear."

Godiva brought a great right forepaw down on the mastiff's back. The crack of the dog's spine wasn't heard above the other sounds but the dying mastiff wriggled away over the sand, and the bear turned its fangs against the elkhound.

The men roared their delight.

The elkhound was thrown almost out of the pit and lay where it fell, for its throat was rent. Godiva pawed at the smallest dog, which was spattered redder than ever with the blood of the bear and the mastiff. The stubborn jaws were locked in Godiva's throat. The bear folded her fore-limbs and squeezed crushingly while she stood and swayed.

Not until the small red dog was lifeless did the jaws relax. Finally the bear was able to brush the bull dog against the pole again and again until it fell off her into the trampled sand like a dislodged burr.

Godiva dropped onto all fours next to the dead dogs but took no interest in them. Agonized and trembling, she began to lick her own raw and bleeding flesh.

There was a murmur of conversation as spectators paid up or collected their wagers. "Too soon, too soon," a man next to Rob grumbled.

"The damned beast still lives and we can yet have some pleasure," another said.

A drunken youth had picked up the pitmaster's lance and began to harry Godiva with it from the rear, poking her in the anus. The men cheered as the bear whirled, roaring, but was jerked up short by the tether on her leg.

"The other eye," someone cried at the rear of the crowd. "Blind the other eye!"

The bear rose again to stand shakily on two limbs. The good eye looked out at them with defiance but with a calm foreknowledge, and Rob was reminded of the woman who had come to him in Northampton with the wasting sickness. The drunkard was jabbing the point of the lance toward the huge head when Rob went to him and ripped the lance from his hands.

"Here, you fucking fool!" Barber called sharply to Rob, and started after him.

"Good Godiva," Rob said. He leveled the lance and drove it deep into the torn chest, and almost at once blood sprang from a corner of the contorted muzzle.

A sound rose from the men that was similar to the snarling made by the dogs when they had closed in.

"He's addled and we shall tend him," Barber called quickly.

Rob allowed Barber and Wat to jostle him out of the pit and beyond the ring of light.

"What kind of stupid shitepoke is this lump of a barber's assistant?" Wat asked, enraged.

"I confess I don't know." Barber's breathing sounded like a bellows. These days his breathing was heavier, Rob realized.

Within the ring of torchlight, the pitmaster was announcing soothingly that there remained a strong badger waiting to be baited, and the complaints turned to ragged cheers.

Rob walked away while Barber apologized to Wat.

He was seated near the wagon by the fire when Barber came lumbering in. Barber opened a bottle of liquor and drank half of it off. Then he dropped heavily into his bed on the other side of the fire and stared.

"You are an arsehole," he said.

Rob smiled.

"If the bets hadn't already been settled they'd have had your blood and I shouldn't have blamed them."

Rob's hand went to the bearskin on which he slept. The pelt had grown rattier than ever and must soon be discarded, he thought, stroking it.

"Goodnight, then, Barber," he said.

Chapter 16

ARMS

It didn't occur to Barber that he and Rob J. would come to disagreement. At seventeen years of age the former apprentice was exactly what he'd been as a whelp, full of work and sweet agreeability.

Except he drove a bargain like a fishwife.

At the end of the first year of employment he asked for one-twelfth share instead of one-twentieth. Barber grumbled but finally agreed because Rob clearly was deserving of larger reward.

Barber noted he scarcely spent his wages and knew he was saving his money to buy arms. One winter's night in the tavern at Exmouth, a gardener tried to sell Rob a dagger.

"Your opinion?" Rob asked, handing it to Barber.

It was a gardener's weapon. "The blade is bronze and will break. The hilt is adequate perhaps, but a handle so gaudily painted can hide defects."

Rob J. handed back the cheap knife.

When they set forth in the spring they traveled the coast and Rob haunted the harbor docks seeking Spaniards, for the best steel weapons came from Spain. But he had bought nothing by the time they had to turn inland.

July found them in upper Mercia. In the township of Blyth their spirits belied the village's name; they awoke one morning to see Incitatus lying on the ground nearby, stiff and unbreathing.

Rob stood and looked bitterly at the dead horse while Barber vented his feelings through cursing.

"You think a disease did him?"

Barber shrugged. "We saw no sign yesterday, but he was old. He wasn't young when I came by him a long time ago."

Rob spent half a day breaking ground and shoveling, for they didn't want Incitatus eaten by dogs and crows. While he dug the great hole,

Barber went out and searched for a replacement. It took him all day and cost him dear, for their horse was vital to them. Finally he bought a bald-faced brown mare, three years old and not quite fully grown.

"Shall we also name her Incitatus?" he asked, but Rob shook his head and they never called her anything but Horse. She was sweet-stepping, but the first morning they had her she threw a shoe, and they returned to Blyth for a new one.

The blacksmith was named Durman Moulton and they found him finishing a sword that made their eyes glisten.

"How much?" Rob asked, with too much eagerness for Barber's bargaining taste.

"This is bought," the craftsman said, but he allowed them to hold it and feel its balance. It was an English broadsword entirely without ornamentation, sharp and true and beautifully forged. If Barber had been younger and not so wise he would have been tempted to bid for it.

"How much for its exact twin, and a matching dagger?"

The total came to more than a year's income for Rob. "And you must pay one-half now, should you place the order," Moulton said.

Rob went to the wagon and returned with a pouch from which he promptly paid over the money.

"We return in one year to claim the arms and pay the balance," he said, and the smith nodded and told him the weapons would be ready.

Despite the loss of Incitatus they enjoyed a prosperous season, but when it was nearly over, Rob asked him for one-sixth.

"One-sixth of my income! To a young herring not yet eighteen years of age?" Barber was genuinely outraged, though Rob took his outburst calmly and said no more.

As the date of their annual agreement approached it was Barber who fretted, since he was aware how greatly his situation had been improved by his journeyman.

In the village of Sempringham he heard a woman patient hiss to her friend: "Get into the line which awaits the younger barber, Eadburga, for they do say he touches you behind the screen. They do say he has healing hands."

They do say he sells a shitload of the Specific, Barber reminded himself wryly.

He didn't fret that the younger man's screen usually had the longer lines in front of it. Indeed, to an employer Rob J. was gold in his pocket.

"One-eighth," he offered finally.

Though he suffered to do so he would have gone to one-sixth, but to his relief Rob nodded.

"One-eighth is just," Rob said.

The Old Man was born out of Barber's mind. Always seeking to improve the entertainment, he invented an old lecher who drinks the Universal Specific Physick and goes after every woman in sight. "And you must play him," he told Rob.

"I'm too large. And too young."

"No, you shall play him," Barber said stubbornly. "For I'm so fat that one look at me would reveal who I am."

They both watched old men for a long time, studying how they walked in pain and the kind of clothing they wore, and they listened when old people spoke.

"Imagine what it must be like to feel your life disappearing," Barber said. "You believe you'll always be able to get hard with a woman. Think about growing old and not being able to do that."

They fashioned a gray wig and a false gray mustache. They couldn't give him wrinkles but Barber covered his face with cosmetics and simulated an old skin made dry and rough by years of sun and wind. Rob bent his long body and developed a hobbling walk, dragging his right leg. When he spoke he made his voice higher and hesitant, as if he had learned to be a little afraid.

The Old Man, dressed in a shabby coat, made his first appearance in Tadcaster, while Barber was discoursing on the remarkable regenerative powers of the Universal Specific. Walking painfully, he tottered up and bought a bottle.

"Doubtless I'm an old fool for wasting my money," the dry old voice said. Opening the container with some difficulty, he drank the physick then and there and made his slow way to the side of a barmaid who had already been instructed and paid.

"Oh, you are a pretty," he sighed, and the girl glanced away quickly as if abashed. "Would you do a kindness, my dear?"

"If I'm able."

"Just place your hand upon my face. Merely a soft warm palm on an old man's cheek. Aaah," he breathed as she complied shyly.

There were titters as he closed his eyes and kissed her fingers.

In a moment his gaze opened wide. "By the blessed St. Anthony," he breathed. "Oh, it's most remarkable."

He limped back to the bank as quickly as possible. "Let me have another," he told Barber, and drank it at once. This time when he returned to the barmaid she moved away and he followed.

"I'm your servant," he said eagerly. "Mistress . . . " Leaning forward, he whispered into her ear.

"Oh, sirrah, you mustn't talk so!" She moved again, and the crowd was convulsed as he followed.

When, a few minutes later, the Old Man limped away with the barmaid on his arm, they roared approval and then, still laughing, hurried to pay Barber their pennies.

Eventually they didn't have to pay a female to play against the Old Man, for Rob quickly learned to manipulate women in the crowd. He could sense when a good wife was taking offense and must be abandoned, or when a more venturesome woman would not feel abused by a juicy compliment or even a quick pinch.

One night in the town of Lichfield he wore the Old Man costume into the public house and soon had the drinkers howling and wiping their eyes over his amorous memories.

"Once I was a rutter. I well recall swiving a plump beauty . . . hair like black fleece, teats you would milk. A sweet thatch like dark swansdown. While on the other side of the wall her fierce father, half my age, slept all gentle and unknowing."

"And what age were you then, Old Man?"

He carefully straightened an aguish back. "Three days younger than now," he said in his dry and dusty voice.

All evening, fools quarreled for the right to furnish him tipple.

That night, for the first time Barber aided his assistant back to their camp instead of being supported there himself.

Barber took refuge in victualing. He spitted capons and barded ducks, gorging on fowl. In Worcester he came upon the slaughtering of a pair of oxen and bought their tongues.

Here was eating!

He boiled the great tongues briefly before trimming and skinning them, then roasted them with onion and wild garlic and turnip, basting with thyme honey and melted lard until outside they were glazed sweet and crisp, and inside were so tender and yielding that the meat scarcely needed to be chewed.

Rob barely tasted the fine rich food, being in a hurry to find a new tavern in which to play the old ass. In each new place the drinkers kept him continually supplied. Barber knew he best liked ale or beer but presently recognized uneasily that Rob would accept mead, pigment, or morat—whatever there was.

Barber watched closely for signs that the hard drinking would hurt his own pocketbook. But no matter how puky or sodden Rob had been the night before, he appeared to do everything as previously, save in one detail.

"I note you no longer take their hands when they come behind your screen," Barber said.

"Nor do you."

"It's not I who has the gift."

"The gift! You have always held that there is no gift."

"Now I think that there is a gift," Barber said. "I believe that it's dulled by drink, and that it flees before the regular use of liquor."

"It was all our fancy, as you said."

"Listen well. Whether or not the gift has fled, you shall take each person's hands when they come behind your screen, for it's evident they like it. Do you understand?"

Rob J. nodded sullenly.

Next morning, on a wooded track they met a fowler. He carried a long cleft stick which he baited with doughballs imbedded with seeds. When birds came to feed on the bait, by pulling on a rope he was able to close the cleft on their legs and capture them, and he was so clever with the device that his belt was hung all around with little white plovers. Barber bought the flock. Plovers were deemed such a delicacy they were commonly roasted without being drawn, but Barber was too picky. He cleaned and dressed each little bird and made a breakfast that was memorable, so that even Rob's thunderous visage lightened.

In Great Berkhamstead they presented their entertainment before a good audience and sold a lot of physick. That night Barber and Rob went to the tavern together to make peace. For a portion of the evening all was well, but they were drinking strong morat that tasted faintly of bitter mulberries, and Barber watched Rob's eyes grow bright and wondered if his own face reddened that way with drink.

Soon Rob went out of his way to jostle and insult a great burly woodcutter.

In a moment they were trying to maim one another. They were of a size and their brawling was savagely earnest, a form of madness. Benumbed with morat, they stood close and struck again and again with all their strength, using fists and knees and feet, and the blows and kicks sounded like hammers on oak.

Finally exhausted, each was able to be dragged apart by a small army of peacemakers, and Barber took Rob J. away.

"Drunken fool!"

"Look who talks," Rob said.

Trembling with rage, Barber sat and regarded his assistant.

"It's true I may also be a drunken fool," he said, "but I have ever known how to avoid trouble. I have never sold poisons. I have nothing to do with magic that casts spells or raises evil spirits. I just buy large amounts of liquor and put on entertainment that allows me to sell small flasks at fine profit. It's a living that depends upon not calling attention to ourselves. Therefore your stupidity must cease and your fists must stay unclenched."

They glared at one another, but Rob nodded.

From that day Rob appeared to do Barber's bidding almost against his will as they moved southward, racing the migrating birds into autumn. Barber chose to bypass the Salisbury Fair, understanding that it would aggravate old wounds for Rob. His effort was to no avail, for when they camped in Winchester instead of Salisbury, that night Rob returned to the campfire reeling. His face had the look of bruised meat and it was evident he'd been brawling.

"We passed an abbey this morning while you were driving the wagon, yet you didn't stop to inquire after Father Ranald Lovell and your brother."

"It does no good to ask. Whenever I ask, no one ever knows them."

Nor did Rob speak any more of finding his sister Anne Mary or Jonathan or Roger, the brother he had last seen as an infant.

He had given them up and now sought to forget them, Barber told himself, struggling to comprehend. It was as if Rob had turned himself into a bear and offered himself anew for baiting in every public house. Meanness was growing in him like a weed; he welcomed the pain brought by drink and fighting, to drive out the pain he suffered when his brothers and sister entered his mind.

Barber couldn't decide whether Rob's acceptance of the loss of the children was a healthy thing or not.

That winter was the most unpleasant they spent in the little house in Exmouth. In the beginning, he and Rob went to the tavern together. Usually they drank and exchanged talk with the local men, and then found women and brought them home. But he couldn't match the younger man's unflagging appetites, nor, to his surprise, did he wish to do so. Now it was Barber, many a night, who lay and watched the shadows and listened, wishing they would for Christ's sweet sake get it over with and shut up and go to sleep.

There was no snow at all that year but it rained incessantly, and the hiss and spatter soon offended the ear and the spirit. On the third day of Christmas week, Rob came home in a fury.

"The damned publican! He's barred me from the Exmouth Inn."

"For no good reason, I trust?"

"For fighting," Rob muttered, scowling.

Rob spent more time in the house but was moodier than ever, and so was Barber. They didn't have long or pleasant conversation. Mostly Barber drank, his familiar answer to the season of bleakness. When he was able, he imitated the hibernating beasts. When he was awake he lay like a great rock in the sagging bed, feeling his flesh pulling him down and listening to his breath whistling and rasping out of his mouth. He had taken a dim view of many a patient whose breathing sounded better than his own.

Made anxious by such thoughts, he rose from bed once a day to cook an enormous meal, seeking in fatty meats protection against chill and foreboding. Usually next to his bed he kept an opened flask and a platter of fried lamb congealed in its own grease. Rob still cleaned house when he was of a mind, but by February the place smelled like a fox's den.

They welcomed the spring eagerly and in March packed the wagon and drove out of Exmouth, moving across the Salisbury Plain and through the low scarpland where begrimed slaves dug through limestone and chalk to grub out iron and tin. They didn't stop in the slave camps because there wasn't a halfpenny to be earned there. It was Barber's thought to travel the border with Wales until Shrewsbury, there to find the River Trent and follow it northeastward. They stopped in all the by-now-familiar villages and little towns. Horse didn't step into a parade prance with anything like the verve that had been shown by Incitatus, but she was handsome and they dressed her mane with scores of ribbons. Business by and large was very good.

At Hope-Under-Dinmore they found a craftsman in leather who had clever hands and Rob bought two scabbards in soft leather to hold the weapons he had been promised.

When they reached Blyth they went at once to the smithy, where Durman Moulton made them a satisfied greeting. The artisan went to a shelf in the dim recesses of his shop and came back carrying two bundles wrapped in soft animal skins.

Rob undid them eagerly and caught his breath.

If it was possible, the broadsword was better than the one they had so admired the previous year. The dagger was equally wrought. While Rob exulted in the sword, Barber hefted the knife and felt its exquisite balancing.

"It is clean work," he told Moulton, who accepted the compliment for what it was.

Rob slipped each blade into its scabbard on his belt, testing the unfamiliar weight. He placed his hands on their hilts and Barber couldn't resist studying him.

He had presence. At eighteen he finally had reached full growth and stood a double span higher than Barber. He was broad in the shoulder and lean, with a mane of curling brown hair, wide-set blue eyes that changed their mood more swiftly than the sea, a large-boned face and a square jaw he kept scraped clean. He half pulled from its sheath the sword that advertised him as freeborn, and slid it down again. Watching, Barber felt a chill of pride and an overpowering apprehension to which he couldn't give a name.

Perhaps it was not incorrect to call it fear.

Chapter 17

A NEW ARRANGEMENT

The first time Rob walked into a public house wearing arms—it was in Beverley—he felt the difference. It was not that men showed him any more respect, but they were more careful with him, and more watchful. Barber kept telling him that he had to be more careful, too, since violent anger was one of Holy Mother Church's eight capital crimes.

Rob grew weary of hearing what would happen if reeve's men should drag him into churchly court, but Barber repeatedly described trials by ordeal, in which the accused were made to test their innocence by grasping heated rocks or white-hot metal, or drinking boiling water.

"Conviction for murder means hanging or beheading," Barber said severely. "Often when someone does manslaughter, thongs are passed under the sinews of his heels and tied to the tails of wild bulls. The beasts are then hunted to death by hounds."

Merciful Christ, Rob thought, Barber has become an elderly lady complete with faint sighs. Does he believe I'll go out and slay the populace?

In the town of Fulford he discovered he had lost the Roman coin he'd carried with him since his father's work crew had dredged it from the Thames. In the blackest of humors, he drank until it was easy to be provoked by a pockmarked Scot who jostled his elbow. Instead of apologizing, the Scot muttered nastily in Gaelic.

"Speak English, you damned dwarf," Rob snarled, for the Scot, though powerfully built, was two heads shorter than he.

Barber's cautions may have taken hold, for he had the sense to unbuckle his weapons. The Scot did likewise at once, and then they closed with one another. Despite the man's lack of height it was a rude surprise to find him unbelievably skillful with his hands and feet. His first kick cracked a rib and then a fist like a rock broke Rob's nose with an unpleasant sound and worse agony.

Rob grunted. "Whoreson," he gasped, and called upon pain and rage to extend his strength. He was barely able to stay in the fight until the Scot was sufficiently used up to make mutual withdrawal possible.

He limped his way back to the camp feeling and looking as though he had been set upon and beaten mercilessly by a band of giants.

Barber was not overly gentle when he set the broken nose with a crackling of gristle. He dabbed liquor on the scrapes and bruises, but his words stung more than the alcohol.

"You're at a crossroads," he said. "You've learned our trade. You've a quick mind and there's no reason you shouldn't prosper, except the quality of your own spirit. For if you continue along your present path, you'll soon be a hopeless drunkard."

"Pronounced so by one who will himself die of the drink," Rob said disdainfully. He grunted as he touched his swollen and bleeding lips.

"I doubt you'll live long enough to die of the drink," Barber said.

No matter how hard Rob searched, the Roman coin was not to be found. The only possession that remained to link him with his childhood was the arrowhead his father had given him. He had a hole bored through the flint and wore it on a short deerskin thong tied around his neck.

Now men tended to move out of his way, for in addition to his size and the professional look of his weapons, he had a motley nose that wandered slightly on a face in various stages of discoloration. Perhaps Barber had been too angry to do his best when he had set the nose, which was never to be straight again.

The rib hurt for weeks whenever he breathed. Rob was subdued as they traveled from the region of Northumbria to Westmoreland, and then back again to Northumbria. He didn't go to public houses or taverns where it was easy to get into fights, but stayed close to the wagon and the evening fire. Whenever they were camped far from a town he took to sampling the physick and developed a taste for metheglin. But on a night when he had drunk heavily of their stock he found himself about to open a flask on whose neck was scratched the letter B. It was a container from the Special Batch of pissed-in liquor, put up to provide revenge on those who became Barber's enemies. Shuddering, Rob threw the flask away; from then on he bought liquor when they stopped at a town and stowed it carefully in a corner of the wagon.

In the town of Newcastle he played the Old Man, taking refuge behind a false beard that hid his bruises. They had a good crowd and sold a lot of physick. After the entertainment, Rob came behind the wagon to remove his disguise so he could set up his screen and begin his examinations; Barber was already there, arguing with a tall, bony man.

"I have followed you from Durham, where I observed you," the man was saying. "Where you go, you draw a crowd. A crowd is what I need, and I propose we travel together and share all earnings."

"You have no earnings," Barber said.

The man smiled. "I do, for my task is hard work."

"You are a fingersmith and a cutpurse, and you'll be caught one day with your hand in a stranger's pocket and that will be the end of you. I do not work with thieves."

"Perhaps the choice isn't yours."

"The choice is his," Rob said.

The man scarcely favored him with a glance. "You must be silent, old man, lest you attract the attention of those able to do you harm."

Rob stepped toward him. The pickpocket's eyes widened in surprise, and he drew a long, narrow knife from inside his clothing and made a little movement toward them both.

Rob's fine dagger seemed to leave the scabbard of its own accord and slip into the man's arm. He wasn't conscious of effort but the thrust must have been forceful, for he could feel the point grate against bone. When he pulled the blade from the flesh it was at once replaced by spouting blood. Rob was amazed that so much gore should appear so quickly from such a skinny crane of a person.

The pickpocket backed away, holding his wounded arm.

"Come back," Barber said. "Let us bind it up for you. We shan't cause you further harm."

But the man was already edging around the wagon and in a moment had scurried off.

"So much bleeding will be noticed. If there are reeve's men in the town they'll take him, and he may well lead them to us. We must leave here quickly," Barber said.

They fled as they had when they had feared the death of patients, not stopping until they were certain they weren't pursued.

Rob made a fire and sat by it, still dressed as the Old Man and too tired to change, eating cold turnip from yesterday's meal.

"There were two of us," Barber said in disgust. "We could have rid ourselves of him."

"He needed a lesson."

Barber faced him. "Listen to me," he said. "You've become a risk."

Rob bridled at the injustice, for he had acted to protect Barber. He felt new anger bubbling in him, and old resentment. "You've never risked anything on me. You no longer provide our money—I do. I earn more for you than that thief could have gathered with his pinching fingers."

"A risk and a liability," Barber said tiredly, and turned away.

They reached the northernmost leg of their route and stopped in border hamlets where the residents didn't rightly know whether they were English or Scots. When he and Barber were playing before an audience they joshed and worked in apparent harmony, but when they weren't on the bank they settled into a cold silence. If they attempted conversation it soon became a quarrel.

The day was past when Barber dared raise a hand to him, but when he was drunk he still had a filthy and abusive tongue that knew no caution.

On a night in Lancaster, camped next to a pond from which moon-painted mist rose like pale smoke, they were plagued by an army of small flylike insects and took refuge in drink.

"Always were a great clumsy lout. Young Sir Dunghill."

Rob sighed.

"I took an orphaned arsehole . . . molded him . . . would be less than nought without me."

One day soon he would begin to practice barber-surgery on his own, Rob decided; he'd been a long time coming to the conclusion that his path must separate from Barber's.

He had found a merchant with a store of sour wine and had bought in quantity; now he tried to drink the abrasive voice silent. But it went on.

". . . ham-handed and slow of wit. How I did labor to teach him to juggle!"

Soon Rob crawled into the wagon to refill his goblet but was followed by the terrible voice.

"Fetch me a bloody stoup."

Fetch it for your miserable self, he was about to answer.

Instead, taken by an irresistible notion, he crept to where the flagons of Special Batch were kept.

He took one and held it to his eyes until he saw the scratch marks that identified what it was. Then he crawled from the wagon, unstoppered the clay bottle, and handed it to the fat man.

Wicked, he thought fearfully. Yet no more wicked than Barber's giving Special Batch to so many through the years.

He watched in fascination as Barber took the flagon, tilted his head back, opened his mouth, and lifted the drink to his lips.

There was yet time to redeem himself. He almost heard his voice calling upon Barber to wait. He would say the bottle had a broken lip and easily replace it with an unmarked bottle of metheglin.

But he kept his silence.

The neck of the bottle entered Barber's mouth.

Swallow it, Rob urged cruelly.

The fleshy neck worked as Barber drank. Then, throwing away the empty flask, he fell back into sleep.

Why did he feel no glee? Through a long and sleepless night he thought on it.

When Barber was sober he could be two men, one of them kindly and with a merry heart, the other a baser person who didn't hesitate to dispense the Special Batch. When he was drunk there was no question, the baser man emerged.

Rob saw with sudden clarity, like a spear of light across a dark sky, that he was transforming himself into the baser Barber. He shivered, and a desolation crept over him as he moved closer to the fire.

Next morning he rose with first light and found the discarded marked bottle and hid it in the woods. Then he restored the fire and by the time Barber stirred, a lavish breakfast awaited him.

"I haven't been a proper man," Rob said when Barber had eaten. He hesitated and then forced himself to go on. "I ask your pardon and absolution."

Barber nodded, astonished into silence.

They harnessed Horse and rode without speaking through half the morning, and at times Rob was aware of the other man's thoughtful eyes on him.

"I have long dwelt on it," Barber said at last. "Next season you must go out as barber-surgeon without me."

Feeling guilty because only the day before he had reached the same conclusion, Rob protested. "It's the damned drink. The stuff transforms each of us cruelly. We must abjure it and we'll get on as before."

Barber appeared moved but shook his head. "It's partly the drink, and partly it is that you're a young hart needing to try his antlers and I'm an old stag. Further, for a stag I am exceedingly huge and breathless," he said drily. "It takes all my strength for me simply to climb the bank, and each day it's more difficult for me to get through the entertainment. I would happily remain in Exmouth forever, to enjoy the soft summer and tend a salad garden, to say nothing of the pleasures I'll gain from my kitchen. While you are gone I can put up a plentiful store of the physick. Too, I'll pay for maintenance of wagon and Horse as heretofore. You shall keep for yourself the proceed from every patient whom you treat, as well as from every fifth bottle of physick sold the first year and every fourth bottle sold each year thereafter."

"Every third bottle the first year," Rob said automatically. "And every second bottle thereafter."

"That's excessive for a youth of nineteen years," Barber said severely. His eyes gleamed. "Let us dwell on it together," he said, "for we are reasonable men."

In the end they agreed on the income from every fourth bottle over the first year, and on every third bottle in years following. The agreement would run for a period of five years, after which they would take stock of it.

Barber was jubilant and Rob couldn't believe his good fortune, for his earnings would be remarkable for one his age. They traveled southward through Northumbria in the highest of spirits and with a renewal of good feeling and comradeship. In Leeds, after their work they spent several hours at marketing; Barber bought prodigiously and declared that he must make a dinner suitable to celebrate their new arrangement.

They left Leeds along a track that rode low beside the River Aire, through mile on mile of ancient trees towering high above green thickets and twisted groves and heathy glades. They camped early among alder beds and willows where the river widened, and for hours he helped Barber create a great meat pie. In it Barber placed the minced and mingled meat of the leg of a roe deer and a loin of veal, a plump capon and a pair of doves, six boiled eggs and half a pound of fat, covering all with a crust that was thick and flaky and oozing oil.

They ate it at great length, and nothing would suit Barber but to begin drinking metheglin when the pie raised his thirst. Remembering his recent vow, Rob drank water and watched as Barber's face reddened and his eyes grew surly.

Presently Barber demanded that Rob carry two boxes of flasks out of the wagon and set them close to him, that he might help himself at will. Rob did so and watched uneasily while Barber drank. Soon Barber began to mutter untowardly about the terms of their agreement, but before things could go thwartly he sank into a sodden sleep.

In the morning, which was bright and sunny and filled with the song of birds, Barber was pale and querulous. He didn't appear to recall his overweening behavior of the previous evening.

"Let's go after trouts," he said. "I could do well with a breakfast of crisp fish and the Aire appears to be likely water." But when he rose from his bed he complained of an ague in his left shoulder. "I'll load the wagon," he decided, "for labor often works to grease an aching joint."

He carried one of the boxes of metheglin back to the wagon, then returned and picked up the other. He was halfway to the wagon when he dropped the box with a thump and a clatter. A puzzled look crept into his face.

He put his hand to his chest and grimaced. Rob saw that pain was making him hunch his shoulders. "Robert," he said politely. It was the first time Rob had heard Barber pronounce his formal name.

He took one step toward Rob, thrusting out both his hands.

But before Rob could reach him he stopped breathing. Like a great tree —no, like an avalanche, like the death of a mountain—Barber toppled and fell, crashing to the earth.

Chapter 18

REQUIESCAT

"I did not know him."

"He was my friend."

"Nor ever have I seen you," the priest said dourly.

"You see me now." Rob had unloaded their belongings from the wagon and hidden them behind a copse of willows, in order to make room for Barber's body. He had driven six hours to reach the small village of Aire's Cross, with its ancient church. Now this mean-eyed cleric asked suspicious and surly questions, as if Barber had pretended to die, solely for his inconvenience.

The priest sniffed in open disapproval when his inquiry revealed what Barber had been in life. "Physician, surgeon, or barber—all of these flout the obvious truth that only the Trinity and the saints have true power to heal."

Rob was burdened with strong emotions and not disposed to listen to such sounds. Enough, he snarled silently. He was conscious of the weapons on his belt but it was as though Barber counseled him to forbear. He spoke softly and pleasingly to the priest and made a sizable contribution to the church.

Finally the priest sniffed. "Archbishop Wulfstan has forbidden priests to entice away another priest's parishioner with his tithes and dues."

"He wasn't another priest's parishioner," Rob said. In the end burial in sacred ground was arranged.

It was fortunate he had taken a full purse with him. The matter couldn't be delayed, for already there was the smell of death. The joiner in the village was shocked when he saw how large a box he must construct. The hole had to be correspondingly generous, and Rob dug it himself in a corner of the churchyard.

Rob had thought Aire's Cross was so named because it marked a ford on the River Aire, but the priest said the hamlet was called after a great rood of polished oak within the church. Before the altar at the foot of this enormous cross was placed Barber's rosemary-strewn coffin. By chance the day was Feast of St. Callistus and the Church of the Rood was well attended. When the Kyrie Eleison was said, the little sanctuary was almost filled.

"Lord have mercy, Christ have mercy," they chanted.

There were only two small windows. Incense fought with the stink, but some air came through the walls of split trees and the thatched roof, causing the rush lights to flicker in their sockets. Six tall tapers struggled against the gloom in a circle around the casket. A white pall covered all but Barber's face. Rob had closed his eyes and he looked asleep, or perhaps very drunk.

"He was father to you?" an old woman whispered. Rob hesitated, then it seemed easiest to nod. She sighed and touched his arm.

He had paid for a Mass of Requiem in which the people participated with touching solemnity, and he saw with satisfaction that Barber wouldn't have been better attended had he belonged to a guild, nor more respectfully prayed away if his pall had been the purple of royalty.

When the Mass was done and the people departed, Rob approached the altar. He knelt four times and signed the cross upon his breast as he had been taught by Mam so long ago, bowing himself separately to God, His Son, Our Lady, and finally to the Apostles and all holy souls.

The priest went about the church and thriftily extinguished the rush lights, and then left him mourning by the bier.

Rob departed neither to eat nor to drink but remained kneeling, seemingly suspended between dancing candlelight and the heavy blackness.

Time passed without his knowledge.

He was startled when loud bells chimed the hour of matins, and he rose to lurch down the aisle on benumbed legs.

"Make your reverence," the priest said coldly, and he did so.

Outside, he walked down the road. Under a tree he passed water, then returned and washed hands and face from the bucket by the door while within the church the priest completed Midnight Office.

Some time after the priest went away for the second time the tapers burned down, leaving Rob alone in darkness with Barber.

Now he allowed himself to think of how the man had saved him when he was a boy in London. He remembered Barber when he was gentle and when he was not; his tender pleasure at preparing and sharing food, and his selfishness; his patience in instruction, and his cruelty; his raunchiness, and his sober advice; his laughter, and his rages; his warm spirit, and his drunkenness.

What had passed between them wasn't love, Rob knew. Yet it had been something that substituted for love sufficiently that, as first light grayed the waxen face, Rob J. wept bitterly, and not entirely for Henry Croft.

Barber was buried after lauds. The priest didn't spend overly long at the graveside. "You may fill it in," he told Rob. As the stone and gravel rattled onto the lid, Rob heard him mutter in Latin, something about the sure and certain hope of the Resurrection.

Rob did what he would have done for family. Remembering his lost graves, he paid the priest to order a stone and specified how it was to be marked.

Henry Croft.
Barber-surgeon.
Died Jul 11 in the yr A.D. *1030.*

"Mayhap *Requiescat in Pace,* or some such?" the priest said.

The only epitaph true to Barber that came to him was *Carpe Diem,* "Enjoy the Day." Yet, somehow . . .

And then he smiled.

The priest was annoyed when he heard the selection. But the formidable young stranger was paying for the stone and insisted, so the cleric carefully wrote it down.

Fumum vendidi. "I sold smoke."

Watching this cold-eyed priest putting away his profit with a satisfied mien, Rob realized that it wouldn't be remarkable if no stone were raised to a dead barber-surgeon. With no one in Aire's Cross to care.

"I shall be back one day soon to see that all is to my satisfaction."

A veil came over the priest's eyes. "Go with God," he said shortly, and went back into the church.

Weary to the bone and hungry, Rob drove Horse to where he had left their things in the willow copse.

Nothing had been disturbed. When he had loaded it all back into the wagon, he sat in the grass and ate. What remained of the meat pie was spoiled, but he chewed and swallowed a stale loaf Barber had baked four days before.

It occurred to him that he was the heir. It was his horse and his wagon.

He had inherited the instruments and techniques, the ratty fur blankets, the juggling balls and the magic tricks, the dazzle and the smoke, the decisions about where to go tomorrow and the day after tomorrow.

The first thing he did was remove the flasks of Special Batch and throw them against a rock, smashing them one by one.

He would sell Barber's weapons; his own were better. But he hung the Saxon horn around his neck.

He clambered onto the front seat of the wagon and sat there, solemn and erect, as though it were a throne.

Perhaps, he thought, he would look around and get himself a boy.

Chapter 19

A WOMAN IN THE ROAD

He traveled on as they always had done, "taking a promenade through the innocent world," Barber would have said. For the first days he couldn't force himself to unpack the wagon or give an entertainment. In Lincoln he bought himself a hot meal at the public house but he did no cooking, mostly feeding on bread and cheese made by others. He didn't drink at all. Evenings, he sat by his campfire and was assailed by a terrible loneliness.

He was waiting for something to happen. But nothing did, and after a bit he came to understand that he would have to live his life.

In Stafford he decided to return to work. Horse picked up her ears and pranced as he banged the drum and announced their presence in the town square.

It was as though he had always worked alone. The people who gathered didn't know there should have been an older man who signaled when to start and stop the juggling and who told the best stories. They gathered about and listened and laughed, watched enthralled as he drew likenesses, bought his doctored liquor, and waited in line to seek treatment behind the screen. When Rob took their hands he discovered the gift was back. A burly blacksmith who looked as though he could lift the world had something in him that was consuming his life, and he wouldn't last long. A thin girl whose wan appearance might have suggested illness had a reservoir of strength and vitality that filled Rob with joy when he felt it. Perhaps, as Barber had declared, the gift had been stifled by alcohol and liberated by abstinence. Whatever the reason for its return, he found himself astir with excitement and eager to be linked to the next pair of hands.

Leaving Stafford that afternoon, he stopped at a farm to buy bacon and saw the barn mouser with a litter of kittens. "Take your pick of the lot," the farmer told him hopefully. "I'll have to drown most of them, for they all consume food."

Rob played with them, dangling a piece of rope in front of their noses, and they were each winsome save for one disdainful little white cat that remained haughty and scornful.

"Do you not wish to come with me, eh?" The kitten was composed and looked to be the goodliest, but when he tried to hold her she scratched him on the hand.

Strangely, it made him all the more determined to take her. He whispered to her soothingly, and it was a triumph when he was able to pick her up and smooth her fur with his fingers.

"This one will do," he said, and thanked the farmer.

Next morning he cooked his own breakfast and fed the cat bread soaked in milk. When he gazed into her greenish eyes he recognized the feline bitchiness there, and he smiled. "I'll name you after Mistress Buffington," he told her.

Perhaps feeding her was the necessary magic. Within hours she was purring to him, lying in his lap as he sat in the wagon seat.

In the middle of the morning he set the cat aside when he drove around a curve in Tettenhall, and came upon a man standing over a woman in the road. "What ails her?" he called, and pulled Horse short. He saw she was breathing; her face was bright with exertion and she had an enormous belly.

"Come her time," the man said.

In the orchard behind him, half a dozen baskets were filled with apples. He was dressed in rags and didn't appear the man to own rich property. Rob guessed he was a cottager, doubtless laboring on a large tract for a landlord in return for a small soccage piece he could work for his own family.

"We were picking earliest fruit when her pains came upon her. She started for home but was quickly caught out. There is no midwife here, for the woman died this spring. I sent a boy running to fetch the leech when it was clear she was in a hard place."

"Well, then," Rob said, and picked up his reins. He was prepared to move on because it was precisely the kind of situation Barber had taught him to avoid; if he could help the woman there would be tiny payment, but if he could not, he might be blamed for what happened.

"It's been time and more now," the man said bitterly, "and still the physician doesn't come. He's a Jew doctor."

Even as the man spoke, Rob saw his wife's eyes roll back in her head as she went into convulsions.

From what Barber had told him of Jew physicians he thought it likely the leech might not come at all. He was snared by the stolid misery in the cottager's eyes and by memories he would have liked to forget.

Sighing, he climbed down from the wagon.

He knelt over the dirty, worn woman and took her hands. "When did she last feel the child move?"

"It's been weeks. For a fortnight she's been feeling poorly, as if she was poisoned." She had had four previous pregnancies, he said. There was a pair of boys at home but the last two babies had been born still.

Rob felt that this child was dead too. He put his hand lightly on the distended stomach and wished devoutly to leave, but in his mind he saw Mam's white face when she had lain on the shitty stable floor, and he had a disturbing knowledge that the woman would die quickly unless he acted.

In the jumble of Barber's gear he found the speculum of polished metal, but he didn't use it as a mirror. When the convulsion had passed he positioned her legs and dilated the cervix with the instrument as Barber had described its use. The mass inside her slid out easily, more putrefaction than baby. He was scarcely aware of her husband sucking in his breath and walking away.

His hands told his head what to do, instead of the other way around.

He got the placenta out and cleansed and washed her. When he looked up, to his surprise he saw that the Jew doctor had arrived.

"You will want to take over," he said. He felt great relief, for there was steady bleeding.

"There is no hurry," the physician said. But he listened interminably to her breathing and examined her so slowly and thoroughly that his lack of faith in Rob was apparent.

Eventually the Jew appeared satisfied. "Place your palm on her abdomen and rub firmly, like this."

Rob massaged her empty belly, wondering. Finally, through the abdomen he could feel the big, spongy womb snap back into a small hard ball, and the bleeding stopped.

"Magic worthy of Merlin and a trick I'll remember," he said.

"There is no magic in what we do," the Jew doctor said calmly. "You know my name."

"We met some years ago. In Leicester."

Benjamin Merlin looked at the garish wagon and then smiled. "Ah. You were a boy, the apprentice. The barber was a fat man who belched colored ribbons."

"Yes."

Rob didn't tell him Barber was dead, nor did Merlin inquire of him. They studied one another. The Jew's hawk face was still framed by a full head of white hair and his white beard, but he was not so thin as he had been.

"The clerk with whom you spoke, that day in Leicester. Did you couch his eyes?"

"Clerk?" Merlin appeared puzzled and then his gaze cleared. "Yes! He is Edgar Thorpe of the village of Lucteburne, in Leicestershire."

If Rob had heard of Edgar Thorpe he had forgotten. It was a difference between them, he realized; much of the time he didn't learn his patients' names.

"I did operate on him and removed his cataracts."

"And today? Is he well?"

Merlin smiled ruefully. "Master Thorpe cannot be called well, for he grows old and has ailments and complaints. But he sees through both eyes."

Rob had hidden the ruined fetus in a rag. Merlin unwrapped it and studied it, then he sprinkled it with water from a flask. "I baptize you in the name of the Father, the Son, and the Holy Spirit," the Jew said briskly, then he rewrapped the little bundle and carried it to the cottage. "The infant has been christened properly," he said, "and doubtless will be allowed to enter the Kingdom of Heaven. You must tell Father Stigand or that other priest at the church."

The husbandman took out a soiled purse, the stolid misery on his face mingling with apprehension. "What do I pay, master physician?"

"What you can," Merlin said, and the man took a penny from the purse and gave it to him.

"Was it a man-child?"

"One cannot tell," the physician said kindly. He dropped the coin into the large pocket of his kirtle and fumbled until he came up with a halfpenny, which he gave to Rob. They had to help the cottager carry her home, a hard ha'penny's worth of work.

When finally they were free they went to a nearby stream and washed off the blood.

"You've watched similar deliveries?"

"No."

"How did you know what to do?"

Rob shrugged. "It had been described to me."

"They say some are born healers. Selected." The Jew smiled at him. "Of course, others are simply lucky," he said.

The man's scrutiny made him uncomfortable. "If the mother had been dead and the babe alive, . . ." Rob said, forcing himself to ask.

"Caesar's operation."

Rob stared.

"You don't know of what I speak?"

"No."

"You must cut through the belly and the uterine wall and take the child."

"Open the mother?"

"Yes."

"Have you done this?"

"Several times. When I was a medical clerk I saw one of my teachers open a live woman to get at her child."

Liar! he thought, ashamed to be listening so eagerly. He remembered what Barber had said about this man and all his kind. "What happened?"

"She died, but she would have died at any rate. I do not approve of opening live women, but I was told of men who had done so with both mother and child surviving."

Rob turned away before this French-sounding man could laugh at him for a fool. But he had taken only two steps when he was compelled to come back.

"Where to cut?"

In the dust of the road the Jew drew a torso and showed two incisions, one a long straight line on the left side, the other up the middle of the belly. "Either," he said, and threw the stick far.

Rob nodded and went away, unable to give him thanks.

Chapter 20

CAPS AT TABLE

He moved out of Tettenhall at once but something was already happening to him.

He was running low on Universal Specific and next day bought a keg of liquor from a farmer, pausing to mix a new batch of physick which that afternoon he began to rid himself of in Ludlow. The Specific sold as well as ever, but he was preoccupied and a little frightened.

To hold a human soul in the palm of your hand like a pebble. To feel somebody slip away, yet by *your actions* to bring her back! Not even a king had such power.

Selected.

Could he learn more? How much could be learned? What must it be like, he asked himself, to learn all that could be taught?

For the first time he recognized in himself a desire to become a physician.

Truly to be able to fight death! He was having new and disturbing thoughts that at times produced rapture and at other times were almost an agony.

Next morning he set out for Worcester, the next town to the south along the Severn River. He didn't remember seeing the river or the track, or recollect guiding Horse, or recall anything else of the journey. When he reached Worcester, the townsfolk gaped as they watched the red wagon; it rolled into the square, made a complete circuit without stopping, and then left the town and traveled back in the direction whence it had come.

The village of Lucteburne in Leicestershire wasn't large enough to support a tavern, but haysel was in progress and when he stopped at a meadow in which four men wielded scythes, the cutter in the swath closest to the road ceased his rhythmic swinging long enough to tell him how to reach Edgar Thorpe's house.

Rob found the old man on his hands and knees in his small garden, harvesting leeks. He perceived at once, with a strange sense of excitement, that Thorpe was able to see. But he was suffering sorely from rheum sickness and, although Rob helped him to regain his feet amid groans and anguished exclamations, it was a few moments before they were able to speak calmly.

Rob brought several bottles of Specific from the wagon and opened one, which pleased his host greatly.

"I am here to inquire into the operation which gave you back your sight, Master Thorpe."

"Indeed? And what is your interest?"

Rob hesitated. "I have a kinsman in need of such treatment, and I inquire in his name."

Thorpe took a swallow of liquor and then sighed. "I hope that he's a strong man with bountiful courage," he said. "Tied to a chair hands and feet, I was. Cruel bindings cut into my head, fixing it against the high back. I'd been fed many a stoup and was close to senseless from drink, but then small hooks were placed beneath my eyelids and lifted by assistants so I couldn't blink."

He closed his eyes and shuddered. The tale obviously had been told many times, for the details were fixed in his memory and related without hesitation, but Rob found them no less fascinating for that.

"Such was my affliction that I could only see, fuzzily, what was directly before me. There swam into my vision Master Merlin's hand. It was holding a blade, which grew larger as it descended, until it cut into my eye.

"Oh, the pain of it sobered me instantly! I was certain he had cut out my eye instead of merely removing the cloudiness and I shrieked at him and importuned him to do nothing more to me. When he persisted I rained curses on his head and said that at last I understood how his despised folk could have killed our gentle Lord.

"When he cut into the second eye the pain was so great that I lost all knowledge. I awoke to the darkness of wrapped eyes and for almost a fortnight suffered grievously. But at length I was able to see as I hadn't done for overly long. So great was the improvement of my sight that I spent two more full years as clerk before the rheum made it sensible to curtail my duties."

So it was true, Rob thought dazedly. Then perhaps the other things Benjamin Merlin had told him were fact as well.

"Master Merlin is the goodliest doctor ever I did see," Edgar Thorpe said. "Except," he added crossly, "for so competent a physician he seems to be meeting untoward difficulty in ridding my bones and joints of great discomfort."

He went to Tettenhall again and camped in a little valley, staying near the town three days like a lovesick swain who lacked the courage to visit a female but couldn't bring himself to leave her alone. The first farmer from whom he bought provision told him where Benjamin Merlin lived, and several times he drove Horse slowly past the place, a low farmhouse with well-kept barn and outbuilding, a field, an orchard, and a vineyard. There were no outward signs that here lived a physician.

On the afternoon of the third day, miles from Merlin's house, he met the physician on the road.

"How do I find you, young barber?"

Rob said he was well and asked after the physician's health. They chatted of weather for a grave moment and then Merlin nodded his dismissal. "I may not tarry, for I must still go to the homes of three sick persons before my day's work is done."

"May I accompany you, and observe?" Rob forced himself to say.

The physician hesitated. He seemed less than pleased by the request. But he nodded, however reluctantly. "Kindly see that you stay out of the way," he said.

The first patient lived not far from where they had met, in a small cottage by a goose pond. He was Edwin Griffith, an old man with a hollow cough, and Rob saw at once that he was failing of advanced chest sickness and soon would be in his grave.

"How do I find you this day, Master Griffith?" Merlin asked.

The old man quailed beneath a paroxysm of coughing and then gasped and sighed. "I am same and with few regrets, save that I wasn't able today to feed my geese."

Merlin smiled. "Perhaps my young friend here might tend to them," he said, and Rob could do nothing but agree. Old Griffith told him where fodder was kept, and soon he was hurrying to the side of the pond with a sack. He was annoyed because this visit was a loss to him, since surely Merlin wouldn't spend time overly with a dying man. He approached the geese gingerly, for he knew how vicious they could be; but they were hungry and single-mindedly made for the feed with a great squabble, allowing him a quick escape.

To his surprise, Merlin was still talking with Edwin Griffith when he

reentered the little house. Rob never had seen a physician work so deliberately. Merlin asked interminable questions about the man's habits and diet,
about his childhood, about his parents and his grandparents and what they
had died of. He felt the pulse at the wrist and again on the neck, and he
placed his ear against the chest and listened. Rob hung back, watching
intently.

When they left, the old man thanked him for feeding the fowl.

It appeared to be a day devoted to tending the doomed, for Merlin led
him two miles away to a house off the town square, in which the reeve's
wife lay wasting away in pain.

"How do I find you, Mary Sweyn?"

She didn't answer but looked at him steadily. It was answer enough, and
Merlin nodded. He sat and held her hand and spoke quietly to her; as he
had done with the old man, he spent a surprising amount of time.

"You may help me to turn Mistress Sweyn," he said to Rob. "Gently.
Gently, now." When Merlin lifted her bedgown to bathe her skeletal body
they noted, on her pitiful left flank, an angry boil. The physician lanced
it at once to give her comfort and Rob saw to his satisfaction that it was
accomplished as he would have done it himself. Merlin left her a flask filled
with a pain-dulling infusion.

"One more to see," Merlin said as they closed Mary Sweyn's door. "He
is Tancred Osbern, whose son brought word this morning that he has done
himself an injury."

Merlin tied his horse's reins to the wagon and sat on the front seat next
to Rob, for the company.

"How fare your kinsman's eyes?" the physician asked blandly.

He might have known that Edgar Thorpe would mention his inquiry,
Rob told himself, and felt the blood rushing into his cheeks. "I didn't intend
to deceive him. I wished to see for myself the results of your couching,"
he said. "And it seemed the simplest way to explain my interest."

Merlin smiled and nodded. As they rode he explained the surgical
method he had used to remove Thorpe's cataracts. "It is not an operation
I would advise anyone doing on his own," he said pointedly, and Rob
nodded, for he had no intention of going off to operate on any person's
eyes!

Whenever they came to a crossroads Merlin pointed the way, until
finally they drew near a prosperous farm. It had the orderly look produced
by constant attention, but inside they found a massive and muscular farmer
groaning on the straw-filled pallet that was his bed.

"Ah, Tancred, what have you done to yourself this time?" Merlin said.

"Hurt t'bloody leg."

Merlin threw back the cover and frowned, for the right limb was twisted at the thigh, and swollen. "You must be in frightful pain. Yet you told the boy to say, 'whenever I arrived.' Next time you are not to be stupidly brave, that I may come at once," he said sharply.

The man closed his eyes and nodded.

"How did you do yourself, and when?"

"Yesterday noon. Fell off damn roof while fixing cursed thatch."

"You will not be fixing the thatch for a while," Merlin said. He looked at Rob. "I shall need help. Find us a splint, somewhat longer than his leg."

"Not to tear up buildings or fences," Osbern growled.

Rob went to see what he could find. In the barn there were a dozen logs of beech and oak, as well as a piece of pine that had been worked by hand into a board. It was too wide, but the wood was soft and it took him little time to split it lengthwise using the farmer's tools.

Osbern glowered when he recognized the splint but said nothing.

Merlin looked down and sighed. "He has thighs like a bull's. We have our work before us, young Cole," he said. Grasping the injured leg by the ankle and the calf, the physician tried to exert a steady pressure, at the same time turning and straightening the twisted limb. There was a small crackling, like the sound made when dried leaves are crushed, and Osbern emitted a great bellowing.

"It is no use," Merlin said in a moment. "His muscles are huge. They have locked themselves to protect the leg and I do not have sufficient strength to overcome them and reduce the fracture."

"Let me try," Rob said.

Merlin nodded, but first he fed a full mug of liquor to the farmer, who was trembling and sobbing with the agony induced by the unsuccessful effort.

"Give me another," Osbern gasped.

When he had swallowed the second cup, Rob grasped the leg as Merlin had done. Careful not to jerk, he exerted steady pressure, and Osbern's deep voice changed to a shrill prolonged scream.

Merlin had grabbed the big man beneath the armpits and was pulling the other way, his face contorted and his eyes popping with the effort.

"I think we're getting it," Rob shouted so Merlin could hear him over the anguished sounds. "It's going!" Even as he spoke, the ends of the broken bone grated past one another and locked into place.

There was a sudden silence from the man in the bed.

Rob glanced to see if he had fainted, but Osbern was lying back limply, his face wet with tears.

"Keep up the tension on the leg," Merlin said urgently.

He fashioned a sling out of strips of rag and fastened it around Osbern's foot and ankle. He tied one end of a rope to the sling and the other end tautly to the door handle, then he applied the splint to the extended limb. "Now you may let go of him," he told Rob.

For good measure, they tied the sound leg to the splinted one.

Within minutes they had comforted the trussed and exhausted patient, left instructions with his pale wife, and taken leave of his brother, who would work the farm.

They paused in the barnyard and looked at one another. Each of them wore a shirt soaked through with perspiration, and both faces were as wet as Osbern's tear-streaked cheeks had been.

The physician smiled and clapped him on the shoulder. "You must come home with me now and share our evening meal," he said.

"My Deborah," Benjamin Merlin said.

The doctor's wife was a plump woman with a figure like a pigeon's, a sharp little nose, and very red cheeks. She had blanched when she saw him and she acknowledged their introduction stiffly. Merlin carried a bowl of spring water into the yard so Rob could refresh himself. As he bathed he could hear the woman inside the house haranguing her husband in a language he had never heard before.

The physician grimaced when he came out to wash. "You must forgive her. She is fearful. Law says we must not have Christians in our homes during holy feasts. This will scarcely be a holy feast. It is a simple supper." He glanced at Rob levelly as he wiped himself dry. "However, I can bring food outside to you, if you choose not to sit at table."

"I'm grateful to be allowed to join you, master physician."

Merlin nodded.

A strange supper.

There were the parents and four small children, three of them males. The little girl was Leah and her brothers were Jonathan, Ruel, and Zechariah. The boys and their father wore caps to table! When the wife brought in a hot loaf Merlin nodded to Zechariah, who broke off a piece and began to speak in the guttural tongue Rob had heard previously.

His father stopped him. "Tonight, *brochot* will be in English as courtesy to our guest."

"Blessed art Thou, O Lord our God, King of the Universe," the boy said sweetly, "Who brings forth bread from the earth." He gave the loaf directly to Rob, who found it good and passed it to others.

Merlin poured red wine from a decanter. Rob followed their example and lifted his goblet as the father nodded to Ruel.

"Blessed art Thou, O Lord our God, King of the Universe, Who creates the fruit of the vine."

The meal was a fish soup made with milk, not as Barber had made it, but hot and zesty. Afterward they ate apples from the Jew's orchard. The youngest boy, Jonathan, told his father with great indignation that rabbits were wasting their cabbages.

"Then you must waste the rabbits," Rob said. "You must snare them so your mother may serve a savory stew."

There was a strange little silence and then Merlin smiled. "We do not eat rabbit or hare, for they are not *kasher.*"

Rob saw that Mistress Merlin appeared apprehensive, as if she feared he wouldn't comprehend or sympathize with their ways.

"It is a set of dietary laws, old as old." Merlin explained that Jews were not allowed to eat animals that didn't chew their cud and have cloven hooves. They couldn't eat flesh together with milk, because the Bible admonished that lamb mustn't be seethed in the flow of its milch-mother's teats. And they were not permitted to drink blood, or to eat meat that had not been thoroughly bled and salted.

Rob's blood turned cold and he told himself that Mistress Merlin had been right: he could not comprehend Jews. Jews were pagans indeed!

His stomach churned as the physician thanked God for their bloodless and meatless food.

Nonetheless he asked if he might camp in their orchard that night. Benjamin Merlin insisted that he sleep under shelter, in the barn which was attached to the house, and presently Rob lay on fragrant straw and listened through the thin wall to the sharp rise and fall of the wife's voice. He smiled mirthlessly in the gloom, knowing the essence of her message despite the unintelligible language.

You do not know this great young brute, yet you bring him here. Can you not see his bent nose and battered face, and the expensive weapons of a criminal? He will murder us in our beds!

Presently Merlin came out to the barn with a great flask and two wooden goblets. He handed Rob a cup and sighed. "She is otherwise a most excellent woman," he said, and poured. "It is difficult for her here, for she feels cut off from many she holds dear."

It was good strong drink, Rob discovered. "What section of France are you from?"

"Like this wine we drink, my wife and I were made in the village of Falaise, where our families live under the benevolent surety of Robert of Normandy. My father and two brothers are vintners and suppliers to the English trade."

Seven years before, Merlin said, he had returned to Falaise from studying in Persia at an academy for physicians.

"Persia!" Rob had no idea where Persia was, but he knew it was very far away. "In what direction does Persia lie?"

Merlin smiled. "It is in the East. Far to the east."

"How came you to England?"

When he returned to Normandy as a new physician, Merlin said, he found that within the protectorate of Duke Robert there were medical practitioners in too goodly a number. Outside of Normandy there was constant strife and the uncertain dangers of war and politics, duke against count, nobles against king. "Twice in my youth I had been to London with my wine merchant father. I remembered the beauty of the English countryside, and all Europe knows of King Canute's gift of stability. So I decided to come to this green and peaceful place."

"And has Tettenhall proved to be a sound choice?"

Merlin nodded. "But there are difficulties. Without those who share our faith we cannot pray to God properly and it is hard to keep the laws of victuals. We speak to our children in their own tongue but they think in the language of England, and despite our efforts, they're ignorant of many of the customs of their people. I am seeking to attract other Jews here from France."

He moved to pour more wine, but Rob covered his cup with his hand. "I'm undone by more than a little drink, and I've need of my head."

"Why have you sought me out, young barber?"

"Tell me about the school in Persia."

"It's in the town of Ispahan, in the western part of the country."

"Why did you go so far?"

"Where else was I to go? My family had no desire to apprentice me to a physician, for though the admission grieves me, over most of Europe my profession is composed of a poor lot of leeches and knaves. There is a large hospital in Paris, the Hôtel Dieu, that is merely a pesthouse for the poor into which screaming men are dragged to die. There is a medical school in Salerno, a sorry place. Through communication with other Jewish merchants my father was aware that in the countries of the East the Arabs have made a fine art of the science of medicine. In Persia the Muslims have a hospital at Ispahan that is truly a healing center. It is in this hospital and in a small academy there that Avicenna makes his doctors."

"Who?"

"The outstanding physician in the world. Avicenna, whose Arab name is Abu Ali at-Husain ibn Abdullah ibn Sina."

Rob made Merlin repeat the foreign melodiousness of the name until he had it memorized.

"Is it hard to reach Persia?"

"Several years of dangerous travel. Sea voyages, then a land voyage over terrible mountains and vast desert." Merlin looked at his guest keenly. "You must put the Persian academies out of mind. How much do you know of your own faith, young barber? Are you familiar with the problems of your anointed Pope?"

He shrugged. "John XIX?" In truth, beyond the Pontiff's name and the fact that he led Holy Church, Rob knew nothing.

"John XIX. He is a Pope who stands astride two giant churches instead of one, like a man seeking to ride two horses. The Western Church ever shows him fealty, but in the Eastern Church there is constant muttering of discontent. Two hundred years ago Photius became a rebellious Patriarch of the Eastern Catholics in Constantinople, and ever since, the movement toward a schism in the Church has gathered strength.

"You may have observed in your own dealings with priests that they mistrust and dislike physicians, surgeons, and barbers, believing that through prayer they themselves are the rightful guardians of men's bodies as well as their souls."

Rob grunted.

"The antipathy of these English priests toward medical men is nothing compared to the hatred which Eastern Catholic priests hold for the Arab physicians' schools and other Muslim academies. Living cheek by jowl with the Muslims, the Eastern Church is engaged in a constant and earnest war with Islam to win men into the grace of the one true faith. The Eastern hierarchy sees in the Arab centers of learning incitement to heathenism and a grievous threat. Fifteen years ago Sergius II, who was then Patriarch of the Eastern Church, declared any Christian attending a Muslim school east of his patriarchate to be sacrilegious and a breaker of the faith, and guilty of heathen practice. He applied pressure on the Holy Father in Rome to join him in this declaration. Benedict VIII was newly elevated to the Seat of Peter, with forebodings of becoming the Pope who oversaw the dissolution of the Church. To appease the discontented Eastern element, he readily granted Sergius' request. The penalty for heathenism is excommunication."

Rob pursed his lips. "It is severe punishment."

The physician nodded. "More severe in that it carries with it terrible retribution under secular law. The legal codes adopted under both King Aethelred and King Canute deem heathenism a principal crime. Those convicted of it have met with awful punishments. Some have been clothed in heavy chains and sent to wander as pilgrims for years until the shackles rust and fall away from their bodies. Several have been burned. Some were hanged, and others were cast into prison where they remain to this day.

"For their part, the Muslims do not yearn to educate members of a hostile and threatening religion, and Christian students have not been admitted to academies in the Eastern Caliphate for years."

"I see," Rob said bleakly.

"Spain may be possible for you. It is in Europe, the absolute western fringe of the Western Caliphate. Both religions are easier there. There are a few Christian students from France. The Muslims have established great universities in cities like Cordova, Toledo, Seville. If you are graduated from one of these, you'll be acknowledged a scholar. And though Spain is hard to reach, it is not nearly so hard as the journey to Persia."

"Why did *you* not go to Spain?"

"Because Jews are permitted to study in Persia." Merlin grinned. "And I wanted to touch the hem of Ibn Sina's garment."

Rob scowled. "I don't wish to travel across the world to become a scholar. I want only to become a sound physician."

Merlin poured more wine for himself. "It puzzles me—you are so young a roebuck, yet wearing a suit of fine stuff and weapons with which I cannot indulge myself. The life of a barber has its rewards. Then why would you become a physician, which will offer more arduous labor and questionable advantage of wealth?"

"I've been taught to dose several ailments. I can snip off a mangled finger and leave a neat stump. But so many people come to me and pay over their coins, and I know nothing of how to help them. I'm ignorant. I tell myself that some might be saved if I knew more."

"And though you study medicine for a score of lifetimes, there will come to you people whose illnesses are mysteries, for the anguish of which you speak is part and parcel of the profession of healing and must be lived with. Still, it's true that the better the training, the more good a doctor may do. You give the best possible reason for your ambition." Merlin drained his cup reflectively. "If the Arab schools are not for you, you must sift the doctors of England until you find the best of the poor, and perhaps you may persuade someone to take you as prentice."

"Do you know of any such physician?"

If Merlin recognized the hint, it went unacknowledged. He shook his head and got to his feet.

"But each of us has earned his rest, and tomorrow we shall face the question refreshed. A good night to you, young barber."

"A good night, master physician."

In the morning there was hot pea gruel in the kitchen and more blessings in Hebrew. The family sat and broke their night's fast together, scrutinizing him covertly while he examined them. Mistress Merlin appeared perpetually cross and in the cruel new light a faint line of dark hairs was visible on her upper lip. He could see fringes peeping out from under the kirtles of Benjamin Merlin and the boy named Ruel. The porridge was good quality.

Merlin inquired politely whether he had had a good night. "I have given thought to our discussion. Unfortunately, I can think of no physician I'm able to recommend as a master and an example." His wife brought to the table a basket of large blackberries, and Merlin beamed. "Ah, you must help yourself to these with your gruel, for they are flavorsome."

"I would like you to take me as your apprentice," Rob said.

To his great disappointment, Merlin shook his head.

Rob said quickly that Barber had taught him a great deal. "I was helpful to you yesterday. Soon I could go alone to visit your patients during severe weather, making things easy for you."

"No."

"You've observed that I've a sense of healing," he said doggedly. "I'm strong and could do heavy work as well, whatever is necessary. A seven-year apprenticeship. Or longer, as long as you like." In his agitation he rose to his feet, jogging the table and sloshing the gruel.

"It is impossible," Merlin said.

He felt baffled; he'd been certain Merlin liked him. "Do I lack the qualities necessary?"

"You have excellent qualities. From what I have seen, you would make an excellent physician."

"What, then?"

"In this most Christian of nations I would not be suffered as your master."

"Who would care?"

"The priests here would care. They already resent me as one forged by the Jews of France and tempered at an Islamic academy, seeing this as cooperation between dangerous pagan elements. Their eyes are on me. I live in dread of the day when my words are interpreted as bewitchery or I forget to christen a newborn."

"If you won't have me," Rob said, "at least suggest a physician to whom I should apply."

"I've told you, I recommend no one. But England is large and there are many doctors I do not know."

Rob's lips tightened and his hand settled on the hilt of his sword. "Last night you told me to sift the best of the poor. Who is the best of the physicians of your acquaintance?"

Merlin sighed and acceded to the bullying. "Arthur Giles of St. Ives," he said coldly, and resumed eating his breakfast.

Rob had no intention of drawing, but the wife's eyes were on his sword and she was unable to stifle a shuddering moan, certain her prophecy was being fulfilled. Ruel and Jonathan were looking at him somberly, but Zechariah began to cry.

He was sick with the shame of how he had repaid their hospitality. He tried to fashion an apology but couldn't, and finally he turned away from the Frenchy Hebrew spooning his gruel and left their house.

Chapter 21

THE OLD KNIGHT

A few weeks earlier he would have sought to rid himself of shame and anger through studying the bottom of a cup, but he had learned to be wary of the drink. It seemed clear that the longer he did without drunkenness, the stronger were the emanations he received from people when he took their hands, and he was placing an increasing value on the gift. So instead of liquor he spent a day with a woman in a glade on the banks of the Severn, a few miles beyond Worcester. The sun had made the grass almost as warm as their blood. She was a seamstress's helper with poor needle-pricked fingers and a hard little body that became slippery when they swam in the river.

"Myra, you feel like an eel!" he shouted, and felt better.

She was trout-quick but he was clumsy, like some great sea monster, when they went down together through the green water. Her hands parted his legs and as she swam through them he stroked the pale tight flanks. The water was chill but they made love twice in the warmth on the bank and he left his ire in her, while a few feet away Horse cropped the grass and Mistress Buffington sat and watched them calmly. Myra had tiny pointed breasts and a bush of the silkiest brown hair. More a plant than a bush, he thought wryly; she was more girl than woman, although it was certain she had been with men before.

"How old are you, dolly?" he asked idly.

"Fifteen year, I'm told."

She was exactly of an age with his sister Anne Mary, he realized, and was saddened to think that somewhere that girl was all grown but unfamiliar to him.

He was struck suddenly by a thought so monstrous that it left him weak and seemed to dim the sunlight.

"Has your name always been Myra?"

159

The question produced an astonished smile. "Why, of course that is my name, Myra Felker. What else would it be?"

"And were you born hereabouts, dolly?"

"Dropped by my mother in Worcester, and here I have lived," she said cheerfully.

He nodded and patted her hand.

Still, he thought in gloomy revulsion, given the situation it wasn't impossible that someday he could bed his own sister all unknowingly. He resolved that in the future he must have nothing to do with young females who might be Anne Mary's age.

The depressing thought ended his holiday mood, and he began to gather up his clothing.

"Ah, must we leave, then?" she said regretfully.

"Yes," he said, "for I must go a long way to get to St. Ives."

Arthur Giles of St. Ives turned out to be a crashing disappointment, although Rob had had no right to high expectation, for clearly Benjamin Merlin had made the recommendation only under duress. The physician was a fat and filthy old man who appeared to be at least slightly mad. He kept goats and must have maintained them within his house part of the time, for the place stank abominably.

"It's the bleeding that cures, young stranger. You must remember that. When all else fails, a good purifying drainage of the blood, and then another and another. That's what cures the bastards," Giles cried. He answered questions willingly, but when they discussed any mode of treatment other than bleeding, it became clear that Rob might profitably have taught the old man. Giles possessed no medical lore, no store of knowledge that might be tapped by a disciple. The physician offered an apprenticeship, and appeared to become furious when it was politely declined. Rob was happy to ride away from St. Ives, for he was better off remaining a barber than becoming a medical creature such as this.

For several weeks he believed he had renounced the impractical dream of becoming a physician. He worked hard at his entertainments, he sold a good deal of the Universal Specific, and was gratified by the thickness of his purse. Mistress Buffington throve on his prosperity as he had benefited from Barber's; the cat ate fine leavings and grew to full size as he watched, a large white feline with insolent green eyes. She thought she was a lioness and got into fights. When they were in the town of Rochester she disappeared during the entertainment and came back into Rob's camp at dusk, badly bitten in the right fore and with most of her left ear gone, her white fur matted with crimson.

He bathed her wounds and tended her like a lover. "Ah, mistress. You must learn to avoid brawling, as I have done, for it avails you nothing." He fed her milk and held her in his lap before the fire.

She rasped his hand with her tongue. It may be that there was a drop of milk on his fingers, or the smell of supper, but he chose to see it as a caress, and he stroked her soft fur in return, grateful for her company.

"If the way were open for me to attend the Muslim school," he told the cat, "I would take you in the wagon and point Horse toward Persia, and nothing would prevent our eventual arrival in that pagan place."

Abu Ali at-Husain ibn Abdullah ibn Sina, he thought wistfully. "To hell with you, you Arab," he said aloud, and went to bed.

The syllables ran through his mind, a haunting and taunting litany. *Abu Ali at-Husain ibn Abdullah ibn Sina, Abu Ali at-Husain ibn Abdullah ibn Sina* . . . until the mysterious repetition overcame the restlessness in his blood and he sank into sleep.

That night he dreamed he was locked in combat with a loathsome old knight, struggling hand to hand with daggers.

The old knight farted and mocked him. He could see rust and lichens on the other's black armor. Their heads were so close that he saw corruption and snot hanging from the bony nose, and looked into terrible eyes and smelled the sickening stench of the knight's breath. They fought desperately. Despite Rob's youth and strength he knew the dark specter's knife to be merciless and his armor infallible. Beyond them could be seen the knight's victims: Mam, Da, sweet Samuel, Barber, even Incitatus and Bartram the bear, and Rob's rage lent him strength, though he could already feel the inexorable blade entering his body.

He awoke to find the outside of his clothing damp with dew and the inside wet from the fear-sweat of the dream. Lying in the morning sun, with a robin singing its exhilaration not five feet away, he knew that although the dream was done, he was not. He was unable to give up the struggle.

Those who were gone wouldn't come back, and that was the way of it. But what better way to spend a lifetime than fighting the Black Knight? The study of medicine was, in its own way, something to love in place of a missing family. He determined, as the cat came and rubbed against him with her good ear, that he would make it come to pass.

The problem was discouraging. He presented entertainments in Northampton and Bedford and Hertford in turn, and in each place he sought out physicians and spoke with them and saw that their combined knowledge of healing was less than Barber's had been. In the town of

Maldon the physician's reputation for butchery was so deadly that when Rob J. asked people to give directions to the leech's home they paled and crossed themselves.

It wouldn't do to apprentice to such as these.

It occurred to him that another Hebrew doctor might be more willing to take him on than Merlin had been. In Maldon's square he stopped where workmen were raising a brick wall.

"Do you have knowledge of any Jews in this place?" he asked the master mason.

The man stared at him, spat, and turned away.

He asked several other men in the square without better results. Finally there was one who examined him curiously. "Why do you seek Jews?"

"I seek a Jew physician."

The man nodded in sympathetic understanding. "May Christ be merciful to you. There are Jews in the town of Malmesbury, and they have a physician there named Adolescentoli," he said.

It was a five-day trip from Maldon to Malmesbury, with stops in Oxford and Alveston to put on entertainments and sell physick. Rob seemed to remember that Barber had spoken of Adolescentoli as a famous physician, and he made his way into Malmesbury hopefully as evening shadows fell over the small and formless village. The inn gave him a plain but heartening supper. Barber would have found the mutton stew unseasoned but it contained plenty of meat, and afterward he was able to pay to have fresh straw spread in a corner of the sleeping room.

Next morning at breakfast he asked the publican to tell him about Malmesbury's Jews.

The man shrugged as if to say, What is there to tell?

"I am curious, for until lately I knew no Jews."

"That is because they are scarce in our land," the publican said. "My sister's husband, who is a ship's captain and has traveled to all places, says they are plentiful in France. He says they are found in every country, and that the farther east one travels, the more thickly are they sprinkled."

"Does Isaac Adolescentoli live among them here? The physician?"

The publican grinned. "No, indeed. It is they who live around Isaac Adolescentoli, basking in his eminence."

"He's celebrated, then?"

"He's a great physician. People come from afar to consult him and stay at this inn," the publican said proudly. "The priests speak against him, of course, but"—he put a finger to his nose and leaned forward—"I know at least two occasions when he was collected in dark of night and bundled off to Canterbury to tend to Archbishop Aethelnoth, who was thought to be dying last year."

He gave directions to the Jewish settlement and soon Rob was riding past the gray stone walls of Malmesbury Abbey, through woods and fields and a steep vineyard in which monks picked grapes. A coppice separated the abbey land from the Jews' homes, perhaps a dozen clustered houses. These must be Jews: men like crows, in loose black caftans and bell-shaped leather hats, were sawing and hammering, raising a shed. Rob drove to a building that was larger than the others, where a wide courtyard was filled with tethered horses and wagons.

"Isaac Adolescentoli?" Rob asked one of several boys attending the animals.

"He's in the dispensary," the boy said, and deftly caught the coin Rob threw to make certain Horse was well tended.

The front door opened into a large waiting room filled with wooden benches, all crammed with ailing humanity. It was like the lines that waited beyond his own treatment screen, but many more people. There were no empty seats, but he found a place against the wall.

Now and again a man came through the little door that led to the rest of the house and collected the patient who sat at the end of the first bench. Everyone would then move one space forward. There appeared to be five physicians. Four were young and the other was a small, quick-moving man of middle age, whom Rob supposed to be Adolescentoli.

It was a very long wait. The room remained crowded, for it seemed that each time someone was led through the waiting room door by a physician, new arrivals entered the front door from the outside. Rob passed the time trying to diagnose the patients.

By the time he was first on the front bench it was midafternoon. One of the young men came through the door. "You may come with me." He had a French accent.

"I want to see Isaac Adolescentoli."

"I am Moses ben Abraham, an apprentice of Master Adolescentoli. I'm able to take care of you."

"I'm certain you would treat me skillfully were I sick. I must see your master on another matter."

The apprentice nodded and turned to the next person on the bench.

Adolescentoli came out in a while and led Rob through the door and down a short corridor; through a door left ajar he glimpsed a surgery with an operating couch, buckets, and instruments. They ended in a tiny room bare of furniture save for a small table and two chairs. "What is your trouble?" Adolescentoli said. He listened in some surprise as, instead of describing symptoms, Rob spoke nervously of his desire to study medicine.

The physician had a dark, handsome face that didn't smile. Doubtless the interview wouldn't have ended differently if Rob had been wiser but he was unable to resist a question: "Have you lived in England long, master physician?"

"Why do you ask?"

"You speak our language so well."

"I was born in this house," Adolescentoli said quietly. "In 70 A.D., five young Jewish prisoners of war were transported from Jerusalem to Rome by Titus following the destruction of the great Temple. They were called *adolescentoli*, Latin for 'the youths.' I am descended from one of these, Joseph Adolescentoli. He won his freedom by enlisting in the Second Roman Legion, with which he came to this island when its inhabitants were little dark coracle men, the black Silures who were the first to call themselves Britons. Has your own family been English that long?"

"I don't know."

"You yourself speak the language adequately," Adolescentoli said silkily.

Rob told him of meeting with Merlin, mentioning only that they had spoken together of medical education. "Did you, too, study with the great Persian physician in Ispahan?"

Adolescentoli shook his head. "I attended the university in Baghdad, a larger medical school with a greater library and faculty. Except, of course, we didn't have Avicenna, whom they call Ibn Sina."

They chatted of his apprentices. Three were Jews from France and the other a Jew from Salerno.

"My apprentices have chosen me over Avicenna or some other Arab," Adolescentoli said proudly. "They don't have a library such as students have in Baghdad, of course, but I own the *Leech Book of Bald*, which lists remedies after the method of Alexander of Tralles and tells how to make salves, poultices, and plasters. They're required to study it with great attention, as well as some Latin writings of Paul of Aegina and certain works of Pliny. And before I'm done with them, each shall know how to perform phlebotomy, cautery, incision of arteries, and the couching of cataracts."

Rob felt an overpowering yearning, not unlike the emotion of a man who gazes upon a woman for whom, instantly, he longs. "I've come to ask you to take me as prentice."

Adolescentoli inclined his head. "I guessed that is why you're here. But I won't take you."

"Can I not persuade you, then?"

"No. You must find yourself a Christian physician as master, or stay a barber," Adolescentoli said, not cruelly but with firmness.

Perhaps his reasons were the same as Merlin's but Rob wasn't to know, for the physician would speak no more. He rose and led the way to the door, and nodded without interest as Rob left his dispensary.

Two towns away, in Devizes, he put on an entertainment and dropped a juggled ball for the first time since he had mastered the knack. People laughed at his banter and bought the physick but there came behind his screen a young fisherman from Bristol, roughly his own age, who was pissing blood and had lost most of his flesh. He told Rob he knew he was dying.

"Is there naught you can do for me?"

"What is your name?" Rob asked him quietly.

"Hamer."

"I think perhaps you have bubo in your insides, Hamer. But I'm not at all certain. I don't know how to cure you or ease your pain." Barber would have sold him more than a few bottles. "This stuff is mostly spirits, bought cheaper elsewhere," he said without knowing why. He had never told that to a patient before.

The fisherman thanked him and went away.

Adolescentoli or Merlin would have known how to do more for him, Rob told himself bitterly. Timorous bastards, he thought, refusing to teach him while the bloody Black Knight grinned.

That evening he was caught out by a sudden wild storm with fierce winds and drenching rain. It was the second day of September and early for fall rains, but that didn't make it less wet or chill. He made his way to the only shelter, the inn at Devizes, fastening Horse's reins to the limb of a great oak in the yard. When he pushed inside he found that too many others had preceded him. Every piece of floor space was taken.

In a dark corner huddled an exhausted man who sat with his arms around a swollen pack such as merchants used for their goods. If Rob had not gone to Malmesbury he wouldn't have given the fellow a second glance, but now he saw from the black caftan and pointed leather cap that this was a Jew.

"It was on such a night that our Lord was slain," Rob said loudly.

Conversation in the inn dwindled as he went on to speak of the Passion story, for travelers love a tale and a diversion. Someone brought him a stoup. When he told of how the populace had denied that Jesus was King of the Jews, the weary man in the corner appeared to shrink.

By the time Rob had reached the part about Calvary, the Jew had taken his pack and slipped out into the night and the storm. Rob broke off the tale and took his place in the warm corner.

But he found no more pleasure in driving away the merchant than he had gained from giving the Special Batch to Barber. The common room of the inn was full of the reek of damp wool clothing and unwashed bodies, and he was soon nauseated. Even before the rain had ceased, he left the inn and went out to his wagon and his animals.

He drove Horse to a nearby clearing and unhitched her. There was dry kindling in the wagon and he managed to light a fire. Mistress Buffington was too young to breed but perhaps she already exuded female scent, for beyond the shadows cast by the fire a tomcat yowled. Rob threw a stick to drive it away and the white cat rubbed against him.

"We are a fine lonely pair," he said.

If it took his lifetime, he would search until he found a worthy physician to whom he might apprentice, he decided.

As for the Jews, he had spoken to only two of their doctors. No doubt there were others. "Perhaps one would apprentice me if I pretended to him that I were a Jew," he told the cat.

Thus it began, as less than a dream—a fantasy in idle chatter; he knew he couldn't be a Jew convincingly enough to undergo the daily scrutiny of a Jewish master.

But he sat before the fire and stared into the flames, and it took form.

The cat offered up her silken belly. "Could I not be a Jew well enough to satisfy Muslims?" Rob asked her, and himself, and God.

Well enough to study with *the greatest physician in the world?*

Stunned by the enormity of the thought, he dropped the cat and she sprang away into the wagon. In a moment she was back, dragging what appeared to be a furry animal. It proved to be the false beard he'd worn during the Old Man nonsense. Rob picked it up. If he could be an old man for Barber, he asked himself, why could he not be a Hebrew? The merchant at the inn in Devizes, and others, could be imitated . . .

"I shall become a counterfeit Jew!" he cried.

It was fortunate no one was passing, to hear him speak aloud and at length to a cat, for it would have been declared that he was a wizard addressing his succubus.

He had no fear of the Church. "I piss on child-stealing priests," he told the cat.

He could grow a full Jew's beard, and he already had the prick for it.

He'd tell folk that, like Merlin's sons, he had been raised isolated from his people, ignorant of their tongue and customs.

He would make his way to Persia!

He would touch the hem of Ibn Sina's garment!

He was excited and terrified, shamed to be a grown man and trembling so. It was like the moment when he'd known he would pass beyond Southwark for the first time.

It was said *they* were everywhere, damn their souls. On the journey he would cultivate them and study their ways. By the time he reached Ispahan he would be ready to play the Jew, and Ibn Sina would have to take him in and share the precious secrets of the Arab school.

PART TWO

The Long Journey

Chapter 22

THE FIRST LEG

More shipping left London for France than from any other port in England, so he made for the city of his birth. All along the way he stopped to work, wanting to set out on such an adventure with as much gold as possible. By the time he reached London he had missed the shipping season. The Thames bristled with the masts of anchored vessels. King Canute had drawn upon his Danish origins and built a great fleet of Viking ships that rode the water like tethered monsters. The fearsome war craft were surrounded by an assorted assemblage: fat knorrs converted to deep-sea fishing boats; the private trireme galleys of the wealthy; squat, slow-sailing grain ships; two-masted merchant packets with triangular lateen-rigged sails; two-masted carracks from Italy; and long, single-masted vessels, the workhorses of the merchant fleets of the northern countries. None of the ships held cargo or passengers, for frigid windstorms already had begun. During the next terrible six months on many mornings salt spray would freeze in the Channel, and sailors knew that to venture out where the North Sea met and merged with the Atlantic Ocean was to ask for drowning in the churning waters.

In the Herring, a mariners' hole on the waterfront, Rob stood and thumped his mug of mulled cider against the tabletop. "I'm searching for snug, clean lodging until spring sailing," he said. "Is anyone here who knows of such?"

A short, wide man, built like a bull dog, studied him as he drained his cup and then nodded. "Aye," he said. "My brother Tom died last voyage. His widow, name of Binnie Ross, is left with two small ones to feed. If you're willing to pay fair I know she would welcome you."

Rob bought him a drink and then followed him a short way to a tiny house near the marketplace at East Chepe. Binnie Ross turned out to be a thin mouse of a girl, all worried blue eyes in a thin, pale little face. The place was clean enough but very small.

"I have a cat and a horse," Rob said.

"Oh, I would welcome the cat," she said anxiously. It was clear she was desperate for the money.

"You might put up the horse for the winter," her brother-in-law said. "There is Egglestan's stables on Thames Street."

Rob nodded. "I know the place," he said.

"She is with young," Binnie Ross said, picking up the cat and stroking her.

Rob could see no extra roundness in the sleek stomach. "How do you know?" he asked, thinking her mistaken. "She's still a young one herself, just born this past summer."

The girl shrugged.

She was right, for within a few weeks Mistress Buffington bloomed. He fed the cat tidbits and provided good food for Binnie and her son. The little daughter was an infant who still took milk at her mother's breast. It pleasured Rob to walk to the marketplace and buy for them, remembering the miracle of eating well after a long time with a rumbling-empty belly.

The infant was named Aldyth and the little boy, less than two years old, was Edwin. Every night Rob could hear Binnie crying. He had been in the house less than a fortnight when she came to his bed in the dark. She said not a word but lay down and put her slender arms around him, silent all through the act. Curious, he tasted her milk and found it sweet.

When they were finished she slipped back to her own bed and next day made no reference to what had happened.

"How did your husband die?" he asked her as she was dishing out the breakfast gruel.

"A storm. Wulf—that is his brother, who brought you here—said my Paul was washed away. He could not swim," she said.

She used him one more night, grinding to him desperately. Then her dead husband's brother, who doubtless had been marshaling his courage to speak to her, came to the house one afternoon. After that Wulf came every day with small gifts; he played with his niece and nephew but it became clear he was paying court to their mother, and one day Binnie told Rob that she and Wulf would be married. It made the house an easier place in which Rob could do his waiting.

During a blizzard he delivered Mistress Buffington of a fine litter: a white female miniature of herself, a white male, and a pair of black and white toms that presumably resembled their sire. Binnie offered to drown the four kittens as a service, but as soon as they were weaned Rob lined a basket with rags and took them to public houses, buying a number of drinks in order to give each of them away.

In March, the slaves who did the brute work of the port were moved back to the waterfront, and long lines of men and drays again began to crowd Thames Street, loading the warehouses and the ships with exports.

Rob asked innumerable questions of traveling men and determined his journey was best started by way of Calais. "That is where my ship is bound," Wulf told him, and took him down to the slip to see the *Queen Emma.* She was not as grand as her name, a great old wooden tub with one towering mast. The stevedores were loading her with slabs of tin mined in Cornwall. Wulf brought Rob to the master, an unsmiling Welshman who nodded when asked if he would take a passenger, and named a price that seemed to be fair.

"I have a horse and a wagon," Rob said.

The captain frowned. "It will cost you dear to move them by sea. Some travelers sell their beasts and carts on this side of the Channel and buy new ones on the other side."

Rob did some pondering, but at length he decided to pay the freight charges, high as they were. It was his plan to work as a barber-surgeon during his travels. Horse and the red wagon were a good rig and he had no faith that he would find another that pleased him as much.

April brought softer weather and finally the first ships began to depart. The *Queen Emma* raised her anchor from the Thames mud on the eleventh day of the month, sent off by Binnie with much weeping. There was a fresh but gentle wind. Rob watched Wulf and seven other sailors haul on the lines, raising an enormous square sail that filled with a crack when it was barely up, and they floated into the outgoing tide. Laden low with its metal cargo, the big boat moved out of the Thames, slipped heavily through the narrows between the Isle of Thanet and the mainland, crept along the coast of Kent, and then doggedly crossed the Channel before the wind.

The green coast became darker as it receded, until England was a blue haze and then a purple smudge that was swallowed by the sea. Rob had no chance to think noble thoughts, for he was pukingly ill.

Wulf, passing him on deck, stopped and spat contemptuously over the side. "God's blood! We are too low in the water to pitch or roll, it is the kindest of weather and the sea is calm. So what ails you?"

But Rob couldn't answer, for he was leaning over in order not to sully the deck. Part of his problem was terror, for he had never been to sea and now was haunted by a lifetime of tales of drowned men, from the husband and sons of Editha Lipton to the unfortunate Tom Ross who had left Binnie a widow. The oily water onto which he was sick appeared inscrutable and bottomless, the likely home of every evil monster, and he rued the reckless-ness with which he had ventured into this strange environment. To make matters worse the wind quickened and the sea developed deep billows. Soon he confidently expected to die and would have welcomed the release. Wulf sought him out and offered dinner of bread and cold fried salt pork. He decided that Binnie must have confessed her visits to Rob's bed and this was her future husband's revenge, to which he hadn't the strength to reply.

The voyage had lasted seven endless hours when another haze lifted itself out of the heaving horizon and slowly became Calais.

Wulf said a hasty goodbye, for he was busy with the sail. Rob led the horse and cart down the gangway and onto firm land that appeared to rise and fall like the sea. He reasoned that the ground in France could not go up and down or he would surely have heard of this oddity; indeed, after he had walked for a few minutes, the earth seemed firmer. But where was he bound? He had no idea as to destination or what his next action should be. The language was a blow. People around him spoke in a rattle of sound, and he could make no sense of it. Finally he stopped and climbed onto his cart and clapped his hands.

"I will hire somebody who has my language," he shouted.

A pinch-faced old man came forward. He had thin shanks and a skeletal frame that warned he wouldn't be of much use in lifting or carrying. But he noted Rob's pale complexion and his eyes twinkled. "May we talk over a soothing glass? Apple spirits do wonders to settle the stomach," he said, and the familiar English was benison to Rob's ears.

They stopped at the first public house and sat at a rough pine table outside the front door.

"I am Charbonneau," the Frenchman said above the waterfront din. "Louis Charbonneau."

"Rob J. Cole."

When the apple brandy came they drank to one another's health and Charbonneau was proven right, for the spirits warmed Rob's stomach and made him one of the living again. "I believe I can eat," he said wonderingly.

Pleased, Charbonneau spoke an order and presently a serving girl brought to their table a crusty bread, a platter of small green olives, and a goat's cheese of which even Barber would have approved.

"You can see why I'm in need of someone's help," Rob said ruefully, "for I can't even ask for food."

Charbonneau smiled. "All my life I've been a sailor. I was a boy when my first ship put into London, and I well remember my longing to hear my native tongue." Half of his time ashore had been spent on the other side of the Channel, he said, where the language was English.

"I'm a barber-surgeon, traveling to Persia to buy rare medicines and healing herbs that will be sent to England." It was what he had decided to tell people, to avoid discussing the fact that his real reason for going to Ispahan was considered a crime by the Church.

Charbonneau lifted his eyebrows. "A long way."

Rob nodded. "I need a guide, someone who can also translate for me, so that I may present entertainments and sell physick and treat the ill as we travel. I'll pay a generous wage."

Charbonneau took an olive from the plate and set it on the sun-warmed table. "France," he said. He took another. "The Saxon-ruled five duchies of Germany." Then another and another, until there were seven olives in a line. "Bohemia," he said, indicating the third olive, "where live the Slavs and the Czechs. Next is the territory of the Magyars, a Christian country but full of wild barbarian horsemen. Then the Balkans, a place of tall, fierce mountains and tall, fierce people. Then Thrace, about which I know little save that it marks the final limit of Europe and contains Constantinople. And finally Persia, where you want to go."

He regarded Rob contemplatively. "My native city is on the border between France and the land of the Germans, whose Teutonic languages I have spoken since childhood. Therefore, if you will hire me, I'll accompany you past—" He picked up the first two olives and popped them into his mouth. "I must leave you in time to return to Metz by next winter."

"Done," Rob said in relief.

Then, while Charbonneau grinned at him and ordered another brandy, Rob solemnly consumed the other olives in the line, eating his way through the remaining five countries, one by one.

Chapter 23

STRANGER IN A STRANGE LAND

France was not as determinedly green as England but there was more sun. The sky seemed higher, the color of France was deep blue. Much of the land was woods, as at home. It was a country of fiercely neat farms, with here and there a somber stone castle similar to the ones Rob was accustomed to seeing in the countryside; but some of the lords lived in great wooden manor houses such as were uncommon in England. There were cattle in the pastures and peasants sowing wheat.

Already Rob saw some wonders. "Many of your farm buildings are roofless," he observed.

"There is less rain here than in England," Charbonneau said. "Some of our farmers thresh the grain in the open barns."

Charbonneau rode a big, placid horse, light gray, almost white. His arms were used-looking and well kept. Each night he tended the mount carefully and cleaned and polished the sword and the dagger. He was good company at the campfire and on the road.

Every farm had orchards, glorious with blossom. Rob stopped at several, seeking to buy spirits; he could find no metheglin but bought a barrel of apple brandy similar to the tipple he had enjoyed in Calais, and found that it made superior Universal Specific.

The best roads here, as everywhere, had been built in earlier times by the Romans for their marching armies, broad highways, connecting and as straight as spear shafts. Charbonneau remarked on them lovingly. "They're everywhere, a network that covers the world. If you wished, you could travel on just this kind of road all the way to Rome."

Nevertheless, at a signpost pointing to a village called Caudry, Rob turned Horse off the Roman road. Charbonneau disapproved.

"Dangerous, these wooded tracks."

"I must travel them to ply my trade. They're the only way to the smaller villages. I blow my horn. It's what I've always done."

Charbonneau shrugged.

Caudry's houses were cone-shaped on top, with roofs of brush or thatched straw. Women were cooking out of doors and most houses had a plank table and benches near the fire, beneath a rude sun shelter laid on four stout poles cut from young trees. It couldn't be mistaken for an English village, but Rob went through the routine as if he were at home.

He handed Charbonneau the drum and told him to thump it. The Frenchman looked amused and then was intently interested as Horse began to prance to the sound of the drum.

"Entertainment today! Entertainment!" Rob called.

Charbonneau got the idea at once and thereafter translated everything as soon as Rob said it.

Rob found the entertainment a droll experience in France. The spectators laughed at the same stories but in different places, perhaps because they had to wait for the translation. During Rob's juggling, Charbonneau stood transfixed, and his sputtered comments of delight seemed to infect the crowd, which applauded vigorously.

They sold a great deal of Universal Specific.

That night at their campfire Charbonneau kept urging him to juggle, but he refused. "You'll get your fill of watching me, never fear."

"It's amazing. You say you've done this since you were a boy?"

"Yes." He told of how Barber had taken him in after his parents had died.

Charbonneau nodded. "You were fortunate. In my twelfth year my father died and my brother Etienne and I were given to a pirate crew as ship's boys." He sighed. "My friend, that was a hard life."

"I thought you said your first voyage took you to London."

"My first voyage on a merchant ship, when I was seventeen. For five years before, I sailed with pirates."

"My father helped defend England against three invasions. Twice when Danes invaded London. And once when pirates invaded Rochester," Rob said slowly.

"My pirates didn't attack London. Once we landed at Romney and burned two houses and took a cow that we killed for meat."

They stared at one another.

"They were bad men. It was what I did to stay alive."

Rob nodded. "And Etienne? What happened to Etienne?"

"When he was old enough he ran from them, back to our town, where he apprenticed himself to the baker. Today he's an old man too, and makes exceptional bread."

Rob grinned and wished him a good night.

Every few days they drove into a different village square, where it was business as usual—the dirty songs, the flattering portraits, the liquorish cures. At first Charbonneau translated Rob's barber-surgeon enticements, but soon the Frenchman was so accustomed to them that he could assemble a crowd on his own. Rob worked hard, driven to fill his cash box because he knew money was protection in foreign places.

June was warm and dry. They bit tiny pieces out of the olive called France, traversing its northern edge, and by early summer were almost at the German border.

"We're getting close to Strasbourg," Charbonneau told him one morning.

"Let us go there, so you may see your people."

"If we do, we'll lose two days' time," Charbonneau said scrupulously, but Rob smiled and shrugged, for he had come to like the elderly Frenchman.

The town proved to be beautiful, abustle with craftsmen who were building a great cathedral that already showed the promise of surpassing the general grace of Strasbourg's wide streets and handsome houses. They rode straight to the bakery, where a voluble Etienne Charbonneau clasped his brother in floury embrace.

Word of their arrival spread on a family intelligence system and that evening Etienne's two handsome sons and three of his dark-eyed daughters, all with children and spouses, came to celebrate; the youngest girl, Charlotte, was unmarried and still lived at home with her father. Charlotte prepared a lavish dinner, three geese stewed with carrots and dried plums. There were two kinds of fresh bread. A round loaf that Etienne called Dog Bread was delicious despite its name, being composed of alternate layers of wheat and rye. "It is inexpensive, the bread of the poor," Etienne said, and urged Rob to try a costlier long loaf baked from meslin, flour blended from many grains ground fine. Rob liked the Dog Bread best.

It was a merry evening, with both Louis and Etienne translating for Rob to the general hilarity. The children danced, the women sang, Rob juggled for his dinner, and Etienne played the pipes as well as he baked bread. When finally the family left, everyone kissed both travelers farewell. Charlotte sucked in her stomach and stuck out her newly ripened chest, and her great warm eyes invited Rob outrageously. That evening as he lay in bed he wondered what life would be like if he were to settle into the bosom of such a family, and in such pleasant surroundings.

In the middle of the night he rose.

"Something?" Etienne asked softly. The baker was sitting in the dark not far from where his daughter lay.

"I have to piss."

"I join you," Etienne said, and the two of them walked outside together and plashed companionably against the side of the barn. When Rob returned to his bed of straw, Etienne settled into the chair and sat watching over Charlotte.

In the morning the baker showed Rob his great round ovens and gave them a sack full of Dog Bread baked twice so it was hard and unspoilable, like ship's biscuit.

Strasbourgians would have to wait for their loaves that day; Etienne shut the bakery and rode with them a little of the way. The Roman road took them to the Rhine River a short ride from Etienne's home and then turned downstream for a few miles to a ford. The brothers leaned from their saddles and kissed. "Go with God," Etienne told Rob, and turned his horse toward home while they splashed across. The swirling water was cold and still faintly brown from the earth that had been washed into it by the spring floods far upstream. The trail up the opposite bank was steep, and Horse had to labor to pull the wagon into the land of the Teutons.

They were in mountains very soon, riding between high forests of spruce and fir. Charbonneau grew ever quieter, which at first Rob attributed to the fact that he hadn't wanted to leave his family and his home, but at length the Frenchman spat. "I do not like Germans, nor do I like to be in their land."

"Yet you were born as near to them as a Frenchman can be."

Charbonneau scowled. "A man can live hard by the sea and still have no love for the shark," he said.

It appeared to Rob to be a pleasant land. The air was cold and good. They went down a long mountain and at the bottom saw men and women cutting and turning the valley hay and getting fodder in, just as farmers were doing in England. They ascended another mountain to small high pastures where children tended cows and goats brought up for summer grazing from the farms below. The track was a high trail, and presently they looked down on a great castle of dark gray stone. Mounted men jousted with padded lances in the tiltyard.

Charbonneau spat again. "It's the keep of a terrible man, landgrave of this place. Count Sigdorff the Even-Handed."

"The Even-Handed? It doesn't seem the name of a man who is terrible."

"He is old now," Charbonneau said. "He earned the name when young, riding against Bamberg and taking two hundred prisoners. He ordered the right hands cut from one hundred and the left hands cut from the other hundred."

They cantered their horses until the castle could no longer be seen.

Before noon they came to a sign that pointed off the Roman road to the village of Entburg and they decided to go there and put on an entertainment. They were only a few minutes along the detour when they came around a bend and saw a man blocking the middle of the track, sitting a skinny brown horse with runny eyes. He was bald, with folds of fat in his short neck. He wore rough homespun over a body that was both fleshy and hard-looking, as Barber had been when Rob first knew him. There was no room to drive the wagon around him, but his weapons were sheathed and Rob reined Horse while they inspected one another.

The bald man said something.

"He wants to know if you have liquor," Charbonneau said.

"Tell him no."

"The whoreson isn't alone," Charbonneau said without altering his tone, and Rob saw that two more men had worked their mounts out from behind the trees.

One was a youth on a mule. When he rode up to the fat man Rob saw a similarity in their features and guessed they were father and son.

The third man sat a huge, clumsy animal that looked like a workhorse. He took a position directly behind the wagon, cutting off escape to the rear. Perhaps he was thirty years old. He was small and mean-looking and was missing his left ear, like Mistress Buffington.

Both of the newcomers were holding swords. The bald man spoke loudly to Charbonneau.

"He says you're to climb down from the wagon and remove your clothing. Know that when you do, they'll kill you," Charbonneau said. "Garments are expensive and they don't want them ruined with blood."

He didn't observe from where Charbonneau had taken the knife. The old man threw it with a grunt of effort and a practiced flip that sent it hard and fast, and it thumped into the chest of the young man with the sword.

Shock came into the fat man's eyes but the smile still hadn't fully faded from his lips when Rob left the wagon seat.

He took a single step onto Horse's broad back and launched himself, dragging the man from the saddle. They struck the ground rolling and clawing, each trying desperately for a crippling hold. Finally Rob was able to jam his left arm under the chin from behind. A meaty fist began to smash at his groin but he twisted and was able to take the hammer blows on a thigh. They were terrible punches that numbed his leg.

Always before he had fought drunk and half mad with rage. Now he was sober, fixing on one cold, clear thought.

Kill him.

Sobbing, he grabbed his left wrist with his free hand and pulled back, trying to throttle the man or crush his windpipe.

Then he moved to the forehead and attempted to pull the head back far enough to ruin the spine.

Break! he begged.

But it was a short, thick neck, padded with fat and ridged with muscle.

A hand with long, black fingernails moved up his face. He strained his head away but the hand raked his cheek, drawing blood.

They grunted and strained, banging one another like obscene lovers.

The hand came back. The man was able to reach a little higher this time, trying for the eyes.

His sharp nails gouged, making Rob scream.

Then Charbonneau was standing over them. He placed the point of his sword deliberately, finding a place between the ribs. He shoved the sword deep.

The bald man sighed, as if in satisfaction. He stopped grunting and moving, and lay heavy. Rob smelled him for the first time.

In a moment he was able to move away from the body. He sat up, nursing his ruined face.

The youth hung over the mule's rump, dirty bare feet cruelly caught. Charbonneau salvaged the knife and wiped it. He eased the dead feet out of the rope stirrups and lowered the body to the ground.

"The third prick?" Rob gasped. He couldn't keep his voice from quavering.

Charbonneau spat. "He ran at first indication we wouldn't become nicely dead."

"Perhaps to the Even-Handed, for reinforcements?"

Charbonneau shook his head. "These are dunghill cutthroats, not a landgrave's men." He searched the bodies, looking as if he had done it before. Around the man's neck was a little bag containing coins. The youth carried no money but wore a tarnished crucifix. Their weapons were poor but Charbonneau threw them into the wagon.

They left the highwaymen where they lay in the dirt, the bald corpse face down in his own blood.

Charbonneau tied the mule to the back of the cart and led the bony captured horse, and they returned to the Roman road.

Chapter 24

STRANGE TONGUES

When Rob asked Charbonneau where he had learned to throw a knife, the old Frenchman said he had been taught by the pirates of his youth. "It was a handy skill to have while fighting the damned Danish and seizing their ships." He hesitated. "And while fighting the damned English and seizing *their* ships," he said slyly. By that time they weren't bothered by the old national rivalries and neither had any doubts left about his companion's worthiness. They grinned at one another.

"Will you show me?"

"If you'll teach me to juggle," Charbonneau said, and Rob agreed eagerly. The bargain was one-sided, for it was too late in life for Charbonneau to master a new and difficult dexterity, and in the little time they had left together he learned only to pop two balls, although he derived much pleasure from tossing and catching them.

Rob had the advantage of youth, and years of juggling had given him strong and wiry wrists, as well as a sharp eye and balance and timing.

"It takes a special knife. Your dagger has a fine blade which would soon be snapped if you started throwing it, or the hilt would be ruined, for the hilt is the center of an ordinary dagger's weight and balance. A throwing knife is weighted in the blade, so that a quick snap of the wrist sends it easily on its way point first."

Rob quickly learned how to throw Charbonneau's knife so it presented its sharp blade first. It was harder to become skilled at hitting targets where he aimed, but he was accustomed to the discipline of practice and threw the knife at a mark on a broad tree whenever he had a chance.

They kept to the Roman roads, which were crowded with a polyglot mixture of people. A French cardinal's party once forced them off the road. The prelate rode past surrounded by two hundred mounted troops and a hundred and fifty servants, and wearing scarlet shoes and hat and a gray cope over a once-white chasuble made darker than the cope by the dust of the road. Pilgrims moved in the general direction of Jerusalem singly or in small or large groups; sometimes they were led or lectured by palmers, religious votaries who signaled that they had accomplished sacred travel by wearing two crossed palm leaves picked in the Holy Land. Bands of armored knights galloped by with shouts and war cries, often drunk, usually pugnacious and always hungry for glory, loot, and deviltry. Some of the religious zealots wore hair shirts and crawled toward Palestine on bloody hands and knees to fulfill vows made to God or a saint. Exhausted and defenseless, they were easy prey. Criminals abounded on the highways, and law enforcement by officials was perfunctory at best; when a thief or highwayman was caught in the act he was executed on the spot by the travelers themselves, without trial.

Rob kept his weapons loose and ready, half expecting the man with the missing ear to lead a pack of riders down on them for vengeance. His size, the broken nose, and the striped facial wounds combined to make him appear formidable, but he realized with amusement that his best protection was the frail-looking old man he had hired because of his knowledge of English.

They bought provision in Augsburg, a bustling trade center founded by the Roman emperor Augustus in 12 B.C. Augsburg was a center of transactions between Germany and Italy, crowded with people and busy with its preoccupation, which was commerce. Charbonneau pointed out Italian merchants, conspicuous in shoes of expensive fabric which rose to curling points at the toes. For some time Rob had seen Jews in increasing number, but in Augsburg's markets he noticed more of them than ever, instantly identifiable in their black caftans and narrow-brim, bell-shaped leather hats.

Rob put on an entertainment in Augsburg but didn't sell as much Specific as he had previously, perhaps because Charbonneau translated with less zest when forced to use the guttural language of the Franks.

It didn't matter, for his purse was fat; at any rate, ten days later when they reached Salzburg, Charbonneau told him that the entertainment in that town would be their final one together.

"In three days' time we come to the Danube River, and there I leave you and turn back to France."

Rob nodded.

"I'm of no further use to you. Beyond the Danube is Bohemia, where the people speak a language strange to me."

"You're welcome to come with me, whether or not you translate."

But Charbonneau smiled and shook his head. "Time for me to go home, this time to stay."

At an inn that night they bought a farewell feast of the food of the land: smoked meat stewed with lard, pickled cabbage, and flour. They didn't like it and got mildly drunk on heavy red wine. He paid off the old man handsomely.

Charbonneau had a last, sobering piece of advice. "A dangerous countryside lies ahead of you. It's said that in Bohemia one can't tell the difference between wild bandits and the hirelings of the local lords. In order to pass through such a land unharmed, you must have the company of others."

Rob promised he would seek to join a strong group.

When they saw the Danube it was a more muscular river than he had expected, fast-flowing and with the menacing oily surface that he knew denoted deep and dangerous water. Charbonneau stayed a day longer than promised, insisting on riding downstream with him to the wild and half-settled village of Linz, where a large log-raft ferry took passengers and freight across a quiet stretch of the wide waterway.

"Well," the Frenchman said.

"Perhaps one day we'll see each other again."

"I don't think so," Charbonneau said.

They embraced.

"Live forever, Rob J. Cole."

"Live forever, Louis Charbonneau."

He got down from the wagon and went to arrange his passage as the old man rode away, leading the bony brown horse. The ferryman was a sullen hulk with a bad cold who kept removing the snot from his upper lip with his tongue. The matter of the fare was difficult because Rob didn't have the Bohemian language, and in the end he felt he had been overcharged. When he returned to the wagon after hard sign-language bargaining, Charbonneau had already ridden out of sight.

On his third day of moving into Bohemia he met up with five fat and ruddy Germans and tried to convey the idea that he wanted to travel with them. His manner was polite; he offered gold and indicated he'd be willing to cook and do other camp chores, but there wasn't a smile from any of them, only hands on the hilts of five swords.

"Fucks," he said finally, and turned away. But he couldn't blame them, for their party already had some strength and he was unknown, a danger.

Horse drew him from the mountains into a great saucer-shaped plateau ringed by green hills. There were cultivated fields of gray earth in which men and women toiled over wheat, barley, rye, and beets, but most of it was mixed forest. In the night, not far away, he heard the howling of wolves. He kept a fire burning although it wasn't cold, and Mistress Buffington mewed at the wild animal sounds, sleeping with the spiny ridge of her back hard against him.

He had depended on Charbonneau for many things, but he found that not the least of these had been companionship. Now he drove down the Roman road and knew the meaning of the word *alone,* for he couldn't speak to any of the people he met.

A week after he and Charbonneau had parted, one morning he came upon the stripped and mutilated body of a man hanging from a tree by the side of the road. The hanged man was slight and ferret-faced and was missing his left ear.

Rob regretted that he wasn't able to inform Charbonneau that others had caught up with their third highwayman.

Chapter 25

THE JOINING

Rob crossed the wide plateau and reentered mountains. They weren't as high as those he had already crossed but they were rugged enough to slow his progress. Twice more he approached groups of travelers on the road and attempted to join with them, but each time he was refused permission to do so. One morning a group of horsemen dressed in rags rode past him and shouted something at him in their strange language, but he nodded a greeting and looked away, for he could see they were wild and desperate. He felt if he were to travel with them he would soon be dead.

Arriving at a large town, he went into the tavern and was overjoyed to find that the publican knew a few words of English. From this man he learned that the town was called Brünn. The people through whose territory he traveled were mostly members of a tribe called the Czechs. He could learn little else, not even where the man had gotten his tiny store of English words, for the simple exchange had overtaxed the publican's linguistic ability. When Rob left the tavern he found a man in the back of his wagon, going through his belongings.

"Get out," he said softly. He pulled his sword but the fellow had leaped from the cart and was off before he could stop him. Rob's money purse was still nailed safely beneath the floor of the wagon, and the only thing missing was a cloth bag full of the paraphernalia used in tricks of magic. It gave him no small comfort to think of the thief's face when he opened the bag.

After that he polished his weapons daily, keeping a thin coat of grease on his blades so they slipped from the scabbards at the slightest pull. At night he slept lightly or not at all, listening for any sound that would indicate someone creeping up on him. He knew he would have little hope if he were attacked by a pack such as the horsemen in rags. He remained alone and vulnerable for nine more long days, until one morning the road emerged from the woods and, to his wonder and delight and burgeoning hope, he saw before him a tiny town that had been engulfed by a large caravan.

The sixteen houses of the village were surrounded by several hundred animals. Rob saw horses and mules of every size and description, saddled or harnessed to wagons, carts, and vans of wide variety. He tethered Horse to a tree. People were everywhere, and as he pushed among them his ears were assaulted by a babble of incomprehensible tongues.

"Please," he said to a man engaged in the arduous task of changing a wheel. "Where is the caravan master?" He helped lift the wheel to the hub but won only a grateful smile and a blank headshake.

"The caravan master?" he asked the next traveler, who was in the process of feeding two span of great oxen with wooden balls fixed to the points of their long horns.

"Ah, *der Meister?* Kerl Fritta," the man said, and gestured down the line.

After that it was easy, for the name Kerl Fritta seemed to be known by all. Whenever Rob uttered it he received a nod and a pointing finger, until finally he came to a place where a table had been set in a field next to a large wagon hitched to six of the largest matched chestnut draft horses he had ever seen. On the table was a naked sword and behind it sat a personage who wore his long brown hair in two thick plaits and was engrossed in conversation with the first of a long line of travelers waiting to speak with him.

Rob stood at the end of the line. "That is Kerl Fritta?" he asked.

"Yes, that is he," answered one of the men.

They stared at one another in delight.

"You're English!"

"Scotch," said the man, with only slight disappointment. "Well met! Well met!" he murmured, grasping both of Rob's hands. He was tall and spare, with long gray hair, and clean-shaven in the Britons' style. He wore a traveling suit of rough black stuff but it was good cloth, and well cut.

"James Geikie Cullen," he said. "Sheep breeder and wool factor, journeying to Anatolia with my daughter in search of better varieties of rams and ewes."

"Rob J. Cole, barber-surgeon. Bound for Persia to buy precious medicinals."

Cullen gazed at him almost fondly. The line moved, but they had enough time to exchange information, and English words never had sounded more euphonious.

Cullen was accompanied by a man dressed in stained brown trousers and a ragged gray kirtle; he said this was Seredy, whom he had hired as servant and interpreter.

To Rob's surprise, he learned that he was no longer in Bohemia but unknowingly had crossed into the country of Hungary two days before. The village they had so transformed was called Vac. Though bread and cheese were available from the inhabitants, provision and other supplies were dear.

The caravan had originated in the town of Ulm, in the duchy of Schwaben.

"Fritta is a German," Cullen confided. "He doesn't appear to go out of his way to be pleasant but it's advisable to get along with him, for there are reliable reports that Magyar bandits are preying on lone travelers and small parties, and there's not another large caravan in this vicinity."

News of the bandits appeared to be general knowledge, and as they moved toward the table other applicants joined the line. Directly behind Rob, to his interest, there were three Jews.

"In such a caravan one must travel with both gentlefolk and vermin," Cullen said loudly. Rob was watching the three men in their dark caftans and leather hats. They were conversing with one another in still another strange language, but it seemed that the eyes of the man closest to him flickered when Cullen spoke, as if he understood what had been said. Rob looked away.

When they reached Fritta's table Cullen took care of his own business and then was kind enough to offer Seredy as Rob's translator.

The caravan master, experienced and quick in conducting such interviews, efficiently learned his name, business, and destination.

"He wants you to understand that the caravan doesn't go to Persia," Seredy said. "Beyond Constantinople you must make another arrangement."

Rob nodded, then the German spoke at length.

"The fee you must pay to Master Fritta is the equal of twenty-two English silver pennies, but he wishes no more of these, for it is in English pennies that my Master Cullen will pay and Master Fritta says he can't easily dispose of too many. Are you able to pay in deniers, he asks."

"I am."

"He'll take twenty-seven deniers," Seredy said too smoothly.

Rob hesitated. He had deniers because he had sold the Specific in France and Germany, but he was ignorant of the fair rate of exchange.

"Twenty-three," a voice said directly behind him, so low he thought he had imagined it.

"Twenty-three deniers," he said firmly.

The caravan master accepted the offer icily, looking straight into his eyes.

"You must provide your own provision and supply. Should you lag or be forced to drop out you'll be left behind," the translator said. "He says the caravan will leave here composed of some ninety separate parties totaling more than one hundred and twenty men. He demands one sentry for each ten parties, so every twelve days you will have to stand guard all night."

"Agreed."

"Newcomers must take a place at the end of the line of march, where the dust is worst and the traveler is most vulnerable. You'll follow Master Cullen and his daughter. Each time somebody ahead of you drops out, you may move up a single place. Each party to join the caravan hereafter will travel behind you."

"Agreed."

"And should you practice your profession of barber-surgeon to the members of the caravan, you must share all earnings equally with Master Fritta."

"No," he said at once, for it was unjust that he should have to give one-half of his earnings to this German.

Cullen cleared his throat. Glancing at the Scot, Rob saw apprehension in his face and remembered what he had said about the Magyar bandits.

"Offer ten, take thirty," the low voice behind him said.

"I'll agree to give up ten percent of my earnings," Rob said.

Fritta uttered a single laconic word which Rob took to be the Teutonic equivalent of "goose shit"; then he made another short sound.

"Forty, he says."

"Tell him twenty."

They agreed on thirty percent. As he thanked Cullen for the use of the interpreter and walked away, Rob glanced quickly at the three Jews. They were men of medium height, with faces tanned to swarthiness. The man who had stood directly behind him had a fleshy nose and large lips over a full brown beard shot with gray. He didn't look at Rob but stepped toward the table with the total concentration of someone who has already tested an adversary.

The newcomers were ordered to take their positions in the line of march during the afternoon and make camp in place that night, for the caravan would set off right after dawn. Rob found his location between Cullen and the Jews, unhitched Horse, and led him to grass a few rods away. The inhabitants of Vac were taking their last opportunity to profit from the windfall by selling provision, and a farmer came by and held up eggs and yellow cheese for which he wanted four deniers, a shocking price. Instead of paying, Rob bartered away three bottles of the Universal Specific and gained his supper.

While he ate he watched his neighbors watching him. In the camp in front of his, Seredy fetched the water but Cullen's daughter did the cooking. She was very tall and had red hair. There were five men in the campsite behind his. When he had finished cleaning up after the meal, he walked to where the Jews were brushing their animals. They had good horses as well as two pack mules, one of which presumably carried the tent they had raised. They watched silently as Rob walked to the man who had stood behind him during his dealing with Fritta.

"I am Rob J. Cole. I wish to thank you."

"For nothing, for nothing." He lifted the brush from the horse's back. "I am Meir ben Asher." He introduced his companions. Two had been with him when Rob had first seen them in the line: Gershom ben Shemuel, who had a wen on his nose and was short and looked as tough as a chunk of wood, and Judah haCohen, sharp-nosed and small-mouthed, with a bear's glossy black hair and the same sort of beard. The other two were younger. Simon ben ha-Levi was thin and serious, almost a man, a beanpole with a wispy beard. And Tuveh ben Meir was a boy of twelve, large for his age as Rob had been.

"My son," Meir said.

No one else talked. They watched him very carefully.

"You are merchants?"

Meir nodded. "Once our family lived in the town of Hameln in Germany. Ten years ago we all moved to Angora, in the Byzantine, from which we travel both east and west, buying and selling."

"What do you buy and sell?"

Meir shrugged. "A little of this, a bit of that."

Rob was delighted with the answer. He had spent hours thinking of spurious details to tell about himself, and now he saw it was unnecessary; businessmen didn't reveal too much.

"Where do *you* travel?" the young man named Simon said, startling Rob, who had decided only Meir knew English.

"Persia."

"Persia. Excellent! You have family there?"

"No, I go there to buy. One or two herbs, perhaps a few medicinals."

"Ah," Meir said. The Jews looked at one another, accepting it instantly.

It was the moment to leave, and he bade them good night.

Cullen had been staring over at them while he talked to the Jews, and when Rob approached his camp the Scot seemed to have lost most of his initial warmth.

He introduced his daughter Margaret without enthusiasm, although the girl greeted Rob politely enough.

Up close, her red hair was something that would be pleasant to touch. Her eyes were cool and sad. Her high round cheekbones seemed large as a man's fist and her nose and jaw were comely but not delicate. Her face and arms were unfashionably freckled and he wasn't accustomed to a woman being so tall.

While he was trying to decide whether she was beautiful, Fritta came along and spoke briefly to Seredy.

"He wishes Master Cole to be a sentry this night," the interpreter said.

So as dusk fell Rob began to walk his post, which started with the Cullens' site and extended through eight camps beyond his own.

As he walked, he saw what a strange mixture the caravan had brought together. Next to a covered cart an olive-skinned woman with yellow hair nursed a baby while her husband squatted near the fire and greased his harnesses. Two men sat and cleaned weapons. A boy fed grain to three fat hens in a crude wooden cage. A cadaverous man and his fat woman glared at one another and quarreled in what Rob believed to be French.

On his third circuit of the area, as he passed the Jews' camp he saw that they stood together and swayed, chanting what he realized was their evening prayer.

A large white moon began to ride up from the forest beyond the village and he felt tireless and confident, for suddenly he was part of an army of more than one hundred and twenty men, and that wasn't the same as traveling through a strange and hostile land by yourself.

Four times during the night he challenged somebody and found it was one of the men going beyond the camp to answer a call of nature.

Toward morning, when he was becoming unbearably sleepy, the Cullen girl came out of her father's tent. She passed close by him without acknowledging his presence. He saw her clearly in the washed light of the moon. Her dress looked very black and her long feet, which must have been wet with dew, looked very white.

He made as much noise as possible while walking in the opposite direction from the one she had taken, but he watched from afar until he saw her safely back, and then he began to walk again.

At first light he quit his post and made a hurried breakfast of bread and cheese. While he ate, the Jews assembled outside their tent for sunrise devotions. Perhaps they would be an annoyance, for they seemed an exceedingly worshipful people. They strapped little black boxes on their foreheads and wound thin leather strips around their forearms until their limbs resembled the barber poles on Rob's wagon, then they lost themselves alarmingly in reverie, covering their heads with prayer shawls. He was relieved when they were done.

He had Horse harnessed too early, and had to wait. Although those at the head of the caravan set out shortly after daybreak, the sun was well up before it was his turn. Cullen led on a rawboned white horse, followed by his servant Seredy riding a scruffy gray mare and leading three packhorses. Why did two people need three pack animals? The daughter sat a proud black. Rob thought the haunches of both the horse and the woman were admirable, and he followed them gladly.

Chapter 26

PARSI

They settled at once into the routine of the journey. For the first three days both the Scots and the Jews regarded him politely and left him alone, perhaps made uneasy by his battered face and the bizarre markings on the wagon. Privacy had never displeased him, and he was content to be left to his thoughts.

The girl rode in front of him constantly, and inevitably he watched her even after they made camp. She appeared to have two black dresses, one of which she washed whenever there was opportunity. She was obviously a sufficiently seasoned traveler not to fret over discomforts but there was about her, and about Cullen, an air of barely concealed melancholy; he assumed from their clothing that they were in mourning.

Sometimes she sang softly.

On the fourth morning, when the caravan was slow to move, she dismounted and led her horse, stretching her legs. He looked down at her walking close by his wagon and smiled at her. Her eyes were enormous, as deep a blue as irises can be. Her high-boned face had long, sensitive planes. Her mouth was large and ripe like everything about her, yet curiously quick and expressive.

"What's the language of your songs?"

"Gaelic. What we call the Erse."

"I thought so."

"Och. How is a Sassenach to recognize the Erse?"

"What is a Sassenach?"

"It's our name for those who live south of Scotland."

"I sense the word isn't a compliment."

"Ah, it is not," she admitted, and this time smiled.

"Mary Margaret!" her father called sharply. She moved to him at once, a daughter accustomed to obeying.

Mary Margaret?

She must be near the age Anne Mary would be now, he realized uneasily. His sister's hair was brown when she was a little girl, but there had been reddish tints . . .

The girl was *not* Anne Mary, he reminded himself firmly. He knew he must stop seeing his sister in every woman who wasn't elderly, for it was the sort of pastime that might become a form of madness.

There was no need to dwell on it, since he had no real interest in James Cullen's daughter. There were more than enough soft things in the world, and he decided that he'd stay away from this one.

Her father evidently determined to give him a second chance at conversation, perhaps because he hadn't seen him talking again to the Jews. On their fifth night on the road James Cullen came to visit, bearing a jug of barley liquor, and Rob said words of welcome and accepted a friendly pull from the bottle.

"You know sheep, Master Cole?"

Cullen beamed when he said he didn't, ready to educate him.

"There are sheep and there are sheep. In Kilmarnock, site of the Cullen holding, ewes often run as small as twelve stone in weight. I'm told that in the East we'll find ewes twice that size, with long hair instead of short —denser fleece than the beasts of Scotland, so full of richness that when the wool is spun and made up into goods, it will shed rain."

Cullen said he planned to buy breeding stock when he found the best, and bring it back to Kilmarnock with him.

That would take ready capital, a goodly amount of trading money, Rob told himself, and realized why Cullen needed packhorses. It might be better if the Scot also had bodyguards, he reflected.

"It's a far journey you're on. You'll be a long time away from your sheep holding."

"I left it in the reliable care of trusted kinsmen. It was a hard decision, but . . . Six months before I left Scotland I buried my wife of twenty-two years." Cullen grimaced and put the jug to his mouth for a long swallow.

That would explain their rue, Rob thought. The barber-surgeon in him made him ask what had caused her to die.

Cullen coughed. "There were growths in both her breasts, hard lumps. She just grew pale and weak, lost appetite and will. Finally there was terrible pain. She took a time to die but was gone before I believed it could be so. Her name was Jura. Well . . . I stayed drunk for six weeks but found it no escape. For years I'd engaged in idle talk about buying fine stock in Anatolia, never thinking it would come to pass. I just decided to go."

He offered the jug and didn't seem offended when Rob shook his head. "Piss time," he said, and smiled gently. He had already finished a large amount of the jug's contents and when he attempted to clamber to his feet and leave, Rob had to assist him.

"A good night, Master Cullen. Please come again."

"A good night, Master Cole."

Watching him walk away unsteadily, Rob reflected that he hadn't once mentioned his daughter.

The following afternoon a French factor named Felix Roux, thirty-eighth in the line of march, was thrown when his horse shied at a badger. He struck the ground badly, with the full weight of his body on his left forearm, breaking the bone so the limb hung askew. Kerl Fritta sent for the barber-surgeon, who set the bone and immobilized the arm, a painful procedure. Rob struggled to inform Roux that although the arm would give him hell's pain when he rode, he would still be able to travel with the caravan. Finally he had to send for Seredy to tell the patient how to handle the sling.

He was thoughtful on his way back to his own wagon. He had agreed to treat sick travelers several times a week. Although he tipped Seredy generously, he knew he couldn't continue to use James Cullen's manservant as interpreter.

Back at his wagon, he saw Simon ben ha-Levi sitting on the ground nearby, mending a saddle cinch, and he walked up to the thin young Jew.

"Do you have French and German?"

The youth nodded while holding a saddle strap close to his mouth and biting off the waxed thread.

Rob talked and ha-Levi listened. In the end, since the terms were generous and the time required wasn't great, he agreed to interpret for the barber-surgeon.

Rob was pleased. "How do you have so many languages?"

"We're merchants between nations. We travel constantly, with family connections in the markets of many countries. Languages are part of our business. For example, young Tuveh is studying the language of the Mandarins, for in three years he'll travel the Silk Road and go to work with my uncle's firm." His uncle, Issachar ben Nachum, he said, headed a large branch of their family in Kai Feng Fu, from which every three years he sent a caravan of silks, pepper, and other Oriental exotics to Meshed, in Persia. And every three years since he was a small boy, Simon and other males of his family had traveled from their home in Angora to Meshed, from which they accompanied a caravan of the rich goods back to the East Frankish Kingdom.

Rob J. felt a quickening within him. "You know the Persian language?"

"Of course. Parsi."

Rob looked at him blankly.

"It's called Parsi."

"Will you teach it to me?"

Simon ben ha-Levi hesitated, because this was a different matter. This could take a good deal of his time.

"I'll pay well."

"Why do you want Parsi?"

"I'll need the language when I reach Persia."

"You want to do business on a regular basis? Return to Persia again and again to buy herbs and pharmaceuticals, the way we do for silks and spices?"

"Perhaps." Rob J. shrugged, a gesture worthy of Meir ben Asher. "A bit of this, a little of that."

Simon grinned. He began to scratch out a first lesson in the dirt with a stick, but it was unsatisfactory and Rob went to the wagon and got his drawing things and a clean round of beechwood. Simon started him in the Parsi language exactly as Mam had taught him to read English many years earlier, by teaching him the alphabet. Parsi letters were composed of dots and squiggly lines. Christ's blood! The written language resembled pigeon shit, bird tracks, curled wood shavings, worms trying to fuck each other.

"I'll never learn this," he said, his heart sinking.

"You shall," Simon said placidly.

Rob J. took the piece of wood back to the wagon. He ate his supper slowly, buying time in which to control his excitement, then he sat on the wagon seat and at once began to apply himself.

Chapter 27

THE QUIET SENTRY

They emerged from the mountains to flat land that the Roman road divided with absolute straightness as far as the eye could see. On both sides of the road were fields with black soil. People were beginning to harvest grain and late vegetables; summer was over. They came to an enormous lake and followed its shoreline for three days, stopping overnight to buy provision at a shoreside town called Siofok. Not much of a town, sagging buildings and a crafty, cheating peasantry, but the lake—it was named Balaton—was an unworldly dream, water dark and hard-looking as a gem, giving off white mist as he waited early in the morning for the Jews to say their prayers.

The Jews were funny to watch. Strange creatures, they bobbed while they prayed and it seemed that God was juggling their heads, which went up and down at different times but seemed to work with a mysterious rhythm. When they were finished and he suggested that they swim with him, they made faces because of the chill but suddenly they were babbling to each other in their language. Meir said something and Simon nodded and turned away; he was camp guard. The others and Rob ran to the shore and threw off their clothes, splashing into the shallows like screaming children. Tuveh wasn't a good swimmer and wallowed. Judah haCohen paddled feebly and Gershom ben Shemuel, who had a shocking-white round belly despite his sun-darkened face, floated on his back and bellowed incomprehensible songs. Meir was a surprise. "Better than the *mikva!*" he shouted, gasping.

"What's the *mikva?*" Rob asked, but the stocky man plunged beneath the surface and then began to move out from shore with strong, even strokes. Rob swam after him, thinking he would rather be with a female. He tried to recall women with whom he had swum. There were perhaps half a dozen and he had made love to each, before or after the swimming.

Several times it had been in the water with the wetness lapping all around them . . .

He hadn't touched a woman for five months, his longest period of abstention since Editha Lipton had guided him into the sexual world. He kicked and flailed in the water, which was very cold, trying to rid himself of the ache to fuck.

When he overtook Meir, he sent a great splash into the other man's face. Meir sputtered and coughed. "Christian!" he shouted ominously.

Rob splashed him again and Meir closed with him. Rob was taller but Meir was *strong!* He pushed Rob under, but Rob locked his fingers in the full beard and pulled the Jew under with him, down and down. As they sank it seemed as though tiny flecks of rime left the brown water and clung to him, cold on cold, until he felt clothed in a skin of icy silver.

Down.

Until, at the same moment, each panicked and decided he would drown for playfulness. They pushed apart to rise, and broke the surface gasping for air. Neither vanquished, neither victor, they swam back to shore together. When they left the water they trembled with a foretaste of autumn chill as they struggled to force wet bodies into their clothes. Meir had noted his circumcised penis and looked at him.

"A horse bit the tip off," Rob said.

"A mare, no doubt," Meir said solemnly; he muttered something to the others in their language, causing them to grin at Rob. The Jews wore curiously fringed garments next to their flesh. Naked, they had been as other men; clad, they reassumed their foreignness and were exotic creatures again. They caught Rob studying them but he didn't ask them to explain the strange undergarments, and no one volunteered.

After they left the lake behind, the scenery suffered. Traveling down a straight and unending road, passing mile after mile of unchanging forest or a field that looked like all the other fields, soon became almost unbearable in its monotony. Rob J. took refuge in his imagination, visualizing the road as it had been soon after it was built, one *via* in a vast network of thousands that had allowed Rome to conquer the world. First there would have come scouts, an advance cavalry. Then the general in his chariot driven by a slave, surrounded by trumpeters both for panoply and signaling. Then on horseback the *tribuni* and the *legati,* the staff officers. They were followed by the legion, a forest of bristling javelins—ten cohorts of the most efficient fighting killers in history, six hundred men to a cohort, each one hundred legionnaires led by a centurion. And finally thousands of slaves doing what other brutes of labor could not, hauling the *tormenta,* the giant machinery of war that was the real reason for building the roads: enormous battering rams for leveling walls and fortifications, wicked *catapulta* to make the sky rain darts on an enemy, giant *ballista,* the slings of the gods, to send boulders through the air or launch great beams as if they were arrows. Finally, the carts laden with *impedimenta,* the baggage, would be trailed by wives and children, whores, traders, couriers, and government officials, the ants of history, living off the spoils of the Roman feast.

Now that army was legend and dream, those camp followers ancient dust, that government long gone, but the roads remained, indestructible highways that were sometimes so straight as to lull the mind.

The Cullen girl was walking near his wagon again, her horse tied to one of the pack animals.

"Will you join me, mistress? The wagon will be a change for you."

She hesitated, but when he extended his hand she took it and allowed him to pull her up.

"Your cheek has healed nicely," she observed. She colored but seemed unable to keep from talking. "There's only the slightest silver line from the last of the scratches. With luck it will fade so there will be no scar."

He felt his own face go hot and wished she wouldn't examine his features.

"How did you come by the injury?"

"An encounter with highwaymen."

Mary Cullen drew a deep breath. "I pray God to preserve us from such." She looked at him thoughtfully. "Some are saying that Kerl Fritta himself started the rumors of Magyar bandits, in order to put fear into travelers and bring them flocking to join his caravan."

Rob shrugged. "It's not beyond Master Fritta to have done so, I think. The Magyars don't appear threatening." On either side of the road, men and women were harvesting cabbages.

They fell into a silence. Each bump in the road jostled them so he was constantly aware of the possibility of a soft hip and a firm thigh, and the scent of the girl's flesh was like a faint warm spice lured out of berry bushes by the sun.

He who had cozened females the length and breadth of England heard his voice thicken when he tried to talk. "Have you always had your middle name of Margaret, Mistress Cullen?"

She regarded him in astonishment. "Always."

"Can't ever remember another name?"

"When I was a child my father called me Turtle, because sometimes I did this." She blinked both her eyes slowly.

He was unnerved from wanting to touch her hair. Under the broad cheekbone of the left side of her face was a tiny scar, unseen unless you studied her, and it didn't mar her appearance. He looked quickly away.

Ahead, her father twisted in the saddle and saw his daughter riding in the wagon. Cullen had witnessed Rob several more times in the company of the Jews, and his displeasure was in his voice when he called Mary Margaret's name.

She prepared to leave. "What is *your* middle name, Master Cole?"

"Jeremy."

Her nod was serious but her eyes mocked him. "Has it always been Jeremy, then? You can't remember any other name?"

She gathered her skirts in one hand and leaped to the ground lightly as an animal. He caught a glimpse of white legs and slapped the reins against Horse's back, furious with the knowledge that he was an object of amusement to her.

That evening after supper he sought out Simon for his second lesson and discovered that the Jews owned books. St. Botolph's school, which he had attended as a boy, had owned three books, a Canon of the Bible and a New Testament, both in Latin, and in English a menology, a list of holy feast days prescribed for general observance by the King of England. Every page was vellum, made by treating the skins of lambs, calves, or kids. Each letter had been transcribed by hand, a monumental task that caused books to be expensive and rare.

The Jews appeared to have a great number of books—later he found that there were seven—in a small chest of worked leather.

Simon selected one that was written in Parsi and they spent the lesson examining it, Rob searching out specific letters in the text as Simon called for them. He had learned the Parsi alphabet quickly and well. Simon praised him and read a passage of the book so Rob could hear the melodiousness of the language. He stopped after each word and had Rob repeat it.

"What is this book called?"

"It is the Qu'ran, their Bible," Simon said, and he translated:

> *"Glory to God Most High, full of Grace and Mercy;*
> *He created All, including Man.*
> *To Man He gave a special place in His Creation.*
> *He honored Man to be His Agent,*

And to that end, imbued him with understanding,
Purified his affections, and gave him spiritual insight.

"I shall give you a list each day, ten Persian words and expressions," Simon said. "You must commit them to your memory for the following day's lesson."

"Give me twenty-five words every day," Rob said, for he knew he would have his teacher only as far as Constantinople.

Simon smiled. "Twenty-five, then."

Next day Rob learned the words easily, for the road was still straight and smooth and Horse was able to plod with loose reins while his master sat in the driver's seat and studied. But Rob saw a wasted opportunity, and after that day's lesson he asked Meir ben Asher's permission to carry the Persian book to his own wagon, so he might study it all through the empty day of travel.

Meir refused firmly. "The book must never leave our sight. You may read it only in our close company."

"May not Simon ride in the wagon with me?"

He felt certain Meir was about to say no again, but Simon spoke up. "I could use the time to prove the account books," he said.

Meir considered.

"This one is going to be a fierce scholar," Simon said quietly. "There's already in him a ravenous appetite for study."

The Jews regarded Rob in a way that was somehow different than heretofore. Finally Meir nodded. "You may take the book to your wagon," he said.

That night he fell asleep wishing it were the next day, and in the morning he awoke early and eager, with a sense of anticipation that was almost painful. The waiting was more difficult because he could witness every one of the Jews' slow preparations for the day: Simon going into the woods to empty bladder and bowels, yawning Meir and Tuveh ambling to the brook to wash, all of them bobbing and muttering at morning prayer, Gershom and Judah serving up their bread and gruel.

No lover ever awaited maiden with more yearning impatience. "Come, come, you slow-foot, you Hebrew dawdler," he muttered, going over his day's lesson of Persian vocabulary one final time.

When finally Simon came he was laden with the Persian book, a heavy account ledger, and a peculiar wooden frame containing columns of beads strung on narrow wooden rods.

"What's that?"

"An abacus. A counting device, useful when doing sums," Simon said.

After the caravan got under way it was apparent that the new arrangement was workable. Despite the relative smoothness of the road, the wagon wheels rolled over stones and writing was impractical; but it was easy to read, and each of them settled into his work as they moved through mile after mile of countryside.

The Persian book made no sense at all to him, but Simon had told him to read the Parsi letters and words until he felt at ease with the pronunciations. Once he came upon a phrase Simon had given him on the list, *Koc-homedy*, "You come with good intent," and he felt triumphant, as if he had scored a minor victory.

Sometimes he looked up and watched Mary Margaret Cullen's back. Now she rode close to her father's side, no doubt at his insistence, for Rob had noted Cullen glowering at Simon when he climbed onto the wagon. She rode with a very straight back and her head erect, as if she had balanced on a saddle all her life.

He learned his list of words and phrases by noon. "Twenty-five isn't enough. You must give me more."

Simon smiled and gave him another fifteen words to learn. The Jew spoke little, and Rob became accustomed to the *click-click-click* of the abacus beads flying under Simon's fingers.

In the middle of the afternoon, Simon grunted and Rob knew he had discovered an error in one of the accounts. The ledger obviously contained the record of a great many transactions; it dawned on Rob that these men were bringing home to their family the profits of the mercantile caravan they had taken from Persia to Germany, which explained why they never left their campsite unguarded. In the line of march in front of him was Cullen, taking a considerable amount of cash to Anatolia in order to buy sheep. Behind him were these Jews, almost certainly carrying a greater sum. If bandits knew about rich plums such as these, he thought uneasily, they would raise an army of outlaws and even so large a caravan wouldn't be safe from attack. But he wasn't tempted to leave the caravan, for to travel alone was to ask for death. So he put all such fears from his mind and day after day sat on the wagon seat with the reins loose and his eyes fixed, as if eternally, on the Sacred Book of Islam.

There followed a special time. The weather held, with skies so autumnal that their blue depth minded him of Mary Cullen's eyes, of which he saw little because she kept her distance. Doubtless she was so ordered by her father.

Simon finished checking the account book and had no excuse for coming to sit on his wagon seat each day, but their routine had been established and Meir had become relaxed about parting with the Persian book.

Simon trained him assiduously to become a merchant prince.

"What is the basic Persian unit of weight?"

"It is the *man,* Simon, about one-half of a European stone."

"Tell me the other weights."

"There is the *ratel,* the sixth part of a *man.* The *dirham,* the fiftieth part of a *ratel.* The *mescal,* half a *dirham.* The *dung,* the sixth part of a *mescal.* And the *barleycorn,* which is one-fourth of a *dung.*"

"Very good. Good, indeed!"

When he wasn't being quizzed, Rob couldn't refrain from eternal questions.

"Simon, please. What is the word for money?"

"*Ras.*"

"Simon, if you would be so kind . . . what is this term in the book, *Sonab a caret?*"

"Merit for the next life, that is to say, in Paradise."

"Simon—"

Simon groaned and Rob knew he was becoming a nuisance, whereupon he held back the questions until the need to ask another popped into his head.

Twice a week they saw patients, Simon interpreting for him and watching and listening. When Rob examined and treated he was the expert and Simon became the one who asked questions.

A foolishly grinning Frankish drover came to see the barber-surgeon and complained about tenderness and pain behind his knees, where there were hard lumps. Rob gave him a salve of soothing herbs in sheep's fat and told him to come back again in a fortnight, but within a week the drover was back in line. This time he reported the same kind of lumps in both armpits. Rob gave him two bottles of the Universal Specific and sent him away.

When everyone else had gone, Simon turned to him. "What is the matter with the big Frank?"

"Perhaps the lumps will go away. But I think they won't, I think he'll get more lumps because he has the bubo. If that is so, soon he's going to die."

Simon blinked. "Is there nothing you can do?"

He shook his head. "I'm an ignorant barber-surgeon. Perhaps somewhere there is a great physician who could help him."

"I wouldn't do what you do," Simon said slowly, "unless I could learn everything there is to know."

Rob looked at him but said nothing. It shocked him that the Jew could see at once and so clearly what it had taken him such a long time to realize.

That night he was awakened roughly by Cullen. "Hurry, man, for Christ's sake," the Scot said. A woman was screaming.

"Mary?"

"No, no. Come with me."

It was a black night, no moon. Just past the Jews' camp somebody had lighted pitch torches and in the flickering illumination Rob saw that a man lay dying.

He was Raybeau, the cadaverous Frenchman who occupied the position three places behind Rob in the line of march. In his throat was an open, grinning rictus and next to him on the ground was a dark and glistening puddle, his escaped life.

"He was our sentry tonight," Simon said.

Mary Cullen was with the shrieking female, Raybeau's ponderous wife with whom he had constantly quarreled. Her husband's slit throat was slippery under Rob's wet fingers. There was a liquid rattling and Raybeau strained for a moment toward the sound of her anguished calling before he twisted and died.

In a moment they started at the sound of galloping. "It's only mounted pickets sent out by Fritta," Meir said quietly from the shadows.

The entire caravan was aroused and armed, but soon Fritta's riders returned with word that there had been no large raiding party. Perhaps the murderer had been a lone thief, or a scout for the bandits; in either case, the cutthroat was gone.

For the remainder of the night they slept little. In the morning Gaspar Raybeau was buried hard by the Roman road. Kerl Fritta intoned the Service of Interment in hurried German, and then people left the grave and nervously prepared to resume their journey. The Jews loaded their pack mules so their burdens wouldn't tear loose if the animals had to be galloped. Rob saw that among the things packed on each mule was a narrow leather bag that appeared to be heavy; he thought he could guess the contents of the bags. Simon didn't come to the wagon but rode his horse next to Meir, ready to fight or flee if either was necessary.

The following day they came to Novi Sad, a bustling Danube River town where they learned that a group of seven Frankish monks traveling to the Holy Land had been set upon by bandits three days before and robbed, sodomized, and killed.

For the next three days they traveled as if attack were imminent, but they followed the wide, sparkling river to Belgrade without incident and took on provision in the farmers' market there, including small sour red plums of exceptional flavor and little green olives that Rob ate with relish. He had his supper at a tavern but found it not to his liking, being a mixture of many greasy meats chopped together and tasting of rancid fats.

A number of persons had left the caravan at Novi Sad and more at Belgrade, and others joined it, so that the Cullens, Rob, and the party of Jews moved forward in the line of march and no longer were part of the vulnerable rear.

Soon after they left Belgrade they entered foothills that quickly became meaner mountains than any they hitherto had crossed, the steep slopes studded with boulders like bared teeth. In the higher elevations, sharper air brought winter suddenly into their minds. These mountains would be hell in the snow.

Now he couldn't drive with slack reins. Going up inclines he had to urge Horse with gentle little flicks of the leather and going downhill he helped by holding her back. When his arms ached and his spirits were raw he reminded himself that the Romans had moved their *tormenta* over this range of brooding peaks, but the Romans had had hordes of expendable slaves and Rob J. had one tired mare who required the most skillful driving. At night, dull with weariness, he dragged himself to the Jews' camp and sometimes there was a lesson of sorts. But Simon didn't ride in the wagon again and some days Rob did not succeed in learning ten Persian words.

Chapter 28

THE BALKANS

Now Kerl Fritta came into his own and for the first time Rob looked at him with admiration, for the caravan leader seemed to be everywhere, helping with wagon breakdowns, urging and exhorting people the way a good drover encourages dumb beasts. The way was stony. On October first they lost half a day while men of the caravan were impressed to remove rocks that had fallen across the trail. Accidents happened frequently now and Rob set two broken arms in the space of a week. A Norman merchant's horse bolted and his wagon overturned on him, smashing his leg. He had to be carried on a litter slung between two horses until they came to a farmhouse whose occupants agreed to nurse him. They left the injured man there, Rob devoutly hoping that the farmer didn't murder him for his belongings as soon as the caravan was out of sight.

"We've passed beyond the land of the Magyar and are now in Bulgaria," Meir told him one morning.

It mattered little, since the hostile nature of the rocks was unchanged and the wind continued to batter them on the high places. As the weather grew raw the people of the caravan began to wear a variety of outer garments, most of them warmer than they were fashionable, until they were a strange-looking collection of ragged and padded creatures.

On a sunless morning, the pack mule Gershom ben Shemuel was leading behind his horse stumbled and fell, front limbs splayed painfully until the left one snapped audibly under the considerable weight of the pack on the animal's back. The doomed mule screamed in agony like a human being.

"Help him!" Rob called, and Meir ben Asher drew a long knife and helped him in the only way possible, by slitting the quivering throat.

They began at once to unpack the bundle that was on the dead mule. When they came to the narrow leather bag Gershom and Judah had to lift it off together, and an argument ensued in their own language. The remaining pack mule already bore one of the heavy leather bags and Rob was able to see that Gershom was protesting, with justification, that the second bag would quickly overtax the animal.

In the stalled caravan to their rear there were outraged shouts from those who didn't countenance falling behind the main body.

Rob ran back to the Jews. "Throw the bag into my wagon."

Meir hesitated, then he shook his head. "No."

"Then go to hell," Rob said roughly, enraged at the implied lack of trust.

Meir said something and Simon ran after him. "They'll lash the pack onto my horse. May I ride in the wagon? Only until we're able to buy another mule."

Rob motioned him onto the seat and climbed up himself. He drove for a long time in silence, for he wasn't in a mood for Persian lessons.

"You don't understand," Simon said. "Meir must keep the bags with him. It isn't his money. Some belongs to the family and most is owed to investors. The money is his responsibility."

The words made him feel better. But it continued to be a bad day. The way was hard and the presence of a second person in the wagon increased Horse's labor so that she was visibly fatigued when dusk caught them on a mountaintop and they were required to make camp.

Before he or Simon could eat their supper they had to go to see patients. The wind was so strong it forced them behind Kerl Fritta's wagon. Only a handful of people were there to see him, and to his surprise, and Simon's, among them was Gershom ben Shemuel. The tough, chunky Jew lifted his caftan and dropped his trousers and Rob saw an ugly purple boil on the right cheek of his arse.

"Tell him to bend over."

Gershom grunted as the point of Rob's scalpel bit, making yellow pus spurt, and he groaned and cursed in his own language as Rob squeezed the boil until all the putrescence was gone and only bright blood appeared.

"He won't be able to sit a saddle. Not for several days."

"He must," Simon said. "We can't leave Gershom."

Rob sighed. The Jews were proving to be a trial today. "You can take his horse and he'll ride in the back of my wagon."

Simon nodded.

The smiling Frankish drover was next. This time new tiny buboes covered his groin. The lumps in his armpits and behind his knees were larger and more tender than they had been, and when Rob asked, the big Frank said they had begun to pain him.

He took the drover's hand into his own. "Tell him he's going to die."

Simon glared. "Be damned," he said.

"Tell him I say he's going to die."

Simon swallowed and began to speak softly in German. Rob watched the smile dwindle from the big, stupid face, then the Frank pulled his hands from Rob's grasp and raised the right one, turning it into a fist the size of a small ham. He spoke in a growl.

"Says you're a fucking liar," Simon said.

Rob stood and waited, his eyes meeting the drover's, and finally the man spat at his feet and shambled away.

Rob sold spirits to two men with ragged coughs and then treated a whimpering Magyar with a disjointed thumb—he had caught it in the saddle girth and his horse had moved.

Then he left Simon, wanting to escape this place and these people. The caravan was spread out; everyone had sought a large boulder to camp behind, as protection from the wind. He walked beyond the final wagon and saw Mary Cullen standing on a rock above the trail.

She was unearthly. She stood holding open her heavy sheepskin coat with both arms spread wide, her head back and her eyes closed as if she were being purified by the full wash of the wind that swept against her with all the strength of water in full flow. The coat billowed and flapped. Her black gown was plastered against her long body, outlining heavy breasts and rich nipples, a soft roundness of belly and a wide navel, a sweet cleft joining strong thighs. He felt a strange warm tenderness that surely was part of a spell, for she looked like a witch. Her long hair streamed behind her, playing like writhing red fire.

He couldn't tolerate the thought of her opening her eyes and seeing him watching her, and he turned and walked away.

At his own wagon he gloomily contemplated the fact that its interior was too fully packed to carry Gershom lying on his stomach. The only way to supply the needed space was to abandon the bank. He carried out the three sections and stared at them, remembering the countless times he and Barber had stood on the little stage and entertained their audience. Then he shrugged and, picking up a large rock, smashed the bank into firewood. There were coals in the firepot and he coaxed a fire to life in the lee of the wagon. In the growing darkness he sat and fed the pieces of the bank to the flames.

It was unlikely that the name Anne Mary would have been changed to Mary Margaret. And a baby's brown hair, even though it had reddish tints, wouldn't have grown into such an auburn magnificence, he told himself as Mistress Buffington came and mewed and lay next to him close to the fire and out of the wind.

* * *

Midmorning on October twenty-second, hard white grains filled the air, flying before the wind and stinging when they struck bare skin.

"Early for this shit," Rob said morosely to Simon, who was back in the wagon seat, Gershom having toughened his cheek and returned to his horse.

"Not for the Balkans," Simon said.

They were into loftier and more rugged steeps, mostly forested with beech, oak, and pine, but with entire slopes as bare and rocky as though an angry deity had wiped away part of the mountain. There were tiny lakes made by high waterfalls that plummeted into deep gorges.

Ahead of him, Cullen father and Cullen daughter were twin figures in their long sheepskin coats and hats, indistinguishable save that he was able to watch the bulky figure on the black horse and know it was Mary.

The snow didn't accumulate and the travelers struggled against it and made headway, but not fast enough for Kerl Fritta, who raged up and down the line of march, urging greater speed.

"Something has put fear of Christ in Fritta," Rob said.

Simon gave him the quick, guarded glance Rob had noted among the Jews whenever he mentioned Jesus. "He must get us to the town of Gabrovo before the heavy snows. The way through these mountains is the great pass called the Balkan Gate, but it's already closed. The caravan will winter in Gabrovo, close to the entrance to the gate. In that town there are inns and houses which take in travelers. No other town near the pass is large enough to harbor a caravan as large as this one."

Rob nodded, able to see advantages. "I can study my Persian all winter."

"You won't have the book," Simon said. "We shan't stay in Gabrovo with the caravan. We go to the town of Tryavna, a short distance away, where there are Jews."

"But I must have the book. And I need your lessons!"

Simon shrugged.

That evening, after he had tended to Horse, Rob went to the Jews' camp and found them examining some special cleated horseshoes. Meir handed one to Rob. "You should have a set made for your mare. They keep the animal from slipping on snow and ice."

"Can I not come to Tryavna?"

Meir and Simon exchanged a glance; it was apparent they had discussed him. "It's not in my power to grant you the hospitality of Tryavna."

"Who has such power?"

"The Jews there are led by a great sage, the *rabbenu* Shlomo ben Eliahu."

"What is a *rabbenu?*"

"A scholar. In our language *rabbenu* means 'our teacher' and is a term of the highest honor."

"This Shlomo, this sage. Is he a haughty man, cold to strangers? Stiff and unapproachable?"

Meir smiled and shook his head.

"Then may I not go to him and ask to be allowed to stay near your book and Simon's lessons?"

Meir looked at Rob and didn't pretend to be happy with the question. He was silent for a long moment, but when it was clear that Rob was prepared to wait stubbornly for a reply, he sighed and shook his head. "We will take you to the *rabbenu,*" he said.

Chapter 29

TRYAVNA

Gabrovo was a bleak town of makeshift stick buildings. For months Rob had been yearning for a meal he hadn't cooked himself, a fine meal served to him at the table of a public house. The Jews paused in Gabrovo to visit a merchant, just long enough for Rob to visit one of the three inns. The meal was a terrible disappointment, the meat heavily salted in a vain attempt to hide the fact it was spoiled, and the bread hard and stale, with holes in it from which, no doubt, weevils had been picked. The accommodations were as unsatisfactory as the fare. If the remaining two hostelries were no better, the other members of the caravan faced a hard winter, for every available room was crammed with sleeping pallets and they would slumber cheek by jowl.

It took Meir's group less than an hour to travel to Tryavna, which proved to be much smaller than Gabrovo. The Jewish quarter—a group of thatch-roofed buildings of weather-silvered boards, huddling together as if for mutual comfort—was separated from the rest of the town by hibernating vineyards and brown fields in which cows cropped the stubs of cold-withered grass. They turned into a dirt courtyard, where boys took charge of their animals. "You'd best wait here," Meir told Rob.

It wasn't a long wait. Soon Simon came for him and led him into one of the houses, down a dark corridor that smelled of apples and into a room furnished only with a chair and a table piled with books and manuscripts. In the chair sat an old man with snowy hair and beard. He was round-shouldered and stout, with drooping dewlaps and large brown eyes that were watery with age but managed to peer into Rob's very core. There were no introductions; it was like coming before a lord.

"The *rabbenu* has been told you're traveling to Persia and need the language of that country for business," Simon said. "He asks whether the joy of scholarship isn't reason enough to study."

"Sometimes there *is* joy in study," Rob said, speaking directly to the old man. "For me, mostly there is hard work. I'm learning the language of the Persians because I hope it will get me what I want."

Simon and the *rabbenu* jabbered.

"He asked if you are generally so honest. I told him you're sufficiently forthright to tell a dying man he is dying, and he said, 'That is honest enough.' "

"Tell him I have money and will pay for food and shelter."

The sage shook his head. "This isn't an inn. Those who live here must work," Shlomo ben Eliahu said through Simon. "If the Ineffable One is merciful, we'll have no need for a barber-surgeon this winter."

"I don't have to work as a barber-surgeon. I'm willing to do anything useful."

The *rabbenu*'s long fingers rooted and scrabbled in his beard while he considered. Finally he announced his decision.

"Whenever slaughtered beef is declared not to be *kasher*," Simon said, "you'll take the meat and sell it to the Christian butcher in Gabrovo. And during the Sabbath, when Jews may not labor, you'll tend the fires in the houses."

Rob hesitated. The elderly Jew looked at him with interest, caught by the gleam in his eyes.

"Something?" Simon murmured.

"If Jews may not labor on your Sabbath, isn't he damning my soul by arranging for me to do so?"

The *rabbenu* smiled at the translation.

"He says he trusts you do not yearn to become a Jew, Master Cole?"

Rob shook his head.

"Then he is certain you may work without fear on Jews' Sabbath, and bids you welcome to Tryavna."

The *rabbenu* led them to where Rob would bed at the rear of a large cow barn. "There are candles in the study house. But no candles may be lighted for reading here in the barn, because of the dry hay," the *rabbenu* said sternly through Simon, and put him to work at once mucking out stalls.

That night he lay on the straw with his cat on guard at his feet like a lion. Mistress Buffington deserted him occasionally to terrorize a mouse but always came back. The barn was a dark, moist palace, warmed to comfort by the great bovine bodies, and as soon as he became accustomed to the eternal lowing and the sweet stench of cow shit he slept contentedly.

* * *

Winter came to Tryavna three days after Rob did. Snow began to fall during the night and for the next two days alternated between a wind-driven bitter sleet and fat flakes that floated down so big they looked like sweet things to eat. When it ended he was given a great wooden snow shovel and helped remove the drifts from before all the doors, wearing a leather Jew's hat he found on a peg in the barn. Above him the looming mountains glittered white in the sun and the exertion in the cold air made him optimistic. When the shoveling was done there was no other work and he was free to go to the study house, a frame building into which the cold oozed and was pitifully fought by a token fire so inadequate that it wasn't unusual for people to forget to feed it. The Jews sat around rough tables and studied hour after hour, quarreling loudly and sometimes bitterly.

They called their language the Tongue. Simon told him it was a mixture of Hebrew and Latin, plus a few idioms from the countries in which they traveled or lived. It was a language designed for disputants; when they studied together they hurled words at one another.

"What are they arguing about?" he asked Meir, amazed.

"Points of the law."

"Where are their books?"

"They don't use books. Those who know the laws have memorized them from hearing them from the mouths of their teachers. Those who haven't yet memorized the laws are learning them by listening. It's always been thus. There is Written Law, of course, but it is there only to be consulted. Every man who knows Oral Law is a teacher of legal interpretations as his own teacher taught them, and there are a multitude of interpretations because there are so many different teachers. That's why they argue. Each time they debate, they learn a little bit more about the law."

From the start in Tryavna they called him Mar Reuven, Hebrew for Master Robert. Mar Reuven the Barber-Surgeon. Being called *Mar* set him apart from them as much as anything else, for they called each other *Reb*, an honorific indicating commendable scholarship but ranking below that of someone designated a *rabbenu*. In Tryavna there was but one *rabbenu*.

They were a strange people, different from him in appearance as well as custom. "What's the matter with his hair?" a man named Reb Joel Levski the Herdsman asked Meir. Rob was the only one in the study house without *peoth*, the ceremonial hair locks that curled beside each ear.

"He knows no better. He's a *goy*, an Other," Meir explained.

"But Simon told me this Other is circumcised. How can that be?" said Reb Pinhas ben Simeon the Dairyman.

Meir shrugged. "An accident," he said. "I've discussed it with him. It has nothing to do with the covenant of Abraham."

For several days Mar Reuven was stared at. In turn he did some staring of his own, for they seemed more than passing strange to him with their headwear and earlocks and bushy beards and dark clothing and heathenish ways. He was fascinated with their habits during prayer. They were so individualized. Meir donned his prayer shawl modestly and unobtrusively. Reb Pinhas unfolded his *tallit* and shook it out almost arrogantly, held it in front of him by two corners, and with an upward motion of his arms and a flick of his wrists sent it billowing over his head, to settle over his shoulders as soft as a blessing.

When Reb Pinhas prayed he bobbed back and forth with the urgency of his desire to send his supplication to the Almighty. Meir swayed gently when he recited the prayers. Simon rocked with a tempo somewhere in between, ending each forward motion with a little shudder and a slight shaking of the head.

Rob read and studied his book and the Jews, behaving too much like the rest of them to stay a novelty. For six hours every day—three hours following the morning prayer service, which they called *shaharit,* and three hours after the evening service, *ma'ariv*—the study house was jammed, for most of the men studied before and after completing the day's work by which they earned their living. Between these two periods, however, it was relatively quiet, with only one or two tables occupied by fulltime scholars. Soon he sat among them at ease and unnoticed, oblivious to the Jewish babble as he worked on the Persian Qu'ran, beginning to make real progress at last.

When their Sabbath came he tended the fires. It was his heaviest day of work since the snow shoveling but still so easy he was able to study for part of the afternoon. Two days later he helped Reb Elia the Carpenter put new rungs into wooden chairs. Other than that there was no labor but the study of Persian until, near the end of his second week in Tryavna, the *rabbenu*'s granddaughter Rohel taught him to milk. She had white skin and long black hair that she wore braided about her heart-shaped face, a small mouth with a womanly swelling of the lower lip, a tiny birthmark on her throat, and large brown eyes that always seemed to be on him.

While they were in the dairy one of the cows, a foolish thing that believed she was a bull, mounted another cow and began to move as if she owned a penis and had entered the other beast.

The color mounted from Rohel's neck into her face, but she smiled and gave a little laugh. She leaned forward on her stool and placed her head against a milch cow's warm flank, her eyes closed. Skirt tautened, she reached between her spread knees and grasped the thick teats beneath the swollen udders. Her fingers rippled, pressing swiftly in turn. When milk drummed into the bucket Rohel drew a breath and sighed. Her pink tongue crept out to wet her lips and she opened her eyes and looked at Rob.

Rob stood alone in the shadowy gloom of the cow barn, holding a piece of blanket. It smelled strongly of Horse and was only a little larger than a prayer shawl. With a quick movement he sent the blanket over his head to settle about his shoulders as nicely as if it were Reb Pinhas' *tallit*. Repetition was giving him a confident motion in donning the prayer shawl. Cattle lowed as he stood and practiced a prayerful swaying, sedate but purposeful. He preferred to emulate Meir in prayer rather than more energetic worshipers like Reb Pinhas.

That was the easy part. Their language, strange-sounding and complex, would take a long time to master, especially while he was exerting such an effort to learn Persian.

They were a people of amulets. On the upper third of the right-hand doorpost of every door in every house was nailed a little wooden tube called a *mezuzah*. Simon said each tube contained a tiny rolled parchment; inscribed on the front in square Assyrian letters were twenty-two lines from Deuteronomy 6:4–9 and 11:13–21, and on the back was the word *Shaddai*, "Almighty."

As Rob had observed during the journey, each morning except on the Sabbath each adult male strapped two small leather boxes to his arm and head. These were called *tefillin* and contained portions of their holy book, the Torah, the box bound to the forehead being close to the mind, the other fastened to the arm, hard by the heart.

"We do it to obey the instructions in Deuteronomy," Simon said. " '*And these words, which I command thee this day, shall be upon thy heart . . . And thou shalt bind them for a sign upon thy hand, and they shall be for frontlets between thine eyes.*' "

The trouble was Rob couldn't tell, simply by watching, how the Jews put on the *tefillin*. Nor could he ask Simon to show him, for it would have been strange for a Christian to want to be taught a rite of Jewish worship. He was able to count that they wrapped ten loops of the leather around their arms, but what they did with the hand was complicated, for the leather strip was wound between the fingers in special ways he couldn't determine.

Standing in the cold, ripe-smelling barn, he wrapped his left arm with a piece of old rope instead of the leather *tefillin* strip, but what he did to his hand and fingers with the rope never made any sense.

Still, the Jews were natural teachers and he learned something new every day. In the school of St. Botolph's Church the priests had taught him that the God of the Old Bible was Jehovah. But when he referred to Jehovah, Meir shook his head.

"Know that for us the Lord our God, Blessed be He, has seven names. This is the most sacred." With a piece of charcoal from the fireplace he drew on the wooden floor, writing the word in both Persian and in the Tongue: *Yahweh*. "It is never spoken, for the identity of the Most High is inexpressible. It is mispronounced by Christians, as you've done. But the name isn't Jehovah, do you understand?"

Rob nodded.

At night on his bed of straw he reviewed new words and customs, and before sleep overwhelmed him he remembered a phrase, a fragment of a blessing, a gesture, a pronunciation, an expression of ecstasy on a face during prayer, and he stored these things into his mind against the day when they would be needed.

"You must stay away from the *rabbenu*'s granddaughter," Meir told him, frowning.

"I have no interest in her." Days had passed since they had talked in the dairy, and he hadn't been near her since.

In truth, he had dreamed of Mary Cullen the night before and had awakened at dawn to lie stunned and hot-eyed, trying to recall details of the dream.

Meir nodded, his face clearing. "Good. One of the women has observed her watching you with too much interest, and told the *rabbenu*. He asked me to have a talk with you." Meir placed a forefinger against his nose. "One quiet word to a wise man is better than a year of pleading with a fool."

Rob was alarmed and disturbed, for he had to stay in Tryavna to observe the ways of the Jews and study Persian. "I don't want trouble over a woman."

"Of course not." Meir sighed. "The problem is the girl, who should be married. She has been betrothed since childhood to Reb Meshullum ben Moses, the grandson of Reb Baruch ben David. You know Reb Baruch? A tall, spare man? Long face? Thin, pointed nose? He sits just beyond the fire in the study house?"

"Ah, that one. An old man with fierce eyes."

"Fierce eyes because he's a fierce scholar. If the *rabbenu* weren't the

rabbenu, Reb Baruch would be the *rabbenu*. They were always rival scholars and the closest of friends. When their grandchildren were still babies
they arranged a match with great joy, to unite their families. Then they had
a terrible falling-out that ended their friendship."

"Why did they quarrel?" asked Rob, who was beginning to feel sufficiently at home in Tryavna to enjoy a bit of gossip.

"They slaughtered a young bull in partnership. Now, you must understand that our laws of *kashruth* are ancient and complex, with rules and
interpretations about how things must be and how things must not be. A
tiny blemish was discovered on the lung of the animal. The *rabbenu* quoted
precedents that said the blemish was insignificant and in no way spoiled the
meat. Reb Baruch cited other precedents that indicated the meat was ruined
by the blemish and couldn't be eaten. He insisted he was right and resented
the *rabbenu* for questioning his scholarship.

"They argued until finally the *rabbenu* lost patience. 'Cut the animal in
half,' he said. 'I'll take my portion, and let Baruch do whatever he pleases
with his.'

"When he brought his half of the bull home, he intended to eat it. But
after deliberating, he complained, 'How can I eat the meat of this animal?
One half lies on Baruch's garbage pile, and I should eat the other half?' So
he threw away his half of the beef as well.

"After that, they seemed to oppose each other all the time. If Reb
Baruch said white, the *rabbenu* said black, if the *rabbenu* said meat, Reb
Baruch said milk. When Rohel was twelve and a half years old, the age
when her elders should have begun talking seriously about a wedding, the
families did nothing because they knew that any meetings would end in
quarreling between the two old men. Then young Reb Meshullum, the
prospective bridegroom, went on his first foreign business trip with his
father and other men of his family. They traveled to Marseilles with a stock
of copper kettles and stayed almost a year, trading and making a fine profit.
Counting the time of traveling they were gone two years before they
returned last summer, bringing a caravan shipment of well-made French
garments. And still the two families, held apart by the grandfathers, do not
arrange for the marriage to take place!

"By now," Meir said, "it's common knowledge that the unfortunate
Rohel might as well be considered an *agunah*, a deserted wife. She has
breasts but suckles no babies, she's a woman grown but she has no husband,
and it has become a major scandal."

They agreed that it would be best for Rob to avoid the dairy during the
hours of milking.

* * *

It was well that Meir had spoken to him, for who knew what might have happened if he had not been made to see clearly that their winter's hospitality didn't include the use of their women. At night he had tortured voluptuous visions of long, full thighs, red hair, and pale young breasts with tips like berries. He felt certain the Jews would have a prayer asking forgiveness for spilled seed—they had a prayer for everything—but he had none and he hid the evidence of his dreams under fresh straw and tried to lose himself in his work.

It was hard. All around him was a humming sexuality encouraged by their religion—they believed it a special blessing to make love on the eve of the Sabbath, for instance, perhaps explaining why they so dearly loved the end of the week! The young men talked freely of such matters, groaning to one another if a wife was untouchable; Jewish married couples were forbidden to copulate for twelve days after the flow of menses began, or seven days after it ceased, whichever period was longer. Their abstinence wasn't over until the wife marked its end by purifying herself through immersion in the ritual pool, called the *mikva*.

This was a brick-lined tank in a bathhouse built over a spring. Simon told Rob that to be ritually fit, the *mikva* water had to come from a natural spring or a river. The *mikva* was for symbolic purification, not cleanliness. The Jews bathed at home, but each week just before the Sabbath, Rob joined the males in the bathhouse, which contained only the pool and a great roaring fire in a round hearth over which hung cauldrons of boiling water. Bathing stripped to the skin in the steamy warmth, they vied for the privilege of pouring water over the *rabbenu* while they questioned him at length.

"*Shi-ailah, Rabbenu, shi-ailah!*" A question, a question!

Shlomo ben Eliahu's answer to each problem was deliberate and thoughtful, full of scholarly precedents and citations, sometimes translated for Rob in far too much detail by Simon or Meir.

"*Rabbenu,* is it truly written in the Book of Guidance that every man must dedicate his oldest son to seven years of advanced study?"

The naked *rabbenu* explored his navel reflectively, tugged at an ear, scrabbled in his full white beard with long pale fingers. "It is *not* so written, my children. On the one hand"—he poked upward with his right forefinger — "Reb Hananel ben Ashi of Leipzig *was* of this opinion. On the other hand"—up went his left forefinger—"according to the *rabbenu* Joseph ben Eliakim of Jaffa, this applies only to the first sons of priests and Levites. But"—he pushed the air at them with both palms—"both of these sages lived hundreds of years ago. Today we are modern men. We understand that learning is not just for a firstborn, with all other sons to be treated as if they were mere women. Today we are accustomed to every youth spending his fourteenth, fifteenth, and sixteenth year in the advanced study of Talmud, twelve to fifteen hours a day. After that, those few who are called may devote their lives to scholarship, while the others may go into business and study only six hours a day thereafter."

Well. Most of the questions that were translated for the visiting Other were not the sort that would start his heart to hammering or even, in truth, maintain his constant attention. Nevertheless, Rob enjoyed Friday afternoons in the bathhouse; never had he felt so at home in the company of unclothed men. Perhaps it had something to do with his bobbed prick. If he had been among his own kind, by now his organ would have been the subject of rude stares, snickering, questions, lewd speculation. An exotic flower growing by itself is one thing, but it is quite another when it is surrounded by an entire field of other flowers of similar configuration.

In the bathhouse the Jews were lavish in feeding wood to the fire and he liked the combination of wood smoke and steamy dampness, the sting of the strong yellow soap whose manufacture was supervised by the *rabbenu*'s daughter, the careful mixing of boiling water with cold spring water to create a lovely warmth for bathing.

He never went into the *mikva,* understanding that it was forbidden. He was content to loll in the vaporous bathhouse, watching the Jews steel themselves to enter the tank. Muttering the blessing that accompanied the act or singing it loudly, according to their personalities, they walked down the six dank stone steps into the water, which was deep. As it covered their faces they blew vigorously or held their breath, for the act of purification made it necessary to immerse oneself so totally that every hair of the body was wet.

Even if invited, nothing could have convinced Rob to enter the chill dark mystery of the water, a place of their religion.

If the God called Yahweh truly existed, then perhaps He was aware that Rob Cole was planning to pass himself off as one of His children.

He felt that if he entered the inscrutable waters something would pull him into the world beyond, where all the sins of his nefarious plan were known and Hebrew serpents would gnaw his flesh, and perhaps he would be personally chastised by Jesus.

Chapter 30

WINTER IN THE STUDY HOUSE

That Christmas was the strangest in his twenty-one years. Barber hadn't raised him to be a true believer, but the goose and the pudding, the nibbling of the headcheese called brawn, the singing, the toasting, the holiday slap on the back—these were a part of him, and this year he felt a yawning loneliness. The Jews didn't ignore him on that day from meanness; Jesus was simply not in their world. Doubtless Rob could have found his way to a church, but he didn't. Strangely, the fact that no one wished him a joyous Christ's Day made him more of a Christian in his own mind than ever he had been.

A week later, at dawn of Our Lord's new year of 1032, he lay on his bed of straw and wondered at what he had become, and where it would take him. When he wandered the British isle he had thought himself the very devil of a traveler, but already he had traveled a far greater distance than was encompassed by his home island, and an endless unknown world still lay before him.

The Jews celebrated that day, but because it was a new moon, not because it was a new year! He learned to his befuddlement that by their heathen calendar it was mid-annum of the year 4792.

It was a country for snow. He welcomed each snowfall and soon it was an accepted fact that after each storm the big Christian with his great wooden shovel would do the work of several ordinary shovelers. It was his only physical activity; when he wasn't shoveling snow he was learning Parsi. He was sufficiently advanced to be able to think slowly in the Persian language now. A number of the Jews of Tryavna had been to Persia and he spoke Parsi with anyone he could trap. "The accent, Simon. How is my accent?" he asked, irritating his tutor.

"Any Persian who wishes to laugh will do so," Simon snapped, "because to Persians you'll be a *foreigner*. Do you expect miracles?" The Jews in the study house exchanged smiles at the foolishness of the giant young *goy*.

Let them smile, he thought; he found them a more interesting study than they found him. For example, he quickly learned that Meir and his group weren't the only strangers in Tryavna. Many of the other males in the study house were travelers waiting out the rigors of the Balkan winter. To Rob's surprise, Meir told him that none of them paid as much as a single coin in return for more than three months' food and shelter.

Meir explained. "It is this system that allows my people to trade among the nations. You've seen how difficult and dangerous it is to travel the world, yet every Jewish community sends merchants abroad. And in any Jewish village in any land, Christian or Muslim, a Jewish traveler is taken in by Jews and given food and wine, a place in the synagogue, a stable for his horse. Each community has men in foreign parts sustained by someone else. And next year, the host will be the guest."

The strangers quickly fit into the life of the community, even to relishing the local babble. Thus it was that one afternoon in the study house, while Rob was conversing in the Persian tongue with an Anatolian Jew named Ezra the Farrier—gossip in Parsi!—he learned that a dramatic confrontation would take place the next day. The *rabbenu* served as *shohet*, the community slaughterer of meat animals. Next morning he would slaughter two beasts of his own, young beeves. A small group of the community's most prestigious sages served as *mashgiot*, ritual inspectors who saw to it that the complicated law, down to the finest detail, was observed during the butchering. And scheduled to preside as a *mashgiah* during the *rabbenu*'s slaughtering was his onetime friend and latter-day bitter antagonist, Reb Baruch ben David.

That evening Meir gave Rob a lesson from the Book of Leviticus. These were the animals Jews were allowed to eat of all those on earth: any creature that both chewed its cud and had a split hoof, including sheep, cattle, goats, and deer. Animals that were *treif*—not *kasher*—included horses, donkeys, camels, and pigs.

Of birds they were permitted to eat pigeons, chickens, tame doves, tame ducks, and tame geese. Winged creatures which were an abomination included eagles, ostriches, vultures, kites, cuckoos, swans, storks, owls, pelicans, lapwings, and bats.

"Never in my life have I tasted so fine a meat as cygnet lovingly larded, barded in salt pork, and then roasted slowly over the fire."

Meir looked faintly repulsed. "You won't get it here," he said.

The next morning dawned clear and cold. The Study House was nearly empty after *shaharit*, the early prayer service, for many wandered to the *rabbenu*'s barnyard to watch *shehitah*, the ritual butchering. Their breath made small clouds that hung in the still, frosty air.

Rob stood with Simon. There was a small stir when Reb Baruch ben David arrived with the other *mashgiah*, a bent old man named Reb Samson ben Zanvil, whose face was set and stern.

"He's older than either Reb Baruch or the *rabbenu* but is not as learned," Simon whispered. "And now he fears he'll be caught between the two if an argument should arise."

The *rabbenu*'s four sons led the first animal from the barn, a black bull with a deep back and heavy hindquarters. Lowing, the bull tossed his head and pawed the earth, and they had to enlist help from the bystanders in controlling him with ropes while the inspectors went over every inch of his body.

"The tiniest sore or break in the skin will disqualify an animal for meat," Simon said.

"Why?"

Simon looked at Rob in annoyance. "Because it is the law," he said.

Finally satisfied, they led the bull to a feeding trough filled with sweet hay. The *rabbenu* picked up a long knife. "See the blunt, square end of the knife," Simon said. "It's made without a point so there's less likelihood it will scratch the animal's skin. But the knife is razor-sharp."

They all stood in the cold while nothing happened. "What are they waiting for?" Rob whispered.

"The precisely right moment," Simon said, "for the animal must be motionless at the instant of the death cut, or it is not *kasher.*"

Even as he spoke, the knife flashed. The single clean stroke severed the gullet and the windpipe and the carotid arteries in the neck. A red stream sprang in its wake, and the bull's consciousness vanished as the blood supply to the brain was cut off at once. The bovine eyes dimmed and the bull went to its knees, and in a moment was dead.

There was a pleased murmur from those who watched but it was as quickly stilled, for Reb Baruch had taken the knife and was examining it.

Watching, Rob could see a struggle that tightened the fine old features. Baruch turned to his elderly rival.

"Something?" the *rabbenu* said coldly.

"I fear," Reb Baruch said. He proceeded to show, midway down the cutting edge of the blade, an imperfection, the tiniest of nicks in the keenly honed steel.

Old and gnarled, his face dismayed, Reb Samson ben Zanvil hung back, certain that as the second *mashgiah* he would be called upon for a judgment he didn't want to make.

Reb Daniel, the father of Rohel and the *rabbenu*'s oldest son, began a blustering argument. "What nonsense is this? Everyone knows of the care with which the *rabbenu*'s ritual knives are sharpened," he said, but his father put up his hand for silence.

The *rabbenu* held the knife up to the light and ran a practiced finger just beneath the razor-sharp edge. He sighed, for the nick was there, a human error that made the meat ritually unfit.

"It's a blessing that your eyes are sharper than this blade and continue to protect us, my old friend," he said quietly, and there was a general relaxing, like a releasing of pent-up breath.

Reb Baruch smiled. He reached out and patted the *rabbenu*'s hand, and the two men looked at one another for a long moment.

Then the *rabbenu* turned away and called for Mar Reuven the Barber-Surgeon.

Rob and Simon stepped forward and listened attentively. "The *rabbenu* asks you to deliver this *treif* bull's carcass to the Christian butcher of Gabrovo," Simon said.

He took Horse, for she was in sore need of the exercise, hitching her to their flatbed sleigh onto which a number of willing hands loaded the slaughtered bull. The *rabbenu* had used an approved knife for the second animal, which was judged to be *kasher*, and the Jews already were dismembering it when Rob shook the reins and directed Horse away from Tryavna.

He drove to Gabrovo slowly and with great enjoyment. The butcher shop proved to be exactly where it had been described, three houses below the town's most prominent building, which was an inn. The butcher was large and heavy, an advertisement of his trade. Language did not prove a barrier.

"Tryavna," Rob said, pointing to the dead bull.

The fat red face became wreathed in smiles. "Ah. *Rabbenu*," the butcher said, and nodded vigorously. Uncarting the creature proved to be hard but the butcher went off to a tavern and returned with a pair of helpers, and with rope and effort at length the bull was unloaded.

Simon had told him the price was fixed and there would be no haggling. When the butcher handed Rob the few paltry coins it became clear why the man smiled with joy, for he had practically stolen a whole excellent beef, simply because there had been a nick in the slaughtering blade! Rob would never be able to understand people who, for no valid reason, could treat good cowflesh as if it were trash. The stupidity of it made him angry and filled him with a kind of shame; he wanted to explain to the butcher that he was a Christian and not one of those who behaved so foolishly. But he could only accept the coins in the name of the Hebrews and place them in his purse pocket for safekeeping.

His business done, he went directly to the tavern of the nearby inn. The dark public house was long and narrow, more like a tunnel than a room, its low ceiling blackened by the smoky fire around which nine or ten men loafed, drinking. Three women sat at a small table nearby and waited watchfully. Rob inspected them while he had a drink—a brown raw whiskey that wasn't at all to his liking. They were clearly tavern whores. Two were well past their prime, but the third was a young blonde with a wicked-innocent face. She saw the purpose of his glance and smiled at him.

Rob finished his drink and went to their table. "I don't suppose you have English," he murmured, and it was a safe guess. One of the older women said something and the other two laughed. But he took out a coin and gave it to the younger one. It was all the communication they needed. She tucked the coin into her pocket, left the table without another word to her companions, and went to where her cloak hung on a peg.

He followed her outside and in the snowy street he met Mary Cullen.

"Hello! Are you and your father having a good winter?"

"We are having a wretched winter," she said, and he noted that she looked it. Her nose was reddened and there was a cold sore on the tender fullness of her upper lip. "The inn is always freezing and the food is very bad. Are you really living with Jews?"

"Yes."

"How can you?" she said thinly.

He had forgotten the color of her eyes and their effect on him was disarming, as if he had chanced upon bluebirds in the snow. "I sleep in a warm barn. The food is excellent," he told her with great satisfaction.

"My father tells me there is a special Jew's stink called *foetor judaicus*. Because they rubbed Christ's body with garlic after he died."

"Sometimes we all smell. But to immerse themselves from head to foot each Friday is the custom of their kind. I trust that they bathe more often than most."

She colored, and he knew that it must be difficult and rare to obtain bath water in an inn such as there was in Gabrovo.

She regarded the woman who patiently waited for him a short distance away. "My father says that anyone who will consent to live with Jews never can be a proper man."

"Your father seemed a nice man. But perhaps," he said thoughtfully, "he is an arse." They began walking away from one another at the same moment.

He followed the blond woman to a room nearby. It was untidy with the soiled garments of women and he suspected that she shared the room with the two others. He watched her as she undressed. "It's cruelty to look on you after seeing that other one," he said, knowing she knew not a word of what he said. "She may not always have a pleasant tongue, but . . . it's not beauty, exactly, yet few women can compare to Mary Cullen in appearance."

The woman smiled at him.

"You're a young whore but already you look old," he said to her. The air was cold, and she shucked her clothing and slipped quickly between the filthy fur covers to escape the chill, but not before he saw more than he liked. He was a man who appreciated the musk-lure of women but what rose from her was sour stink, and her body hair had a hard and plastered look as if juices had dried and redried untold times without feeling the plain honest wetness of water. Abstinence had produced such hunger in him that he would have fallen on her, but the brief glimpse of her bluish body had shown him overused, caked flesh he didn't want to touch.

"God damn that red-haired witch," he said morosely.

The woman looked up at him in puzzlement.

"It isn't your fault, dolly," he told her, reaching into his purse. He gave her more than she would have been worth even if value-giving had been attempted, and she pulled the coins under the furs and clutched them next to her body. He hadn't begun to take anything off, and he straightened his clothing and nodded to her and went out into fresher air.

As February waned he spent more time than ever in the study house, poring over the Persian Qu'ran. He found himself constantly amazed by the Qu'ran's unremitting hostility toward Christians and bitter loathing of Jews.

Simon explained it. "Mohammed's early teachers were Jews and Syriac Christian monks. When first he reported that the Angel Gabriel had visited him, and that God had named him Prophet and instructed him to found a new and perfect religion, he expected these old friends to flock after him with glad cries. But the Christians preferred their own religion and the Jews, startled and threatened, actively joined those who disclaimed Mohammed's preachings. For the rest of his life he never forgave them, but spoke and wrote of them with revilement."

Simon's insights made the Qu'ran come alive for Rob. He was almost halfway through the book and he labored over it, aware that soon they would travel again. When they reached Constantinople he and Meir's group would go different ways, not only separating him from his teacher Simon but, more important, depriving him of the book. The Qu'ran gave him intimations of a culture remote from his own, and the Jews of Tryavna gave him a glimpse of still a third way of life. As a boy he had thought that England was the world, but now he saw that there were other peoples; in some traits they were alike, but they differed from one another in important ways.

The encounter at the slaughtering had reconciled the *rabbenu* with Reb Baruch ben David, and their families began at once to plan for the wedding of Rohel to young Reb Meshullum ben Nathan. The Jewish Quarter hummed with excited activity. The two old men walked about in the highest spirits, often together.

The *rabbenu* made Rob a gift of the old leather hat and loaned him, for study, a tiny section of the Talmud. The Hebrew Book of Laws had been translated into Parsi. Though Rob welcomed the opportunity to see the Persian language in another document, the meaning of the segment was beyond him. The fragment dealt with a law called *shaatnez:* although Jews were allowed to wear linen and to wear wool, they weren't allowed to wear a mixture of linen and wool, and Rob couldn't understand why.

Anyone he asked either didn't know or shrugged and said it was the law.

That Friday, naked in the steamy bathhouse, Rob found his courage as the men gathered about their sage.

"*Shi-ailah, Rabbenu, shi-ailah!*" he cried. A question, a question!

The *rabbenu* paused in soaping his great sloping belly and grinned at the young stranger, and then spoke.

"He says, 'Ask it, my son,' " Simon said.

"You are forbidden to eat meat with milk. You are forbidden to wear linen with wool. You are forbidden to touch your wives half the time. Why is so much forbidden?"

"To necessitate faith," the *rabbenu* said.

"Why should God make such strange demands of the Jews?"

"To keep us separate from you," the *rabbenu* said, but his eyes twinkled and there was no malice in the words, and Rob gasped as Simon poured water over his head.

* * *

Everyone participated when Rohel, the granddaughter of the *rabbenu*, was married to Reb Baruch's grandson, Meshullum, on the second Friday of the month of Adar.

Early that morning everyone assembled outside the house of Daniel ben Shlomo, the bride's father. Inside, Meshullum paid a handsome bride price of fifteen gold pieces. The *ketubah*, or wedding contract, was signed and Reb Daniel presented a handsome dowry, returning the bride price to the couple and adding an additional fifteen gold pieces, a wagon, and a span of horses. Nathan, the groom's father, gave the fortunate couple a pair of milch cows. When they left the house, a radiant Rohel walked past Rob as if he were invisible.

The entire community escorted the pair to the synagogue, where they recited seven blessings under a canopy. Meshullum stamped on a fragile glass to illustrate that happiness is transient and Jews must not forget the destruction of the Temple. And then they were man and wife, and a day-long celebration was under way. A flutist, a fifer, and a drummer provided music and the Jews sang lustily, *My beloved is gone down to his garden, to the beds of spices, to feed in the gardens and to gather lilies,* which Simon told Rob was from the Scriptures. The two grandfathers spread their arms in joy, snapped their fingers, closed their eyes, threw back their heads and danced. The wedding celebration lasted until the early hours of the morning and Rob ate too heavily of meat and rich puddings and had too much to drink.

That night he brooded as he lay on his straw in the warm blackness of the barn, his cat at his feet. He remembered the blond woman in Gabrovo with less and less disgust and willed himself not to think of Mary Cullen. He thought resentfully of skinny young Meshullum, lying at that moment with Rohel, and hoped the boy's prodigious scholarship would enable him to appreciate his good fortune.

He woke well before dawn and felt rather than heard the changes in his world. By the time he had slept again and awakened and risen from his bed, the sounds were clearly audible: a dripping, a tinkling, a rushing, a roar that grew in volume as more and more ice and snow gave way and joined the waters of the unlocked earth, sweeping down the mountainsides and signifying the coming of spring.

Chapter 31

THE WHEAT FIELD

When her mother died, Mary Cullen's father had told her he would mourn Jura Cullen for the rest of his life. She had willingly joined him in wearing black and avoiding public pleasures, but when a full year of mourning ended on the eighteenth of March, she told her father it was time for them to return to the routines of ordinary living.

"I continue to wear black," James Cullen said.

"I shall not," she said, and he nodded.

She had carried all the way from home a bolt of light woollen stuff woven from their own fleece, and she inquired carefully until she found a fine seamstress in Gabrovo. The woman nodded when she conveyed what she wanted, but indicated that the cloth, of a nondescript natural color, had best be dyed before cutting. The roots of the madder plant could give red shades, but with her hair that would make her stand out like a beacon. The center wood of oak would give gray, but after her steady diet of black, gray was too subdued. Maple or sumac bark would give yellow or orange, frivolous colors. It would have to be brown.

"I've gone all my life wearing nut-husk brown," she grumbled to her father.

Next day he brought her a small pot of a yellowish paste, like slightly turned butter. "It is dye, and fiercely expensive."

"Not a color I admire," she said carefully.

James Cullen smiled. "It's called India blue. It dissolves in water and you must be careful not to get it on your hands. When the wet cloth is taken from the yellow water it changes color in the air and thereafter the dye is fast."

It produced a rich, deep blue cloth such as she had never seen, and the seamstress cut and sewed a dress and a cloak. She was pleased with the garments but folded them and put them away until the morning of the tenth of April, when hunters brought the news to Gabrovo that the way through the mountains was open at last.

By early afternoon, people who had been awaiting the thaw throughout the countryside had begun to hasten into Gabrovo, the departure town for the great pass known as the Balkan Gate. Provisioners set up their wares, and milling mobs began to shout for the right to buy supplies.

Mary had to make the innkeeper's wife a gift of money to persuade her to heat water over the fire at such a frenzied time and carry it upstairs to the women's sleeping chambers. First Mary knelt over the wooden tub and washed her hair, now long and thick as a winter pelt, then she squatted in the tub and scrubbed herself until she glowed.

She dressed in the newly made garments and went to sit outside. Drawing a wooden comb through her hair as it dried sweet in the sun, she saw that the principal street of Gabrovo was crowded with horses and wagons. Presently a large pack of men, wildly drunk, galloped their horses through the town, uncaring about the havoc caused by the pounding hooves of their mounts. A wagon was overturned as horses bucked and shied, their eyes rolling in fright. While men cursed and fought to hold the reins and horses whickered and screamed, Mary ran inside before her hair was fully dried.

She had their belongings packed and ready by the time her father appeared with his manservant, Seredy.

"Who were the men who stormed through the town?" she asked.

"They call themselves Christian knights," her father said coldly. "There are almost eighty of them, Frenchmen from Normandy on pilgrimage to Palestine."

"They are very dangerous, lady," Seredy said. "They wear mail vests but they travel with wagons laden with full armor. They stay drunk and . . ." He averted his eyes. "They ill-treat women of all sorts. You must stay close to us, lady."

She thanked him gravely, but the thought of having to depend upon Seredy and her father to protect her from eighty drunken and brutal knights would have been amusing were it not grim.

Mutual protection was the best reason for traveling in a large caravan, and they lost no time in loading the pack animals and leading them to a large field on the eastern edge of the town, where the caravan was assembling. When they rode past Kerl Fritta's wagon, Mary saw that he had already set up a table and was doing a brisk business in recruiting.

It was something of a homecoming, for they were greeted by a number of people they had known on the earlier portion of the trip. The Cullens found their place well toward the middle of the line of march because so many new travelers had formed up behind them.

She kept a careful watch, but it was almost nightfall before she saw the party for which she'd been waiting. The same five Jews with whom he had left the caravan returned on horseback. Behind them she saw the little brown mare; Rob J. Cole drove the garish wagon toward her and suddenly she could feel her heart beating in her chest.

He looked as well as ever and appeared glad to be back, and he greeted the Cullens as cheerfully as if he and she had not walked angrily away from one another last time they had met.

When he had taken care of his horse and came into their camp, it was only neighborly of her to mention that the local merchants had scarcely anything left to sell, lest he was short of provision.

He thanked her kindly but said he had bought supplies in Tryavna with no difficulty. "Do you have enough yourself?"

"Yes, for my father bought early." She was vexed that he made no mention of the new dress and cloak, though he studied her for the longest time.

"They are the exact shade of your eyes," he said finally.

She wasn't certain but took it for a compliment. "Thank you," she said gravely and, as her father approached, forced herself to turn away to study Seredy setting up the tent.

Another day went by without the caravan's departure, and up and down the line there was grumbling. Her father went to see Fritta and came back to tell her the caravan master was waiting for the Norman knights to leave. "They have caused great mischief and Fritta wisely prefers to have them ahead of us instead of harrying our rear," he said.

But the following morning the knights hadn't departed and Fritta decided he had waited long enough. He gave the signal that started the caravan on the last long leg toward Constantinople, and finally the ripple of forward movement reached the Cullens. The previous autumn they had followed a young Frank and his wife and two small children. The Frankish family had wintered away from the town of Gabrovo; it had been their declared intent to resume the trip with the caravan, but they hadn't appeared. Mary knew that something terrible must have occurred and prayed Christ to watch over them. She now rode behind two fat French brothers who had told her father they hoped to make their fortunes buying Turkish rugs and other treasures. They chewed garlic for health and often twisted in the saddle to stare stupidly at her body. It entered her mind that, driving his wagon behind her, the young barber-surgeon might be watching her too, and at times she was wicked enough to move her hips more than demanded by the motion of the horse.

The giant serpent of travelers soon wound to the pass that led through the high mountains. The sheer mountainside fell away below the twisting trail, down to the glittering river, swollen with the melt of snows that had imprisoned them all winter.

On the other side of the great defile were foothills that gradually turned into rolling land. They slept that night in a vast plain of shrubby growth. Next day they traveled due south and it became clear that the Balkan Gate separated two unique climes, for the air was softer this side of the pass and with every hour they traveled it grew warmer.

That night they stopped outside the village of Gornya, camping in plum orchards with the permission of the farmers, who sold some of the men a fiery plum liquor as well as green onions and a fermented milk drink so thick it had to be eaten with a spoon. Early the following morning, while they were still encamped, Mary heard a rumbling as of distant thunder. But it quickly grew louder and soon the wild screams and shouts of men were part of the noise.

As she came out of the tent she saw that the white cat had left the barber-surgeon's wagon and stood transfixed in the road. The French knights galloped past like demons in a nightmare and the cat was lost in a dust cloud, but not before Mary had seen what the first hooves had done. She wasn't conscious of screaming but knew she was running toward the road before the dust had settled.

Mistress Buffington no longer was white. The cat had been trodden into the dust and Mary lifted the poor broken little body and for the first time became aware that he'd come out of his wagon and stood over her.

"You'll ruin your new dress with the blood," he said roughly, but his pale face was stricken.

He took the cat and a spade and went away from the camp. When he returned she didn't approach him, but she noted from afar that his eyes were reddened. Putting a dead animal into the ground wasn't the same as burying a person, but it wasn't strange to her that he was able to weep over a cat. Despite his size and strength, his vulnerable gentleness was the quality that drew her.

For the next several days she let him be. The caravan stopped heading due south and turned east again, but the sun continued to shine hotter each day. It was already clear to Mary that the new clothing which had been made for her in Gabrovo was largely a waste, for the weather was too warm for wool. She rummaged through the summer clothing in her baggage and found some lighter garments but they were too fine for traveling and would quickly be ruined. She settled on a cotton undergarment and a rough, sacklike work dress to which she gave a minimum of form by knotting a cord around her waist. She placed a broadbrimmed leather hat upon her head, although her cheeks and nose were already freckled.

That morning, when she got off her horse and started to walk for exercise as she was wont to do, he smiled at her. "Come ride with me in my wagon."

She came without fuss. This time there was no awkwardness, just a deep gladness to sit on the seat next to him.

He dug behind the seat and came up with a leather hat of his own, but such a head covering as the Jews wore.

"Wherever did you get it?"

"It was given me in Tryavna by their holy man."

Presently they saw her father sending him such a sour look they both began to laugh.

"I'm surprised he allows you to visit," he said.

"I've convinced him you are harmless."

They looked at one another comfortably. His was a handsome face despite the homely fact of his broken nose. She realized that however impassive his large features might remain, the key to his feelings was his eyes, deep and steady and somehow older than his years. She felt in them a great loneliness to match her own. How old was he? Twenty-one years? Twenty-two?

She realized with a start that he was speaking of the farming plateau over which they were passing.

". . . mostly fruits and wheat. Winters here must be short and mild, for the crops are advanced," he said, but she wasn't to be robbed of the intimacy they had gained in the last moments.

"I hated you that day in Gabrovo."

Another man might have protested or smiled, but he made no response.

"Because of the Slav woman. How could you go with her? I hated her, too."

"Don't waste your hatred on either of us, for she was pitiable and I didn't lie with her. Seeing you spoiled such for me," he said simply.

She never doubted he would tell her truth, and something warm and triumphant started to grow in her like a flower.

Now they could talk about trifles—their route, the way animals must be driven to make them endure, the difficulty of finding cooking wood.

They sat together all afternoon and talked quietly about everything except the white cat and themselves, and his eyes said other things to her without words.

She knew it. She was frightened for several reasons but there was no place on earth she would rather be than sitting next to him on the uncomfortable, swaying wagon under the battering sun, and she went obediently but reluctantly when at last her father's peremptory call summoned her away.

Now and again they passed a small flock of sheep, which were mostly scruffy, though her father invariably stopped to inspect them and went with Seredy to interrogate the owners. Always the shepherds advised that for truly wonderful sheep he must go beyond to Anatolia.

By early May they were a week's travel from Turkey, and James Cullen made no attempt to conceal his excitement. His daughter was dealing with an excitement of her own, but she was making every effort to conceal it from him. Although there was always a chance to cast a smile or a glance in the barber-surgeon's direction, sometimes she forced herself to steer clear of him two days in a row, for she was afraid that if her father sensed her feelings he would order her to stay away from Rob Cole.

One night as she was cleaning up after supper, Rob appeared in their camp. He nodded to her politely and went directly to her father, holding out a flask of brandy as a peace offering.

"Sit you down," her father said reluctantly. But after the two men had shared a drink her father became friendlier, no doubt because it was pleasant to sit in fellowship and converse in English, and also because it was difficult not to warm to Rob J. Cole. Before long, James Cullen was telling their visitor what lay before them.

"I'm told of a breed of Eastern sheep, lean and narrow-backed, but with tails and rear legs so fat the animal may live on stored reserves when food is scarce. Their lambs have a silky fleece of rare and unusual luster. Wait a moment, man, let me show you!" He disappeared into the tent and came out with a hat made of lambskin. The fleece was gray and tightly curled.

"Finest quality," he said eagerly. "The fleece stays this curly only until the fifth day of the lamb's life, but then the fur remains wavy until the beastie is two months old."

Rob inspected the hat and assured her father it was a fine skin.

"Oh, it *is*," Cullen said, and put the hat on his head, which made them laugh because it was a warm night and a fur hat was made for snow. He put it back in the tent and then the three of them sat before the fire and her father gave her a sip or two from his glass. The brandy was hard to swallow but made the world safe for her.

Thunder rumbled and shook the purpled sky and sheet lightning illuminated them for long seconds during which she could see the hard planes of Rob's face, but the vulnerable eyes that made him beautiful were hidden from her.

"A strange land, with regular thunder and lightning and never a drop of rain," her father said. "I well mark the morning you were born, Mary Margaret. There was thunder and lightning then as well, but there was a teeming Scots rain that fell as though the heavens had opened and were never to close."

Rob leaned forward. "That would have been in Kilmarnock, where you have your family holding?"

"No, it was not, 'twas in Saltcoats. Her mother was a Tedder of Saltcoats. I had taken Jura to her old Tedder home because in her heaviness she had a great longing for her mother, and we were celebrated and coddled for weeks and overstayed her time. She was caught out with labor, and so it was that instead of in Kilmarnock like a proper Cullen, Mary Margaret was born in her grandfather Tedder's house overlooking the Firth of Clyde."

"Father," she said gently. "Master Cole can have no interest in the day of my birth."

"On the contrary," Rob said, and he asked question after question of her father and listened at length.

She sat and prayed that the lightning would not resume, for she had no wish for her father to see that the barber-surgeon's hand rested on her bare arm. His touch was like thistledown but her flesh was all stirred feelings and dither bumps, as though the future had brushed her or the night were chill.

On the eleventh of May the caravan reached the western bank of the Arda River and Kerl Fritta decided to camp there an extra day to allow for wagon repairs and the buying of supplies from nearby farmers. Her father took Seredy and paid a guide to go with them across the river into Turkey, impatient as a boy to begin his search for the fat-tailed sheep.

An hour later, she and Rob mounted double on her saddleless black horse and rode away from the noise and confusion. As they passed the Jews' encampment she saw the thin young one ogling. Simon it was, the youth who served as Rob's teacher; he grinned and nudged one of the others in the ribs to watch them ride by.

She scarcely cared. She felt dizzy, perhaps because of the heat, for the morning sun was a fireball. She put her arms around his chest so as not to fall off the horse and closed her eyes and leaned her head against his broad back.

A distance from the caravan they passed two sullen peasants leading a donkey laden with firewood. The men stared but didn't return their greeting. Perhaps they had come from afar, for there were no trees in that place, only broad fields empty of workers because planting was long since over and the crops weren't yet ripe enough to be reaped.

When they came to a brook, Rob tethered the horse to a bush and they left their shoes and waded down a dazzling brightness. On both sides of the reflecting water grew a wheat field and he showed her how the tall stalks shaded the ground and made it invitingly dark and cool.

"Come," he said, "it's like a cave," and crawled into it as if he were a great child.

She followed more slowly. Nearby a small living thing rustled through the tall ripening grain and she gave a start.

"Just a tiny mouse, already frightened off," he said. As he moved to her in the cool, dappled place, they contemplated one another.

"I don't want to, Rob."

"Well, then you won't, Mary," he said, although she could see in his eyes how thwarted he felt.

"Could you merely kiss me, please?" she asked humbly.

So their first overt intimacy became a clumsy, moody kiss doomed by her apprehension.

"I don't like the other. I've done it, you see," she said all in a rush, and the moment she had dreaded was accomplished.

"You've experience, then?"

"Only once, with my cousin in Kilmarnock. He hurt me awfully."

He kissed her eyes and her nose, her mouth softly, while she fought her doubts. After all, who *was* this? Stephen Tedder had been someone she had known all her life, her cousin and her friend, and he had caused her true agony. And afterward had roared with laughter at her discomfort, as if it were clumsily funny of her to have let him do such a thing to her, like allowing him to push her onto her bottom in a mud slough.

And while she was thinking these unpleasant thoughts, this Englishman had changed the nature of his kisses, his tongue caressing the inside of her lips. It was not unpleasant and when she tried to imitate him, he sucked her tongue! But she began to tremble again when he undid her bodice.

"I just want to kiss them," he said urgently, and she had the odd experience of looking down at his face moving toward her teats, which she had to acknowledge with grudging satisfaction were heavy but high and firm, already flushed with rosy color.

His tongue gently rasped the pink border and made it all bumps. It moved in narrowing circles until it was flicking her hardened rose-colored nipple, which he drew on as if he were a babe when it was between his lips, all the while stroking her behind the knees and inside her legs. But when his hand went to the mound she went all rigid. She could feel the muscles in her thighs and stomach lock, she was that tense and fearful until he took his hand away.

He fumbled his clothing and then found her hand and made her a gift. She had glimpsed men before by accident, coming upon her father or one of the workers urinating behind a bush. And she had witnessed more on those occasions than when she had been with Stephen Tedder; so she had never *seen*, and now she couldn't refrain from studying him. She hadn't expected it to be so . . . *thick*, she thought accusingly, as if it were his fault. Gaining courage, she stroked the cods and gave a low laugh when it made him twitch. It was the bonniest thing!

So she was soothed as they fondled each other, until she was trying on her own to consume his mouth. Soon their bodies were all warm fruits and it wasn't so terrible when his hand left off making her buttocks feel firm and round and came back between her legs to dabble richly.

She was at a loss about what to do with her hands. She put a finger between his lips and felt his saliva and teeth and tongue, but he pulled away to suck her breasts again and kiss her belly and thighs. He found his way into her first with one finger and then with two, wooing the little pea in quickening circles.

"Ah," she said faintly, lifting her knees.

But instead of the martyrdom for which her mind was prepared, she was amazed to feel the warmth of his breath on her. And his fish of a tongue swam into her wetness between the hairy folds she herself was shamed to touch! How ever shall I face this man again? she asked herself, but the question was quickly gone, strangely and wonderfully vanished, for she was already shuddering and bucking wickedly, her eyes closed and her silent mouth half open.

Before she had returned to her senses he had insinuated himself. They were truly linked, he was an extension of snug, silken warmth in her very core. There was no pain, only a certain feeling of tightness that presently eased as he moved slowly.

Once, he stopped. "All right?"

"Yes," she said, and he resumed.

Directly she found herself moving her body to meet his. Soon it became impossible for him to exercise restraint and he moved faster and from a greater distance, jarringly. She wanted to reassure him, but as she studied him through slitted eyes she saw him rear his head back and arch into her.

How singular to feel his great trembling, to hear his snarl of what seemed to be overwhelming relief as he emptied into her!

For a long time then in the dimness of the man-tall grain they scarcely moved. They were quiet together, one of her long limbs flung across him and the sweat and the liquids drying.

"You might get to like it," he said finally. "Like malt ale."

She pinched his arm as sharply as she could. But she was pensive. "*Why* do we like it?" she asked. "I have watched horses. Why do animals like it?"

He appeared startled. Years later, she would understand that the question separated her from any woman he had known, but now all she knew was that he was studying her.

She couldn't bring herself to say so, but he was already separated from other males in her mind. She sensed he had been remarkably kind to her in a way she didn't fully comprehend, save that she had a prior boorishness as comparison.

"You thought more of me than of yourself," she said.

"I didn't suffer."

She stroked his face and held her hand there while he kissed her palm. "Most men . . . most people are not so. I know it."

"You must forget the damned cousin in Kilmarnock," he told her.

Chapter 32

THE OFFER

Rob gained some patients from among the newcomers and was amused when he was told that when Kerl Fritta had recruited them he boasted that his caravan was doctored by a masterful barber-surgeon.

It gave his spirits a special lift to see those he had treated during the first part of the journey, for never before had he tended to the health needs of anyone for so long a time.

People told him the big grinning Frankish drover whom he had treated for bubo had died of the disease in Gabrovo in midwinter. He had known it would happen and had told the man of his coming fate, yet the news threw him into gloom.

"What's gratifying is an injury I know how to mend," he told Mary. "A broken bone, a gaping wound, when the person is hurt and I'm secure in what must be done to make him well. It's the mysteries I loathe. Diseases about which I know nothing at all, perhaps less than the afflicted. Ailments that appear out of the air and defy all reasonable explanation or plan of treatment. Ah, Mary, I know so little. I know nothing at all, yet I'm all they have."

Without understanding everything he said, she comforted him. For her part, she drew no small comfort from him; one night she came to him bleeding and racked with cramp, and she spoke of her mother. Jura Cullen had started her monthly course on a fine summer's day and the flow had turned to gush and then to hemorrhage. When she died Mary had been too torn by grief to cry, and now each month when her flux came she expected it to kill her.

"Hush! It wasn't ordinary monthly bleeding, it had to be something more. You know that's true," he said, holding a warm and soothing palm to her belly and solacing her with kisses.

A few days later, riding with her on the wagon, he found himself talking

238

of things he had never told anyone: the deaths of his parents, the separation of the children and their loss. She wept as though she could never stop, twisting in the seat so her father wouldn't see.

"How I love you!" she whispered.

"I love you," he said slowly and to his own amazement. He had never said the words to anyone.

"I never want to leave you," she said.

After that, when they were on the trail often she turned in the saddle on her black gelding and looked at him. Their secret sign was the fingers of the right hand touched to the lips, as if to brush away an insect or a bit of dust.

James Cullen still sought forgetfulness in the bottle and sometimes she came to Rob after her father had been drinking and was sleeping soundly. He tried to discourage her from doing this because the sentries usually were nervous and it was dangerous to move about the camp at night. But she was a headstrong woman and came anyway, and he was always glad.

She was a quick learner. Very soon they knew each other's every feature and blemish like old friends. Their largeness was part of the magic and sometimes when they moved together he thought of mammoth beasts coupling to thunder. It was as new to him as to her, in a way; he had had a lot of females but never had made love before. Now he wanted only to give her pleasure.

He was troubled and struck dumb, unable to understand what had befallen him in so short a time.

They pushed ever deeper into European Turkey, a part of the country known as Thrace. The wheat fields became rolling plains of rich grasslands and they began to see flocks of sheep.

"My father is coming alive," Mary told him.

Whenever they came to sheep Rob saw James Cullen and the indispensable Seredy galloping out to talk with the shepherds. The brown-skinned men carried long crooks and wore long-sleeved shirts and loose trousers pulled tight at the knees.

One evening Cullen came alone to call on Rob. He settled himself by the fire and cleared his throat uncomfortably.

"I wouldn't have you think me blind."

"I hadn't supposed you were," Rob said, but with respect.

"Let me tell you about my daughter. She has some learning. She has Latin."

"My mother had Latin. She taught some to me."

"Mary has a good deal of Latin. It is an excellent thing to have in foreign lands, because with it one can talk with officials and churchmen. I sent her to the nuns at Walkirk for teaching. They took her because they thought they would lure her into the order, but I knew better. She doesn't take to languages, but after I told her she must have Latin, she worked at it. Even then I dreamed of traveling to the East for fine sheep."

"Can you get sheep back to your home alive?" Rob doubted it.

"I can do it. I'm a good man with the sheep," Cullen said with pride. "It was always just a dream, but when my wife died I decided we would go. My kinsmen said I was fleeing because I was mad with grief, but it was more than that."

They sat in a thick silence.

"You've been to Scotland, boy?" Cullen asked finally.

He shook his head. "Closest I've come is the English north and the Cheviot Hills."

Cullen snorted. "Close to the border perhaps, but not even close to the *real* Scotland. Scotland is higher, you see, and the rocks are bonier. The mountains have good streams full of fish and plenty of water left over for grass. Our holding is in rugged hills, a very large holding. Vast flocks."

He paused, as though to choose his words carefully. "The man who marries Mary will take them over, be he the right sort," he said finally.

He leaned toward Rob. "In four days' time we'll reach the town of Babaeski. There my daughter and I shall leave the caravan. We'll swing due south to the town of Malkara, where there is a large animal market at which I expect to buy sheep. And then travel to the Anatolian Plateau, where I place my highest hopes. I would be content if you were to accompany us." He sighed and gave Rob a level look. "You're strong and in health. You've courage, else you wouldn't venture so far to do business and better your position in the world. You are not what I would have chosen for her, but she wants you. I love her and wish her happiness. She is all I have."

"Master Cullen," he said, but the sheep raiser stopped him.

"It's not something to be offered or acted upon lightly. You want to think on it, man, as I have."

Rob thanked him politely, as if he had been offered an apple or a sweetmeat, and Cullen returned to his own camp.

He spent a sleepless night, staring at the sky. He was not so great a fool not to recognize that she was rare. And miraculously, she loved him. He would never meet such a woman again.

And *land*. Good God, land.

He was offered a life such as his father had never dreamed, nor any of their forebears. There would be assured labor and income, respect and responsibilities. Property to be handed down to sons. A different existence than he had ever known was being *handed* to him—a loving female with whom he was besotted, and an assured future as one of the world's few, those who owned land.

He tossed and turned.

Next day she came with her father's razor and proceeded to trim his hair.

"Not near the ears."

"It is there it has gotten especially unruly. And why don't you shave? The stubble makes you look wild."

"I'll trim it when it's longer." He pulled the cloth from his neck. "You know that your father spoke to me?"

"He spoke to me first, of course."

"I'm not going to Malkara with you, Mary."

Only her mouth indicated what she was feeling, and her hands. Her hands appeared to be in repose against her skirt but grasped the razor so tightly the knuckles showed white through her translucent skin.

"Will you be joining us elsewhere?"

"No," he said. It was difficult. He was unaccustomed to speaking honestly to women. "I'm going to Persia, Mary."

"You do not want me."

The stunned bleakness in her voice made him realize how unprepared she was for such an eventuality.

"I want you, but I've turned it over and over in my mind and it isn't possible."

"Why, impossible? Have you already a wife?"

"No, no. But I'm going to Ispahan, in Persia. Not to seek opportunity in commerce, as I had told you, but to study medicine."

Her confusion was in her face, asking what medicine was, compared to the Cullen holding.

"I must be a physician." It seemed an unlikely excuse. He felt a strange kind of shame, as though he were acknowledging a vice or other weakness. He made no attempt to explain, for it was complicated and he didn't understand it himself.

"Your work gives you misery. You know that to be fact. You came to me and told me so, complaining that it torments you."

"What torments me is my own ignorance and inability. In Ispahan, I can learn to help those for whom now I do nothing."

"Cannot I be with you? My father could come with us and buy sheep there." The pleading in her voice and the hope in her eyes caused him to steel himself against comforting her.

He explained the Church's ban against attending Islamic academies, and he told her what he intended to do.

She had paled as she gained understanding. "You are risking eternal damnation."

"I cannot believe my soul will be forfeit."

"A Jew!" She wiped the razor clean on the cloth with preoccupied movements and returned it to its little leather bag.

"Yes. So you see, it's something I must do alone."

"What I see is a man who is mad. I have closed my eyes to the fact that I know nothing about you. I think you have said farewells to many women. It is true, is it not?"

"This is not the same." He wanted to explain the difference but she wouldn't allow it. She had listened well and now he saw the depth of the wound he had made.

"Do you not fear I'll tell my father you've used me, so he may pay to see your death? Or that I'll hasten to the first priest I meet and whisper the destination of a Christian who makes mockery of Holy Mother Church?"

"I've given you truth. I could neither cause your death nor betray you, and I'm certain you must treat me the same way."

"I'll not be waiting for any physician," she said.

He nodded, loathing himself for the bitter veil over her eyes as she turned away.

All day he watched her riding very erect in the saddle. She didn't turn around to look at him. That evening he observed Mary and Master Cullen talking seriously and at length. Evidently she told her father only that she had decided not to marry, for a while later Cullen shot a grin at Rob that was both relieved and triumphant. Cullen conferred with Seredy, and just before dark the servant brought two men into the camp, whom Rob took to be Turks from their clothing and appearance.

Later he guessed they had been guides, for when he awoke the next morning, the Cullens were gone.

As was customary in the caravan, everyone who had traveled behind them moved up one place. That day, instead of following her black gelding, he now drove behind the two fat French brothers.

He felt guilt and sorrow but also experienced a sense of relief, for he had never considered marriage and had been ill prepared. He pondered whether his decision had been made out of true commitment to medicine or if he had merely fled matrimony in weak panic, as Barber would have done.

Perhaps it was both, he decided. Poor stupid dreamer, he told himself in disgust. You'll grow tired one day, older and needier of love, and doubtless you will settle for some slovenly sow with a terrible tongue.

Conscious of a great loneliness, he yearned for Mistress Buffington to be alive again. He tried not to think of what he had destroyed, hunching over the reins and staring in distaste at the obscene arses of the French brothers.

Thus for a week he felt as he had after a death had occurred. When the caravan reached Babaeski he experienced a deepening of guilty grief, realizing that here they would have turned off together to accompany her father and start a new life. But when he thought of James Cullen he felt better about being alone, for he knew the Scot would have been a troublesome father-in-law.

Still, he didn't stop thinking of Mary.

He began to come out of his moodiness two days later. Traveling through a countryside of grassy hills, he heard a distinctive noise coming toward the caravan from far away. It was a sound such as angels might make and eventually it drew near and he saw his first camel train.

Each camel was hung with bells that chimed with every strange, lurching step the beasts took.

Camels were larger than he had expected, taller than a man and longer than a horse. Their comic faces seemed both serene and sinister, with great open nostrils, floppy lips, and heavily lidded liquid eyes half hidden behind long lashes that gave them an oddly feminine appearance. They were tied to one another and laden with enormous bundles of barley straw piled between their twin humps.

Perched atop the straw bundle of every seventh or eighth camel was a skinny, dark-skinned drover wearing only a turban and a ragged breechcloth. Occasionally one of these men urged the beasts forward with a "Hut! Hut! Hut!" that his ambling charges seemed to ignore.

The camels took possession of the rolling landscape. Rob counted almost three hundred animals before the last of them diminished into specks in the distance and the wonderful tinkling whisper of their bells faded away.

The undeniable sign of the East hurried the travelers along their way as they began to follow a narrow isthmus. Although Rob couldn't see water, Simon told him that to their south lay the Sea of Marmara and to their north the great Black Sea, and the air had taken on an invigorating salt tang that reminded him of home and filled him with a new sense of urgency.

The following afternoon, the caravan crested a rise and Constantinople lay before him like a city of his dreams.

Chapter 33

THE LAST CHRISTIAN CITY

The moat was wide and as they clattered across the drawbridge Rob could see carp large as pigs in the green depths. On the inside bank was an earthen breastwork and twenty-five feet beyond, a massive wall of dark stone, perhaps a hundred feet high. Sentries walked the top from battlement to battlement.

Fifty feet farther and there was a second wall, identical to the first! This Constantinople was a fortress with four lines of defense.

They passed through two sets of great portals. The huge gate of the inside wall was triple-arched and adorned with the noble statue of a man, doubtless an early ruler, and some strange animals in bronze. The beasts were massive and bulky, with big floppy ears raised in anger, short tails to the rear, and what appeared to be longer tails growing rampantly out of their faces.

Rob pulled at Horse's reins so he could study them, and behind him Gershom hooted and Tuveh groaned. "You must move your arse, *Inghiliz*," Meir shouted.

"What are these?"

"Elephants. You have never seen elephants, you poor foreigner?"

He shook his head, twisting on the wagon seat as he drove away so he could study the creatures. So it was that the first elephants he saw were the size of dogs and frozen in metal that bore the patina of five centuries.

Kerl Fritta led them to the caravanserai, an enormous transportation yard through which travelers and freight entered and left the city. It was a vast level space containing warehouses for the storage of the varied goods, and pens for animals and rest houses for humans. Fritta was a veteran guide and, bypassing the noisy horde in the caravanserai yard, he directed his charges into a series of khans, man-made caverns dug into adjoining hillsides to provide coolness and shelter for caravans. Most of the travelers would spend only a day or two at the caravanserai, recuperating, making wagon repairs or swapping horses for camels, then they would follow a Roman road south to Jerusalem.

"We'll be gone from here within hours," Meir told Rob, "for we are within ten days' travel of our home in Angora and eager to be freed of our responsibility."

"I'll stay a while, I think."

"When you decide to leave, go to see the *kervanbashi*, the Chief of Caravans here. His name is Zevi. When he was a young man he was a drover and then a caravan master who took camel trains over all the routes. He knows the travelers and," Simon said proudly, "he is a Jew and a good man. He'll see that you journey in safety."

Rob grasped wrists with each of them in turn.

Farewell, chunky Gershom, whose tough arse I lanced.

Farewell, sharp-nosed, black-bearded Judah.

Goodbye, friendly young Tuveh.

Thank you, Meir.

Thank you, thank you, Simon!

He said goodbye to them with regret, for they had shown him kindness. The parting was more difficult because it took him from the book that had led him into the Persian language.

Presently he drove alone through Constantinople, an enormous city, perhaps larger than London. When seen from afar it had appeared to float in the warm clear air, framed between the dark blue stone of the walls and the different blues of the sky above and the Sea of Marmara to the south. Seen from within, Constantinople was a city full of stone churches that loomed over narrow streets crowded with riders on donkeys, horses, and camels, as well as sedan chairs and carts and wagons of every description. Burly porters dressed in a loose uniform of rough brown stuff carried incredible burdens on their backs or on platforms that they wore on their heads like hats.

In a public square Rob paused to study a lone figure that stood atop a tall column of porphyry, overlooking the city. From the Latin inscription he was able to learn that this was Constantine the Great. The teaching brothers and priests of St. Botolph's school in London had given him a thorough grounding in the subject of this statue; priests were greatly taken with Constantine, for he was the first Roman emperor to become a Christian. Indeed, his conversion had been the making of the Christian Church, and when he had captured the metropolis called Byzantium from the Greeks by force of arms and made it his own—Constantinople, city of

Constantine—it became the jewel of Christianity in the East, a place of cathedrals.

Rob left the area of commerce and churches and entered the neighborhoods of narrow wooden houses built cheek by jowl, with overhanging second stories that might have been transported from any number of English towns. It was a city rich in nationalities, as befit a place that marked the end of one continent and the beginning of another. He drove through a Greek quarter, an Armenian market, a Jewish sector, and suddenly, instead of listening to one impenetrable babble after another, he heard words in Parsi.

Straightaway he asked for and found a stable, run by a man named Ghiz. It was a good stable and Rob saw to Horse's comfort before leaving her, for she had served him well and deserved a lazy rest and lots of grain. Ghiz pointed Rob toward his own home at the top of the Path of the Three Hundred and Twenty-nine Steps, where a room was for rent.

The room proved worth the climb, for it was light and clean and a salt breeze blew through the window.

From it he looked down over the hyacinth Bosporus, on which sails were like moving blossoms. Past the far shore, perhaps half a mile away, he could see looming domes and minarets keen as lances and realized they were the reason for the earthworks, the moat, and the two walls surrounding Constantinople. A few feet from his window the influence of the Cross ended and the lines were manned to defend Christendom from Islam. Across the strait, the influence of the Crescent began.

He stayed at the window and stared over at Asia, into which he would delve deep and soon.

That night Rob dreamed of Mary. He awoke to melancholy and fled the room. Off a square called August's Forum he found public baths, where he took the chill waters briefly and then sat lolling in the *tepidarium*'s hot water like Caesar, soaping himself and breathing steam.

When he emerged, toweled dry and glowing from the last cold plunge, he was enormously hungry and more optimistic. In the Jewish market he bought little fishes fried brown and a bunch of black grapes that he ate while he searched for what he needed.

In many of the booths he saw the short linen undergarments every Jew had worn at Tryavna. The little vests bore the braided embellishments called *tsitsith* which, Simon had explained, allowed Jews to carry out the biblical admonition that all their lives they must wear fringes on the corners of garments.

He found a Jewish merchant who spoke Persian. He was a doddering man with a down-turned mouth and there were food stains on his caftan, but in Rob's eyes he was the first threat of exposure.

"It's a gift for a friend, he is my size," Rob muttered. The old man paid him small attention, intent on the sale. Finally he came up with a fringed undergarment that was large enough.

Rob didn't dare buy everything at once. Instead, he went to the stables and saw that Horse was fine.

"Yours is a decent wagon," Ghiz said.

"Yes."

"I might be willing to buy."

"Not for sale."

Ghiz shrugged. "An adequate wagon, though I would have to paint it. But a poor beast, alas. Without spirit. Without the proud look in her eyes. You would be fortunate to have that animal off your hands."

He saw at once that Ghiz's interest in the wagon was a diversion to direct attention from the fact that he had taken a fancy to Horse.

"Neither is for sale."

Still, he had to fight a smile at the idea that so clumsy a diversion had been attempted on one for whom diversion had been a stock in trade. The wagon was close at hand and it amused him, while the stableman was busy in a stall, to make certain unobtrusive preparations.

Presently he drew a silver coin from Ghiz's left eye.

"O Allah!"

He convinced a wooden ball to vanish when covered by a kerchief, then he caused the kerchief to change color, and change color again, green to blue to brown.

"In the Prophet's name . . ."

Rob drew a red ribbon from between his teeth and presented it with as pretty a flourish as if the stableman were a blushing girl. Caught between wonderment and fear of this infidel *djinni*, Ghiz gave in to delight. And thus part of the day was spent pleasantly in magic and juggling, and before he was through, he could have sold Ghiz anything.

With his evening meal he was served a flask of fiery brown drink, too thick and cloying and too plentiful. At the next table was a priest, and Rob offered him some of the drink.

Priests here wore long flowing black robes and tall, cylindrical cloth hats with stiff little brims. This one's robe was fairly clean but his hat bore the greasy story of a long career. He was a red-faced, pop-eyed man of middle age, eager to converse with a European and improve his facility with Western languages. He knew no English but tried Rob in the Norman and Frankish tongues and finally settled for speaking Persian, a trifle sulkily.

His name was Father Tamas and he was a Greek priest.

His mood sweetened over the liquor, which he drank in large draughts.

"Are you to settle in Constantinople, Master Cole?"

"No, in a few days I'll travel East in hopes of acquiring medicinal herbs to take back to England."

The priest nodded. It would be best to venture East without delay, he said, for the Lord had ordained that one day there would be a righteous war between the One True Church and the Islamic savage. "Have you visited our Cathedral of St. Sofia?" he demanded, and was aghast when Rob smiled and shook his head. "But, my new friend, you must, before you leave! You must! For it is the churchly marvel of the world. It was raised at the order of Constantine himself, and when that worthy emperor first entered the cathedral he fell upon his knees and exclaimed, 'I have built better than Solomon.'

"It is not without reason that the head of the Church makes his quarters within the magnificence of the Cathedral of St. Sofia," Father Tamas said.

Rob looked at him in surprise. "Has Pope John moved to Constantinople from Rome, then?"

Father Tamas contemplated him. When he seemed satisfied that Rob was not laughing at his expense, the Greek priest smiled frostily. "John XIX remains Patriarch of the Christian Church in Rome. But Alexius IV is Patriarch of the Christian Church in Constantinople, and here he is our only shepherd," he said.

The liquor and the ocean air combined to give him a deep and dreamless sleep. Next morning he allowed himself to repeat the luxury of the Augustine Baths, and in the street bought a breakfast of bread and fresh plums as he walked to the Jews' bazaar. At the market he selected carefully, for he had given thought to each item. He had observed a few linen prayer shawls in Tryavna but the men he had respected most there had worn wool; now he bought wool for himself, a four-cornered shawl adorned with fringes similar to those on the undergarment he had found the day before.

Feeling passing strange, he bought a set of phylacteries, the leather straps they placed on their forehead and wound around an arm during the morning prayers.

He had made each of the purchases from a different merchant. One of them, a sallow young man with gaps in his mouth from missing teeth, had a particularly large display of caftans. The man didn't know Parsi but gestures served them well. None of the caftans was large enough, but the merchant motioned that Rob must wait, and then he hurried to the booth of the old man who had sold Rob the *tsitsith*. Here there were larger caftans, and within a few moments Rob had purchased two of them.

Leaving the bazaar with his possessions in a cloth bag, he took a street on which he hadn't walked and soon saw a church so magnificent it could only be the Cathedral of St. Sofia. He entered enormous brazen doors and found himself in a huge openness of lovely proportion, with a reaching of pillar into arch, of arch into vault, of vault into a dome so high it made him smaller than life. The vast space of the nave was illuminated by thousands of wicks whose soft clear burning in cups of oil was reflected by more glitter than he was accustomed to in a church, icons framed in gold, walls of precious marbles, too much gilt and blaze for an English taste. There was no sign of the Patriarch but, looking down the nave, he saw priests at the altar in richly brocaded chasubles. One of the figures was swinging a censer and they were singing a Mass but were so far away that Rob couldn't smell the incense or make out the Latin.

The greater part of the nave was deserted and he sat in the rear surrounded by empty carven benches, beneath the contorted figure hanging from a cross that loomed in the lamp-lit gloom. He felt that the staring eyes penetrated his depths and knew the contents of the cloth bag. He hadn't been raised in piety, yet in this calculated rebellion he was strangely moved to religious feeling. He knew he had entered the cathedral precisely for this moment, and he rose to his feet and for a time stood in silence and met the challenge of those eyes.

Finally he spoke aloud. "It needs be done. But I am not forsaking you," he said.

He was less certain a short time later, after he had climbed the hill of stone steps and was again in his room.

On the table he propped the small square of steel in whose polished surface he had been accustomed to shaving, and he took his knife to the hair that now fell long and tangled over his ears, trimming until what was left were the ceremonial earlocks they called *peoth*.

He disrobed and put on the *tsitsith* fearfully, half expecting to be stricken. It seemed to him that the fringes crawled over his flesh.

The long black caftan was less intimidating. It was only an outer garment, with no connection to their God.

The beard was still undeniably sparse. He arranged his earlocks so they hung loosely beneath the bell-shaped Jew's hat. The leather cap was a fortunate touch because it was so obviously old and used.

Still, when he had left the room again and entered the street he knew it was madness and it wouldn't work; he expected anyone who looked at him to howl with laughter.

I shall need a name, he thought.

It wouldn't do to be called Reuven the Barber-Surgeon as he had been known in Tryavna; to succeed in the transformation he required more than a piss-weak Hebrew version of his *goy* identity.

Jesse . . .

A name he remembered from Mam's reading the Bible aloud. A strong name he could live with, the name of the father of King David.

For his patronymic he chose Benjamin, in honor of Benjamin Merlin, who had, albeit unwillingly, shown him what a physician could be.

He would say he came from Leeds, he decided, because he remembered the look of the Jewish-owned houses there and could speak in detail of the place if need should arise.

He resisted an urge to turn and flee, for coming toward him were three priests and with something akin to panic he recognized that one of them was Father Tamas, his dining companion of the previous evening.

The three proceeded as unhurriedly as pacing crows, deep in conversation.

He forced himself to walk toward them. "Peace be unto you," he said when they were abreast.

The Greek priest slid his glance disdainfully over the Jew and then turned back to his companions without replying to the greeting.

When they had passed him, Jesse ben Benjamin of Leeds indulged in a smile. Calmly now and with more confidence he continued on his way, striding with his palm pressed against his right cheek, as the *rabbenu* of Tryavna had been wont to walk when deep in thought.

PART THREE

Ispahan

Chapter 34

THE LAST LEG

Despite the change in his appearance he still felt like Rob J. Cole when he went to the caravanserai at midday. A large train to Jerusalem was in the process of organization and the great open space was a confusing maelstrom of drovers leading laden camels and asses, men trying to back wagons into line, riders on horseback milling dangerously close, while animals screamed their protests and harried humans raised their voices in condemnation of the beasts and one another. A party of Norman knights had claimed the only shade, on the northern side of the storehouses, where they lounged on the ground and hurled drunken insults at passers-by. Rob J. didn't know if they were the men who had killed Mistress Buffington, but they might well have been, and he avoided them with distaste.

He sat on a bale of prayer rugs and watched the Chief of Caravans. The *kervanbashi* was a burly Turkish Jew who wore a black turban over grizzled hair that still contained traces of its former red color. Simon had told him that this man, name of Zevi, could be invaluable in helping to arrange safe travel. Certainly, all quailed before him.

"Woe be unto you!" Zevi roared at an unfortunate drover. "Hie you from this place, dullard. Lead your animals away, for are they not to follow the beasts of the merchants of the Black Sea? Have I not told you twice? Cannot you ever recall your true place in the line of march, O misbegotten?"

It seemed to Rob that Zevi was everywhere, settling arguments between merchants and transporters, conferring with the caravan master concerning the route, checking bills of lading.

As Rob sat and watched, a Persian sidled up to him, a small man, so skinny he had hollows in his cheeks. From his beard, to which flecks of food still clung, it was evident he had eaten millet gruel that morning, and he wore a dirty orange turban, too small for his head.

"Where do you travel, Hebrew?"

"I hope to leave soon for Ispahan."

"Ah, Persia! You wish a guide, *effendi?* For I was born in Qum, a hart hunt from Ispahan, and I know every stone and bush along the way."

Rob hesitated.

"Everyone else will take you the long, hard way, along the coast. Then through the Persian mountains. That is because they avoid the shortest route through the Great Salt Desert, fearing it. But I can take you straight across the desert to water, avoiding all robbers."

He was strongly tempted to agree and leave at once, remembering how well Charbonneau had served. But there was something furtive about the man and in the end he shook his head.

The Persian shrugged. "If you change your mind, master, I am a bargain as a guide, very cheap."

A moment later one of the highborn French pilgrims, passing the bale where Rob was sitting, staggered and fell against him.

"You shit," he said, and spat. "You Jew."

Rob stood, his color mounting. He saw that the Norman was already reaching for his sword.

Suddenly Zevi was upon them. "A thousand pardons, my lord, ten thousand pardons! I shall tend to this one," he said, and shoved the astonished Rob away before him.

When they were clear, Rob listened to the rattle of words that came from Zevi and shook his head.

"I don't speak the Tongue well. Nor did I need your help with the Frenchman," he said, searching for the words in Parsi.

"Indeed? You'd have been killed, young ox."

"It was my own affair."

"No, no! In a place crowded with Muslims and drunken Christians, killing a single Jew would be like eating a single date. They would have killed many of us and therefore it was very much my affair." Zevi stared at him furiously. "What kind of *Yahud* is it who speaks Persian like a camel, doesn't speak his own tongue, and seeks to brawl? What is your name and where are you from?"

"I am Jesse, son of Benjamin. A Jew of Leeds."

"Where in hell is Leeds?"

"England."

"An *Inghiliz!*" Zevi said. "Never before have I met a Jew who was an *Inghiliz.*"

"We're few and scattered. There is no community there. No *rabbenu,* no *shohet*, no *mashgiah*. No study house or synagogue, so we seldom hear the Tongue. That is why I have so little of it."

"Bad, to raise your children in a place where they don't feel their own God or hear their own language." Zevi sighed. "Often it is hard to be a Jew."

When Rob asked whether he knew of a large, protected caravan bound for Ispahan, he shook his head.

"I have been approached by a guide," Rob said.

"A Persian turd with a little turban and a dirty beard?" Zevi snorted. "That one would take you straight into the hands of evil men. You would be left lying in the desert with your throat cut and your belongings stolen. No," he said, "you will be better off in a caravan of our own people." He thought for a long moment. "Reb Lonzano," he said finally.

"Reb Lonzano?"

Zevi nodded. "Yes, it may be that Reb Lonzano is the answer." Not far away an altercation broke out between drovers and someone called his name. He grimaced. "Those sons of camels, those diseased jackals! I have no time now, you must come back after this caravan has departed. Come to my office late in the afternoon, in the hut behind the main hostelry. All things may be decided then."

When he returned a few hours later he found Zevi in the hut that served as his retreat in the caravanserai. With him were three Jews. "This is Lonzano ben Ezra," he told Rob.

Reb Lonzano, middle-aged and the senior, was clearly the leader. He had brown hair and a brown beard that hadn't yet grayed, but any youthfulness gained thereby was offset by his lined face and serious eyes.

Both Loeb ben Kohen and Aryeh Askari were perhaps ten years younger than Lonzano. Loeb was tall and lanky and Aryeh stockier and square-shouldered. Both had the dark, weather-beaten faces of traveling merchants but they kept them carefully neutral, awaiting Lonzano's verdict concerning him.

"They are tradesmen bound for their home in Masqat, across the Persian Gulf," Zevi said, and then turned to Lonzano. "Now," he said sternly, "this pitiable one has been brought up like a *goy*, all unknowing in a far-away Christian land, and he needs to be shown that Jews can be kind to Jews."

"What is your business in Ispahan, Jesse ben Benjamin?" Reb Lonzano asked.

"I go there to study, to become a physician."

Lonzano nodded. "The *madrassa* in Ispahan. Reb Aryeh's cousin, Reb Mirdin Askari, is a student of medicine there."

Rob leaned forward eagerly and would have asked questions, but Reb Lonzano would suffer no diversions. "Are you solvent and able to pay fair portion of the expenses of travel?"

"I am."

"Willing to share work and responsibilities along the way?"

"Most willing. In what do you trade, Reb Lonzano?"

Lonzano scowled. Clearly, he felt that the interviewing should be directed by him, not at him. "Pearls," he said unwillingly.

"How large is the caravan with which you travel?"

Lonzano allowed the barest hint of a smile to twitch the corners of his mouth. "*We* are the caravan with which we travel."

Rob was confounded. He turned to Zevi. "How can three men offer me protection from bandits and other perils?"

"Listen to me," Zevi said. "These are *traveling* Jews. They know when to venture and when not. When to hole up. Where to go for protection or help, any place along the way." He turned to Lonzano. "What say you, friend? Will you take him along, or will you not?"

Reb Lonzano looked at his two companions. They were silent and their bland expressions didn't change, but they must have conveyed something, for when he looked back at Rob he nodded.

"All right, you are welcome to join us. We leave at dawn tomorrow from the Bosporus slip."

"I'll be there with my horse and wagon."

Aryeh snorted and Loeb sighed.

"No horse, no wagon," Lonzano said. "We sail on the Black Sea in small boats, to eliminate a long and dangerous land journey."

Zevi placed a huge hand on his knee. "If they are willing to take you, it is an excellent opportunity. Sell the horse and wagon."

Rob made up his mind, and nodded.

"*Mazel!*" Zevi said in quiet satisfaction, and poured red Turkish wine to seal their bargain.

From the caravanserai he made straight for the stable, and Ghiz gasped when he saw him. "You are *Yahud?*"

"I am *Yahud.*"

Ghiz nodded fearfully, as if convinced that this magician was a *djinni* who could alter his identity at will.

"I have changed my mind, I shall sell you the wagon."

The Persian threw him a sullen offer, a fraction of the cart's worth.

"No, you shall pay a fair price."

"You may keep your frail wagon. Now, should you wish to sell the horse . . ."

"I am making you a gift of the horse."

Ghiz narrowed his eyes, trying to see danger.

"You must pay a fair price for the wagon, but the horse is a gift."

He went to Horse and rubbed her nose for the last time, thanking her silently for the faithful way in which she had served him. "Bear this in mind always. This animal works willingly but she must be fed well and regularly and kept clean so she is never afflicted with sores. If she is in health when I return here, all will go well with you. But if she has been abused . . ."

He held Ghiz's gaze, and the stableman blanched and looked away. "I shall treat her well, Hebrew. I shall treat her very well!"

The wagon had been his only home for these many years. And it was like saying goodbye to the last of Barber.

It was necessary to leave most of its contents, a bargain for Ghiz. He took his surgical instruments and an assortment of medicinal herbs. The little pine grasshopper box with the perforated lid. His arms. A few other things.

He thought he had exerted discipline, but he was less certain the following morning when he carried a great cloth bag through the still-dark streets. He reached the Bosporus slip as light was graying, and Reb Lonzano looked sourly at the bundle that bowed his back.

They were taken across the Bosporus Strait in a *teimil,* a long, low skiff that was little more than a hollowed tree trunk that had been oiled and outfitted with a single pair of oars manned by a sleepy youth. On the far shore they were landed at Uskudar, a town of shacks clustered along the waterfront, facing slips whose moorings were crowded with boats of all sizes and descriptions. To Rob's dismay he learned that they faced an hour's walk to the little bay where the boat was moored that would take them through the Bosporus and along the coast of the Black Sea. He shouldered his ponderous bundle and followed after the other three men.

Presently he found himself walking alongside Lonzano.

"I have heard from Zevi what happened between you and the Norman at the caravanserai. You must keep a tighter rein on your temper, lest you endanger the rest of us."

"Yes, Reb Lonzano."

At length he heaved a sigh as he shifted his bag.

"Is anything wrong, *Inghiliz?*"

Rob shook his head. Holding his bundle on his aching shoulder as the salt sweat ran into his eyes, he thought of Zevi and grinned.

"It is hard to be a Jew," he said.

Finally they reached a deserted inlet and Rob saw, bobbing on the swell, a wide, squat cargo vessel with a mast and three sails, one large and two small.

"What sort of boat is that?" he asked Reb Aryeh.

"A keseboy. A good boat."

"Come!" called the captain. He was Ilias, a homely blond Greek with a sun-darkened face in which a gap-toothed grin gleamed whitely. Rob thought him too indiscriminating a businessman, for already waiting to board were nine shaven-headed scarecrows with no eyebrows or lashes.

Lonzano groaned. "Dervishes, Muslim begging monks."

Their cowls were filthy rags. From the girdle of rope tied around each waist hung a cup and a sling. In the center of each forehead was a round dark mark like a scabby callus; Reb Lonzano told Rob later that it was the *zabiba*, common to devout Muslims who pressed their heads into the ground during prayer five times a day.

One of them, perhaps the leader, placed his hands to his breast and bowed to the Jews. "*Salaam.*"

Lonzano returned the bow. "*Salaam aleikhem.*"

"Come! Come!" the Greek called, and they waded into the welcoming coolness of the surf to where the boat crew, two youths in loincloths, waited to help them up the rope ladder into the shallow-draft keseboy. There was no deck or structure, simply an open space taken up by the cargo of lumber, pitch, and salt. Since Ilias insisted that a center aisle be left to allow the crew to manipulate the sails, little room remained for the passengers, and after their bundles had been stowed, the Jews and the Muslims were jammed together like so many salt herrings.

As the two anchors were lifted the dervishes began to bellow. Their leader, whose name was Dedeh—he had an aged face and, in addition to the *zabiba*, three dark marks on his forehead that appeared to have been made by burning—threw back his head and cried into the sky, "*Allah Ek-beeeer.*" The drawn-out sound seemed to hover over the sea.

"*La ilah illallah,*" chorused his congregation of disciples.

"*Allah Ek-beeer.*"

The keseboy drifted offshore, found the wind with much flapping of her sails, and then moved steadily eastward.

* * *

He was jammed in between Reb Lonzano and a skinny young dervish with a single burn mark on his forehead. The young Muslim smiled at him presently and, digging into his pouch, came up with four battered bits of bread, which he distributed to the Jews.

"Thank him for me," Rob said. "I don't want any."

"We must eat it," Lonzano said. "Otherwise they will take grave offense."

"It is made of a noble flour," the dervish said easily in Persian. "Truly an excellent bread."

Lonzano glared at Rob, doubtless peeved because he didn't speak the Tongue. The young dervish watched them eat the bread, which tasted like solidified sweat.

"I am Melek abu Ishak," the dervish said.

"I am Jesse ben Benjamin."

The dervish nodded and closed his eyes. Soon he was snoring, which Rob saw as a sign of his wisdom, for traveling in a keseboy was exceedingly dull. Neither the seascape nor the nearby land ever appeared to change in any detail.

Still, there were things to think about. When he asked Ilias why they hugged the shoreline, the Greek smiled. "They cannot come and get us in shallow water," he explained. Rob followed his pointing finger and saw, far out, tiny white puffs that were the great sails of a ship.

"Pirates," the Greek said. "They hope perhaps we'll be blown out to sea. Then they would kill us and take my cargo and your money."

As the sun grew higher a stench of unwashed bodies began to dominate the atmosphere in the boat. Much of the time it was dissipated by the sea breeze but when it wasn't, it was markedly unpleasant. He determined that it came from the dervishes and tried to lean away from Melek abu Ishak, but there was no place to go. Still, there were advantages to traveling with Muslims, for five times a day Ilias brought the keseboy to the shore in order to allow them to prostrate themselves in the direction of Mecca. These intervals were opportunities for the Jews to have hurried meals ashore or to scurry behind bushes and dunes to empty bladders and bowels.

His English skin had long since been tanned on the trail, but now he felt the sun and the salt curing it into leather. As night fell the absence of the sun was a blessing, but sleep soon threw the sitters from their perpendicular positions and he was pinned between the dead weights of a noisily slumbering Melek on his right and an oblivious Lonzano on his left. When finally he could take no more he used his elbows and received fervent imprecations from both sides.

The Jews prayed in the boat. Rob put on his *tefillin* each morning when the others did, winding the leather strip around his left arm the way he had practiced with the rope in the barn at Tryavna. He wrapped the leather around every other finger, bending his head over his lap and hoping no one would notice he didn't know what he was doing.

Between landings, Dedeh led his dervishes in prayer afloat:

"God is greatest! God is greatest! God is greatest! God is greatest!"

"I confess that there is no God but God! I confess that there is no God but God!"

"I confess that Mohammed is the Prophet of God! I confess that Mohammed is the Prophet of God!"

They were dervishes of the Order of Selman, the Prophet's barber, sworn to lives of poverty and piety, Melek told Rob. The rags they wore signified renunciation of the luxuries of the world. To wash them would indicate abnegation of their faith, which explained the stink. The shaving of all body hair symbolized removing the veil between God and his servants. The cups carried in their rope belts were a sign of the deep well of meditation, their slings were to drive away the devil. The burns in the forehead aided in penitence, and they gave bits of bread to strangers because Gabriel had brought bread to Adam in Paradise.

They were on *ziaret,* pilgrimage to the saintly tombs in Mecca.

"Why do you wind leather about your arms in the morning?" Melek asked him.

"It's the Lord's commandment," he said, and he told Melek of how the order was given in the Book of Deuteronomy.

"Why do you cover your shoulders with shawls when you pray, sometimes but not always?"

He knew too few answers; he had picked up only superficial knowledge from observing the Jews of Tryavna. He fought to conceal his agony at being questioned. "Because the Ineffable One, Blessed be He, has instructed us to do these things," he said gravely, and Melek nodded and smiled.

When he turned away from the dervish he saw that Reb Lonzano was studying him with his heavily lidded eyes.

Chapter 35

SALT

The first two days were calm and easy, but on the third day the wind freshened and produced a heavy sea. Ilias skillfully maintained the keseboy between the dangers of the pirate ship and the pounding surf. At sunset sleek dark shapes rose from the blood-colored waters and curved and lunged alongside and under their boat. Rob shuddered and knew genuine fear, but Ilias laughed and said they were porpoises, harmless and playful creatures.

By dawn the swells rose and fell in steep hills and seasickness returned to Rob like an old friend. His retching was contagious even to hardened sailors and soon the boat was filled with sick and heaving men praying in a variety of languages for God to put an end to their misery.

At the worst of it Rob begged to be abandoned ashore, but Reb Lonzano shook his head.

"Ilias will no longer stop to allow the Muslims to pray on land, for here there are Turkoman tribes," he said. "Any strangers they don't kill are made their slaves, and in each of their tents are one or two mistreated unfortunates who are in chains for life."

Lonzano told the story of his cousin who, along with two strapping sons, had attempted to move a caravan of wheat into Persia. "They were taken. They were bound and buried up to their necks in their own wheat and left to starve, not a pretty way to die. Finally the Turkomans sold the wasted bodies to our family for Jewish burial."

So Rob stayed in the boat and thus, like a series of bad years, passed an interminable four days.

Seven days after they had left Constantinople, Ilias piloted the keseboy into a tiny harbor around which were clustered some forty houses, a few of them rickety wooden structures but most built of sun-hardened clay blocks. It was an inhospitable-looking port, but not to Rob, who ever after would remember the town of Rize with gratitude.

"Imshallah! Imshallah!" exclaimed the dervishes as the keseboy touched the dock. Reb Lonzano recited a blessing. With darkened skin, a thinner body, and a concave belly, Rob leaped from the boat and walked carefully over the heaving earth away from the hated sea.

Dedeh bowed to Lonzano, Melek blinked his eyes at Rob and smiled, and the dervishes went away.

"Come," Lonzano said. The Jews plodded as though they knew where they were going. Rize was a sorry place. Yellow dogs ran out and barked at them. They passed giggling children with sores in their eyes, a slatternly woman cooking something over an open fire, two men asleep in the shade as close as lovers. An old man spat as they went by.

"Their main business is selling livestock to people who arrive by boat and continue through the mountains," Lonzano said. "Loeb has a perfect knowledge of beasts and will buy for all."

So Rob gave over money to Loeb, and presently they came to a small hut next to a large pen containing donkeys and mules. The dealer was a wall-eyed man. The third and fourth fingers of his left hand were missing and in removing them somebody had done a crude job, but he had stumps that were useful to him as he pulled halters, separating the animals for Loeb's inspection.

Loeb didn't bargain or fuss. Often he scarcely seemed to glance at an animal. Sometimes he paused to check eyes, teeth, withers, and hocks.

He proposed to buy only one of the mules and the seller gasped at his offer. "Not enough!" he said angrily, but when Loeb shrugged and walked away, the sullen man stopped him and accepted his money.

At another dealer's they bought three animals. The third dealer they visited took a long look at the beasts they led and nodded slowly. He separated animals from his herd for them.

"They know each other's stock and he sees that Loeb will take only the best," Aryeh said. Soon all four members of the Jewish party had a tough, durable little donkey for riding and a strong mule to serve as pack animal.

Lonzano said they were only one month's travel from Ispahan if all went well, and the knowledge gave Rob new strength. They spent a day traversing the coastal plain and three days in foothills. Then they were in the higher hills. Rob liked mountains, but these were arid and rocky peaks where foliage was sparse. "It is because most of the year there is no water," Lonzano said. "In the spring there are wild and dangerous floods and then the rest of the time it is dry. When there is a lake, it is likely to be salt water, but we know where to find sweet water."

In the morning they prayed, and afterward Aryeh spat and looked at Rob in contempt. "You don't know shit. You are a stupid *goy.*"

"*You* are the stupid one and you speak like a swine," Lonzano told Aryeh.

"He doesn't even know how to lay on the *tefillin!*" Aryeh said sullenly.

"He has been brought up among strangers and if he doesn't know, this is our opportunity to teach. I, Reb Lonzano ben Ezra ha-Levi of Masqat, shall give him some of the ways of his people."

Lonzano showed Rob how to lay on the phylacteries correctly. The leather was wound three times around the upper arm, making the Hebrew letter *shin,* then it was wrapped seven times down the forearm and across the palm and around the fingers in such a way as to spell out two more letters, *dalet* and *yud,* forming the word *Shaddai,* one of the Unutterable's seven names.

During the wrapping there were prayers, among them a passage from Hosea 2:21–22: *And I will betroth thee unto Me forever . . . in righteousness and in justice, and in loving kindness and in compassion. And I will betroth thee unto Me in faithfulness, and thou shalt know the Lord.*

Repeating them, Rob began to tremble, for he had promised Jesus that despite donning the outer appearance of a Jew he would remain faithful. Then he recalled that Christ had been a Jew and doubtless during his lifetime had laid on the phylacteries thousands of times while saying these same prayers. The heaviness in his heart lifted and so did his fear, and he repeated the words after Lonzano while the straps around his arm empurpled his hand in a way that was most interesting, for it indicated that blood had been trapped in the fingers by the tight binding, and he found himself wondering whence the blood had traveled and where it would go from the hand when the straps were removed.

"Another thing," Lonzano said as they unwrapped the phylacteries. "You mustn't neglect to seek divine guidance because you don't have the Tongue. It is written that if a person cannot say a prescribed supplication, he should at least think of the Almighty. That, too, is prayer."

They were not a dashing sight, for if a man isn't short there is a certain lack of proportion when he rides an ass. Rob's feet barely cleared the ground, but the donkey was easily capable of bearing his weight over long distances and was an agile beast, perfectly suited for going up and down mountains.

He didn't like Lonzano's pace, for the leader had a thornbush switch and kept tapping his donkey's flanks with it, urging it on.

"Why so fast?" he growled finally, but Lonzano didn't bother to turn.

It was Loeb who answered. "Bad people live near here. They'll kill any travelers and especially have a hatred for Jews."

The route was all in their heads; Rob knew nothing of it and if any mishap should occur to the other three, it was doubtful he would survive this bleak and hostile environment. The trail rose and fell precipitously, writhing between the dark and brooding peaks of eastern Turkey. Late in the afternoon of the fifth day they reached a small stream moving moodily between rock-strewn banks.

"The Coruh River," Aryeh said.

The water in Rob's flask was almost gone but Aryeh shook his head when he started for the river.

"It runs salty," he said bitingly, as if Rob should have known, and they rode on.

Rounding a bend at dusk, they came upon a boy tending goats. He sprang away when he saw them.

"Shall we go after him?" Rob said. "Perhaps he runs to tell bandits we are here."

Now Lonzano looked at him and smiled, and Rob saw that the tension was leaving his face. "That was a Jewish boy. We're coming to Bayburt."

The village had less than a hundred people, about one-third of them Jews. They lived behind a stout, high wall built into the mountainside. By the time they reached the gate in the wall it had been opened. It closed behind them at once and was locked, and when they dismounted they had security and hospitality within the walls of the Jewish quarter.

"*Shalom*," the Bayburt *rabbenu* said without surprise. He was a small man who would have looked perfectly natural astride a donkey. He had a full beard and a wistful expression about the mouth.

"*Shalom aleikhum*," Lonzano said.

Rob had been told in Tryavna of the Jewish system of travel, but now he saw it as a participant. Boys led their animals away for care, other boys collected their flasks to wash them and fill them with sweet water from the town well. Women brought wet cloths that they might wash, and they were led to fresh bread and soup and wine before gathering in the synagogue with the men of the town for *ma'ariv*. After the prayers they sat with the *rabbenu* and some of the town leaders.

"Your face is familiar, no?" the *rabbenu* said to Lonzano.

"I've enjoyed your hospitality before. I was here six years ago with my brother Abraham and our father of blessed memory, Jeremiah ben Label. Our father was taken four years ago when a small scratch on his arm mortified and poisoned him. The will of the Most High."

The *rabbenu* nodded and sighed. "May he rest."

A grizzled Jew scratched his chin and broke in eagerly. "Do you recall me, perhaps? Yosel ben Samuel of Bayburt? I stayed with your family in Masqat, ten years ago this spring. I brought copper pyrites on a caravan of forty-three camels and your uncle ... Issachar? ... helped me sell the pyrites to a smelter and obtain a load of sea sponges to take back with me for a fine profit."

Lonzano smiled. "My Uncle Jehiel. Jehiel ben Issachar."

"Jehiel, just so! It was Jehiel. Is he in health?"

"He was in health when I left Masqat," Lonzano said.

"Well," the *rabbenu* said, "the road to Erzurum is controlled by a scourge of Turkish bandits, may the plague take them and all forms of catastrophe dog their steps. They murder, they exact ransom, whatever they please. You must go around them, over a small track through the highest mountains. You won't lose your way, for one of our youths will guide you."

So it was that early the next day their animals turned off the traveled track shortly after leaving Bayburt and picked their way over a stony path that in places was only a few feet wide, with sheer drops down the mountainside. The guide stayed with them until they were safely back on the main trail.

The following night they were in Karakose, where there were only a dozen Jewish families, prosperous merchants who were under the protection of a strong warlord, Ali ul Hamid. Hamid's castle was built in the shape of a heptagon on a high mountain overlooking the town. It had the appearance of a galleon-of-war, dismantled and dismasted. Water was brought to the fortress from the town on asses, and cisterns were kept full in case of siege. In return for Hamid's protection, the Jews of Karakose were pledged to keep the castle's magazines full of millet and rice. Rob and the three Jews didn't glimpse Hamid but left Karakose gladly, not wishing to remain where safety lay at the caprice of a single powerful man.

They were passing through territory that was extremely difficult and dangerous, but the travel network was working. Each night they had a renewed supply of sweet water, good food and shelter, and advice about the countryside ahead. The worry lines in Lonzano's face all but disappeared.

On a Friday afternoon they reached the tiny mountainside village of Igdir and stayed an extra day in the small stone houses of the Jews there in order that they need not travel on the Sabbath. Fruit was grown in Igdir and they gorged gratefully on black cherries and quince preserves. Now even Aryeh relaxed and Loeb was gracious to Rob, showing him a secret sign language with which Jewish merchants in the East conducted their negotiations without speaking. "It's done with the hands," Loeb said. "The straight finger stands for ten, the bent finger for five. The finger grasped so only the tip is showing is one, the whole hand counts for one hundred, the fist for one thousand."

He and Loeb rode side by side the morning they left Igdir, bargaining silently with their hands, making deals for nonexistent shipments, buying and selling spices and gold and kingdoms to while away the time. The trail was rocky and difficult.

"We're not far from Mount Ararat," Aryeh said.

Rob considered the towering, unwelcoming peaks and the sere terrain. "What must Noah have thought on leaving the ark?" he said, and Aryeh shrugged.

At Nazik, the next town, they were delayed. The community was built down the length of a large rocky defile, with eighty-four Jews living there and perhaps thirty times as many Anatolians. "There will be a Turkish wedding in this town," they were told by the *rabbenu*, a skinny old man with stooped shoulders and strong eyes. "They have already begun to celebrate and they are excited in a mean way. We do not dare leave our quarter."

Their hosts kept them locked within the Jewish section for four days. There was plenty of food in the quarter, and a good well. The Jews of Nazik were pleasant and polite, and although the sun was fierce there the travelers slept in a cool stone barn on clean straw. From the town Rob heard sounds of fighting and drunken revelry and the breaking of furniture, and once a hail of stones came raining down on the Jews from the other side of the wall, but no one was injured.

At the end of four days all was quiet and one of the *rabbenu*'s sons ventured forth to find that the Turks were exhausted and docile following the wild celebration, and the following morning Rob left Nazik gladly with his three fellow travelers.

There followed a trek through country devoid of Jewish settlement or protection along the way. Three mornings after they left Nazik they came to a plateau containing a great body of water surrounded by a wide perimeter of white cracked mud. They got down from their donkeys.

"This is Urmiya," Lonzano told Rob, "a shallow salt lake. In the spring, streams carry minerals here from the mountainsides. But no stream empties the lake, and so the summer sun drinks the water and leaves the salt around the edges. Take a pinch of salt and place it on your tongue."

He did, gingerly, and made a face.

Lonzano grinned. "You are tasting Persia."

It took him a moment to get the meaning. "We are in Persia?"

"Yes. This is the border."

He was disappointed. It seemed a long way to travel for . . . this. Lonzano was perceptive. "Never mind, you will be enamored of Ispahan, I guarantee it. We had best remount, we still have long days to ride."

But first Rob pissed into Lake Urmiya, adding his English Special Batch to Persia's saltiness.

Chapter 36

THE HUNTER

Aryeh made his loathing plain. He was careful to watch his words in front of Lonzano and Loeb, but when the other two were out of earshot his comments to Rob were apt to be cutting. Even when speaking to the other two Jews, he was often less than pleasant.

Rob was larger and stronger. Sometimes it took an act of will to keep from striking Aryeh.

Lonzano was perceptive. "You must ignore him," he told Rob.

"Aryeh is a . . ." He didn't know the Persian word for bastard.

"Even at home Aryeh wasn't the most pleasant of men, but he does not have the soul to be a traveler. When we departed from Masqat he'd been married less than a year and he had a new son he didn't want to leave. He has been sullen ever since." He sighed. "Well, we all have families, and often it is hard to be a traveler far from home, especially on the Sabbath or a holy day."

"How long have you been gone from Masqat?" Rob asked.

"This time it is twenty-seven months."

"If this merchant's life is so hard and lonely, why do you follow it?" Lonzano looked at him. "It is how a Jew survives," he said.

They circled the northeast corner of Lake Urmiya and soon were in high, bare-earth mountains again. They stayed overnight with Jews in Tabriz and Takestan. Rob could see little difference between most of these places and the villages he had seen in Turkey. They were bleak mountain towns built on stony rubble, with people sleeping in the shade and stray goats near the community well. Kashan was like that too, but Kashan had a lion on its gate.

A real lion, huge.

"This is a famous beast, measuring forty-five spans from nose to tail,"

Lonzano said proudly, as if it were his lion. "It was slain twenty years ago by Abdallah Shah, father of the present ruler. It played havoc on the cattle of this countryside for seven years and finally Abdallah tracked and killed it. In Kashan there is a celebration each year on the anniversary of the hunt."

Now the lion had dried apricots instead of eyes and a piece of red felt for a tongue, and Aryeh scornfully pointed out that it was stuffed with rags and dried weeds. Generations of moths had eaten the sun-hardened pelt down to bare leather in spots, but its legs resembled columns and its teeth were still its own, large and sharp as lance-heads, so that when Rob touched them he felt a chill.

"I wouldn't like to meet him."

Aryeh smiled his superior smile. "Most men go through life without seeing a lion."

The *rabbenu* of Kashan was a chunky man with sandy hair and beard. His name was David ben Sauli the Teacher, and Lonzano said he already had a reputation as a scholar despite the fact that he was still a young man. He was the first *rabbenu* Rob had seen wearing a turban instead of a leather Jew's hat. When he spoke to them the worry lines came back into Lonzano's face.

"It isn't safe to follow the route south through the mountains," the *rabbenu* told them. "A strong force of Seljuks is in your way."

"Who are the Seljuks?" Rob said.

"They are a herdsmen nation that lives in tents instead of towns," Lonzano said. "Killers and fierce fighters. They raid the lands on both sides of the border between Persia and Turkey."

"You can't go through the mountains," the *rabbenu* said unhappily. "Seljuk soldiers are crazier than bandits."

Lonzano looked at Rob and Loeb and Aryeh. "Then we have but two choices. We can remain here in Kashan and wait for the trouble with the Seljuks to pass, which may take many months, perhaps a year. Or we can skirt the mountains and the Seljuks, approaching Ispahan through desert and then forest. I haven't traveled on that desert, the Dasht-i-Kavir, but I have been over other deserts and know them to be terrible." He turned to the *rabbenu*. "Can it be crossed?"

"You would not have to cross the entire Dasht-i-Kavir. Heaven forbid," the *rabbenu* said slowly. "You need only to cut across a corner, a journey of three days, going east and then south. Yes, it is sometimes done. We can tell you how to go."

The four regarded one another. Finally Loeb, the inarticulate one, broke the thick silence. "I don't want to stay here for a year," he said, speaking for all of them.

Each of them bought a large goatskin waterbag and filled it before leaving Kashan. It was heavy when full. "Do we need this much water for three days?" Rob asked.

"Accidents occur. We could be on the desert a longer time," Lonzano said. "And you must share your water with your beasts, for we are taking donkeys and mules into the Dasht-i-Kavir, not camels."

A guide from Kashan rode with them on an old white horse as far as the point where an almost invisible track branched off from the road. The Dasht-i-Kavir began as a clay ridge that was easier to travel over than the mountains. At first they made good time, and for a little while their spirits lifted. The nature of the ground changed so gradually it disarmed them, but by midday, when the sun beat on them like brass, they were struggling through deep sand so fine that the hooves of the animals sank into it. All the riders dismounted, and men and beasts floundered forward in equal misery.

It was dreamlike to Rob, an ocean of sand extending in every direction as far as he could see. Sometimes it formed into hills like the great sea waves he dreaded, elsewhere it was like the flat smooth waters of a still lake, merely rippled by the west wind. There was no life he could detect, no bird in the air, no beetle or worm on the earth, but in the afternoon they passed bleaching bones heaped like a careless pile of kindling behind an English cottage, and Lonzano told Rob the remains of animals and men had been collected by nomadic tribes and piled there as a reference point. This sign of people who could be at home in such a place was unnerving and they tried to keep their animals quiet, knowing how far a donkey's braying would carry on the still air.

It was a salt desert. At times the sand they walked on wound between morasses of salt mud like the shores of Lake Urmiya. Six hours of such a march thoroughly exhausted them and when they came to a small hill of sand which cast a shadow before the shallow sun, men and beasts crowded together to fit into the well of comparative coolness. After an hour of shade they were able to resume walking until sunset.

"Perhaps we had best travel by night and sleep in the heat of day," Rob suggested.

"No," Lonzano said quickly. "When I was young, once I crossed the Dasht-i-Lut with my father and two uncles and four cousins. May the dead rest. Dasht-i-Lut is a salt desert, like this one. We decided to travel by night and soon had trouble. During the hot season, the salt lakes and swamps of the wet season dry quickly, in places leaving a crust on the surface. We found that men and animals broke through the crust. Sometimes beneath it there is brine or quicksand. It is too dangerous to go by night."

He wouldn't answer questions about his youthful experience on the Dasht-i-Lut, and Rob didn't press him, sensing it was a subject best left alone.

As darkness fell they sat or sprawled on the salty sand. The desert that had broiled them by day became cold by night. There was no fuel, nor would they have kindled a fire lest it be seen by unfriendly eyes. Rob was so tired that despite his discomfort he fell into a deep sleep that lasted until first light.

He was struck by the fact that what had seemed like ample water in Kashan had dwindled in the dry wilderness. He limited himself to small sips as he ate his breakfast of bread, giving far more to his two animals. He poured their portions into the leather Jew's hat and held it while they drank, enjoying the sensation of placing the wet hat on his hot head when they were finished.

It was a day of dogged plodding. When the sun was highest, Lonzano began to sing a phrase from the Scriptures: *Arise, shine, for thy light is come, and the glory of the Lord is risen upon thee.* One by one the others picked up the refrain, and for a while they praised God with juiceless throats.

Presently there was an interruption. "Horsemen coming!" Loeb shouted.

Far off to the south they saw a cloud such as would be raised by a large host and Rob was afraid that these were the desert people who had left the travel marker of bones. But as the sight swept nearer they saw that it was only a cloud.

By the time the hot desert wind reached them the donkeys and the mules had turned their backs to it with the wisdom of instinct. Rob huddled as best he could behind the beasts and the wind clattered over them. Its first effects were those of fever. The wind carried sand and salt that burned his skin like flakes of hot ash. The air became even heavier and more oppressive than before, and the men and the animals waited doggedly as the storm made them part of the land, coating them with a frosting of sand and salt two fingers thick.

That night he dreamed of Mary Cullen. He sat with her and knew tranquility. There was happiness on her face and he was aware her fulfillment came from him, which made him glad. She began to work embroidery and, without his understanding how or why, it turned out that she was Mam, and he experienced a rush of warmth and security he hadn't known since he was nine years old.

Then he awoke, hawking and spitting drily. There was sand and salt in his mouth and ears, and when he got up and walked it rubbed abrasively between his buttocks.

It was the third morning. *Rabbenu* David ben Sauli had instructed Lonzano to walk east for two days and then south for a day. They had gone in the direction Lonzano believed to be east, and now they turned in the direction Lonzano believed to be south.

Rob had never been able to tell east from south, north from west. He asked himself what would become of them if Lonzano didn't truly know south or truly know east, or if the Kashan *rabbenu*'s directions weren't accurate.

The piece of the Dasht-i-Kavir they had set out to cross was like a small cove in a great ocean. The main desert was vast and, for them, uncrossable.

Supposing that, instead of crossing the cove, they were heading straight toward the heart of the Dasht-i-Kavir?

If that was the case, they were doomed.

It occurred to him to wonder whether the God of the Jews was claiming him because of his masquerade. But Aryeh, although less than likable, wasn't evil, and both Lonzano and Loeb were most worthy; it wasn't logical that their God would destroy them to punish one *goy* sinner.

He was not the only one entertaining thoughts of despair. Sensing their mood, Lonzano attempted to start them singing again. But Lonzano's was the only voice raised in the refrain and eventually he stopped singing, too.

Rob poured a sparing final portion for each of his animals and let them drink from his hat.

What remained in his leathern bottle was about six mouthfuls of water. He reasoned that if they were nearing the end of Dasht-i-Kavir it wouldn't matter, while if they were traveling in the wrong direction this small amount of water was insufficient to save his life.

So he drank it. He forced himself to take it in small sips, but it was gone in a very brief time.

As soon as the goatskin was empty he began to suffer thirst more severely than ever. The swallowed water seemed to scald him internally, followed by a terrible headache.

He willed himself to walk but found his steps faltering. *I cannot*, he realized with horror.

Lonzano began to clap his hands fiercely. "*Ai*, di-di-di-di-di-di, *ai*, di-di *di,* di!" he sang, and went into a dance, shaking his head, whirling, lifting his arms and knees to the rhythm of the song.

Loeb's eyes glinted with tears of anger. "Stop it, you fool!" he shouted. But in a moment he grimaced and joined in the singing and clapping, cavorting along behind Lonzano.

Then Rob. And even sour Aryeh.

"*Ai,* di-di-di-di-di-di, *ai,* di-di *di,* di!"

They sang through dry lips and danced on feet that no longer had feeling. Eventually they fell silent and ceased the mad prancing, but they continued to plod, moving one numbed leg after the other, not daring to face the possibility that they were indeed lost.

Early in the afternoon they began to hear thunder. It rumbled in the distance for a long time before it heralded a few drops of rain, and shortly afterward they saw a gazelle and then a pair of wild asses.

Their own animals suddenly quickened. The beasts moved their legs faster and then began to trot of their own volition, scenting what lay ahead, and the men mounted the donkeys and rode again as they left the extreme boundary of the sand over which they had struggled for three days.

The land evolved into a plain, first with sparse growth and then more verdant. Before dusk they came to a pond where reeds grew and swallows dipped and wheeled. Aryeh tasted the water and nodded. "It is good."

"We mustn't let the beasts drink too much at once or they will founder," Loeb cautioned.

They watered the animals carefully and tied them to trees, then they drank and tore off their clothes and lay in the water, soaking among the reeds.

"When you were in the Dasht-i-Lut did you lose men?" Rob said.

"We lost my cousin Calman," Lonzano said. "A man of twenty-two years."

"Did he fall through the salt crust?"

"No. He abandoned all self-discipline and drank his water. Then he died of thirst."

"May he rest," Loeb said.

"What are the symptoms of a man dying of thirst?"

Lonzano was obviously offended. "I don't wish to think on it."

"I ask because I'm to be a physician, and not out of curiosity," Rob said, and saw that Aryeh was gazing at him with dislike.

Lonzano waited a long moment and then nodded. "My cousin Calman became confused with the heat and drank with abandon until his water was gone. We were lost and every man took care of his own water. We weren't allowed to share. After a while, he began to vomit weakly but there was no liquid to bring up. His tongue turned quite black and the roof of his mouth was a grayish white. His mind wandered, he believed he was in his mother's house. His lips were shriveled, his teeth were exposed, and his mouth hung open in a wolfish grin. He alternately panted and snored. That night under cover of darkness I disobeyed and dripped a little water on a rag and squeezed it into his mouth, but it was too late. After the second day without water, he died."

They lay silent in the brown water.

"*Ai*, di-di-di-di-di-di, *ai*, di-di- *di*, di!" Rob sang finally. He looked into Lonzano's eyes and they grinned at one another.

A mosquito settled on Loeb's leathery cheek and he slapped himself. "The beasts are ready for more water, I think," he said, and they left the lake and finished tending to their animals.

Next day they were back on their donkeys at dawn, and to Rob's intense pleasure they soon found themselves passing countless little lakes surrounded by garlands of meadow. The lakes exhilarated him. The grass was as high as a tall man's knee and had a delicious odor. It was full of grasshoppers and crickets, as well as tiny gnats that burned when they bit him and immediately left an itching welt. A few days earlier, he would have rejoiced at seeing any insect, but now he ignored the large and brilliant butterflies of the meadows while he slapped at bites and called down heaven's curses on gnats and mosquitoes.

"Oh, God, what is that?" Aryeh cried.

Rob followed his pointing finger and in full sunlight he perceived an immense cloud rising to the east. He watched with growing alarm as it approached, for it looked like the dust cloud they had seen when the hot wind struck them in the desert.

But from this cloud came the unmistakable sound of hooves, as of a great army sweeping down on them.

"The Seljuks?" he whispered, but no one answered.

Pale and expectant, they waited and watched as the cloud came nearer and the sound grew deafening.

At a distance of about fifty paces there was a clatter as if a thousand practiced horsemen had reined up at a word of command.

At first he could see nothing. Then the dust thinned and he saw wild asses, in countless number and in prime condition, and ranged in a well-formed line. The asses stared in intent curiosity at the men and the men gazed at them.

"*Hai!*" Lonzano shouted, and the herd wheeled as one and renewed its flight, moving northward and leaving behind a message about the multiplicity of life.

They passed smaller herds of asses and enormous herds of gazelles, sometimes feeding together and obviously seldom hunted, because they paid the men little mind. More ominous were the wild pigs that seemed to abound. Occasionally Rob glimpsed a hairy sow or a boar with wicked tusks, and on all sides he heard the animals grunting as they rustled and rooted in the tall grass.

Now they all sang when Lonzano suggested it, in order to warn the pigs of their approach and prevent startling them and provoking a charge. Rob's skin crawled and his long legs, hanging over the sides of the little donkey and dragging through the deep grass, felt exposed and vulnerable, but the pigs gave way before the male loudness of the singing and made them no trouble.

They came to a swift-moving stream that was like a great ditch, its sides almost vertical and rampant with fennel, and though they traveled upstream and downstream there was no easy place to cross; finally they just drove their animals into the water. It was very difficult, with donkeys and mules trying to climb the overgrown far bank and slipping back. The air was rich with curses and the sharp smell of crushed fennel, and it took them a while to complete the fording. Beyond the river they entered a forest, following a track like the ones Rob had known at home. The country was wilder than English woods; the high canopy of treetops interlocked and shut out the sun, yet the undergrowth was greenly rank and teeming with wildlife. He identified deer and rabbits and a porcupine, and in the trees were doves and what he thought was a kind of partridge.

It was the sort of track Barber would have liked, he thought, and wondered how the Jews would react if he were to blow the Saxon horn.

They had rounded a curve in the track and Rob was taking his turn in the lead when his donkey shied. Above them, on a large branch, crouched a wildcat.

The donkey reared and behind them the mule caught the scent and screamed. Perhaps the panther could sense overwhelming fear. As Rob scrabbled for a weapon the animal, which appeared monstrous to him, sprang.

A bolt, long and heavy and fired with tremendous force, slammed into the beast's right eye.

The great claws raked the poor donkey as the cat crashed into Rob and unseated him. In a moment he was stretched on the ground choking on the muskiness of the cat. The animal lay athwart him so that he was facing the hindquarter, noting the lustrous black fur, the matted arsehole, and the great right rear paw that rested inches from his face, with obscenely large, swollen-looking footpads. The claw somehow had been ripped recently from the second of the four toes, which was raw and bloody and indicated to him that at the other end of the cat there were eyes that were not dried apricots and a tongue that was not red felt.

People came out of the forest. Nearby stood their master, still holding his longbow.

The man was dressed in a plain red calico coat quilted with cotton, rough hose, shagreen shoes, and a carelessly wound turban. He was perhaps forty years old, with a strong build, erect bearing, short dark beard, aquiline beak of a nose, and a killer's light still in the eyes as he watched his beaters pulling the dead panther off the huge young man.

Rob scrambled to his feet, trembling, willing himself to control his bowels. "Catch the fucking donkey," he demanded of no one in particular. Neither the Jews nor the Persians understood, for he had spoken in English. At any rate the donkey was turned back by the strangeness of the woods, in which perhaps other dangers lurked, and now returned to stand and quiver like her owner.

Lonzano came to his side and grunted in recognition. Then everyone was kneeling in the prostration rite that later was described to Rob as *ravi zemin*, "face upon the ground," and Lonzano pulled him down without gentleness and made certain, with a hand on the back of his neck, that his head was properly lowered.

The sight of this instruction gained the hunter's attention; Rob heard the sound of his footsteps and then glimpsed the shagreen shoes, stopped a few inches from his obeisant head.

"It is a large dead panther and a large untutored *Dhimmi*," an amused voice said, and the shoes moved away.

The hunter and the servants bearing his prey departed without another word, and after a time the kneeling men rose.

"You are all right?" Lonzano said.

"Yes, yes." His caftan was ripped but he was unharmed. "Who is he?"

"He is Alā-al-Dawla, *Shahanshah*. The King of Kings."

Rob stared at the road down which they had departed. "What is a *Dhimmi?*"

"It means 'Man of the Book.' It is what they call a Jew here," Lonzano said.

Chapter 37

REB JESSE'S CITY

He and the three Jews parted ways two days later at Kupayeh, a crossroads village of a dozen crumbling brick houses. The detour through Dasht-i-Kavir had taken them a bit too far east, but he had less than a day's journey west to Ispahan, while they still faced three weeks of hard travel south and a crossing of the Straits of Hormuz before they were home.

He knew that without these men and the Jewish villages that had given him haven, he wouldn't have reached Persia.

Rob and Loeb embraced. "Go with God, Reb Jesse ben Benjamin!"

"Go with God, friend."

Even sour Aryeh affected a crooked smile as they wished each other a safe journey, no doubt as happy to say goodbye as Rob was.

"When you attend the school for physicians you must tender our love to Aryeh's kinsman, Reb Mirdin Askari," Lonzano said.

"Yes." He took Lonzano's hands. "Thank you, Reb Lonzano ben Ezra."

Lonzano smiled. "For one who is almost an Other you've been an excellent companion and a worthy man. Go in peace, *Inghiliz.*"

"Go you in peace."

To a chorus of good wishes they went in different directions.

Rob rode the mule, for after the attack by the panther he had transferred his bundle to the back of the poor frightened donkey and now led the beast. He made slower time with this arrangement but excitement was rising in him and he wished to travel the last portion deliberately, in order to savor it.

It was well he was in no hurry, for it was a trafficked road. He heard the sound that pleased him so, and soon he overtook a column of belled camels, each burdened with great twin baskets of rice. He traveled behind the rearmost camel, glorying in the musical tinkling of the bells.

The forest ascended to an open plateau; wherever there was sufficient water there were fields of ripened rice and opium poppies, separated by expanses of flat, dry rockiness. The plateau in turn became white limestone hills, cast in a variety of changeable hues by sun and shadow. In several places the limestone had been deeply quarried.

Late in the afternoon the mule crested a hill and Rob looked down upon a little river valley and—twenty months after he had left London!—he saw Ispahan.

His first and predominant impression was of dazzling whiteness with touches of deep blue. It was a voluptuous place full of hemispheres and curves, with great domed buildings glittering in the sunlight, mosques with minarets like airy lances, green open spaces, and mature cyprus and plane trees. The southern quarter of the city was a warm pink where the sun's rays were reflected from sand hills instead of limestone.

Now he couldn't hang back. "*Hai!*" he shouted, and heeled the mule's flanks. The donkey clattering behind, they swung out of line and passed the camels at a fast trot.

A quarter of a mile from the city, the trail turned into a spectacular cobblestoned avenue, the first paved road he had seen since leaving Constantinople. It was very broad, with four wide lanes separated from one another by rows of tall matched plane trees. The avenue crossed the river over a bridge that was really an arched dam creating an irrigation pool. Near a sign that proclaimed the stream to be Zayandeh, the River of Life, naked brown-skinned youths splashed and swam.

The avenue brought him to the great stone wall and a unique arched city gate.

Inside the wall were the large homes of the wealthy, with terraces, orchards, and vineyards. Pointed arches were everywhere—arched doorways, arched windows, arched garden gates. Beyond the rich neighborhood were mosques and larger buildings with vaulted domes, white and round with little points on top, as though their architects had fallen madly in love with the female breast. It was easy to see where the quarried rock had gone; everything was white stone trimmed with dark blue tile set to form geometric designs or quotations from the Qu'ran:

There is no God but He, the most merciful.

Fight for the religion of God.

Woe be unto those who are negligent at their prayer.

The streets were full of turbaned men, but no women. He passed a huge open square; and then, perhaps half a mile later, another. He relished the sounds and the smells. It was unmistakably a *municipium,* a large warren of humanity such as he had known as a boy in London, and for some reason he felt it right and fitting to be riding slowly through this city on the north bank of the River of Life.

From the minarets male voices, some of them distant and thin, others near and clear, began to call the faithful to prayer. All traffic ceased as men faced what was apparently southwest, the direction of Mecca. All the men in the city had fallen to their knees, caressing the ground with their palms and dropping forward so their foreheads were pressed into the cobbles.

Rob stopped the mule and alighted out of respect.

When the prayers were done he approached a man of middle age who was briskly rolling up a small prayer rug he had taken from his nearby oxcart. Rob asked how he might find the Jewish quarter.

"Ah. It is called Yehuddiyyeh. You must continue on down the Avenue of Yazdegerd, until you come to the Jews' market. At the far end of the market there is an arched gate, and on the other side you will find your quarter. You cannot miss it, *Dhimmi.*"

The place was lined with stalls that sold furniture, lamps and oil, breads, pastries giving off the scent of honey and spices, clothing, utensils of every sort, vegetables and fruits, meats, fish, chickens plucked and dressed or alive and squawking—everything necessary to material life. He saw displays of prayer shawls, fringed garments, phylacteries. In a letter-writer's booth an old man with a lined face sat hunched over inkpot and quills, and a woman told fortunes under an open tent. Rob knew he was in the Jewish quarter because there were women vending in the stalls and shopping in the crowded market with baskets over their arms. They wore loose black dresses and their hair was bound in cloths. A few had face veils, like Muslim women, but most did not. The men were dressed like Rob, with full, bushy beards.

He wandered slowly, enjoying the sights and sounds. He passed two men arguing over the price of a pair of shoes, as bitterly as enemies. Others were joking, shouting at one another. It was necessary to talk loud in order to be heard.

On the other side of the market he passed through the arched gate and wandered down close, narrow bystreets, then descended a winding and rugged declivity to a large district of wretched houses, irregularly built, divided by small streets with no attempt at uniformity. Many of the houses were attached to one another, but here and there a house was set apart, with a small garden; although these were humble by English standards, they stood out from the neighboring structures as though they were castles.

Ispahan was old, but Yehuddiyyeh seemed much older. The streets were convoluted, and from them ran alleys. The houses and synagogues were of stone or ancient brick that had faded to a pale rose. Some children led a goat past him. People stood in groups, laughing and talking. Soon it would be time for the evening meal, and the cooking smells from the houses made his mouth water.

He wandered through the quarter until he found a stable, where he arranged for the animals' care. Before he left them he cleaned the claw scratches on the donkey's flank, which were healing nicely.

Not far from the stable he found an inn run by a tall old man with a handsome smile and a crooked back, named Salman the Lesser.

"Why the Lesser?" Rob couldn't refrain from asking.

"In my native village of Razan my uncle was Salman the Great. A renowned scholar," the old man explained.

Rob rented a pallet in a corner of the large sleeping room.

"You wish food?"

It enticed him, small pieces of meat broiled on skewers, thick rice that Salman called *pilah*, small onions blackened by the fire.

"Is it *kasher?*" he asked cleverly.

"Of course it is *kasher,* you need not fear to eat it!"

After the meat Salman served honey cakes and a pleasing drink he called a *sherbet*. "You come from afar," he said.

"Europe."

"Europe! Ah."

"How did you know?"

The old man grinned. "The way you speak the language." He saw Rob's face. "You'll learn to speak it better, I'm certain. How is it to be a Jew in Europe?"

Rob didn't know how to answer, then he thought of what Zevi had said. "It's hard to be a Jew."

Salman nodded soberly.

"How is it to be a Jew in Ispahan?"

"Oh, it's not bad here. The people are instructed in the Qu'ran to revile us, and so they call us names. But they're accustomed to us and we're used to them. There have always been Jews in Ispahan," Salman said. "The city was started by Nebuchadnezzar, who, according to legend, settled Jews here after taking them prisoner when he conquered Judea and destroyed Jerusalem. Then, nine hundred years later, a shah named Yazdegerd became enamored of a Jewess who lived here, name of Shushan-Dukht, and made her his queen. She made things easier for her own people, and more Jews settled in this place."

Rob told himself he couldn't have chosen a better disguise; he could blend in among them like an ant in an anthill, once he had learned their ways.

So that after dinner he accompanied the innkeeper to the House of Peace, one of the dozens of synagogues. It was a square building of ancient stone whose cracks were filled with a soft brown moss, though there was no dampness. It had only narrow loopholes instead of windows, and a door so low that Rob had to stoop to enter. A dark passage led to the interior, where lamps showed pillars supporting a roof too high and dark for his eyes to make it out. Men sat in the main portion, while women worshiped behind a wall in a small recess at the side of the building. Rob found it easier to perform the *ma'ariv* worship in the synagogue than in the company of only a few Jews on the trail. Here there was a *hazzan* to lead the prayer and an entire congregation to mumble or sing as each individual chose, so he joined in the swaying with less self-consciousness about his poor Hebrew and the fact that often he couldn't keep up with the prayers.

On the way back to the inn, Salman smiled at him shrewdly. "Perhaps you would like some excitement, a young man such as yourself, eh? At night here the *maidans,* the public squares in the Muslim sections of the city, come alive. There are females and wine, and music and entertainments such as you cannot imagine, Reb Jesse."

But Rob shook his head. "I should like that, another time," he said. "Tonight I keep my head clear, for tomorrow I transact a matter of the utmost importance."

That night he didn't sleep but tossed and turned, wondering whether Ibn Sina was a man with whom one could talk easily.

In the morning he found a public bath, a brick structure built over a natural warm spring. With strong soap and clean cloths, he scrubbed himself free of the accumulated grime of travel, and when his hair had dried he took a surgical knife and trimmed his beard, peering at the reflection in his polished steel square. The beard had filled out, and he thought he looked a proper Jew.

He wore the better of his two caftans. Setting his leather hat squarely on his head, he went into the street and asked a man with withered limbs to direct him to the school for physicians.

"You mean the *madrassa,* the place of teaching? It is next to the hospital," the beggar said. "On the Street of Ali, near the Friday Mosque in the center of the city." In return for a coin the lame man blessed his children down to the tenth generation.

It was a long walk. He had opportunity to observe that Ispahan was a place of business, for he glimpsed men laboring over their crafts, shoemakers and metalsmiths, potters and wheelwrights, glass blowers and tailors. He passed several bazaars in which goods of all sorts were sold. Eventually he came to the Friday Mosque, a massive square structure with a splendid minaret on which birds fluttered. Beyond it was a marketplace with a preponderance of bookstalls and small eating places, and presently he saw the *madrassa*.

On the outer perimeters of the school, nestled among more bookshops placed to serve the needs of the scholars, were long, low buildings that contained living quarters. Around them children ran and played. Young men were everywhere, most of them wearing green turbans. The *madrassa* buildings were constructed of blocks of white limestone, after the manner of most of the mosques. They were widely spaced, with gardens in between. Beneath a chestnut tree heavy with unopened spiky fruit, six young men sat on folded legs and gave their attention to a white-bearded man who wore a sky-blue turban.

Rob drifted close to them. ". . . Socrates' syllogisms," the lecturer was saying. "A proposition is logically inferred to be true from the fact that two other propositions are true. For example, from the fact that, one, all men are mortal, and, two, Socrates is a man, it can be logically concluded that, three, Socrates is mortal."

Rob grimaced and moved on, touched by doubt; there was much he didn't know, too much he didn't understand.

He paused before a very old building with an attached mosque and lovely minaret to ask a green-turbaned student in which building medicine was taught.

"Third building down. Here, they teach theology. Next door, Islamic law. There is where they teach medicine," he said, pointing to a domed building of white stone. It was so slavishly similar to the prevailing architecture of Ispahan that ever after Rob was to think of it as the Big Teat. Next to it was a large one-story building whose sign proclaimed it to be the *maristan*, "the place for sick people." Intrigued, instead of entering the *madrassa* he walked up the *maristan*'s three marble steps and through its wrought-iron portal.

There was a central courtyard containing a pool in which colored fish swam, and benches under fruit trees. Corridors radiated from the courtyard like the rays of the sun, with large rooms off each corridor. Most of the rooms were filled. He had never seen so many ill and injured people gathered in one place, and he wandered in amazement.

The patients were grouped according to affliction: here, a long room filled with men who suffered from fractured bones; here, victims of fevers; here—he wrinkled his nose, for clearly this was a room reserved for patients with diarrhea and other diseases of the excretory process. Yet even in this room the atmosphere wasn't as oppressive as it might have been, for there were large windows, with the flow of air impeded only by light cloths which had been stretched over the windows to keep insects away. Rob noted slots at the tops and bottoms of the casements so shutters could be slipped into place during the winter season.

The walls were whitewashed and the floors were of stone, which was easy to clean and made the building cool compared to the considerable heat outside.

In each room, a small fountain splashed!

Rob paused before a closed door, held by the sign on it: *dar-ul-maraftan,* "abode of those who require to be chained." When he opened the door he saw three naked men, their heads shaved and their arms bound, chained to a high window from iron bands fastened around their necks. Two sagged, asleep or unconscious, but the third man stared and began to howl like a beast, tears wetting his slack cheeks.

"I am sorry," Rob said gently, and left the maniacs.

He came to a hall of surgical patients and had to resist the temptation to stop at each pallet and lift the dressings to examine the stumps of amputees and the wounds of the injured.

To be exposed to this many interesting patients every day, and to be taught by great men! It would be like spending one's early life in the Dasht-i-Kavir, he thought, and then discovering that you owned an oasis.

The sign on the doorway to the next hall was too much for his limited Persian, but as he entered it was easy to see that it was devoted to the diseases and injuries of the eye.

Nearby, a stalwart male nurse quailed before a tongue-lashing.

"It was a mistake, Master Karim Harun," the nurse said. "I thought you told me to remove the bandages of Eswed Omar."

"You donkey's prick," the other man said in disgust. He was young and athletically slender, and Rob saw with surprise that he wore the green turban of a student, for his manner was as assured as that of a physician who owned the hospital floor he trod. He wasn't in any way feminine but was aristocratically handsome, the most beautiful man Rob had ever seen, with glossy black hair and deep-set brown eyes that flashed with anger. "It was *your* mistake, Rūmi. I told you to change the dressings of Kuru Yezidi, not those of Eswed Omar. *Ustad* Juzjani couched the eyes of Eswed Omar himself and ordered me to see that his bandages weren't disturbed for five days. I passed the order to you and you failed to obey it, you shit. Therefore, if Eswed Omar should fail to see with the utmost clarity, and should the wrath of al-Juzjani fall on me, I'll slit your fat ass like a roast of lamb."

He noticed Rob, standing there transfixed, and scowled. "What is it *you* want?"

"To speak with Ibn Sina about entering the school for physicians."

"Doubtless you do. But the Prince of Physicians isn't awaiting you?"

"No."

"Then you must go to the second floor of the building next door and see *Hadji* Davout Hosein, the deputy governor of the school. The governor is Rotun bin Nasr, distant cousin of the Shah and a general in the army, who accepts the honor and never comes to the school. *Hadji* Davout Hosein administers, it is he you must see." The student named Karim Harun then turned back to the nurse with a scowl. "Now, do you think you can change Kuru Yezidi's dressings, O you green object on a camel's hoof?"

At least some of the medical students lived in the Big Teat, for the shadowy first-floor corridor was lined with tiny cells. Through an open door near the stairway landing Rob saw two men who seemed to be cutting a yellow dog that lay on the table, perhaps dead.

On the second floor he asked a man in a green turban to direct him to the *hadji* and was ushered, ultimately, into the office chamber of Davout Hosein.

The deputy governor was a small, thin man, not yet old, who wore an air of self-importance, a tunic of good gray stuff, and the white turban of one who has made his way to Mecca. He had little dark eyes and on his forehead a very distinct *zabiba* bore witness to the fervor of his piety.

After they had exchanged *salaams* he listened to Rob's request and studied him narrowly. "You've come from England, you say? In Europe? . . . Ah, what part of Europe is that?"

"The north."

"The north of Europe. How long did it take you to reach us?"

"Not quite two years, *Hadji.*"

"Two years! Extraordinary. Your father is a physician, a graduate of our school?"

"My father? No, *Hadji.*"

"Hmmm. An uncle, perhaps?"

"No. I shall be the first physician in my line."

Hosein frowned. "Here we have scholars descended from long lines of physicians. You have letters of introduction, *Dhimmi?*"

"No, Master Hosein." He felt rising panic. "I am a barber-surgeon, I already have had some training . . ."

"No references from some of our distinguished graduates?" Hosein asked, astounded.

"No."

"We don't accept for education any person who appears."

"This isn't a passing fancy. I have traveled a terrible distance because of my determination to be trained in medicine. I have learned your language."

"Poorly, I may say." The *hadji* sniffed. "We do not simply train in medicine. We do not produce tradesmen, we fashion educated men. Our students learn theology, philosophy, mathematics, physics, astrology, and jurisprudence as well as medicine, and upon being graduated as well-rounded scientists and intellectuals they may take their choice of careers in teaching, medicine, or the law."

Rob waited with a sinking feeling.

"Surely you must comprehend? It is impossible."

He comprehended almost two years.

Turning his back on Mary Cullen.

Sweating under the burning sun, shivering in glacial snows, beaten by storm and rain. Through salt desert and treacherous forest. Laboring like a bloody ant over mountain after mountain.

"I will not leave without speaking with Ibn Sina," he said firmly.

Hadji Davout Hosein opened his mouth but saw something in Rob's eyes that made him close it. He paled and nodded quickly. "Please to wait here," he said, and left the room.

Rob sat there alone.

After a time, four soldiers came. None was as large as he but they were muscular. They carried short, heavy wooden batons. One of them had a pocked face and kept smacking his baton into the meaty palm of his left hand.

"What is your name, Jew?" the man with the pocked face asked, not impolitely.

"I am Jesse ben Benjamin."

"A foreigner, a European, *Hadji* said?"

"Yes, from England. A place a great distance from here."

The soldier nodded. "Did you not refuse to leave at *Hadji*'s request?"

"That is true, but—"

"It is time to leave now, Jew. With us."

"I will not leave without speaking with Ibn Sina."

The spokesman swung his baton.

Not my nose, he thought in anguish.

But blood began to pour at once, and all four of them knew where and how to use the clubs with economic efficiency. They hemmed him in so he couldn't swing his arms.

"To hell!" he said in English. They couldn't have understood but the tone was unmistakable, and they hit harder. One of the blows cracked him above the temple and he was suddenly dizzy and nauseated. He tried at the very least to succeed in being sick in *Hadji*'s office chamber but the pain was too great.

They knew their job very well. When he was no longer a threat, they stopped using the batons in order to beat him very skillfully with their fists.

They made him walk out of the school, one of them supporting him under each arm. They had four large brown horses tethered outside and they rode while he staggered between two of the beasts. Whenever he fell, which happened three times, one of them dismounted and kicked him hard in the ribs until he got to his feet. It seemed a long walk but they went just beyond the *madrassa* grounds to a small brick building, shabby and unprepossessing, part of the lowest branch of the Islamic court system, as he would learn. Inside there was only a wooden table, behind which sat a cross-looking man, bushy-haired, full-bearded, and wearing black clerical robes not unlike Rob's caftan. He was in the process of opening a melon.

The four soldiers led Rob to the table and stood respectfully while the justice used a dirty fingernail to scrape the seeds from the melon into an earthen bowl. Then he sliced the melon and ate it slowly. When it was gone he wiped first his hands and then the knife on his robe and turned toward Mecca and thanked Allah for the food.

Having finished praying, he sighed and looked at the soldiers.

"A crazy European Jew who has disturbed the public tranquility, *mufti*," the soldier with the pocked face said. "Taken on complaint of *Hadji* Davout Hosein, against whom he threatened violent deeds."

The *mufti* nodded and dug a bit of melon from between his teeth with a fingernail. He looked at Rob. "You are not a Muslim, and you are accused by a Muslim. The word of an unbeliever may not be accepted against one of the faithful. Do you have a Muslim who will speak in your defense?"

Rob tried thickly to talk but no sound came, though his legs buckled with the effort. The soldiers yanked him erect.

"Why do you behave like a dog? Ah, well. An infidel, after all, unused to our ways. Therefore, it requires mercy. You shall hand him over to be kept in the *carcan* at the discretion of the *kelonter,*" the *mufti* told the soldiers.

It added two words to Rob's Persian vocabulary, which he pondered as the soldiers half dragged him from the court and again herded him between their mounts. He guessed correctly on one of the definitions; though he didn't know it then, the *kelonter,* whom he supposed to be some kind of jailkeeper, was the provost of the city.

When they arrived at a great and grim jail, Rob thought that *carcan* surely meant prison. Inside, the pockfaced soldier turned him over to two guards who hustled him past forbidding dungeons of foul dankness, but they emerged finally from the windowless dark into the open brilliance of an inner court where two long lines of stocks were occupied by groaning or unconscious human misery. The guards marched him along the line until they came to an empty device, which one of them unlocked.

"Thrust your head and right arm into the *carcan,*" he ordered.

It was instinct and fear that made Rob pull back, but they were technically correct in interpreting it as resistance.

They struck him until he fell and then began to kick him, as the soldiers had done. Rob could do nothing but curl himself into a ball to hide his groin and throw up his arms to protect his head.

When they were finished savaging him, they shoved and maneuvered him like a sack of meal until his neck and right arm were positioned, then they slammed down the heavy upper half of the *carcan* and nailed it closed before abandoning him, more unconscious than not, to hang hopeless and helpless under the unshaded sun.

Chapter 38

THE *CALAAT*

They were peculiar stocks indeed, made of a rectangle and two squares of wood fastened in a triangle, the center of which gripped Rob's head so that his crouching body was half suspended. His right hand, the eating hand, had been placed over the end of the longest piece and a wooden cuff nailed over his wrist, for while in the *carcan* a prisoner wasn't fed. The left hand, the wiping hand, was unfettered, for the *kelonter* was civilized.

At intervals he drifted into consciousness to stare at the long double row of stocks, each containing a wretch. In his line of sight at the other end of the courtyard was a large wooden block.

Once he dreamed of people and demons in black robes. A man knelt and placed his right hand on the block; one of the demons swung a sword that was larger and heavier than an English cutlass and the hand was taken off at the wrist while the other robed figures prayed.

The same dream again and again in the hot sun. And then a difference. A man knelt so the back of his neck was on the block and his eyes bulged at the sky. Rob was afraid they would decapitate him but they took his tongue.

When next Rob opened his eyes he saw neither people nor demons but on the ground and on the block were fresh stains such as are not left by dreams.

It hurt him to breathe. He had been given the most thorough beating of his life and he couldn't tell if there were broken bones.

He hung in the *carcan* and wept weakly, trying to be silent and hoping no one was watching.

Eventually he tried to relieve his ordeal by speaking to his neighbors, whom he could just manage to see by turning his head. It was an effort he learned not to make casually, for the skin of his neck quickly rubbed raw against the wood that held him fast. To his left was a man who had been

288

beaten unconscious and didn't move; the youth on his right studied him curiously but was either a deaf mute, incredibly stupid, or unable to make sense of his broken Persian. After several hours a guard noticed that the man on his left was dead. He was taken away and another put in his place.

By midday Rob's tongue rasped and seemed to fill his mouth. He felt no urge to urinate or void, for any wastes had long ago been sucked from him by the sun. At times he believed himself back in the desert and in lucid moments remembered too vividly Lonzano's description of how a man dies of thirst, the swollen tongue, the blackened gums, the belief that he was in another place.

Presently Rob turned his head and met the new prisoner's eyes. They studied one another and he saw a swollen face and ruined mouth.

"Is there no one of whom we can ask mercy?" he whispered.

The other waited, perhaps puzzled by Rob's accent. "There is Allah," he said finally. He was not himself easily understood because of his split lip.

"But no one here?"

"You are a foreigner, *Dhimmi?*"

"Yes."

The man directed his hatred at Rob. "You have seen a *mullah,* foreigner. A holy man has sentenced you." He appeared to lose interest and turned his face away.

The waning of the sun was a blessing. Evening brought such a coolness as to be almost joyful. His body was numb and he no longer felt muscular pain; perhaps he was dying.

During the night the man next to him spoke again. "There is the Shah, foreign Jew," the man said.

Rob waited.

"Yesterday, the day of our torture, was Wednesday, *Chaban Shanbah.* Today is *Panj Shanbah.* And each week on the morn of *Panj Shanbah,* in order to attempt a perfect soul-cleansing before *Jom'a,* the Sabbath, Alā-al-Dawla Shah holds audience during which anyone may approach his throne in the Hall of Pillars to complain of injustice."

Rob couldn't stifle the reluctant stir of hope. "Anyone?"

"Anyone. Even a prisoner may demand to be brought to place his case before the Shah."

"No, you must not!" a voice bawled from the darkness. Rob couldn't tell from which *carcan* the sound came.

"You must put it out of your mind," the unknown voice said. "For the Shah almost never reverses a *mufti*'s judgment or a sentence. And the *mullahs* eagerly await the return of those who waste the Shah's time with a wagging tongue. It is then that tongues are taken and bellies are ripped, as this devil surely knows, this evil son of a bitch who gives you false advice. You must place your faith in Allah and not in Alā Shah."

The man on his right was laughing slyly, laughing as if caught out in a practical joke.

"There is no hope," the voice said from the darkness.

His neighbor's mirth had turned into a paroxysm of coughing and wheezing. When he caught his breath the man said viciously, "Yes, we may look for hope in Paradise." No one spoke again.

Twenty-four hours after Rob was placed in the *carcan* he was released. He tried to stand but fell, and lay in agony as blood reentered his muscles.

"Go," a guard said finally, and kicked at him.

He struggled to his feet and limped out of the jail, hurrying from that place. He walked to a great square with plane trees and a splashing fountain from which he drank and drank, surrendering to a thirst without end. Then he plunged his head into the water until his ears rang and he felt that some of the prison stink had been washed away.

Ispahan's streets were crowded and people glanced at him as they passed.

A fat little vendor in a tattered tunic was fanning flies from a pot cooking on a brazier in his donkey cart. The aroma from the pot brought such a weakness it gave Rob a fright. But when he opened his purse-pocket, instead of sufficient funds to keep him for months, it contained one small bronze coin.

He had been robbed while unconscious. He cursed bleakly, not knowing whether the thief had been the pockfaced soldier or a jail guard. The bronze coin was a mockery, a wry joke on the thief's part, or perhaps it had been left through some twisted religious sense of charity. He gave it to the vendor, who ladled out a small portion of a greasy rice *pilah*. It was spicy and contained bits of bean and he swallowed it too quickly, or perhaps his body had been overtaxed by deprivation and sun and the *carcan*. Almost at once he cast up the contents of his stomach into the dusty street. His neck was bleeding where it had been tormented by the stocks and there was a pounding behind his eyes. He moved into the shade under a plane tree and stood there thinking of green England, his own Horse and cart with money beneath the floorboards and Mistress Buffington sitting next to him for company.

The crowd was denser now, a flood of people flowing through the street, all headed in the same direction.

"Where are they going?" he asked the food vendor.

"To the Shah's audience," the man said, staring askance at the battered Jew until Rob moved away.

Why not? he asked himself. Did he have another choice?

He joined in the tide that swept down the Avenue of Ali and Fatima, crossed the four-laned Avenue of the Thousand Gardens, turned into the immaculate boulevard marked Gates of Paradise. They were young and old and in-between, *hadjis* in white turbans, students in green turbans, *mullahs*, beggars whole and maimed and wearing rags and cast-off turbans of all colors, young fathers holding babies, porters bearing sedan chairs, men on horseback and on donkeys. Rob found himself trailing a dark-caftaned gaggle of Jews and hobbled just behind them, an errant gosling.

They passed through the small coolness of an artificial woods, for trees were not plentiful in Ispahan, and then, although they were still well within the town walls, past numerous fields on which sheep and goats grazed, separating royalty from its city. Now they approached a great green lawn with two stone pillars at either end like portals. When the first house of the royal court came into view Rob thought it the palace, for it was larger than King's House in London. But there was house after house of the same size, mostly built of brick and stone, many with towers and porches and each with terraces and extensive gardens. They passed vineyards, stables, and two racing tracks, orchards and gardened pavilions of such beauty he wanted to leave the crowd and wander in the perfumed splendor, but knew it was doubtless forbidden.

And then a structure so formidable, and at the same time so sweepingly graceful that he didn't credit it, all breast-shaped roofs and girded battlements on which sentries with glittering helms and shields paced beneath long colored pennants that fluttered in the breeze.

He plucked at the sleeve of the man in front of him, a stocky Jew whose fringed undergarment peeped from his shirt. "What is the fortress?"

"Why, the House of Paradise, home of the Shah!" The man peered at him worriedly. "You are bloodied, friend."

"Nothing, a small accident."

They poured down the long approach road, and as they drew near he saw that the main section of the palace was protected by a wide moat. The drawbridge was raised, but on the near side of the moat, next to a plaza that served as the palace's great portal, was a hall through whose doors the crowd entered.

Inside was a space half as large as the Cathedral of St. Sofia in Constantinople. The floor was marble; the walls and the lofty ceilings were stone, cleverly chinked so daylight softly illuminated the interior. It was the Hall of Pillars, for next to all four walls were stone columns, elegantly wrought and fluted. Where each column joined the floor, its base had been carved into the legs and paws of a variety of animals.

The hall was half filled when Rob arrived, and immediately people entered behind him, pressing him in among the party of Jews. Roped-off sections left open aisles down the length of the hall. Rob stood and watched, noting everything with a new intensity, for his time in the *carcan* had impressed upon him that he was a foreigner; actions that he would think of as natural the Persians might consider bizarre and threatening, and he was aware his life might depend on correctly sensing how they behaved and thought.

He observed that men of the upper class, wearing embroidered trousers and tunics and silk turbans and brocaded shoes, rode into the hall on horseback through a separate entrance. Each was halted approximately one hundred and fifty paces from the throne by attendants who took his horse in return for a coin, and from that privileged point they proceeded on foot among the poor.

Petty officials in gray clothing and turbans now passed among the people and called out requests for the identities of those with petitions, and Rob made his way to the aisle and laboriously spelled out his name to one of these aides, who recorded it on a curiously thin and unsubstantial-looking parchment.

A tall man had entered the raised portion at the front of the hall, on which sat a large throne. Rob was too far away to see detail, but the man wasn't the Shah, for he seated himself at a smaller throne below and to the right of the royal place.

"Who is that?" Rob asked the Jew to whom he had spoken previously.

"It is the Grand Vizier, the holy Imam Mirza-aboul Qandrasseh." The Jew looked at Rob uneasily, for it had not gone unnoticed that he was a petitioner.

Alā-al-Dawla Shah strode onto the platform, undid a sword belt, and placed the scabbard on the floor as he took the throne. Everyone in the Hall of Pillars performed the *ravi zemin* while the Imam Qandrasseh invoked the favor of Allah upon those who would seek justice of the Lion of Persia.

At once the audience began. Rob could hear clearly neither the suppli-cants nor the enthroned, despite the hush that suddenly fell. But whenever a principal spoke, his words were repeated in loud voices by others sta-tioned at strategic locations in the hall, and in this way the words of the participants were faithfully brought to all.

The first case involved two weather-beaten shepherds from the village of Ardistan, who had walked two days to reach Ispahan to bring their dispute before the Shah. They were in fierce disagreement over the ownership of a new kid. One man owned the dame, a doe that had long been barren and unreceptive. The other said he had readied the doe for successful mounting by the male goat and therefore now claimed half-ownership of the kid.

"Did you use magic?" the Imam asked.

"Excellency, I did but reach in with a feather and make her hot," the man said, and the crowd roared and stamped its feet. In a moment the Imam indicated that the Shah found in favor of the feather wielder.

It was an entertainment for most of those present. The Shah never spoke. Perhaps he conveyed his wishes to Qandrasseh by signal, but all questions and decisions appeared to come from the Imam, who did not suffer fools.

A severe schoolteacher, with his hair oiled and his little beard cut to a perfect point, and dressed in an ornate embroidered tunic that looked like a rich man's castoff, presented a petition for the establishment of a new school in the town of Nain.

"Are there not already two schools in the town of Nain?" Qandrasseh asked sharply.

"They are poor schools taught by unworthy men, Excellency," the teacher replied smoothly. A small murmur of disapproval arose from the crowd.

The teacher continued to read the petition, which advised the hiring of a governor for the proposed school, with such detailed, specific, and irrelevant requirements for the position that a tittering occurred, for it was obvious the description would fit only the reader himself.

"Enough," Qandrasseh said. "This petition is sly and self-serving, therefore an insult to the Shah. Let this man be caned twenty times by the *kelonter*, and may it please Allah."

Soldiers appeared flourishing batons, the sight of which made Rob's bruises throb, and the teacher was led away, protesting volubly.

There was little enjoyment in the next case—two elderly noblemen in expensive silk clothing who had a mild difference of opinion concerning grazing rights. It prompted what seemed an interminable soft-voiced discussion of ancient agreements made by men long dead, while the audience yawned and whispered complaints about the ventilation in the crowded hall and the aching in their tired legs. They showed no emotion when the verdict was reached.

"Let Jesse ben Benjamin, a Jew of England, come forward," someone called.

His name hung in the air and then bounced echo-like through the hall as it was repeated again and again. He limped down the long carpeted aisle, aware of his filthy torn caftan and the battered leather Jew's hat that matched his ill-used face.

At last he approached the throne and performed the *ravi zemin* three times, as he had observed to be proper.

When he straightened he saw the Imam in *mullah* black, his nose a hatchet imbedded in a willful face framed by an iron-gray beard.

The Shah wore the white turban of a religious man who had been to Mecca, but into its folds had been slipped a thin gold coronet. His long white tunic was of smooth, light-looking stuff worked with blue and gold thread. Dark blue wrappings covered his lower legs and his pointed shoes were blue embroidered with blood-red. He appeared vacuous and unseeing, the picture of a man who was inattentive because he was bored.

"An *Inghiliz,*" observed the Imam. "You are at present our only *Inghiliz,* our only European. Why have you come to our Persia?"

"As a seeker of truth."

"Do you wish to embrace the true religion?" asked Qandresseh, not unkindly.

"No, for we already agree there is no Allah but He, the most merciful," Rob said, blessing the long hours spent under the tutelage of Simon ben ha-Levi, the scholarly trader. "It is written in the Qu'ran, 'I will not worship that which you worship, nor will you worship that which I worship . . . You have your religion and I my religion.'"

He must be brief, he reminded himself.

Unemotionally and keeping his language spare, he recounted how he had been in the jungle of western Persia when a beast had sprung upon him.

The Shah seemed to begin to listen.

"In the place of my birth, panthers do not exist. I had no weapon, nor did I know how to fight such a creature."

He told how his life had been saved by Alā-al-Dawla Shah, hunter of wildcats like his father Abdallah Shah who had slain the lion of Kashan. The people closest to the throne began to applaud their ruler with sharp little cries of approbation. Murmurs rippled through the hall as the repeaters passed the story out into the crowds who were too far from the throne to have heard it.

Qandresseh sat motionless but Rob thought from his eyes that the Imam was not pleased with the story nor the reaction it drew from the crowd.

"Now hasten, *Inghiliz*," he said coolly, "and declare what it is that you request at the feet of the one true Shah."

Rob took a steadying breath. "Since it is also written that one who saves a life is responsible for it, I ask the Shah's help in making my life as valuable as possible." He recounted his futile attempt to be accepted as a student in Ibn Sina's school for physicians.

The story of the panther had now spread to the far corners of the hall, and the great auditorium shook under the steady thunder of stamping feet.

Doubtless Alā Shah was accustomed to fear and obedience but perhaps it had been a long time since he had been spontaneously cheered. From the look of his face, the sound came to him like the sweetest music.

"Hah!" The one true Shah leaned forward, his eyes shining, and Rob knew he was remembered in the incident of the killing of the panther.

His eyes held Rob's for a moment and then he turned to the Imam and spoke for the first time since the beginning of the audience.

"Give the Hebrew a *calaat*," he said.

For some reason, people laughed.

"You shall come with me," the grizzled officer said. He would be an old man before many years, but for now he was still powerful and strong. He wore a short helm of polished metal, a leather doublet over a brown military tunic, and sandals with leather thongs. His wounds spoke for him: the ridges of healed sword cuts stood out whitely on both massive brown arms, his left ear was flattened, and his mouth was permanently crooked because of an old piercing wound below his right cheekbone.

"I am Khuff," he said. "Captain of the Gates. I inherit chores such as yourself." His eyes went to Rob's raw neck and he smiled. "The *carcan?*"

"Yes."

"The *carcan* is a bastard," Khuff said admiringly.

They left the Hall of Pillars and walked toward the stables. Now on the long green field men galloped their horses at one another, wheeling and brandishing long shafts like reversed shepherd's crooks, but no one fell.

"They seek to strike each other?"

"They seek to strike a ball. It is ball-and-stick, a horsemen's game." Khuff studied him. "There is much you don't know. Do you understand about the *calaat?*"

Rob shook his head.

"In ancient times when someone found favor in the eyes of a Persian king, the monarch would remove a *calaat*, an item of his own clothing, and bestow it as a token of his pleasure. The custom has come down through the ages as a sign of royal favor. Now the 'royal garment' consists of a living, a suit of clothes, a house, and a horse."

Rob felt numb. "Then am I rich?"

Khuff grinned at him as though he were a fool. "A *calaat* is a singular honor but varies widely in its sumptuousness. An ambassador from a nation that has been Persia's close ally in war would be given the most costly raiment, a palace close in splendor to the House of Paradise, and a remarkable steed whose harness and trappings are encrusted with precious stones. But you are not an ambassador."

Behind the stables was a vast stock pen that enclosed a swirling sea of horses. Barber had always said that in selecting a horse one should look for an animal with a head like a princess and a hind like a fat whore. Rob saw a gray that fit the description perfectly and had additional regality in the eyes.

"Can I have that mare?" he asked, pointing it out. Khuff didn't bother to answer that it was a horse for a prince, but a wry smile did strange things to his twisted mouth. The Captain of the Gates unhitched a saddled horse and mounted. He rode into the milling mass and skillfully separated from the herd an adequate but dispirited brown gelding with short, sturdy legs and strong shoulders.

Khuff showed him a large tulip brand on the horse's near thigh. "Alā Shah is the only horse breeder in Persia, and this is his mark. This horse may be traded for another bearing the tulip but must never be sold. If he should die, cut off the skin with the mark on it and I will exchange it for another horse."

Khuff gave him a purse containing fewer coins than Rob might earn by selling the Specific at a single entertainment. In a nearby warehouse the Captain of the Gates searched until he found a serviceable saddle from the army's stores. The clothing he issued was similarly well made but plain, consisting of loose trousers that fastened at the waist with a drawstring; linen wrappings that went around each leg outside the pants, like bandages worn from ankle to knee; a loose shirt called a *khamisa* that hung over the trousers, knee-length; a tunic called a *durra;* two coats for the different seasons, one short and light, the other long and lined with sheepskin; a cone-shaped turban support called a *qalansuwa;* and a brown turban.

"Do you have green?"

"This is better. The green turban is poor, heavy stuff, worn by students and the poorest of the poor."

"Nevertheless I want it," Rob insisted, and Khuff gave him the cheap green turban and a hard look of scorn.

Minions with watchful eyes leaped to do the captain's bidding when he called for his personal horse, which turned out to be an Arab stallion bearing resemblance to the gray mare Rob had coveted. Riding the placid brown gelding and carrying a cloth bag laden with his new garments, he rode behind Khuff like a squire, all the way to Yehuddiyyeh. For a long time they wended the narrow streets of the Jewish quarter, until finally Khuff reined up at a small house of old, dark-red brick. There was a small stable, merely a roof on four poles, and a tiny garden in which a lizard blinked at Rob and then vanished into a crack in the stone wall. Four overgrown apricot trees cast their shade on thornbushes that would have to be cut out. Inside the house were three rooms, one with an earthen floor and two with floors of the same red brick as the walls, worn into shallow troughs by the feet of many generations. The dried mummy of a mouse lay in a corner of the dirt-floored room and the faint, cloying stink of its decay hung in the air.

"Yours," Khuff said. He nodded once and then went away.

Even before the sound of his horse had vanished, Rob's knees gave way. He sank to the dirt floor, then he allowed himself to lie back and know no more than the dead mouse.

He slept for eighteen hours. When he woke he was cramped and aching, like an old man with frozen joints. He sat in the silent house and watched the dust motes in the sunlight that shone through the smoke hole in the roof. The house was in slight disrepair—there were cracks in the clay plaster of the walls and one of the windowsills was crumbling—but it was the first dwelling that had been truly his since his parents died.

In the small barn, to his horror his new horse stood waterless, unfed, and still saddled. After removing the saddle and carrying water in his hat from a nearby public well, he hurried to the stable where his mule and donkey were boarded. He bought wooden buckets, millet straw, and a basket of oats and bore them home on the donkey.

When the animals were tended, he took his new clothes and walked toward the public baths, stopping first at the inn of Salman the Lesser.

"I've come for my belongings," he told the old innkeeper.

"They've been kept safe, though I mourned for your life when two nights passed and you didn't return." Salman stared at him fearfully. "A story is being told of a foreign *Dhimmi*, a European Jew, who went before the audience and won a *calaat* from the Shah of Persia."

Rob nodded.

"It was indeed you?" Salman whispered.

Rob sat heavily. "I haven't eaten since you fed me last."

Salman lost no time in setting food before him. He tried his stomach gingerly on bread and goat's milk and then, feeling nothing but famine, graduated to four boiled eggs, more bread in quantity, a small hard cheese, and a bowl of *pilah*. Strength began to steal back into his limbs.

At the baths he soaked long, soothing his bruises. When he put on his new clothing he felt like a stranger, though not so much of a stranger as he had felt the first time he put on the caftan. He managed the leg bindings with difficulty, but wrapping the turban would require instruction and for the time being he retained the leather Jew's hat.

Back at the house, he rid himself of the dead mouse and assessed his situation. He had a modest prosperity but that wasn't what he had requested of the Shah, and he felt a vague apprehension that was presently interrupted by the arrival of Khuff, still surly, who unrolled a flimsy parchment and proceeded to read it aloud.

ALLAH

Edict of the King of the World, High and Majestic Lord, Sublime and honorable beyond all comparison; magnificent in Titles, the unshakeable Basis of the Kingdom, Excellent, Noble and Magnanimous; the Lion of Persia and Most Powerful Master of the Universe. Directed to the Governor, the Intendant, and other Royal Officers of the Town of Ispahan, the Seat of the Monarchy and the Theater of Science and Medicine. They are to know that Jesse son of Benjamin, Jew and Barber-Surgeon of the Town of Leeds in Europe, has come into our Kingdoms, the best govern'd of all the Earth and a well-known refuge of the oppress'd, and has had the Facility and the Glory to appear before the Eyes of the Most High, and by humble petition beg the assistance of the true Lieutenant of the true Prophet who is in Paradise, to wit, our most Noble Majesty. They are to know that Jesse son of Benjamin of Leeds is assured of Royal Favor and Good Will and is hereby granted a Royal Garment with Honors and Beneficences and that All should treat him accordingly. You must also know that this Edict is made on rigorous Penalties and that there is no infringing it without being expos'd to Capital Punishment. Done on the third Panj Shanbah of the Month of Rejab in the name of our most high Majesty by his Pilgrim of the Noble and Sacred Holy Places, and his Chief and Superintendent of the Palace of Women of the most High, the Imam Mirza-aboul Qandrasseh, Vizier. *It is necessary to arm one's self with the Assistance of the most High God, in all Temporal Affairs.*

"But, of the *school?*" Rob could not resist asking hoarsely.

"I do not deal with the school," the Captain of the Gates said, and departed as hurriedly as he had come.

A short time later two burly porters delivered to Rob's door a sedan chair bearing the *hadji* Davout Hosein and a quantity of figs as a token of sweet fortune in the new house.

They sat among the ants and the bees on the ground in the ruins of the tiny apricot garden and ate the figs.

"They are still excellent apricot trees," the *hadji* said, studying them judiciously. He explained at great length how the four trees could be brought back through assiduous pruning and irrigation and application of the horse's manure.

Finally Hosein fell silent.

"Something?" Rob murmured.

"I have the honor to extend the greetings and felicitations of the honorable Abu Ali at-Husain ibn Abdullah ibn Sina." The *hadji* was sweating and so pale that the *zabiba* on his forehead was especially pronounced. Rob took pity on him, but not so much that it diminished the exquisite pleasure of the moment, sweeter and richer than the dizzying fragrance of the small apricots that littered the ground beneath his trees, as Hosein rendered to Jesse son of Benjamin an invitation to enroll in the *madrassa* and study medicine at the *maristan*, where he might aspire eventually to become a physician.

PART FOUR

The Maristan

Chapter 39

IBN SINA

Rob J.'s first morning as a student dawned hot, a sullen day. He dressed carefully in the new clothes but decided it was too warm for leg wrappings. He had struggled without success to learn the secret of winding the green turban and finally he gave a coin to a street youth who showed him how to strap the folded cloth tightly around the *qalansuwa* and then tuck it in neatly. But Khuff had been right about the heaviness of the cheap stuff; the green turban weighed almost a stone, and in the end he took the unfamiliar burden from his head and put on the leather Jew's hat, a relief.

It made him instantly identifiable as he approached the Big Teat, where a group of young men in green turbans stood talking.

"Here is your Jew now, Karim," one of them called.

A man who had been sitting on the steps rose and approached him, and he recognized the handsome, lanky student he had observed castigating a nurse during his first visit to the hospital.

"I am Karim Harun. And you are Jesse ben Benjamin."

"Yes."

"The *hadji* has assigned me to show you around the school and the hospital and to answer your questions."

"You will wish you were back in the *carcan*, Hebrew!" somebody called, and the students laughed.

Rob smiled. "I do not think so," he said. It was obvious that the entire school had heard of the European Jew who had gone to jail and then won admittance to the medical school on the intervention of the Shah.

They began with the *maristan*, but Karim walked much too fast, a cranky and perfunctory guide who evidently wished to complete an unwelcome task as quickly as possible. But Rob J. was able to learn that the hospital was divided into male and female sections. Men had male nurses, women had female nurses and female porters. Physicians and a patient's husband were the only men allowed to approach the women.

There were two rooms devoted to surgery, and a long, low-ceilinged chamber filled with shelves of neatly labeled jars and flasks. "This is the *khazanat-ul-sharaf,* the 'treasure house of drugs,' " Karim said. "On Mondays and Thursdays, physicians hold a clinic at the school. After patients are examined and treated, the druggists make up physick prescribed by the physicians. *Maristan* druggists are accurate to the smallest grain, and honest. Most druggists in the town are whores who will sell a bottle of piss and swear it is rose water."

In the school building next door, Karim showed him examining rooms, lecture halls and laboratories, a kitchen and a refectory, and a large bath for use of faculty and students. "There are forty-eight physicians and surgeons, but not all are lecturers. Including yourself, there are twenty-seven students of medicine. Each clerk is apprenticed to a series of different physicians. The apprenticeships vary in length for different individuals, and so does the entire clerkship. You become a candidate for oral examination whenever the bastardly faculty decides you are ready. If you pass, they address you as *Hakim.* If you fail, you remain a student and must work toward another chance."

"How long have you been here?"

Karim glowered, and Rob knew he had asked the wrong question.

"Seven years. I've taken examinations twice. Last year, I failed the section on philosophy. My second attempt was three weeks ago, when I made a poor thing of questions on jurisprudence. What should I care about the history of logic or the precedents of the law? I'm already a good physician." He sighed bitterly. "In addition to classes in medicine you must attend lectures in law, theology, and philosophy. You may choose your own classes. It's best to return often to the same lecturers," he disclosed grudgingly, "for some of them are merciful during the oral examinations if they've become familiar with you.

"Everyone in the *madrassa* must attend morning lectures in each discipline. But in the afternoon, law students prepare briefs or attend the courts, would-be theologians hie themselves to mosques, future philosophers read or write, and medical students serve as clerks at the hospital. Physicians visit the hospital in the afternoon and students attach themselves to these men, who permit them to examine patients and propose treatment. The physicians ask endless instructive questions. It's a splendid opportunity to learn or"—he smiled sourly—"to make yourself a complete arsehole."

Rob studied the handsome, unhappy face. Seven years, he thought numbly, and nothing but uncertain prospects ahead. And this man no doubt had entered the study of medicine with far better preparation than his own sketchy background!

But fears and negative feelings vanished when they entered the library, which was called the House of Wisdom. Rob had never imagined so many books in one place. Some manuscripts were scribed on animalskin vellums, but most were made of the same lighter material on which his *calaat* had been written. "Persia has a poor parchment," he observed.

Karim snorted. "Not parchment at all. It is called paper, an invention of the slanted-eyes to the east, who are very clever infidels. You don't have paper in Europe?"

"I've never seen it there."

"Paper is but old rags beaten and sized with animal glue and then pressed. It is inexpensive, afforded even by students."

The House of Wisdom dazzled Rob as no other sight he had ever seen. He walked quietly about the room and touched the books, noting the authors, only a few of them names he knew.

Hippocrates, Dioscorides, Ardigenes, Rufas of Ephesus, the immortal Galen . . . Oribasius, Philagrios, Alexander of Tralles, Paul of Aegina . . .

"How many books are here?"

"The *madrassa* owns almost one hundred thousand books," Karim said proudly. He smiled at the disbelief in Rob's eyes. "Most of them were translated into Persian in Baghdad. In the university at Baghdad is a school for translators, where books are transcribed onto paper in all the languages of the Eastern Caliphate. Baghdad has an enormous university with six hundred thousand books in its library, and more than six thousand students and famous teachers. But there is one thing our little *madrassa* has that they lack."

"What is that?" Rob asked, and the senior student led him to a wall in the House of Wisdom entirely devoted to the works of one author.

"Him," Karim said.

That afternoon in the *maristan* Rob saw the man the Persians called the Chief of Princes. At first glimpse, Ibn Sina was a disappointment. His red physician's turban was faded and carelessly wound and his *durra* was shabby and plain. Short and balding, he had a bulbous, veined nose and the beginning of dewlaps beneath his white beard. He looked like any aging Arab until Rob noted his keen brown eyes, sad and observant, stern and curiously alive, and felt at once that Ibn Sina saw things not visible to ordinary men.

Rob was one of seven students who, with four physicians, trailed behind Ibn Sina as he made his way through the hospital. That day the Chief Physician paused not far from the pallet of a wizened man with skinny limbs.

"Who is student clerk of this section?"

"I, Master. Mirdin Askari."

So this was Aryeh's cousin, Rob told himself. He looked with interest at the swarthy young Jew whose long jaw and square white teeth gave him a homely, likable face, like that of an intelligent horse.

Ibn Sina nodded toward the patient. "Tell us of that one, Askari."

"He is Amahl Rahin, a camel driver who came to the hospital three weeks ago with intense pain in the lower back. At first we suspected he had injured his spine while drunk but the pain soon extended into his right testicle and right thigh."

"How of the urine?" Ibn Sina asked.

"Until the third day his urine was clear. Light yellow in color. On the morning of the third day his urine showed blood, and that afternoon he passed six urinary calculi, four like grains of sand and two of them stones the size of small peas. Since then he has had no further pain and his urine is clear, but he will take no food."

Ibn Sina frowned. "What have you offered him?"

The student appeared puzzled. "The usual fare. *Pilah* of several sorts. Hens' eggs. Mutton, onions, bread . . . He will touch nothing. His bowels have ceased to function, his pulse is fainter, and he grows progressively weak."

Ibn Sina nodded and looked at them. "What ails him, then?"

Another of the medical clerks gathered his courage. "I think, Master, that his intestines have become twisted, blocking the passage of food through his body. Sensing this, he will allow no nourishment to enter his mouth."

"Thank you, Fadil ibn Parviz," Ibn Sina said with courtesy. "But in such an injury the patient will eat, only to cast up his food." He waited. When no other observations were forthcoming, he approached the man on the pallet.

"Amahl," he said, "I am Husayn the Physician, son of Abd-Ullah who was son of al-Hasan who was son of Ali who was son of Sina. These are my friends and would be thine. Where are you from?"

"The village of Shaini, Master," the man whispered.

"Ah, a man of Fars! I have spent happy days in Fars. The dates of the oasis in Shaini are large and sweet, is it not so?"

Tears formed in Amahl's eyes, and he nodded dumbly.

"Askari, go now and fetch our friend dates and a bowl of warm milk."

In a short time the food was brought, and the physicians and the students watched as the man began to eat the fruit hungrily.

"Slowly, Amahl. Slowly, my friend," Ibn Sina warned. "Askari, you shall see to the change in our friend's diet."

"Yes, Master," the Jew said as they walked away.

"This must be remembered about the sick people in our care. They come to us but they do not become us, and very often they do not eat what we eat. Lions do not relish hay because they visit the kine.

"Dwellers in the desert subsist mainly on sour curds and similar preparations of milk. The inhabitants of the Dar-ul-Maraz eat rice and dry foods. The Khorasanis want only soup thickened with flour. The Indians eat peas, pulse, oil, and hot spices. The people of Transoxiania take wine and meat, especially horse flesh. The people of Fars and Arabistan eat mainly dates. The Bedouins are accustomed to meat, camel's milk, and locusts. The people of Gurgan, the Georgians, the Armenians, and the Europeans are wont to take spirits with meals and to eat the flesh of cows and pigs."

Ibn Sina looked flintily at the men gathered about him. "We terrify them, young masters. Ofttimes we cannot save them and sometimes our treatment kills them. Let us not starve them as well."

The Chief of Princes walked away from them, his hands behind his back.

Next morning, in a small amphitheater with rising tiers of stone seats, Rob attended his first lecture at the *madrassa.* Out of nervousness he was early, and he was seated alone in the fourth row when half a dozen clerks entered together.

At first they paid him no attention. From their conversation it was evident that one of them, Fadil ibn Parviz, had been notified he would be examined for his fitness to become a physician, and his fellow clerks were reacting with envious gibes.

"Only one week before your examination, Fadil?" said a short, plump clerk. "You will piss green with fear, I think!"

"Shut your fat face, Abbas Sefi, you Jew's nose, you Christian's prick! You needn't be afraid of the examination, for you'll be a clerk even longer than Karim Harun," Fadil said, and they all laughed.

"*Salaam,* what have we here?" Fadil said, noticing Rob for the first time. "What's your name, *Dhimmi?*"

"Jesse ben Benjamin."

"Ah, of jail fame! The Jew barber-surgeon of the Shah's *calaat.* You'll find it takes more than a royal decree to make a physician."

The hall was filling. Mirdin Askari was picking his way up the stone tiers to a vacant place, and Fadil called to him.

"Askari! Here's another Hebrew arrived to be made into a leech. You'll soon quite outnumber us."

Askari looked over at them coolly, disregarding Fadil as he might have ignored a bothersome insect.

Further comment was cut off by the arrival of the lecturer, a worried-looking teacher of philosophy named Sayyid Sa'di.

Rob received an inkling of what he had assumed by fighting to become a medical clerk, for Sayyid looked about the room and noted a face that was strange to him.

"You, *Dhimmi*, what is your name?"

"I am Jesse ben Benjamin, master."

"Jesse ben Benjamin, tell us how Aristotle described the relationship between the body and the spirit."

Rob shook his head.

"It is in his work, *On the Soul*," the lecturer said impatiently.

"I don't know *On the Soul*. I've never read Aristotle."

Sayyid Sa'di stared at him with concern. "You must begin to do so at once," he said.

Rob understood little that Sayyid Sa'di spoke about in his lecture.

When the class was over and the amphitheater was emptying, he made his way to Mirdin Askari. "I bring you the best wishes of three men of Masqat, Reb Lonzano ben Ezra, Reb Loeb ben Kohen, and your cousin, Reb Aryeh Askari."

"Ah. Was their trip successful?"

"I believe it was."

Mirdin nodded. "Good. You are a Jew from Europe, I hear. Well, Ispahan will seem strange to you, but most of us are from other places." Their fellow medical clerks, he said, included fourteen Muslims from countries of the Eastern Caliphate, seven Muslims from the Western Caliphate, and five Eastern Jews.

"I'm only the sixth Jewish clerk, then? I would have thought us more numerous, from what Fadil ibn Pardiz said."

"Oh, Fadil! Even one Jewish medical clerk would be too many to please Fadil. He's an Ispahani. Ispahanis consider Persia the only civilized nation and Islam the only religion. When Muslims exchange insults, they call each other 'Jew' or 'Christian.' When they're in a good mood, they consider it the soul of wit to call another Mohammedan '*Dhimmi*.'"

Rob nodded, remembering that when the Shah had called him "Hebrew" people had laughed. "It makes you angry?"

"It makes me work my mind and arse hard. So I can smile when I leave the Muslim clerks far behind me in the *madrassa.*" He looked at Rob curiously. "They say you're a barber-surgeon. Is it true?"

"Yes."

"I wouldn't talk about it," Mirdin said cautiously. "Persian physicians believe barber-surgeons to be . . ."

"Less than admirable?"

"They are not in favor."

"I don't care what's in favor. I make no apology for what I am."

He thought he saw a flicker of approval in Mirdin's eyes, but if so it was gone in a moment.

"Nor should you," Mirdin said. He nodded coolly and made his way out of the amphitheater.

A lesson in Islamic theology taught by a fat *mullah* named Abul Bakr was only slightly better than the philosophy class. The Qu'ran was divided into one hundred and fourteen chapters called *suras.* The *suras* varied in length from a few lines to several hundred verses, and to Rob's dismay he learned he could not be graduated from the *madrassa* until he had memorized the important *suras.*

During the next lecture, by a master surgeon named Abu Ubayd al-Juzjani, he was ordered to read *Ten Treatises on the Eye* by Hunayn. Al-Juzjani was small and swarthy and fearsome, with an unblinking stare and the disposition of a newly awakened bear. The rapid accumulation of assigned scholarly work chilled Rob, but he was interested in al-Juzjani's lecture about the opacity that covered the eyes of so many people and robbed them of vision. "It is believed such blindness is caused by a pouring-out of corrupt humor into the eye," al-Juzjani said. "For this reason early Persian physicians called the ailment *nazul-i-ab,* or 'descent of water,' which has been vulgarized into waterfall disease or cataract."

The surgeon said most cataracts began as a small spot in the lens that scarcely interfered with vision but gradually spread until the entire lens became milky white, causing blindness.

Rob watched as al-Juzjani couched the eyes of a dead cat. Soon thereafter, his assistants passed among the clerks and distributed animal corpses so they might try the procedure on dogs and cats and even hens. Rob was given a brindle cur with a fixed stare, a permanent snarl, and no front paws. His hands were unsteady and he had no real idea of what to do. But he took courage from recalling how Merlin had rid Edgar Thorpe of his blindness because he had been taught this operation at this school, perhaps even in this very room.

Suddenly al-Juzjani was leaning over him and peering at the eye of his dead dog. "Place your needle upon the spot at which you intend to couch and make a mark there," he said sharply. "Then move the tip of the needle toward the outer angle of the eye, level with and slightly above the pupil. This would make the cataract sink below it. If you are operating on the right eye, you hold the needle in your left hand, and vice versa."

Rob followed the instructions, thinking of the men and women who had come behind his barber-surgeon's screen through the years with opaque eyes, and for whom he had been able to do nothing.

To hell with Aristotle and the Qu'ran! This was why he had made his way to Persia, he told himself exultantly.

That afternoon he was among a group of clerks following al-Juzjani through the *maristan* like acolytes trailing a bishop. Al-Juzjani visited patients and taught and commented and questioned the students as he changed dressings and removed stitches. Rob saw that he was a surgeon of skill and diversity; his patients in the hospital that day were recovering from cataract surgery, a crushed and amputated arm, the excision of buboes, circumcisions, and the closing of a wound in the face of a boy whose cheek had been perforated by a sharp stick.

When al-Juzjani was through, Rob made the trip through the hospital again, this time behind *Hakim* Jalal-ul-Din, a bonesetter whose patients were rigged with complex systems of retractors, couplers, ropes, and pulleys that Rob regarded with awe.

He had waited nervously to be called upon or questioned, but neither physician had acknowledged his existence. When Jalal was done, Rob aided the porters in feeding patients and cleaning up slops.

He went in search of books when he was finished at the hospital. Copies of the Qu'ran could be found in ample number in the *madrassa* library, and he discovered *On the Soul.* But he learned that the single copy of Hunayn's *Ten Treatises on the Eye* had been taken by someone else, and half a dozen students had applied before him to study the book.

The keeper of the House of Wisdom was a kindly man named Yussuf-ul-Gamal, a calligrapher who spent his spare time with quill and ink, making extra copies of books bought from Baghdad. "You have waited too long. Now it will be many weeks before *Ten Treatises on the Eye* will be available to you," he said. "When a book is advised by a lecturer you must hurry to me at once or others will get here first."

Rob nodded wearily. He carried the two books home, stopping along the way at the Jewish market to buy a lamp and oil from a spare woman with a strong jaw and gray eyes.

"You're the European?"

"Yes."

She beamed. "We are neighbors. I am Hinda, wife of Tall Isak, three houses north of you. You must visit."

He thanked her and smiled, warmed.

"For you, the lowest price. My finest price for a Jew who wormed a *calaat* out of that king!"

At the inn of Salman the Lesser he stopped for a meal of *pilah*, but was dismayed when Salman brought two more neighbors to meet the Jew who had won the *calaat*. They were burly young men, stonecutters by trade—Chofni and Shemuel b'nai Chivi, sons of the widowed Nitka the Midwife, who lived at the end of his street. The brothers patted his back, bade him welcome, tried to buy him wine. "Tell us of the *calaat*, tell us of Europe!" Chofni cried.

Their fellowship was tempting, but he escaped to the loneliness of his house. When he had tended the animals he read the Aristotle in the garden and found it difficult, for meaning eluded him and he was smitten by his ignorance.

As darkness fell he moved indoors and lighted the lamp, and then he turned to the Qu'ran. The *suras* appeared to be arranged according to length, with the longest chapters first. But which were the important *suras* that must be memorized? He hadn't an idea. And there were so many introductory passages; were *they* important?

He was desperate and felt he must begin somewhere.

Glory to God Most High, full of Grace and Mercy; He created All, including Man . . .

He read the passages again and again, but before more than a few verses had been committed to memory, his heavy lids closed. Fully dressed, he sank into deep sleep on the lamplit floor, like a man seeking to escape a sore and vexatious wakefulness.

Chapter 40

AN INVITATION

Rob was awakened each morning by the rising sun glinting through his chamber's narrow window, reflected golden off the tile roofs of Yehud-diyyeh's crazily leaning houses. People appeared in the streets at daybreak, the men going to morning prayers in the synagogues, the women hurrying to tend stalls in the market or to shop early for the best produce of the day.

In the house next door to the north lived a shoemaker named Yaakob ben Rashi, his wife Naoma, and their daughter Lea. The house to the south was occupied by a bread baker named Micah Halevi, his wife Yudit, and three small children, all females. Rob had lived in Yehuddiyyeh only a few days before Micah sent Yudit to Rob's house to deliver a round, flat loaf for his breakfast, still warm and crisp from the oven. Everywhere he went in Yehuddiyyeh, people had a kind word for the foreign Jew who had won the *calaat*.

He was less popular in the *madrassa*, where the Muslim students never called him by name and took open pleasure in addressing him as *Dhimmi*, and where even the Jewish students called him "European."

If his experience as a barber-surgeon wasn't generally admired, it was still useful in the *maristan*, where within three days it was apparent that he could bandage, bleed, and set simple fractures with a skill equal to a graduate of the school. He was relieved of the chore of collecting slops and given duties that more directly involved the care of sick people, and that made his life a little more bearable.

When he asked Abul Bakr which of the one hundred and fourteen *suras* of the Qu'ran were the important ones, he couldn't get an answer. "All are important," the fat *mullah* said. "Some are more important in the eyes of one scholar, others are more important to another scholar."

"But I can't be graduated from this place unless I have memorized the

312

important *suras!* If you don't tell me which they are, how am I to know?"

"Ah," the theology lecturer said. "You must study Qu'ran, and Allah (exalted is He!) will reveal them."

He felt the weight of Mohammed on his back, the eyes of Allah on him always. Everywhere he turned in the school, there inescapably was Islam. A *mullah* sat in every class to make certain Allah (great and mighty is He!) was not profaned.

Rob's first class with Ibn Sina was an anatomy lesson at which they dissected a large pig, forbidden to Muslims as food but permitted for study.

"The pig is a particularly good anatomy subject, because its internal organs are identical to man's," Ibn Sina said, deftly cutting away the skin.

This one was full of tumors.

"These smooth-surfaced growths are likely to cause no harm. But some have grown so fast . . . see, like these—" Ibn Sina said, tipping the heavy carcass so they could better observe, "—that clumps of flesh have crowded against one another like the sections in a head of cauliflower. The cauliflower tumors are deadly."

"Do they appear in humans?" Rob asked.

"We do not know."

"Couldn't we look for them?"

Now the room was silent, the other students contemptuous of the stranger and infidel devil, the assisting instructors watchful. The *mullah* who had slaughtered the pig had lifted his head from his prayer book.

"It is written," Ibn Sina said carefully, "that the dead shall rise and be greeted by the Prophet (may God bless him and greet him!), to live again. Against that day, their bodies must be unmutilated."

After a moment, Rob nodded. The *mullah* returned to his prayers, and Ibn Sina resumed his anatomy lesson.

That afternoon *Hakim* Fadil ibn Parviz was in the *maristan,* wearing a physician's red turban and receiving the congratulations of the medical clerks because he had passed the examination. Rob had no reason to like Fadil but he was excited and glad nevertheless, for any student's success might one day be his own.

Fadil and al-Juzjani were the physicians who made the rounds of patients that day, and Rob followed them along with four other clerks: Abbas Sefi, Omar Nivahend, Suleiman-al-Gamal, and Sabit bin Qurra. At the last moment al-Juzjani and Fadil were joined by Ibn Sina and Rob could feel the general heightening of nervousness, the small excitement that always occurred with the presence of the Chief Physician.

Soon they came to the place for tumor patients. On the pallet closest to the entrance lay a still, hollow-eyed figure, and they paused well away from him. "Jesse ben Benjamin," al-Juzjani said. "Tell us of this man."

"He is Ismail Ghazali. He doesn't know his age but says he was born in Khur during the great spring floods there. I have been told that was thirty-four years ago."

Al-Juzjani nodded approvingly.

"He has tumors in his neck, under his arms, and in his groin that cause him great pain. His father died of similar disease when Ismail Ghazali was a small boy. It agonizes him to urinate. When he does, his water is deep yellow with casts like small red threads. He cannot eat more than a few spoonfuls of gruel without vomiting, so he has been fed lightly and as often as he will accept nourishment."

"Have you bled him this day?" al-Juzjani asked.

"No, *Hakim.*"

"Why have you not?"

"It is unnecessary to cause him further pain." Perhaps if Rob hadn't been thinking of the pig and wondering whether Ismail Ghazali's body was consumed by cauliflower growths, he would not have trapped himself. "By nightfall he will be dead."

Al-Juzjani stared.

"Why do you think this?" Ibn Sina asked.

All eyes were on Rob, but he knew better than to attempt an explanation. "I know it," he said finally, and Fadil forgot his new dignity and guffawed.

Al-Juzjani's face reddened with anger, but Ibn Sina raised his hand to the other physician and indicated that they should continue.

The incident drained Rob's optimistic excitement. That evening he found study to be impossible. The school was a mistake, he told himself. There was nothing that could make him what he was not, and perhaps it was time to acknowledge he wasn't meant to be a physician.

Yet next morning he went to the school and attended three lectures, and in the afternoon he forced himself to follow al-Juzjani on his inspection of patients. As they set off, to Rob's anguish Ibn Sina joined them as he had on the previous day.

When they arrived at the tumor section, a stripling youth lay on the pallet closest to the door.

"Where is Ismail Ghazali?" al-Juzjani asked the nurse.

"Taken during the night, *Hakim.*"

Al-Juzjani made no comment. As they continued on their way, he treated Rob with the icy contempt due an alien *Dhimmi* who had made a fortunate guess.

But when they had completed their visitations and had been dismissed, Rob felt a hand on his arm and turned to look into the old man's unsettling eyes.

"You will come to share my evening meal," Ibn Sina said.

Rob was nervous and expectant that evening as he followed the Chief Physician's directions, riding the brown horse along the Avenue of the Thousand Gardens to the lane leading to Ibn Sina's home. It proved to be an enormous twin-towered residence of stone set among the terraced orchards and vineyards. Ibn Sina, too, had been given a "royal garment" by the Shah, but his *calaat* had come when he was famous and venerated, and the gift had been princely.

Rob was admitted to the walled estate by a gateman who expected him and took his horse. The path to the house was of stone crushed so fine that his footsteps sounded like whispering. As he approached the house, a side door opened and a woman emerged. Young and graceful, she wore a red velvet coat full at the waist and with tinsel edges, over a loose cotton gown of yellow-printed flowers, and although diminutive she walked like a queen. Beaded bracelets clutched her ankles where the scarlet trousers were fastened tightly and ended in woollen fringes over sweet bare heels. Ibn Sina's daughter—if indeed that was who she was—scrutinized him with large dark eyes as curiously as he assessed her, before averting her veiled face from a male, according to Islam.

Behind her came a turbaned figure, enormous as a bad dream. The eunuch's hand was on the jeweled hilt of the dagger in his belt, and he didn't avert his eyes but watched Rob balefully until he saw his charge safely through a door in a garden wall.

Rob was still gazing after them when the front door, a single great stone slab, opened on oiled hinges and a manservant admitted him into spacious coolness.

"Ah, young friend. You are welcome to my house."

Ibn Sina led the way through a series of large rooms whose tiled walls were adorned with rich woven hangings the colors of the earth and the sky. The carpets on the stone floors were thick as turf. In an atrium garden in the heart of the house, a table had been set close to a splashing fountain.

Rob felt awkward, for a servant had never before helped him to be seated. Another brought an earthen tray of flat bread and Ibn Sina sang his

Islamic prayer with unmusical ease. "Do you wish your own blessing?" he asked with grace.

Rob broke one of the flat loaves and it was easily done, for he had become accustomed to the Hebrew thanksgiving: "Blessed art Thou, O Lord our God, King of the Universe, who brings forth bread from the earth."

"Amen," Ibn Sina said.

The meal was simple and excellent, sliced cucumbers with mint and heavy soured milk, a light *pilah* prepared with bits of lean lamb and chicken, stewed cherries and apricots, and a refreshing *sherbet* of fruit juices.

When they had eaten, a man whose ringed nose marked him a slave brought wet cloths for their hands and faces, while other slaves cleared the table and lighted smoky torches to drive away insects.

A bowl of plump pistachios was brought and they sat and cracked the nuts with their teeth and chewed companionably.

"Now." Ibn Sina leaned forward and his remarkable eyes, that could convey so many things, shone bright and attentive in the torchlight. "Let us speak of the reason you knew Ismail Ghazali would die."

Rob told him how, when he was nine years old, by taking his mother's hand he had become aware that she would die. And of how, in the same way, he had learned of his father's impending death.

And he described the others since, the occasional person whose hand in his had brought the piercing dread and awful revelation.

Ibn Sina questioned him patiently as he reported each case, plumbing his memory and making certain that no detail was overlooked. Slowly, the reserve in the old man's face disappeared.

"Show me what you do."

Rob took Ibn Sina's hands and looked into his eyes, and in a little while he smiled. "For now, you need have no fear of death."

"Nor do you," the physician said quietly.

A moment passed and then, *Good Christ!* Rob thought. "Is it truly something *you* can feel as well, Chief Physician?"

Ibn Sina shook his head. "Not as you feel it. In me, it manifests itself as a certainty somewhere deep inside—strong instinct that a patient will or will not die. Down through the years I have talked with other physicians who share this intuition, and we are a larger brotherhood than you may imagine. But never have I met one in whom this gift is stronger than in you. It is a responsibility, and to be equal to it you must make an excellent physician of yourself."

It brought unpleasant reality, and Rob sighed ruefully. "I may end up no physician, for I am not a scholar. Your Muslim students have been force-fed on classical learning all their lives, and the . . . other Jewish clerks were weaned on the fierce scholarship of their study houses. Here in the university they build on these foundations, while I build on two paltry years of schooling, and vast ignorance."

"Then you must build harder and faster than the others," Ibn Sina said without sympathy.

Despair made Rob bold. "Too much is demanded in the school. And some of it I neither want nor need. Philosophy, Qu'ran—"

The old man broke in scornfully. "You make a common error. If you have not studied philosophy, how can you reject it? Science and medicine teach of the body, while philosophy teaches of the mind and the soul, and a physician requires all these as he needs food and air. As for theology, I had memorized the Qu'ran by the age of ten. It is of my faith and not of your own but it will not harm you, and memorizing ten Qu'rans would be small price if it would gain you medical knowledge.

"You have the mind, for we see you grasp a new language, and we detect your promise in a dozen other ways. But you must not fear to allow learning to become a part of you, so that it is as natural as breathing. You must stretch your mind, wide enough to take in all we can give you."

Rob was silent and watchful.

"I've a gift of my own, as strong as yours, Jesse ben Benjamin. I can detect a man in whom there may be a physician, and in you I feel a need to heal, so strong that it burns. But it is not enough to have such a need. A physician is not declared by *calaat*, which is fortunate since there are already too many ignorant physicians. That is why we have the school, to winnow the chaff from the wheat. And when we see a clerk who is worthy, we make his testing especially severe. If our trials are too much for you, then you must forget us and go back to being a barber-surgeon and selling your spurious ointments—"

"Physick," Rob said, glaring.

"Your spurious physick, then. For to be *hakim* must be earned. If you desire it, you must punish yourself for the sake of learning, seek every advantage in keeping up with the other clerks and in excelling them. You must study with the fervor of the blessed or the cursed."

Rob drew a breath, his eyes still locked hotly with Ibn Sina's, and told himself he hadn't struggled across the world to fail.

He rose to take his leave and was struck by a thought. "Do you own Hunayn's *Ten Treatises of the Eye,* Chief Physician?"

Now Ibn Sina smiled. "I do," he said, and hurried to fetch the book and give it to his student.

Chapter 41

THE *MAIDAN*

Early on a hurried morning three soldiers called upon him. He tensed and readied himself for anything, but this time they were all politeness and respect and their batons remained sheathed. Their leader, whose breath revealed he had breakfasted on green onions, bowed deeply.

"We are sent to inform you, master, that there will be a formal session of the court tomorrow after Second Prayer. Recipients of a *calaat* are expected."

Thus, on the following morning Rob found himself once again under the arched and gilded roofs of the Hall of Pillars.

This time the masses of people were absent, which Rob thought a pity, for the *Shahanshah* was resplendent. Alā wore a turban, a flowing tunic, and pointed shoes of purple, trousers and leg wrappings of crimson, and a heavy crown of worked gold. The Vizier, the Imam Mirza-aboul Qandrasseh, sat a smaller throne nearby, dressed as always in *mullah* black.

The *calaat* beneficiaries stood away from the thrones as observers. Rob couldn't see Ibn Sina and recognized no one nearby save for Khuff, Captain of the Gates.

The floor surrounding Alā was spread with carpets lustrous with threads of silk and gold. Seated on cushions on both sides of the throne and facing it was a host of richly caparisoned men.

Rob went to Khuff and touched his arm. "Who are they?" he whispered.

Khuff looked at the foreign Hebrew with scorn but answered patiently, as he was trained to do. "The empire is divided into fourteen provinces, in which there are five hundred and forty-four Considerable Places—cities, walled towns, and castles. These are the *mirzes, chawns, sultans,* and *beglerbegs* who govern the principalities over which Alā-al-Dawla Shah holds sway."

Perhaps the ceremonies would soon begin, for Khuff hurried away and stationed himself inside the door.

The ambassador from Armenia was the first of the envoys to ride into the hall. He was a man still young, with black hair and beard but otherwise a gray eminence, riding a gray mare and wearing silver foxes' tails on a gray silk tunic. One hundred and fifty paces from the throne he was stopped by Khuff, who helped him dismount and conducted him to the throne for the kissing of Alā's feet.

That accomplished, the ambassador presented the Shah with lavish gifts from his own sovereign, including a large crystal lantern, nine small crystal looking-glasses set into gold frames, one hundred and twenty yards of purple cloth, twenty bottles of fine scent, and fifty sables.

Barely interested, Alā welcomed the Armenian to the court and bade him thank his most gracious lord for the gifts.

Next, in rode the ambassador from the Khazars, to be met by Khuff, and the whole performance was played again, save that the gift of the Khazar king was three fine Arabian horses and a chained baby lion that was not tamed, so that in its fright the beast shat upon the gold and silk carpet.

The hall was still, awaiting the Shah's reaction. Alā did not frown or smile, but waited as slaves and servants hastened to remove the offending matter, the gifts, and the Khazar. The courtiers at the Shah's feet sat on their cushions like inanimate statues, their eyes on the King of Kings. They were shadows, ready to move with Alā's body. At last there was an imperceptible signal and a general relaxing as the next envoy, from the Amīr of Qarmatia, was announced and rode a reddish-brown horse into the hall.

Rob continued to stand and gaze respectfully, but within himself he turned from the court and began to do his lessons, silently reviewing. The four elements: earth, water, fire and air; the qualities recognized by touch: cold, heat, dryness, and moisture; the temperaments: sanguineous, phlegmatic, choleric, and saturnine; the faculties: natural, animal, and vital.

He pictured the separate parts of the eye as Hunayn listed them, named seven herbs and medications that were recommended for agues and eighteen for fevers, even recited several times the first nine stanzas of the Qu'ran's third sura, entitled "The Family of 'Imran."

He was becoming pleased with this preoccupation when it was interrupted, and he saw that Khuff was engaged in a tight exchange of words with an imperious white-haired old man on a nervous chestnut stallion.

"I am presented last because I am of the Seljuk Turks, a deliberate slight to my people!"

"Someone must be last, Hadad Khan, and this day it is Your Excellency," the Captain of the Gates said calmly.

In a high fury, the Seljuk attempted to move the large horse past Khuff and ride to the throne. The grizzled old soldier chose to pretend that the steed and not the rider was at fault. "Ho!" Khuff shouted. He grasped the bridle and struck the horse sharply and repeatedly across the nose with his baton, causing the animal to whinny and step back.

Soldiers controlled the chestnut as Khuff helped Hadad Khan to dismount with hands that were not overly gentle, and walked the ambassador to the throne.

The Seljuk performed the *ravi zemin* perfunctorily and in a shaking voice offered the greetings of his leader, Toghrul-beg, presenting no gifts.

Alā Shah said no word to him, but dismissed him coldly with a wave of his hand, and the proceedings were done.

Save for the Seljuk ambassador and the shitting lion, Rob thought the court had been exceedingly dull.

It would have pleased him to make the little house in Yehuddiyyeh better than it had been when Alā Shah bestowed it on him. The work would have taken a few days at most, but an hour had become a precious commodity, and so the windowsills went unrepaired, the cracked walls remained unplastered, the apricot trees were not pruned, and the garden was rank with weeds.

From Hinda, the woman merchant in the Jewish market, he bought three *mezuzot*, the little wooden tubes containing tiny rolled parchments of Scripture. They were part of his disguise; he affixed them to the right-hand post of each of his doors, no less than one handbreadth from the top, as he remembered *mezuzot* had been placed in the Jewish houses of Tryavna.

He described what he wanted to an Indian carpenter and drew sketches in the earth, and with no difficulty the man made him a rough-hewn olivewood table and a pine chair in the European style. He bought a few cooking utensils from a coppersmith. Otherwise, he bothered so little about the house he might have been living in a cave.

Winter was coming. The afternoons were still hot but the night air that drifted through the windows turned raw, announcing the change in season. He found several inexpensive sheepskins in the Armenian market and bedded in them gratefully.

On a Friday evening, his neighbor Yaakob ben Rashi the shoemaker prevailed upon Rob to come to his home for the Sabbath meal. It was a modest but comfortable house, and at first Rob enjoyed the hospitality. Naoma, Yaakob's wife, covered her face and said the blessing over the tapers. The buxom daughter, Lea, served the good meal of river fish, stewed fowl, *pilah,* and wine. Lea mostly kept her eyes modestly downcast, but several times she smiled at Rob. She was of marriageable age and twice during the dinner her father made careful hints about a sizable dowry. There seemed to be general disappointment when Rob thanked them and left early to return to his books.

His life developed a pattern. Daily religious observance was compulsory for *madrassa* students but Jews were allowed to attend their own services, so each morning he went to the House of Peace Synagogue. The Hebrew of the *shaharit* prayers had become familiar but many of them were still as untranslatable as nonsense syllables; nonetheless, the swaying and chanting was a soothing way to begin his day.

Mornings were taken up by lectures in philosophy and religion that he attended with grim purposefulness, and a host of medical courses.

He was getting better at the Persian language, but there were times during a lecture when he was forced to ask the meaning of a word or an idiom. Sometimes the other students explained but often they didn't.

One morning Sayyid Sa'di, the philosophy teacher, mentioned the *gashtagh-daftaran.*

Rob leaned toward Abbas Sefi, who sat next to him. "What is *gashtagh-daftaran?*"

But the plump medical clerk merely cast him an annoyed look and shook his head.

Rob felt a poke in his back. When he turned he saw Karim Harun on the stone tier behind and above him. Karim grinned. "An order of ancient scribes," he whispered. "They recorded the history of astrology and early Persian science." The seat next to him was empty and he pointed to it.

Rob moved. From then on, when he attended a lecture he looked about; if Karim was there, they sat together.

The best part of his day was the afternoon, when he worked in the *maristan.* This became even better in his third month at the school, when it was his turn to examine new patients. The admission process amazed him with its complexity. Al-Juzjani showed him how it was done.

"Listen well, for this is an important task."

"Yes, *Hakim.*" He had learned always to listen well to al-Juzjani, for almost at once he had known that, next to Ibn Sina, al-Juzjani was the best physician in the *maristan.* Half a dozen people had told him al-Juzjani had been Ibn Sina's assistant and lieutenant most of their lives, but al-Juzjani spoke with his own authority.

"You must make note of the patient's entire history, and at first opportunity you will review it in detail with a senior physician."

Each ill person was asked about his occupation, habits, exposure to contagious diseases, and chest, stomach, and urinary complaints. All clothing was removed and a physical scrutiny was done, including appropriate inspection of sputum, vomit, urine, and feces, an assessment of the pulse, and an attempt to detect fever by the warmth of the skin.

Al-Juzjani showed him how to run his hands over both the patient's arms at the same time, then both legs, then each side of the body together, so that any defect, swelling, or other irregularity would be revealed because it felt different from the normal limb or side. And how to strike the patient's body with sharp, short blows of the fingertips in an attempt to discover illness by hearing an abnormal sound. Much of this was new and strange to Rob, but he quickly became familiar with the routine and found it easy because he had worked with patients for years.

His difficult time began early in the evening, after he had arrived back in his house in Yehuddiyyeh, for that is when the battle began between the need to study and the need to sleep. Aristotle proved to be a sapient old Greek and Rob learned that if a subject was captivating, studying changed from a chore to a pleasure. It was a momentous discovery, perhaps the single thing that allowed him to work as doggedly as necessary, for Sayyid Sa'di quickly assigned him readings from Plato and Heraclitus; and al-Juzjani, as casually as if he were requesting another log on the fire, asked him to read the twelve books dealing with medicine in Pliny's *Historia naturalis*—"as preparation for reading all of Galen next year"!

There was constantly Qu'ran to memorize. The more he consigned to his memory, the more resentful he became. Qu'ran was the official compilation of the preachings of the Prophet, and Muhammed's message had been essentially the same for years on end. The book was repetition upon repetition, and filled with calumny against Jews and Christians.

But he persevered. He sold the donkey and the mule so he wouldn't have to spend time tending and feeding them. He ate his meals quickly and without pleasure, and frivolity had no place in his life. Each night he read until he could read no more, and he learned to put minuscule amounts of oil in his lamps, so they would burn themselves out after his head dropped into his arms and he slept over his books at the table. Now he knew why God had given him a great, strong body and good eyes, for he taxed himself to the limit of his endurance as he sought to make himself a scholar.

* * *

One evening, aware only that he could study no more and must escape, he fled the little house in Yehuddiyyeh and plunged into the night life of the *maidans.*

He had grown accustomed to the great municipal squares as they were during the day, sunbaked open spaces with a few people strolling or curled asleep in a patch of shade. But he found that by night the squares became seamy and alive, riotous celebrations jam-packed with the males of common-class Persia.

Everyone appeared to be talking and laughing at once, producing a clamor louder than several Glastonbury Fairs. A group of singing jugglers used five balls and were droll and adept, making him want to join them. Muscular wrestlers, their heavy bodies gleaming with animal grease to make it difficult for opponents to gain a hold, struggled while onlookers screamed advice at them and made wagers. Puppeteers performed a lewd play, acrobats leaped and somersaulted, hucksters of a variety of food and wares vied for the passing trade.

Rob stopped in a torchlit bookstall, where the first volume he examined was a collection of drawings. Each sketch showed the same man and woman, cleverly depicted in a variety of lovemaking positions he had never met even in his imagination.

"The entire sixty-four in pictures, master," the bookseller said.

Rob hadn't the slightest idea what the sixty-four were. He knew it was against Islamic law to sell or own pictures of the human form because Qu'ran said Allah (exalted is He!) was the one and only creator of life. But he was captivated by the book and bought it.

He went next to a refreshment place where the air was thick with babble and ordered wine.

"No wine. This is *chai-khana,* a tea house," the effeminate waiter said. "You may have *chai* or *sherbet,* or rose water boiled with cardamons."

"What is *chai?*"

"Excellent drink. It comes from India, I think. Or perhaps it is carried to us down the Silk Road."

Rob ordered *chai* and a dish of sweetmeats.

"We have a private place. You wish a boy?"

"No."

When the refreshment came the drink was very hot, an amber-colored liquid with a flat, mouth-puckering taste; Rob couldn't decide whether he liked it, but the sweetmeats were very good. From the upper galleries of the arcades near the *maidan* came plangent melody, and when he looked across the square he saw that the music was being played on polished copper trumpets eight feet long. He sat in the dimly lighted *chai-khana,* gazing out at the crowd and drinking *chai* after *chai,* until a storyteller began to regale the patrons with a tale of Jamshid, the fourth of the hero kings. Mythology attracted Rob not much more than pederasty, and he paid the waiter and wove his way through the crowd until he was at the edge of the *maidan.* For a while he stood and watched the mule-drawn carriages that were driven slowly around and around the square, for he had heard of them from other students.

Finally he hailed a well-kept coach with a lily painted on its door.

Inside, it was dark. The woman waited until the mules had begun to draw the carriage before she moved.

Soon he could see her well enough to know that the plump body was old enough to have mothered him. During the act he liked her, for she was an honest whore; she made no simulations of passion or pretense of enjoyment, but cared for him gently and with skill.

Afterward, the woman pulled a cord, signifying completion, and the pimp on the box drew the mules to a halt.

"Take me to Yehuddiyyeh," Rob called. "I'll pay for her time."

They lay companionably in the swaying coach. "What are you called?" he asked.

"Lorna." Well trained, she didn't ask his name.

"I am Jesse ben Benjamin."

"Well met, *Dhimmi,* " she said shyly, and touched the tightened muscles in his shoulders. "Why are these like knots of rope? What do you dread, a great young man like you?"

"I fear I'm an ox when I must be a fox," he said, smiling in the dark.

"You are no ox, as I have learned," she said drily. "What is your trade?"

"I study in the *maristan,* to be a physician."

"Ah. Like the Chief of Princes. My own cousin has been his first wife's cook as long as Ibn Sina has been in Ispahan."

"You know his daughter's name?" he said after a moment.

"There is no daughter, Ibn Sina has no children. He has two wives, Reza the Pious, who is old and sickly, and Despina the Ugly, who is young and beautiful, but Allah (exalted is He!) has blessed neither woman with issue."

"I see," Rob said.

He used her once more in comfortable fashion before the carriage reached Yehuddiyyeh. Then he directed the driver to his door and paid them well for making it possible for him to go inside and light his lamps and face his best friends and worst enemies, the books.

Chapter 42

THE SHAH'S ENTERTAINMENT

He was in a city and surrounded by people but it was a solitary existence. Each morning he came into contact with the other clerks, and each evening he left them. He knew that Karim and Abbas and some of the others lived in cells at the *madrassa* and he assumed that Mirdin and the other Jewish students lived somewhere in Yehuddiyyeh, but he had no idea what any of their lives were like away from the school and the hospital. Much like his own, he supposed, filled with reading and study. He was too busy to be lonely.

He spent only twelve weeks admitting new patients to the hospital, then he was assigned to something he loathed, for apprentice physicians took turns servicing the Islamic court on days when sentences were carried out by the *kelonter*.

His stomach roiled the first time he returned to the jail and walked past the *carcans*.

A guard led him to a dungeon where a man lay tossing and moaning. Where the prisoner's right hand should have been, a hempen cord bound a coarse blue rag to a stump, above which the forearm was dreadfully swollen.

"Can you hear me? I am Jesse."

"Yes, lord," the man muttered.

"What is your name?"

"I am Djahel."

"Djahel, how long since they took your hand?"

The man shook his head in bewilderment.

"Two weeks," the guard said.

Removing the rag, Rob found a packing of horse dung. As a barber-surgeon he had often seen dung used in this way and he knew it was seldom beneficial and perhaps was harmful. He shook it off.

The top of the forearm next to the amputation was ligated with another piece of hemp. Owing to the swelling, the cord had sunk into the tissue and the arm was beginning to turn black. Rob cut the cord and washed the stump slowly and carefully. He anointed it with a mixture of sandalwood and rose water and packed it in camphor in place of the dung, leaving Djahel groaning but relieved.

That was the best part of his day, for he was led from the dungeons to the prison courtyard for the beginning of the punishments.

They were much as he had witnessed them during his own confinement, save that while in the *carcan* he had been able to retreat into unconsciousness. Now he stood stonily among *mullahs* who chanted prayers while a muscular guard lifted an oversized curved sword. The prisoner, a gray-faced man who had been convicted of fomenting treason and sedition, was forced to kneel and lay his cheek against the block.

"I love the Shah! I kiss his sacred feet!" the kneeling man screamed in a vain attempt to avert the sentence, but no one answered him and the sword was already whistling. The blow was clean and the head rolled to come to rest against a *carcan*, the eyes still protruding in anguished fear.

The remains were removed and then a young man who had been caught with another's wife had his belly opened. This time the same executioner wielded a long, slim dagger, a ripping from left to right that efficiently spilled the adulterer's bowels.

Fortunately, there were no murderers, who would have been drawn and quartered, then set out to be consumed by dogs and carrion birds.

Rob's services began to be required after the minor punishments.

A thief who was not yet a man soiled himself in his fright and pain as his hand was taken. There was a jar of hot pitch but Rob didn't need it, for the force of the amputation sealed the stump, which he had only to wash and dress.

He had a messier time with a fat, weeping woman who had been convicted of mocking the Qu'ran for the second time and thus was deprived of her tongue. The red poured through her hoarse, wordless screaming until he succeeded in pinching off a blood vessel.

Within him there was a lush blossoming of hatred for Muslim justice and Qandrasseh's court.

"This is one of your most important tools," Ibn Sina told the medical students solemnly. He held up the urine glass, which he had told them was properly called a *matula*. It was bell-shaped, with a wide, curved lip designed to catch urine. Ibn Sina had trained a glass-blower to make the *matulae* for his doctors and students.

Rob had known that if urine contained blood or pus, something was wrong. But Ibn Sina already had lectured for two weeks on urine alone!

Was it thin or viscous? The subtleties of odor were weighed and discussed. Was there the treacly hint of sugar? The chalky smell that suggested the presence of stones? The sourness of a wasting sickness? Or merely the rank grassiness of someone who has eaten asparagus?

Was the flow copious, which meant the body was flushing out the disease, or sparing, which could signify that internal fevers were drying up the system's fluids?

As to color, Ibn Sina taught them to look at urine with an artist's eye for the palette, twenty-one nuances of color, from clear through yellow, dark ocher, red and brown, to black, showing the various combinations of *contenta*, or undissolved components.

Why all this fuss about piss? Rob asked himself wearily. "Why is the urine so important?" he asked.

Ibn Sina smiled. "It comes from within, where important things happen." The master physician read them a selection from Galen which indicated that the kidneys were the organs for separating out the urine:

Any butcher knows this from the fact that he sees every day the position of the kidneys and the duct (called the ureter) which runs from each kidney into the bladder and by studying this anatomy he reasons what their use is and the nature of their functions.

The lecture left Rob enraged. Physicians shouldn't need to consult with butchers, or learn from dead sheep and pigs how humans were constructed. If it was so bloody important to know what was happening within men and women, *why didn't they look within men and women?* If Qandrasseh's *mullahs* could be blithely evaded for coupling or a drunken binge, why didn't physicians dare to ignore the holy men to gain knowledge? No one spoke of eternal mutilation or the quickening of the dead when a religious court cut off a prisoner's head or hand or tongue or slit his belly.

Early next morning two of Khuff's palace guardsmen, driving a mule cart laden with food supplies, stopped in Yehuddiyyeh to fetch Rob.

"His Majesty will go visiting today, master, and commands your company," one of the soldiers said.

What now? Rob asked himself.

"The Captain of the Gates urges you to hurry." The soldier cleared his throat discreetly. "Perhaps it would be best if the master were to change into his best clothing."

"I am wearing my best clothing," Rob said, and they sat him in the back of the cart atop some sacks of rice and hurried him away.

They traveled out of the city in a line of traffic consisting of courtiers on horseback and in sedan chairs, mingled with all manner of wagons transporting equipment and supplies. Despite his homely perch Rob felt regal, for he had never before been conveyed over roads newly graveled and freshly watered. One side of the road, where the soldiers said only the Shah would travel, was strewn with flowers.

The journey ended at the home of Rotun bin Nasr, general of the army, distant cousin to Alā Shah and honorary governor of the *madrassa.* "That is he," one of the soldiers told Rob, pointing out a beaming fat man, voluble and posturing.

The handsome estate had extensive grounds. The party would begin in a commodious groomed garden, in the center of which a great marble fountain splashed. All around the pool tapestries of silk and gold had been spread, strewn with cushions of rich embroidery. Servants hurried everywhere, carrying trays of sweetmeats, pastries, perfumed wines, and scented waters. Outside a gate at one side of the garden, a eunuch bearing an unsheathed sword guarded the Third Gate, leading to the *haram.* Under Muslim law only the master of a house was allowed in the women's apartment and any male transgressor could have his belly ripped, so Rob was happy to move away from the Third Gate. The soldiers had made it clear that he wasn't expected to unload the cart or otherwise work, and he meandered outside the garden into an adjacent open area crowded with beasts, noblemen, slaves, servants, and an army of entertainers who appeared all to be rehearsing at the same time.

A nobility of four-legged creatures had been assembled. Tethered twenty paces apart were a dozen of the finest white Arabian stallions he had ever seen, nervous and proud, with brave dark eyes. Their trappings were worthy of close inspection, for four of the bridles were adorned with emeralds, two with rubies, three with diamonds, and three with a mixture of colored stones he couldn't identify. The horses were clad in low-hanging, blanketlike garments of gold brocade set with pearls, and tethered with tresses of silk and gold to rings atop thick gold nails that had been driven into the ground.

Thirty paces from the horses were wild beasts: two lions, a tiger, and a leopard, all magnificent specimens, each on its own large piece of scarlet tapestry, tethered in the same manner as the horses and with a golden water bowl.

In a pen beyond, half a dozen white antelopes with long horns straight as arrows—unlike any deer in England!—stood together and nervously eyed the cats, which blinked at them sleepily.

But Rob spent little time with these animals and disregarded gladiators, wrestlers, bowmen, and the like, pushing past them toward a huge object that immediately captured his attention, until finally he stood within touching distance of his first live elephant.

It was even more massive than he had expected, far larger than the brazen elephant statues he had seen in Constantinople. The beast stood half again higher than a tall man. Each of its four legs was a stout column ending in a perfectly round foot. Its wrinkled hide seemed too large for its body and was gray, with large pink splotches like patches of lichen on a rock. Its arched back was higher than the shoulder or the rump, from which dangled a thick rope of tail with a frazzled end. The enormous head caused its pink eyes to seem tiny in comparison, although they weren't smaller than a horse's eyes. On the sloping forehead were two little humps, as if horns were unsuccessfully striving to break through. Each gently waving ear was almost as large as a warrior's shield, but the most extraordinary feature of this extraordinary creature was its nose, which was longer and thicker by far than its tail.

The elephant was cared for by a small-boned Indian in a gray tunic and white turban, sash, and trousers, who told Rob upon questioning that he was Harsha, a *mahout* or elephant tender. The elephant was Alā Shah's personal combat mount and was named Zi, short for Zi-ul-Quarnayn or "Two-Horned One," in honor of the wicked bone protuberances, curved and as long as Rob was tall, that extended from the monster's upper jaw.

"When we go into battle," the Indian said proudly, "Zi wears his own mail and long, sharp swords are fixed on his tusks. He is trained to the onslaught, so that the charge of His Excellency on his trumpeting war elephant is sight and sound to chill any enemy's blood."

The *mahout* kept servants busy carrying buckets of water. These were emptied into a large gold vessel from which the animal sucked water into its nose and then sprayed it into its mouth!

Rob stayed near the elephant until a flourish of drums and cymbals announced the arrival of the Shah, then he returned to the garden with the other guests.

Alā Shah wore simple white clothing, in contrast to the guests, who might have been costumed for an affair of state. He acknowledged the *ravi zemin* with a nod and took his place on a sumptuous chair above the cushions near the pool.

The entertainment began with a demonstration by swordsmen wielding scimitars with such strength and grace that the assemblage fell quiet and gave their attention to the clash of steel on steel, the stylized circling of a combat exercise as ritualized as a dance. Rob noted that the scimitar was lighter than the English sword and heavier than the French; it required both a duelist's skill at the thrust and strong wrists and arms for hacking. He was sorry when the display came to an end.

Acrobat-magicians made a great and busy show of planting a seed in the earth, watering it, and covering it with a cloth. Behind a screen of tumbling bodies, just at the climax of their acrobatics, one of them swept off the cloth, jabbed a leafy twig into the ground, and covered it again. Both the diversion and the deception were nakedly apparent to Rob, who had been watching for them, and he was amused when finally the cloth was removed and people applauded "the magical growing tree."

Alā Shah was visibly restless as wrestling began. "My longbow," he called.

When it arrived he strung and unstrung it, showing his courtiers how easily he bent the heavy weapon. Those nearest him murmured their admiration at his strength, while others took advantage of the relaxed mood to converse, and now Rob learned the reason for his invitation; as a European, he was as much a displayed oddity as any of the animals or the entertainers, and the Persians regaled him with questions.

"Do you have a Shah in your country, that place . . .?"

"England. Yes, a king. His name is Canute."

"Are the men of your country warriors and horsemen?" an old man with wise eyes asked curiously.

"Yes, yes, great warriors, fine horsemen."

"What of the weather and climate?"

Colder and wetter than here, he told them.

"What of the food?"

"It is different from yours, not so many spices. We do not have *pilah*."

It shocked them. "No *pilah*," the old man said with contempt.

They surrounded him, but out of inquisitiveness rather than friendship, and he felt an isolation in their midst.

Alā Shah rose from his chair. "Let us to the horses!" he exclaimed impatiently, and the crowd streamed after him to a nearby field, leaving the wrestlers still grunting and tugging at one another.

"Ball-and-stick, ball-and-stick!" someone called, and there was immediate applause.

"So, let us play," the Shah agreed, and chose three men to be his teammates and four men to oppose them.

The horses that were led onto the field by grooms were tough little ponies at least a hand smaller than the pampered white stallions. When all were mounted, each player was given a long, limber stick that ended in a crook.

At each end of the long field were two stone columns, about eight paces apart. Each team cantered its horses to these goals and lined up in front of them, the riders facing one another like opposing armies. An army officer who would serve as judge stood off to the side and rolled a wooden ball, about the size of an Exmouth apple, into the center of the field.

The people began to shout. The horses hurtled toward one another at a dead gallop, the riders screaming and brandishing their sticks.

God, Rob J. thought in terror. Look out, look out! Three of the horses came together with a sickening sound and one of them went down and rolled over, sending its rider flying. The Shah brought his stick around and stroked the wooden ball soundly, and the horses plunged after it with flying sward and a pounding of hooves.

The fallen horse was neighing shrilly as it struggled to stand on a broken hock. A dozen grooms came and cut its throat and dragged it from the field before its rider had gained his feet. He was holding his left arm and grinning through clenched teeth.

Rob thought the arm might be broken, and approached the injured man. "Shall I help you?"

"You are a physician?"

"A barber-surgeon and a student at the *maristan.*"

The noble grimaced at him in amazed disgust. "No, no. We must summon al-Juzjani," he said, and they led him away.

Another horse and man had joined the game at once. The eight riders apparently had forgotten they were playing and not fighting a battle. They battered their mounts against one another, and in their attempts to flail at the ball and drive it between the goalposts, they struck dangerously close to their opponents and the horses. Even their own mounts weren't safe from their sticks, for the Shah often stroked at the ball close behind his horse's flying hooves and beneath the beast's belly.

The Shah was given no quarter. Men who undoubtedly would have been slain if they had directed a cross look at their sovereign lord now apparently were doing their best to maim him, and from the grunts and whispers of the spectators, Rob J. judged that they wouldn't have been displeased if Alā Shah were struck or thrown.

He was not. Like the others, the Shah rode recklessly, but with a skill numbing to watch, directing his pony without using his hands, which held the stick, and with little apparent gripping of his legs. Instead, Alā maintained a strong, confident seat and rode as if he were an extension of his horse. It was a standard of horseback riding Rob had never met, and he thought with hot embarrassment of the old man who had asked about English horsemanship and had been assured of its excellence.

The horses were a wonder, for they followed after the ball without slackening speed but could wheel instantly and gallop in the opposite direction, and time and again only this fine control prevented horses and riders from careening into the stone goalposts.

The air became choked with dust and the spectators screamed themselves hoarse. Drums were pounded and cymbals jangled ecstatically when someone scored, and presently the Shah's team had driven the ball between the posts five times to their opponents' three, and the game was over. Alā's eyes glistened with satisfaction as he dismounted, for he had scored twice himself. In celebration, as the ponies were led away two young bulls were staked in the center of the field and two lions were turned loose upon them. The contest was puzzlingly unfair, for no sooner had the great cats been released than the bulls were pulled down by their handlers and brained with axes, the felines then being allowed to tear the still-quivering flesh.

Realization came to Rob that this human assistance was given because Alā Shah was the Lion of Persia. It would have been unseemly and the most evil of portents if, by mischance during his own entertainment, a mere bull had gained victory over the symbol of the stalwart might of the King of Kings.

In the garden, four veiled females swayed and danced to the music of pipers while a poet sang of the *houri*, the fresh and sensuous virgin women of Paradise.

The Imam Qandrasseh could have had no objection; though occasionally the curve of a buttock or a thrusting of breast could be seen in the loose stuff of their voluminous black dresses, only the gesturing hands were uncovered, and the feet, rubbed red with henna at which the assembled nobles stared hungrily, reminded of other hennaed places hidden by the black cloth.

Alā Shah rose from his chair and walked away from those around the pool, past the eunuch holding his naked sword, and into the *haram*.

Rob seemed to be the only one staring after the king as Khuff, the Captain of the Gates, came up and began to guard the Third Gate with the eunuch. The level of bright conversation rose; nearby, General Rotun bin Nasr, the host of the king's entertainment and the master of the house, laughed too loudly at his own joke, as if Alā had not just gone in to his wives in full view of half the court.

Is this, then, what may be expected of the Most Powerful Master of the Universe? Rob asked himself.

In an hour the Shah was back, looking benign. Khuff slipped away from the Third Gate and gave an imperceptible sign, and the feasting began.

The finest white plate was set on cloths of Qum brocade. Bread of four sorts was brought, and eleven kinds of *pilah* in silver basins so large a single dish would have served the assemblage. The rice in each basin was of a different color and flavor, having respectively been prepared with saffron, or sugar, or peppers, or cinnamon, or cloves, or rhubarb, or pomegranate juice, or the juice of citrons. Four of the enormous trenchers each contained twelve fowl, two contained braised haunches of antelope, one was heaped high with broiled mutton, and four contained whole lambs that had been cooked on a spit to a tender, juicy crackliness.

Barber, Barber, a pity you are not here!

For one who had been taught the appreciation of savory food by such a master, in recent months Rob had had more than his share of hurried, spartan meals in order to devote himself to the scholar's life. Now he sighed and tasted everything with a will.

As the long shadows turned to dusk, slaves fixed great tapers to the horny carapaces of living tortoises and lighted them. Four oversized kettles were carried in, each hauled from the kitchen on poles; one was full of hens' eggs made into a cream pudding, one held a rich clear soup with herbs, another was filled with hashed meat made pungent with spices, and the last with slabs of fried fish of a type unfamiliar to Rob, the meat white and flaky like plaice but with the delicacy of trout.

Shadows turned to darkness. Night birds cried; otherwise the only sounds were soft murmurings, belches, the tearing and crunching of food. Once in a while a tortoise sighed and moved, and the light cast by its candle shifted and flickered, like the moon's glow shivering on water.

And still they ate.

There was a plate of winter salad, root herbs preserved in brine. And a bowl of summer salad, including Roman lettuce and bitter, peppery greens he had never tasted before.

A deep porringer was set before each person and filled with a sweet-and-sour *sherbet*. And now servants bore in goatskins of wine, and cups, and dishes of pastries and honeyed nuts and salted seeds.

Rob sat alone and sipped the good wine, neither speaking nor addressed, watching and listening to everything with the same curiosity with which he had tasted the food.

The goatskins were emptied of wine and full ones were brought, an inexhaustible supply from the Shah's own storehouse. People rose and went off to relieve themselves or to vomit. Some were sodden and inert from drink.

The tortoises moved together, perhaps out of nervousness, pooling the light in a corner and leaving the rest of the garden in darkness. Accompanied by a lyre, a boy eunuch with a high, sweet voice sang of warriors and love, ignoring the fact that near him two men were fighting.

"Slit of a whore," one of them snarled drunkenly.

"Face of a Jew!" the other spat.

They grappled and rolled, till they were separated and dragged off.

Eventually the Shah became nauseated and then unconscious, and was carried to his carriage.

After that Rob slipped away. There was no moon and the way from Rotun bin Nasr's estate was hard to follow. Out of a deep and bitter urge, he walked on the Shah's side of the road and once stopped to piss long and satisfyingly on the strewn flowers.

Horsemen and driven conveyances passed him but no one offered a ride, and it took him hours to return to Ispahan. The sentry had grown accustomed to stragglers returning from the Shah's entertainment, and the soldier waved him wearily through the gate.

Halfway across Ispahan Rob stopped and sat on a low wall and contemplated this strangest of cities, where everything was forbidden by the Qu'ran and committed by the people. A man was allowed four wives but most men seemed willing to risk death to sleep with other women, while Alā Shah openly fucked whomever he pleased. Taking wine was proscribed by the Prophet as a sin, yet there was a national craving for wine and a large percentage of the populace drank to excess, and the Shah owned a vast storehouse of fine vintages.

Musing on the puzzle that was Persia, he went home on unsteady legs under pearling skies and to the lovely sound of the *muezzin* from the minaret of the Friday Mosque.

Chapter 43

THE MEDICAL PARTY

Ibn Sina was accustomed to the pious doomsaying of Imam Qandrasseh, who could not control the Shah but who had been warning his advisers with increasing stridency that wine-drinking and licentiousness would bring retribution from a force higher than the throne. To this end the Vizier had been collecting intelligence from abroad and presenting a pattern of evidence that Allah (all-powerful is He!) was furious with sinners all over the earth.

Travelers along the Silk Road had brought word of disastrous earthquakes and pestilential fogs in the part of China watered by the Kiang and Hoai rivers. In India, a year of drought had been followed by plentiful spring rain, but the burgeoning crops were devoured by a plague of locusts. Great storms had battered the coast of the Arabian Sea, causing flooding that drowned many, while in Egypt there was famine due to the failure of the Nile to rise to the requisite level. In Maluchistan, a smoking mountain opened and spewed forth a river of molten rock. Two *mullahs* in Nain reported that demons appeared to them in their sleep. Exactly one month before the fast of *Ramadan* there was a partial eclipse of the sun, and then the heavens appeared to burn; strange celestial fires were observed.

The worst portent of Allah's displeasure came from the royal astrologers, who reported with great trepidation that within two months there would be a grand conjunction of the three superior planets, Saturn, Jupiter, and Mars, in the sign of Aquarius. There were disputes about the exact date when this would occur, but no disagreement about its gravity. Even Ibn Sina heard the news gravely, for he knew that Aristotle had written of the menace inherent in the conjunction of Mars and Jupiter.

So it seemed preordained when Qandrasseh summoned Ibn Sina one bright, terrible morning and told him pestilence had broken out in Shīrāz, the largest city in the territory of Anshan.

"What pestilence?"

"The Death," the Imam said.

Ibn Sina blanched and hoped the Imam was wrong, for the Death had been absent from Persia for three hundred years. But his mind went directly to the problem. "Soldiers must be ordered down the Spice Road at once, to turn back all caravans and travelers coming from the south. And we must send a medical party to Anshan."

"We do not gain very much from Anshan in taxes," the Imam said, but Ibn Sina shook his head.

"It is in our self-interest to contain the disease, for the Death moves readily from place to place."

By the time he had returned to his own home, Ibn Sina had decided he couldn't send a group of his own colleagues, for if the plague should reach Ispahan the physicians would be needed in their own territory. Instead, he would select one physician and a party of apprentices.

The emergency should be used to temper the best and the strongest, he decided. After some consideration, Ibn Sina took quill, ink, and paper and wrote:

> *Hakim* Fadil ibn Parviz, leader
> Suleiman-al-Gamal, third-year clerk
> Jesse ben Benjamin, first-year clerk
> Mirdin Askari, second-year clerk

The party should also contain some of the school's weakest candidates, in order to give them a single, Allah-sent opportunity to redeem their unfavorable records and go on to become physicians. To this end he added to the list the names:

> Omar Nivahend, third-year clerk
> Abbas Sefi, third-year clerk
> Ali Rashid, first-year clerk
> Karim Harun, seventh-year clerk.

When the eight young men were assembled and the Chief Physician told them he was sending them to Anshan to fight the Death, they couldn't look at him or at one another; it was a form of embarrassment.

"You must each wear arms," Ibn Sina said, "for it is impossible to determine how people will act when there is a plague."

There was a long, shuddering sigh from Ali Rashid. He was sixteen years old, a round-cheeked boy with soft eyes, so homesick for his family in Hamadhān that he wept day and night and couldn't apply himself to his studies.

Rob forced himself to concentrate on what Ibn Sina was saying.

". . . We cannot tell you how to fight it, for it hasn't appeared in our lifetimes. But we have a book compiled three centuries ago by physicians who survived plagues in different places. We shall give this book to you. Doubtless it contains many theories and remedies of little value, but among them might be information that will be effective." Ibn Sina stroked his beard. "Against the possibility that the Death is caused by atmospheric contamination from putrid effluvia, I think you must kindle huge fires of aromatic woods in the vicinity of both the sick and the healthy. The healthy should wash in wine or vinegar and sprinkle their houses with vinegar, and they should sniff camphor and other volatile substances.

"You who will care for the sick should do these things also. You would do well to hold vinegar-soaked sponges to your noses when you approach the afflicted, and to boil all water before drinking, to clarify it and separate off the impurities. And you must manicure your hands daily, for the Qu'ran says the Devil hides beneath the fingernails."

Ibn Sina cleared his throat. "Those who survive this plague must not return immediately to Ispahan, lest you bring it here. You will go to a house which stands at Ibrahim's Rock, one day's distance to the east of the town of Nain, and three days' east of here. There you will rest for a month before coming home. Is it understood?"

They nodded. "Yes, Master," *Hakim* Fadil ibn Parviz said tremulously, speaking for all in his new position. Young Ali was weeping silently. Karim Harun's handsome face was dark with foreboding.

Finally Mirdin Askari spoke up. "My wife and children . . . I must make arrangements. To be certain they'll be all right if . . ."

Ibn Sina nodded. "Those of you with responsibilities have only brief hours to make these arrangements."

Rob hadn't known Mirdin was married and a father. The Jewish clerk was private and self-reliant, sure of himself in the classroom as well as in the *maristan*. But now his lips were bloodless, and moved in silent prayer.

Rob J. was as frightened as any at being sent on this errand from which there might be no return, but he struggled for courage. At least he would no longer have to serve as leech at the jail, he told himself.

"One thing more," Ibn Sina said, gazing at them with a parent's eyes. "You must keep careful notes, for those who will fight the next plague. And you must leave them where they will be found if something should happen to you."

* * *

Next morning, as the sun bloodied the tops of the trees they clattered over the bridge across the River of Life, each man on a good horse and leading either a packhorse or a mule.

After a while Rob suggested to Fadil that one man be sent ahead as scout and another ride far back as rear guard. The young *hakim* pretended to consider and then he bawled out the orders.

That night Fadil agreed at once when Rob suggested the same system of alternating sentries that had been employed by Kerl Fritta's caravan.

Seated around a thornbush fire, they were by turns jocular and grim.

"I believe Galen was never so wise as when he considered a physician's best choice of action during plague," Suleiman-al-Gamal said darkly. "Galen said a physician should flee the plague, to live to treat another day, and that is exactly what he did himself."

"I believe the great physician Rhazes said it better," Karim said.

> *"Three little words the plague dispel:*
> *Quick, far and late, where'er you dwell.*
> *Start quick, go far and right away,*
> *And your return till late delay."*

Their laughter was too loud.

Suleiman was their first sentry. It should have been no great surprise the following morning when they awoke to discover he had slipped away during the night, taking his horses with him.

It shook them and filled them with gloom. When they made camp the following evening, Fadil named Mirdin Askari to be sentry, a good choice; Askari guarded them well.

But the sentry at their third camp was Omar Nivahend, who emulated Suleiman and fled with his horses during the night.

Fadil called a meeting as soon as the second desertion was discovered.

"It's no sin to be afraid of the Death, else each of us is eternally damned," he said. "Nor, if you agree with Galen and Rhazes, is it a sin to flee—though I side with Ibn Sina in thinking a physician should fight pestilence instead of showing it his heels.

"What *is* a sin is to leave your companions unguarded. And it is worse to steal off with a pack animal bearing supplies needed by the sick and the dying." He gazed at them levelly. "Therefore, I say that if anyone else wishes to leave us, let him go now. And I promise on my honor that he will be allowed to do so without shame or prejudice."

They could hear each other's breathing. No one came forward.

Rob spoke up. "Yes, anyone should be allowed to go. But if the departure leaves us sentryless and unguarded, or if he takes with him supplies needed by the patients toward whom we travel, I say we must ride after such a deserter and kill him."

Again there was a silence.

Mirdin licked his lips. "I agree," he said.

"Yes," Fadil said.

"I agree also," said Abbas Sefi.

"And I," Ali whispered.

"And I!" said Karim.

Each of them knew it was no empty promise, but a solemn vow.

Two nights later, it was Rob J.'s turn to serve as sentry. They had made camp in a stony defile where moonshine created monsters of the looming rocks. It was a long and lonely night that gave him opportunity to think of sad things he otherwise managed to crowd out of his mind, and he dwelt on his brothers and his sister, and on those who were dead. He had long thoughts about the woman he had allowed to drift through his fingers.

Toward morning he was standing in the shadow of a great rock, not far from the sleeping men, when he became aware that one of them was awake and appeared to be making preparations for leaving.

Karim Harun stole through the encampment, taking care not to disturb the sleepers. When he was clear, he began to run lightly down the trail, and soon he was out of sight.

Harun had neither taken supplies nor left the party unguarded, and Rob made no attempt to stop him. But he felt a bitter disappointment, for he had begun to like the handsome and sardonic clerk who had been a medical student for so many years.

Perhaps an hour later he drew his sword, alerted by the sound of pounding footsteps coming toward him in the gray light. He stood and confronted Karim, who stopped in front of him and gaped at the ready blade, his chest heaving and his face and tunic wet with sweat.

"I saw you leave. I believed you had run away."

"I did." Karim fought for breath. "I ran away . . . and I ran back. I am a runner," he said, and smiled as Rob J. put away his sword.

Karim ran every morning, returning to them drenched in sweat. Abbas Sefi told comical stories and sang filthy songs and was a cruel mimic. *Hakim* Fadil was a wrestler, and in their camps at night the leader threw them all, having trouble only with Rob and with Karim. Mirdin was the best cook among them and cheerfully accepted the duty of preparing the evening meals. Young Ali, who had Bedouin blood, was a dazzling horseman and loved nothing better than serving as scout, ranging far ahead of the party; soon his eyes shone with enthusiasm instead of tears and he displayed a youthful energy that endeared him to all.

Their growing companionship was pleasant and the long ride might have been enjoyable except that, in camp and during rest pauses, *Hakim* Fadil read to them from the Plague Book that Ibn Sina had entrusted to him. The book offered hundreds of suggestions by various authorities, all of whom claimed to know how to fight the plague. A man named Lamna of Cairo insisted that an infallible method was to give the patient his own urine to drink, at the same time reciting specified imprecations to Allah (glorified is He!).

Al-Hajar of Baghdad suggested the sucking of an astringent pomegranate or plum at the time of an epidemic, and Ibn Mutillah of Jerusalem strongly recommended the eating of lentils, Indian peas, pumpkin seeds, and red clay. There were so many suggestions that each was made worthless to the bewildered medical party. Ibn Sina had written an addendum to the book, in which he had listed practices that seemed reasonable to him: the lighting of fires to create acrid smoke, washing down walls with limewater, sprinkling vinegar, and giving victims fruit juices to drink. In the end, they agreed to follow the regimen suggested by their teacher and to ignore all other advice.

During a pause in the middle of the eighth day Fadil read from the book that, of every five physicians who had treated the Death during the Cairo plague, four had themselves died of the disease. A quiet melancholy took hold of them as they resumed the ride, as if they had been informed of the sealing of their fate.

Next morning they came to a small village and learned it was Nardiz and that they had entered the district of Anshan.

The villagers treated them respectfully when *Hakim* Fadil announced they were physicians from Ispahan, sent by Alā Shah to help those afflicted by the plague.

"We do not have the pestilence, *Hakim*," the head of the village said thankfully. "Although rumors have reached us of death and suffering in Shīrāz."

Now they traveled expectantly, but they passed village after village and saw healthy people. In a mountain valley at Naksh-i-Rustam, they came to great rock-hewn tombs, the burial place of four generations of Persian kings. Here, overlooking their windswept valley, Darius the Great, Xerxes, Ataxerxes, and Darius II had lain for fifteen hundred years during which wars, pestilences, and conquerors had come and faded into nothingness. While the four Muslims paused for Second Prayer, Rob and Mirdin stood before one of the tombs in wonder as they read the inscription:

> I AM XERXES THE GREAT KING, THE KING OF KINGS,
> THE KING OF COUNTRIES OF MANY RACES,
> THE KING OF THE GREAT UNIVERSE, THE SON OF DARIUS THE KING,
> THE ACHAEMENIAN.

They rode past a great ruined place of broken fluted columns and strewn stone. Karim told Rob it was Persepolis, destroyed by Alexander the Great nine hundred years before the birth of the Prophet (may God bless him and greet him!).

A short distance from the ancient remains of the town they came to a farm. It was quiet save for the bleating of a few sheep grazing beyond the house, a pleasant sound that carried cleanly through the sunlit air. A shepherd seated beneath a tree appeared to be watching them, and when they rode up to him they saw he was dead.

The *hakim* just sat his horse like the rest of them, staring at the body. When Fadil failed to take the lead, Rob dismounted and examined the man, whose flesh was blue and already hard and stiff. He had been dead too long for his staring eyes to be closed, and an animal had been gnawing at his legs and had eaten away his right hand. The front of his tunic was black with blood. When Rob took his knife and cut open the garment he could find no sign of plague but there was a stab wound over the heart, large enough to have been made by a sword.

"Search," Rob said.

The house proved to be deserted. In the field beyond, they found the remains of several hundred slaughtered sheep, many of the bones already picked clean by wolves. All about, the field was greatly trampled, and it was apparent that an army had stopped there long enough to kill the shepherd and take meat.

Fadil, his eyes glassy, didn't give a direction or an order.

Rob lay the body on its side and they mounded it over with stones and large rocks to preserve the rest of it from the beasts, then they were glad to ride from that place.

Eventually they came to a fine estate, a sumptuous house surrounded by cultivated fields. It too appeared deserted, but they dismounted.

After Karim had knocked loudly and long, a peephole in the center of the door was opened and an eye stared out at them.

"Begone."

"We are a medical party from Ispahan, bound for Shīrāz," Karim said.

"I am Ishmael the Merchant. I can tell you few remain alive in Shīrāz. Seven weeks ago, an army of Seljuk Turkomen came to Anshan. Most of us fled before the Seljuks, taking women, children, and animals within the Shīrāz walls. The Seljuks beleaguered us. The Death already had broken out among them and they gave up the siege within a few days. But before they departed they sent the bodies of two of their plague-dead soldiers over the walls by catapult, into the crowded town. As soon as they were gone, we hastened to take the two corpses outside the wall and burn them, but it was too late, and the Death appeared among us."

Now *Hakim* Fadil found his tongue. "Is it a fearsome pestilence?"

"No worse can be imagined," said the voice behind the door. "Some persons appear to be immune to the disease, as was I, thanks be to Allah (whose mercy abounds!). But most who were within the walls are dead or dying."

"What of the physicians of Shīrāz?" Rob asked.

"There were in the town two barber-surgeons and four physicians, all other leeches having fled as soon as the Seljuks departed. Both barbers and two of the physicians labored among the people until they too were dead, and quickly. One leech was down with the disease and only a single physician remained to care for the afflicted when I abandoned the city myself, not two days since."

"Then it appears that we are badly needed in Shīrāz," Karim said.

"I have a large clean house," the man said, "stocked with ample supplies of food and wine, vinegar and lime, and a plentiful store of hemp plant to chase away troubles. I would open this house to you, for it is my protection to let in healers. In but a little while, when the pestilence has run its course, we can enter Shīrāz to our mutual profit. Who will join my safety?"

There was a silence.

"I," Fadil said hoarsely.

"Do not do this, *Hakim,*" Rob said.

"You are our leader and our only physician," Karim said.

Fadil didn't appear to hear them. "I shall come inside, merchant."

"I shall come inside too," Abbas Sefi said.

Both men slid from their horses. There was the sound of a heavy bar being eased slowly free. They glimpsed a pale, bearded face as the door opened only far enough to allow the two men to slip inside, then it was slammed again and barred.

Those outside stood like men adrift on the open sea. Karim looked at

Rob. "Perhaps they are right," he muttered. Mirdin said nothing, his face troubled and uncertain. The youth Ali was about to weep again.

"The Plague Book," Rob said, remembering that Fadil carried it in a large purse he wore on a strap around his neck. He went to the door and hammered on it.

"Go away," Fadil said. He sounded terrified; doubtless he feared to open the door lest they fall on him.

"Hear me, you shitepoke," Rob said, seized by fury. "If we are not given Ibn Sina's Plague Book, wood and brush will be gathered and piled high against the walls of this house. And I will delight in setting it afire, you false physician."

In a moment the drawing of the bar was heard again. The door opened and the book was thrown out to fall in the dust at their feet.

Rob picked it up and mounted. His fury didn't last as he rode away, for part of him yearned to be with Fadil and Abbas Sefi in the merchant's safe place.

He traveled a long time before he could bring himself to turn in the saddle. Mirdin Askari and Karim Harun were far back, but coming after him. The youth, Ali Rashid, brought up the rear, leading Fadil's packhorse and Abbas Sefi's mule.

Chapter 44

THE DEATH

The trail traversed a marshy plain almost in a straight line and then became tortuous in a rocky chain of bare mountains that they crossed for two days. Finally descending toward Shīrāz on the third morning, they saw smoke from afar. As they drew near, they came upon men burning bodies outside the wall. Beyond Shīrāz they could see the slopes of its famous gorge, Teng-i-Allahu Akbar, or Pass of God Is Most Great. Rob noticed dozens of large black birds soaring above the pass and knew that at last they had found the pestilence.

No sentry was at the gate when they passed into the city.

"Were the Seljuks inside the walls, then?" Karim said, for Shīrāz had a raped look. It was a pleasantly arranged city of pink stone, with many gardens, but everywhere raw stumps marked where once large trees had given shade and green majesty, and even the rosebushes of the gardens had been taken to feed the funeral pyres.

Dreamlike, they rode down empty streets.

At last they spied a man with a stumbling gait, but when they hailed him and moved to approach, he fled behind some houses.

Soon they found another pedestrian, and this time they boxed him in with their horses when he tried to run away, and Rob J. drew his sword.

"Answer and we do you no harm. Where are the physicians?"

The man was terrified. He held before his mouth and nose a small packet, probably of aromatic herbs. "The *kelonter*'s," he gasped, pointing down the street.

On the way they passed a charnel wagon. Its two burly collectors, their faces more heavily veiled than if they'd been women, stopped to pick up the small body of a child from where it had been left at the side of the street. There were three adult cadavers, one male and two female, in the wagon.

At the municipal offices, they presented themselves as the medical party from Ispahan and were stared at with astonishment by a tough man with

344

a military look and an old man, enfeebled; both had the slack faces and staring eyes of long sleeplessness.

"I am Dehbid Hafiz, the *kelonter* of Shīrāz," the younger man told them. "And this is *Hakim* Isfari Sanjar, our last physician."

"Why are your streets empty?" Karim said.

"We were fourteen thousand souls," Hafiz said. "With the coming of the Seljuks, an additional four thousand scurried behind the protection of our wall. After the outbreak of the Death, one-third of all those in Shīrāz fled the city, including," he said bitterly, "every rich man and the entire government, content to leave their *kelonter* and his soldiers to guard their property. Nearly six thousand have died. Those who are not yet stricken cower inside their homes and pray to Allah (merciful is He!) that they may remain so."

"How do you treat them, *Hakim?*" Karim asked.

"Nothing avails against the Death," the old doctor said. "A physician may hope only to bring some small comfort to the dying."

"We are not yet physicians," Rob said, "but medical apprentices sent to you by our master Ibn Sina, and we shall do your bidding."

"I give you no bidding, you shall do as you may," *Hakim* Isfari Sanjar said roughly. He waved his hand. "I give you only advice. If you would stay alive as I have, each morning with your breakfast you must eat a piece of toast soaked in vinegar of wine, and each time you speak with any person, you must first take a drink of wine," he said, and Rob J. realized that what he had mistaken for the infirmity of old age was instead an advanced state of drunkenness.

Records of the Ispahan Medical Party.

If this compendium is found after our deaths, generous reward will be realized upon its delivery to Abu Ali at-Husain ibn Abdullah ibn Sina, Chief Physician of the *maristan*, Ispahan. Inscribed on the 19th Day of the Month of Rabia I, in the 413th Year After the Hegira.

We have been in Shīrāz four days during which 243 have died. The pestilence begins as a mild fever followed by headache, sometimes severe. The fever becomes extremely high just before the appearance of a lesion in the groin, in an armpit, or behind an ear, commonly called a bubo. There is mention in the Plague Book of such buboes, which *Hakim* Ibn al-Khatīb of Andalusia said were inspired by the Devil and always in the shape of a serpent. Those observed here are not serpent-shaped but round and full, like the lesion of a tumor. They may be as large as a plum, but most are the size of a lentil. Often there is vomiting of blood, which always means death is imminent. Most victims die within two days of the appearance of a bubo. Some few are fortunate in that the bubo suppurates. When this occurs it is as if an evil humor passes from the patient, who may then recover.

(signed)
Jesse ben Benjamin
Clerk

They found an established pesthouse in the jail, the prisoners having been freed. It was packed with the dead, the dying, and the newly afflicted, so many it was impossible to comfort any. The air was filled with groans and cries, and heavy with the stench of bloody vomit, unwashed bodies, and human waste.

After conferring with the other three clerks, Rob went to the *kelonter* and requested the use of the Citadel, in which soldiers had been housed. This granted, he went from patient to patient in the jail, assessing them, holding their hands.

The message that flowed into his own hands was generally dreadful: the cup of life turned into a sieve.

Those close to death were moved to the Citadel. Since this was a large percentage of the victims, those not yet moribund could be nursed in a cleaner and less crowded place.

It was Persian winter, cold nights, warm afternoons. The peaks of the mountains were dazzling with snow and in the mornings the clerks needed their sheepskin coats. Above the gorge, black vultures soared in growing numbers.

"Your men are throwing bodies down the pass instead of burning them," Rob J. told the *kelonter*.

Hafiz nodded. "I have forbidden it, but I believe you are right. Wood is scarce."

"Every body must be burned. Without exception," Rob told him firmly, for it was something about which Ibn Sina had been adamant. "You must do what is necessary to make certain."

That afternoon three men were beheaded for dumping bodies in the pass, execution adding to the death all around them. It wasn't what Rob had intended, but Hafiz was resentful.

"Where are my men to get wood? All our trees are gone."

"Send soldiers into the mountains to cut trees," Rob said.

"They would not come back."

So Rob delegated young Ali to take soldiers into houses that had been deserted. Most of the houses were of stone but they had wooden doors, wooden shutters, stout roof beams. Ali drove the men to rip and tear, and the pyres roared outside the city wall.

They tried to follow Ibn Sina's instructions about breathing through vinegar-soaked sponges, but the sponges hampered their work and were soon discarded. Heeding the example of *Hakim* Isfari Sanjar, each day they choked down vinegar-soaked toast and drank a good deal of wine. Sometimes by nightfall they were as drunk as the old *hakim*.

In his cups, Mirdin told them of his wife Fara and his small sons Dawwid and Issachar who awaited his safe return to Ispahan. He spoke with nostalgia of his father's house by the Arabian Sea, where his family traveled the coast buying seed pearls. "I like you," he said to Rob. "How can you be friend to my terrible cousin Aryeh?"

Now Rob understood Mirdin's initial coolness. "A friend of Aryeh? I am not a friend of Aryeh. Aryeh is a shit!"

"He *is*, he is a shit, exactly!" Mirdin cried, and they rocked with laughter.

Handsome Karim drawled stories of sexual conquest and promised he would find young Ali the most beautiful pair of teats in the Eastern Caliphate when they returned to Ispahan. Karim ran every day, through the city of death. Sometimes he jeered at them until they ran with him, hurling themselves through the empty streets past vacant houses, past houses in which the nervous undiseased huddled, past houses before which bodies had been placed to await the charnel wagon—running from the dreadful sight of reality. For they were touched by more than wine. Surrounded by death, they were young and alive, and they tried to bury their terror by pretending they were immortal and inviolate.

Records of the Ispahan Medical Party.

Inscribed on the 28th Day of the Month of Rabia I, in the 413th Year After the Hegira.

Blood-letting, cupping, and purging appear to have little effect. The relationship of the buboes to dying of this plague is interesting, for it continues to hold true that in the event the bubo bursts or steadily evacuates its green smelly discharge, the patient is likely to survive.

It may be that many are killed by the terribly high fever that eats the fat from their bodies. But when the buboes suppurate, the fever drops precipitously and recuperation begins.

Having observed this, we have labored to ripen the buboes that they might open, applying poultices of mustard and lily bulbs; poultices of figs and boiled onions, pounded and mixed with butter; and a variety of drawing plasters. Sometimes we have cut open the buboes and treated them like ulcers, with but little success. Often these swellings, affected partly by the distemper and partly by their being too violently drawn, become so hard no instrument can cut them. These we have attempted to burn with caustics, with poor results. Many died raving mad with the torment and some during the very operation, so that we may be said to have tortured these poor creatures even to death. Yet some are saved. These might have lived without our presence in this place, but it is our comfort to believe we have been of assistance to a few.

(signed)
Jesse ben Benjamin
Clerk

"You bone-pickers!" the man screamed. His two servants dumped him unceremoniously on the pesthouse floor and fled, doubtless to steal his belongings, a commonplace thievery in a plague that appeared to corrupt souls as fast as bodies. Children with buboes were being abandoned without hesitation by their terror-crazed parents. Three men and a woman had been beheaded that morning for looting, and a soldier was flayed for fucking a dying female. Karim, who had led soldiers armed with buckets of limewater to cleanse houses in which there had been pestilence, said every vice was for sale and reported witnessing so much rutting that it was clear many were grasping at life through a wildness of the flesh.

Just before midday the *kelonter,* who never entered the pesthouse himself, sent a white and trembling soldier to bring Rob and Mirdin to the street, where they found Kafiz sniffing a spice-studded apple to ward off disease. "Be advised that the count of those who died yesterday was down to thirty-seven," he told them triumphantly. It was a dramatic improvement, for on the most virulent day, in the third week after the outbreak, 268 had perished.

Kafiz told them that by his reckoning Shīrāz had lost 801 men, 502 women, 3,193 children, 566 male slaves, 1,417 female slaves, 2 Syrian Christians, and 32 Jews.

Rob and Mirdin exchanged a knowing glance, neither of them having missed the *kelonter*'s listing of the victims in their order of importance.

Young Ali came walking down the street. Something odd, for the boy would have passed them without a sign had not Rob called his name.

Rob went to him and saw that his eyes were strange. When he touched Ali's head, the familiar terrible burning chilled his heart.

Ah, God.

"Ali," he said gently. "You must come inside with me now."

They had already seen many die, but witnessing the swiftness with which the disease possessed Ali Rashid, it was as if Rob and Karim and Mirdin suffered in the youth's pain.

From time to time Ali lurched in sudden spasm, as if something had bitten him in the stomach. Agony made him shudder with convulsion and arch his body into queer, contorted positions. They bathed him with vinegar and in the early afternoon they had hope, for he was almost cool to the touch. But it was as if the fever had gathered itself and when the fresh assault came he was hotter than before, his lips cracked, his eyes rolling up into his head.

Among all the cries and groans his were almost lost, but the other three clerks heard the terrible sounds clearly because circumstances had made them his family.

When night came, they took turns sitting by his bed.

The boy was lying racked on the tumbled pallet when Rob came to relieve Mirdin before dawn. His eyes were dull and unknowing and fever had wasted his body and transformed the round adolescent face, from which high cheekbones and a hawkish beak had emerged to give a glimpse of the Bedouin man he might have become.

Rob took Ali's hands and experienced the dwindling.

Now and again, as an escape from the helplessness of doing nothing, he moved his fingers to Ali's wrists and felt the pulse beats, weak and blurred like the wing strokes of a struggling bird.

By the time Karim came to relieve Rob, Ali was gone. They could no longer make a pretense of immortality. It was obvious that one of them soon would be next and they began to know the true meaning of fear.

They accompanied Ali's body to the pyre and each prayed in his own way as it burned.

That morning they began to witness the turning; it was obvious that fewer were brought to the pesthouse with the illness. Three days later the *kelonter,* barely able to suppress the wishfulness in his voice, reported that on the preceding day only eleven persons had died.

Walking near the pesthouse, Rob noted a large group of dead and dying rats and saw a singular thing when he inspected them: the rodents had the plague, for almost all of them displayed a small but indisputable bubo. Locating one that had died so recently that the warm furry body still crawled with fleas, he laid it on a large flat rock and opened it with his knife as neatly as though al-Juzjani or some other anatomy teacher were peering over his shoulder.

Records of the Ispahan Medical Party.

Inscribed on the Fifth Day of the Month of Rabia II, 413th Year After the Hegira.

Various animals have died as well as men, word having reached us that horses, cows, sheep, camels, dogs, cats, and birds have perished of the pestilence in Anshan.

Dissections of six plague-killed rats were of interest. External signs were similar to those found in human victims, with staring eyes, contorted muscles, gaping lips, protruding tongue of blackish color, bubo in the groin area or behind an ear.

Upon dissection of these rats it becomes clear why surgical removal of the bubo is most often unsuccessful. The lesion is likely to have deep, carrot-like roots which, after the main body of the bubo has been removed, remain imbedded in the victim to wreak their havoc.

On opening the abdomens of the rats I found the lower orifices of all six stomachs and the upper bowels to be quite discolored by green gall. The lower intestines were speckled. The livers of all six rodents were shriveled and in four of the rats the hearts were shrunken.

In one of the rats the stomach was, so to say, internally peeled.

Do these effects occur to the organs of human victims of this plague?

Clerk Karim Harun says Galen wrote that man's internal anatomy is precisely identical to the pig's and the ape's, but dissimilar to the rat's.

Thus, while we do not know the causal events of plague death in humans, we may be bitterly certain they are occurring internally and thus are barred from our inspection.

(signed)
Jesse ben Benjamin
Clerk

Working in the pesthouse two days later, Rob felt an uneasiness, a heaviness, a weakness in the knees, a difficulty in breathing, a burning within as though he had eaten heavily of spices, although he hadn't.

These sensations stayed with him and grew as he worked all through the afternoon. He fought to ignore them until, looking into a victim's face

—inflamed and distorted, the brilliant eyes starting out of the man's head —Rob felt he was seeing himself.

He went to Mirdin and Karim.

The answer was in their eyes.

Before he would allow them to lead him to a pallet he insisted on fetching the Plague Book and his notes and giving them to Mirdin. "If neither of you should survive, these must be left by the last man where they can be found and sent to Ibn Sina."

"Yes, Jesse," Karim said.

Rob felt calm. A mountain had been moved from his shoulders; the worst had happened and therefore he had been freed from the terrible prison of dread.

"One of us will stay with you," good, grieving Mirdin said.

"No, there are many here who need you."

But he could sense them hovering and watching him.

He determined to note each separate stage of the disease, marking it well in his mind, but got only as far as the onset of high fever and a headache so formidable it made the skin of his entire body sensitive. The covers became heavy and irritating and he threw them off. Sleep overcame him.

He dreamed he sat and conversed with tall, spare Dick Bukerel, the long-dead Chief Carpenter of his father's guild. When he awoke he could feel the heat becoming more oppressive, the frenzy within him increasing.

During a fitful night he was troubled by dreams more violent, in which he wrestled a bear that gradually grew thinner and taller until he was the Black Knight, while everyone who had been taken by the plague stood by and witnessed the thrashing struggle in which neither could pin the other.

In the morning he was awakened by soldiers dragging their miserable load from the pesthouse out to the charnel wagon. It was a familiar sight to him as medical clerk, but seeing it as one of the afflicted was different. His heart beat throbbingly, there was a far-off buzzing in his ears. The heaviness in all his limbs was worse than before he had gone to bed, and a fire raged within him.

"Water."

Mirdin hastened to fetch some, but as Rob shifted himself to drink, he caught his breath in anguish. He hesitated before looking at the place where he felt the pain. Finally he uncovered it and he and Mirdin exchanged a fearful look. Under his left arm there was a hideous bubo of a livid purple hue.

He grasped Mirdin's wrist. "You shan't cut it! And you mustn't burn it with caustics. Do you promise?"

Mirdin ripped his hand free and pushed Rob J. back down onto the pallet. "I promise, Jesse," he said gently, and hurried away to fetch Karim.

Mirdin and Karim pulled his hand behind his head and tied it to a post, leaving the bubo exposed. They heated rose water and soaked rags to make compresses, changing the poultices faithfully when they cooled.

He grew hotter with fever than he had ever been, man or child, and all the pain in his body concentrated in the bubo, until his mind turned away from the unremitting agony and wandered.

He sought coolness in the shade of a wheat field and kissed her, touched her mouth, kissed her face, the red hair falling over him like a dark mist.

He heard Karim praying in Persian and Mirdin in Hebrew. When Mirdin came to the *Shema*, Rob followed along. *Hear, O Israel, the Lord our God, the Lord is One. And thou shalt love the Lord thy God with all thy heart . . .*

He feared to die with Jewish scripture on his lips and strove for a Christian prayer. The one that came to mind was a chant of his boyhood priests.

> *Jesus Christus natus est.*
> *Jesus Christus crucifixus est.*
> *Jesus Christus sepultus est.*
> *Amen.*

His brother Samuel sat on the floor close by the pallet, doubtless a guide come to fetch him. Samuel appeared the same, down to the wry and quizzical expression on his face. He scarcely knew what to say to Samuel; Rob had grown to manhood but Samuel was still the boy he had been when he died.

The pain was even more intense. The pain was terrible.

"Come, Samuel," he cried. "Let us be gone!"

But Samuel only sat and stared at him.

Presently there was such a sweet and sudden easing of the pain in his arm that the relief was as sharp as a fresh hurt. He could not allow himself false hope, and he forced himself to wait patiently for someone to come.

After what seemed an inordinately long time, he was aware of Karim leaning over him.

"Mirdin! Mirdin! All praise to Allah, the bubo has opened!"

Two grinning faces hovered above him, the one darkly handsome, the other homely with the goodness of saints.

"I'll put in a wick so it will drain," Mirdin said, and for a while they became too busy for thanksgiving.

It was as if he had come through the stormiest of seas and now drifted in the calmest and most peaceable of backwaters.

The recovery was as swift and uneventful as he had seen in other survivors. There was a weakness and shakiness, natural following the high fevers; but clarity returned to his mind and there was no further mixing of past and present events.

He fretted, wishing to make some small use of himself, but his caretakers would have none of it and kept him supine upon his pallet.

"It means all to you, this practice of medicine," Karim observed keenly one morning. "I knew it, and therefore made no objection when you seized leadership of our little party."

Rob opened his mouth to protest but closed it quickly, for it was true.

"I was infuriated when Fadil ibn Parviz was made the leader," Karim said. "He does well in examinations and is highly regarded by faculty, but as a working physician he is a calamity. Further, he began his apprenticeship two years after I started my own and he is a *hakim* while I am still a clerk."

"Then how could you accept me as leader, who hasn't yet apprenticed a full year?"

"You are different, taken out of the competition by your enslavement to healing."

Rob smiled. "I've seen you, these hard weeks. Aren't you owned by the same master?"

"No," Karim said calmly. "Oh, don't misunderstand, I desire to be the best of doctors. But at least as strongly, I need to become rich. Wealth isn't your strongest ambition, is it, Jesse?"

Rob shook his head.

"When I was a child in the village of Carsh, which is in the province of Hamadhān, Abdallah Shah, the father of Alā Shah, led a great army across our countryside to move against bands of Seljuk Turks. Wherever Abdallah's army stopped, misery came, a plague of soldiers. They took crops and animals, food that meant survival or disaster to their own people. When the army moved on, we starved.

"I was five years old. My mother held her newborn daughter by the feet and dashed her head against the rocks. They say many resorted to cannibalism, and I believe it.

"First my father died, and then my mother. For a year I lived in the streets with beggars and was a beggar boy. Finally I was taken in by Zaki-Omar, a man who had been my father's friend. He was a noted athlete. He educated me and taught me to run. And for nine years he fucked my arse."

Karim fell silent a moment, the stillness broken only by the soft moaning of a patient across the room.

"When he died, I was fifteen. His family threw me out, but he had made arrangements for my entrance to the *madrassa* and I came to Ispahan, free for the first time. I made up my mind that when I have sons they will be safe, and that kind of safety comes from wealth."

As children they had met similar catastrophes half a world apart, Rob thought. Had he been slightly less fortunate, or had Barber been a different sort of a man . . .

The conversation was interrupted by the arrival of Mirdin, who sat on the floor on the other side of the pallet from Karim. "Nobody died in Shīrāz yesterday."

"Allah," Karim said.

"No one died!"

Rob took each of them by the hand.

Presently Karim and Mirdin clasped hands too. They were beyond laughter, beyond tears, like old men who had shared a lifetime. Linked, they sat and looked at one another, savoring survival.

It was ten more days before they pronounced Rob strong enough to travel. Word of the plague's end had spread. It would be years before there were trees in Shīrāz again but people were beginning to come back, and some brought lumber. They passed a house on whose windows carpenters were hanging shutters, several more where men were putting up doors.

It was good to leave the city behind and head north.

They traveled without haste. When they came to the house of Ishmael the Merchant, they dismounted and knocked, but no one answered.

Mirdin wrinkled his nose. "There are dead nearby," he said quietly.

Entering the house, they found the decomposed bodies of the merchant and *Hakim* Fadil. There was no sign of Abbas Sefi, who doubtless had fled the "safe refuge" when he saw that the other two were stricken.

So they had one last responsibility before they left the land of the plague, and they spoke prayers and burned the two bodies, building a hot fire with the merchant's expensive furniture.

Where eight had left Ispahan with the medical party, three rode back from Shīrāz.

Chapter 45

A MURDERED MAN'S BONES

When he got back there seemed an unreality about Ispahan, full of healthy people laughing or squabbling. For a time it was strange for Rob to walk among them, as if the world were tipped on end.

Ibn Sina was saddened but not surprised to learn of the desertions and deaths when they got home. He received the record book from Rob eagerly. During the month in which the three clerks had waited in the house at Ibrahim's Rock, to make certain they didn't bring home the plague, Rob had written at length, resulting in a detailed account of their work in Shīrāz.

He made it plain in his reports that the other two clerks had saved his life, and he had written of them with warm praise.

"Karim too?" Ibn Sina asked him bluntly when they were alone.

Rob hesitated, for it seemed presumptuous of him to evaluate a fellow student. But he drew a breath and answered the question. "He may have trouble with the examinations but he is already a wonderful physician, calm and resolute during disaster and tender with those in torment."

Ibn Sina seemed satisfied. "And now you must go to the House of Paradise and report to Alā Shah, for the king is eager to discuss the presence of a Seljuk army in Shīrāz," he said.

Winter was dying but not dead, and the palace was cold. Khuff's hard boots rang on the stone floors as Rob followed him down dark corridors.

Alā Shah sat alone at a great table.

"Jesse ben Benjamin, Majesty." The Captain of the Gates withdrew as Rob performed the *ravi zemin*.

"You may sit with me, *Dhimmi*. You must pull the tablecloth over your lap," the king instructed. When Rob did so, it was a pleasant shock. The table was set over a grill in the floor, through which heat drifted pleasantly from ovens below.

355

He knew he mustn't look at the monarch too long or too directly, but he had already noted evidence that confirmed the marketplace gossip of the Shah's continuing dissipation. Alā's eyes burned like a wolf's and the flat planes of the lean, hawkish face looked slack, doubtless the result of consuming too much wine too steadily.

Before the Shah was a board divided into alternately light and dark squares, set with elaborately carved bone figures. Next to it were cups and a pitcher of wine. Alā poured for them both and downed his wine quickly.

"Drink it, drink it, I would make you a merry Jew." The red eyes were commanding.

"I ask your kind permission to leave it. It doesn't make me merry, Majesty. It makes me surly and wild, so I can't enjoy wine like more fortunate men."

The Shah's attention had been gained. "It causes me to awake each morning with a powerful pain behind the eyes and a trembling of the hands. You are the physician. What is the remedy?"

Rob smiled. "Less wine, Highness, and more riding out in the pure Persian air."

The sharp eyes searched his face for insolence and found none. "Then you must ride out with me, *Dhimmi.*"

"I am at your service, Majesty."

Alā waved his hand to show it was understood. "Now, let us speak of the Seljuks in Shīrāz. You must tell all."

He listened attentively while Rob recounted at length what he knew about the force that had invaded Anshan.

Finally he nodded. "Our enemy to the northwest encircled us and sought to establish themselves to our southeast. Had they conquered and occupied all of Anshan, Ispahan would have been a morsel between grinding Seljuk jaws." He slapped the table. "Allah be blessed for bringing them the plague. When they come again, we will be ready."

He pulled the large checkered board so that it sat between them. "You know this pastime?"

"No, Sire."

"Our ancient pursuit. When you lose it is called *shahtreng,* the 'anguish of the king.' But mostly it is known as the Shah's Game, for it is about war." He smiled, amused. "I shall teach you the Shah's Game, *Dhimmi.*"

He handed one of the elephant figures to Rob and let him feel the creamy smoothness. "Carved from an elephant's tusk. You see, we both have an equal array. The king stands in the center, his faithful companion, the general, in attendance. On each side of them is an elephant, casting comfortable shadows as dark as indigo about the throne. Two camels are next to the elephants, with men of fast intent mounted on them. Then come two horses with their riders, ready to fight on the day of combat. At each end of the battle lines a *rukh,* or warrior, raises his cupped hands to his lips, drinking his enemies' blood. In front move the foot soldiers, whose duty is to come to the assistance of the others in the fighting. If a foot soldier presses through to the other end of the field of battle, that hero is placed beside the king, like the general.

"The brave general never moves in the battle more than one square from his king. The mighty elephants run through three squares and observe the whole battlefield two miles wide. The camel runs snorting and stamping through three squares, thus and so. The horses also move over three squares, and in jumping them one of the squares remains untouched. To all sides rage the vindictive *rukhs,* crossing the whole field of battle.

"Each piece moves in its own area, and makes neither less nor more than its appointed move. If anyone approaches the king in battle he cries aloud, 'Remove, O Shah!' and the king must retreat from his square. Should the opposing king, horse, *rukh,* general, elephant, and army close the road before him, he must look about him on all four sides with knit brows. If he see that his army has been overthrown, his road barred by water and the ditch, the enemy to left and right, before and behind, he shall die of weariness and thirst, the fate ordained by the revolving firmament for a loser in war." He poured himself more wine, drank it down, and glowered at Rob. "Do you comprehend?"

"I believe so, Sire," Rob said cautiously.

"Then let us begin."

Rob made mistakes, moving some of the pieces incorrectly, and each time Alā Shah corrected him with a growl. The game didn't last long, for very quickly his forces were slain and his king taken.

"Another," Alā said with satisfaction.

The second contest was concluded almost as swiftly as the first, but Rob began to see that the Shah anticipated his moves because he had set ambushes and lured him into traps, just as though they were fighting a real war.

When the second game was finished, Alā waved his hand in dismissal.

"A proficient player can ward off defeat for days," he said. "Who wins at the Shah's Game is fit to govern the world. But you have done well, your first time. It is no disgrace for you to suffer *shahtreng,* for after all you are but a Jew."

* * *

How satisfying to be in the little house in Yehuddiyyeh again, and to slip back into the hard routines of the *maristan* and the lecture halls!

To Rob's great pleasure he wasn't sent back to serve as jail surgeon, but instead was apprenticed in fractures for a time, to serve with Mirdin as clerks under *Hakim* Jalal-ul-Din. Slim and saturnine, Jalal appeared to be a typical leader of Ispahan's medical society, respected and prosperous. But he differed from most of the Ispahan doctors in several important aspects.

"So you are Jesse the Barber-Surgeon, of whom I have heard?" he said when Rob reported to him.

"Yes, Master Physician."

"I can't share the general scorn for barber-surgeons. Many are thieves and fools, true enough, but also among their number are men who are honest and clever. Before I became a physician I was of another profession despised by Persian doctors, a traveling bonesetter, and after I became *hakim* I am the same man I was before. But though I don't damn you as a barber, still you must work hard for my respect. If you don't earn it, I shall kick your arse from my service, European."

Both Rob and Mirdin were happy to work hard. Jalal-ul-Din was famous as a bone specialist and had developed a wide variety of padded splints and traction devices. He taught them to use fingertips as if they were eyes that could peer beneath bruised and crushed flesh, visualizing the injury until the best course of treatment was clear. Jalal was especially skillful in manipulating chips and fragments until they were back in their rightful places, where nature could make them part of bones once again.

"He appears to have a curious interest in crime," Mirdin grumbled after their first few days as Jalal's assistants. And it was true, for Rob had noted that the physician spoke inordinately long about a murderer who had shriven his guilt that week in Imam Qandrasseh's court.

One Fakhr-i-Ayn, a shepherd, had confessed that two years earlier he had sodomized and then slain a fellow shepherd named Qifti al-Ullah, burying his victim in a shallow grave outside the city walls. The murderer was condemned by the court and promptly executed and quartered.

A few days later, when Rob and Mirdin reported to Jalal, he told them that the body of the murdered man was to be removed from its crude grave and reburied in a Muslim cemetery with benefit of Islamic prayer to insure his soul's admission to Paradise.

"Come," Jalal said. "It is a rare opportunity. Today we shall be grave-diggers."

He didn't disclose whom he had bribed, but soon the two clerks and the physician, leading a laden mule, accompanied a *mullah* and a *kelonter*'s soldier to the lonely hillside which the late Fakhr-i-Ayn had pointed out to authorities.

"Have a care," Jalal said as they used their spades.

Presently they saw the bones of a hand, and soon after that removed the entire skeleton, laying the bones of Qifti-al-Ullah on a blanket.

"Time for food," Jalal announced, and led the donkey to the shade of a tree a distance from the grave. The animal's pack was opened to give forth roast fowl, sumptuous *pilah,* large desert dates, honey cakes, a jug of *sherbet.* The soldier and the *mullah* fell to eating eagerly, and Jalal and his clerks left them to the heavy meal and the nap that would surely follow.

The three of them hurried back to the skeleton. The earth had done its task and the bones were clean save for a rusty stain around the place where Fakhr's dagger had punched through the sternum. They knelt over the bones, murmuring, scarcely aware that the remains once had been a man named Qifti.

"Note the femur," Jalal said, "the largest and strongest bone in the body. Is it not apparent why it is difficult to set a break that occurs in the thigh?

"Count the twelve pairs of ribs. Do you note how the ribs form a cage? The cage protects the heart and the lungs, is that not marvelous?"

It was remarkably different to be studying human bones instead of a sheep's, Rob thought; but it was only a small part of the story. "The human heart and lungs—have you seen them?" he asked Jalal.

"No. But Galen says they are very much like the pig's. We have all seen the pig's."

"What if they are not the same?"

"They are the same," Jalal said crankily. "Let us not waste this golden chance for study, for soon those two will return. Do you witness how the upper seven pair of ribs are attached to the breastplate by flexible connective stuff? The next three are united by a common tissue, and the last two pairs have no attachment to the front at all. Is Allah (great and mighty is He!) not the cleverest designer, *Dhimmis?* Is it not a wondrous framework on which He has built his people?"

They squatted in the hot sun over their scholarly feast, making an anatomy lesson of the murdered man.

Afterward, Rob and Mirdin spent time in the academy's baths, washing away the funereal feeling and easing muscles unaccustomed to digging. It was here that Karim found them, and at once Rob saw from his friend's face that something was wrong.

"I am to be reexamined."

"But surely that is what you want!"

Karim glanced at two faculty members conversing at the other end of the room and lowered his voice. "I'm afraid. I'd almost given up hope for another examining. This will be my third—if I fail this time all will be over." He looked at them bleakly. "At least now I'm able to be a clerk."

"You will trot through the examination like a runner," Mirdin said.

Karim waved off any attempt at lightheartedness. "I'm not concerned with the medical portion. It's the portion on philosophy, and the portion on the law."

"When?" Rob asked.

"In six weeks."

"That gives us time, then."

"Yes, I will study philosophy with you," Mirdin said calmly. "Jesse and you will work on the law."

Inside, Rob groaned, for he scarcely considered himself a jurist. But they had been through the plague together and were linked by similar boyhood catastrophes; he knew they must try. "We begin tonight," he said, reaching for a cloth to dry his body.

"I have never heard of anyone staying apprentice for seven years and then being made a physician," Karim said, and he made no attempt to hide his terror from them, a new level of intimacy.

"You will pass," Mirdin said, and Rob nodded.

"I must," Karim said.

Chapter 46

THE RIDDLE

Two weeks in a row, Ibn Sina invited Rob to dine with him.

"Hoo, the Master has a favorite clerk," Mirdin gibed, but there was pride and not jealousy in his smile.

"It's good that he takes an interest," Karim said seriously. "Al-Juzjani has had Ibn Sina's sponsorship since they were young men, and al-Juzjani became a great physician."

Rob scowled, unwilling to share the experience even with them. He couldn't describe what it was like to have an entire evening as the sole beneficiary of Ibn Sina's mind. One evening they had talked of the heavenly bodies—or, to be precise, Ibn Sina had talked and Rob had listened. Another evening, Ibn Sina had held forth for hours on the theories of the Greek philosophers. He knew so much and could teach it effortlessly!

In contrast, before Rob could teach Karim, he had to learn. He determined that for six weeks he would stop attending all lectures save for selected ones on the law, and he drew books on law and jurisprudence from the House of Wisdom. Tutoring Karim in law would not simply be a selfless act of friendship, for it was an area Rob had neglected. In helping Karim he would be preparing himself for the day when his own ordeal of testing would begin.

In Islam there were two branches of law: *Fiqh,* or legal science, and *Shari'a,* the law as divinely revealed by Allah. When there was added to these *Sunna,* truth and justice as revealed by the exemplary life and sayings of Mohammed, the result was a complex and complicated body of learning that might make scholars quail.

Karim was trying, but it was obvious he was sorely tried. "It's too much," he said. The strain was apparent. For the first time in seven years, except for the period in which they had fought the plague in Shīrāz, he wasn't going to the *maristan* daily, and he confessed to Rob that he felt

361

strange and ripped out of his element without his daily routine of caring for patients.

Each morning, before he met with Rob to study the law and then with Mirdin to study the philosophers and their teachings, Karim ran in the first gray light. Once Rob tried to run with him but he was soon left behind; Karim ran as if trying to outdistance his fears. Several times, Rob rode the brown horse and paced the runner. Karim sped through the stirring city, past the grinning sentries at the main gate of the wall, across the River of Life and into the countryside. Rob didn't think he knew or cared where he was running. His feet rose and fell and his legs moved with a steady, mindless rhythm that appeared to lull and comfort him as if it were an infusion of *buing,* the strong hempseed they gave to people with hopeless pain. The daily expenditure of effort bothered Rob.

"It takes Karim's strength," he complained to Mirdin. "He should save all his energy for studying."

But wise Mirdin pulled his nose and stroked his long equine jaw and shook his head. "No, without the running I think he would not be able to get past this hard time," he said, and Rob was wise enough to defer, for he had great faith that Mirdin's everyday wisdom was as formidable as his scholarship.

One morning he was summoned, and rode the brown horse down the Avenue of the Thousand Gardens until he came to the dusty lane leading to Ibn Sina's handsome house. The gateman took his horse, and by the time he had walked to the stone door Ibn Sina was there to greet him.

"It is my wife. I would be grateful if you would examine her."

Rob bowed, confused; Ibn Sina had no lack of distinguished colleagues who would be pleased and honored to examine the woman. But he followed him to a door leading to a stone stairway like the inside of a snail shell, and they ascended the north tower of the house.

The old woman lay on a pallet and stared through them with dull and unseeing eyes. Ibn Sina knelt by her.

"Reza."

Her dry lips were cracked. He moistened a square of cloth in rose water and wiped her mouth and face tenderly. Ibn Sina had a lifetime of experience in how to make a sickroom comfortable, but not even clean surroundings and newly changed garments and the fragrant wisps of smoke rising from incense dishes could mask the stink of her illness.

The bones seemed almost to violate her transparent skin. Her face was waxen, her hair thin and white. Perhaps her husband was the greatest physician in the world but she was an old woman in the final stages of bone sickness. Large buboes were visible on her skinny arms and lower legs. Her ankles and feet were swollen with gathered fluids. Her right hip was largely deteriorated and Rob knew that if he were to lift the bed gown he would find that more of the advanced growths had invaded other external parts of her body just as, from the odor, he was certain they had spread to her intestines.

It wasn't to confirm a terrible and obvious diagnosis that Ibn Sina had summoned him. Now he knew what was required of him and he took both her frail hands in his, talking to her softly. He took longer than necessary, gazing into her eyes, which for a moment seemed to clear. "Da'ud?" she whispered, and her grip on his hands strengthened.

Rob looked at Ibn Sina questioningly.

"Her brother, dead these many years."

The vacancy returned to her eyes, the fingers clutching his grew slack. Rob returned her hands to the pallet and they withdrew from the tower.

"How long?"

"Not long, *Hakim-bashi.* I believe a matter of days." Rob felt clumsy; the other man was far too senior to him for the standard condolences. "Is there nothing, then, that can be done for her?"

Ibn Sina's mouth twisted. "I am left to showing her my love with stronger and stronger infusions." He took his apprentice to the front door and thanked him, then returned to his afflicted wife.

"Master," someone said to Rob.

When he turned he saw the huge eunuch who guarded the second wife. "You will follow, please?"

They passed through a doorway in the garden wall, the opening so small each of them had to stoop, into another garden outside the south tower.

"What is it?" he asked the slave curtly.

The eunuch made no reply. Something drew Rob's glance and he looked to where a veiled face stared down at him through a small window.

Their eyes held and then hers moved away in a swirl of veils and the window was empty.

Rob turned to the slave and the eunuch smiled slightly and shrugged.

"She bade me bring you here. She desired to look upon you, master," he said.

Perhaps Rob might have dreamed of her that night but there was no time. He studied the laws of ownership of property and, as the oil in his lamp was burning low, he heard the clopping sound of hooves that came down his street and appeared to stop outside his door.

There was a tapping.

He reached for his sword, thinking of thieves. It was far too late for callers. "Who is there?"

"Wasif, master."

Rob knew no Wasif but thought he recognized the voice. Holding the weapon ready, he opened the door and saw he had been right. It was the eunuch, holding the reins of a donkey.

"Were you sent by the *hakim?*"

"No, master. I am sent by her, who wishes you to come."

He had no reply. The eunuch knew better than to smile, but there was a glint behind the grave eyes that took in the *Dhimmi*'s amazement.

"Wait," Rob said rudely, and shut the door.

He came out after a hasty washing-up and, mounting the brown horse without a saddle, wended through the dark streets behind the huge slave, whose splayed feet dragged furrows in the dust as he rode astride the poor donkey. They plodded past silent houses in which people slept, turning into the lane whose deeper dust muffled the animals' hooves, and then into a field that extended behind the wall of Ibn Sina's estate.

A gate in the wall took them close to the door of the south tower. The eunuch opened the tower gate and, bowing, motioned for Rob to go on alone.

It was like the fantasies he had had on a hundred nights while lying alone and aroused. This dark stone passage was twin to the stairway in the north tower, circling like the whorls of a nautilus shell, and when he emerged at the top he found himself in a commodious *haram*.

In the lamplight he saw that she waited on a large cushioned pallet, a Persian woman who had prepared herself to make love, her hands and feet and cunnus red with henna and slick with oil. Her breasts were a disappointment, scarcely larger than a boy's.

Rob removed her veil.

She had black hair, also treated with oil and pulled back tight against her round skull. He had imagined the forbidden features of a Queen of Sheba or a Cleopatra and was startled to find instead a haunting young girl with a trembling mouth that she now licked nervously with a flick of pink tongue. It was a heart-shaped, lovely face with a pointed chin and a short, straight nose. From the thin right nostril dangled a small metal ring just large enough to admit his little finger.

He had been in this country too long: her uncovered facial features were more exciting to him than her shaven body.

"Why are you called Despina the Ugly?"

"Ibn Sina decreed it. It is to fool the Evil Eye," she said as he sank to the pallet beside her.

Next morning he and Karim studied *Fiqh* again, the laws of marriage and divorce.

"Who makes the marriage settlement?"

"The husband makes the marriage contract and presents it to the wife, and he writes the *mahr,* the amount of the dowry, into the agreement."

"How many witnesses are needed?"

"I don't know. Two?"

"Yes, two. Who has the greater rights in the *haram,* the second wife or the fourth wife?"

"All wives have equal rights."

They turned to the laws of divorce, and the grounds: barrenness, shrewish behavior, adultery.

Under *Sharī'a,* the penalty for adultery was stoning, but this had given way, two centuries before. An adulterous woman of a rich and powerful man might still be executed in the *kelonter's* jail by beheading, but the adulterous wives of the poor often were given a severe striping with a cane and then divorced or not, depending upon the husband's wishes.

Karim had little trouble with *Sharī'a,* for he had been raised in a devout household and knew the laws of piety. It was *Fiqh* that haunted him. There were so many laws, about so many things, that he knew he couldn't remember them all.

Rob thought about it. "If you can't recall the exact wording of the *Fiqh,* then you should turn to *Sharī'a* or *Sunna.* All the law is based on the sermons and writings of Mohammed. Therefore, if you can't remember the law, give them an answer from religion or from the life of the Prophet and perhaps they will be satisfied." He sighed. "It is worth trying. And in the meantime we'll pray, and memorize as many of the laws of the *Fiqh* as we are able."

Next afternoon at the hospital he followed al-Juzjani through the halls and paused with the others at the pallet of a skinny little rat of a boy, Bilāl. Close by sat a peasant with dumb, accepting eyes.

"Distemper," al-Juzjani said. "An example of how colic can suck the soul. What is his age?"

Cowed but flattered to be addressed, the father ducked his head. "He is in the ninth season, lord."

"How long ill?"

"Two weeks. It is the side sickness and has killed two of his uncles and my father. Terrible pain. Come and gone, come and gone. But three days ago it came and did not leave."

The nurse, who addressed al-Juzjani fawningly and doubtless wished they would finish with the child and move on, said he had been fed only *sherbets* of sweetened juices. "Everything he swallows, he spews or shits."

Al-Juzjani nodded. "Examine him, Jesse."

Rob pulled down the blanket. The boy had a scar under the chin but it was fully healed and not part of his illness. He placed a palm on the thin cheek and Bilāl tried to move but didn't have the strength. Rob patted his shoulder.

"Hot."

He ran his fingertips slowly down the body. When he reached the stomach, the boy screamed.

"The belly is soft on the left and hard on the right side."

"Allah tried to protect the site of the distemper," al-Juzjani said.

As gently as possible Rob used his fingertips to outline the area of pain from the navel across the right half of the abdomen, regretting the torture he produced each time he pressed the belly. He turned Bilāl and they saw that the rectum was red and tender.

When he had replaced the blanket he took the small hands and heard the old Black Knight laughing at him again.

"Will he die, lord?" the father asked matter-of-factly.

"Yes," Rob said, and the man nodded.

Nobody smiled at the opinion. Since they had returned from Shīrāz, Mirdin and Karim had told certain stories that had been repeated. Rob had noticed that now no one hooted when he dared to say somebody would die.

"Aelus Cornelius Celsus has described the side sickness in his writings and should be read," *Hakim* al-Juzjani said, and turned to the next pallet.

When the last patient had been visited, Rob went to the House of Wisdom and asked Yussuf-ul-Gamal, the librarian, to help him find what the Roman had written of the side sickness. He was fascinated to learn that Celsus had opened the bodies of the dead to advance his knowledge. Still, there wasn't much knowledge of this particular complaint, which Celsus described as distemper in the large intestine near the cecum, accompanied by violent inflammation and pain on the right side of the abdomen.

When he was through reading, he went again to where Bilāl lay. The father was gone. A stern *mullah* perched over the boy like a great raven, intoning from the Qu'ran while the child stared at his black robes, his eyes stark.

Rob pulled the pallet so the little one was looking away from the *mullah*.

On a low table the nurse had left three Persian pomegranates round as balls, to be eaten with the evening meal, and he took them now and popped them one at a time until he had them flowing over his head from hand to hand. Just like olden days, Bilāl. He was a very unpracticed juggler now but with only three objects there was no trouble and he made the fruits play tricks.

The boy's eyes were as round as the flying objects.

"What we need is melody!"

He didn't know any Persian songs and he required something lively. There emerged from his mouth Barber's raucous old dolly song.

> *"Your eyes caressed me once,*
> *Your arms embrace me now . . .*
> *We'll roll together by and by*
> *So make no fruitless vow!"*

Not a suitable song for a child to die by, but the *mullah*, glaring at his antics in disbelief, was supplying solemnity and prayer while Rob supplied some of the joyousness of life. They didn't understand the words at any rate, so there was no disrespect. He gave Bilāl several choruses and then saw the child leap into a final convulsion that arched his small body into a bow. Still singing, Rob felt the final pulse flutter into nothingness in Bilāl's throat.

He shut the eyes, cleaned the snot from the nose, straightened and bathed the body. He combed Bilāl's hair and tied the jaw closed with a cloth.

The *mullah* still sat cross-legged, chanting from the Qu'ran. His eyes glared: he was able to pray and hate at the same time. Doubtless he would make complaint that the *Dhimmi* had committed sacrilege, but Rob told himself that the report would not show that just before he died, Bilāl had smiled.

Four nights out of seven the eunuch Wasif came for him and he stayed in the tower *haram* until the early hours of morning.

They gave language lessons.

"A prick."

She laughed. "No, your *lingam*. And this, my *yoni.*"

She said they were adequately matched. "A man is either as a hare, a bull, or a horse. You are as a bull. A woman is either as a deer, a mare, or an elephant, and I am as a deer. That is good. It would be difficult for a hare to bring joy to an elephant," she said seriously.

She was the teacher, he the student, as if he were a boy again and had never made love. She did things he recognized from the pictures in the book he had bought in the *maidan* and a number that weren't depicted in the book. She showed him *kshiraniraka*, the milk-and-water embrace. The position of the wife of Indra. The *auparishtaka* mouth congress.

In the beginning he was intrigued and delighted as they progressed through the Turnabout, the Knocking at the Door, the Coition of the Blacksmith. He became cranky when she tried to teach him the proper sounds to make when coming, the choice of *sut* or *plat* as substitution for the groan.

"Do you never simply relax and fuck? It is worse than memorizing *Fiqh.*"

"It is more pleasurable after it is learned," she said, offended.

He was unaffected by the reproach in her voice. Also, he had decided that he liked women to keep their hair.

"Isn't the old man sufficient?"

"He was more than enough, once. His potency was famous. He loved drink and women, and when the mood was on him he would do a snake. A *female* snake," she said, and her eyes glittered with tears as she smiled. "But he hasn't lain with me for two years. When she became very sick, he stopped."

Despina said she had belonged to Ibn Sina all her life. She had been born to two of his slaves, an Indian woman and a Persian who had been his trusted servant. Her mother died when she was six. The old man had married her at her father's death, when she was twelve, and had never freed her.

Rob fingered her nose ring, symbol of her slavery. "Why has he not?"

"As his property as well as his second wife, I am doubly protected."

"What if he were to come here now?" He thought of the single stairway.

"Wasif stands below and would divert him. Besides, my husband sits next to Reza's pallet and doesn't let go of her hand."

Rob looked at Despina and nodded and felt the guilt that had been growing without his knowledge. He liked the small and beautiful olive-skinned girl with tiny breasts and a plump little belly and a hot mouth. He was sorry about the life she led, a prisoner in this comfortable jail. He knew Islamic tradition kept her shut up most of the time within the house and the gardens and he didn't blame her for anything, but he had come to love the shabby old man with the magnificent mind and the big nose.

He got up and began to put on his clothing. "I would be your friend."

She wasn't stupid. She watched him with interest. "You've been here almost every night and have had your fill of me. If I send Wasif in two weeks' time, you will come."

He kissed her on the nose just above the ring.

Riding the brown horse slowly home in the moonlight, he wondered whether he was a great fool.

Eleven nights later, Wasif knocked at his door.

Despina was almost right, he was powerfully tempted and wanted to nod in agreement. The old Rob J. would have hurried to reinforce a story that for the rest of his life could have been pulled forth whenever men tippled and bragged—of how he had gone to the young wife again and again while the old husband sat in another part of the house.

Rob shook his head. "Tell her I can't come to her any more."

Wasif's eyes glittered beneath great, black-dyed lids, and he smiled scornfully at the timid Jew and rode his donkey away.

Reza the Pious died three mornings later as the *muezzins* of the city chanted First Prayer, a suitable time for the ending of a religious life.

In the *madrassa* and the *maristan* people spoke of how Ibn Sina prepared the woman's body with his own hands, and of the simple burial, which he had allowed only a few praying *mullahs* to attend.

Ibn Sina didn't come to the school or the hospital. No one knew where he was.

A week after Reza's death, one evening Rob saw al-Juzjani drinking in the central *maidan*.

"Sit, *Dhimmi*," al-Juzjani said, and signaled for more wine.

"*Hakim*, how is the Chief Physician?"

It was as if the question was unasked. "He thinks you are something different. A special clerk," al-Juzjani said resentfully.

If he were not a medical clerk, and if al-Juzjani were not the great al-Juzjani, Rob would have thought the other man jealous of him.

"If you are not a special clerk, *Dhimmi*, you will reckon with me." Al-Juzjani fixed him with a shining stare, and Rob realized the surgeon was quite drunk. They fell silent as the wine was served.

"I was seventeen years old when we met in Jurjān. Ibn Sina was only a few years older, but Allah! It was like looking straight into the sun. My father struck the bargain. Ibn Sina was to apprentice me in medicine, I would be his factotum."

Al-Juzjani drank reflectively. "I attended him. He taught me mathematics, using the *Almagest* as text. And he dictated several books to me, including the first part of *The Canon of Medicine*, fifty pages every golden day.

"When he left Jurjān I followed, to half a dozen places. In Hamadhān, the Amīr made him vizier but the army rebelled and Ibn Sina was thrown into prison. At first they said they'd kill him, but he was released—the lucky son of a mare! Soon the Amīr was tormented by colic and Ibn Sina cured him, and the vizierate was given to him a second time!

"I stayed with him whether he was a physician or a prisoner or a vizier. He had become as much my friend as my master. Every night pupils would gather in his house, while by turns I read aloud from his book called *Healing* and someone else read from the *Canon.* Reza made sure we always had good food. When we were finished we drank lots of wine and went out and found women. He was the merriest of companions and played the way he worked. He had dozens of beautiful cunts—perhaps he fucked remarkably, as he did everything else better than most men. Reza always knew but she loved him anyway."

He looked away. "Now she is buried and he is consumed. So that he sends old friends from him, and every day he walks the city alone, bestowing gifts to the poor."

"*Hakim,*" Rob said gently.

Al-Juzjani stared.

"*Hakim,* shall I see you to your home?"

"Foreigner. I would like you to leave me now."

So Rob nodded and thanked him for the wine, and then he went away.

Rob waited a week and then rode to the house in full daylight and left his horse with the man at the gate.

Ibn Sina was alone. His eyes were at peace. He and Rob sat together comfortably, talking sometimes, and sometimes not.

"Were you already a physician when you wed her, Master?"

"I became *hakim* at sixteen. We were wed when I was ten, the year I memorized the Qu'ran, the year I began the study of healing herbs."

Rob was awed. "At that age I was struggling to become a faker and a barber-surgeon." He told Ibn Sina how Barber had apprenticed him as an orphaned boy.

"What had been your father's work?"

"A carpenter."

"I know of European guilds. I had heard," Ibn Sina said slowly, "that in Europe there are very few Jews and they are not allowed in the guilds."

He knows, Rob thought in anguish. "A few are allowed," he muttered.

Ibn Sina's eyes seemed to pierce him gently. Rob couldn't rid himself of the certainty that he was undone.

"You yearn so desperately to learn the healing art and science."

"Yes, Master."

Ibn Sina sighed, nodded, looked away.

No doubt, Rob noted with relief, his fear had been mistaken; for soon they talked of other things.

Ibn Sina recalled the first time he had seen Reza as a boy. "She was from Bukhārā, a girl four years older than I. Our fathers were tax collectors both, and the marriage was amicably arranged save for brief difficulty because her grandfather objected that my father was an Ismaili and used hashish during holy worship. But presently we were wed. She was steadfast all my life."

The old man turned his eyes on Rob. "You still have the fire in you. What do you want?"

"To be a good physician." The kind only you make, he added silently. But he believed Ibn Sina understood.

"You are already a healer. As for worthiness . . ." Ibn Sina shrugged. "To be a good physician, you must be able to answer an unanswerable riddle."

"What is the question?" Rob J. asked, intrigued.

But the old man smiled in his sorrow. "Perhaps one day you may discover it. That is part of the riddle," he said.

Chapter 47

THE EXAMINATION

On the afternoon of Karim's examination, Rob went through his customary activities with special energy and attention, attempting to divert his mind from the scene he knew would soon take place in the meeting room just off the House of Wisdom.

He and Mirdin had recruited Yussuf-ul-Gamal, the kindly librarian, as their accomplice and spy. While going about his duties in the library Yussuf was able to witness the identities of the examiners. Mirdin waited outside for the news, which he promptly brought to Rob.

"It is Sayyid Sa'di for philosophy," Yussuf had told Mirdin before hurrying back inside for more. That wasn't bad; the philosopher was difficult but would not go out of his way to fail a candidate.

But from then on, the news was terrifying.

Nadir Bukh, the autocratic, spade-bearded legalist who had failed Karim on his first examination, would test for the law! The *mullah* Abul Bakr would question on matters of theology, and the Prince of Physicians himself would examine on medicine.

Rob had hoped that Jalal would sit on the board for surgery, but Rob could see Jalal at his usual duties, tending to patients; and presently Mirdin came rushing in and whispered that the last member had arrived and it was Ibn al-Natheli, whom none of them knew well.

Rob concentrated on his work, helping Jalal put traction on a dislocated shoulder, using a clever device of ropes of Jalal's own design. The patient, a palace guard who had been thrown from his pony during a game of ball-and-stick, finally lay like a wild animal in rope restraints, pop-eyed with the sudden release from pain.

"Now you will lie for several weeks, at ease while others struggle with the onerous duties of soldiering," Jalal said cheerfully. He directed Rob to administer astringent drugs and to order an acid diet until they could be certain the guardsman had not developed inflammation or a hematoma.

The binding of the shoulder with cloths, not too tight but sufficient to restrain movement, was Rob's last chore. When he was finished he went to the House of Wisdom and sat and read Celsus, trying to hear what was being said in the examining room and gaining only the unintelligible murmur of voices. Finally he abandoned the effort and went to wait on the steps of the medical school, where presently he was joined by Mirdin.

"They are still inside."

"I hope it is not drawn out," Mirdin said. "Karim isn't the sort who can deal with too long a testing."

"I am not certain he can deal with any testing. He puked for an hour this morning."

Mirdin sat beside Rob on the steps. They spoke about several patients and then lapsed into silence, Rob scowling, Mirdin sighing.

After a longer time than they would have thought possible, Rob stood. "Here he is," he said.

Karim threaded his way toward them through the clusters of students.

"Can you tell from his face?" Mirdin said.

Rob couldn't, but well before Karim reached them, he shouted the news. "You must call me *hakim,* clerks!"

They charged down the steps.

The three of them embraced, danced, and shouted, pummeling one another and making such a row that *Hadji* Davout Hosein, passing, showed them a face pale with indignation that students of his academy should behave in such a fashion.

The rest of the day and the evening became a time they would remember for the remainder of their days.

"You must come to my rooms for refreshment," Mirdin said.

It was the first time he had asked them to his home, the first time they opened their private worlds to one another.

Mirdin's quarters were two rented rooms in a joined house hard by the House of Zion Synagogue, on the other side of Yehuddiyyeh from Rob's neighborhood.

His family was a sweet surprise. A shy wife, Fara: short, dark, low-arsed, steady-eyed. Two round-faced sons, Dawwid and Issachar, who clung to their mother's robes. Fara served sweetcakes and wine, obviously in readiness for the celebration, and after a number of toasts the three friends went forth again and found a tailor who measured the new *hakim* for his black physician's robes.

"This is a night for the *maidans!*" Rob declared, and at eventide they were in a dining place overlooking the great central square of the city, eating a fine Persian meal and calling for more of a musky wine which Karim scarcely needed, being drunk on physicianhood.

They dwelled over each question of the examination, and each answer.

"Ibn Sina kept asking me questions about medicine. 'What are the various signs obtained from sweat, candidate? . . . Very good, Master Karim, very complete . . . And what are the general signs that we use for prognosis? Will you now discuss proper hygiene for a traveler on the land and then on the sea?' It was almost as though he were aware that medicine was my strength and the other fields my weakness.

"Sayyid Sa'di bade me discuss Plato's concept that all men desire happiness, which I am grateful, Mirdin, that we studied so completely. I answered at length, with many references to the Prophet's concept that happiness is Allah's reward for obedience and faithful prayer. And that was one danger dealt with."

"And what of Nadir Bukh?" Rob asked.

"The lawyer." Karim shuddered. "He asked me to discuss the *Fiqh* regarding punishment of criminals. I couldn't think. So I said that all punishment is based on the writings of Mohammed (may he be blessed!), which declare that in this world we all depend upon one another proximately, though our ultimate dependence is always on Allah now and forever. Time separates the good and pure from the evil and rebellious. Every individual who strays will be punished and every one who obeys will be in complete consonance with God's Universal Will, on which *Fiqh* is based. The command of the soul thus rests wholly with Allah, who works to punish all sinners."

Rob was staring. "What does that *mean?*"

"I don't know now. I didn't know then. I saw Nadir Bukh chewing the answer to see if it contained meat he hadn't recognized. He seemed about to open his mouth to demand clarification or ask further questions, in which case I should have been doomed, but then Ibn Sina asked me to expound upon the humor of blood, whereupon I gave back his own words from the two books he has written on the subject, and *the questioning was over!*"

They roared until they wept, and drank and drank again.

When finally they could drink no more they staggered to the street beyond the *maidan* and hailed the donkey coach with the lily on the door. Rob sat in the driver's seat with the pimp. Mirdin fell asleep with his head in the ample lap of the whore named Lorna, and Karim rested his head upon her bosom and sang gentle songs.

Fara's quiet eyes were round with concern when they half-carried her husband into his rooms.

"He is ill?"

"He is drunk. As are we all," Rob explained, and they returned to the coach. It carried them to the little house in Yehuddiyyeh, where he and Karim dropped to the floor as soon as they were inside the door, falling asleep in their clothes.

During the night he was awakened by a quiet rasp of sound and knew Karim was weeping.

At dawn he was awakened again, by the rising of his visitor.

Rob groaned. He should not drink at all, he thought gloomily.

"Sorry to disturb. I must go and run."

"Run? Why, on this of all mornings? After last night?"

"To prepare for *chatir.*"

"What is *chatir?*"

"A footrace."

Karim slipped out of the house. There was the *slap-slap-slap* as he began to run, a receding sound, soon gone.

Rob lay on the floor and listened to the barking of cur dogs that marked the progress of the world's newest physician, roaming like a *djinn* through the narrow streets of Yehuddiyyeh.

Chapter 48

A RIDE IN THE COUNTRY

"The *chatir* is our national footrace, an annual event almost as old as Persia," Karim told Rob. "It's held to celebrate the end of *Ramadan*, the month of religious fasting. Originally—so far back in the mists of time that we've lost the name of the king who sponsored the first race—it was a competition to select the Shah's *chatir,* or footman, but through the centuries it has drawn to Ispahan the best runners of Persia and elsewhere and taken on the qualities of a great entertainment."

The course began at the gates of the House of Paradise and wound through the streets of Ispahan for ten and one-half Roman miles, ending at a series of posts in the palace courtyard. On the posts were hung slings, each containing twelve arrows and assigned to a specific runner. Every time a runner reached the posts he took an arrow from his sling and placed it in a quiver on his back, then he retraced his steps for another lap. Traditionally the race began with the call to First Prayer. It was a grueling test of endurance. If the day was hot and oppressive, the last runner to remain in the race was declared the winner. In races run during cool weather men sometimes finished the entire twelve laps, 126 Roman miles, usually collecting the final arrow some time after Fifth Prayer. Although it was rumored that ancient runners had achieved better times, most ran the course in about fourteen hours.

"No one now living can remember a runner who finished in less than thirteen hours," Karim said. "Alā Shah has announced that if a man finishes in twelve hours or less, he will be awarded a magnificent *calaat.* In addition he will earn a reward of five hundred gold pieces and an honorary appointment as Chief of the *Chatirs,* which carries with it a handsome annual stipend."

"This is why you've worked so hard, run so far every day? You think you can win this race?"

Karim grinned and shrugged. "Every runner dreams of winning the *chatir*. Of course I would like to win the race and the *calaat*. Only one thing could be better than being a physician—and that is being a *rich* physician in Ispahan!"

The air turned, becoming so perfectly moist and temperate that it seemed to kiss Rob's skin when he left the house. The whole world seemed in full youth, and the River of Life roared day and night with snowmelt. It was foggy April in London but in Ispahan it was the month of *Shaban*, softer and sweeter than the English May. The neglected apricot trees in the little yard burst into whiteness of stunning beauty, and one morning Khuff rode up to Rob's door and collected him, telling him Alā Shah wished his company on a ride that day.

Rob was apprehensive about spending time with the mercurial monarch, and surprised the Shah had remembered his promise that they would ride together.

At the stables of the House of Paradise he was told to wait. He waited a considerable time; eventually Alā came, followed by such a retinue Rob could scarcely credit it.

"Well, *Dhimmi!*"

"Majesty."

Alā Shah waved off the *ravi zemin* impatiently and they were quickly into the saddle.

They rode deep into the hills, the Shah on a white Arabian stallion that fairly flew with easy beauty, Rob riding behind him. Presently the Shah settled into an easy canter and waved him alongside.

"You are an excellent physician to prescribe riding, Jesse. I have been drowning in the shit of the court. Is it not pleasing to be away from all people?"

"It is, Majesty."

Rob stole a look behind them a few moments later. Far back, here came the entire world: Khuff and his guardsmen, keeping a wary eye on the monarch, equerries with spare mounts and pack animals, wagons that rolled and clanked as they were dragged over the rough open ground.

"Do you wish a more spirited animal to ride?"

Rob smiled. "It would be a waste of Your Majesty's generosity. This horse is suited to my mastery, Excellency." Actually, he had grown fond of the brown gelding.

Alā snorted. "It is clear you are no Persian, for no Persian would lose an opportunity to better his mount. In Persia riding is all, and man-children emerge from their dames with tiny saddles between their legs." He dug his heels exuberantly into the Arabian's flanks. The horse sprang past a dead tree and the Shah turned in the saddle and fired his enormous longbow over his left shoulder, roaring with laughter when the great bolt of an arrow missed its mark.

"Do you know the story behind this exercise?"

"No, Sire. I saw it done by horsemen at your entertainment."

"Yes, it is often performed by us, and some are excellently skilled at it. It is called the Parthian shot. Eight hundred years ago, the Parthians were just one of the peoples of our land. They lived east of Media, in a territory that was mostly terrible mountains and an even more terrible desert, the Dasht-i-Kavir."

"I know the Dasht-i-Kavir. I crossed a bit of it to come to you."

"Then you know the kind of people it would take to live on it," Alā said, reining the stallion strongly to keep it by the gelding's side.

"There was a struggle for the control of Rome. One of the contenders was the aging Crassus, governor of Syria. He needed a military conquest to equal or surpass the exploits of his rivals, Caesar and Pompey, and he decided to challenge the Parthians.

"The Parthian army, one-quarter the size of Crassus' dread Roman legions, was led by a general named Suren. It consisted mostly of bowmen on small, fast Persian horses and a tiny force of cataphracts, armored horse soldiers wielding long, deadly lances.

"Crassus' legions came straight at Suren, who retreated into the Dasht-i-Kavir. Rather than turn north into Armenia, Crassus gave chase, plunging into the desert. And something wonderful happened.

"The cataphracts attacked the Romans before they had a chance to complete their classic defensive square. After the first charge the lancers withdrew and the archers moved in. They used Persian longbows like mine, more powerful than the Romans'. Their arrows pierced Roman shields, breastplates, and greaves, and to the amazement of the legions, the Parthians kept loosing arrows accurately over their shoulders as they retreated."

"The Parthian shot," Rob said.

"The Parthian shot. At first the Romans kept their morale, expecting the arrows soon would be depleted. But Suren brought in new supplies of arrows on baggage camels, and the Romans couldn't fight their customary war at close quarters. Crassus sent his son on a diversionary raid and the youth's head was returned to him on the end of a Persian lance. The Romans fled under cover of night—the most powerful army in the world! Ten thousand escaped, led by Cassius, future assassin of Caesar. Ten thousand were captured. And twenty thousand, including Crassus, were killed. Parthian casualties were insignificant, and since that day every Persian schoolboy has practiced the Parthian shot."

Alā gave the stallion his head and tried it again, this time shouting with delight as the arrow slammed solidly into the bole of a tree. Then he raised his bow high in the air, his signal for the others in the party to come up.

A thick rug was carried to them and unrolled and over it soldiers quickly raised the king's tent. Soon, while three musicians softly played dulcimers, food was brought.

Alā sat and motioned for Rob to join him. They were served breasts of various game fowls baked in savory spices, a tart *pilah*, bread, melons which must have been kept in a cave through the winter, and three kinds of wine. Rob ate with pleasure while Alā tasted little food but drank steadily, all three wines.

When Alā ordered the Shah's Game a board was brought at once and the pieces set up. This time Rob remembered the different moves but the Shah had an easy time defeating him thrice in succession, despite having called for more wine and quickly dispatching it.

"Qandrasseh would enforce the edict against wine drinking," Alā said.

Rob didn't know a safe reply.

"Let me tell you of Qandrasseh, *Dhimmi*. Qandrasseh understands— wrongly, wrongly!—that the throne exists principally to punish those who overstep the Qu'ran. The throne exists to enlarge the nation and make it all-powerful, not to worry about the mean sins of villagers. But the Imam believes he is Allah's terrible right hand. It is not enough that he has risen from being the head of a tiny mosque in Media until he is Vizier to the Shah of Persia. He is distant kin to the Abbasid family, in his veins flows the blood of the Caliphs of Baghdad. He would like one day to rule in Ispahan, striking out from my throne with a religious fist."

Now Rob could not have answered had the words been there, for he was stricken with terror. The Shah's wine-loosened tongue had put him at highest risk, for if Alā, sobering, should regret his words it would be no great task to arrange the witness's swift disposal.

But Alā showed no discomfiture. When a sealed jug of wine was brought, he tossed it to Rob and led him back to the horses. They made no attempt to hunt but simply rode through the lazy day and grew hot and nicely tired. The hills were bright with flowers, cuplike blossoms of red and yellow and white, on thick stalks. They weren't plants he had seen in England. Alā couldn't tell him their names but said each came not from a seed but from a bulb like an onion.

"I am taking you to a place you must never show to any man," Alā said, and led him through brush until they were at the ferny mouth of a cave. Just inside, amid a stench like slightly rotting eggs, was warm air and a pool of brown water lined with gray rocks blotched with purple lichens. Already Alā was undressing. "Well, do not tarry. Off with your clothes, you foolish *Dhimmi!*"

Rob did so with nervous reluctance, wondering whether the Shah was a man who loved the bodies of men. But Alā already was in the water and assessing him unabashedly but without lust.

"Bring the wine. You are not exceptionally hung, European."

He realized it would not be politic to point out that his organ was larger than the king's.

The Shah was more sensitive than Rob had credited, for Alā was grinning at him. "I don't need to be made like a horse, for I can have any woman. I never do a woman twice, do you know that? That is why a host does not hold more than one entertainment for me, unless he gets a new wife."

Rob settled gingerly into hot water odorous with mineral deposits, and Alā opened the wine jug and drank, then leaned back and closed his eyes. Sweat sprang from his cheeks and forehead until the part out of the water was as wet as the portion of his body that was submerged. Rob studied him, wondering what it was like to be supreme.

"When did you lose your maidenhead?" Alā asked, eyes still closed.

Rob told him of the English widow who had taken him into her bed.

"I, too, was twelve years old. My father ordered his sister to begin to come to my bed, as is our custom with young princes, very sensible. My aunt was tender and instructive, almost a mother to me. For years I thought that after every fucking came a bowl of warm milk and a sweetmeat."

They soaked in contented silence. "I would be King of Kings, European," Alā said finally.

"You are King of Kings."

"That is what I am called."

Now he opened his eyes and looked directly at Rob, an unblinking brown stare. "Xerxes. Alexander. Cyrus. Darius. All great, and if each was not Persian by birth, they were Persian kings when they died. Great kings over great empires.

"Now there is no empire. In Ispahan, I am the king. To the west, Toghrul-beg rules over vast tribes of nomadic Seljuk Turks. To the east, Mahmud is the sultan of the mountainous fasts of Ghazna. Beyond Ghazna, two dozen weak rajahs rule in India but they are a threat only to one another. The only kings strong enough to matter are Mahmud, Toghrul-beg, and I. When I ride forth, the *chawns* and *beglerbegs* who rule the towns and cities rush outside their walls to meet me with tribute and fawning compliments.

"But I know the same *chawns* and *beglerbegs* would pay the same homage to either Mahmud or Toghrul-beg if they should ride that way with their armies.

"Once in ancient days there was a time like now, when there were small kingdoms and kings who fought for the prize of a vast empire. Finally only two men held all the power. Ardashir and Ardewan met in single combat while their armies watched. Two great, mailed figures circling each other in the desert. It ended when Ardewan was bludgeoned to death and Ardashir was the first man to take the title *Shahanshah*. Would you not like to be that kind of King of Kings?"

Rob shook his head. "I want only to be a physician."

He could see puzzlement on the Shah's face. "Something new. All my life no one has failed to take an opportunity to flatter me. Yet you would not exchange places with the king, it is clear.

"I have made inquiries. They say that as an apprentice you are remarkable. That great things are expected when you become *hakim*. I shall need men who can do great things but do not lick my arse.

"I will use guile and the power of the throne to stave off Qandrasseh. The Shah has always had to fight to keep Persia. I will use my armies and my sword against other kings. Before I am through, Persia will be an empire again and I shall truly be *Shahanshah*."

His hand clamped Rob's wrist. "Will you be my friend, Jesse ben Benjamin?"

Rob knew he had been lured and trapped by a clever hunter. Alā Shah was recruiting his future loyalty for his own purposes. And it was being done coldly and with forethought; clearly, there was more to this monarch than the drunken profligate.

He would not have chosen to be involved in politics and he regretted riding out into the country that morning. But it was done, and Rob was very aware of his debts.

He took the Shah's wrist. "You have my allegiance, Majesty."

Alā nodded. He leaned back again, into the heat of the pool, and scratched his chest. "So. And do you like this, my special place?"

"It is sulfurous as a fart. Sire."

Alā was not a man to guffaw. He merely opened his eyes and smiled. Eventually he spoke again. "You may bring a woman here if you like, *Dhimmi*," he said lazily.

* * *

"I don't like it," Mirdin said when he heard that Rob had ridden with Alā. "He is unpredictable and dangerous."

"It's a great opportunity for you," Karim said.

"An opportunity I don't desire."

To his relief, days went by and the Shah didn't summon him again. He felt the need for friends who were not kings and spent much of his free time with Mirdin and Karim.

Karim was settling into the life of a young physician, working at the *maristan* as he had before, save that now he was paid a small stipend by al-Juzjani for daily examination and care of the surgeon's patients. With more time to himself and a bit more money to spend, he was frequenting the *maidans* and the brothels. "Come with me," he urged Rob. "I'll bring you to a whore with hair black as a raven's wing and fine as silk."

Rob smiled and shook his head.

"What kind of woman do you want?"

"One with hair red as fire."

Karim grinned at him. "They don't come that way."

"You need wives," Mirdin told them placidly, but neither of them heeded him. Rob turned his energies to his studies. Karim continued his solitary womanizing, and his sexual appetite was becoming a source of merriment to the hospital staff. Knowing his story, Rob was aware that within the beautiful face and the athlete's body was a friendless little boy seeking female love to blot out terrible memories.

Karim ran more than ever now, at the start and end of each day. He trained hard and constantly and not only by running. He taught Rob and Mirdin to use the curved sword of Persia, the scimitar, a heavier weapon than Rob was used to and one requiring strong, supple wrists. Karim made them exercise with a heavy rock in each hand, turning the rocks up and down, before and behind, to make their wrists quick and strong.

Mirdin was not a good athlete and couldn't become a swordsman. But he accepted his clumsiness cheerfully, and he was so endowed with intellectual power it scarcely seemed to matter that he wasn't fierce with a sword.

They saw little of Karim after dark—abruptly, he stopped asking Rob to accompany him to brothels, confiding that he had begun an affair with a married woman and was in love. But with increasing frequency Rob was invited to Mirdin's rooms near the House of Zion Synagogue for the evening meal.

On a chest in Mirdin's home he was amazed to see a checkered board such as he had seen only twice before. "Is it the Shah's Game?"

"Yes. You know it? My family has played it forever."

Mirdin's pieces were wooden, but the game was identical to that Rob had played with Alā, save that instead of being intent on swift and bloody victory, Mirdin was quick to teach. Before long, under his patient tutelage, Rob began to grasp the fine points.

Homely Mirdin offered him small glimpses of peace. On a warm evening, after a simple meal of Fara's vegetable *pilah*, he followed Mirdin to wish six-year-old Issachar a good night.

"*Abba*. Is our Father in Heaven watching me?"

"Yes, Issachar. He sees you always."

"Why cannot I see Him?"

"He is invisible."

The boy had fat brown cheeks and serious eyes. His teeth and jaw already were too large and he would have his father's inelegance, but also his sweetness.

"If He is invisible, how does He know what He looks like?"

Rob grinned. Out of the mouth of babes and sucklings, he thought. Answer that, O Mirdin, scholar of oral and written law, master of the Shah's Game, philosopher and healer . . .

But Mirdin was equal to it. "The Torah tells us He has made man in His own image, after His likeness, and therefore He does but glance at you, my son, and sees Himself." Mirdin kissed the child. "A good night, Issachar."

"A good night, *Abba*. A good night, Jesse."

"Rest well, Issachar," Rob said, and kissed the boy and followed his friend from the sleeping chamber.

Chapter 49

FIVE DAYS TO THE WEST

A large caravan arrived from Anatolia and a young drover came to the *maristan* with a basket of dried figs for the Jew named Jesse. The youth was Sadi, eldest son of Dehbid Hafiz, *kelonter* of Shīrāz, and the figs were a gift symbolizing his father's love and gratitude for the plague-fighters of Ispahan.

Sadi and Rob sat and drank *chai* and ate the delectable figs, which were large and meaty, full of crystals of sugar. Sadi had bought them in Midyat from a drover whose camels had carried them from Izmir, across the whole of Turkey. Now he would drive the camels east again, bound for Shīrāz, and he was caught up in the great adventure of travel and proud when the *Dhimmi* healer requested that he carry a gift of Ispahan wines to his distinguished father, Dehbid Hafiz.

The caravans were the only source of news, and Rob questioned the youth closely.

There had been no further sign of the plague when the caravan had departed Shīrāz. Seljuk troops had been sighted once in the mountainous eastern part of Media but they appeared to be a small party and did not attack the caravan (praise be to Allah!). In Ghazna the people were afflicted with a curious itching rash and the caravan master would not stop there lest the drovers lie with the local women and contract the strange disease. In Hamadhān there was no plague but a Christian foreigner had brought a European fever to Islam and the *mullahs* had forbidden the populace from all contact with the infidel devils.

"What are the signs of this disease?"

Sadi ibn Dehbid demurred, for he was no physician and didn't bother his head with such matters. He knew only that no one save the Christian's daughter would go near him.

"The Christian has a daughter?"

Sadi could not describe the sick man or his daughter but said that Boudi the Camel Trader, who was with the caravan, had seen them both.

Together they sought out the camel trader, a sly-eyed, wizened man who spat red saliva from between teeth blackened from chewing betel nut.

Boudi barely remembered the Christians, he said, but when Rob pressed a coin on him his memory improved until he recalled that he had seen them five days' travel to the west, half a day beyond the town of Datur. The father was middle-aged, with long gray hair and no beard. He had worn foreign clothing black as a *mullah*'s robes. The woman was young and tall and had curious hair a little lighter in color than henna.

Rob looked at him in dismay. "How ill did the European appear?"

Boudi smiled pleasantly. "I do not know, master. Ill."

"Were there servants?"

"I saw no one attending them."

Doubtless the hirelings had run off, Rob told himself. "Did she appear to have sufficient food?"

"I myself gave her a basket of pulse and three loaves of bread, master."

Now Rob fixed him with a stare that frightened Boudi. "Why did you give her foodstuffs?"

The camel trader shrugged. He turned and rummaged in a sack, and pulled out a knife, hilt first. There were fancier knives to be found in every Persian marketplace but it was the proof, for the last time Rob had seen it, this dagger had swung from the belt of James Geikie Cullen.

He knew if he confided in Karim and Mirdin they would insist on accompanying him, and he wanted to go alone. He left word for them with Yussuf-ul-Gamal. "Tell them I'm called off on a personal matter and will explain on my return," he said to the librarian.

Of others, he told only Jalal.

"Going away for a time? But why?"

"It's important. It involves a woman . . ."

"Of course it does," Jalal muttered. The bonesetter was cranky until he found that there were enough apprentices to serve the clinic without discomforting him, and then he nodded.

Rob left next morning. It was a long trip and undue haste would have worked against him, yet he kept the brown gelding moving, for always in his mind was the picture of a woman alone in a foreign wilderness with her sick father.

It was summer weather and the runoff waters of spring already had evaporated under the coppery sun, so that the salty dust of Persia coated him and insinuated itself into his saddle pack. He ate it in his food and drank a thin film of it in his water. Everywhere he saw wildflowers turned brown, but he passed people tilling the rocky soil by turning the little moisture to irrigate the vines and date trees, as had been done for thousands of years.

He was grimly purposeful and no one challenged or delayed him, and at dusk of the fourth day he passed the town of Datur. Nothing could be done in the dark, but next morning he was riding at sunrise. At midmorning in the tiny village of Gusheh, a merchant accepted his coin, bit it, and then told him everyone knew of the Christians. They were in a house off Ahmad's *wadi*, a short ride due west.

The *wadi* eluded him but he came upon two goatherds, an old man and a boy. At his question about the whereabouts of Christians, the old man spat.

Rob drew his weapon. He had an almost-forgotten ugliness in him. The old man could sense it and, with his eyes on the broadsword, he raised his arm and pointed.

Rob rode in that direction. When he was out of range, the younger goatherd put a stone in his sling and launched it. He could hear it rattling in the rocks behind him.

He came upon the *wadi* suddenly. The old riverbed was mostly dry but had been flooded earlier in the season, for in shady places there was still green growth. He followed it a good way before he saw the little house built of mud and stone. She was standing outside boiling a wash and when she saw him she sprang away like a wild thing, into the house. By the time he was off his horse, she had dragged something heavy against the door.

"Mary."

"Is it you?"

"Yes."

There was a silence, then a grating sound as she moved the rock. The door opened a crack, and then wider.

He realized she had never seen him in the beard or the Persian garb, although the leather Jew's hat was the one she knew.

She was holding her father's sword. The ordeal was in her face, which was thin, making her eyes and the large cheekbones and long thin nose all the more prominent. There were blisters on her lips, which he recalled happened to her when she was exhausted. Her cheeks were sooty except for two lines washed by tears from the smoky fire. But she blinked and he could see her become as sensible as he remembered.

"Please. Will you help him?" she said, and led Rob quickly into the house.

* * *

His heart sank when he saw James Cullen. He didn't need to take the sheepman's hands to know he was dying. She must have known too, but she looked at him as though she expected him to heal her father with a touch.

There hung over the house the fetid stink of Cullen's insides.

"He has had the flux?"

She nodded wearily and recited the details in a flat voice. The fever had begun weeks before with vomiting and a terrible pain in the right side of his abdomen. Mary had nursed him carefully. After a time his temperature had subsided and to her great relief he had begun to get well. For several weeks he had made steady gains and was almost recovered, and then the symptoms had recurred, this time with even greater severity.

Cullen's face appeared pale and sunken, and his eyes dull. His pulse was barely perceptible. He was racked with alternating fever and chills, and had both diarrhea and vomiting.

"The servants thought it was the plague. They ran away," she said.

"No. Not the plague." The vomitus wasn't black and there were no buboes. Small consolation. His abdomen had hardened on the right side until it was boardlike. When Rob pressed on it, Cullen—although he appeared to be lost in the deep softness of coma—screamed.

Rob knew what it was. The last time he had seen it, he had juggled and sang so a little boy could die without fright.

"A distemper of the large intestine. Sometimes they call it the side sickness. It is a poison that began in his gut and has spread through his body."

"What has caused it?"

He shook his head. "Perhaps the bowel has become kinked or there is an obstruction." They both recognized the hopelessness of his ignorance.

He worked hard over James Cullen, trying anything that might possibly help. He gave enemas of milky chamomile tea and when they didn't do anything he administered doses of rhubarb and salts. He applied hot packs to the abdomen, but by then he knew it was no use.

He stayed next to the Scot's bed. He would have sent Mary into the next room to get some of the rest she had denied herself, but he knew the end was near and reasoned she would have plenty of time to rest later.

In the middle of the night Cullen just gave a little leap, a small start.

"It's all right, Da," Mary whispered, rubbing his hands, and there was a slipping away, so quiet and easy that for a little while neither she nor Rob knew that her father was no longer alive.

* * *

She had given up shaving him a few days before he died and there was gray beard to be scraped from his face. Rob combed his hair and held the body in his arms while she washed it, dry-eyed. "I am glad to do this. I wasn't allowed to help with my mother," she said.

Cullen had a long scar on the right thigh. "He got that chasing a wild boar into the brush, when I was eleven. He had to spend the winter in the house. We made a crèche together for Yuletide and it was then I came to know him."

After her father had been prepared, Rob carried more water from the brook and heated it on the fire. While she bathed he dug a grave, which proved devilishly hard, for the soil was mostly stone and he hadn't a proper tool. In the end he used Cullen's sword and a stout sharpened branch for prying, and his bare hands. When the grave was ready, he fashioned a rood of two sticks lashed together with the dead man's belt.

She wore the black dress in which he had first seen her. He carried Cullen in a winding sheet that was a wool blanket they had brought from their home, so beautiful and warm he regretted placing it in the grave.

It required a Holy Mass of Requiem and he couldn't even speak a proper burial prayer, not trusting himself to get the Latin right. But a psalm that had been one of Mam's came to mind.

> "The Lord is my shepherd; I shall not want.
> He maketh me to lie down in green pastures; He leadeth me beside the still waters.
> He restoreth my soul; He guideth me in the paths of righteousness for His name's sake.
> Yea, though I walk through the valley of the shadow of death, I will fear no evil, for Thou art with me; Thy rod and Thy staff, they comfort me.
> Thou preparest a table before me in the presence of mine enemies; Thou hast anointed my head with oil; my cup runneth over.
> Surely goodness and mercy shall follow me all the days of my life; and I shall dwell in the house of the Lord for ever."

He closed the grave and fixed the cross. When he walked away she remained kneeling, her eyes closed and her lips moving with words only her own mind could hear.

He gave her time to be alone in the house. She had told him about turning loose their two horses to forage for themselves on the thin growth in the *wadi*, and he rode out to find the animals.

He saw they had built a pen with a thornbush fence. Inside he found the bones of four sheep, probably killed by animals and eaten. Doubtless Cullen had bought many more sheep that had been stolen by humans.

Crazy Scot! He never could have brought a flock all the way to Scotland. And now he would not bring himself home either, and his daughter was left alone in an unfriendly land.

At one end of the stony little valley Rob discovered the remains of Cullen's white horse. Perhaps it had broken a leg and had been easy prey; the carcass was almost consumed, but he recognized the work of jackals and went back to the fresh grave and armored it in heavy, flat stones that would prevent the beasts from digging up the body.

He came upon her black mount at the other end of the *wadi,* as far from the jackals' feast as it had been able to get. It wasn't difficult to put a halter on the horse, which appeared eager for the safety and security of servitude.

When he returned to the house he found her composed but pale. "What would I have done, had you not appeared?"

He smiled at her, remembering the barricaded door and the sword in her hand. "What was needed."

She was tightly controlled. "I would like to return to Ispahan with you."

"I want that." His heart leaped, but he was chastened by her next words.

"There is a caravanserai there?"

"Yes. Busily trafficked."

"Then I'll join a protected caravan traveling west. And make my way to a port where I may be able to book passage home."

He went to her and took her hands, the first time he had touched her. Her fingers were rough from work, unlike a *haram* woman's hands, but he didn't want to release them. "Mary, I made a terrible mistake. I can't let you go again."

Her steady eyes contemplated him.

"Come with me to Ispahan, but live there with me."

It would have been easier if he hadn't felt constrained to speak guiltily of Jesse ben Benjamin and the need for pretense.

It was as if a current ran between their fingers, but he saw anger in her eyes, a kind of horror. "So many lies," she said quietly. She pulled herself away from him and went outside.

He went to the door and watched her walking away from the house over the broken ground of the riverbed.

She was gone long enough for him to worry, but she returned.

"Tell me why it is worth the deception."

He forced himself to put it into words, an embarrassment he undertook because he wanted her and knew the truth was her due.

"It's being chosen. As though God has said, 'In the creation of human beings I made mistakes and I charge you with working to correct some of my errors.' It isn't a thing I desired. It sought me out."

His words frightened her. "Surely that is blasphemy, to set yourself as one who corrects God's mistakes?"

"No, no," he said gently. "A good physician is but His instrument."

She nodded, and now he thought he saw in her eyes a glimmer of understanding, perhaps even envy.

"I would always share you with a mistress."

Somehow she had sensed Despina, he thought foolishly. "I want only you," he said.

"No, you want your work and it will come first, before family, before anything. But I have loved you so, Rob. And want to be your wife."

He put his arms around her.

"Cullens are married in the Church," she said into his shoulder.

"Even if we could find a priest in Persia he wouldn't marry a Christian woman and a Jew. We must tell people we were married in Constantinople. When I finish my medical training we'll return to England and be properly wed."

"And meantime?" she said bleakly.

"A hand-held marriage." He took both of her hands in his.

They regarded one another soberly. "There should be words, even with a hand-held marriage," she said.

"Mary Cullen, I take you for my wife," he said thickly. "I promise to cherish and protect you, and you have my love." He wished the words were better but he was deeply moved and didn't feel in control of his tongue.

"Robert Jeremy Cole, I take you for husband," she said clearly. "I promise to go where you go and ever to seek your well-being. You have had my love since first I saw you."

She gripped his hands so hard they hurt and he could feel her vitality, a throbbing. He was aware that the fresh grave outside made joy indecent, yet he felt a wild mixture of emotions and he told himself their vows had been better than many he had heard in a church.

He packed her belongings on the brown horse and she rode the black. He would trade the pack off between the animals, transferring it each morning. On the rare occasions when the way was smooth and flat, both he and Mary sat the one horse, but most of the time she rode and he led the way on foot. It made for slow travel, but he wasn't in a hurry.

She was more given to silence than he recalled and he made no move to touch her, sensitive to her grief. Camping in a brushy clearing by the side of the road on the second night of their trip to Ispahan, he lay awake and listened to her finally weeping.

"If you're God's helper, correcting mistakes, why could you not save him?"

"I don't know enough."

The weeping had been a long time coming and now she couldn't stop. He took her into his arms. While they lay with her head on his shoulder, he began to kiss her wet face and finally her mouth, which was soft and welcoming and tasted as he remembered. He rubbed her back and stroked the lovely hollow at the base of her spine and then, as their kiss hardened and he felt her tongue, he groped through her underclothing.

She was weeping again but open to his fingers and spreading to accept him.

What he felt more than passion was an overriding regard for her and a thanksgiving. Their joining was a delicate, tender rocking in which they scarcely moved at all. It went on and on, on and on, until it ended exquisitely for him; seeking to heal he was healed, and seeking to comfort he was comforted, but to bring her some measure of solace he had to finish her with his hand.

Afterward he held her and talked softly, telling her of Ispahan and Yehuddiyyeh, and the *madrassa* and the hospital, and Ibn Sina. And of his friends the Muslim and the Jew, Mirdin and Karim.

"Do they have wives?"

"Mirdin has a wife. Karim has a lot of women."

They fell asleep wrapped in one another.

He was awakened in the harsh gray light of morning by the creaking of saddle leather, the slow thudding of hooves in the dusty road, someone's ragged coughing, men talking as they sat their walking beasts.

Looking over her shoulder through the thorny brush that separated their hiding place from the road, he watched a force of mounted soldiers riding past. They were fierce-looking, carrying the same eastern swords as Alā's men but with bows that were shorter than the Persian variety. They wore ragged robes and once-white turbans stained dark with sweat and dirt, and they exuded a stink that reached Rob where he lay in agony, waiting for one of his horses to give him away or for a rider to glance through the bushes and see him and the sleeping woman.

A familiar face came into view and he recognized Hadad Khan, the hot-tempered Seljuk ambassador to the court of the Alā Shah.

These were Seljuks, then. And riding next to white-haired Hadad Khan was another figure known to him, a *mullah* named Musa Ibn Abbas, chief aide to the Imam Mirza-aboul Qandrasseh, the Persian Vizier.

Rob saw a total of six other *mullahs* and counted ninety-six horse soldiers. There was no knowing how many had ridden past while he slept.

Neither his horse nor Mary's whinnied or made any other sound to reveal their presence, and eventually the last Seljuk rode past and Rob dared to breathe, listening to their sounds growing fainter.

Presently he kissed his wife to waken her and then lost no time breaking their rude camp and starting on their way, for he had found a reason for hurrying.

Chapter 50

THE *CHATIR*

"Married?" Karim said. He looked at Rob and grinned.

"A wife! I didn't expect you would heed my advice," Mirdin said, beaming. "Who arranged this match?"

"No one. That is," Rob said hastily, "there was a nuptial agreement more than a year ago, but it wasn't acted upon until now."

"What is her name?" Karim asked.

"Mary Cullen. She's a Scot. I met her and her father in a caravan on my eastward journey." He told them something of James Cullen, and of his illness and death.

Mirdin seemed scarcely to be listening. "A Scot. That is a European?"

"Yes. She comes from a place north of my own country."

"She is a Christian?"

Rob nodded.

"I must see this European woman," Karim said. "Is she a pretty female?"

"She's so beautiful!" Rob blurted, and Karim laughed. "But I want you to judge for yourself." Rob turned to include Mirdin in the invitation, but saw that his friend had walked away.

Rob didn't relish reporting to the Shah what he had seen, but he knew he had committed his loyalty and had little choice. When he appeared at the palace and asked to see the king, Khuff smiled his hard smile.

"What is your errand?"

The Captain of the Gates hurled a glance like a stone when Rob shook his head in silence.

But Khuff bade him wait and went to tell Alā that the foreign *Dhimmi* Jesse wished to see him, and presently the old soldier ushered Rob in to the royal presence.

Alā smelled of drink but listened soberly enough to Rob's report that his Vizier had sent pietist disciples to meet and confer with a party of the Shah's enemies.

"There has been no report of attacks in Hamadhān," Alā said slowly. "It was not a Seljuk raiding party, therefore doubtless they met to discuss treachery." He examined Rob through veiled eyes. "To whom have you spoken of this?"

"To no man, Majesty."

"Let it remain so."

Instead of further talk, Alā placed the board of the Shah's Game between them. He was visibly pleased to encounter a more difficult opponent than heretofore he had met in Rob.

"Ah, *Dhimmi*, you grow skilled and cunning as a Persian!"

Rob was able to hold him off for a time. In the end, Alā ground him into the dust and it was as always, *shahtreng*. But each recognized that their game had turned a corner. It was more of a struggle now, and Rob might have been able to hold out even longer if he were not so eager to return to his bride.

Ispahan was the most beautiful city Mary had ever seen, or perhaps it was because she was there with Rob. She was pleased with the little house in Yehuddiyyeh, although the Jewish quarter was shabby. The house wasn't as large as the house in which she and her father had lived by the *wadi* in Hamadhān, but it was of sounder construction.

At her insistence Rob bought plaster and a few simple tools and she vowed to repair the house while he was gone, her first day alone. The full heat of the Persian summer was on them, and the long-sleeved black dress of bereavement soon was sodden with perspiration.

In the middle of the morning the most handsome man she had ever seen knocked at the door. He was carrying a basket of black plums, which he set down so he could reach out to touch her red hair, frightening her. He was chuckling and looked awed, dazzling her with his perfect white teeth in his tanned face. He spoke at length; it sounded eloquent and graceful and full of feeling, but it was in Persian.

"I am sorry," she said.

"Ah." He understood at once and touched his chest. "Karim."

She lost her fright and was delighted. "So. You are my husband's friend. He's spoken of you."

He beamed and led her, protesting in words she couldn't understand, to a chair where she sat and ate a sweet plum while he mixed plaster to exactly the correct consistency and spread it on three cracks in the interior walls, and then replaced a windowsill. Shamelessly, she also allowed him to help her cut out the large, wicked thornbushes in the garden.

Karim was still there when Rob came home and she insisted that he share their meal, which then they had to delay until darkness had fallen, for it was *Ramadan,* the ninth month, the month of fasting.

"I like Karim," she told Rob when he had gone. "When shall I meet the other one—Mirdin?"

He kissed her and shook his head. "I don't know," he said.

Ramadan seemed a most peculiar holiday to Mary. It was Rob's second *Ramadan* in Ispahan, and he told her it was a somber month, supposed to be devoted to prayer and shriving, but food seemed foremost on everyone's mind because Muslims were proscribed from taking nourishment or liquid from dawn to sunset. Vendors of food were absent from the markets and the streets, and the *maidans* remained dark and silent all month, though friends and families assembled at night to eat and fortify themselves for the next day's fasting.

"We were in Anatolia last year during *Ramadan,*" Mary said wistfully. "Da bought lambs from a herdsman and gave a feast for our Muslim servants."

"We could give a *Ramadan* dinner."

"It would be pleasant, but I am in mourning," she reminded him.

Indeed, she was torn by conflicting emotions, at times racked by such grief that she felt crippled by the pain of her loss, at other times giddily aware she was the most fortunate of women in her marriage.

On the few occasions when she ventured from the house, it seemed to her that people stared at her with enmity. Her black mourning dress wasn't dissimilar from the costume of the other women of Yehuddiyyeh, but doubtless her uncovered red hair marked her as a European. She tried wearing her wide-brimmed traveling hat, but she saw women point her out in the street just the same, and their coldness toward her was unabated.

Under other circumstances she might have felt loneliness, for in the midst of a teeming city she was able to communicate with but one person; but instead of isolation she felt a privacy that was complete, as though only she and her new husband peopled the world.

In that waning month of *Ramadan* they were visited solely by Karim Harun, and several times she saw the young Persian physician running, running through the streets, a sight that made her catch her breath, for it was like watching a roe deer. Rob told her about the footrace, the *chatir,* which would be held on the first day of the three-day holiday called *Bairam* that celebrated the end of the long fast.

"I've promised to attend Karim during the running."

"Will you be his only attendant?"

"Mirdin will be there too. But I believe he will need the two of us." There was a question in his voice and she knew he was troubled that she might consider it a disrespect toward her father.

"Then you must," she said firmly.

"The race itself isn't a celebration. It could not be considered wrong for one in mourning merely to look on."

She thought about it as *Bairam* approached and in the end decided her husband was right, and that she would watch the *chatir*.

Early on the first morning of the month of *Shawwal* there was a heavy mist that gave Karim hope it would be a good day, a runner's day. He had slept fitfully but told himself that doubtless the other competitors had spent the night the same way, trying to keep their minds from dwelling on the race.

He rose and cooked himself a large pot of peas and rice, sprinkling the coarse *pilah* with celery seed that he measured with careful attention. He ate more than he wanted, stoking himself like a fire, and then returned to his pallet and rested while the celery seed did its work, keeping his mind blank and serene with prayer:

> *Allah, make me fleet and sure of foot this day.*
> *Let my chest be like unto a bellows that does not fail*
> *And my legs strong and supple as young trees.*
> *Keep my mind clear and my senses sharp*
> *And my eyes ever fixed on Thee.*

He didn't pray for victory. When he was a boy, Zaki-Omar had told him often enough: "Every yellow dog of a runner prays for victory. How confusing for Allah! It is better to ask Him to grant speed and endurance and use them to take the responsibility for victory or defeat upon oneself."

When he felt the urge he rose and went to the bucket, squatting a long and satisfying time to move his bowels. The amount of celery seed had been correct; when he was through he was emptied but not weakened, and he would not be deterred that day by a cramp in the midst of a lap.

He warmed water and bathed from a bowl by candlelight, wiping himself dry quickly because the dwindling dark contained a coolness. Then he anointed himself with olive oil against the sun, and twice wherever friction might cause pain—nipples, armpits, loins and penis, the crease of buttocks, and finally his feet, taking care to oil the tops of his toes.

He dressed in a linen loincloth and linen shirt, light leather footman's shoes, and a jaunty feathered cap. Around his neck he suspended a bowman's quiver and an amulet in a small cloth bag, and threw a cloak over his shoulders to guard against chill. Then he let himself out of the house.

He walked slowly at first and then more rapidly, feeling warmth beginning to unlock his muscles and joints. There were as yet few people in the streets. No one noticed him as he entered a brushy copse to indulge in one last nervous piss. But by the time he reached the starting point by the drawbridge of the House of Paradise a crowd had gathered there, hundreds of men. He made his way carefully through it until by prearrangement he came upon Mirdin at the very rear, and it was here a short time later that Jesse ben Benjamin found them.

His friends greeted one another stiffly. Some trouble between them, Karim saw. He put it out of his mind at once. This was a time to think only of the race.

Jesse grinned at him and questioningly touched the little bag hanging from his neck.

"My luck," Karim said. "From my lady." But he shouldn't talk before a race, he could not. He gave Jesse and Mirdin a quick smile to show he meant no offense and closed his eyes and brought in blankness, shutting out the loud talk and boisterous laughter all around him. It was harder to shut out the smells of oils and animal grease, body odor and sweaty clothing.

He said his prayer.

When he opened his eyes the mist had turned pearly. Looking through it, he was able to see a perfectly round red disc, the sun. The air had changed and already was heavy. He realized with a pang that it would be a brutally hot day.

Out of his hands. *Imshallah.*

He removed his cloak and gave it to Jesse.

Mirdin was pale. "Allah be with you."

"Run with God, Karim," Jesse told him.

He didn't answer. Now a hush had fallen. The runners and the onlookers were gazing up at the nearest minaret, the Friday Mosque, where Karim could see a tiny, dark-robed figure just entering the tower.

In a moment the haunting call to First Prayer floated to their ears and Karim prostrated himself to the southwest, the direction of Mecca.

When the praying ended everyone was screaming at the top of his lungs, runners and spectators alike. It was frightening and made him tremble. Some shouted encouragement, others called upon Allah; many simply howled, the bloodcurdling sound men might make when attacking an enemy's wall.

Back where he was standing the movement of the front runners could only be sensed but he knew from experience how some were springing forward to be in the first rank, fighting and shoving, heedless of who was trampled and what injuries were inflicted. Even those who were not slow in rising from prayer were at risk, because in the churning maelstrom of bodies, flailing arms would strike faces, feet would kick nearby legs, ankles would be twisted and turned.

It was why he waited in the rear with contemptuous patience as wave after wave of runners moved away ahead of him, assaulting him with their noise.

But finally he was running. The *chatir* had begun and he was in the tail of a long serpent of men.

He was running very slowly. It would take a long time to cover the first five and one-quarter miles, but that was part of his plan. The alternative would have been to station himself in front of the crowd, then, assuming he wasn't injured in the melee, surge forward at a pace guaranteed to move him safely ahead of the pack. But this would have used up too much energy at the outset. He had chosen the safer way.

They ran down the wide Gates of Paradise and turned left to stay for more than a mile on the Avenue of the Thousand Gardens, which dropped and then rose, giving a long hill on the first half of the lap and a short but steeper hill on the return. The course turned right onto the Street of the Apostles, which was only a quarter of a mile long; but the short street fell on the way out and was a laborious run on the return. They padded left again onto the Avenue of Ali and Fatima, and followed it all the way to the *madrassa*.

All kinds of people were in the pack. It was fashionable for young nobles to run for half a lap, and men in silk summer clothing ran shoulder to shoulder with runners in rags. Karim hung back, for at this point it wasn't a race so much as a running mob, full of high spirits over the end of *Ramadan*. It wasn't a bad way for him to begin, for the slow pace allowed his juices to begin to flow gradually.

There were spectators but it was too early for a dense crowd to line the streets; it was a long race and most people would come to watch later. At the *madrassa* he looked at once toward the long roof of the one-storied *maristan*, where the woman who had given him the amulet—it was a lock of her hair in the little bag—had said her husband had arranged for her to watch the *chatir*. She wasn't there yet but two nurses stood on the street in front of the hospital and shouted *"Hakim! Hakim!"* Karim waved as he ran by, knowing they would be disappointed to see him at the end of the pack.

They wound through the *madrassa* grounds and on to the central *maidan*, where two great open tents had been raised. One for courtiers, carpeted and lined with brocades, contained tables bearing all manner of rich victuals and wines. The other tent, for runners of common birth, offered free bread and *pilah* and *sherbet* and appeared no less welcoming, so that here the race lost almost half its contestants, who made for the refreshment with glad cries.

Karim was among those who ran past the tents. They circled the stone ball-and-stick goals and then began to retrace the course to the House of Paradise.

Now they were fewer and strung along a distance, and Karim had room to set his pace.

There were choices. Some held with pushing the first few laps smartly to take advantage of the morning cool. But he had been taught by Zaki-Omar that the secret of completing long distances was to select a pace that would drain his last bit of energy at the completion, and to stay with that speed unvaryingly. He was able to fall into it with the perfect rhythm and regularity of a trotting horse. The Roman mile was one thousand five-foot paces but Karim ran about twelve hundred steps to a mile, each covering a little more than four feet. He held his spine perfectly straight, his head high. The *slap-slap-slap* of his feet against the ground at his chosen pace was like the voice of an old friend.

He began to pass some runners now, though he knew that most were not men in serious contention, and he was running easily when he returned to the palace gates and collected the first arrow to be dropped into his quiver.

Mirdin offered balm to be rubbed into his skin against the sun, which he refused, and water, which he took gratefully but sparingly.

"You are forty-second," Jesse said, and he nodded and sprang away.

Now he ran in the full light of day and the sun was low but already strong, clearly signaling the heat to come. It wasn't unexpected. Sometimes Allah was kind to runners but most *chatirs* were ordeals through the Persian heat. The high points of Zaki-Omar's athletic career had been to win second place in two *chatirs*, once when Karim was twelve years old and again the year he was fourteen. He remembered his terror at seeing the exhaustion in Zaki's red face and popping eyes. Zaki had run as long and as far as he had been able, but in both races there had been one runner who could run longer and farther.

Grimly, Karim removed the thought from his mind.

The hills seemed no worse than they had on the first lap and he ascended them almost without thought. The crowds began to be thicker everywhere, for it was a fine sunny morning and Ispahan was enjoying a holiday. Most businesses were closed and people stood or sat along the route in groups —Armenians together, Indians together, Jews together, learned societies and religious organizations en masse.

When Karim came to the hospital again and still couldn't see the woman who had promised to be there, he felt a pang. Perhaps, after all, her husband had forbidden her to come.

There was a solid clump of spectators in front of the school and they cheered and waved him on.

As he approached the *maidan* he saw it was already as frenzied as if it were a Thursday evening. Musicians, jugglers, fencers, acrobats, dancers, and magicians played to large audiences, while the runners made their way around the outside of the square almost unnoticed.

Karim began to pass spent contenders lying or sitting by the side of the road.

When he collected his second arrow Mirdin again tried to give him an ointment to protect his skin from the sun but he refused it, though he knew with a private shame it was because the ointment was unsightly and he wanted her to see him without it. It would be available if needed since, by prearrangement, on this lap Jesse would begin to follow him on the brown horse. Karim knew himself; the first testing of his soul was coming, for he invariably felt distress after 25 Roman miles.

Problems came almost on schedule. Halfway up the hill on the Avenue of the Thousand Gardens he became aware of a raw place on the heel of his right foot. It was impossible to run such a long race without damaging his feet and he knew he must ignore the discomfort, but soon it was joined by a sticking pain in his right side that grew until he gasped whenever his right foot jarred against the road.

He signaled to Jesse, who was carrying a goatskin of water behind his saddle, but a warm drink tasting of goaty leather did little to ease his discomfort.

But when he drew close to the *madrassa*, at once he spotted on the hospital roof the woman for whom he'd been looking, and it was as if everything that had been troubling him fell away.

Rob, riding behind Karim like a squire trailing his knight, saw Mary as they approached the *maristan* and they smiled at each other. Dressed in her mourning black, she would have been inconspicuous were her face not unadorned, but every other female in sight wore the heavy black street veil. The others on the roof stood slightly apart from his wife, as if afraid lest they be corrupted by her European ways.

There were slaves with the women and he recognized the eunuch Wasif standing behind a small figure disguised by a shapeless black dress. Her face was hidden behind the horsehair veil but he could note Despina's eyes, and where they were turned.

Following her gaze to Karim, Rob saw something that made it difficult for him to breathe. Karim had found Despina too and held her with his glance. As he ran past her, his hand went up and touched the little bag suspended around his neck.

It seemed to Rob a naked declaration to all, but the sound of the cheering didn't change. And although Rob tried to study the crowd for Ibn Sina's presence, he didn't see him among the spectators as they went past the *madrassa*.

Karim ran away from the pain in his side until it dwindled, and he ignored the discomfort in his feet. Now the time of attrition had begun and all along the way men in donkey-drawn wagons were busy picking up runners who couldn't go on.

When he claimed his third arrow he allowed Mirdin to smear him with the ointment, made of óil of roses, oil of nutmeg, and cinnamon. It turned his light-brown skin yellow but was good against the sun. Jesse kneaded his legs while Mirdin applied the salve, then held a cup to his cracked lips, giving him more water than he desired.

Karim tried to protest. "Don't want to have to piss!"

"You're sweating too hard to piss."

He knew it was true, and he drank. In a moment he was away again and running, running.

This time when he passed the school he was aware that she saw an apparition, the melted yellow grease streaked by rivulets of sweat and muddied dust.

Now the sun was high and hot, baking the ground so the heat of the road penetrated the leather of his shoes and seared his soles. Along the route men stood and held out containers of water, and sometimes he paused to drench his head before darting off without thanks or a blessing.

After he had collected the fourth arrow, Jesse left him, to reappear in a short time on his wife's black mount, doubtless leaving the brown horse to water and rest in cool shade. Mirdin waited by the post containing the arrows, studying the other runners, according to their plan.

Karim kept running past men who had collapsed. Someone stood bent over at the waist in the middle of the road, weakly vomiting nothing. A muttering Indian stopped hobbling and kicked off his shoes. He ran half a dozen steps, leaving the red tracks of his bloody feet, and then stood quietly and waited for a wagon.

When Karim passed the *maristan* on the fifth lap Despina was no longer on the roof. Perhaps she had been frightened by his appearance. It didn't matter, for he had seen her and now occasionally he reached up and grasped the little bag containing the thick locks of black hair he had cut from her head with his own hands.

In places the wagons and the feet of the runners and the hooves of the attendants' animals raised a fearful dust that coated his nostrils and throat and made him cough. He began to close down his consciousness until it was small and remote somewhere deep inside, dwelling on nothing, allowing his body to continue to do what it had done so many times.

The call to Second Prayer was a shock.

All along the route, runners and spectators alike prostrated themselves toward Mecca. He lay and trembled, his body unable to believe that the demands on it had halted, however briefly. He wanted to remove his shoes but knew he wouldn't get them back on his swollen feet. When the prayers were finished, for a moment he didn't move.

"How many?"

"Eighteen. Now it is the race," Jesse told him.

Karim started up again, forcing himself to run through the heat shimmer. But he knew it was not yet the race.

It was harder to climb the hills than it had been all morning but he kept to the steady rhythm of his running. This was the worst, with the sun directly overhead and the real testing before him. He thought of Zaki and knew that unless he died he would keep going until at least he had won second place.

Until now he hadn't had the experience, and in another year perhaps his body would be too old for such punishment. It would have to be today.

The thought allowed him to reach within himself and find strength when some of the others were searching and finding nothing, and when he slid the sixth arrow into his quiver, he turned at once to Mirdin. "How many?"

"Six runners are left," Mirdin said wonderingly, and Karim nodded and began to run again.

Now it was the race.

He saw three runners ahead and knew two of them. He was overtaking a small, finely made Indian. Perhaps eighty paces in front of the Indian was a youth whose name Karim didn't know but whom he recognized as a soldier in the palace guard. And far ahead but close enough for him to identify was a runner of note, a man from Hamadhān named al-Harāt.

The Indian had slowed but picked up the pace when Karim drew even, and they went on together, matching stride for stride. He had very dark skin, almost ebony, under which long, flat muscles gleamed in the sun as he moved.

Zaki's skin had been dark, an advantage under a hot sun. Karim's skin needed the yellow salve; it was the color of light leather, the result, Zaki always said, of a female ancestor being fucked by one of Alexander's fair Greeks. Karim thought something like that probably was true. There had been a number of Greek invasions and he knew light-skinned Persian men, and women with snowy breasts.

A little spotted dog had come from nowhere and was pacing them, barking.

When they passed the estates on the Avenue of the Thousand Gardens people held out melon slices and cups of *sherbet* but Karim didn't take any, being fearful of cramps. He accepted water, which he put into his cap before setting it back on his head and reaping momentary relief until the hat dried in the sun with remarkable swiftness.

The Indian grabbed green melon and gobbled as he ran, discarding the rind over his shoulder.

Together they passed the young soldier. He was already out of contention, a full lap behind, for there were only five arrows in his quiver. Two dark red lines ran down the front of his shirt from nipples rubbed raw. Every time he took a step his legs buckled slightly at the knees and it was clear he wouldn't be running much longer.

The Indian looked at Karim and gave a white-toothed grin.

Karim was dismayed to see that the Indian was running easily and his face was alert but relatively unstrained. Runner's intuition said that the man was stronger than Karim and less tired. Perhaps faster, too, if it should come to that.

The spotted dog that had run with them for miles suddenly swerved and cut across their path. Karim jumped to avoid him and felt the brush of the warm fur, but the dog smashed solidly into the other runner's legs and the Indian fell to the ground.

He started up as Karim turned to him, then he sat back in the road. His right foot was twisted crazily and he gazed at his ankle in disbelief, unable to comprehend that his race was done.

"Go!" Jesse shouted to Karim. "I will take care of him. You go!" And

Karim turned and ran as if the Indian's strength were transferred to his own limbs, as if Allah had spoken with the *Dhimmi*'s voice, because he was beginning truly to believe that now might be the time.

He trailed al-Harāt most of the lap. Once, on the Street of the Apostles, he came up close behind and the other runner glanced back. They had known one another in Hamadhān and he saw recognition in al-Harāt's eyes, and an old familiar contempt: Ah, it is Zaki-Omar's bum boy.

Al-Harāt increased his pace and soon led him again by 200 paces.

Karim took the seventh arrow and Mirdin told him of the other runners as he gave water and smeared the yellow ointment.

"You are fourth. In first place is an Afghan whose name I don't know. A man from al-Rayy is second, name of Mahdavi. Then al-Harāt and you."

For a lap and one-half he trailed al-Harāt like one who knew his place, sometimes wondering about the two who were so far ahead they weren't in his sight. In Ghazna, a place of towering mountains, Afghan men ran trails so high the air was thin, and it was said that when they ran at lower altitudes they didn't tire. And he had heard that Mahdavi of al-Rayy also was a good runner.

But while descending the short, steep hill on the Avenue of the Thousand Gardens he saw a dazed runner at the edge of the road, holding his right side and weeping. They passed him by, but soon Jesse brought the news that it had been Mahdavi.

Karim's own side had begun to hurt again and both his feet gave him pain. Call to Third Prayer caught him just beginning the ninth lap. Third Prayer was a time that had worried him, for the sun was no longer high and he feared his muscles would stiffen. But the heat was unrelenting and pressed down like a heavy blanket as he lay and prayed, and he was still sweating when he rose and began to run again.

This time, though he kept his pace, he seemed to overtake al-Harāt as if the Hamadhān man were walking. When he drew abreast, al-Harāt tried to make a race of it but soon his breathing was loud and desperate and he was lurching. The heat had him; as a physician, Karim knew that the man could die if it was the kind of heat sickness that brought on a red face and dry skin, but al-Harāt's face was pale and wet.

Nevertheless he stopped when the other staggered to a halt.

Al-Harāt still had enough contempt in him to glare, but he wanted a Persian to win. "Run, bastard."

Karim left him gladly.

From the high slope of the first descent, gazing down the straight stretch of white road, he caught sight of a small figure moving up the long hill in the distance.

As he watched, the Afghan fell and then got to his feet and began to run again, finally turning out of sight onto the Street of the Apostles. It was hard for Karim to hold himself in rein but he kept to his pace and didn't see the other runner again until he had achieved the Avenue of Ali and Fatima.

They were much closer. The Afghan fell again and got up to run raggedly; he may have been accustomed to thin air but the mountains of Ghazna were cool and the Ispahan heat served Karim, who kept closing the distance.

When they ran past the *maristan* he didn't see or hear the people he knew because he was concentrating on the other runner.

Karim reached him after the fourth and final fall. They had brought the Afghan water and were applying wet cloths as he lay gasping like a landed fish, a squat man with broad shoulders and dark skin. He had slightly slanted brown eyes that were calm as they watched Karim pass him.

Victory brought more anguish than triumph, for now there had to be a decision. He had won the day; did he have it in him to try for the Shah's *calaat?* The "royal garment," five hundred gold pieces, and the honorary but well-paid appointment as Chief of the *Chatirs* would go to any man who completed the entire course of 126 miles in less than twelve hours.

Rounding the *maidan,* Karim faced the sun and studied it. He had run all through the day, almost 95 miles. It should be enough and he ached to turn in his nine arrows and collect the prize of coins, then to join other runners now splashing in the River of Life. He needed to soak in their envy and admiration and in the river itself, a sinking into green waters that was more than earned.

The sun hovered above the horizon. Was there time? Was there strength in his body still? Was it Allah's wish? It would be very close, and perhaps he could not complete another 31 miles before the call to Fourth Prayer signaled the setting of the sun.

Yet he knew that total victory might banish Zaki-Omar from his bad dreams more completely than lying with all the women of the world.

And thus when he had collected another arrow, instead of turning toward the officials' tent he started around for the tenth time. The white dust road before him was vacant, and now he was running against the dark *djinn* of the man to whom he had yearned to be a son and who had made him, instead, a whore.

* * *

When the race had dwindled to the last man and the *chatir* was won, the spectators had begun to disperse; but now all along the way, people saw Karim coming alone and they flocked to regather as they realized he was trying to gain the Shah's *calaat.*

They were sophisticated in matters of the annual *chatir* and knew the toll exacted by running through a day of crippling heat, and they raised such a hoarse roar of love that the sound seemed to pull him around the course, a lap he almost enjoyed. At the hospital he was able to pick out faces beaming with pride, al-Juzjani, the nurse Rūmī, Yussuf the librarian, the *hadji* Davout Hosein, even Ibn Sina. When he sighted the old man his eyes went at once to the roof of the hospital and he saw that she was back and knew that when he was alone with her again, she would be the real prize.

But he began to experience his gravest trouble on the second half of the lap. He was accepting water often and pouring it over his head, and now fatigue made him careless and some of the water splashed onto his left shoe, where almost immediately the wet leather began to abrade the abused skin from his foot. Perhaps it made a tiny alteration in his stride, for soon he developed a cramp in the right hamstring.

Worse, when he came down toward the Gates of Paradise the sun was lower than he expected. It was directly over the far hills, and as he started on what he prayed was the last lap but one, weakening swiftly and fearful that there was insufficient time, he was taken by the deepest melancholy.

Everything became heavy. He stayed with the pace but his feet were transformed into stones, the quiver full of arrows struck him a ponderous blow in the back with every step, and even the little bag containing her locks of hair pushed against him as he ran. He threw water on his head more often and felt himself fading.

But the people of the city had caught a strange fever. Each of them had become Karim Harun. Women screamed as he passed. Men made a thousand vows, shouted his praises, called upon Allah, implored the Prophet and the twelve martyred Imams. Anticipating him by the approaching cheers, they watered the street before he came, scattered flowers in his path, ran alongside and fanned him or sprinkled scented water on his face, his thighs, his arms, his legs.

He felt them enter his blood and bones and he caught their fire. His stride strengthened and steadied.

His feet rose and fell, rose and fell. He kept the pace, but now he didn't hide from the hurt, seeking instead to pierce the smothering fatigue by concentrating on the pain in his side, the pain in his feet, the pain in his legs.

When he took the eleventh arrow, the sun had begun its slide behind the hills and had the shape of half a coin.

He ran through the deepening light, his last dance, up the first short incline, down the steep drop to the Avenue of the Thousand Gardens, through the flat, up the long climb, his heart pounding.

When he attained the Avenue of Ali and Fatima he threw water on his head and couldn't feel it.

Pain ebbed along with every response as he ran on. When he reached the school he didn't look for friends, more concerned with the fact that he had lost the sensory experience of his limbs.

Yet the feet he couldn't feel kept on with their rise and fall, propelling him forward, *slap-slap-slap*.

This time at the *maidan* no one watched the entertainments but Karim didn't hear the roar or see them, running in his silent world to the end of a fully ripened and dwindling day.

When he entered the Avenue of the Thousand Gardens again, he saw a shapeless dying red light on the hills. It seemed to him that he moved slowly, so slowly, across the flat and up the hill—the last hill he must climb!

He swept downward, the most dangerous time, for if his senseless legs made him stumble and sprawl, he wouldn't get up again.

When he made the turn and entered the Gates of Paradise there was no sun. He watched blurred people now who seemed to float above the ground, silently urging him on, but in his mind his vision was clear as a *mullah* entered the narrow, winding stairway of the mosque, climbed to the little platform in the high tower, waited for the last ray's dying . . .

He knew he had only moments.

He tried to will dead legs to longer strides, straining to quicken the ingrained pace.

Ahead of him, a small boy left his father's side and ran out into the road; he froze, staring at the giant who lumbered down on him.

Karim swept the child up and lifted him to his shoulders as he ran, and the roar shook the earth. When he reached the posts with the boy, Alā was waiting, and as he grasped the twelfth arrow the Shah took off his own turban and exchanged it for the runner's feathered cap.

The surge of the crowd was checked by the call of the *muezzins* from minarets all over the city. The people turned toward Mecca and dropped into prayer. The child he still held began to wail and Karim released him. Then the prayer was over, and when he rose, king and nobles were at him like nattering puppies. Beyond, the common people began to scream again and pushed forward to claim him, and it was as if Karim Harun suddenly owned Persia.

PART FIVE

The War Surgeon

Chapter 51

THE CONFIDENCE

"Why do they dislike me so?" Mary asked Rob.

"I don't know." He made no attempt to deny it; she wasn't a fool. When the smallest Halevi daughter toddled toward them from the house next door, her mother Yudit, who no longer brought gifts of warm bread for the foreign Jew, ran to snatch up her daughter wordlessly, fleeing as from corruption. Rob took Mary to the Jewish market and discovered he was no longer smiled upon as the Jew of the *calaat*, no longer the favorite customer of Hinda the woman merchant. They passed their other neighbors Naoma and her stout daughter Lea and the two women looked away coldly, as if Yaakob ben Rashi hadn't hinted to Rob over a Sabbath meal that he might become part of the shoemaker's family.

Wherever Rob walked in Yehuddiyyeh he saw conversing Jews fall silent and stare. He noted the meaningful nudge, the burning resentment in an occasional glance, even a muttered curse on the lips of old Reb Asher Jacobi the Circumciser, bitterness directed against one of their own who had partaken of forbidden fruit.

He told himself he didn't care: what were the people in the Jewish quarter to him, really?

Mirdin Askari was something else again; it wasn't Rob's imagination that Mirdin was avoiding him. These mornings he missed Mirdin's big-toothed smile and comforting companionship, for Mirdin invariably presented a wooden face as he offered a brief greeting and then moved away.

Finally he sought Mirdin out, finding him sprawled in the shade of a chestnut tree on the *madrassa* grounds, reading the twentieth volume of *Al-Hawi* of Rhazes, the final volume. "Rhazes was good. *Al-Hawi* covers all of medicine," Mirdin said uncomfortably.

"I've read twelve volumes. I'll reach the others soon." Rob looked at him. "Is it so bad that I've found a woman to love?"

Mirdin stared back. "How could you marry an Other?"

"Mirdin, she's a jewel."

" 'For the lips of a strange woman drop as a honeycomb, and her mouth is smoother than oil.' She's a Gentile, Jesse! You fool, we're a dispersed and beleaguered people struggling for survival. Each time one of us marries outside our faith it means the end of future generations of us. If you can't see that, you aren't the man I thought you to be and I won't be your friend."

He had been deluding himself—the people of the Jewish quarter did matter, for they had freely given him acceptance. And this man mattered most of all, for he had given friendship and Rob did not have so many friends that he could throw Mirdin away. "I'm *not* the man you thought me to be." He felt a compulsion to speak, believing absolutely that he didn't misplace his trust. "I haven't married outside my faith."

"She's a Christian."

"Yes."

The blood drained from Mirdin's face. "Is this a stupid jest?"

When Rob said nothing he gathered up the book and scrambled to his feet. "Miscreant! Should it be true—if you're not mad—not only do you risk your own neck, you've endangered mine. If you consult *Fiqh* you'll learn that by telling me, you've criminalized me and made me party to the deception unless I inform on you." He spat. "Son of the Evil One, you've placed my children in danger and I curse the day we met."

And Mirdin hurried away.

Day after day passed and the *kelonter*'s men didn't come for him. Mirdin had not informed.

At the hospital, Rob's marriage wasn't a problem. The gossip that he had married a Christian woman had circulated among the *maristan* staff, but he was already regarded as an eccentric—the foreigner, the Jew who had gone from jail to a *calaat*—and this unseemly union was accepted as only one more aberration. Other than that, in a Muslim society where each man was allowed four wives, the taking of a woman caused little stir.

Nevertheless, he felt his loss of Mirdin deeply. These days he saw little of Karim, either; the young *hakim* had been taken up by the nobles of the court and was feted at entertainments day and night. Karim's name was on everyone's lips since the *chatir*.

So Rob was as alone with his bride as she was with him, and he and Mary settled easily into life together. She was what the house had needed; it was a warmer and more comfortable place. Smitten, he spent every spare moment with her, and when they were apart he found himself remembering pink moist flesh, the long, tender line of her nose, the lively intelligence in her eyes.

They rode into the hills and made love in the warm sulfurous waters of Alā's secret pool. He left the ancient Indian picture volume where she would see it, and when he tried the variations the book depicted, he found she had studied it. Some of the practices were pleasing and others brought them hilarity. They laughed often and joyously on the bed mat, playing strange and sensuous private games.

He was ever the scientist. "What causes you to become so wet? You're a well that sucks me in."

She drove an elbow into his ribs.

But she wasn't embarrassed by her own curiosity. "I like it so when it is little—limp and weak and feels like satin. What causes it to change? I had a nurse once who told me it became long and heavy and dense because it filled with pneuma. Do you think that's so?"

He shook his head. "Not air. It fills with arterial blood. I've seen a hanged man whose rigid prick was so full of blood it was red as a salmon."

"I haven't hanged *you*, Robert Jeremy Cole!"

"It has to do with scent and sight. Once, at the end of a brutal journey, I rode a horse that was almost unable to move, so great was his fatigue. But he smelled a mare on the wind, and even before we saw the animal his organ and muscles were like wood and he was running toward her so eagerly I had to pull him back."

He loved her so, she was worth any loss. Still, his heart leaped one evening when a familiar figure appeared at their door and nodded a greeting.

"Come in, Mirdin."

Presented to the visitor, Mary looked at Mirdin curiously; but she provided wine and sweet cakes and left them almost at once, going to feed the animals with the wise instinct he already cherished.

"You're truly a Christian?"

Rob nodded.

"I can take you to a distant town in Fars where the *rabbenu* is my cousin. If you request conversion by the learned men there, perhaps they'll agree. Then there would be no reason for lies and deceits."

Rob looked at him and slowly shook his head.

Mirdin sighed. "If you were a knave you would agree at once. But you're an honest and faithful man as well as an uncommon physician. That's why I can't turn my back on you."

"Thank you."

"Jesse ben Benjamin isn't your name."

"No. My true name is—"

But Mirdin shook his head warningly and held up his hand. "The other name mustn't be spoken between us. You must remain Jesse ben Benjamin."

He looked at Rob appraisingly. "You've blended yourself into Yehuddiyyeh. In some ways you rang false. I told myself it was because your father was a European Jew, an apostate who strayed from our ways and neglected to pass his birthright to his son.

"But you must remain constantly alert lest you make a fatal error. Uncovered, your deceit would bring a terrible sentence from a *mullah*'s court. Doubtless, death. If you should be caught, it might imperil the Jews here. Though your deception is no fault of theirs, in Persia it's easy for the innocent to suffer."

"Are you certain you want to become involved with so much risk?" Rob asked quietly.

"I've thought it out. I must be your friend."

"I'm glad."

Mirdin nodded. "But I have my price."

Rob waited.

"You have to understand what you pretend to be. There's more to being a Jew than donning a caftan and wearing your beard a certain way."

"How shall I gain this understanding?"

"You must study the Lord's commandments."

"I know the Ten Commandments." Agnes Cole had taught them to each of her children.

Mirdin shook his head. "The ten are a fraction of the laws that make up our Torah. The Torah contains 613 commandments. These are what you must study, along with the Talmud—the commentaries dealing with each law. Only then will you see the soul of my people."

"Mirdin, that's worse than *Fiqh*. I'm being smothered by scholarship," he said desperately.

Mirdin's eyes glinted. "It's my price," he said.

Rob saw he was serious.

He sighed. "Be damned. All right."

Now for the first time Mirdin smiled. He poured himself some of the wine and, ignoring the European table and chairs, sank to the floor and sat with his legs folded beneath him. "So let us begin. The first commandment is, 'Thou shalt be fruitful and multiply.' "

It occurred to Rob that it was exceedingly pleasant to see Mirdin's warm, homely face here in his house. "I'm trying, Mirdin," he said, grinning at his friend. "I'm doing the best I can!"

Chapter 52

SHAPING JESSE

"Her name is Mary, like Yeshua's mother," Mirdin told his wife in the Tongue.

"Her name is Fara," Rob said to Mary in English.

The two wives studied each other.

Mirdin had brought Fara to visit, along with their brown-skinned little boys, Dawwid and Issachar. The women couldn't converse, lacking common language. Nevertheless, soon they were communicating certain thoughts amid giggling, hand signals, eye-rolling, and exclamations of frustration. Perhaps Fara became Mary's friend at her husband's command but from the start the two women, dissimilar in every way, shared a bond of mutual esteem.

Fara showed Mary how to pin up her long red hair and cover it with a cloth before leaving the house. Some of the Jewish women wore veils in the Muslim style but many simply covered their hair, and that single act made Mary inconspicuous. Fara guided her to market stalls where the produce was fresh and the meat good, and pointed out merchants to be avoided. Fara taught her to *kasher* meat, soaking and salting it to remove excess blood. And how to place meat, capsicum powder, garlic, laurel leaves, and salt in a covered earthen pot which was then heaped with hot coals and allowed to bake slowly all through the long *shabbat* to become spicy and tender, a delectable dish called *shalent* that became Rob's favorite meal.

"Oh, I would so like to *talk* with her, to ask her questions and tell her things!" Mary said to Rob.

"I'll give you lessons in the Tongue."

But she would have none of the Jews' language or the Persians'. "I'm not quick with foreign words, as you are," she said. "It took years for me to learn English, and I had to work like a slave to gain command of Latin. Will we not go soon to where I may hear my own Gaelic?"

"When the time is proper," he said, but he made her no promise of when that would be.

Mirdin undertook to manage Jesse ben Benjamin's reacceptance by Yehuddiyyeh.

"Jews since King Solomon—no, before Solomon!—have taken Gentile wives and survived within the Jewish community. But always they've been men who made it clear through their daily living that they continued to cleave to their people."

At Mirdin's suggestion it became their custom to meet twice a day for prayer in Yehuddiyyeh, for *shaharit* in the morning at the little synagogue called the House of Peace, which Rob favored, and for *ma'ariv* at day's end in the House of Zion Synagogue near Mirdin's home. Rob found it no hardship. He had always gained tranquility from the swaying and reverie and rhythmic chanted prayer. As the Tongue grew ever more natural to him, he forgot that he came to the synagogue as part of a disguise and sometimes he felt that his thoughts might reach God. He prayed not as Jesse the Jew or as Rob the Christian, but as one reaching for understanding and comfort. At times this happened while he said a Jewish prayer but he was as likely to find a moment of communion in a relic from his boyhood; sometimes, while all about him men babbled blessings so ancient they may well have been used by a Judean carpenter's son, he petitioned one of Mam's saints or prayed to Jesus or to His mother.

Gradually, fewer glares were directed at him, and then none, as the months passed and those in Yehuddiyyeh became accustomed to the sight of the big English Jew holding a fragrant citron and waving palm branches in the House of Peace Synagogue during the harvest festival of *Sukkot*, fasting alongside the others at *Yom Kippur*, dancing in the procession that followed the scrolls in celebration of the Lord's giving the Torah to the people. Yaakob ben Rashi told Mirdin it was obvious that Jesse ben Benjamin was seeking to atone for his rash marriage to an alien woman.

Mirdin was shrewd and knew the difference between protective coloration and total commitment of a man's soul. "I ask one thing," he said. "You must never allow yourself to be the tenth man."

Rob J. understood. If religious folk waited for a *minyan*, the congregation of ten male Jews that would allow them to worship in public, it would be a terrible thing to deceive them for the sake of his illusion. He made the promise promptly, and he was always careful to keep it.

Almost every day, he and Mirdin made time to study the commandments. They used no book. Mirdin knew the precepts as oral law. "It's generally agreed that 613 commandments can be gleaned from the Torah," he said. "But there's no agreement on their exact form. One scholar may count a precept as a separate commandment, another scholar may count it as part of the previous law. I'm giving you the version of the 613 commandments that was passed down the long generations of my family and taught me by my father, Reb Mulka Askar of Masqat."

Mirdin said 248 *mitzvot* were positive commandments, such as the directive that a Jew must care for the widow and the orphan, and 365 were negative commandments, such as the admonition that a Jew must not accept a bribe.

Learning the *mitzvot* from Mirdin was more enjoyable than Rob's other studies because he knew there would be no examinations. He enjoyed sitting over a cup of wine and listening to the Jewish law, and he soon found that their sessions helped him in his study of Islamic *Fiqh*.

He worked harder than ever but savored his days. He knew that life in Ispahan was far easier for him than for Mary. Though he returned to her eagerly at the end of each day, every morning he left her for the *maristan* and the *madrassa* with a different kind of eagerness. That was the year of studying Galen and he immersed himself in descriptions of anatomical phenomena he couldn't see by looking at a patient—the difference between arteries and veins, the pulse, the working of the heart like a constantly squeezing fist pushing blood from it during systole, then relaxing and refilling with blood during diastole.

He was taken from apprenticeship to Jalal and turned from the bonesetter's retractors, couplers, and ropes to the surgeon's inventory of tools, for he was assigned to al-Juzjani.

"He dislikes me. All he allows me to do is clean and sharpen instruments," he complained to Karim, who had spent more than a year in al-Juzjani's service.

"It's the way he starts each new clerk," Karim said. "You mustn't be discouraged."

It was easy for Karim to talk about patience these days. Part of his *calaat* had been a large and elegant house, from which he now ran a practice consisting largely of the families of the court. It was fashionable for a nobleman to be able to remark casually that his physician was Persia's hero-athlete, Karim of the *chatir*, and he attracted patients so swiftly that he would have been prosperous even without the prize money and stipend he had been awarded by the Shah. He blossomed out in expensive raiment and came to their house bearing generous gifts, delicacies of food and drink, and once even a thick Hamadhān rug to cover their floor, a wedding gift.

He flirted with Mary with his eyes and said outrageous things to her in Persian which she declared that she was grateful not to comprehend, but she soon became fond of him and treated him like a naughty brother.

At the hospital, where Rob might have expected Karim's popularity to be more restrained, it was not. Clerks clustered about and followed after him as he tended his patients, as though he were the wisest of the wise, and Rob couldn't disagree when Mirdin Askari grinned and remarked that the best way to become a successful doctor was to win the *chatir*.

On occasion al-Juzjani interrupted Rob's work to ask the name of the instrument being cleaned, or its use. There were many more instruments than Rob had used as a barber-surgeon, surgical tools specifically designed for special tasks, and he cleaned and sharpened rounded bistouries, curved bistouries, scalpels, bone saws, ear curettes, probes, little knives for opening cysts, drills for removing foreign bodies lodged in bone . . .

Al-Juzjani's method made sense after all, for at the end of two weeks, when Rob began to assist him in the *maristan* operating room, the surgeon had but to mutter a request and Rob could select the proper tool and hand it over at once.

There were two other surgical clerks who already had apprenticed under al-Juzjani for months. They were allowed to operate on uncomplicated cases, always to the master's caustic comments and close criticism.

It took ten weeks of assisting and observing before al-Juzjani would allow Rob to make a cut, even under supervision. When the opportunity came, it was to remove the index finger of a porter whose hand had been crushed beneath a camel's hoof.

He had learned by watching. Al-Juzjani always applied a tourniquet, using a thin leather thong similar to the ones employed by phlebotomists to raise a vein prior to bleeding. Rob tied the tourniquet deftly and performed the amputation without hesitation, for it was a procedure he had done many times through the years as a barber-surgeon. Always he had worked impeded by blood, however, and he was delighted with al-Juzjani's technique, which allowed him to make a flap and close the stub without wiping and with scarcely more than a drop of ooze.

Al-Juzjani watched closely with his usual scowl. When Rob had finished the surgeon turned away without a word of praise, but neither had he growled nor pointed out a way that would have been better, and as Rob cleaned the table after the operation he felt a glow, recognizing a small victory.

Chapter 53

FOUR FRIENDS

If the King of Kings had made any moves to curtail the powers of his Vizier as a result of the disclosures Rob had made, they were invisible. If anything, Qandrasseh's *mullahs* seemed to be more ubiquitous than ever, and more stringent and energetic in their zeal to see that Ispahan reflected the Imam's Qu'ranic view of Muslim behavior.

Seven months had gone by without a royal summoning. Rob was content that this was so, for between his wife and his medical training, his hours were too few.

One morning, to Mary's alarm he was called for by soldiers, as on the previous occasions.

"The Shah wishes you to ride with him this day."

"It's all right," he assured his wife, and went with them. At the great stables behind the House of Paradise he found an ashen-faced Mirdin Askari. When they conferred, they agreed that behind their summoning was Karim, who had come to be Alā's favorite companion since gaining athletic celebrity.

It was so. When Alā came to the stables Karim walked directly behind the ruler and his face wore the broadest of smiles as he followed the Shah to his two friends.

The grin became less confident as the Shah leaned forward to listen to Mirdin Askari, who was audibly muttering words in the Tongue as he prostrated himself in the *ravi zemin*.

"Come! You must speak Persian and tell us what you are saying," Alā snapped.

"It is a benediction, Sire. A blessing Jews offer when they see the King," Mirdin managed to say. " 'Blessed art Thou, O Lord our God, King of the Universe, who has given of His glory to flesh and man.' "

"The *Dhimmis* offer prayer of thanks when they see their Shah?" Alā said, amazed and pleased.

Rob knew it was a *berakhah* said by the pious upon sighting *any* king but neither he nor Mirdin saw any reason to point this out, and Alā was in a splendid mood as he swung onto his white horse and they rode after him into the quiet countryside.

"I'm told you have taken a European wife," he called to Rob, twisting in the saddle.

"That's true, Excellency."

"I have heard she has hair the color of henna."

"Yes, Majesty."

"A female's hair should be black."

Rob couldn't argue with a king and saw no need; he was grateful to have a woman Alā didn't value.

The day was spent much as the first in which Rob had ridden in the Shah's company, save that now they traveled with two others to share the burden of the monarch's attention, so there was less strain and more pleasure than on the previous occasion. Alā was delighted to discover in Mirdin a profound knowledge of Persian history, and as they rode slowly into the hills the two talked of the ancient sacking of Persepolis by Alexander, which the Persian in Alā decried and the militarist in him applauded. At midmorning in a shady spot Alā practiced against Karim with the scimitar, and while they whirled and the swords clanged and clashed, Mirdin and Rob talked quietly of surgical ligatures, discussing the relative merits of silk, linen thread (which they both agreed decomposed too easily), horsehair and, Ibn Sina's favorite, human hair. At midday there was rich food and drink under the shade of the king's tent, and the three took turns being bested at the Shah's Game, although Mirdin fought valiantly and in one contest almost succeeded in winning, making victory all the more sweet for Alā.

Within Alā's secret cave the four soaked companionably, loosening their bodies in the warm water of the pool and their spirits with an unending supply of fine drink.

Karim rolled the wine on his tongue appreciatively before swallowing and then favored Alā with his smile. "I was a beggar boy. Have I told you that, Excellency?"

Alā returned the smile and shook his head.

"A beggar boy now drinks the wine of the King of Kings."

"Yes. I choose as my friends a beggar boy and a pair of Jews." Alā's laughter was louder and more sustained than theirs. "For my Chief of *Chatirs* I have lofty and noble plans, and I have long liked this *Dhimmi*," he said, giving Rob a friendly, slightly drunken shove. "And now another *Dhimmi* appears to be an excellent man, worthy of notice. You must stay in Ispahan when you finish the *madrassa,* Mirdin Askari, and become a physician to my court."

Mirdin colored in discomfort. "Sire, you do me honor. I beg you not to take offense, but I ask your good will in allowing me to return home to the lands along the great gulf when I become *hakim.* My father is old and ailing. I shall be the first physician in our line, and before he dies I wish him to see me settled in the bosom of our family."

Alā nodded carelessly. "What does it do, this family that lives on the great gulf?"

"Our men have traveled the shores as long as any can remember, buying pearls from the divers, Majesty."

"Pearls! That is good, for I acquire pearls when I can find good ones. You shall be the making of your kinsmen, *Dhimmi,* for you must tell them to search out the largest perfect pearl and bring it to me, and I will buy it and make your family rich."

They were weaving in their saddles by the time they rode home. Alā strove to sit erect and addressed them with a fondness that might or might not survive the painful sobering that was certain to follow. When they reached the royal stables and his attendants and sycophants closed in and hovered, the Shah chose to flaunt them.

"We are four friends!" he shouted within the hearing of half the court. "Just four good men who are friends!"

It was repeated quickly and traveled through the city, as all gossip did that involved the Shah.

"With some friends, wariness is necessary," Ibn Sina cautioned Rob one morning about a week later.

They were at an entertainment given for the Shah by Fath Ali, a wealthy man whose mercantile firm was responsible for selling wines to the House of Paradise and most of the nobles of the court. Rob was happy to see Ibn Sina. Since Rob's marriage, with typical sensitivity the Chief Physician seldom asked for his company in the evening. Now they strolled past Karim, who was surrounded by admiring courtiers, and Rob thought that his friend appeared to be as much a prisoner as an object of adulation.

Their presence was demanded by the fact that each was the recipient of a *calaat,* but Rob was bored with royal entertainments; while they might differ in detail, they were cursed by a general sameness. In addition, he was resentful of the demands on his time. "I would greatly prefer to be working in the *maristan* where I belong," he said.

Ibn Sina looked about cautiously. They were walking alone on the merchant's estate and would have a brief period of freedom, since Alā had entered Fath Ali's *haram* moments before.

"You must never forget that dealing with a monarch is not like dealing with an ordinary man," Ibn Sina said. "A king is not like you or me. He drops a hand carelessly and someone like us is put to death. Or he wiggles a finger and someone is allowed to live. That is absolute power, and no man born of woman is able to resist it. It drives even the best of monarchs slightly mad."

Rob shrugged. "I never seek the Shah's company, nor have I any desire to stew in politics."

Ibn Sina nodded in approval. "There is this about monarchs in the East: they like to choose physicians as their viziers, feeling that healers somehow already have Allah's attention. I know how easy it is to answer the lure of such an appointment and I have drunk the intoxicating wine of power. Twice when I was younger I accepted the title of Vizier in Hamadhān. It was more dangerous than the practice of medicine. After the first time, I narrowly escaped execution. I was thrown into the castle-prison called Fardajān, where I languished for months. After I was released from Fardajān, Vizier or not, I knew I couldn't stay in Hamadhān in safety. With al-Juzjani and my household I made my way to Ispahan, where I have been under Alā's protection ever since."

They turned back, retracing their steps toward the gardens in which the entertainment was being held.

"Fortunate for Persia that Alā allows great physicians to pursue their profession," Rob said.

Ibn Sina smiled. "It fits his plans to be known as a great king who fosters the arts and the sciences," he said drily. "Even when he was a young man, he hungered after an empire of influence. Now he must seek to make it wider, trying to eat up his enemies before they devour him."

"The Seljuks."

"Oh, I should fear the Seljuks most if I were Vizier in Ispahan," Ibn Sina said. "But it is Mahmud of Ghazna whom Alā watches most intently, for the two are cut from the same fabric. Alā has made four raids into India, capturing twenty-eight war elephants. Mahmud is closer to the source, he has raided India more often and has more than fifty war elephants. Alā envies and fears him. It is Mahmud who must be eliminated next if Alā is to proceed with his dream."

Ibn Sina stopped and placed a hand on Rob's arm. "You must take great care. It is said by thoughtful men that Qandrasseh's days are numbered as Vizier. And that a young physician will take his place."

Rob said nothing, but he remembered suddenly that Alā had spoken of having "lofty and noble plans" for Karim.

"If it is true, Qandrasseh will strike without mercy at anyone he may see as the friend or supporter of his rival. It isn't enough to have no political ambitions for yourself. When a physician deals with those in power he must learn to bend and sway or he will not survive."

Rob wasn't certain he would be skilled at bending and swaying.

"Don't be overconcerned," Ibn Sina said. "Alā changes his mind often and swiftly, and one cannot plan on what he will do in the future."

They resumed walking and reached the gardens shortly before the subject of their discussion returned from Fath Ali's haram, looking relaxed and in a good mood.

Halfway through the afternoon, Rob began to wonder whether Ibn Sina ever had been host to an entertainment for his Shah and protector. He went up to Khuff and casually asked the question.

The grizzled Captain of the Gates slitted his eyes in concentration, then he nodded. "A few years since," he said.

Clearly, Alā would have had no interest in the first wife, old Pious Reza, so it was virtually certain that he had claimed sovereign right to Despina. Rob pictured the Shah climbing the circular staircase in the stone tower while Khuff guarded the approach.

Mounting the girl's small, voluptuous body.

Fascinated now, Rob studied the three men, each surrounded by idolizing and deferring nobles. The Shah was ringed by his usual attendance of arse kissers. Ibn Sina, grave and composed, quietly answered questions of scholarly looking men. Karim, as always nowadays, was virtually hidden by the admirers who sought to speak to him, to touch his clothing, to bathe in the excitement and glow of his sought-after presence.

This Persia seemed to seek to make every man a cuckold in turn.

He felt natural and right with surgical instruments in his hand, as if they were interchangeable parts of his own body. Al-Juzjani gave him more and more of his own precious time, showing him with painstaking patience how to do every procedure. The Persians had ways of immobilizing and desensitizing patients. When hemp was soaked in barley water for days and the infusion was swallowed, it allowed someone to remain conscious but deadened the pain. Rob spent two weeks with the master pharmacists of the khazanat-ul-sharaf learning to mix concoctions that put patients to sleep. The substances were unpredictable and hard to control, but sometimes they allowed surgeons to operate without the convulsive shudderings and moans and screams of pain.

The recipes seemed to him more like magic than medicine.

Take the flesh of a sheep. Free it from fat and cut it into lumps, piling the pieces of meat over and around a goodly amount of braised henbane seeds. Set this in an earthenware jar beneath a heap of horse dung until worms are generated. Then place the worms in a glass vessel until they shrivel up. When required for use, take two parts of these and one part of powdered opium, and instill this into the nose of the patient.

Opium was derived from the juice of an Eastern flower, the poppy. It was grown in Ispahan fields but the demand outpaced the supply, for it was used in the mosque rites of Ismaili Muslims as well as in medicines, so some of it was imported from Turkey and from Ghazna. It was the base of all pain-killing formulae.

Take pure opium and nutmeg. Grind and cook them together and allow them to soak in old wine for forty days. Keep on putting the bottle in the sun. Soon it will be a paste. When a pill is made from this and administered to anyone, he will at once fall unconscious and be without sensation.

They used another prescription most of the time, because it was the one that was preferred by Ibn Sina:

Take equal parts of henbane, opium, euphorbia and licorice seeds. Grind each of them separately and mix the whole together in a mortar. Place some of the mixture upon any kind of food and whosoever eats thereof will fall asleep immediately.

Despite Rob's suspicion that al-Juzjani resented his relationship with Ibn Sina, he was soon busily using all the instruments of surgery. Al-Juzjani's other clerks thought the new apprentice had more than his share of choice work and grew surly, taking out their jealousy on Rob by mutterings and mean insults. Rob didn't care, for he was learning more than he had dared dream was possible. One afternoon, having for the first time performed alone the procedure that dazzled him above all others in surgery—the couching of eyes blinded by cataracts—he attempted to thank al-Juzjani, but the surgeon interrupted him brusquely.

"You've the knack for cutting flesh. It's not something many clerks have, and my special instruction is selfish, for I'll get a great amount of work from you."

It was true. Day after day he did amputations, repaired every kind of wound, tapped into abdomens to relieve the pressure of accumulated fluids in the peritoneal cavity, removed piles, stripped varicose veins . . .

"I think you begin to like cutting too much," Mirdin said shrewdly as they sat together in Mirdin's house one evening over the Shah's Game. In the next room, Fara listened while Mary put her sons to sleep with a lullaby in the Erse, the language of the Scots.

"I am drawn to it," Rob admitted. Lately he had given thought to becoming a surgeon after winning the designation of *hakim*. In England surgeons were considered below physicians in status, but in Persia they were addressed by the special title of *ustad* and enjoyed equal respect and prosperity.

But he had reservations. "Surgery is satisfying so far as it goes. But we're limited to operating on the outside of the bag of skin. The inside of the body is a mystery handed down in books more than a thousand years old. We know almost nothing about the internal body."

"That's the way it must be," Mirdin said placidly, and took a *rukh* with one of his own foot soldiers. "Christians, Jews, and Muslims agree it is sin to desecrate the human form."

"I don't speak of desecration. I speak of surgery, I speak of dissection. The ancients didn't cripple their science with admonitions of sin, and what little we now know came from the early Greeks, who had the freedom to open the body and study it. They dissected the dead and observed how man is fashioned within. For a brief moment in those long-ago days their brilliance illuminated all of medicine, and then the world fell into darkness." He brooded and the game suffered, so that Mirdin quickly captured the other *rukh* and one of his camels.

"I think," Rob said at length, almost idly, "that during all these long centuries of dark ignorance, there have been small, secret fires."

Now Mirdin's attention was drawn from the board.

"Men who have had the strength to dissect dead humans in stealth. Defying the priests in order to do the Lord's work as physicians."

Mirdin stared. "Dear God. They would be treated as witches."

"They would not have been able to report their knowledge, but at least they would have gained it for themselves."

Mirdin now looked alarmed.

Rob smiled at him. "No, I would not," he said gently. "I have enough trouble pretending to be a Jew. I simply do not have the necessary variety of courage."

"We must show gratitude for tiny blessings," Mirdin said drily. He had been made sufficiently uneasy and diverted so that now he played poorly, giving up an elephant and two horses in swift succession, but Rob hadn't yet learned enough about pressing through to victory. Quickly and coolly Mirdin rallied his forces and, within a dozen moves, to Rob's chagrin he was once again forced to experience *shahtreng*, the anguish of the king.

Chapter 54

MARY'S EXPECTATIONS

Mary had no female friend other than Fara, but the Jewess was enough. The two women learned to sit for hours and talk to one another, communications devoid of the questions and answers characterizing most social conversation. Sometimes Mary talked and Fara listened to an outpouring of Gaelic she didn't understand, sometimes Fara spoke the Tongue to an uncomprehending Mary.

The words were curiously unimportant. What mattered was the play of emotions across the facial features, the expressions of the hands, what was in the voice, secrets conveyed by the eyes.

Thus they shared their feelings and for Mary it was an advantage, for she spoke of things she wouldn't have mentioned to one she had known so short a time. She revealed her sorrow over the loss of her father; her loneliness for the Christian Mass; the power of her longing when she awoke from dreaming of the young and beautiful woman Jura Cullen once had been, and then had to lie in the little Yehuddiyyeh house as, like a cold and loathsome creature, the realization crept into her mind that her mother was long dead. And she spoke of things she wouldn't have mentioned no matter how long she and Fara had been friends: of how she loved him so much that sometimes it caused a trembling she couldn't control; of moments when desire flooded her with such warmth that for the first time she understood mares in heat; of how she would never again watch a ram mounting a ewe without thinking of her limbs around Rob, his taste in her mouth, the smell of his firm warm flesh in her nostrils, the hot magical extension of her husband making her one with him as they strove to get him into the core of her body.

She didn't know if Fara spoke of such things but her eyes and ears told her that betimes what Mirdin's wife talked about was intimate and important, and the two dissimilar women became linked by love and high regard, a bond of friendship.

427

One morning Mirdin laughed and clapped Rob's shoulder in delight. "You've obeyed the commandment to multiply. She's expecting a child, you European ram!"

"It isn't so!"

"It is so," Mirdin said firmly. "You'll see. In this, Fara is never wrong."

Two mornings later Mary paled after eating her breakfast and spewed up the food and drink, requiring Rob to clean and scrape the packed-earth floor and carry in fresh sand. That week she began regularly to be plagued by vomiting, and when her monthly flow was absent, no doubt remained. It should have been no surprise, for they'd been unflagging in their love-making; but she'd long since begun to think that perhaps God didn't favor the union.

Her periods ordinarily were difficult and painful and she was pleased to be relieved of them, but the frequent nausea made the exchange no great bargain. Rob held her head and cleansed her when she was sick and thought of the coming child with both delight and foreboding, nervously wondering what sort of creature would grow from his seed. Now he unclothed his wife with more ardor than ever, for the scientist in him gloried in the chance to note the changes down to the slightest detail, the widening and purpling in the areolae of her nipples, the greater fullness of her breasts, the first gentle curving of belly, a rearrangement of expressions caused by the subtle swelling of her mouth and nose. He insisted that she lie on her stomach so he could judge the accumulation of fat in the hips and buttocks, the slight thickening of her legs. At first Mary enjoyed the attention but gradually she lost patience.

"The toes," she grumbled. "What of the toes."

He studied her feet gravely and reported that the toes were unchanged.

The attractions of surgery were spoiled for Rob by a spate of geldings.

The making of eunuchs was a commonplace procedure, and two types of castrations were performed. Handsome men, selected to guard the entrances of *harams*, where they would have little contact with the women of a house, suffered only the loss of their testicles. For general service inside the *harams*, ugly men were prized, with premiums paid for such disfigurements as a mashed or naturally repelling nose, a misshapen mouth, thick lips, and black or irregular teeth; in order to render such men completely functionless sexually, their genitalia were entirely removed and they were compelled to carry a quill for use whenever they wished to pass water.

Often young boys were castrated. Sometimes they were sent to a school for the training of eunuchs in Baghdad, where they were taught to be singers and musicians or thoroughly grounded in the practices of business or in purchasing and administration, turning them into highly prized servants, valuable pieces of property like Ibn Sina's eunuch slave, Wasif.

The technique for gelding was basic. In his left hand the surgeon grasped the object to be amputated. Holding a sharp razor in his right hand, he removed the parts with a single sweep of the blade, for speed was essential. At once a poultice of warm ashes was clapped to the bleeding area, and the male was permanently altered.

Al-Juzjani had explained to him that when castration was performed as a punishment, sometimes the poultice of ashes wasn't administered and the patient was allowed to bleed to death.

Rob came home one evening and looked at his wife and tried not to consider that none of the men or boys he had operated on would ever make a woman swell with life. He put his hand on her warm abdomen, which had not really grown much larger yet.

"Soon it will be like a green melon," she said.

"I want to see it when it is a watermelon."

He had gone to the House of Learning and read about the fetus. Ibn Sina had written that after the womb shuts over the semen, life is formed in three stages. According to the Master of Physicians, in the first stage, the clot is transformed into a small heart; in the second stage, another clot appears and develops into the liver; and in the third stage, all of the chief organs are formed.

"I've found a church," Mary said.

"A Christian church?" he said, and was amazed when she nodded.

He hadn't known of a church in Ispahan.

The week before, she and Fara had gone to the Armenian market to buy wheat. They had made a wrong turn down an alley, narrow and smelling of piss, and she had come upon the Church of Archangel Michael.

"Eastern Catholics?"

She nodded again. "It's a tiny, sad church, attended by a handful of the poorest Armenian laborers. Doubtless it is tolerated because it's too weak to be a threat." She'd returned twice, alone, to stand and envy the ragged Armenians who entered and left the church.

"Mass would be in their language. We couldn't even offer the responses."

"But they celebrate the Eucharist. Christ is present on their altar."

"We would risk my life to attend. Go to the synagogue with Fara to pray, but offer your own silent prayers. When I'm in the synagogue I pray to Jesus and the saints."

She lifted her head and for the first time he saw the smoldering behind her eyes.

"I need no Jews to allow me to pray," she said hotly.

Mirdin agreed with him about rejecting surgery as a profession. "It's not only the gelding, although that is terrible. But in places where there are no medical clerks to service the *mullahs'* courts, the surgeon is called upon to tend prisoners after punishments. Better to use our knowledge and skills against illness and hurt than to trim the stubs and stumps of what could have been healthy limbs and organs."

Sitting in the early morning sun on the stone steps of the *madrassa*, Mirdin sighed when Rob told him about Mary and her yearnings for a church. "You must pray your own prayers with her when you're alone. And you must take her to your own people as soon as you're able."

Rob nodded, studying the other man thoughtfully. Mirdin had been bitter and hateful when he had thought Rob a Jew who had rejected his own faith. But since gaining the knowledge that Rob was an Other, he had shown the essence of friendship.

"Have you considered," Rob said slowly, "how each faith claims that it alone has God's heart and ear? We, you, and Islam—each vows it is the true religion. Can it be that we're all three wrong?"

"Perhaps we're all three right," Mirdin said.

Rob felt a welling of affection. Soon Mirdin would be a physician and return to his family in Masqat and when Rob was *hakim* he too would go home. Doubtless, they would never meet again.

When he met Mirdin's eyes he was certain his friend shared his thoughts.

"Shall we see each other in Paradise?"

Mirdin stared at him gravely. "I shall meet you in Paradise. Solemn vow?"

Rob smiled. "Solemn vow."

They clasped wrists.

"I think of the separation between life and Paradise as a river," Mirdin said. "If there are many bridges that cross the river, should it be of great concern to God which bridge the traveler chooses?"

"I believe not," Rob said.

The two friends parted warmly and hurried off, each to his own labor.

Rob sat in the surgery with two other clerks and listened to al-Juzjani warn them of the need for discretion regarding the operation that would follow. He wouldn't give the patient's identity in order to protect her reputation, but he let it be known that she was the close relative of a powerful and famous man, and that she had cancer of the breast.

Because of the gravity of the disease, the theological prohibition known as *aurat*—which forbade any but a woman's husband to look upon her body from neck to knee—would be disregarded to enable them to operate.

The woman had been plied with opiates and wine and was carried in to them unconscious. She was full-formed and heavy, with wisps of gray hair escaping from the cloth that bound her head. She was loosely veiled and fully draped save for her breasts, which were large, soft, and flaccid, indicating a patient no longer young.

Al-Juzjani ordered each of the clerks in turn to palpate both breasts gently in order to learn what a breast tumor feels like. It was detectable even without palpation, a visible growth in the side of the left breast, as long as Rob's thumb and three times as thick.

He was very interested in watching; he had never seen a human breast opened before. Blood welled as al-Juzjani pressed the knife into the yielding flesh and cut well below the bottom of the lump, desiring to get it all. The woman moaned and the surgeon worked quickly, eager to finish before she awoke.

Rob saw that the inside of the breast contained muscle, cellular gray flesh, and clumps of yellow fat like that in a dressed chicken. He could clearly make out several pink lactiferous ducts running to join at the nipple like the branches of a river merging at a bay. Perhaps al-Juzjani had nicked one of the ducts; reddened liquid welled from the nipple like a drop of rosy milk.

Al-Juzjani had the tumor out and was sewing rapidly. If such a thing were possible, Rob would have said the surgeon was nervous.

She is related to the Shah, he told himself. Perhaps an aunt; maybe even the very woman of whom the Shah had told him in the cave, the aunt who had inducted Alā into sexual life.

Groaning and almost fully awake, she was carried away as soon as the breast was closed.

Al-Juzjani sighed. "There is no cure. The cancer will kill her in the end, but we can attempt to slow its progress." He saw Ibn Sina outside and went to report on the operation while the clerks tidied the surgery.

Soon Ibn Sina entered the surgery and spoke briefly to Rob, patting his shoulder before taking leave of him.

He was dazed by what the Chief Physician had told him. He left the surgery and walked toward the *khazanat-ul-sharaf*, where Mirdin was working. They met in the corridor leading from the pharmacy. Rob saw in Mirdin's face all the emotions that were churning within him. "You also?"

Mirdin nodded. "In two weeks?"

"Yes." He tasted panic. "I'm not ready for testing, Mirdin. You've been here four years, but I've been here only three years and I'm not yet ready."

Mirdin forgot his own nervousness, and smiled. "You are ready. You've been a barber-surgeon and all who have taught you have come to know what you are. We have two weeks to study together, and then we shall have our examination."

Chapter 55

THE PICTURE OF A LIMB

Ibn Sina was born in a tiny settlement called Afshanah, outside the village of Kharmaythan, and soon after his birth his family moved to the nearby city of Bukhārā. While he was still a small boy his father, a tax collector, arranged for him to study with a teacher of Qu'ran and a teacher of literature, and by the time he was ten he had memorized the entire Qu'ran and absorbed much of Muslim culture. His father met a learned vegetable peddler named Mahmud the Mathematician, who taught the child Indian calculation and algebra. Before the gifted youth grew his first facial hairs he had qualified in law and delved into Euclid and geometry, and his teachers begged his father to allow him to devote his life to scholarship.

He began the study of medicine at eleven and by the time he was sixteen he was lecturing to older physicians and spending much of his time in the practice of law. All his life he would be both jurist and philosopher, but he noted that although these learned pursuits were given deference and respect by the Persian world in which he lived, nothing mattered more to an individual than his well-being and whether he would live or die. At an early age, fate made Ibn Sina the servant of a series of rulers who used his genius to guard their health, and though he wrote dozens of volumes on law and philosophy—enough to win him the affectionate sobriquet of Second Teacher (First Teacher being Mohammed)—it was as the Prince of Physicians that he gained the fame and adulation that followed him wherever he traveled.

In Ispahan, where he had gone at once from political refugee to *hakim-bashi*, Chief Physician, he found a city with a large supply of physicians, and more men constantly becoming healers by means of simple declaration. Few of these would-be physicians shared the dogged scholarship or intellectual genius that had marked his own entry into medicine, and he realized that a means was needed to determine who was qualified to practice and who was not. For more than a century, examinations had been given to potential physicians in Baghdad, and Ibn Sina convinced the medical community that in Ispahan the qualifying examination at the *madrassa* should create or reject physicians, with himself as chief medical examiner.

Ibn Sina was the foremost physician in the Eastern and Western Caliphates, yet he worked in an educational environment that did not have the prestige of the largest facilities. The academy at Toledo had its House of Science, the university in Baghdad had its school for translators, Cairo boasted a rich and solid medical tradition that went back many centuries. Each of these places had a famous and magnificent library. In contrast, in Ispahan there was the small *madrassa* and a library that depended on the charity of the larger and richer institution in Baghdad. The *maristan* was a smaller, paler version of the great Azudi hospital in Baghdad. The presence of Ibn Sina had to make up for a lack of institutional size and grandeur.

Ibn Sina admitted to the sin of pride. While his own reputation was so towering as to be untouchable, he was sensitive about the standing of the physicians he trained.

On the eighth day of the month of *Shawwa*, a caravan from Baghdad brought him a letter from Ibn Sabur Yāqūt, the chief medical examiner of Baghdad. Ibn Sabur was coming to Ispahan and would visit the *maristan* the first half of the month of *Zulkadah*. Ibn Sina had met Ibn Sabur before and steeled himself to withstand the condescension and constant smug comparisons of his Baghdad rival.

Despite all the costly advantages medicine enjoyed in Baghdad, he knew that the examining there was often notoriously lax. But here at the *maristan* were two medical clerks as sound as any he had seen. And at once he knew how he could send word back to the Baghdad medical community about the kind of physicians Ibn Sina made in Ispahan.

Thus, because Ibn Sabur Yāqūt was coming to the *maristan*, Jesse ben Benjamin and Mirdin Askari were called to the examining that would grant or deny their right to be called *hakim*.

Ibn Sabur Yāqūt was as Ibn Sina remembered him. Success had made his eyes slightly imperious beneath his puffy lids. There was more gray in his hair than had been there when the two of them had met in Hamadhān twelve years before, and now he wore a flamboyant, costly costume of particolored stuff that proclaimed his position and prosperity but, despite its exquisite workmanship, couldn't hide the fact that he had added greatly to his girth since his younger days. He toured the *madrassa* and the *maristan* with a smile on his lips and lofty good humor, sighing and commenting that it must be luxury to be able to deal with problems on so small a scale.

The distinguished visitor seemed pleased to be asked to sit on the examining board that would question two candidate clerks.

The scholastic community of Ispahan didn't have a depth of excellence but there was sufficient brilliance at the top of most disciplines to make it easy for Ibn Sina to enlist an examining board that would have been respected in Cairo or Toledo. Al-Juzjani would question on surgery. The Imam Yussef Gamali of the Friday Mosque would test on theology. Musa Ibn Abbas, a *mullah* who was on the staff of the Imam Mirza-aboul Qandrasseh, Vizier of Persia, would test on law and jurisprudence. Ibn Sina himself would deal with philosophy; and in medicine, the visitor from Baghdad was subtly encouraged to present his most difficult questions.

Ibn Sina was unbothered by the fact that both his candidates were Jews. Some Hebrews, of course, were dullards who made poor doctors, but in his experience the most intelligent of the *Dhimmis* who came to medicine had already traveled half the distance, for inquiry and intellectual argument and a delving after truths and proofs were part of their religion, ingrained in them in their study houses long before they became medical clerks.

Mirdin Askari was summoned first. The homely, long-jawed face was alert but calm, and when Musa Ibn Abbas asked a question regarding the laws of property he answered without flamboyance but fully and completely, citing examples and precedents in *Fiqh* and *Sharī'a*. The other examiners sat a little straighter when Yussef Gamali's questions merged law with theology, but any thought that the candidate was at a disadvantage because he was not a True Believer was dispelled by Mirdin's profundity. He used examples from Mohammed's life and recorded thoughts as his arguments, acknowledging the legal and social differences between Islam and his own religion where they were relevant, and where they were not, weaving Torah into his answers as a shoring up of Qu'ran, or Qu'ran as a buttressing of Torah. He used his mind like a sword, Ibn Sina thought, feinting, parrying, now and then sinking a point home as if it were made of cold steel. So many-layered was his scholarship that, although each man who listened shared erudition with him to a greater or lesser degree, nonetheless it numbed them and filled them with an admiration for the revealed mind.

When his chance came, Ibn Sabur loosed question after question like arrows. The answers always were given without hesitation, but they were never the opinion of Mirdin Askari. Instead, they were citations from Ibn Sina or Rhazes or Galen or Hippocrates, and once Mirdin quoted from *On Low Fevers* by Ibn Sabur Yāqūt, and the physician from Baghdad kept his face impassive as he sat and listened to his own words come back at him.

The examining went on far longer than most, until finally the candidate fell silent and looked at them and no more questions came from the seated men.

Ibn Sina dismissed Mirdin gently and sent for Jesse ben Benjamin.

He could feel a subtle change in the atmosphere as the new candidate came in, tall and broad enough to be a visual challenge to older, ascetic men, with skin leathered by the sun of West and East, wide-set brown eyes that held a wary innocence, and a fierce broken nose that made him look more like a spear-carrier than a physician. His large, square hands seemed fashioned to bend iron but Ibn Sina had seen them stroke fevered faces with great gentleness and cut into bleeding flesh with an absolutely controlled knife. His mind had long been a physician's.

Ibn Sina purposely had brought Mirdin to testing first, to set the stage and because Jesse ben Benjamin was different from the clerks to whom these authorities were accustomed, with qualities that couldn't be revealed in an academic examination. He had covered material prodigiously in three years but his scholarship wasn't as deep as Mirdin's. He had presence, even now in his nervousness.

He was staring at Musa Ibn Abbas and appeared white about the mouth, more nervous than Askari had been.

The Imam Qandrasseh's aide had noted the stare, which was almost rude, and abruptly the *mullah* began with a political question whose dangers he didn't bother to hide.

"Does the kingdom belong to the mosque or to the palace?"

Rob did not answer with the swift and unhesitating surety that had been so impressive in Mirdin. "It is spelled out in Qu'ran," he said in his accented Persian. "Allah says in *Sura* Two, 'I am setting in the earth a viceroy.' And in *Sura* Thirty-eight, a Shah's task is stated in these words: 'David, behold, We have appointed thee a viceroy in the earth, therefore judge between men justly, and follow not caprice, lest it lead thee astray from the way of God.' Therefore, the kingdom belongs to God."

In giving the kingdom to God, the reply had avoided the choice between Qandrasseh and Alā, yet it was a good and clever answer. The *mullah* did not argue.

Ibn Sabur asked the candidate to differentiate between smallpox and measles.

Rob quoted from Rhazes' treatise entitled *Division of Diseases*, pointing out that the premonitory symptoms of smallpox are fever and pain in the back, while in measles the heat is greater and there is marked mental distress. He cited Ibn Sina as if the physician were not there, saying that Book Four of the *Qānūn* suggests that the rash of measles usually emerges all at once, while the rash of smallpox appears spot after spot.

He was steady and unwavering and didn't try to draw into his answer his experience with the plague, as a lesser man might have done. Ibn Sina knew him to be worthy; of all the examiners, only he and al-Juzjani knew the magnitude of the effort this man had put into the past three years.

"What if you must treat a fractured knee?" al-Juzjani asked.

"If the leg is straight, one must immobilize it by binding it between two rigid splints. If it is bent, *Hakim* Jalal-ul-Din has devised a way of splinting which serves well for a knee as well as for a fractured or dislocated elbow." There was paper and ink and a quill next to the visitor from Baghdad, and the candidate moved to these materials. "I can draw a limb so that you may see the placement of the splint," he said.

Ibn Sina was horrified. Though the *Dhimmi* was a European, surely he must know that one who drew a picture of a human form, in whole or in part, would burn in the hottest of hell's fires. It was sin and transgression for a strict Muslim even to glance at such a picture. Given the presence of the *mullah* and the Imam, the artist who mocked God and seduced their morality by re-creating man would go to an Islamic court and never be named a *hakim*.

The seated examiners reflected a variety of emotions. Al-Juzjani's face indicated vast regret, a small smile trembled on Ibn Sabur's mouth, the Imam was perturbed, the *mullah* already angry.

The quill flew between inkpot and paper. It made a quick scratching and in a moment it was too late, the drawing was done. Rob handed it to Ibn Sabur and the man from Baghdad studied it, transparently disbelieving. When he passed it to al-Juzjani, the surgeon could not prevent a grin.

It seemed to take a long time to reach Ibn Sina but when the paper arrived he saw that the limb depicted was . . . a limb! The bent branch of an apricot tree without doubt, for it was drawn in leaf. A knotted gnarl cleverly took the place of the injured knee joint, and the ends of the splint were shown tied well above and below the knot.

There were no questions regarding the splint.

Ibn Sina looked at Jesse, taking care to mask both his relief and his affection. He vastly enjoyed glancing at the face of the visitor from Baghdad. Settling back, he began to ask his student the most intriguing philosophical question he could formulate, secure that the *maristan* of Ispahan could afford to show off just a little more.

* * *

Rob had been shaken when he recognized Musa Ibn Abbas as the Vizier's aide, whom he had seen in secret meeting with the Seljuk ambassador. But he had quickly realized that on that occasion he himself hadn't been observed, and the *mullah*'s presence on the examining committee posed no special threat.

When the examination was finished he went directly to the wing of the *maristan* that contained the surgical patients, for he and Mirdin had agreed that simply to sit and wait together to learn their fate would be too hard. The interval was best spent working, and he threw himself into a variety of tasks, examining patients, changing dressings, removing stitchings—the homely jobs to which he had become accustomed.

Time passed, but there was no word.

Presently Jalal-ul-Din came into the surgery—which surely must mean the examiners had dispersed. Rob was tempted to ask if Jalal knew their decision but couldn't bring himself to do so. As Jalal gave his customary greeting he offered no indication that he was aware of the clerk's agony of waiting.

The day before, they had labored together over a herdsman who had been savaged by a bull. The man's forearm had snapped like a willow in two places when the beast trod on it, and then the bull had gored his victim before being diverted by other herdsmen.

Rob had trimmed and sewn the torn muscles and flesh of the shoulder and arm and Jalal had reduced the fractures and applied splints. Now after they examined their patient, Jalal complained that the bulky rag dressings made a clumsy juxtaposition with the splints.

"Can the dressings not be removed?"

It puzzled Rob, for Jalal knew better. "It is too soon."

Jalal shrugged. He looked at Rob warmly and smiled. "It must be as you say, *Hakim*," he said, and left the chamber.

Thus was Rob informed. It dizzied him, so that for a time he stood without moving.

Eventually he was claimed by his routine. Four sick men remained to be seen and he went on, forcing himself to give the care of a good physician, as though his mind were the sun focusing on each of them small and hot through the crystal of his concentration.

But when the last patient had been tended he allowed his feelings to take him again, the purest pleasure he had experienced in his life. Walking almost drunkenly, he hurried home to tell Mary.

Chapter 56

THE COMMAND

Rob had become *hakim* six days before his twenty-fourth natal day, and the glow lasted for weeks. To his satisfaction, Mirdin didn't suggest that they go to the *maidans* to celebrate their new status as physicians; without making too much of it, he felt that the change in their lives was too important to be marked by an evening of drunkenness. Instead, the two families met at the Askaris' house and rejoiced together over an evening meal.

Rob and Mirdin went to watch each other being measured for the *hakim*'s black gown and hood.

"Will you go back to Masqat now?" Rob asked his friend.

"I'll stay here several more months, for there are things I still must learn in the *khazanat-ul-sharaf*. And you? When will you return to Europe?"

"Mary can't travel safely while pregnant. We'd best wait until the child has been born and is strong enough to withstand the journey." He smiled at Mirdin. "Your family will celebrate in Masqat when their physician comes home. Have you sent word that the Shah wishes to buy a great pearl from them?"

Mirdin shook his head. "My family travels the villages of the pearl-fishers and buys tiny seed pearls. They then sell them by the measuring cup, to merchants who sell them in turn to be sewn into garments. My family would be hard pressed indeed to raise the sums needed to buy great pearls. Nor would they be eager to deal with the Shah, for kings seldom are willing to pay fairly for the large pearls they love so well. For my part, I would hope that Alā has forgotten the 'great good fortune' he has bestowed on my kinsmen."

"Members of the court inquired after you last evening and missed your presence," Alā Shah said.

439

"I cared for a desperately ill woman," Karim replied.

In truth, he had gone to Despina. Each of them had been desperate. It was the first time in five nights that he had been able to escape the fawning demands of spoiled courtiers, and he had valued every moment with her.

"There are ill people in my court who need your wisdom," Alā said peevishly.

"Yes, Excellency."

Alā had made it clear that Karim had the favor of the throne, but Karim already was tired of the members of noble families who often came to him with imagined complaints, and he missed the bustle and genuine labor of the *maristan*, where he could be ever useful as a physician instead of an ornament.

Yet each time he rode into the House of Paradise and was saluted by the sentries he was newly moved. He thought often of how astounded Zaki-Omar would have been to see his boy riding with the King of Persia.

". . . I am making plans, Karim," the Shah was saying. "Formulating great events."

"May Allah smile on them."

"You must send for your friends, the pair of Jews, to meet with us. I would speak to all three of you."

"Yes, Majesty," Karim said.

Two mornings later Rob and Mirdin were summoned to ride out with the Shah. It gave them a chance to be with Karim, whose time these days was fully occupied in the company of Alā. In the stable yard of the House of Paradise, the three young physicians reviewed the examinations, to Karim's pleasure, and when the Shah arrived they mounted and rode behind him into the countryside.

It was by now a familiar excursion, save that on this day they were overlong practicing the Parthian shot, which only Karim and Alā could perform with even a random hope of success. They dined well and spoke of nothing serious until all four of them were seated in the hot water of the cavern pool, drinking wine.

That was when Alā told them calmly that he would lead a large raiding party out of Ispahan in five days' time.

"To raid where, Majesty?" Rob asked.

"The elephant pens of southwest India."

"Sire, may I go with you?" Karim asked at once, his eyes alight.

"I hope that all three of you may come," Alā said.

He spoke to them at length, flattering them by making them privy to his most secret plans. To the west the Seljuks clearly were preparing for war. In Ghazna, the Sultan Mahmud was more truculent than ever and eventually would have to be dealt with. This was a time for Alā to build his forces. His spies reported that in Mansura a weak Indian garrison guarded many elephants. A raid would be a valuable training maneuver and, more important, might provide him with priceless animals which, covered in mail, made awesome weapons that could turn the tide of a battle.

"There is another goal," Alā said. He reached to his scabbard lying next to the pool and pulled out a dagger whose blade was of an unfamiliar blue steel, patterned with little swirls.

"The metal of this knife is found only in India. It is unlike any metal we have. It takes a better edge than our own steel and holds it longer. It is so hard, it will cut into ordinary weapons. We shall look for swords made of this blue steel, for with enough of them, an army would conquer." He passed the dagger so each could examine its tempered keenness.

"Will you come with us?" he asked Rob.

Both knew it was a command and not a request; the note had now come due and it was time for Rob to pay his debt.

"Yes, I'll come, Sire," he said, trying to sound glad. He was light-headed with more than wine and could feel his pulse racing.

"And you, *Dhimmi?*" Alā said to Mirdin.

Mirdin was pale. "Your Majesty has granted me permission to return to my family in Masqat."

"Permission! Of course you have had permission. Now it is for you to decide whether you will accompany us or not," Alā said stiffly.

Karim hastily seized the goatskin and splashed wine into their goblets. "Come to India, Mirdin."

"I'm not a soldier," he said slowly. He looked at Rob.

"Come with us, Mirdin," Rob heard himself urge. "We've discussed fewer than a third of the commandments. We could study together along the way."

"We'll need surgeons," Karim said. "Besides, is Jesse the only Jew I have met in my life who is willing to fight?"

It was good-natured rough teasing, but something tightened in Mirdin's eyes.

"It isn't true. Karim, you're stupid with wine," Rob said.

"I will go," Mirdin said, and they shouted in pleasure.

"Think of it," Alā said with satisfaction. "Four friends together, raiding India!"

* * *

Rob went to Nitka the Midwife that afternoon. She was a thin, severe woman, not quite old, with a sharp nose in a sallow face and snapping raisin eyes. She offered him refreshment half-heartedly and then listened without surprise to what he had to say. He explained only that he must go away. Her face told him the problem was part of her normal world: the husband travels, the wife is left at home to suffer alone.

"I've seen your wife. The red-haired Other."

"She is a European Christian. Yes."

Nitka stared pensively and then appeared to make up her mind. "All right. I'll attend her when her time comes. If there is a difficulty, I'll live in your house during the final weeks."

"Thank you." He handed her five coins, four of them gold. "Is it enough?"

"It is enough."

Instead of going home, he left Yehuddiyyeh again and went uninvited to the house of Ibn Sina.

The Chief Physician greeted him and then heard him gravely.

"What if you should die in India? My own brother Ali was killed taking part in a similar raid. Perhaps the possibility has not occurred to you because you are young and strong and see only life for yourself. But if death should take you?"

"I'm leaving my wife with money. Little of it is mine, most was her father's," he said scrupulously. "If I die, will you arrange travel back to her home for her and the child?"

Ibn Sina nodded. "You must be careful to make such work unnecessary for me." He smiled. "Have you given thought to the riddle I have challenged you to guess?"

Rob stood in wonder that such a mind still could play childish games. "No, Chief Physician."

"No matter. If Allah wills, there will be plenty of time for you to guess the riddle." His tone changed and he said brusquely, "And now, sit closer, *Hakim.* I think we would do well to talk for a time of the treatment of wounds."

Rob told Mary as they lay abed. He explained that there was no choice; that he was pledged to repay Alā and that, at any rate, his presence in the raiding party was a command. "Needless to say, neither Mirdin nor I would chase a mad adventure if it could be avoided," he said.

He didn't go into detail about possible mishaps but told her he had arranged for Nitka's services for the birthing, and that Ibn Sina would help her in the event of any other problem.

She must have been terrified but she didn't carry on. He thought he detected anger in her voice when she asked questions, but that may have been a trick of his own guilt, for deep within himself he recognized that part of him was excited about going soldiering, happy to live a childhood dream.

Once in the night he placed his hand lightly on her belly and felt the warm flesh that was already rising, beginning to show.

"You may not be able to see it the size of a watermelon, as you said you wished to do," she said in the darkness.

"Doubtless I'll return by then," he told her.

Mary retreated into herself as the day of departure came, becoming again the harder woman he had found alone and fiercely protecting her dying father in Ahmad's *wadi*.

When it was time for him to go she was outside, wiping down her black horse. She was dry-eyed as she kissed him and watched him leave, a tall woman with a growing middle who held her large body now as if she were always tired.

Chapter 57

THE CAMELEER

It would have been a small force for an army but it was large for a raiding party, six hundred fighting men on horses and camels and twenty-four elephants. Khuff commandeered the brown horse as soon as Rob rode up to the mustering place on the *maidan*.

"Your horse will be returned to you when we come back to Ispahan. We will use only mounts that have been trained not to shy at the scent of elephants."

The brown horse was turned into the herd that would be taken to the royal stables and to Rob's consternation and Mirdin's great amusement he was given a scruffy gray female camel that looked at him coldly as she chewed her cud, her rubbery lips twisting and her jaws grinding in opposite directions.

Mirdin was given a brown male camel; he had ridden camels all his life and showed Rob how to twist the reins and bark a command to cause the single-humped dromedary to bend its front legs and drop to its knees, then fold its hind legs and fall to the ground. The rider sat sidesaddle and jerked the reins as he voiced another command, and the beast unfolded itself, reversing the order of its descent.

There were two hundred and fifty foot soldiers, two hundred horse soldiers, and one hundred and fifty on camels. Presently Alā came, a splendid sight. His elephant was a yard taller than any of the others. Gold rings adorned the wicked tusks. The *mahout* sat proudly on the bull's head and directed his progress with feet dug in behind the elephant's ears. The Shah sat erect in a cushion-lined box on the great convex back, a splendid sight in dark blue silks and a red turban. The people roared. Perhaps some of them were cheering the hero of the *chatir*, for Karim sat a nervous gray Arabian stallion with savage eyes, riding directly behind the royal elephant.

Khuff shouted a hoarse, thunderous command and his horse trotted

444

after the king's elephant and Karim, and then the other elephants fell into line and moved out of the square. After them came the horses and then the camels, and then hundreds of pack asses whose nostrils had been surgically slit so they could take in more air when they labored. The foot soldiers were last.

Once again Rob found himself three-quarters of the way back in the line of march, which seemed to be his customary position when traveling with large assemblages. That meant he and Mirdin had to cope with constant clouds of dust; anticipating this, each had exchanged his turban for the leather Jew's hat, which afforded better protection from both dust and sun.

Rob found the camel alarming. When she knelt and he settled his considerable weight on her back she whined loudly and then grunted and groaned as she clambered to her feet. He couldn't believe the ride: he was higher than when on a horse; he bounced and swayed, and there was less fat and flesh to pad his seat.

As they crossed the bridge over the River of Life, Mirdin glanced over at him and grinned. "You shall learn to love her!" he shouted to his friend.

Rob never learned to love his camel. When given a chance the beast spat ropy globs at him and snapped like a cur so that he had to tie its jaws, and aimed vicious backward kicks at him such as are employed by an ugly-tempered mule. He was wary of the animal at all times.

He enjoyed traveling with soldiers in front and behind; they might have been an ancient Roman cohort, and he was pleased to fancy himself part of a legion bringing its own kind of enlightenment where it went. The fantasy was dispelled late each afternoon, for they didn't make a neat Roman camp. Alā had his tent and soft carpets and musicians, and cooks and hands aplenty to do his will. The others picked a spot on the ground and rolled up in their clothing. The stink of the excretions of animals and men was ever present, and if they came to a brook it was foul before they left it.

At night, lying in the dark on the hard ground, Mirdin continued to teach him the laws according to the Jewish God. The familiar exercise of teaching and learning helped them forget discomfort and apprehension. They went through commandments by the dozens, making excellent progress and causing Rob to observe that going to war could be an ideal environment for study. Mirdin's calm, scholarly voice seemed a reassurance that they would see a better day.

For a week they used their own stores and then all provisions were gone, according to plan. One hundred of the foot soldiers were assigned as foragers and moved ahead of the main party. They scoured the country-side with skill and it was a daily sight to see the men leading goats or herding sheep, carrying squawking fowl or laden with produce. The finest was chosen for the Shah and the rest distributed, so that each night there was cooking over a hundred fires and the raiders ate well.

A daily medical call was held at each new encampment; it was within sight of the king's tent to discourage malingerers, but still the line was long. One evening Karim came to them there.

"Do you want to work? We're in need of help," Rob said.

"It's forbidden. I'm to stay close to the Shah."

"Ah," Mirdin said.

Karim gave them his crooked smile. "Do you want more food?"

"We have enough," Mirdin said.

"I can get what you want. It will take several months to reach the elephant pens at Mansura. You may as well make your life on the march as comfortable as possible."

Rob thought of the story Karim had told him during the plague in Shīrāz. Of how an army passing through the province of Hamadhān had brought a bitter end to Karim's parents. He wondered how many babies would be brained against the rocks to save them from starvation, because of the passing of this army.

Then he felt ashamed of his animosity toward his friend, for the raid into India wasn't Karim's fault. "There is something I'd like to ask for. Ditches should be dug on the four perimeters of each new camp, to be used as latrines."

Karim nodded.

The suggestion was implemented at once, along with an announcement that the new system was an order of the surgeons. It didn't make them popular, for now each evening weary soldiers were assigned to ditch-digging, and anyone who awoke in the night with cramps gripping his bowels had to stumble about in the darkness seeking a trench. Violators who were caught received canings. But there was less of a stench and it was pleasant not having to worry about stepping in human shit as they broke camp every morning.

Most of the troops viewed them with bland contempt. It hadn't escaped general notice that Mirdin had reported to the raiding party without a weapon, requiring Khuff to issue him a clumsy excuse for a guardsman's sword, which usually he forgot to wear. Their leather caps also set them apart, as did their habit of rising early and walking from the camp to don prayer shawls and recite benedictions and wind leather thongs around their arms and hands.

Mirdin was bemused. "There are no other Jews here to scrutinize and suspect you, so why do you pray with me?" He grinned when Rob shrugged. "I think a small part of you has become a Jew."

"No." He told Mirdin how, on the day he had assumed a Jewish identity, he had gone to the Cathedral of St. Sofia in Constantinople and promised Jesus that he would never forsake Him.

Mirdin nodded, no longer grinning. They were wise enough not to pursue the subject. They were aware of things about which they could never agree because they had been raised in differing beliefs regarding God and the human soul, but they were content to avoid these pitfalls and share their friendship as reasoning men, as physicians, and now as bumbling soldiers.

When they reached Shīrāz, by prearrangement the *kelonter* came to them outside the city with a pack train laden with provender, a sacrifice that saved the Shīrāz district from being indiscriminately stripped by the foragers. After he had paid his homage to the Shah the *kelonter* embraced Rob and Mirdin and Karim and they sat with him and drank wine and remembered the days of the plague.

Rob and Karim rode back with him as far as the city gates. Turning back, they succumbed to a flat, smooth stretch of road and the wine in their veins and began to race their camels. It was a revelation to Rob, for what had been a rolling, cumbersome walking gait turned into something else when the camel ran. The beast's stride lengthened so that each step was a pushing leap that carried her and her rider through the air in a level, hurtling rush. Rob sat her easily and enjoyed various sensations; he floated, he soared, he became the wind.

Now he understood why the Persian Jews had coined a Hebrew name for the variety which the general populace had adopted—*gemala sarka,* the flying camels.

The gray female strove desperately, and for the first time Rob felt affection for her. "Come, my dolly! Come, my girl!" he shouted as they sped toward the camp.

Mirdin's brown male won but the contest left Rob in high spirits. He begged extra forage from the elephant keepers and gave it to her and she bit him on the forearm. The bite didn't break the skin but it was nasty, a purpled bruise that gave him pain for days, and that was when he gave the camel her name, Bitch.

Chapter 58

INDIA

Below Shīrāz they found the Spice Road and followed it until, to avoid the mountainous inland terrain, they moved to the coast near Hormuz. It was winter but the gulf air was warm and perfumed. Sometimes after they had made camp late in the day the soldiers and their animals bathed in the warm saltiness from hot sandy beaches while sentries kept a nervous watch for sharks. The people they saw now were as likely to be blacks or Baluchis as Persians. They were fisher folk or, at the oases that sprang from the coastal sand, farmers who grew dates and pomegranates. They lived in tents or in mud-plastered stone houses with flat roofs; now and then the raiders moved through a *wadi* where families lived in caves. Rob thought it a poor land, but Mirdin grew exhilarated as they traveled, looking about with soft eyes.

When they reached the fishing villag of Tīz, Mirdin took Rob by the hand and led him to the water's edge. "There, on the other side," he said, pointing out at the azure gulf. "There is Masqat. From here, a boat could bring us to my father's house in a few hours."

It was tantalizingly close, but next morning they broke camp and went farther away from the Askari family with every step.

Almost a month after they had departed from Ispahan they moved beyond Persia. Changes were made. Alā ordered three rings of sentries around the camp at night, and each morning a new watchword was passed to every man; anyone who tried to get into their camp without knowing the word would be killed.

Once on the soil of the foreign land of Sind the soldiers gave way to their instinct for marauding, and one day the foragers drove women back to the camp the way they drove animals. Alā said he would allow them to have females in the camp for this night only and then no more. It would be difficult enough for six hundred men to approach Mansura undetected,

448

and he wanted no rumors to go before them because of women taken along their way.

It would be a wild night. They saw Karim selecting four of the women with great care.

"Why does he need four?" Rob asked.

"He doesn't select them for himself," Mirdin said.

It was true. They observed Karim leading the women to the king's tent.

"Is this why we struggled to help him pass the examination and become a physician?" Mirdin said bitterly. Rob didn't answer.

The raiders passed the other females from man to man, choosing lots for turns. Groups stood and watched the rutting and cheered, the sentries being relieved so they could come and share in these first spoils.

Mirdin and Rob sat off to one side with a goatskin of bitter wine. For a time they attempted study, but it wasn't the occasion to review the Lord's laws.

"You've taught me more than four hundred commandments," Rob said wonderingly. "Soon we'll be finished with them."

"I've merely listed them. There are sages who devote their lives to trying to understand the commentaries on just one of the laws."

The night was filled with screams and drunken sounds.

For years Rob had governed himself well in avoiding strong drink, but now he was lonely and in sexual need undampened by the ugliness taking place about him, and he drank too eagerly.

In a little while he was truculent. Mirdin, amazed that this was his mild and reasoning friend, gave him no excuse. But a passing soldier jostled him and would have been the object of his anger if Mirdin hadn't soothed and cozened, coddling Rob like a spoiled child and leading him to a sleeping place.

When he awoke in the morning the women were gone and he paid for his foolishness by having to ride the camel with a terrible head. Ever the medical student, Mirdin added to his pain by questioning him at length, at last coming away with a greater understanding that to some men wine must be treated as if it were a poison and a bewitchery.

Mirdin hadn't thought to bring a weapon to battle but he had brought the Shah's Game and it was a blessing, for they played each evening until darkness came. Now finally the contests became hard-fought and close, and on occasion when luck was with him, Rob won.

Over the game board he confided his concern for Mary.

"Doubtless she's fine, for Fara says that having babes is something women have learned to do long since," Mirdin said cheerfully.

Rob wondered aloud whether the child would be daughter or son.

"How long after her menses had stopped did the fucking take place?" He shrugged.

"It is written by al-Habib that if intercourse takes place on the first to fifth day after the end of bleeding, it will be a boy. If from the fifth to the eighth day after her period, a girl." He hesitated, and Rob knew it was because al-Habib also had written that if the mating occurred after the fifteenth day, there was a possibility the child would be a hermaphrodite.

"Al-Habib also writes that brown-eyed fathers make sons and blue-eyed fathers make daughters. Yet I come from a land where most men have blue eyes, and they have always had many sons," Rob said crossly.

"Doubtless al-Habib wrote only of normal folk such as are found in the East," Mirdin said.

Sometimes, instead of playing the Shah's Game they reviewed Ibn Sina's teachings on the treatment of battle wounds, or they inspected their supplies and made certain they were in readiness as surgeons. It was fortunate that they did, for one evening they were invited to Alā's tent to share the king's evening meal and answer his questions about their preparations. Karim was there, greeting his friends uncomfortably; it soon became apparent he had been ordered to question them and judge their efficiency.

Servants brought water and cloths that they might wash their hands before eating. Alā dipped his hands in a beautifully chased golden bowl and wiped them dry on pale blue linen towels worked with Qu'ranic phrases in gold thread.

"Tell us how you'll treat slash wounds," Karim said.

Rob told what Ibn Sina had taught: oil was to be boiled and poured into the wound as hot as possible, to ward off suppuration and evil humors.

Karim nodded.

Alā had been listening palely. Now he gave firm instructions that if he himself were mortally struck, they were to dose him with soporifics to ease the pain the very moment after a *mullah* had led him in final prayer.

The meal was simple by royal standards, spit-roasted fowl and summer greens gathered along the way, but it was better prepared than the fare to which they were accustomed, and it was served on plates. Afterward, while three musicians played dulcimers, Mirdin tested Alā at the Shah's Game but was easily bested.

It was a welcome change in their routine, but Rob was not unhappy to leave the presence of the king. He didn't envy Karim, who nowadays often rode on the elephant named Zi, seated in the box with the Shah.

But Rob hadn't lost his fascination with elephants and watched them closely at every opportunity. Some were laden with bundles of war mail similar to the armor worn by human warriors. Five of the elephants carried twenty extra *mahouts* brought along by Alā as excess baggage in the hopeful expectation that on the trip back to Ispahan they would be occupied in tending the elephants taken at Mansura. All the *mahouts* were Indians captured in previous raids, but they had been excellently treated and lavishly rewarded, as befit their value, and the Shah was certain of their loyalty.

The elephants took care of their own foraging. At the end of each day their small, dark keepers accompanied them to vegetation where they ate their fill of grass, leaves, small branches, and bark, often gaining their food by knocking down trees with startling ease.

One evening the feeding elephants frightened from the trees a chattering band of manlike, furry little creatures with tails, which Rob knew from his reading to be monkeys. After that they saw monkeys every day, and a variety of bright-plumaged birds and occasional serpents on the ground and in the trees. Harsha, the Shah's *mahout*, told Rob that some of the snakes were deadly. "If someone is bitten, a knife must be used to open the site of the bite and all the poison must be sucked away and spat out. Then a small animal should be killed and the liver tied to the wound to draw it." The Indian warned that the person doing the sucking must not have a sore or a cut in his mouth. "If he does, the poison will enter and he will die in half an afternoon."

They passed Buddhas, great sitting gods at which some of the men jeered uncomfortably but which nobody defiled, for though they told each other that Allah was the one true God, there was an amused, subtle menace in the ageless figures that made them realize they were a long way from their homes. Looking up at the looming stone gods, Rob fought them off with a silent recitation of the Paternoster from St. Matthew. That evening perhaps Mirdin fought them off as well, for, lying on the ground surrounded by the Persian army, he taught an especially enthusiastic lesson in the Law.

It was the night when they reached the five hundred and twenty-fourth commandment, on the face of it a puzzling edict: "If a man has committed a sin worthy of death, and he be put to death, and thou hang him on a tree, his body shall not remain all night upon the tree but thou shalt surely bury him the same day."

Mirdin told him to mark the words well. "Because of them, we don't study human dead as did the heathen Greeks."

Rob's skin prickled and he sat up.

"The sages and scholars draw three edicts from this commandment," Mirdin said. "First, if a convicted criminal's body is to be treated with such respect, then the body of a respected citizen certainly should also be swiftly interred without being subjected to shame or disgrace. Second, whoever keeps his dead unburied overnight transgresses a negative commandment. And third, the body must be interred whole and uncut, for if one leaves out even a small amount of tissue, it's as if no burial took place at all."

"This is what's done the mischief," Rob said wonderingly. "Because this law forbids leaving a murderer's body unburied, Christians and Muslims and Jews have kept physicians from studying that which they seek to heal!"

"It's God's commandment," Mirdin said sternly.

Rob lay back and studied the darkness. Nearby, a foot soldier snored loudly and beyond that unpleasant sound someone hawked and spat. For the hundredth time he asked himself what he was doing in their midst. "I think your way is disrespect for the dead. To throw them into the earth with such haste, as if you can't wait to get them out of sight."

"It's true we don't fuss over the corpse. After the funeral we honor the memory of the person through *shiva*, seven days in which the mourners stay inside their house in grief and prayer."

Frustration welled, and Rob felt as savage as if he had wallowed in strong drink. "It makes little sense. It's an ignorant commandment."

"You shall not say that God's word is ignorant!"

"I'm not speaking of God's word. I'm talking of man's interpretation of God's word. That has kept the world in ignorance and darkness for a thousand years."

For a moment Mirdin was silent. "Your approval isn't required," he said finally. "Nor is wisdom or decency. Our agreement was simply that you would study God's laws."

"Yes, I agreed to study. I didn't agree to close off my mind or withhold my judgment."

This time Mirdin didn't reply.

Two days later, they came at last to the banks of a great river, the Indus. There was an easy ford a few miles north but the *mahouts* told them that sometimes it was guarded by soldiers, so they traveled south a few miles to another ford, deeper but still passable. Khuff set a party of men to building rafts. Those who were able swam to the far bank with the animals. Those who were not swimmers poled across on the rafts. Some of the elephants walked on the river bottom, submerged save for their trunks, which extended out of the water and gave them air! When the river became too deep even for them, the elephants swam as well as horses.

On the other side the raiders reassembled and began to move north again, toward Mansura, making a wide sweep around the guarded ford.

Karim summoned Mirdin and Rob to the Shah, and for a time they rode with Alā on Zi's back. Rob had to concentrate on the king's words, for the world was different atop an elephant.

Alā's spies had reported to him in Ispahan that Mansura was but lightly guarded. The old Rajah of that place, who had been a fierce commander, had recently died and it was said his sons were poor soldiers who under-manned their garrisons.

"Now I must send out scouts to confirm this," Alā said. "You shall go, for it occurs to me that two *Dhimmi* merchants can approach Mansura without raising comment."

Rob resisted the impulse to glance at Mirdin.

"You must keep your eyes open for elephant traps near the village. Sometimes these people build wooden frames through which project sharp iron spikes, and bury them in shallow trenches outside their walls. These devastate the elephants, and we must know that they are not in use here before we commit our beasts."

Rob nodded. When one rode an elephant all things appeared possible. "Yes, Majesty," he told the Shah.

The raiders made camp, where they would wait until the scouts returned. Rob and Mirdin left their camels, which were obviously military beasts bred for speed and not for burden, and led two asses away from the encampment.

It was a fresh, sunny morning. In the overripe forest savage birds challenged and shrieked, and a company of monkeys scolded them from a tree.

"I should like to dissect a monkey."

Mirdin was still angry with him, and was finding even less enjoyment in becoming a secret observer than in being a soldier. "Why?" he demanded.

"Why, to discover what I may," Rob said, "even as Galen dissected Barbary apes to learn."

"I thought you had determined to be a physician."

"That is being a physician."

"No, that is being a dissector. *I'll* be a physician, spending all my days caring for the people of Masqat in time of sickness, which is what a physician does. *You* can't fix your mind whether to be a surgeon or a dissector or a physician or a . . . a midwife with balls! You want it all!"

Rob smiled at his friend but said nothing more. He had little defense, for to a great extent what Mirdin accused him of was true.

They traveled for a time in silence. Twice they passed Indian men, a farmer up to his ankles in the muck of a roadside irrigation ditch, and two men in the road lugging a pole from which hung a basket filled with yellow plums. This pair hailed them in a language neither Rob nor Mirdin could comprehend and they could but answer with a smile; Rob hoped they wouldn't walk as far as the encampment, for now anyone who came upon the raiders would at once become a slave or a corpse.

Presently half a dozen men leading donkeys came toward them around a bend in the road and Mirdin grinned at Rob for the first time, for these travelers wore dusty leather Jew's hats like their own, and black caftans that bore witness to hard journeying.

"*Shalom!*" Rob called when they were close enough.

"*Shalom aleikhem!* And well met."

Their spokesman and leader said he was Hillel Nafthali, spice merchant of Ahwaz. He was bluff and smiling, with a livid strawberry birthmark that covered the cheek under his left eye, and he appeared willing to spend the entire day in introductions and the recital of pedigrees. One of the men with him was his brother Ari, one was his son, and the other three were husbands of his daughters. He didn't know Mirdin's father but had heard of the pearl-buying Askari family of Masqat, and the exchange of names went on and on until finally they reached a distant Nafthali cousin with whom Mirdin had acquaintance, thus satisfying both sides that they were not strangers.

"You've come from the north?" Mirdin said.

"We've been to Multan. A small errand," Nafthali said with a satisfaction that indicated the magnitude of the transaction. "Where do you travel?"

"Mansura. Business, a bit of this, a bit of that," Rob said, and the men nodded with respect. "Do you know Mansura well?"

"Very well. In fact, we spent last night there with Ezra ben Husik, who deals in peppercorns. A most worthy man, always excellent hospitality."

"Then you have observed the garrison there?" Rob said.

"The garrison?" Nafthali gazed at them, puzzled.

"How many soldiers are stationed in Mansura?" Mirdin asked quietly.

Understanding dawned, and Nafthali drew back, appalled. "We do not become involved in such things," he said in a low voice, almost a whisper.

They began to turn away, in a moment they would be gone. Rob knew it was time for a show of faith. "You must not continue very far down this road on peril of your life. Nor must you turn back to Mansura."

They gazed at him palely.

"Then where shall we go?" Nafthali said.

"Lead your animals off the road and hide in the woods. Stay hidden as long as necessary—until you have heard a great many men going by. When they have all passed, return to the road and go to Ahwaz as fast as you are able."

"We thank you," Nafthali said bleakly.

"Is it safe for us to approach Mansura?" Mirdin asked.

The spice merchant nodded. "They are accustomed to seeing Jewish traders."

Rob was unsatisfied. Remembering the sign language that Loeb had taught him on the way east to Ispahan, the secret signals by which Jewish merchants in the East conducted their business without conversation, he held out his hand and turned it, the signal for *How many?*

Nafthali gazed at him. Finally he placed his right hand on his left elbow, the sign for hundreds. Then he spread all five fingers. Hiding the thumb of his left hand, he spread the other fingers and placed them on his right elbow.

Rob had to be certain he understood. "Nine hundred soldiers?"

Nafthali nodded. *"Shalom,"* he said with quiet irony.

"Peace be with you," Rob said.

The forest ended and they could see Mansura. The village lay in a small valley at the bottom of a stony slope. From the height they could see the garrison and its arrangement: barracks, training grounds, horse corrals, elephant pens. Rob and Mirdin took careful note of the locations and impressed them in their memories.

Both the village and the garrison were enclosed in a single stockade made of logs set into the ground side by side, with sharpened tops to make the barricade difficult to climb.

When they drew near the wall Rob jabbed one of the asses with a stick and then, followed by shouting and laughing children, he pursued the animal around the outside of the wall while Mirdin went the other way, ostensibly to cut off the creature's escape.

There was no sign of elephant traps.

They didn't tarry, but turned west again at once. It didn't take long to return to the encampment.

The watchword of the day was *mahdi*, which meant "savior"; after they had given it to three lines of sentries they were allowed to follow Khuff into the presence of the Shah.

Alā scowled when hearing of nine hundred soldiers, for he had been led by his spies to expect far fewer defenders at Mansura. Yet he was undaunted. "If we are able to surprise, advantage will yet be on our side."

Drawing on the ground with sticks, Rob and Mirdin indicated the details of the fortifications and the location of the elephant pens, while the Shah listened attentively and made his plans.

All morning the men had been tending equipment, oiling harness, whetting blades to edges of perfect sharpness.

The elephants were given wine in their buckets. "Not much. Just enough to make them sullen and ready to fight," Harsha told Rob, who nodded wonderingly. "It is given to them only before battle."

The beasts appeared to understand. They moved about restlessly and their *mahouts* had to be alert as the elephants' mail was unpacked, draped, and fastened. Special long, heavy swords with sockets instead of hilts were fitted onto the tusks, and now added to their aura of brute strength was a wicked new lethality.

There was a burst of nervous activity when Alā ordered out the entire force.

They moved down the Spice Road, slowly, slowly, for timing was all, and Alā wanted them to arrive at Mansura with day's end. No one spoke. They met only a few unfortunates along the way, who were taken at once, bound, and guarded by foot soldiers so they could not give alarm. When they came to the place in the road where Rob last had seen the Jews of Ahwaz, he thought of the men hiding somewhere nearby and listening to the sounds of the animals' hooves and the marching feet and the soft jangling of the elephants' mail.

They emerged from the forest as dusk began to claim the world, and under cover of the gloom Alā deployed his forces along the top of the hill. Behind each elephant, on which four archers sat back to back, were sword-wielding men on camels and horses, and after the cavalry would come foot soldiers with lances and scimitars.

Two elephants, naked of battle gear and bearing only their *mahouts*, moved away on signal. Those atop the hill watched them slowly descending through the peaceful gray light. Beyond them, cooking fires glowed throughout the village as the women prepared the evening meal.

When the two elephants reached the stockade they lowered their heads against the timbers.

The Shah raised his arm.

The elephants moved forward. There was a cracking and a series of thuds as the wall fell. Now the Shah's arm came down and the Persians began to move.

The elephants ran down the hill eagerly. Behind them, the camels and horses began to lope and then to gallop. From the village there arose the first faint cries.

Rob had drawn his sword and was using it to tap Bitch's flanks, but she needed no urging. First there was just the swift thudding of hooves and the music of the mail, then six hundred voices began to scream their battle cry and the beasts joined, the camels moaning, the elephants trumpeting wild and shrill.

The hairs rose on the back of Rob's neck, and he was howling like an animal when Alā's raiders fell upon Mansura.

Chapter 59

THE INDIAN SMITH

Rob had swift impressions, like glimpsing a series of drawings. The camel made its way through the splintered ruin of the wall at top speed. As he rode through the village the fear in the faces of the people frantically scurrying gave him a strange feeling of his own invulnerability, a carnal knowledge compounded of both power and shame, like the feeling he had experienced long ago in England when he had baited the old Jew.

When he reached the garrison a fierce battle already was in progress. The Indians fought on the ground, but they knew elephants and how to attack them. Foot soldiers carrying long pikes tried to jab out the elephants' eyes and Rob saw that they had been successful against one of the armorless elephants that had pushed down the wall. The *mahout* was gone, doubtless slain, and the beast had lost both eyes and stood blind and trembling, screaming piteously.

Rob found himself staring into a grimacing brown face, seeing the drawn-back sword, watching the blade come forward. He didn't remember deciding to use his broadsword like a thin French blade; he simply shoved and the point entered the Indian's throat. The man fell away and Rob turned to a figure struggling at him from the other side of the camel and began hacking.

Some of the Indians had axes and scimitars and tried to take the elephants out by chopping at their trunks or their treelike legs, but it was an unequal contest. The elephants attacked, their ears in their rage spread wide like sails. Bending their trunks inward and folded beneath their deadly sworded tusks, they surged like ramming ships, falling upon the Indians in charges that overturned many. The giant animals raised their feet high, as in a savage dance, and brought them down in stampings that shook the earth. Men caught beneath the driving hooves were pulped like trodden grapes.

458

He was imprisoned in a hell of killing and fearful sounds, gruntings, trumpetings, screams, curses, shouts, the groans of the dying.

Zi, being the largest elephant and royally caparisoned, attracted more attackers than any other, and Rob saw that Khuff stood and fought near his Shah. Khuff had lost his horse. He wielded his heavy sword, whirling it around his head and shouting great oaths and insults, and atop the elephant Alā sat and used his longbow.

The battle roiled, the men laboring with a fury, all caught up in the serious work of butchery.

Plunging the camel after a lancer who parried and ran, Rob came across Mirdin on foot, the sword at his side looking as if it had not been used. He held a wounded man under the arms and was dragging him out of the fighting, oblivious to all else.

The sight was like a shock of icy water. Rob blinked and jerked the camel's reins, sliding off before Bitch had truly knelt. He went to Mirdin and helped him bear the fallen man, who was already gray from a wound in the neck.

From that time, Rob forgot about killing and strove as a physician.

The two surgeons laid the wounded in a village house, bringing them in one by one while the slaughter went on. All they could do was collect those who were down, for their carefully prepared supplies were on the backs of half a dozen asses scattered who knew where, and now there was no opium or oil, no great bundles of clean rags. When cloths were needed to stanch the flow of blood, Rob or Mirdin cut them from the clothing of one of the dead.

Very soon the fighting became a massacre. The Indians had been surprised, and while half of them had been able to find arms and use them, the others had resisted with sticks and rocks. They were easily slain, yet most fought desperately in the sure knowledge that if they surrendered they faced shameful execution or lives as slaves or eunuchs in Persia.

The bloodletting carried into the darkness. Rob drew his sword and, carrying a torch, went to a nearby house. Inside was a small, slim man, his wife, and two small children. The four dark faces turned toward him, their eyes fixed on his sword. "You must go unseen," Rob told the man, "while there is still time."

But they didn't know Persian and the man said something in their strange tongue.

Rob went to the door and pointed out into the night at the distant forest, and then returned and made urgent shooing movements with his hands.

The man nodded. He looked terrified; perhaps there were beasts in the forest. But he gathered his family and soon they had slipped through the door.

In that house Rob found lamps, and in others he discovered oil and rags and brought them back to the wounded.

Late in the night, as the last of the fighting ended, Persian swordsmen killed all enemy wounded and the looting and raping began. He and Mirdin and a handful of soldiers walked the field of battle with torches. They didn't bring in the dead or anyone clearly dying, but sought Persians who might be saved. Soon Mirdin found two of the precious pack asses and, working by lamplight, the surgeons began to treat wounds with hot oil and sew and dress them. They cut off four ruined limbs, but all but one of those patients died. Thus they worked through the terrible night.

They had thirty-one patients and when dawn brought light to the grisly village they found seven more who were wounded but alive.

After First Prayer, Khuff brought orders that the surgeons were to tend to the wounds of five elephants before resuming work on the soldiers. Three of the animals had been cut in the legs, one had an arrow through the ear, and the trunk of another had been severed, so that at Rob's recommendation she and the elephant that had been blinded were put down by lancers.

After the morning meal of *pilah,* the *mahouts* moved into the elephant pens of Mansura and began to sort the animals there, talking to them softly and moving them about by tugging their ears with the hooked goads called *ankushas.*

"Here, my father."

"Move, my daughter. Steady, my son! Show me what you can do, my children."

"Kneel, mother, and let me ride on your beautiful head."

With tender cries the *mahouts* separated the trained beasts from those which still were half wild. They could take only docile animals that would obey them on the march back to Ispahan. The wilder ones would be released and allowed to return to the forest.

The voices of the *mahouts* were joined by a competing sound, a buzzing, for blowflies already had found the corpses. Soon, with the rising heat of day, the smell would be intolerable. Seventy-three Persians had perished. Only one hundred and three Indians had surrendered and lived, and when Alā offered them opportunity to become military bearers they accepted with eager relief; in a few years they might earn trust and be allowed to carry arms for Persia, and they preferred being soldiers to becoming eunuchs. Now they were at work digging a mass grave for the Persian dead.

Mirdin looked at Rob. *Worse than I had feared*, his eyes said. Rob agreed but was comforted that it was over and now they would go home.

But Karim came to see them. Khuff had killed an Indian officer, Karim said, but not before the Indian's sword had sliced almost halfway through the softer steel of Khuff's oversized blade. Karim brought Khuff's sword to show them how deeply it had been cut. The captured Indian sword was fashioned out of the precious swirl-patterned steel and now Alā wore it. The Shah personally had overseen the interrogation of prisoners until he learned that the sword had been made by a craftsman named Dhan Vangalil in Kausambi, a village three days to the north of Mansura.

"Alā has decided to march on Kausambi," Karim said.

They would capture the Indian smith and take him to Ispahan, where he would make weapons of rippled steel to help the Shah conquer his neighbors and restore the great and far-flung Persia of ancient days.

It was said easily but proved more difficult.

Kausambi was another small village on the west bank of the Indus, a place of a few dozen rickety wooden houses leaning into four dusty streets, each of which led to the military garrison. Again they succeeded in keeping their attack a surprise, creeping up through the forest that kept the village pinned against the riverbank. When the Indian soldiers recognized the assault they exploded from the place like a pack of startled monkeys, streaming away into the wilderness.

Alā was delighted, thinking that enemy cowardice had given him the easiest of victories. He lost no time in putting his sword to a throat and telling the terrified villager to lead them to Dhan Vangalil. The sword-maker turned out to be a wiry man with unsurprised eyes and gray hair and a white beard that sought to hide a young-old face. Vangalil agreed readily to go to Ispahan to serve Alā Shah; but he said he would choose death unless the Shah allowed him to bring his wife, two sons, and a daughter, as well as various supplies needed to make the rippled steel, including a large stack of square ingots of hard Indian steel.

The Shah agreed at once. Before they could depart that place, however, scouting parties came back with disturbing news. The Indian troops, far from fleeing, had set up positions in the forest and along the road and were waiting to fall upon anyone seeking to leave Kausambi.

Alā knew the Indians couldn't contain them indefinitely. As had been the case at Mansura, the hidden soldiers were poorly armed; further, they were forced to live off the wild fruits of the land. The Shah's officers told him that doubtless runners had been sent to bring Indian reinforcements, but the nearest known military force of any size was in Sehwan, six days away.

"You must go into the forest and clean them out," Alā ordered.

The five hundred Persians were divided into ten units of fifty fighters each, all foot soldiers. They left the village and beat the brush to find their enemy as though they were hunting wild pigs. When they came upon Indians, the fighting was fierce and bloody and prolonged.

Alā ordered all casualties to be removed from the forest lest they be counted by the enemy and give him knowledge of dwindling strength. And so the Persian dead were laid in the gray dust of a street in Kausambi, to be buried in mass graves by the prisoners from Mansura. The first body to be brought in, at the very start of the forest fighting, was that of the Captain of the Gates. Khuff was dead from an Indian arrow in the back. He had been a strict, unsmiling man but a fixture and a legend. The scars on his body could be read like a history of hard campaigns for two Shahs. All that day, Persian soldiers came to look at him.

They were coldly angered by his death and this time they took no prisoners, killing even when an Indian wished to surrender. In turn, they faced the frenzy of hunted men who knew they would be shown no mercy. The warfare was unrelievedly ugly, either jagged arrows or men doing their worst with sharp metal, all slashing and stabbing and screaming.

Twice a day the wounded were assembled in a clearing and one of the surgeons went out under heavy guard and gave first treatment and brought the patients back to the village. The fighting lasted three days. Of the thirty-eight wounded at Mansura, eleven had died before the Persians had departed that village and sixteen more had perished in the three-day march to Kausambi. To the eleven wounded who survived in the care of Mirdin and Rob, thirty-six new maimed were added during the three days of the forest battle. Forty-seven more Persians were killed.

Mirdin performed one more amputation and Rob three, one of them involving only the fixing of a skin flap over a stub made perfectly below the elbow when an Indian sword took a soldier's forearm. At first they treated wounds the way Ibn Sina had taught: they boiled oil and poured it as hot as possible into the wound to ward off suppuration. But on the morning of the last day Rob ran out of oil; remembering how Barber had tended lacerations with metheglin, he took a goatskin of wine and bathed each new wound with strong drink before dressing it.

That morning the last outburst of fighting had begun immediately after dawn. At midmorning a new group of wounded arrived and bearers carried in someone wrapped from head to ankles in a purloined Indian blanket.

"Only wounded here," Rob said sharply.

But they set him down and stood, waiting uncertainly, and he noticed suddenly that the dead man was wearing Mirdin's shoes.

"Had he been an ordinary soldier we would have placed him in the street," one of them said. "But he is *hakim,* so we have brought him to *hakim.*"

They said they were on the way back when a man sprang from the brush with an ax. The Indian had struck only Mirdin and then was himself cut down.

Rob thanked them and they went away.

When he removed the blanket from the face he saw it was indeed Mirdin. The face was contorted and seemed puzzled and sweetly cranky.

Rob closed the tender eyes and bound the long, homely jaw shut. He didn't think, moving as if drunk. From time to time he left to comfort the dying or care for the wounded, but always he came back and sat. Once he kissed the cold mouth but didn't believe Mirdin knew. He felt the same way when he tried to hold Mirdin's hand. Mirdin was no longer there.

He hoped Mirdin had crossed one of his bridges.

Eventually Rob left him and tried to stay away, working blindly. A man was brought in with a maimed right hand and he did the last amputation of the campaign, taking the hand just above the joint of the wrist. When he came back to Mirdin at midday, flies had gathered.

He removed the blanket and saw that the ax had cleaved Mirdin open at the chest. When Rob bent over the great wound, he was able to pry it wider with his hands.

He was bereft of awareness of either the odors of death within the tent or the scent of the hot crushed grass underfoot. The groans of the wounded, the buzzing of flies, and the far-off shouts and battle sounds faded from his ears. He lost the knowledge that his friend was dead and forgot the crushing burden of his grief.

For the first time he reached inside a man's body and touched the human heart.

Chapter 60

FOUR FRIENDS

Rob washed Mirdin and cut his nails, combed his hair and wrapped him in his prayer shawl, from which half of one of the fringes was cut away, according to custom.

He sought out Karim, who blinked as if slapped upon hearing the news. "I don't want him in the mass grave," Rob said. "His family will certainly come here to get him and bring him home to Masqat for burial among his people in sacred ground."

They chose a place directly in front of a boulder so large elephants couldn't move it, taking precise bearings and pacing off the distance from the rock to the edge of the nearby road. Karim used his privilege to obtain parchment, quill, and ink, and after they had dug the grave Rob carefully mapped it. He would redraw a good chart and send it to Masqat. Unless there was incontrovertible evidence that Mirdin had died, Fara would be considered an *agunah*, a deserted wife, and she would never be permitted to marry again. That was the law; Mirdin had taught it to him.

"Alā will want to be here," he said.

He watched Karim approach the Shah. Alā was drinking with his officers, bathing in the warm glow of victory. Rob saw him listen to Karim for a moment and then wave him away impatiently.

Rob felt a surge of hatred, remembering the king's voice in the cave, and what he had told Mirdin: *We are four friends.*

Karim returned and said shamefacedly that they must proceed; he muttered broken fragments of Islamic prayer as they filled in the hole, but Rob didn't try to pray. Mirdin deserved sorrowing voices raised in *Hashkavot*, the burial chant, and the *Kaddish*. But the *Kaddish* had to be said by ten Jews and he was a Christian pretending to be a Jew, standing numb and silent as the earth closed over his friend.

* * *

That afternoon the Persians could find no more Indians in the forest to kill.

The way from Kausambi was open. Alā appointed a hard-eyed veteran named Farhad to be his new Captain of the Gates, and the officer began to bawl orders calculated to whip the force into readiness to leave.

Amid general jubilation, Alā made an accounting. He had gained his Indian swordmaker. He had lost two elephants at Mansura but had taken twenty-eight there. In addition, four young, healthy elephants had been found by the *mahouts* in a pen in Kausambi; they were work animals, untrained for battle but still valuable. The Indian horses were scrubby little animals ignored by the Persians, but they had discovered a small herd of fine fast camels in Mansura and dozens of pack camels in Kausambi.

Alā was aglow with the success of his raids.

One hundred and twenty of the six hundred who had followed the Shah out of Ispahan were dead, and Rob had the responsibility for forty-seven wounded. Many of these were grievously injured and would die during travel, but there was no question of leaving them behind in the ravaged village. Any Persian found there would be killed when fresh Indian forces came.

Rob sent soldiers through every house to collect rugs and blankets, which were fastened between poles to make litters. When they left at dawn the following morning, Indians carried the litters.

It was three and a half days of hard, tense travel to a place where the river could be forded without fighting. In the early stages of the crossing two men were swept away and drowned. In the middle of the Indus the current was shallow but swift and the *mahouts* placed the elephants upstream to break the force of the water like a living wall, yet another demonstration of the true value of these animals.

The terribly wounded died first, those with perforated chests or slashed bellies, and a man who had been stuck in the neck. In one day alone, half a dozen succumbed. Fifteen days of travel brought them into Baluchistan, where they camped in a field and Rob placed his wounded in an open-sided barn. Seeing Farhad, he sought an audience, but Farhad was all posturing and pompous delay. Fortunately Karim overheard and at once brought him to the tent to see the Shah.

"I have twenty-one left. But they must lie in one place for a time or they will die too, Majesty."

"I cannot wait for wounded," Alā said, eager for his triumphal march through Ispahan.

"I ask your permission to stay here with them."

The Shah stared. "I will not spare Karim to remain with you as *hakim*. He must return with me."

Rob nodded.

They gave him fifteen Indians and twenty-seven armed soldiers to bear litters, and two *mahouts* and all five of the injured elephants so the animals might continue to receive his care. Karim arranged for sacks of rice to be unloaded. Next morning the camp was filled with the usual frenzied bustle. Then the main body moved out onto the trail and, when finally the last of them had gone, Rob was left with his patients and his handful of men in a sudden lack of noise that was at the same time welcome and discomfiting.

The rest benefited his patients, out of the sun and the dust, and spared the constant jolting and shaking of travel. Two men died on their first day in the barn and another on the fourth day, but those who hung on were the tough ones who clutched at survival, and Rob's decision to pause in Baluchistan allowed them to live.

At first the soldiers resented the duty. The other raiders soon would be back in Ispahan to safety and triumphant acclaim, while they had been given prolonged risk and a dirty job. Two members of the armed guard slipped away during the second night and were not seen again. The weaponless Indians did not attempt to flee, nor did the other members of the guard. Soldiers by profession, they soon realized that next time any of them might be struck down, and they were grateful that the *hakim* would risk himself to help their kind.

He sent out hunting parties every morning and small game was brought back and dressed and stewed with some of the rice Karim had left them, and his patients gained in strength even as he watched.

He treated the elephants as he did the men, changing their dressings regularly and bathing their wounds in wine. The great beasts stood and allowed him to hurt them, as if they understood he was their benefactor. The men were as stolid as the animals, even when wounds mortified and he was forced to cut stitches and rip open mending flesh so he could clean away the pus and bathe the wound in wine before closing it again.

He witnessed a strange fact: in virtually every case he had treated with the boiling oil, the wounds had become angry, swollen, and full of suppuration. Many of these patients had died, while most of the men whose wounds were treated after the oil had run out were without pus, and these men lived. He began to keep records, suspecting that this single observation perhaps had made his presence in India worth something. He was almost out of wine, but he had not manufactured the Universal Specific without having learned that where there were farmers, kegs of strong drink could be obtained. They would buy more along the way.

When finally they left the barn at the end of three weeks, four of his patients were well enough to ride. Twelve of the soldiers were burdenless and thus could trade off with those who carried litters, allowing some to rest at all times. Rob led them off the Spice Road at first opportunity and took a circuitous route. The longer way would add almost a week to their travel, which made the soldiers sullen. But he wouldn't risk his tiny caravan by following the Shah's larger force through a countryside in which hatred as well as starvation had been sown by the ravaging Persian foragers.

Three of the elephants still limped and were not given loads, but Rob rode on the back of the elephant whose trunk had received minor slashes. He was happy to leave Bitch and would be content never to ride a camel again. In contrast, the elephant's broad back offered comfort and stability and a king's view of the world.

But the easy travel allowed unlimited opportunity for him to think, and the memory of Mirdin was with him every step of the way, so that the ordinary wonders of a journey—a sudden flight of thousands of birds, a sunset that set the sky to flaming, the way one of the elephants stepped on the lip of a steep ditch to crumble it and then sat like a child to slide down the resulting earth ramp—these things were noticed but brought little joy.

Jesus, he thought. *Or Shaddai, or Allah, whoever You may be. How can You allow such waste?*

Kings led ordinary men into battle and some who survived were poor stuff and some were purely evil, he thought bitterly. Yet God had permitted one to be cut down who had had the qualities of saintliness and a mind scholars envied and coveted. Mirdin would have spent his life seeking only to heal and serve mankind.

Not since the burial of Barber had Rob been so moved and shaken by a death, and he was still brooding and in despair when they reached Ispahan.

They approached in late afternoon, so that the city was as he first had seen it, white buildings, blue-shadowed, with roofs of reflected pink from the sand hills. They rode directly to the *maristan,* where the eighteen wounded men were handed over to others for care.

Then they went to the stables of the House of Paradise, where he rid himself of responsibility for the animals, the troops, and the slaves.

When that was done, he asked for his brown gelding. Farhad, the new Captain of the Gates, was nearby and overheard, and he ordered the groom not to waste time trying to locate one horse in the milling herd. "Issue the *hakim* another mount."

"Khuff said I would get back the same horse." Not everything had to change, he told himself.

"Khuff is dead."

"Nevertheless." To his own great surprise, Rob's voice and stare became hard. He had come from carnage that had sickened him but now he yearned for something to strike, violence as a release. "I wish the same horse."

Farhad knew men and recognized the challenge in the *hakim*'s voice. He had nothing to gain from brawling with this *Dhimmi* and a great deal to lose. He shrugged and turned away.

Rob rode beside the groom, back and forth through the herd. By the time he saw the gelding he was ashamed of his ugly conduct. They separated the horse from the others and put a saddle on it while Farhad hovered and didn't hide his contempt that this flawed beast was what the *Dhimmi* had been prepared to fight for.

But the brown horse trotted eagerly through the dusk to Yehuddiyyeh.

Hearing noises among the animals, Mary took her father's sword and the lamp and opened the door between house and stable.

He had come home.

The saddle was already off the brown horse and he was in the act of backing the gelding into the stall. He turned, and in the poor light she saw he had lost considerable weight; he looked almost like the thin, half-wild boy she had met in Kerl Fritta's caravan.

He reached her in three steps and held her without speaking, then his hand touched her flat belly.

"Did it go well?"

She gave a shaky laugh, for she was weary and torn. Only by five days had he missed hearing her frantic screams. "Your son was two days in coming."

"A son."

He placed his large palm against her cheek. At his touch the flooding relief made her tremble, so that she came close to spilling oil from the lamp and the flame flickered. When he was away she had made herself hard and strong, a leather woman, but it was deepest luxury to trust again that someone else was shielding and capable. Like turning from leather back into silk.

She set down the sword and took his hand, leading him inside to where the infant lay asleep in a blanket-lined basket.

Suddenly she saw the round-faced bit of humanity through Rob's eyes, tiny red features swollen from birthing travail, fuzz of darkish hair atop his head. She felt annoyance at the kind of man this was, for she couldn't tell if he was disappointed or overjoyed. When he looked up, mixed with pleasure there was agony in his face.

"How is Fara?"

"Karim came and told her. I observed *shiva* with her, seven days. Then she took Dawwid and Issachar and joined a caravan bound for Masqat. With God's aid, by now they are among kinsmen."

"It will be hard for you without her."

"Harder for her," she said bitterly.

The child began a thin wailing and Rob picked him from the basket and gave his little finger, which was taken hungrily.

Mary wore a loose dress with a drawstring at the neck, sewn for her by Fara. She opened the garment and lowered it beneath her full breasts, then took the babe from him. Rob lay down alongside them on the mat as she began to nurse. He moved his head onto her free breast and soon she felt his cheek's wetness.

She had never known her father to weep, or any man, and Rob's convulsive shaking frightened her. "My dear. My Rob," she murmured.

Instinctively, her free hand gently directed him until his mouth was on the nipple. He was a more tentative suckler than his son and when he drew on her and swallowed, she was vastly moved but tenderly amused: for once, part of *her* body was entering *him*. She thought fleetingly of Fara and, with no little guilt, thanked the Virgin that it had not been her husband who had been taken. The two pairs of lips on her, one tiny and the other large and so familiar, filled her with a tingling warmth. Perhaps it was the Blessed Mother or the saints working their magic, but for a time the three of them became one.

Finally Rob sat up, and when he leaned over and kissed her, she tasted her own warm richness.

"I am not a Roman," he said.

PART SIX

Hakim

Chapter 61

THE APPOINTMENT

The morning after his return Rob studied his man-child in the light of day and saw that the babe was beautiful, with deep blue English eyes and large hands and feet. He counted and gently flexed each tiny finger and toe and rejoiced in the slightly bowed little legs. A strong infant.

The child smelled like an olive press, having been oiled by his mother. Then he smelled less pleasing and Rob changed a baby's cloth for the first time since tending his brothers and sister. Deep within him he still yearned to find William Stewart, Anne Mary, and Jonathan Carter one day. Wouldn't it be joy to show this nephew to the long-lost Coles?

He and Mary quarreled about circumcision.

"It will do him no harm. Here every man is circumcised, Muslim and Jew, and it's an easy way for him to be more easily accepted."

"I don't wish him to be more easily accepted in Persia," she said wearily. "I wish him to be accepted at home, where men aren't bobbed and knobbed but are left to nature."

He laughed and she began to cry. He comforted her and then, when he could, escaped to confer with Ibn Sina.

The Prince of Physicians greeted him warmly, thanking Allah for his survival and speaking sadly of Mirdin. Ibn Sina listened with close attention to Rob's report of treatments and amputations performed at the two battles, being especially interested in his comparisons between the efficacy of hot oil versus wine baths for cleansing open wounds. Ibn Sina showed himself more interested in scientific truth than in his own infallibility. Even though Rob's observations contradicted what he himself had said and written, he insisted that Rob write his findings. "Also, this thing concerning wine in wounds should be your first lecture as a *hakim*," he said, and Rob found himself agreeing with his mentor.

Then the old man looked at him. "I would like you to work with me, Jesse ben Benjamin. As assistant."

He had never dreamed of this. He wanted to tell the Chief Physician that he had come to Ispahan—from so great a distance, through other worlds, surmounting so many problems—only to touch the hem of Ibn Sina's garment.

Instead, he nodded. *"Hakim-bashi,* I would like that."

Mary made no difficulty when he told her. She had been in Ispahan long enough so it didn't occur to her that her husband could refuse such an honor, for in addition to a comfortable salary there would be the immediate prestige and respect of association with a man who was venerated like a demigod, loved above royalty. When Rob saw her joy for him, he took her into his arms. "I *will* take you home, I promise you, Mary. But not for a time yet. Please trust me."

She did. Yet she recognized that if they were to remain for a longer time, she must change. She determined to make an effort to bend to the country. Reluctantly, she gave in concerning the matter of the child's circumcision.

Rob went to Nitka the Midwife for advice. "Come," she said, and led him two streets away to Reb Asher Jacobi the *mohel.*

"So, a circumcision," the *mohel* said. "The mother . . ." Musing, he looked at Nitka through narrowed eyes, his fingers scrabbling in his beard. "An Other!"

"It doesn't have to be a *brit,* with all the prayers," Nitka said impatiently. Having taken the serious step of delivering the Other's manchild, she slipped easily into the role of defender. "If the father asks for the seal of Abraham on the child, it is a blessing to circumcise him, isn't it so?"

"Yes," Reb Asher admitted. "Your father. Will he hold the child?" he asked Rob.

"My father is dead."

Reb Asher sighed. "Will other family members be present?"

"Only my wife. There are no other family members here. I'll hold the child myself."

"A time of celebration," Nitka said gently. "Would you mind? My sons Shemuel and Chofni, a few neighbors . . ."

Rob nodded.

"I'll attend to it," Nitka said.

Next morning she and her two burly stonecutter sons were the first to arrive at Rob's house. Hinda, the disapproving merchant from the Jewish market, came with her Tall Isak, a gray-bearded scholar with bemused eyes. Hinda was still unsmiling but she brought a gift, a swaddling garment.

Yaakob the Shoemaker and Naoma, his wife, gave a flagon of wine. Micah Halevi the Baker came, his wife Yudit carrying two large loaves of sugared bread.

Holding the sweet little body supine in his lap, Rob had doubts when Reb Asher cut the foreskin from the tiny penis. "May the lad grow in vigor —of mind and body—to a life of good works," the *mohel* declared, as the baby shrieked. The neighbors lifted bowls of wine and cheered, and Rob gave the boy the Jewish name Mirdin ben Jesse.

Mary hated every moment. An hour later when everyone had gone home and she and Rob were alone with their child, she wet her fingers in barley water and touched her screaming son lightly on the forehead, the chin, and one earlobe and then the other.

"In the name of the Father and the Son and the Holy Spirit, I christen you Robert James Cole," she said clearly, naming him for his father and his grandfather.

After that, when they were alone she called her husband Rob, and it was the child to whom she referred as Rob J.

To the Most Respected Reb Mulka Askari, Pearl Merchant of Masqat, Greetings.

Your late son Mirdin was my friend. May he rest.

We were surgeons together in India, from whence I have brought these few things, sent to you now via the kind hands of Reb Moise ben Zavil, merchant of Qum, whose caravan is bound this day for your city with a manifest of olive oil.

Reb Moise will give to you a parchment chart showing the precise location of Mirdin's grave in the village of Kausambi, that his bones some day may be moved if that is your wish. I also send the *tefillin* which daily he wound on his arm and which he told me you gave to him when he entered into *minyan* on reaching his fourteenth year. In addition, I send the pieces and board of the Shah's Game, over which Mirdin and I spent many a happy hour.

There were no other belongings with him in India. He was, of course, buried in his *tallit*.

I pray the Lord may bring some measure of understanding to your bereavement and to ours. With his passing a light went from my life. He was the finest man ever I have valued. I know that Mirdin is with *Adashem,* and I hope that one day I may be worthy to be with him again.

Please convey my affection and respect to his widow and stalwart

young sons and inform them that my wife has given birth to a healthy
son, Mirdin ben Jesse, and sends them her loving wishes for a good life.
Yivorechachah Adonai V'Yishmorechah, May the
Lord Bless You and Keep You. I am
Jesse ben Benjamin, *hakim*

Al-Juzjani had been Ibn Sina's assistant for years. He had achieved
greatness in his own right as a surgeon and was the most notable success
among the former assistants, but all of them had done well. The *hakim-bashi* worked his assistants hard, and the position was like an extension of
training, an opportunity to continue to learn. From the beginning Rob
did far more than follow Ibn Sina about and fetch things for him, as
sometimes the assistants of other great men were called upon to do. Ibn
Sina expected to be consulted when there was a problem or his opinion
was required, but the young *hakim* had his confidence and was expected
to act on his own.

For Rob it was a happy time. He lectured in the *madrassa* concerning
wine baths for open wounds; few people attended, for a visiting physician
from al-Rayy lectured that morning on the subject of physical love. Persian
doctors always crowded into lectures dealing with the sexual, a curiosity
to Rob, for in Europe the subject wasn't a physician's responsibility. Still,
he attended many such lectures himself, and whether because of what he
learned or despite it, his marriage prospered.

Mary healed quickly from the birthing. They followed the prescriptions
of Ibn Sina, who cautioned that abstinence should prevail between man and
wife for six weeks following a birth and advised that the new mother's
pudenda should be gently treated with olive oil and massaged with a mixture of honey and barley water. The treatment worked wonderfully well.
The six weeks' wait seemed an eternity, and when it was over, Mary turned
to him just as eagerly as he embraced her.

Several weeks later, the milk in her breasts began to dwindle. It came
as a shock because her supply had been copious; she had told him she had
milky rivers in her, milk enough to supply the world. When she had given
suck it had relieved the painful pressure in her breasts, but too soon the
pressure was gone and now the pain came from hearing little Rob J.'s thin,
hungry wailing. They saw that a wet nurse would be necessary, and Rob
talked with midwives and through them found a strong, homely Armenian
woman named Prisca who had more than enough milk for her new daughter and the *hakim*'s son. Four times a day Mary carried the child to the
leather shop of Prisca's husband Dikran and waited while little Rob J. took
the teat. At night Prisca came to the house in Yehuddiyyeh and stayed in

the other room with the two babies while Mary and Rob tried to be stealthy about lovemaking and then enjoyed the luxury of uninterrupted sleep.

Mary was fulfilled and happiness made her luminous. She bloomed with a new assurance. Sometimes it seemed to Rob that she took full credit for the small and noisy creature they had created together, but he loved her all the more.

In the first week of the month of *Shaban* the caravan of Reb Moise ben Zavil came through Ispahan again on the way to Qum and the merchant delivered gifts from Reb Mulka Askari and his daughter-in-law Fara. Fara had given the child Mirdin ben Jesse six small linen garments, sewn with love and care. The pearl merchant had sent back to Rob the Shah's Game that had belonged to his dead son.

It was the last time Mary wept for Fara. When she had dried her eyes, Rob set up Mirdin's figures on the board and taught her the game. After that, they played often. He didn't expect much, for it was a warriors' game and she was but a woman. But she learned quickly and would capture one of his pieces with a whoop and battle cry that would have been credible in a Seljuk marauder. Her swift skill in moving a king's army, if unnatural in a female, nevertheless wasn't a great shock, for he had learned long since that Mary Cullen was an extraordinary creature.

The advent of *Ramadan* caught Karim unprepared, so intent upon sinfulness that the purity and shriving implicit in the month of fasting seemed impossible to achieve and too painful to contemplate. Not even the prayers and the fasting could banish his thoughts of Despina and his unflagging yearning for her. Indeed, because Ibn Sina spent several evenings a week in various mosques and breaking the fast with *mullahs* and Qu'ranic scholars, *Ramadan* provided a secure time for the lovers to meet. Karim saw her as often as ever.

During *Ramadan*, Alā Shah too was diverted by prayer meetings and other demands on his time, and one day Karim had an opportunity to return to the *maristan* for the first time in months. Happily, it was a day when Ibn Sina was away from the hospital, caring for one of the members of the court who was down with fever. Karim knew the taste of guilt; Ibn Sina always had treated him fairly and well, and he had no desire to spend time with Despina's husband.

The visit to the hospital was a cruel disappointment. Medical clerks followed him through the halls as usual—perhaps even in greater number than before, for his legend had grown. But he knew none of the patients; anyone he had treated here was either dead or long since recovered. And though once he had walked these halls with a sure confidence in his own skills, he found himself fumbling as he asked nervous questions, uncertain of what he was looking at in patients who were the responsibilities of others.

He managed to survive the visit without making himself out to be a fool, but he had the grim awareness that unless he could spend time in the true practice of medicine, the abilities he had gained so painfully through many years soon would be gone.

He had no choice. Alā Shah had assured him that what lay ahead for them both would make medicine seem pale by comparison.

That year Karim didn't run in the *chatir*. He hadn't trained and he was heavier than a runner should be. He watched the race with Alā Shah.

The first day of *Bairam* dawned even hotter than the day when he had won, and the race was very slow. The king had renewed his offer of *calaat* to anyone who could repeat Karim's feat and finish all twelve laps of the city before Final Prayer, but it was clear that no one would run 126 Roman miles that day.

It developed into a race by the fifth lap, dwindling to a struggle between al-Harat of Hamadhān and a young soldier named Nafis Jurjis. Each of them had set too quick a pace the previous year and had ended the race in collapse. Now, to avoid this, they ran too slowly.

Karim shouted encouragement to Nafis. He told Alā that this was because Nafis had survived the Indian raids with them. In truth, although he liked the young soldier, it was because he didn't want al-Harat to win, for he had known al-Harat as a child in Hamadhān, and when they met Karim still sensed his contempt for Zaki-Omar's bum boy.

But Nafis wilted after collecting his eighth arrow and the race was al-Harat's alone. It was already late afternoon and the heat was brutal; sensibly, al-Harat signaled that he would finish the lap and claim his victory.

Karim and the Shah rode the final lap well ahead of the runner so they could be at the finishing line to greet him, Alā on his savage white stallion and Karim astride his head-tossing Arabian gray. Along the route Karim's spirits rose, because the people knew it would be a long time, if ever, before a runner ran another *chatir* such as he had run. They embraced him for this with roars of joy, and for being a hero of Mansura and Kausambi. Alā beamed, and Karim knew he could look upon poor al-Harat with benevolence, for the runner was a farmer of poor land and Karim soon would be Vizier of Persia.

When they passed the *madrassa* he saw the eunuch Wasif on the hospital roof and next to him the veiled Despina. At sight of her Karim's heart leaped and he smiled. It was better to go by her like this, on a priceless horse and dressed in silk and linen, than to stagger past stinking of sweat and blind with fatigue!

Not far from Despina a woman without a veil grew impatient with the heat and, removing her black cloth, shook her head as if in imitation of Karim's horse. Her hair fell and fanned forth, long and billowing. The sun glinted in it gloriously, revealing different shades of gold and red. Next to him he heard the Shah speak.

"It is the *Dhimmi*'s wife? The European woman?"

"Yes, Majesty. The woman of our friend Jesse ben Benjamin."

"I thought it must be she," Alā said.

The king watched the bareheaded female until they had ridden past her. He asked no further questions, and soon Karim was able to engage him in conversation concerning the Indian smith Dhan Vangalil and the swords he was making for the Shah with his new furnace and forge behind the stables of the House of Paradise.

Chapter 62

AN OFFER OF REWARD

Rob continued to start each day at the House of Peace Synagogue, partly because the strange mixture of chanted Jewish prayer and silent Christian prayer had become pleasing and nurturing.

But mostly because in some strange way his presence in the synagogue was the fulfillment of a debt he owed to Mirdin.

Yet he was unable to enter the House of Zion, Mirdin's synagogue. And though scholars sat daily and argued the law at the House of Peace, and it would have been a simple matter to suggest that somebody tutor him in the eighty-nine commandments he hadn't examined, he hadn't the heart to finish that task without Mirdin. He told himself that five hundred and twenty-four commandments would serve a spurious Jew as well as six hundred and thirteen, and he turned his mind to other things.

The Master had written on every subject. While a student, Rob had had a chance to read many of his works on medicine, but now he sampled other kinds of writing by Ibn Sina and felt ever more in awe of him. He had written on music and poetry and astronomy, on metaphysics and Eastern thought, on philology and the active intellect, and commentaries on all the books of Aristotle. While a prisoner in the castle of Fardajān he wrote a book called *Guidance*, summarizing all the branches of philosophy. There was even a military manual, *The Management and Provisioning of Soldiers, Slave Troops, and Armies*, which would have served Rob well if he had read it before going to India as a field surgeon. He had written on mathematics, on the human soul, and on the essence of sorrow. And again and again he had written about Islam, the religion given him by his father and which, despite the science that permeated his being, he was able to accept on faith.

This is what made him beloved of the people. They saw that despite the luxurious estate and all the fruits of royal *calaat*, despite the fact that the learned and glorious men of the world came to seek him out and plumb his mind, despite the fact that kings vied for the honor of being recognized as the Master's sponsor—despite all these things, even as the lowliest wretch among them, Ibn Sina raised his eyes heavenward and exclaimed:

La ilaha illa-l-Lah;
Muhammadun rasulu-l-Lah.

There is no God but God;
Mohammed is the prophet of God.

Each morning before First Prayer a crowd of several hundred gathered in front of his house. They were beggars, *mullahs,* shepherds, merchants, poor and rich, men of every sort. The Prince of Physicians carried out his own prayer rug and worshiped with his admirers, then when he rode to the *maristan* they walked alongside his horse and sang of the Prophet and chanted verses from the Qu'ran.

Several evenings a week pupils gathered at his house. Customarily there were medical readings. Every week for a quarter of a century al-Juzjani had read aloud from Ibn Sina's works, most frequently from the famous *Qān-ūn.* Sometimes Rob was asked to read aloud from Ibn Sina's book entitled *Shifa.* Then a lively discussion period would follow, a combination drinking party and clinical debate, often heated and sometimes hilarious but always illuminating.

"How does the blood get to the fingers?" al-Juzjani might cry in despair, repeating a clerk's question. "Do you forget Galen said the heart is a pump that sets the blood into motion?"

"Ah!" Ibn Sina would interject. "And the wind sets a sailing ship into motion. But how does it find its way to Bahrain?"

Frequently when Rob took his leave he was able to glimpse the eunuch Wasif standing hidden in the shadows near the door to the south tower. One evening Rob slipped away and went to the field behind the wall of Ibn Sina's estate. He wasn't surprised to find Karim's gray Arabian stallion tethered there, tossing his head impatiently.

Walking back to his own unhidden horse, Rob studied the apartment atop the south tower. Through the window slits in the round stone wall the yellow light flickered and teased, and without envy or regret he recalled that Despina liked to make love by the light of six candles.

Ibn Sina inducted Rob into mysteries. "There is within us a strange being—some call it the mind, others the soul—which has great effect on our bodies and our health. I first saw evidence of this as a young man in Bukhārā, when I was beginning to be interested in the subject that led me to write *The Pulse*. I had a patient, a youth of my own age called Achmed; his appetite had flagged and he had lost weight. His father, a wealthy merchant of that place, was distressed and begged for my help.

"When I examined Achmed I could see nothing wrong. But as I tarried with him a strange thing occurred. My fingers were on the artery in his wrist while we chatted in friendly fashion about various towns in the area of Bukhārā. The pulse was slow and steady until I mentioned the village of Efsene, where I was born. Then there was such a tremolo in his wrist that I became frightened!

"I knew that village well, and I began to mention various streets, to no great effect until I came to the Lane of the Eleventh Imam, whereupon his pulse quickened and danced again. I no longer knew all the families in that lane, but further questioning and prodding produced the information that on that street lived Ibn Razi, a worker in copper, and that he had three daughters, the eldest of whom was Ripka, very beautiful. When Achmed spoke of this female, in his wrist the fluttering reminded me of an injured bird.

"I spoke to his father, saying that healing for him lay in marriage with this Ripka. It was arranged and came to pass. Shortly thereafter, Achmed's appetite returned. When last I saw him, some years past, he was a fat and contented man.

"Galen tells us that the heart and all the arteries pulsate with the same rhythm, so that from one you can judge of all, and that a slow and regular pulse signifies good health. But since Achmed, I have found that the pulse also may be used to determine the state of a patient's agitation or peace of mind. I have done so many times, and the pulse has proven to be The Messenger Who Never Lies."

So Rob learned that, in addition to the gift that allowed him to gauge vitality, he could monitor the pulse to garner information about the patient's health and mood. There was ample opportunity to practice. Desperate people flocked to the Prince of Physicians seeking miracle cures. Rich or poor, they were treated the same, but only a few could be accepted as patients by Ibn Sina and Rob, and most were turned over to other physicians.

Much of Ibn Sina's clinical practice consisted of the Shah and valued members of Alā's entourage. Thus one morning Rob was dispatched to the House of Paradise by the Master, who informed him that Siddha, the wife of the Indian swordmaker Dhan Vangalil, was ill with a colic.

As translator Rob sought out the services of Alā's personal *mahout*, the

Indian named Harsha. Siddha proved to be a pleasant, round-faced woman with graying hair. The Vangalil family worshiped Buddha, so the prohibition of *aurat* did not apply and Rob could palpate her stomach without worrying about being denounced to the *mullahs*. After examining her at length he determined that her problem was one of diet, for Harsha told him that neither the smith's family nor any of the *mahouts* was furnished with a sufficient supply of cumin, turmeric, or peppers, spices to which they had been accustomed all their lives, and on which their digestions were dependent.

Rob set the matter right by personally seeing to the distribution of the spices. He had already won the regard of some of the *mahouts* by tending to the battle wounds of their elephants, and now he won the gratitude of the Vangalils as well.

He brought Mary and Rob J. to visit them, hoping that the mutual problems of people transplanted into Persia would serve as a basis for friendship. Alas, the sympathetic spark that had ignited immediately between Fara and Mary didn't reappear. The two women eyed one another uncomfortably with rigid politeness, Mary trying not to stare at the round black *kumkum* painted in the middle of Siddha's forehead. Rob didn't bring his family to visit the Vangalils again.

But he returned to them alone, fascinated by what Dhan Vangalil could accomplish with steel.

Over a shallow hole in the ground Dhan had constructed a smelting furnace, a clay wall surrounded by a thicker outer wall of rock and mud, the whole girdled with bands of sapling. It stood the height of a man's shoulders and a pace wide, tapering to a slightly narrower diameter at the top to concentrate the heat and reinforce the walls against collapse.

In this oven Dhan made wrought iron by burning alternating layers of charcoal and Persian ore, pea to nut size. Around the oven a shallow trench had been dug. Sitting on the outer lip with his feet in the trench, he operated bellows made from the hide of a whole goat, forcing precisely controlled amounts of air into the glowing mass. Above the hottest part of the fire, ore was reduced to bits of iron like drops of metal rain. They settled through the furnace and collected at the bottom in a blob-like mixture of charcoal, slag, and iron, called the bloom.

Dhan had sealed a removal hole with clay that he now broke away so he could drag out the bloom, which was refined by strong hammering requiring many reheatings in his forge. Most of the iron in the ore went into slag and waste, but that which was reduced made a very good grade of wrought iron.

But it was soft, he explained to Rob through Harsha. The bars of Indian steel, carried from Kausambi by the elephants, were very hard. He melted several of these in a crucible and then quenched the fire. After cooling, the steel was extremely brittle and he shattered it and stacked it on pieces of the wrought iron.

Now, sweating among his anvils, tongs, chisels, punches, and hammers, the skinny Indian displayed biceps like serpents as he wedded the soft and hard metals. He forge-welded multiple layers of iron and steel, hammering as if possessed, twisting and cutting, overlapping, folding the sheet and hammering again and again, mixing his metals like a potter wedging clay or a woman kneading bread.

Watching him, Rob knew he could never learn the complexities, the variables needing subtle skills passed down long generations of Indian smiths; but he gained an understanding of the process through asking innumerable questions.

Dhan made a scimitar and cured the weapon in soot dampened with a citron vinegar, resulting in an acid-etched, "watermarked" blade with a blue, smoky undertone. Fashioned out of the iron alone, it would have been soft and dull; made only from the hard Indian steel, it would have been brittle. But this sword took a fine edge that could cut a dropped thread in midair, and it was a supple weapon.

The swords Alā had ordered Dhan to make weren't meant for kings. They were unembellished soldiers' arms, to be stockpiled against a future war in which superior scimitars might give Persia a needed advantage.

"He will run out of the Indian steel before many more weeks," Harsha observed.

Yet Dhan offered to make Rob a dagger, out of gratitude for what the *hakim* had done for his family and the *mahouts.* Rob refused regretfully; the weapons were beautiful but he wanted no more to do with killing. But then he couldn't resist opening his bag and showing Dhan a scalpel, a pair of bistouris, and two knives used for amputations, one blade curved and thin and the other large and serrated for cutting through bone.

Dhan smiled broadly, showing the gaps of many missing teeth, and nodded his head.

A week later, Dhan handed over instruments in patterned steel that would take the keenest edge and hold it like no other surgical tools Rob had ever seen.

They would outlast his own life, he knew. It was a princely gift and called for a generous gift in return, but he was too overwhelmed to think of that for the moment. Dhan saw his enormous pleasure and basked in it. Unable to communicate with words, the two men embraced. Together they oiled the steel objects and wrapped them individually in rags, then Rob carried them off in a leather bag.

Filled with delight, he was riding away from the House of Paradise when he met a returning hunting party led by the king. In his rough hunting clothes Alā looked exactly as he had when Rob had first glimpsed him, years before.

He drew up his horse and bowed, hoping they would pass him by, but a moment later Farhad cantered up smartly.

"He wishes you to approach."

The Captain of the Gates wheeled his mount and Rob followed him back to the Shah.

"Ah, *Dhimmi*. You must ride with me for a time." Alā signaled that the soldiers who accompanied him were to hang back, and he and Rob walked their animals toward the palace.

"I have not rewarded your service to Persia."

Rob was surprised, having thought all awards for service during the Indian raids long since were past. Several officers had been promoted for valor and soldiers had been given purses. Karim had been praised so lavishly in public by the Shah that market gossip had him soon to be named to any number of exalted posts. Rob was content to have been overlooked, happy that the raids were now history.

"I have it in mind to present you with another *calaat*, calling for a larger house and extensive grounds, an estate suitable for a royal entertainment."

"No *calaat* is necessary, Sire." In a dry voice he thanked the Shah for his generosity. "My presence was a small way of repaying my enormous gratitude to you."

It would have been more graceful for him to speak of love for the monarch, but he could not and Alā didn't seem to take his words to heart, in any case.

"Nevertheless, you deserve reward."

"Then I ask my Shah to reward me by allowing me to stay in the small house in Yehuddiyyeh where I am comfortable and happy."

The Shah looked hard at him. Finally he nodded. "Leave me, *Dhimmi*." He dug his heels into the white horse and the stallion sprang away. Behind, his escort hastened to gallop after him, and in a moment the horse soldiers were streaming past Rob with a pounding and a clatter.

Thoughtfully, he turned the brown horse and made his way homeward again to show the patterned steel instruments to Mary.

Chapter 63

A CLINIC IN IDHAJ

That year winter came hard and early to Persia. One morning all the mountain peaks were white, and the next day huge chill winds swept a mixture of salt, sand, and snow into Ispahan. In the markets the merchants covered their goods with cloths and longed for spring. Bulky in ankle-length sheepskin *cadabis,* they huddled over charcoal braziers and kept themselves warm with gossip about their king. Though much of the time they reacted to Alā's exploits with a chuckle or a wry, resigned glance, the latest scandal brought a pinched gravity to many faces that was not a result of the raw winds.

In the light of the Shah's daily drinking and debauchery, the Imam Mirza-aboul Qandrasseh had sent his friend and chief aide, the *mullah* Musa Ibn Abbas, to reason with the king and remind him that strong drink was an abomination to Allah, forbidden by the Qu'ran.

Alā had been drinking for hours when he received the Vizier's delegate. He listened to Musa gravely. When he perceived the subject of the message and caught the careful admonishing tone, the Shah stepped down from his throne and approached the *mullah.*

Disconcerted but not knowing how else to behave, Musa continued to speak. Presently, with no change of expression, the king had dribbled wine over the old man's head, to the astonishment of all present—courtiers, servants, and slaves. Throughout the remainder of the lecture he had dripped strong drink all over Musa, wetting his beard and his clothing, then dismissed him with a wave of his hand, sending him back to Qandrasseh sodden and totally humiliated.

It was a show of contempt for the holy men of Ispahan and was widely interpreted as proof that Qandrasseh's time as Vizier was coming to an end. The *mullahs* had grown accustomed to the influence and privileges Qandrasseh had given them, and next morning in every mosque in the city dark

486

and disturbing prophecies were heard concerning the future of Persia.

Karim Harun came to consult with Ibn Sina and Rob about Alā.

"He isn't like that. He can be the most unselfish of companions, merry and lovable. You saw him in India, *Dhimmi*. He is the bravest of fighters and if he is ambitious, wanting to be a great *Shahanshah*, then it is because he is even more ambitious for Persia."

They listened to him silently.

"I've tried to keep him from drinking," Karim said. He looked miserably at his former teacher and his friend.

Ibn Sina sighed. "He is most dangerous to others early in the morning, when he awakens with the sickness of yesterday's wine in him. Give him senna tea then, to purge the poisons and take the ache from his head, and sprinkle ground Armenian stone in his food to rid him of melancholia. But nothing will protect him from himself. When he drinks you must stay out of his presence if you can." He regarded Karim gravely. "You must also take care as you go about the city, for you are known as the Shah's favorite and are generally regarded as the Qandrasseh's rival. Now you have powerful enemies with a great stake in stopping your climb to power."

Rob caught Karim's eye. "You must take care to lead a blameless life," he said meaningfully, "for your enemies will pounce on any weakness."

He recalled the self-loathing he had felt when he had made the Master a cuckold. He knew Karim; despite his ambition and his love for the woman, Karim had a basic goodness and Rob could guess at the anguish he felt in betraying Ibn Sina.

Karim nodded. As he took his leave he grasped Rob's wrist and smiled. Rob smiled back; it was impossible not to respond. Karim still had his handsome charm, though it was no longer carefree. Rob saw great tension and restless uncertainty in Karim's face, and he looked after his friend with pity.

Little Rob's blue eyes regarded the world fearlessly. He had begun to make crawling motions and his parents rejoiced when he learned to drink from a cup. At Ibn Sina's suggestion Rob tried feeding him camel's milk, which the Master said was the most healthful food for a child. It was strong-smelling and had yellowish lumps of butterfat but the little boy swallowed it hungrily. From then on, the woman Prisca no longer suckled him. Each morning Rob fetched camel's milk from the Armenian market in a stone crock. The former wet nurse, always holding one of her own children, peered from her husband's leather stall to watch for him every morning.

"Master *Dhimmi!* Master *Dhimmi!* How is my little boy?" Prisca called, and she gave him a luminous smile each time he assured her that the child was fine.

Because of the bitter air, patients in number came to the physicians with catarrh and aching bones and inflamed and swollen joints. Pliny the Younger had written that to cure a cold the patient should kiss the hairy muzzle of a mouse, but Ibn Sina pronounced Pliny the Younger not fit to be read. He had his own favorite remedy against the affliction of phlegm and the rigors of rheumatism. He carefully instructed Rob to assemble two *dirhams* each of castoreum, galbanum of Ispahan, stinking asafetida, asafetida, celery seed, Syrian fenugreek, galbanum, caltrop, harmel seed, opopanax, rue gum, and kernel of pumpkin seed. The dry ingredients were pounded. The gums were steeped in oil for a night and then pounded, and over them was poured warm honey bereft of froth, the wet mixture then being kneaded with the dry ingredients and the resulting paste put into a glazed vessel.

"The dose is one *mithqal*," Ibn Sina said. "It is efficacious if God wishes."

Rob went to the elephant pens, where the *mahouts* were snuffling and coughing, dealing less than cheerfully with a season unlike the mild winters they had known in India. He visited them three days in a row and gave them fumitory and sagepenum and Ibn Sina's paste, with results so indecisive he would have preferred to dose them with Barber's Universal Specific. The elephants didn't look splendid as they had in battle; now they were draped like tents, festooned with blankets in an attempt to keep them warm.

Rob stood with Harsha and watched Zi, the Shah's great bull elephant, cramming himself with hay.

"My poor children," Harsha said softly. "Once, before Buddha or Brahman or Vishnu or Shiva, the elephants were all-powerful and my people prayed to them. Now they are so much less than gods that they are captured and made to do our will."

Zi shivered as they watched, and Rob prescribed that the beasts be given buckets of warmed drinking water to heat them from within.

Harsha was doubtful. "We have been working them and they labor well despite the cold."

But Rob had been learning about elephants in the House of Wisdom. "Do you know about Hannibal?"

"No," the *mahout* said.

"A soldier, a great leader."

"Great as Alā Shah?"

"At least as great, but from a time long gone. With thirty-seven elephants he led an army over the Alps—high, terrible mountains, steep and snow-covered—and he didn't lose an animal. But cold and exposure weakened them. Later, crossing smaller mountains, all but one of the elephants died. The lesson is that you must rest your beasts and keep them warm."

Harsha nodded respectfully. "Do you know that you are followed, *Hakim?*"

Rob was startled.

"That one there, sitting in the sun."

He was just a man huddling in the fleece of his *cadabi,* seated with his back to the wall to hide from the cold wind.

"Are you certain?"

"Yes, *Hakim,* I saw him follow you yesterday too. Even now, he keeps you in his sight."

"When I leave here can you follow after him cleverly, so we may discover who he is?"

Harsha's eyes gleamed. "Yes, *Hakim.*"

Late that evening Harsha came to Yehuddiyyeh and tapped on Rob's door.

"He followed you home, *Hakim.* When he left you here, I followed him to the Friday Mosque. I was very clever, O Honorable, I was invisible. He entered the *mullah*'s house wearing the ragged *cadabi* and after a short time emerged clad in black robes, and he went into the mosque in time for Final Prayer. He is a *mullah, Hakim.*"

Rob thanked him thoughtfully and Harsha went away.

The *mullah* had been sent by Qandrasseh's friends, he was certain. Doubtless they had followed Karim to his meeting with Ibn Sina and Rob and then had watched to determine the extent of Rob's involvement with the prospective Vizier.

Perhaps they concluded he was harmless, for next day he watched carefully but could see no one who might have been trailing after him and, so far as he could tell, in the days that followed he wasn't spied on again.

It remained chill, but spring was coming. Only the tips of the purple-gray mountains were white with snow, and in the garden the stark branches of the apricot trees were covered with tiny black buds, perfectly round.

Two soldiers came one morning and fetched Rob to the House of Paradise. In the cold stone throne room small knots of blue-lipped members of the court stood about and suffered. Karim was not among them. The Shah sat at the table over the floor grille through which oven heat drifted.

After the *ravi zemin* was out of the way he motioned for Rob to join him, and the warmth trapped by the heavy felt tablecloth proved to be pleasant.

The Shah's Game was already set up, and without conversation Alā made his first move.

"Ah, *Dhimmi*, you have become a hungry cat," he said presently.

It was true; Rob had learned to attack.

The Shah played with a scowl on his face, eyes intent on the board. Rob used his two elephants to do damage and quickly gained a camel, a horse and rider, three foot soldiers.

The onlookers followed the game in rapt, expressionless silence. Doubtless some were horrified and some delighted by the fact that a European nonbeliever appeared to be besting the Shah.

But the king had vast experience as a sneaking general. Just as Rob began to think himself a fine fellow and a master of strategy, Alā offered sacrifices and drew his enemy in. He employed his own two elephants more adroitly than Hannibal had used his thirty-seven, until Rob's elephants were gone, and his horsemen. Still Rob fought doggedly, calling upon all Mirdin had taught him. It was a respectable time before he was *shahtreng*. When it was over, the courtiers applauded the king's victory and Alā allowed himself to look pleased.

The Shah slipped a heavy ring of massy gold from his finger and placed it in Rob's right hand. "About the *calaat*. We now give it. You shall have a house large enough for a royal entertainment."

With a *haram*. And Mary in the *haram*.

The nobles watched and listened.

"I shall wear this ring with pride and gratitude. As for the *calaat*, I am quite happy with your Majesty's past generosity and I shall remain in my house."

His voice was respectful but it was too firm and he did not turn his eyes away quite fast enough to prove humility. And all who were present heard the *Dhimmi* say these things.

By the following morning, it had reached Ibn Sina.

Not for nothing had the Chief Physician twice been a vizier. He had informants in the court and among the servants at the House of Paradise, and from several sources he heard about the rash stupidity of his *Dhimmi* assistant.

As always in time of crisis, Ibn Sina sat and thought. He was aware that his presence in Alā's capital city was a source of royal pride, enabling the Shah to compare himself to the Baghdad caliphs as a monarch of culture and a patron of learning. But Ibn Sina was also aware that his influence had limits; a direct appeal would not save Jesse ben Benjamin.

All his life Alā had dreamed of being one of the greatest Shahs, a king with an undying name. Now he was preparing for a war that could take him either to immortality or to oblivion, and it was impossible at this moment for him to allow anyone to obstruct his will.

Ibn Sina knew that the king would have Jesse ben Benjamin killed.

Perhaps orders already had been given for unidentified assailants to fall upon the young *hakim* in the streets, or he might be arrested by soldiers and tried and sentenced by an Islamic court. Alā was capable of political craft and would use the execution of this *Dhimmi* in a manner that would serve him best.

For years Ibn Sina had studied Alā Shah and he understood the workings of the king's mind. He knew what must be done.

That morning in the *maristan* he summoned his staff. "Word has reached us that in the town of Idhaj are a number of patients too sick to travel here to the hospital," he said, which was true. "Therefore," he told Jesse ben Benjamin, "you must ride to Idhaj and hold a clinic for the treatment of these people."

After they discussed herbs and drugs that must be taken with him on a pack ass, and medicines that could be found in that town, and the histories of certain patients they knew to be ill there, Jesse said goodbye and left without delay.

Idhaj was a slow, uncomfortable three-day ride to the south, and the clinic would take at least three days. It would give Ibn Sina more than enough time.

Next afternoon, he went alone into Yehuddiyyeh and rode directly to his assistant's house.

The woman answered the door holding her child. Surprise and brief confusion showed in her face when she saw the Prince of Physicians standing on her threshold, but she recovered quickly and showed him inside with proper courtesy. It was a plain home but kept well, and it had been made comfortable, with wall hangings and rugs on the earthen floors. With commendable dispatch she placed an earthen plate of sweet seed cakes before him, and a *sherbet* of rose water flavored with cardamon.

He hadn't counted on her ignorance of the language. When he tried to talk with her it was quickly obvious that she had only a few words of Persian.

He wanted to converse at length and with persuasion, wanted to tell her that when first he had recognized the quality of her husband's mind and instincts, he had hungered after the large young foreigner the way a miser lusts for a treasure or a man desires a woman. He had wanted the European for medicine because it was clear to him that God had fashioned Jesse ben Benjamin to be a healer.

"He will be a shining light. He is almost realized, but it is too soon, he is not yet there.

"All kings are mad. To one with absolute power, it is no more difficult to take a life than to bestow a *calaat*. Yet if you flee now, it will be a resentment for the rest of your lives, for he has come so far, dared so much. I know he is no Jew."

The woman sat and held the child, watching Ibn Sina with growing tension. He tried speaking Hebrew with no success, then Turkish and Arabic in quick succession. He was a philologist and a linguist but knew few European languages, for he learned a tongue only in pursuit of scholarship. He spoke to her in Greek without response.

Then he turned to Latin and saw her head move slightly and her eyes blink.

"*Rex te venire ad se vult. Si non, maritus necabitur.*" He repeated it: The king wishes you to come to him. If you do not, your husband will be slain.

"*Quid dicas?*" What do you say? she said.

He repeated it very slowly.

The child was beginning to fuss in her arms, but the woman paid her baby no heed. She stared at Ibn Sina, her face drained of color. It was a face like stone but he saw it contained an element he hadn't noted before. The old man understood people and for the first time his anxiety abated, for he recognized the woman's strength. He would make the arrangements and she would do what was necessary.

Slaves bearing a sedan chair came for her. She didn't know what to do with Rob J., so she brought him along; it was a happy solution, for in the *haram* of the House of Paradise the child was received by a number of delighted women.

She was taken to the baths, an embarrassment. Rob had told her it was a religious obligation for Muslim women to remove their pubic hair every ten days by means of a lime-and-arsenic depilatory. Similarly, the hair of the armpits was plucked or shaved, once a week by a married woman, every two weeks by a widow, and once a month by a virgin. The women attending her stared in undisguised disgust.

After she had been washed, three trays of scents and dyes were offered but she used only a bit of perfume.

She was led to a room and instructed to wait. It was furnished only with a large pallet, pillows, and blankets, and a closed cabinet on which stood a basin of water. Somewhere nearby, musicians played. She was cold. When she had waited what seemed a long time, she picked up a blanket and wrapped herself.

Presently Alā came. She was terrified but he smiled at seeing her standing cowled in the blanket.

He waggled his finger for her to remove it, and then motioned impatiently that she was to take off the robe too. She knew she was thin compared to most Eastern females, and Persian women had gone out of their way to inform her that freckles were Allah's just punishment on someone so shameless she did not wear the veil.

He touched the heavy red hair on her head, lifted a handful to his nostrils. She hadn't perfumed her hair and its lack of scent made him grimace.

For a moment Mary was able to escape by worrying about her child. When Rob J. was older, would he remember having been brought to this place? The glad cries and soft cooing of the women? Their tender faces beaming down at him? Their hands caressing him?

The king's hands were still at her head. He was speaking in Persian, whether to himself or to her she couldn't tell. She dared not even shake her head to signify she didn't understand, lest he interpret the gesture as disagreement.

He went straight to an examination of her body patch. He was most curious about her hair.

"Henna?"

She understood the single word and assured him the color wasn't henna, in language which of course he didn't comprehend. He pulled a strand gently through his fingertips and tried to wash out the red.

In a moment he took off his single loose cotton garment. His arms were muscular and he was thick in the waist, with a protruding, hairy belly. His entire body was hairy. His pizzle seemed smaller than Rob's and darker.

In the sedan chair on the way to the palace she had had fantasies. In one, she had wept and explained that Christian women were forbidden by Jesus to perform this act outside of marriage; and as though it were a story about one of the saints, he had taken pity on her tears and, out of kindness, had sent her home. In another vision, having been forced into this to save her husband, she had been freed to enjoy the most lascivious physical release of her lifetime, a ravishment by a supernatural lover who, although able to command the most beautiful women in Persia, had selected her.

Reality resembled neither imagining. He examined her breasts, touching the nipples; perhaps the coloring differed from those he was accustomed to. The chill air had made her breasts hard but they didn't maintain his interest. When he pushed her to the mat she silently begged the help of the blessed Mother of God whose namesake she was. She was an unwilling receptacle, kept dry by fear and anger at this man who had come close to ordering the death of her husband. There were none of the sweet caresses with which Rob warmed her and turned her bones to water. Instead of being a vertical stick Alā's organ was drooping and he had difficulty in pushing into her, resorting to olive oil that he splashed irritably on her instead of himself. Finally he squeezed greasily inside and she lay with her eyes closed.

She had been bathed but discovered he had not. He wasn't vigorous. He seemed almost bored, grunting softly as he worked. In a very few moments he gave an unroyal little shudder for so large a man and a disgusted moan. Then the King of Kings pulled out with a small sucking of oil and strode from the room without a word or a glance.

She lay in sticky humiliation where he had left her, not knowing what to do next. She would not allow herself to weep.

Eventually she was called for by the same women and taken to her son. She dressed hurriedly and scooped up Rob J. Sending her home, the women placed a rope bag of green melons in the sedan chair. When she and Rob J. reached Yehuddiyyeh she thought of leaving the melons in the road, but it seemed easier to carry them into the house and let the sedan chair go on its way.

The melons in the marketplaces were poor, because they were stored in caverns throughout the Persian winter and many spoiled. These were in excellent condition and perfectly ripe when Rob returned from his mission to Idhaj, and they proved to have an uncommonly fine flavor.

Chapter 64

THE *BEDOUI* GIRL

Strange. To enter the *maristan,* that cool, sacred place with its stinks of illness and its rough medicinal smells and groanings and cries and bustling sounds, the song of the hospital. It still made Rob catch his breath, still made his heart pound to enter the *maristan* and find trailing behind him, like baby geese following their mother, a gaggle of students.

Following him, who not long before had trailed others!

To stop and allow a clerk to recite a history of affliction. Then to approach a pallet and speak with the patient, watching, examining, touching, smelling out disease like a fox snuffling to find an egg. Trying to outwit the fucking Black Knight. At length, to discuss the sick or injured person with the group, receiving opinions often worthless and absurd but sometimes wonderful. For the clerks, a learning; for Rob, an opportunity to mold these minds into a critical instrument that analyzed and proposed treatment and rejected and proposed again, so that sometimes as a result of teaching them he reached conclusions that otherwise would have eluded him.

Ibn Sina urged him to lecture, and when he did, others came to hear him but he never was truly at ease before them, standing and sweating earnestly while discoursing on a subject he had carefully reviewed in the books. He was aware of how he must look to them, bigger than most and with his broken English nose, and aware of how he sounded, for now he was fluent enough with the language to be conscious of his accent.

Similarly, because Ibn Sina demanded he be a writer, he fashioned a short article on the wine treatment of wounds. He labored over the essay but took no joy from it even when it was finished and transcribed and placed in the House of Learning.

He knew he must pass on learning and skills, as these things had been passed to him, but Mirdin had been wrong: Rob did not want to do everything. He would not fashion himself after Ibn Sina. He had no ambition to be philosopher and educator and theologian, no need to write or preach. He was forced to learn and seek so he could know what to do when he must act. For him, the challenge came each time he held a patient's hands, the same magic he had first felt when he was nine years old.

One morning a girl named Sitara was brought into the *maristan* by her father, a *bedoui* tentmaker. She was very sick, nauseous and vomiting and racked by terrible pain in the lower right part of her rigid belly. Rob knew what was wrong but had no idea how to treat the side sickness. The girl groaned and could barely answer but he questioned her at length, seeking to learn something that might show him the way.

He purged her, tried hot packs and cold compresses, and that night he told his wife about the *bedoui* girl and asked Mary to pray for her.

Mary was saddened by the thought of a young girl stricken as James Geikie Cullen had been stricken. It brought to mind the fact that her father lay in an unvisited grave in Ahmad's *wadi* in Hamadhān.

Next morning Rob let blood from the *bedoui* girl and gave drugs and herbs, but all he did was to no avail. He saw her turn febrile and glassy-eyed and begin to fade like a leaf after frost. She died on the third day.

He went over the details of her short life painstakingly.

She had been healthy prior to the series of painful attacks that had killed her. A twelve-year-old virgin who had reached her womanly bleeding but recently . . . what had she in common with a small male child and his middle-aged father-in-law? Rob could see nothing.

Yet all three had been killed in precisely the same way.

The breach between Alā and his Vizier, the Imam Qandrasseh, became more public at the Shah's audience. The Imam was seated on the smaller throne below Alā's right hand, as was customary, but he addressed the Shah with such cold courtesy that his message was clear to all who attended.

That night Rob sat in Ibn Sina's home and they played at the Shah's Game. It was more a lesson than a contest, like a grown man playing with a child. Ibn Sina seemed to have thought out the entire game in advance. He moved the pieces without hesitation. Rob could not contain him but perceived the need for planning ahead, and this foresight quickly became a part of his own strategy.

"Small groups of people are gathered in the streets and in the *maidans*, speaking softly," Rob said.

"They become worried and confused when the priests of Allah are in conflict with the lord of the House of Paradise, for they fear the quarrel will destroy the world." Ibn Sina took a *rukh* with his horseman. "It will pass. It always passes, and those who are blessed will survive."

They played for a time in silence and then he told Ibn Sina of the death of the *bedoui* girl, recounting the symptoms and describing the two other cases of abdominal distemper that haunted him.

"Satira was my mother's name." Ibn Sina sighed. But he had no explanation for the girl's death. "There are many answers we have not been given."

"They will not be given unless we seek them out," Rob said slowly.

Ibn Sina shrugged and chose to change the subject by relating court news, disclosing that a royal expedition was being sent to India. Not raiders this time, but merchants empowered by the Shah to buy Indian steel or the ore from which to smelt it, for Dhan Vangalil did not have any steel left to make the patterned blue blades that Alā valued so highly.

"He has told them not to return without a full caravan of ore or hard steel, if they must go to the end of the Silk Road to get it."

"What is at the end of the Silk Road?" Rob asked.

"Chung-Kuo. An enormous country."

"And beyond that?"

Ibn Sina shrugged. "Water. Oceans."

"Travelers have told me that the world is flat and is surrounded by fire. That one can venture only so far before dropping into the fire that is Hell."

"Travelers' babble," Ibn Sina said scornfully. "It is not true. I have read that outside the inhabited world all is salt and sand, like the Dasht-i-Kavir. It is also written that much of the world is ice." He gazed pensively at Rob. "What is beyond your own country?"

"Britain is an island. Beyond it is an ocean and then Denmark, the land of the Northmen from which our king came. Beyond *that,* it is said there is a land of ice."

"And if one goes north from Persia, beyond Ghazna is the land of the Rus—and beyond that is a land of ice. Yes, I think it true that much of the world is covered with ice," Ibn Sina said. "But there is no fiery Hell at the edges, for thinking men have known always that the earth is round as a plum. You have voyaged on the sea. When sighting a distant oncoming ship, the first thing seen on the horizon is the tip of the mast, and then more and more of the craft as it sails over the curved surface of the world."

He finished Rob off on the game board by trapping his king, almost absentmindedly, and then summoned a slave to bring wine *sherbet* and a bowl of pistachios. "Do you not recall the astronomer Ptolemy?"

Rob smiled; he had read only enough astronomy to satisfy the requirements of the *madrassa*. "An ancient Greek who did his writing in Egypt."

"Just so. He wrote that the world is round. Suspended beneath the concave firmament, it is the center of the universe. Around it circle the sun and the moon, making the night and the day."

"This ball of a world, with its surface of sea and land, mountains and rivers and forests and deserts and places of ice—is it hollow or solid? And if it is solid, what is the nature of its interior?"

The old man smiled and shrugged, in his element now and enjoying himself. "We cannot know. The earth is enormous, as you understand, who have ridden and walked over a vast piece of it. And we are but tiny men who cannot burrow deeply enough to answer such a question."

"But if you were able to look within the center of the earth—would you?"

"Of course!"

"Yet you are able to peer inside the human body, but you do not."

Ibn Sina's smile faded. "Mankind is close to savagery and must live by rules. If not, we would sink into our own animal nature and perish. One of our rules forbids the mutilation of the dead, who will one day be rescued from their graves by the Prophet."

"Why do people suffer from abdominal distemper?"

Ibn Sina shrugged. "Open the belly of a hog and study the puzzle. The pig's organs are identical to the organs of man."

"You are certain of this, Master?"

"Yes. So it has been written since the time of Galen, whose fellow Greeks would not let him cut up humans. The Jews and the Christians have a similar prohibition. All men share this abhorrence of dissection." Ibn Sina looked at him with tender concern. "You have overcome much to become a physician. But you must practice your healing within the rule of religion and the general will of men. If you do not, their power will destroy you," he said.

Rob rode home gazing at the sky until the points of light swam before his eyes. Of the planets he could find only the moon and Saturn, and a glowing that might have been Jupiter, for it shed a steady brilliance amidst the starry glittering.

He realized Ibn Sina was not a demigod. The Prince of Physicians was simply an aging scholar caught between medicine and the faith in which he had been piously reared. Rob loved the old man all the more for his human limitations but he had a sense of being somehow cheated, like a small boy realizing the frailties of his father.

When he reached Yehuddiyyeh he was reflective while he saw to the needs of the brown horse. Inside the house Mary and the child were asleep, and he undressed with quiet care and then lay awake, thinking on what might cause distemper of the abdomen.

In the middle of the night Mary awoke urgently and ran outside, where she retched and was ill. He followed; obsessed by the disease that had taken her father, he was aware that vomiting was its first sign. Though she objected, he examined her when she reentered the house, but her abdomen was soft and there was no fever.

At last they returned to their pallet.

"Rob!" she called at length. And again: "My Rob," a cry of distress, as from a nightmare.

"Hush, or you will wake him," he whispered. He was surprised, for he hadn't known her to have bad dreams. He stroked her head and comforted her, and she pulled him to her with a desperate strength.

"I'm here, Mary. I'm here, O my love." He spoke soft, quiet things to her until she calmed, endearments in English and Persian and the Tongue.

Once again a short time later she started but then she touched his face and sighed and cradled his head in her arms, and Rob lay with his cheek on his wife's soft breast until the sweet slow thudding of her heart pulled him also into his rest.

Chapter 65

KARIM

The warming sun drew pale green shoots out of the earth as spring surged into Ispahan. Birds flashed through the air carrying straw and nesting twigs in their beaks, and the runoff gushed from brooks and *wadis* into the River of Life, which roared as its waters rose. It was as if Rob had taken the hands of the earth into his own and could feel nature's boundless, eternal vitality. Among other evidences of fertility was Mary's. Her nausea continued and worsened, and this time they didn't need Fara to tell them she was pregnant. He was delighted but Mary was moody, quicker to show irritation than heretofore. He spent more time than ever with his son. The little face lighted when Rob J. saw him, and the baby crowed and wriggled like a tail-wagging puppy. Rob taught him to yank at his father with joy.

"Pull Da's beard," he said, and felt pride in the strength of the tugging.

"Pull Da's ears."

"Pull Da's nose."

The same week that the child took his first tentative, unsteady steps, he also began to talk. It was no wonder that his first word was Da. The sound of the small creature addressing him filled Rob with such awed love that he found his good fortune hard to believe.

On a mild afternoon he persuaded Mary to walk to the Armenian market with him while he carried Rob J. At the market he set the baby down near the leather booth so Rob J. could take several shaky steps toward Prisca, and the former wet nurse screamed with delight and swept the child into her arms.

On the way home through Yehuddiyyeh they smiled and greeted this one and that, for if no woman had taken Mary into her heart since Fara had left, neither did anyone curse the European Other any more, and the Jews of the quarter had grown accustomed to her presence.

Later, while Mary was cooking their *pilah* and Rob was pruning one of the apricot trees, two of the small daughters of Mica Halevi the Baker ran from the house next door and played in the garden with his son. Rob delighted in the sound of their childish shrieks and foolishness.

There were worse people than the Jews of Yehuddiyyeh, he told himself, and worse places to be than Ispahan.

One day, hearing that al-Juzjani was to teach a class in dissection of a pig, Rob volunteered to assist. The animal in question proved to be a stout boar with tusks as fierce as a small elephant's, mean porcine eyes, a long body covered with coarse gray bristles, and a robust hairy pizzle. The pig had been dead for a day or so and smelled it, but it had been fed on grain and the predominant odor when the stomach was opened was of beery fermentation, slightly sour. Rob had learned that such odors were not bad or good; all smells were of interest, since each told a story. But neither his nose nor his eyes nor his searching hands taught him anything about abdominal distemper as he searched the belly and gut for signs. Al-Juzjani, more interested in teaching his class than in allowing Rob access to his pig, was justifiably irritated by the amount of time he spent grubbing.

After the class, no wiser than before, Rob went to meet with Ibn Sina in the *maristan*. He knew at first sight of the Chief Physician that something untoward had taken place.

"My Despina and Karim Harun. They have been arrested."

"Sit, Master, and ease yourself," he said gently, for Ibn Sina was shaken and puzzled and old-looking.

It was the realization of Rob's most dreadful fears. He forced himself to ask the questions that were required and was not surprised to learn that the charges were adultery and fornication.

Qandrasseh's agents had followed Karim to Ibn Sina's house that morning. *Mullahs* and soldiers had burst into the stone tower and found the lovers.

"What of the eunuch?"

For the time it takes to blink, Ibn Sina looked at him and Rob hated himself, aware of all that was revealed by his question. But Ibn Sina only shook his head.

"Wasif is dead. Had they not killed him by stealth, they would not have gained entrance to the tower."

"How can we help Karim and Despina?"

"Only Alā Shah can help them," Ibn Sina said. "We must petition him."

As Rob and Ibn Sina rode through the streets of Ispahan the people turned their eyes away, unwilling to shame Ibn Sina with their pity.

At the House of Paradise they were greeted by the Captain of the Gates with the courtesy usually shown to the Prince of Physicians, but they were ushered into an anteroom instead of the Shah's presence.

Farhad left them and returned presently to tell them the king regretted he could not spend time with them that day.

"We shall wait," Ibn Sina said. "Perhaps an opportunity will present itself."

Farhad was glad to see the mighty fallen; he smiled at Rob as he bowed.

All that afternoon they waited, and then Rob took Ibn Sina home.

In the morning they returned. Again Farhad was careful to be courteous. They were led to the same anteroom and allowed to languish, but it became clear the king wouldn't see them.

Nevertheless, they waited.

Ibn Sina seldom spoke. Once, he sighed. "She has ever been as a daughter to me," he said. And, after a time: "It is easier for the Shah to treat Qandrasseh's bold stroke as a small defeat than to challenge the Vizier."

Throughout the second day they sat in the House of Paradise. Gradually they understood that, despite the eminence of the Prince of Physicians and the fact that Karim was Alā's favorite, the king would do nothing.

"He is willing to concede Karim to Qandrasseh," Rob said bleakly. "As though they were playing the Shah's Game and Karim is a piece that will not be grievously missed."

"In two days there will be an audience," Ibn Sina said. "We must make it easy for the Shah to help them. I will make public request that the king grant them mercy. I am the woman's husband and Karim is the beloved of the people. They will roar to support my request to save their hero of the *chatir*. The Shah will allow it to appear that he grants mercy because of the will of his subjects." If this happened, Ibn Sina said, Karim might be given twenty strokes and Despina beaten and sentenced to confinement for life in her master's house.

But as they left the House of Paradise they came upon al-Juzjani, who had been awaiting them. The master surgeon loved Ibn Sina as much as any man. Out of that love, he brought him bad news.

Karim and Despina had been taken before an Islamic court. Testimony had been given by three witnesses, each an ordained *mullah*. Doubtless to avoid torture, neither Despina nor Karim had attempted to offer a defense.

The presiding *mufti* had sentenced each of them to death on the following morning.

"The woman Despina will be decapitated. Karim Harun will have his belly ripped."

They gazed at one another in dismay. Rob waited for Ibn Sina to tell al-Juzjani how Karim and Despina yet might be saved, but the old man shook his head. "We cannot avert the sentence," he said heavily. "We can only make certain their end is merciful."

"Then there are things to be done," al-Juzjani said quietly. "Bribes to be paid. And instead of the medical clerk in the *kelonter*'s prison we must substitute a physician we trust."

Despite the warmth of the spring air, Rob was chilled. "Let it be me," he said.

That night he was sleepless. He rose before dawn and rode the brown horse through the dark city. At Ibn Sina's house he half expected to see the eunuch Wasif in the gloom. There was neither light nor life in the tower rooms.

Ibn Sina gave him a jar of grape juice. "It is heavily infused with opiates and a powder of pure hempseed called *buing*," he said. "Herein lies the risk. They must drink a lot of it. But if either of them drinks too much to walk when they are summoned, you shall die with them."

Rob nodded to show he understood. "God's mercy."

"God's mercy," Ibn Sina said. He was chanting from the Qu'ran before Rob left the room.

At the prison he told the sentry he was the physician and was given an escort. They went first to the women's cells, in one of which a woman could be heard alternately singing and sobbing.

He was afraid the terrible sound came from Despina but it didn't; in a tiny cell, she waited. She was unwashed and unperfumed and her hair hung in lank locks. Her small, finely made body was clad in a dirty black garment.

He set down the jar of *buing* and went to her and lifted her veil.

"I have brought something for you to drink."

To him she would ever after be *femina*, a combination of Anne Mary his sister, Mary his wife, the whore who had serviced him in the carriage on the *maidan*, and every female put upon by the world.

There were unshed tears in her eyes but she refused the *buing*.

"You must drink. It will help you."

She shook her head. Soon I will be in Paradise, the fearful eyes begged him to believe. "Give it to him," she whispered, and Rob bade her goodbye.

The footsteps echoed as he followed the soldier along a corridor, down two short flights of stairs, into another stone tunnel and then another tiny cell.

His friend was pale.

"So, European."

"So, Karim."

They embraced, holding each other hard.

"Is she . . . ?"

"I've seen her. She is well."

Karim sighed. "I hadn't talked with her for weeks! It was just to hear her voice, you understand? I was certain I wasn't followed, that day."

Rob nodded.

Karim's mouth trembled. Offered the jar, he grasped it and drank deeply, finishing two-thirds of the liquid before handing it back.

"It will work. Ibn Sina mixed it himself."

"The old man you worship. Often I dreamed of poisoning him so I could have her."

"Every man has wicked thoughts. You wouldn't carry them out." For some reason it seemed vital that Karim should know this before the narcotic took effect. "You understand?"

Karim nodded. Rob watched closely, fearful he had drunk too much *buing*. If the infusion worked quickly, a *mufti*'s court would reconvene to kill a second physician.

Karim's eyes drooped. He remained awake but chose not to talk. Rob stayed with him in silence until finally he heard footsteps approaching.

"Karim."

He blinked. "Is it now?"

"Think of winning the *chatir*," Rob said gently. The footsteps stopped, the door opened; they were three soldiers and two *mullahs*. "Think of the happiest day of your life."

"Zaki-Omar could be a kindly man," Karim said. He favored Rob with a small, vacant smile.

Two of the soldiers took his arms. Rob followed directly behind them, out of the cell, down the stone corridor, up the two flights of stairs, into the courtyard where the sun smote a brassy blow. The morning was soft and beautiful, an ultimate cruelty. He could see Karim's knees buckle as he walked but any observer would think it was caused by fear. They went past the double row of *carcan* victims to the blocks, scene of his nightmares.

Something awful already lay next to a black-gowned form on imbrued ground, but the *buing* cheated the *mullahs;* Karim did not see her.

The executioner seemed scarcely older than Rob, a short, beefý man with huge arms and indifferent eyes. His strength and skill and the keenest whetted blades were what Ibn Sina's money had bought.

Karim's eyes were glazed as the soldiers brought him forward. There were no goodbyes; the executioner's stroke was swift and certain. The point came up into the heart and brought death at once as the wielder had been bribed to do, and Rob heard his friend make a sound like a loud discontented sigh.

It was left to Rob to see that Despina and Karim were carried from the prison to a cemetery outside the city walls. He paid well for prayer to be chanted over both new graves, a bitter irony: the praying *mullahs* were found among those who had witnessed the deaths.

When the funeral was over, Rob finished the infusion that remained in the jar and allowed the brown horse to carry him back unguided.

But as they neared the House of Paradise he reined up and studied it. The palace was particularly beautiful that day, its colorful pennons streaming and fluttering in the spring breeze and the sun glittering on the guidons and halberds and making dazzle of the sentries' weapons.

He could hear Alā's voice. *We are four friends . . . We are four friends . . .*

He shook his fist. *"UN–WOR–THYYYY!"*

The sound rolled toward the wall, reaching and startling the sentries.

Their officer came down to the outermost guard. "Who is it? Can you tell?"

"Yes. I believe it is the *hakim* Jesse. The *Dhimmi.*"

They studied the figure on the horse, observing him shaking his fist once more, noting the wine jar and the horse's slack reins.

The officer knew the Jew as one who had stayed behind the returning force of Indian raiders to tend the wounds of soldiers. "His face is full of drink." He grinned. "But he is not a bad shit, that one. Let him be," he said, and they watched the brown horse carry the physician toward the city gates.

Chapter 66

THE GRAY CITY

So he was the last surviving member of the Ispahan Medical Party. To think of both Mirdin and Karim beneath the earth was to suck on an infusion of rage and regret and sadness; yet, perversely, their deaths made his days sweet as a loving kiss. He savored life's ordinary juices. A deep breath, a long piss, a slow fart. To chew stale bread when he was hungry, sleep when he was tired. To touch his wife's clumsy girth, listen to her snore. To bite his son's stomach until the gurgling howl of infantile laughter brought tears to his eyes.

This, despite the fact that Ispahan had become a somber place.

If Allah and the Imam Qandrasseh could bring low the hero athlete of Ispahan, then what ordinary man would now dare break the Islamic rules set down by the Prophet?

Whores disappeared and the *maidans* no longer were riotous at night. *Mullahs* patrolled the streets of the city in pairs, alert for a veil that covered too little of a woman's face, a man slow in responding with prayer to a *muezzin*'s call, a refreshment-house owner stupid enough to sell wine. Even in Yehuddiyyeh, where females always were careful to cover their hair, many Jewish women began to wear the heavy Muslim veils.

Some sighed in private, missing the music and gaiety of remembered nights, but others expressed satisfaction, and at the *maristan* the *hadji* Davout Hosein thanked Allah during a morning's prayer. "Mosque and state were born of one womb, joined together and never to be sundered," he said.

Each morning more worshipers than ever came to Ibn Sina's home and joined him in prayer, but now when he was through with worship the Prince of Physicians returned inside his house and wasn't seen until it was time to pray again. He gave himself fully to grieving and introspection and didn't come to the *maristan* to teach or to treat patients. Some who objected to being touched by a *Dhimmi* were treated by al-Juzjani, but these were not many and Rob was busy all the time now, tending to Ibn Sina's patients as well as his own responsibilities.

One morning a skinny old man with stinking breath and dirty feet wandered into the hospital. Qasim ibn Sahdi had legs like a knob-kneed crane and a moth-eaten wisp of white beard. He didn't know his age and he had no home because for most of his life he had made his way as a menial in one caravan after another.

"I have traveled everywhere, master."

"To Europe, whence I came?"

"*Almost* everywhere." He had no family, he said, but Allah watched over him. "I reached here yesterday with a caravan of wool and dates from Qum. On the route I was stricken with a pain like a wicked *djinn.*"

"Where, pain?"

Qasim, groaning, clutched at his right side.

"Has your gorge risen?"

"Lord, I am pukingly ill and know a terrible weakness. Yet as I dozed, Allah spoke, saying that nearby was one who would heal me. And when I awoke I asked people if there was a place of healing nearby and I was directed to this *maristan.*"

He was led to a pallet, where he was bathed and fed lightly. He was the first patient with abdominal distemper whom Rob had been able to observe in an early stage of the disease. Perhaps Allah knew how to make Qasim well, but Rob did not.

He spent hours in the library. Finally courtly Yussuf-ul-Gamal, the Keeper of the House of Wisdom, asked him what it was that he sought so assiduously.

"The secret of abdominal illness. I am trying to find accounts of ancients who opened the human belly before it was forbidden to do so."

The venerable librarian blinked and nodded gently. "I shall try to help you. Let me see what I am able to find," he said.

Ibn Sina wasn't available and Rob went to al-Juzjani, who didn't have Ibn Sina's patience.

"Often people die of distemper," al-Juzjani said, "but some come to the *maristan* complaining of pain and burning in the lower right abdomen, and the hurting goes away and the patients are sent home."

"Why?"

Al-Juzjani shrugged and gave him an annoyed glance and would spend no more time on the subject.

Qasim's pain disappeared too after a few days, but Rob didn't want to release him. "Where shall you go?"

The old drover shrugged. "I shall find a caravan, *Hakim,* for they are my home."

"Not all who come here are able to leave. Some die, you understand that."

Qasim nodded seriously. "All men must die in the end."

"To wash the dead and prepare them for burial is to serve Allah. Could you do such work?"

"Yes, *Hakim.* For it is God's labor, as you say," he said solemnly. "Allah brought me here and it may be that He wishes me to stay."

There was a small storeroom next to the two rooms that served as the hospital's charnel house. They cleaned it out together and this became Qasim ibn Sahdi's living quarters.

"You will take your meals here after the patients are fed, and you may bathe in the *maristan* baths."

"Yes, *Hakim.*"

Rob gave him a sleeping mat and a clay lamp. The old man unrolled his worn prayer rug and declared the room the finest home he had ever had.

It was almost two weeks before Rob's busy schedule allowed him to meet Yussuf-ul-Gamal in the House of Wisdom. He brought a gift of appreciation for the librarian's help. All the vendors were displaying large, fat pistachios but Yussuf had few teeth for chewing nuts and instead Rob had bought a reed basket filled with soft desert dates.

He and Yussuf sat and ate the fruit late one night in the House of Wisdom. The library was deserted.

"I have gone back in time," Yussuf said. "Far as I am able. Into antiquity. Even the Egyptians, whose embalming fame you know, were taught it was evil and a disfigurement of the dead to open the abdomen."

"But . . . when they made their mummies?"

"They were hypocrites. They paid despised men called *paraschistes* to sin by making the forbidden initial incision. As soon as they made the cut the *paraschistes* fled lest they be stoned to death, an acknowledgment of guilt that allowed the respectable embalmers to empty the abdomen of organs and get on with their preservation."

"Did they study the organs they removed? Did they leave behind written observations?"

"They embalmed for five thousand years, altogether eviscerating almost three-quarters of a billion human beings who had died of every ill, and they stored the viscera in vessels of clay, limestone, or alabaster, or simply threw them away. But there is no evidence that they ever studied the organs.

"The Greeks—now that was different. And it happened in the same Nile region." Yussuf helped himself to more dates. "Alexander the Great stormed through this Persia of ours like a beautiful, youthful god of war, nine hundred years before the birth of Mohammed. He conquered the ancient world, and at the northwestern end of the Nile River delta, on a strip of land between the Mediterranean Sea and Lake Mareotis, he founded a graceful city to which he gave his own name.

"Ten years later he was dead of a swamp fever, but Alexandria already was a center of Greek culture. In the breakup of the Alexandrian empire, Egypt and the new city fell to Ptolemy of Macedonia, one of the most scholarly of Alexander's associates. Ptolemy established the Museum of Alexandria, the world's first university, and the great Alexandria Library. All branches of knowledge prospered, but the school of medicine attracted the most promising students of the entire world. For the first and only time in man's long history, anatomy became the keystone, and dissection of the human body was practiced on an extensive scale for the next three hundred years."

Rob leaned forward eagerly. "Then it is possible to read their descriptions of the diseases that afflict the internal organs?"

Yussuf shook his head. "The books of their magnificent library were lost when Julius Caesar's legions sacked Alexandria thirty years before the start of the Christian era. The Romans destroyed most of the writings of the Alexandrian physicians. Celsus collected what little was left and tried to preserve it in his work entitled *De re medicina,* but there is only one brief mention of 'distemper seated in the large intestine principally affecting that part where I mentioned the cecum to be, accompanied by violent inflammation and vehement pains, particularly on the right side.' "

Rob grunted in disappointment. "I know the quotation. Ibn Sina uses it when he teaches."

Yussuf shrugged. "So my delving into the past leaves you exactly where you were when I began. The descriptions you are seeking do not exist."

Rob nodded gloomily. "Why do you suppose that the only brief moment in history when physicians opened human beings came with the Greeks?"

"They did not have the advantage of a single strong God who forbade them to desecrate the work of His creation. Instead, they had all those fornicators, those weak and squabbling gods and goddesses." The librarian spat a mouthful of date seeds into his cupped palm and smiled sweetly. "They could dissect because they were, after all, only barbarians, *Hakim,* " he said.

Chapter 67

TWO ARRIVALS

Her pregnancy was too far advanced to permit her to ride, but Mary went on foot in order to buy the foodstuffs needed for her family, leading the donkey which bore her purchases and Rob J., who rode in a sling on the animal's back. The burden of her unborn child tired her and vexed her back, and she moved slowly from one marketplace to another. As she generally did when she attended the Armenian market, she stopped in the leather shop to share a *sherbet* and a hot loaf of thin Persian bread with Prisca.

Prisca always appeared happy to see her former employer and the baby she had suckled, but today she was especially voluble. Mary had been trying hard to learn the Persian tongue, but she could make out only a few words.

Stranger. From afar. Same as the hakim. *Like you.*

It was with no enlightenment and mutual frustration that the two women parted, and that evening Mary was irked as she reported the incident to her husband.

He knew what Prisca had been trying to tell her, for the rumor had quickly reached the *maristan.* "A European is newly arrived in Ispahan."

"From what country?"

"England. He's a merchant."

"An Englishman?" She stared. Her face was flushed, and he noted the interest and excitement in her eyes and the way her hand remained unnoticed at her breast.

"Why have you not gone to him at once?"

"Mary . . ."

"But you must! Do you know where he is staying?"

"He's in the Armenian quarter, that's why Prisca knew of him. It's said that at first he would consent to stay only with Christians." Rob smiled. "But when he saw the hovels in which the few, poor Armenian Christians live, he quickly rented a finer house from a Muslim."

510

"You must write a message. Ask him to come to us for an evening meal."

"I don't even know his name."

"What matter? Hire a messenger. Anyone in the Armenian quarter will direct him," she said. "Rob! He will have *tidings.*"

The last thing he wanted was dangerous contact with an English Christian. But he knew he couldn't deny her this opportunity to hear of places closer to her heart than Persia, so he sat and wrote the letter.

"I am Bostock. Charles Bostock."

At a glance, Rob remembered. On his first return to London after becoming the barber-surgeon's boy, he and Barber had ridden for two days in the protection of Bostock's long line of packhorses laden with salt from the brine works at Arundel. In camp they had juggled and the merchant had given Rob tuppence to spend when he reached London.

"Jesse ben Benjamin. Physician of this place."

"Your invitation was writ in English. And you speak my language."

The answer could only be the one Rob had established in Ispahan. "I was reared in the town of Leeds." He was more amused than concerned. Fourteen years had passed. The puppy he had once been had grown into a strange sort of a dog, he told himself, and there was little likelihood that Bostock could connect that juggling boy with this over-tall Jewish physician to whose Persian home Bostock had been drawn.

"And this is my wife Mary, who is a Scot from the north country."

"Mistress."

Mary had ached for finery but her ponderous belly had made her best blue dress an impossibility and she wore a loose, tentlike black gown. But her scrubbed red hair gleamed richly. She wore an embroidered headband and her only piece of jewelry, a little crochet of seed pearls that hung between her brows.

Bostock still had long hair held back with bows and ribbons, but now his hair was more gray than yellow. The ornate red velvet suit he wore, complete with soiled embroidery, was too warm for the clime and too costly for the occasion. Never were eyes so sharply weighing, Rob thought, so obviously calculating the worth of every animal, the house, their raiment, each piece of furniture. And with a mixture of curiosity and distaste assessing the swarthy and bearded Jew, the Celtic red-haired wife so perfectly ripe with child, and the sleeping baby who was further proof of the shameful union of this mixed pair.

Despite his unhidden displeasure the visitor yearned to hear English as eagerly as they, and all three soon were chattering. Rob and Mary could not restrain themselves and their questions poured forth.

"Have you intelligence of Scots' lands?"

"Was it good times or bad when you departed London?"

"Was it peace there?"

"Was Canute still the king?"

Bostock was made to sing for his supper, though the latest news was almost two years old. He knew naught of the lands of the Scots nor of the north of England. Times had remained prosperous and London was growing apace, with more dwellings being raised each year and the ships straining the facilities of the Thames. Two months before he had left England, Bostock reported, King Canute had died a natural death, and the day he had landed in Calais he learned of the death of Robert I, Duke of Normandy.

"Bastards now rule on both sides of the Channel. In Normandy, Robert's illegitimate son William, although he is still a boy, has become Duke of Normandy with the help of his dead father's friends and kinsmen.

"In England, succession rightfully belonged to Harthacnut, the son of Canute and Queen Emma, but for years Harthacnut has made an un-British life in Denmark and so the throne has been usurped by his younger half-brother. Harold Harefoot, whom Canute had acknowledged to be his bastard son out of a little-known Northampton woman named Aelfgifu, is now the King of England."

"Where are Edward and Alfred, the two princes Emma bore by King Aethelred before her marriage to King Canute?" Rob asked.

"They are in Normandy under the protection of Duke William's court, and it may be presumed that they are gazing across the Channel with great interest," Bostock said.

Starved as they were for details of home, by now the smells of Mary's meal had made all three hungry for food as well, and the merchant's eyes warmed somewhat when he saw what she had prepared in his honor.

A brace of pheasants, well oiled and frequently basted, stuffed in the Persian manner with rice and grapes, and pot-cooked slowly and long. A summer salad. Sweet melons. An apricot-and-honey tart. Not least, a skin of good pinkish wine, bought at expense and peril. Mary had gone with Rob to the Jewish market, where at first Hinda had vehemently denied she had wine, glancing about fearfully to see who had overheard their request. After much pleading and the exchange of three times the ordinary cost, a wineskin had been dug from the middle of a bag of grain and Mary had carried it home hidden from the *mullahs* in the sling next to her sleeping child.

Bostock devoted himself to the meal but presently, after a great belch, declared that he would be leaving for Europe in a few days' time.

"Reaching Constantinople on churchly business, I couldn't resist continuing eastward. Know you that the King of England will elevate to thane any merchant-adventurer who dares to make three trips to open foreign parts to English trade? Well, that is true, and it's a fine way for a free man to attain noble rank and at the same time gain high profits. 'Silks,' I thought. If I might follow the Silk Road I could bring back cargo that would allow me to buy London! I was happy to reach Persia, where I have bought, instead of silks, rugs and fine weavings. But I shall never return here, for there's little profit in it—I must pay a small army to get them back to England."

When Rob sought to find similarity in their eastward routes of travel, Bostock revealed that from England he had gone first to Rome. "Combining business with an errand for Aethelnoth, the Archbishop of Canterbury. At the Lateran Palace, Pope Benedict IX promised me ample reward for *expeditiones in terra et mari* and commanded me in the name of Christ Jesus to ply my merchant's way to Constantinople, there to deliver papal letters to Patriarch Alexius."

"A papal legate!" Mary exclaimed.

Less a legate than a messenger, Rob surmised drily, though it was plain Bostock enjoyed Mary's wonder.

"For six hundred years, Eastern Church has disputed Western Church," the merchant said, thick with importance. "In Constantinople Alexius is viewed as the Pope's equal, to Holy Rome's aversion. The Patriarch's damned bearded priests marry—they *marry!* And they neither pray to Jesus and Mary nor treat the Trinity with sufficient awe. Thus the letters of complaint are carried to and fro."

The ewer was empty and Rob took it into the next room to replenish it from the wineskin.

"Are you a Christian?"

"I am," she said.

"Then how have you become chattel to this Jew? Were you taken by pirates or Muslims and sold to him?"

"I am his wife," she said clearly.

In the next room Rob paused in the task of filling the ewer with wine and listened, his lips drawn in a mirthless grin. So great was the Englishman's contempt for him that Bostock didn't bother to lower his voice.

"I would accommodate my caravan for you and the child. You could have a litter and bearers until you've given birth and are able to sit a horse."

"It is not a possibility, Master Bostock. I am my husband's, gladly and by agreement," Mary said, but she thanked him coolly.

He replied with grave courtesy that it was Christian duty, what he would want another man to offer his own daughter if, Jesus forbid, she might find herself in similar circumstances.

Rob Cole returned wishing to do Bostock bodily harm, but Jesse ben Benjamin behaved with Eastern hospitality, pouring wine for his guest instead of throttling him. Conversation was resentful and sparse, however. The English merchant departed almost immediately after he was done eating, and Rob and Mary were left with one another.

They were occupied with their own thoughts as they gathered up the ruins of the meal.

Finally she said, "Shall we ever go home?"

He was astonished. "Of course we shall."

"Bostock was not my only chance?"

"I swear it."

Her eyes glistened. "He's right to hire a protecting army. The journey is so dangerous . . . how shall two children travel so far and survive?"

There was more of her than fit, but he took her carefully into his arms. "After we reach Constantinople we will be Christians, and we will join a strong caravan."

"And between here and Constantinople?"

"I learned the secret as I traveled here." He helped her to lower herself to the mat. It was difficult for her now, because no matter how she lay, soon some part of her ached. He held her and stroked her head, talking to her as though telling a comforting story to a child. "From Ispahan to Constantinople I shall remain Jesse ben Benjamin. And we shall be taken in by Jewish village after Jewish village, and fed and safeguarded and guided, like a man crossing a dangerous stream by stepping from one safe rock to another." He touched her face. Placing his palm on the great warm stomach he felt the unborn child move and was filled with gratitude and pity. That is how it would happen, he assured himself. But he couldn't tell her when it would come to pass.

He had become accustomed to sleeping with his body curled around the huge hardness of her stomach but one night he was awakened to feel wetness as well as warmth, and when he had gathered his wits he struggled into his clothes and ran for Nitka the Midwife. Although she was accustomed to people hammering on her door while the world slept, she emerged cranky and snappish, ordering him to be quiet and patient.

"She has cast out her water."

"All right, all right," she grumbled.

Soon they made a caravan through the black street, Rob lighting the way with a torch, Nitka following with a great bag of washed rags, trailed by her two burly sons grunting and gasping under the weight of the birthing chair.

Chofni and Shemuel set the chair next to the fireplace like a throne and Nitka ordered Rob to kindle a fire, for in the middle of the night the air was cool. Mary climbed into the chair like a naked queen. When the sons left they carried away Rob J. for safekeeping during his mother's labor. In Yehuddiyyeh neighbors did such things for one another, even when one of them was a *goya*.

Mary lost her royal bearing with the first pain, and the grunting, grinding cry that issued from her throat filled Rob with dismay. The chair was of stout construction so it could withstand any amount of bucking and thrashing and Nitka went about the task of folding and stacking her rags, obviously undisturbed as Mary gripped the handles at the side of the chair and sobbed.

Her legs trembled all the time but during the terrible cramping they shook and jerked. After the third pain Rob stood behind her and pulled her shoulders against the back of the chair. Mary showed her teeth and snarled like a wolf; he wouldn't have been surprised if she had bitten him or howled.

He had cut off men's limbs and become inured to every foul disease, but he felt the blood rushing from his head. The midwife looked at him hard and, taking a fold of flesh on his arm between her wiry fingers, she squeezed. The painful pinch restored his senses and he did not disgrace himself.

"Out," Nitka said. "Out, out!"

So he went into the garden and stood in the dark, listening to the sounds that followed him out of the house. It was cool and quiet; he thought briefly about vipers coming out of the stone wall and decided he didn't care. He lost track of time, but eventually knew that the fire would be in need of tending, so he went back inside to replenish it.

When he looked at Mary, her knees were spread wide.

"Now you will bear down," Nitka commanded sternly. "Work, my friend. Work!"

Transfixed, he saw the crown of the baby's head appear between his wife's thighs, like the pate of a monk with a wet red tonsure, and he fled for the garden again. He was there a long time until he heard the thin wail, then he went back in and saw the infant.

"Another boy," Nitka said briskly, clearing mucus from the tiny mouth with the tip of her little finger.

The thick, ropy umbilicus looked blue in the thin light of dawn.

"It was much easier than the first time," Mary told him.

Nitka cleaned and comforted, and gave Rob the afterbirth to bury in the garden. The midwife accepted generous payment with a satisfied nod and went home.

When they were alone in their bedchamber they embraced, then Mary asked for water and christened the child Thomas Scott Cole.

Rob held and examined him: slightly smaller than his older brother had been, but not a runt. A lusty, ruddy man-child with round brown eyes and a patch of dark hair that already contained glints of his mother's redness. He decided that in the eyes and the shape of the head, the wide mouth and the long, narrow little fingers, the new child bore close resemblance to his brothers William Stewart and Jonathan Carter when they were newly born. It was always easy to tell a Cole baby, he told Mary.

Chapter 68

THE DIAGNOSIS

Qasim had been keeper of the dead for two months when the pain returned to his abdomen.

"What is it like?" Rob asked him.

"It is bad, *Hakim.*"

But obviously it wasn't as bad as it had been before. "Is it a dull pain, or sharp?"

"It is as if a *djinn* lives within me and claws at my insides, twisting and tearing." The former drover succeeded in terrifying himself; he gazed beseechingly at Rob for reassurance that this was not indeed the case.

He wasn't feverish as he had been during the attack that had brought him to the *maristan,* nor was his abdomen rigid. Rob prescribed frequent dosing with a honey-and-wine infusion, which Qasim took to eagerly since he was a drinker and had been sorely tried by the enforced religious abstinence.

Qasim spent several pleasant weeks, slightly inebriated as he lazed about the hospital exchanging views and opinions. There was much to gossip about. The latest news was that Imam Qandrasseh had deserted the city, despite his obvious political and tactical victory over the Shah.

It was rumored Qandrasseh had fled to the Seljuk Turks, and that when he returned it would be with an attacking Seljuk army to depose Alā and place a strict Islamic religionist—perhaps himself?—on the throne of Persia. In the meantime, life was unchanged and pairs of somber *mullahs* continued to patrol the streets, for the wily old Imam had left his disciple, Musa Ibn Abbas, as keeper of the faith in Ispahan.

The Shah remained in the House of Paradise as if in hiding. He didn't hold audiences. Rob hadn't heard from Alā since Karim had been put to death. There was no summoning to entertainment, no hunting or games or invitations to the court. When a physician was required at the House of Paradise in place of the indisposed Ibn Sina, al-Juzjani or someone else was demanded, but never Rob.

But a gift for the new son had come from the Shah.

It arrived following the Hebrew naming of the baby. This time Rob knew enough to invite the neighbors himself. Reb Asher Jacobi the *mohel* asked that the child might grow in vigor to a life of good works, and cut off the foreskin. The babe was given suck on a wine sop to quiet his yowl of pain and in the Tongue was declared to be Tam, son of Jesse.

Alā had bestowed no gift when little Rob J. was born, but now he sent a handsome small rug, light blue wool interwoven with lustrous silk threads of the same shade and embossed in darker blue with the crest of the royal Samanid family.

Rob thought it a handsome rug and would have laid it on the floor next to the cradle, but Mary, who was pettish following the birth, said she didn't want it there. Instead, she bought a sandalwood chest that would protect it from moths and put it away.

Rob participated in an examining board. He knew he was there in Ibn Sina's absence and it shamed him that someone might think him presumptuous enough to assume he could take the place of the Prince of Physicians.

But there was no help for it, so he did his best. He prepared for the board as though he were a candidate himself and not an examiner. He asked thoughtful questions designed not to undo a candidate but to bring out knowledge, and he listened attentively to the answers. The board examined four candidates and made three physicians. There was embarrassment over the fourth man. Gabri Beidhawi had been a medical clerk for five years. He had failed the testing twice before, but his father was a rich and powerful man who had flattered and cozened the *hadji* Davout Hosein, the administrator of the *madrassa*, and Hosein had requested that Beidhawi be tested again.

Rob had been a student with Beidhawi and knew him for a lazy wastrel, careless and callous in treating patients. During the third examining he showed himself to be ill prepared.

Rob knew what Ibn Sina would have done. "I reject the candidate," he said firmly and with little regret. The other examiners hastened to concur, and the board was adjourned.

Several days after the examinations, Ibn Sina came to the *maristan*.

"Welcome back, Master!" Rob said, gladdened.

Ibn Sina shook his head. "I haven't returned." He appeared tired and worn, and he told Rob he had come for an evaluation which he wished performed by al-Juzjani and Jesse ben Benjamin.

They sat with him in an examining room and talked with him, gathering the history of his complaint as he had taught them to do.

He had waited at home, hoping soon to resume his duties, he told them. But he had never recovered from the twin shocks of losing first Reza and then Despina, and he had begun to look and feel poorly.

He had felt lassitude and weakness, an inability to make the effort required for the simplest of tasks. At first he had attributed his symptoms to acute melancholia. "For we all know well that the spirit can do terrible and strange things to the body."

But lately his bowel movements had become explosive and his stools had been besmeared with mucus, pus, and blood; and so he had requested this medical examination.

They performed the search as though they would never have another chance to inspect a human being. They overlooked nothing. Ibn Sina sat with sweet patience and allowed them to prod and press and thump and listen and question.

When they were through, al-Juzjani was pale but put on an optimistic face. "It is the bloody flux, Master, brought on by the aggravation of your emotions."

But Rob's intuition had told him something else. He looked at his beloved teacher. "I believe it is schirri, the early stages."

Ibn Sina blinked once. "Cancer of the intestine?" he said, as calmly as if talking to a patient he had never met.

Rob nodded, trying not to think of the slow torture of the disease.

Al-Juzjani was ruddy with rage at being overruled, but Ibn Sina soothed him. That is why he had asked for the two of them, Rob realized—he had known al-Juzjani would be so blinded with love he would be unable to find a loathsome truth.

Rob's legs felt weak. He took Ibn Sina's hands in his own, and their eyes met and held. "You are still strong, Master. You must keep your bowels open, to guard against the accumulation of black bile that would cause the cancer to grow."

The Chief Physician nodded.

"I pray I've made an error in diagnosis," Rob said.

Ibn Sina favored him with a small smile. "Prayer can do no hurt."

He told Ibn Sina he would like to visit him soon and pass an evening with the Shah's Game, and the old man said Jesse ben Benjamin would always be welcome in his house.

Chapter 69

GREEN MELONS

On a dry and dusty day near the end of the summer, out of the haze to the northeast came a caravan of one hundred and sixteen belled camels. The beasts, all in a line and spewing ropy saliva under the exertion of carrying heavy loads of iron ore, wound into Ispahan late in the afternoon. Alā had hoped Dhan Vangalil would use the ore to make many weapons of blue patterned steel. Tests by the swordsmith, alas, subsequently would prove the iron in the ore to be too soft for that purpose, but by nightfall news brought by the caravan had created a stir of excitement among some in the city.

A man named Khendi, the caravan's captain of drovers, was summoned to the palace to repeat details of the intelligence for the Shah's own ears, and then he was taken to the *maristan* to tell his tale to the doctors there.

Over a period of months Mahmud, the Sultan of Ghazna, had become gravely ill, with fever and so much pus in his chest that it caused a broad, soft bulge in his back, and his physicians had decided that if Mahmud was to live, this lump would have to be drained.

One of the details Khendi brought was that the Sultan's back had been smeared with a thin wash of potter's clay.

"Why was that?" one of the newest physicians asked.

Khendi shrugged, but al-Juzjani, who served as their leader in Ibn Sina's absence, knew the answer. "The clay must be watched attentively, for the first patch to dry indicates the hottest part of the skin and is therefore the best place for cutting."

When the surgeons opened the Sultan corruption sprang forth, Khendi said, and to rid Mahmud of the remaining pus, they inserted drains.

"Did the cutting scalpel have a round blade or a pointed one?" al-Juzjani asked.

"Did they dose him for the pain?"

"Were the drains fashioned of tin or of linen wicks?"

"Was the pus dark or white?"

"Were there traces of blood in it?"

"Lords! My lords, I am a drovers' captain and not a *hakim!*" Khendi exclaimed in anguish. "I have the answers to none of these questions. I know only one thing more, masters."

"And what is that?" al-Juzjani asked.

"Three days after they cut him, lords, the Sultan of Ghazna was dead."

They had been two young lions, Alā and Mahmud. Each had come early to his throne to follow a strong father, and each had kept the other in sight while their kingdoms watched, aware that one day they would clash, that Ghazna would eat Persia or Persia would eat Ghazna.

It had never come to pass. They had circled each other warily and at times their forces had skirmished, but each had waited, sensing the time was not right for total war. Yet Mahmud never was out of Alā's thoughts. Often the Shah dreamed of him. It was always the same dream, with their armies massed and eager and Alā riding out alone toward Mahmud's fierce Afghan tribesmen, hurling down the single combat call to the Sultan as Ardashir had roared challenge to Ardewan, the survivor to claim his destiny as the true and proven King of Kings.

Now Allah had intervened and Alā would never meet Mahmud in combat. In the four days after the arrival of the camel caravan, three experienced and trusted spies rode separately into Ispahan and spent time in the House of Paradise, and from their reports the Shah began to perceive a clear picture of what had occurred in the capital city of Ghazni.

Immediately following the Sultan's death, Mahmud's son Muhammad had attempted to mount the throne but was thwarted by his brother Abu Said Masūd, a young warrior with the firm support of the army. Within hours, Muhammad was a shackled prisoner and Masūd had been declared Sultan. Mahmud's funeral was a wild affair, part grim leavetaking and part frenzied celebration, and when it was through Masūd had called his chieftains together and declared his intention to do what his father never had done: the army was put on notice that it would march against Ispahan within days.

It was intelligence that would finally bring Alā out of the House of Paradise.

The planned invasion was not unwelcome to him, for two reasons. Masūd was impetuous and untried, and Alā was pleased by the chance to pit his generalship against the stripling's. And because there was something in the Persian soul that loved war, he was shrewd enough to realize that the conflict would be embraced by his people as a foil to the pious restrictions under which the *mullahs* had forced them to live.

He held military meetings that were small celebrations, with wine and women making their appearances at the proper times, as in days gone by. Alā and his commanders pored over their charts and saw that from Ghazna there was only one route that was feasible for a large force. Masūd must cross the clay ridges and foothills to the north of the Dasht-i-Kavir, skirting the great desert until his army was deep into Hamadhān. Thence they would turn south.

But Alā decided that a Persian army would march to Hamadhān and meet them before they could fall upon Ispahan.

The preparations of Alā's army was the sole topic of conversation, not to be escaped even in the *maristan,* though Rob tried. He didn't think of the impending war because he wished no part of it. His debt to Alā, while it had been considerable, was paid. The raids in India had convinced him he never wanted to go soldiering again.

So he worried and waited for a royal summons that didn't come.

In the meantime he worked hard. Qasim's abdominal pains had disappeared; to the former drover's delight Rob continued to prescribe a daily portion of wine and returned him to his duties in the charnel house. Rob was caring for more patients than ever, for al-Juzjani had taken on many of the duties of Chief Physician and had turned over a number of his patients to other physicians, Rob among them.

He was stunned to hear that Ibn Sina had volunteered to lead the surgeons who would accompany Alā's army north. Al-Juzjani, who had gotten over his anger or hidden it, told him.

"A waste, to send such a mind to war."

Al-Juzjani shrugged. "The Master wishes one last campaign."

"He is old and won't survive."

"He has looked old forever but he hasn't yet lived sixty years." Al-Juzjani sighed bitterly. "I believe he hopes an arrow or a spear will find him. It wouldn't be tragedy to meet a quicker death than now appears to lie in store for him."

The Prince of Physicians quickly let it be known that he had chosen a party of eleven to accompany him as surgeons to the Persian army. Four were medical students, three were the newest of the young doctors, and four were veteran physicians.

Now al-Juzjani became Chief Physician in title as well as in fact. It was a grim promotion in that it caused the medical community to realize that Ibn Sina would not be back as their leader.

To Rob's surprise and consternation he was named to fill some of the duties al-Juzjani had performed for Ibn Sina, although there were a number of more experienced physicians al-Juzjani could have selected. Also, since five of the twelve who had gone with the army were teachers, he was told he would be expected to lecture more often and to teach when he visited his patients in the *maristan.*

In addition, he was made a permanent member of the examining board and was asked to serve on the committee that oversaw the cooperation between the hospital and the school. His first meeting on the committee was held in the lavish home of Rotun bin Nasr, governor of the school. The title was an honorific and the governor didn't bother to attend, but he had made his home available and had left orders that a fine meal should be served to the gathered physicians.

The first course consisted of slices of large green-fleshed melons of singular flavor and melting sweetness. Rob had tasted this type of melon only once before and was about to remark on it when his former teacher, Jalal-ul-Din, grinned widely at him. "We may thank the governor's new bride for the delicious fruit."

Rob didn't understand.

The bonesetter winked. "Rotun bin Nasr is a general and the Shah's cousin, as you may know. Alā visited here last week to plan the war and no doubt met the youngest wife. After royal seeds have been planted, there is always a gift of Alā's special melons. And if the seeds result in a male crop, then there is a princely gift, a Samanid rug."

He didn't manage to get through the meal but pleaded illness and left the meeting. With his mind in turmoil he rode straight to the house in Yehuddiyyeh. Rob J. was off playing in the garden with his mother but the infant was in the cradle and Rob took Tam into his arms and inspected him.

Just a small, new baby. The same child he had loved when he left the house that morning.

He returned the boy and went to the sandalwood chest and removed the carpet bestowed by the Shah. He spread it on the floor next to the cradle.

When he glanced up, Mary was in the doorway.

They looked at one another. It became a fact then, and the pain and pity he experienced for her was wrenching.

He went to her, intending to take her into his arms, but instead he found that both of his hands were gripping her very tightly. He tried to speak but no words came.

She tore away and kneaded her upper arms.

"You have kept us here. I have kept us alive," she said with contempt. The sadness in her eyes had changed to something cold, the reverse of love.

That afternoon she moved out of his chamber. She bought a narrow pallet and set it down between the sleeping places of her children, next to the carpet of the Samanid princes.

Chapter 70

QASIM'S ROOM

Unable to sleep all that night, he felt bewitched, as if the ground had disappeared beneath his feet and he must walk a long way on air. It wasn't unusual for someone in his situation to kill the mother and the child, he reflected, but he knew Tam and Mary were safe in the next room. He was haunted by mad thoughts but he wasn't mad.

In the morning he rose and went to the *maristan*, where all was not well either. Four of the nurses had been taken into the army by Ibn Sina as litter bearers and collectors of the wounded, and al-Juzjani had not yet found four more who met his standards. The nurses who were left in the *maristan* were overworked and sullen, and Rob visited his patients and did his physician's work unassisted, sometimes pausing to clean up what a nurse had not had time to set right, or bathe a feverish face or fetch water to ease a dry and thirsty mouth.

He came upon Qasim ibn Sahdi lying whey-faced and groaning, the floor next to him soiled with vomitus.

Ill, Qasim had left his room next to the charnel house and given himself a place as a patient, aware that Rob would find him as he made his way through the *maristan*.

He had been afflicted several times within the past week, Qasim said. "But why have you not told me!"

"Lord, I had my wine. I took my wine and the pain went away. But now the wine doesn't help, *Hakim,* and I cannot bear it."

He felt feverish but not burning, and his abdomen was tender but soft. Sometimes in his pain he panted like a dog; his tongue was coated and his breath was strong.

"I'll make you an infusion."

"Allah will bless you, lord."

Rob went directly to the pharmacy. In the red wine Qasim loved he steeped opiates and *buing*, then hurried back to his patient. The eyes of the old keeper of the charnel house were filled with fearful portent as he swallowed the potion.

Through the thin fabric screens of the open windows, sounds had been invading the *maristan* in increasing volume, and when Rob went outside he saw that the city had turned out to bid its army farewell.

He followed the people to the *maidans.* This army was too large to be contained in the squares. It spilled over and filled the streets throughout the central portion of the city. Not hundreds, as in the raiding party that had gone to India, but thousands. Long ranks of heavy infantry, longer ranks of lightly armed men. Javelin hurlers. Lancers on horses, and sword cavalry on ponies and camels. The press of the crowd was tremendous, as was the hubbub: cries of farewell, weeping, the screams of women, obscene badinage, commands, words of farewell and encouragement.

He pushed his way forward like a man swimming against the human tide, through the stink, an amalgam of human odor and camel sweat and horseshit. The sun-glitter on the polished weapons was blinding. At the head of the line were the elephants. Rob counted thirty-four. Alā was committing all the war elephants he owned.

Rob didn't see Ibn Sina. He had made his farewells to several of the departing physicians in the *maristan,* but Ibn Sina hadn't come to say goodbye nor had he summoned Rob, and it was obvious he preferred no words of leavetaking.

Here came the royal musicians. Some blew long golden trumpets and others rang silver bells, heralding the swaying approach of the great elephant Zi, a ponderous force. The *mahout* Harsha was dressed in white and the Shah clad in the blue silks and red turban that was his costume for going to war.

The people roared in ecstasy at seeing their warrior king. As he raised his hand in royal greeting, they knew he was promising them Ghazna. Rob studied the Shah's rigid back; at that moment, Alā was not Alā—he had become Xerxes, he had become Darius, he had become Cyrus the Great. He was all conquerors to all men.

We are four friends. We are four friends. Rob felt dizzy, thinking of the occasions when it would have been so easy to kill him.

He was far back in the crowd. Even if he had been up front, he would have been cut down the moment he hurled himself at the king.

He turned away. He didn't wait with the others to see the departing parade of those bound to glory or to death. He struggled out of the crowd and walked unseeingly until he came to the banks of Zayendeh, the River of Life.

He took from his finger the ring of massy gold Alā had given him for his service in India and dropped it into the brown water. Then, while in the distance the crowd roared and roared, he walked back to the *maristan.*

Qasim had been dosed heavily with the infusion but he appeared to be very ill. His eyes were vacant, his countenance pale and sunken. Though the day was warm he was shivering, and Rob covered him with a blanket. Soon the blanket was soaked and when he felt Qasim's face, it was hot.

By late afternoon the pain had become so powerful that when Rob touched his abdomen, the old man screamed.

Rob didn't go home. He stayed in the *maristan,* returning often to Qasim's pallet.

That evening, in the midst of Qasim's agony, there was complete relief. For a time his breathing was quiet and even, and he slept. Rob dared hope, but within a few hours he was reclaimed by fever and his body became ever hotter, his pulse rapid and at times barely perceptible.

He tossed and thrashed in delirium. "Nuwas," he called. "Ah, Nuwas." Sometimes he spoke to his father or to his uncle Nili, and again and again to the unknown Nuwas.

Rob took his hands and his heart sank; he didn't let go, for now he could offer only his presence and the meager comfort of a human touch. At length the labored breathing simply slowed and then stopped. He was still holding the callused hands when Qasim died.

He placed one arm beneath the knobby knees and the other under the bare bony shoulders and carried the body into the charnel house, then he went into the room next door. It stank; he would have to see that it was scrubbed. He sat among Qasim's belongings, which were few: one extra garment, shabby; a prayer rug, tattered; some paper sheets and a tanned leather on which Qasim had paid a scribe to copy several prayers from the Qu'ran. Two flasks of forbidden wine. A loaf of stale Armenian bread and a bowl of rancid green olives. A cheap dagger with a nicked blade.

It was past midnight and most of the hospital slept. Now and again a patient cried out or wept. Nobody saw him remove Qasim's meager belongings from the little room. While he was carrying in the wooden table he met a nurse, but the shortage of help had given the man courage to look the other way and hurry past the *hakim* before he could be given more work than he already had.

In the room, under two of the legs at one end Rob placed a board so the table tilted, and on the floor under the lower end he set a basin. He needed ample light and he prowled the hospital, stealing four lamps and a dozen candles, which he set around the table as though it were an altar. Then he brought Qasim from the charnel house and laid him on the table.

Even as Qasim lay dying, Rob had known he would break the commandment.

Yet now the moment was at hand and he found it difficult to breathe. He wasn't an ancient Egyptian embalmer who could call in a despised *paraschiste* to open the body and absorb the sin. The act and the sin, if any, must be his own.

He picked up a curved, probe-tipped surgical knife called a bistoury and made the incision, slicing open the abdomen from the groin to the sternum. The flesh parted crisply and began to ooze blood.

He didn't know how to proceed and he flayed the skin away from the sternum, then he lost his nerve. In all his life he had had but two peer friends and each had died by having his body cavity cruelly violated. If he were caught he would die the same way but in addition there would be flaying, the ultimate agony. He left the little room and nervously prowled the hospital, but those who were awake paid him no heed. He still felt as though the ground had opened up and he walked on air, but now he believed he was peering deep into the abyss.

He fetched a small-toothed bone saw to the makeshift little laboratory and sawed through the sternum in imitation of the wound that had killed Mirdin in India. At the bottom of the incision he cut from the groin to the inside of the thigh, making a large, clumsy flap that he was able to fold back, exposing the abdominal cavity. Beneath the pink belly the stomach wall was red meat and whitish strands of muscle, and even in skinny Qasim there were yellow globules of fat.

The thin inner lining of the abdominal wall was inflamed and covered with a coagulable substance. The organs appeared healthy to his dazzled eyes except for the small intestine, which was reddened and angry in many places. Even the smallest vessels were so filled with blood they looked as if they had been injected with red wax. A little pouchy part of the gut was unusually black and adhered to the abdominal lining; when he attempted to separate them gently by pulling, the membranes broke and exposed two or three spoonfuls of pus, the infection that had caused Qasim so much pain. He suspected that Qasim's agony had stopped when the diseased tissue had ruptured. A thin, dark-colored, fetid fluid had escaped from the inflammation into the cavity of the abdomen. He dipped a fingertip into it and sniffed it with interest, for this might be the poison that had produced fever and death.

He wanted to examine the other organs but he was afraid.

He sewed up the opening carefully, so that if the holy men were right and Qasim ibn Sahdi should be resurrected from the grave, he would be whole. Then he crossed the wrists and tied them and used a large cloth to bind the old man's loins. He carefully wrapped the body in a shroud and returned it to the charnel house to await burial in the morning.

"Thank you, Qasim," he said somberly. "May you rest."

Taking a single candle to the *maristan* baths, he scrubbed himself clean and changed his garments. But still he fancied the odor of death remained on him and he rinsed his hands and arms in perfume.

Outside, in the darkness, he was still afraid. He could not believe what he had done.

It was almost dawn when he settled himself onto his pallet. In the morning he slept deeply and Mary's face turned to stone as she breathed another woman's flowery scent that seemed to foul their house.

Chapter 71

IBN SINA'S ERROR

Yussuf-ul-Gamal beckoned Rob into the scholarly shade of the library. "I want to show you a treasure."

It was a thick book, an obviously new copy of Ibn Sina's masterwork, *Canon of Medicine.*

"This *Qānūn* isn't owned by the House of Wisdom. It is a copy made by a scribe of my acquaintance. It is for sale."

Ah. Rob picked it up. It was lovingly done, the letters black and crisp on each ivory-colored page. It was a codex, a book with many gatherings —large sheets of vellum folded and then cut so each page could be freely turned. The gatherings had been finely stitched between covers of soft tanned lambskin.

"It is costly?"

Yussuf nodded.

"How much?"

"He will sell for eighty silver *bestis.* Because he needs money."

He pursed his lips, aware he didn't have that much. Mary had a large sum, her father's money, but he and Mary no longer . . .

Rob shook his head.

Yussuf sighed. "I felt *you* should own it."

"When must it be sold?"

Yussuf shrugged. "I can keep it for two weeks."

"All right, then. Keep it."

The librarian looked at him doubtfully. "Will you have the money then, *Hakim?*"

"If it is God's will."

Yussuf smiled. "Yes. *Imshallah.*"

He placed a stout hasp and a heavy lock on the door of the chamber next to the charnel house. He brought in a second table, a steel, a fork, a small

530

knife, several sharp scalpels, and the kind of chisel stonecutters call a quarrel; a drawing board, paper and charcoals and leads; thongs, clay and wax, quills, and an inkstand.

One day he took several strong students to the market and brought back the fresh carcass of a hog, with no little effort. No one appeared to think it odd when he said he would do some dissecting in the little room.

That night, alone, he carried in the corpse of a young woman who had died a few hours before and placed her on the empty table. Her name had been Melia.

This time he was more eager and less afraid. He had thought about his fear and didn't think he was driven to his actions by witchery or the work of a *djinn.* He believed he had been allowed to become a physician to work toward the protection of God's finest creation, and that the Almighty wouldn't frown at his learning more about so complex and interesting a creature.

Opening both the pig and the woman, he prepared to make a careful comparison of the two anatomies.

Because he began his double inspection in the area where abdominal distemper takes place, he was brought up short at once. The pig's cecum, the pouchlike gut from which the large intestine began, was substantial, almost eighteen inches long. But the woman's cecum was tiny in comparison, only two or three inches long and as wide as Rob's little finger. And halloo! . . . attached to this tiny cecum was . . . something. It looked like nothing so much as a pink worm, uncovered in the garden, picked up and placed within the woman's belly.

The pig on the other table did not have a wormlike attachment, and Rob had never observed a similar appendage on a pig's bowel.

He drew no swift conclusions. He thought at first that the small size of the woman's cecum might be an anomaly, and that the wormlike thing was a rare tumor or some other growth.

He prepared the corpse of Melia for burial as carefully as he had done with Qasim, and returned her to the charnel house.

But in the nights that followed he opened the bodies of a stripling youth, a middle-aged woman, and a six-week-old male infant. In each case, with rising excitement, he found that the same tiny appendage was there. The "worm" was a part of every person—one tiny proof that the organs of a human being were not the same as the organs of a swine.

Oh, you damned Ibn Sina. "You bloody old man," he whispered. "You're wrong!"

Despite what Celsus had written, despite what had been taught for a thousand years, men and women were unique. And if this was so, who knew how many magnificent mysteries might be uncovered and answered simply by looking for them within the bodies of human beings.

All his life Rob had been alone and lonely until he had met her, and now he was lonely again and could not bear it. One night when he came into the house he lay down next to her between the two sleeping children.

He made no move to touch her but she turned like a wild creature. Her hand found his face with a stinging blow. She was a large female and strong enough to do hurt. He took her hands and pinned them to her sides.

"Madwoman."

"Do not come to me from Persian harlots!"

It was the aromatic, he realized. "I use it because I've been dissecting animals in the *maristan.*"

She said nothing for a moment but then she tried to move free. He could feel the familiar body against him as she struggled and the scent of her red hair was in his nostrils.

"Mary."

She became calmer; perhaps it was what was in his voice. Still, when he moved to kiss her it wouldn't have surprised him to be bitten on the mouth or the throat, but he was not. It took him a moment to realize she was kissing him back. He stopped holding her hands and was infinitely grateful to touch breasts that were rigid but not with death.

He couldn't tell if she was weeping or merely aroused because she was making little moaning sounds. He tasted her milky nipples and nuzzled her navel. Beneath this warm belly shiny pink and gray viscera were coiled and twined like sea creatures in congress, but her limbs were not stiff and cold and in the mound first one of his fingers and then two found heat and slipperiness, the stuff of life.

When he thrust inside her they came together like clapping hands, pounding and slamming as if trying to destroy something they couldn't face. Exorcising the *djinn.* Her nails punished his back as she banged straight at him. There was only a quiet grunting and the *slap-slap-slap* of their mating until finally she cried out and then he cried out, and Tam bawled and Rob J. awoke with a scream, and together the four of them laughed or wept, the adults doing both.

Eventually things were sorted out. Little Rob J. returned to sleep and the infant was brought to the breast, and as she fed him, in a quiet voice she told Rob of how Ibn Sina had come to her and instructed her about what she must do. And so he heard how the woman and the old man had saved his life.

He was surprised and shocked to hear of Ibn Sina's involvement.

As for the rest, her experience was close to what he had already guessed, and after Tam fell asleep he held her in his arms and told her she was his own chosen woman for always, and smoothed the red hair and kissed the nape of her white neck where freckles didn't dare appear. When she slept too he lay and stared at the dark ceiling.

In the days that followed she smiled a lot and it saddened and angered him to see the trace of fear in the smiles, though by his actions he tried to show his love and gratitude.

One morning, caring for a sick child in the house of a member of the court, he saw next to the sleeping pallet the small blue carpet of Samanid royalty. When he looked at the boy he observed swarthy skin, a nose already hooked, a certain quality in the eyes. It was a familiar face, made even more familiar whenever he looked at his own younger son.

He broke with his schedule and went home and picked up little Tam and held him to the light. The face was brother to that of the sick child's.

And yet Tam did also sometimes look remarkably like Rob's lost brother Willum.

Before and after the time he had spent in Idhaj on Ibn Sina's errand, he and Mary had made love. Who was to say this was not fruit of his own seed?

And he changed the child's wet cloth and touched the small hand and kissed the so-soft cheek, and returned him to his cradle.

That night he and Mary made tender and considerate love that brought them release but wasn't the same as once it was. Afterward he went out and sat in the moon-washed garden next to the autumnal ruins of the flowers on which she had lavished her care.

Nothing ever remains the same, he realized. She wasn't the young woman who had followed him so trustingly into a field of wheat, and he wasn't the youth who had led her there.

And that was not the least of the debts for which he yearned to repay Alā Shah.

Chapter 72

THE TRANSPARENT MAN

Out of the east there arose a dust cloud of such proportion that the lookouts confidently expected an enormous caravan, or perhaps even several great caravans merged into a single train.

Instead, an army approached the city.

When it reached the gates it was possible to identify the soldiers as Afghans from Ghazna. They stopped outside the walls and their commander, a young man wearing a dark blue robe and snowy turban, entered Ispahan accompanied by four officers. No one was there to stop him. Alā's army having followed him to Hamadhān, the gates were guarded by a handful of aged troopers, old men who melted away at the foreign army's approach, so that Sultan Masūd—for it was he—rode into the city unchallenged. At the Friday Mosque the Afghans dismounted and went inside, where reportedly they joined the congregation at Third Prayer and then sequestered themselves for several hours with the Imam Musa Ibn Abbas and his coterie of *mullahs*.

Most of the inhabitants of Ispahan didn't see Masūd, but as the Sultan's presence was made known, Rob and al-Juzjani were among those who went to the top of the wall and looked down upon the soldiers of Ghazna. They were tough-looking men in ragged trousers and long loose shirts. Some of them wore the ends of their turbans wrapped about their mouths and noses to keep out the dust and sand of travel, and quilted bed mats were rolled behind the small saddles of their shaggy ponies. They were in high spirits, fingering arrows and shifting their longbows as they looked upon the rich city with its unprotected women, the way wolves would look at a warren of hares, but they were disciplined and waited without violence while their leader was in the mosque. Rob wondered if among them was the Afghan who had run so well against Karim in the *chatir*.

"What can Masūd want with the *mullahs?*" he asked al-Juzjani.

"Doubtless his spies have told him of Alā's troubles with them. I think he intends to rule here some day soon and bargains with the mosques for blessings and obedience."

It may have been so, for soon Masūd and his aides returned to their troops and there was no pillaging. The Sultan was young, hardly more than a boy, but he and Alā could have been kinsmen: they had the same proud, cruel predator's face. They watched him unwind the clean white turban, which was then carefully stowed away, and put on a filthy black turban before he resumed the march.

The Afghans rode to the north, following the route taken by Alā's army.

"The Shah was wrong in thinking they would come by way of Hamadhān."

"I think the main Ghazna force is in Hamadhān already," al-Juzjani said slowly.

Rob realized he was right. The departing Afghans were far fewer in number than the Persian army and there were no war elephants among them; they had to have another force. "Then Masūd is springing a trap?"

Al-Juzjani nodded.

"We can ride to warn the Persians!"

"It is too late, or Masūd wouldn't have left us alive. At any rate," al-Juzjani said with irony, "it little matters whether Alā defeats Masūd or Masūd defeats Alā. If the Imam Qandrasseh truly has gone to lead the Seljuks to Ispahan, ultimately neither Masūd nor Alā will prevail. The Seljuks are fearsome, and they are as numerous as the sands of the sea."

"If the Seljuks come, or if Masūd returns to take this city, what will become of the *maristan?*"

Al-Juzjani shrugged. "The hospital will close for a while and we'll all scurry to hide from disaster. Then we'll come out of our holes and life will be same as before. With our Master I have served half a dozen kings. Monarchs come and go, but the world continues to need physicians," he said.

Rob asked Mary for the money for the book, and the *Qānūn* became his. It filled him with awe to hold it in his hand. Never had he owned a book before, but so great was his delight in proprietorship of this book that he vowed there would be others.

Yet he didn't spend overly long reading it, for Qasim's room drew him.

He dissected several nights a week and began to use his drawing materials, hungry to do more but unable because he required a minimum of sleep in order to function in the *maristan* during the day.

In one of the corpses he studied, that of a young man who had been knifed in a wineshop brawl, he found the little cecum appendage enlarged and with its surface reddened and rough, and he surmised he was looking at the earliest stage of the side sickness, when the patient would begin to get the first intermittent pangs. He now had a picture of the progress of the illness from onset to death, and he wrote in his casebook:

Perforating abdominal distemper has been witnessed in six patients, each of whom died.

The first decided symptom of the disease is sudden abdominal pain.

The pain is usually intense and rarely slight.

Occasionally it is accompanied by an ague and more often by nausea and vomiting.

The abdominal pain is followed by fever as the next constant symptom.

A circumscribed resistance is felt on palpation of the right lower belly, with the area often agonized by pressure and the abdominal muscles tense and rigid.

The condition comes to an appendage of the cecum which in appearance is not unlike a fat, pink earthworm of common variety. Should this organ become angry or infected it turns red and then black, fills with pus and finally bursts, its contents escaping into the general abdominal cavity.

In that event death follows rapidly, as a rule within half an hour to thirty-six hours of the onset of high fever.

He cut and studied only those parts of the body that would be covered by the burial shroud. This excluded the feet and the head, a frustration because he was no longer content with examining a pig's brain. His respect for Ibn Sina remained unbounded, but he had become aware that in certain areas his mentor had himself been taught incorrectly about the skeleton and the musculature and had passed on the misinformation.

Rob worked patiently, uncovering and sketching muscles like wire and like strands of rope, some beginning in a cord and ending in a cord, some with flat attachment, some with round attachment, some with cord only at one end, and some that were compound muscles with two heads, their special value apparently being that if one head is injured the other will take over its function. He began in ignorance and gradually, in a constant state of fevered and dreamlike excitement, he learned. He made sketches of bone and joint structure, shape, and position, realizing that such drawings would be invaluable in teaching young doctors how to deal with sprains and fractures.

Always when he finished working he shrouded and returned the bodies and took his drawings away with him. He no longer felt that he peered into the pit of his own damnation, but he never lost the awareness of the terrible end that awaited him if he were discovered. Dissecting in the uneven, flickering lamplight of the airless little room, he started at every noise and froze in terror on the rare occasion when someone walked past the door.

He had good reason for his fear.

Early one morning he removed from the charnel house the body of an elderly woman who had died only a short time before. Outside the door he looked up to see a nurse coming toward him, carrying the body of a man. The woman's head lolled and one arm swung as Rob stopped wordlessly and gazed at the nurse, who bent his head politely.

"Shall I help you with that one, *Hakim?*"

"She's not heavy."

Preceding the nurse, he went back inside and they laid the two bodies side by side and left the charnel house together.

The pig he had dissected had lasted only four days, rapidly reaching a state of ripeness that made disposal a necessity. Yet opening the human stomach and gut released odors far worse than the sickly-sweet stench of porcine rot. Despite soap and water, the smell permeated the place.

One morning he bought a new hog. That afternoon he walked past Qasim's room to discover the *hadji* Davout Hosein rattling the locked door.

"Why is it locked? What is inside?"

"It's a room in which I am dissecting a pig," Rob said calmly.

The deputy governor of the school gazed at him in disgust. These days, Davout Hosein looked at everything with stern suspicion, for he had been delegated by the *mullahs* to police the *maristan* and the *madrassa* for infractions of Islamic law.

Several times that day, Rob observed him hovering watchfully.

That evening Rob went home early. Next morning when he came to the hospital he saw that the lock on the door of the little room had been forced and broken. Inside, things were as he had left them—but not quite. The pig lay covered on the table. His instruments had been disarranged but none was missing. They had found nothing to incriminate him, and he was safe for the moment. But the intrusion had chilling implications.

He knew sooner or later he would be discovered, but he was learning precious facts and seeing marvelous things and was not ready to stop.

He waited two days, in which the *hadji* left him alone. An old man died in the hospital while holding a quiet conversation with him. That night he opened the body to see what had accomplished so peaceful a death and found that the artery which had fed the heart and the lower members was parched and shrunken, a withered leaf.

In a child's body he saw why cancer had received its name, noting how the hungry crablike growth had extended its claws in every direction. In another man's body he found that the liver, instead of being soft and of a rich red-brown, had turned into a yellowish object of woody hardness.

The following week he dissected a woman several months pregnant and sketched the womb in the swollen belly like an inverted drinking glass cradling the life that had been forming in it. In the drawing he gave her the face of Despina, who would never give life to a child. He labeled it the Pregnant Woman.

And one night he sat by the dissection table and created a young man to whom he gave the features of Karim, an imperfect likeness but a recognizable one to anybody who had loved him. Rob drew the figure as if the skin were made of glass. What he couldn't see for himself in the body on the table he drew as Galen had claimed it existed. He knew some of this unsubstantiated detail would be inaccurate, but still the drawing was remarkable even to him, showing organs and blood vessels as if the eye of God were peering through man's solid flesh.

When it was completed he exultantly signed his name and the date and labeled the drawing the Transparent Man.

Chapter 73

THE HOUSE IN HAMADHĀN

All this time there had been no news of the war. By prearrangement four caravans laden with supplies had gone out in search of the army, but they were never seen again and it was supposed they had found Alā and had been absorbed into the fighting. And then one afternoon just before Fourth Prayer a rider came, bearing the worst possible intelligence.

As had been surmised, by the time Masūd had paused in Ispahan his main force already had found the Persians and was engaging them. Masūd had sent two of his senior generals, Abū Sahl al-Hamdūnī and Tāsh Far-rāsh, to lead his army along the expected route. They planned and executed the frontal attack perfectly. Splitting their force in two, they hid behind the village of al-Karaj and sent forth their scouts. When the Persians drew close enough, Abū Sahl al-Hamdūnī's host streamed from around one side of al-Karaj and Tāsh Farrāsh's Afghans came around the other side. They fell upon Alā Shah's men on two flanks, which rapidly drew together until the Ghazna army was reunited across a giant semicircular line of combat, like a net.

After their initial surprise the Persians fought bravely but they were outnumbered and outmaneuvered, and they lost ground steadily for days. Finally they discovered that at their back was another Ghazna force led by Sultan Masūd. Then the fighting grew ever more desperate and savage, but the end was inevitable. In front of the Persians was the superior force of the two Ghazna generals. Behind them, the cavalry of the Sultan, small in number and vicious, waged a conflict similar to the historic battle between the Romans and the ancient Persians, but this time Persia's enemy was the ephemeral harrying force. The Afghans struck again and again and always melted away to reappear in another rear sector.

Finally, when the bloodied Persians had been sufficiently weakened and confused, under cover of a sandstorm Masūd launched the full power of all three of his armies in all-out attack.

539

Next morning, the sun disclosed sand swirling over the bodies of men and beasts, the better part of the Persian army. Some had escaped and it was rumored Alā Shah was among them, the messenger said, but this wasn't certain.

"What has befallen Ibn Sina?" al-Juzjani asked the man.

"Ibn Sina left the army well before it reached al-Karaj, *Hakim.* He had been afflicted by a terrible colic that rendered him helpless, and so with the Shah's permission the youngest physician among the surgeons, one Bibi al-Ghurī, took him to the city of Hamadhān, where Ibn Sina still owns the house that had been his father's."

"I know the place," al-Juzjani said.

Rob knew al-Juzjani would go there. "Let me come too," he said.

For a moment jealous resentment flickered in the older physician's eyes, but reason quickly won and he nodded.

"We shall leave at once," he said.

It was a hard and gloomy trip. They pushed their horses hard, not knowing if they would find him alive when they arrived. Al-Juzjani was made dumb by despair and this wasn't to be wondered at; Rob had loved Ibn Sina for relatively few years, while al-Juzjani had worshiped the Prince of Physicians all his life.

It was necessary for them to circle to the east to avoid the war, which for all they knew, was still being fought in the territory of Hamadhān. But when they reached the capital city that gave the territory its name, Hamadhān appeared sleepy and peaceable, with no hint of the great slaughter that had taken place only a few miles away.

When Rob saw the house it seemed to him that it suited Ibn Sina better than the grand estate in Ispahan. This mud-and-stone house was like the clothing Ibn Sina always wore, unprepossessing, shabby and comfortable.

But within was the stench of illness.

Al-Juzjani jealously asked Rob to wait outside the chamber in which Ibn Sina lay. Moments later Rob heard a low murmur of voices and then, to his surprise and alarm, the unmistakable sound of a blow.

The young physician named Bibi al-Ghurī emerged from the chamber. His face was white and he was weeping. He pushed past Rob without greeting and rushed from the house.

Al-Juzjani came out a short while later, followed by an elderly *mullah.*

"The young charlatan has doomed Ibn Sina. When they arrived here, al-Ghurī gave the Master celery seed to break the wind of the colic. But instead of two *dānaqs* of seed he gave five *dirhams,* and ever since then Ibn Sina has passed great amounts of blood."

There were six *dānaqs* to a *dirham;* that meant that fifteen times the recommended dosage of the brutal cathartic had been given.

Al-Juzjani looked at him. "I myself served on the examining board that passed al-Ghurī," he said bitterly.

"You weren't able to look into the future and see this mistake," Rob said gently.

But al-Juzjani wasn't to be consoled. "What a cruel irony," he said, "that the great physician should be undone by an inept *hakim!*"

"Is the Master aware?"

The *mullah* nodded. "He has freed his slaves and given his wealth to the poor."

"May I go in?"

Al-Juzjani waved his hand.

Inside the chamber, Rob was shocked. In the four months since he had last seen him, Ibn Sina's flesh had melted. His closed eyes were sunken, his face looked caved in, and his skin was waxen.

Al-Ghurī had done him harm, but mistreatment had only served to hasten the inevitable result of the stomach cancer.

Rob took his hands and felt so little life that he found it hard to speak. Ibn Sina's eyes opened. They bore into his; he felt they could see his thoughts, and there was no need for dissembling. "Why is it, Master," he asked bitterly, "that despite all a physician is able to do, he is as a leaf before the wind, and the real power lies only with Allah?"

To his mystification, a brilliance illuminated the wasted features. And suddenly he knew why Ibn Sina was attempting to smile.

"That is the riddle?" he asked faintly.

"It is the riddle . . . my European. You must spend the rest of your life . . . seeking . . . to answer it."

"Master?"

Ibn Sina had closed his eyes again and didn't answer. For a time Rob sat next to him in silence.

"I could have gone elsewhere without dissembling," he said in English. "To the Western Caliphate—Toledo, Cordova. But I'd heard of a man. Avicenna, whose Arab name seized me like a spell and shook me like an ague. Abu Ali at-Husain ibn Abdullah ibn Sina."

He couldn't have understood more than his name, yet he opened his eyes again and his hands put a slight pressure on Rob's.

"To touch the hem of your garment. The greatest physician in the world," Rob whispered.

He scarcely remembered the tired, world-whipped carpenter who had been his natural father. Barber had treated him well but had stopped short of affection. This was the only father his soul had known. He forgot about the things he had scorned and was conscious only of a need.

"I ask your blessing."

The halting words Ibn Sina spoke were pure Arabic but it was unnecessary to understand them. He knew Ibn Sina had blessed him long before.

He kissed the old man goodbye. When he left, the *mullah* had settled by the bed again and was reading aloud from the Qu'ran.

Chapter 74

THE KING OF KINGS

He rode back to Ispahan by himself. Al-Juzjani had remained in Hama-dhān, making it plain that he wished to be alone with his dying Master in the final days.

"We shall never see Ibn Sina again," Rob told Mary gently when he returned home, and she averted her face and wept like a child.

As soon as he had rested he hurried to the *maristan*. Without either Ibn Sina or al-Juzjani the hospital was disorganized and full of loose ends, and he spent a long day examining and treating patients, lecturing on wounds and—a distasteful chore—meeting with the *hadji* Davout Hosein regarding the general administration of the school.

Because of the uncertain times, many of the students had left their apprenticeships and returned to their homes outside the city. "This leaves few medical clerks to do the work of the hospital," the *hadji* grumbled. Fortunately, the patient population was correspondingly low, people instinctively feeling more concern about impending military violence than about illness.

That night Mary's eyes were red and swollen and she and Rob clung to one another with a tenderness that had almost been forgotten.

In the morning when he left the little house in Yehuddiyyeh he could feel change in the air like dampness before an English storm.

In the Jewish market most of the shops were uncharacteristically empty, and Hinda was frantically packing up the goods in her stall.

"What is it?" he said.

"The Afghans."

He rode to the wall. When he climbed the stairs he found the top lined with strangely silent people and at once saw the reason for their fear, for the host of Ghazna lay assembled in great strength. Masūd's foot warriors filled half the small plain outside the western wall of the city. The horsemen and camel soldiers were encamped across the foothills, and war elephants were tethered on the higher slopes near the tents and booths of the nobles and commanders, whose standards snapped in the dry wind. In the midst of the camp, floating above all, was the serpentine banner of the Ghaznavids, a black leopard's head on an orange field.

Rob estimated this Ghazna army to be four times as large as the one Masūd had led through Ispahan on his way west.

"Why haven't they entered the city?" he asked a member of the *kelonter*'s police force.

"They have pursued Alā here and he is within the city walls."

"Why should that hold them outside?"

"Masūd says Alā must be betrayed by his own people. He says if we deliver the Shah, they will spare our lives. If we do not, he promises a mountain of our bones in the central *maidan.*"

"Will Alā be delivered?"

The man glared and spat. "We are Persians. And he is the Shah."

Rob nodded. But he did not believe.

He descended the wall and rode the horse back to the house in Yehuddiyyeh. The English sword had been stored away, wrapped in oily rags. He strapped it to his side and bade Mary to take out her father's sword and barricade the door behind him.

Then he remounted the horse and rode to the House of Paradise.

On the Avenue of Ali and Fatima, people stood in worried groups. There were fewer persons in the four-laned Avenue of the Thousand Gardens and no one in the Gates of Paradise. That usually immaculate royal boulevard showed signs of neglect; caretakers had not groomed or pruned the landscaping of late. At the far end of the road was a solitary sentry.

The guard stepped out to challenge as Rob approached.

"I am Jesse, *hakim* at the *maristan.* Summoned by the Shah."

The guard was little more than a boy and looked uncertain, even frightened. Finally he nodded and stepped aside so the horse might pass.

Rob rode through the artificial woods created for kings, past the green field for ball-and-stick, past the two racing tracks and the pavilions.

He stopped behind the stables, at the living quarters that had been given to Dhan Vangalil. The Indian weapons-maker and his elder son had been taken to Hamadhān with the army. Rob didn't know if the two men had survived, but their family was gone. Their little house was deserted and someone had kicked in the clay walls of the smelting furnace Dhan had built with such care.

He rode down the long graceful approach road to the House of Paradise. The battlements were empty of sentries. His mount's hooves clattered hollowly across the drawbridge, and he tethered the horse outside the great doors.

Inside the House of Paradise his footsteps echoed through the empty corridors. Finally he came to the audience chamber in which he had always come before the king, and he saw that Alā sat in a corner alone on the floor, his legs crossed. Before him was a ewer half-filled with wine, and a board set up with a problem in the Shah's Game.

He looked as rank and untended as some of the gardens outside. His beard was untrimmed. There were purple smudges under his eyes and he was thinner, making his nose more of a harsh beak than ever. He stared up at Rob standing before him with his hand on the hilt of his sword.

"Well, *Dhimmi?* Have you come to avenge yourself?"

It was a moment before Rob realized Alā was talking of the Shah's Game and already rearranging the pieces on the game board.

He shrugged and took his hand from the hilt, arranging the sword so he could be comfortable as he sat on the floor opposite the king.

"Fresh armies," Alā said without humor, and opened by moving an ivory foot soldier.

Rob moved a black soldier. "Where is Farhad? Was he slain in the fighting?" He had not expected to find Alā alone. He had thought he would have to kill the Captain of the Gates first.

"Farhad was not slain. He has fled." Alā took a black soldier with his white horseman, and at once Rob used one of his ebony horsemen to capture a white foot soldier.

"Khuff would not have deserted you."

"No, Khuff would not have run away," Alā agreed absently. He studied the board. Finally, at the end of the battle line he picked up and moved the *rukh* warrior carved in ivory with killer's hands cupped to his lips, drinking his enemy's blood.

Rob baited a trap and sucked Alā in, giving up an ebony horseman in exchange for the white *rukh.*

Alā stared.

After that the king's moves were more deliberate and he spent more time in contemplation. His eyes gleamed as he gained the other white horseman but cooled when he lost his elephant.

"What of the elephant Zi?"

"Ah, *that* was a good elephant. I lost him too at the Gate of al-Karaj."

"And the *mahout* Harsha?"

"Killed before the elephant died. A lance through the chest." He drank wine without offering any to Rob, directly from the pitcher and spilling some on his already filthy tunic. He wiped his mouth and beard with the back of his hand. "Sufficient talk," he said, and settled into play, for the slight advantage was with the ebony pieces.

Alā turned grim attacker and tried all the ruses that once had worked so well, but Rob had spent the last years pitted against finer minds; Mirdin had shown him when to be daring and when to be cautious and Ibn Sina had taught him to anticipate, to think so far ahead that now it was as though he led Alā down the very paths in which annihilation of the ivory pieces was a certainty.

Time passed, and a sheen of sweat appeared on Alā's face, though the stone walls and stone floor kept the room cool.

It seemed to Rob that Mirdin and Ibn Sina played as part of his mind.

Of the ivory pieces there came to be on the board only the king, the general, and a camel; and soon, his eyes holding the Shah's, Rob took the camel with his own general.

Alā placed his general before the king piece, blocking the line of attack. But Rob had five pieces left: the king, the general, a *rukh*, a camel, and a foot soldier, and he quickly moved the unthreatened foot soldier to the opposite side of the board, where the rules allowed him to exchange it for his other *rukh*, no longer lost.

In three moves he had sacrificed the newly reclaimed *rukh* in order to capture the ivory general.

And in two more moves his own ebony general periled the ivory king. "Remove, O Shah," he said softly.

He repeated the words three times, while he positioned his pieces so there was no place for Alā's beleaguered king to turn.

"*Shahtreng,*" he said finally.

"Yes. The agony of the king." Alā swept the remaining pieces from the board.

Now they examined one another and Rob's hand was back on the hilt of his sword.

"Masūd has said if the people don't deliver you up, the Afghans will murder and pillage in this city."

"The Afghans will murder and pillage in this city whether they give me up or don't give me up. There is only one chance for Ispahan." He clambered to his feet, and Rob rose so a commoner would not be seated while the ruler stood.

"I will challenge Masūd to combat, king against king."

Rob desired to kill him, not to admire or like him, and he frowned.

Alā bent the heavy bow few men could have bent, and strung it. He pointed to the sword of patterned steel Dhan Vangalil had made, where it hung on the far wall. "Fetch my weapon, *Dhimmi.*"

Rob brought it and watched him strap it on. "You go against Masūd now?"

"Now appears a good time."

"You wish me to attend you?"

"No!"

Rob saw shocked disdain at the suggestion that the King of Persia would be squired by a Jew. Instead of being angry, he felt relief; for it had been said impulsively and regretted as soon as uttered, since he could see no sense or glory in dying alongside Alā Shah.

Yet the hawk's face softened and Alā Shah paused before leaving. "It was a manly offer," he said. "Consider what you would like as reward. When I return, I shall issue you a *calaat.*"

Rob climbed a narrow stone stairway to the highest battlements of the House of Paradise, and from this aerie he could see the houses of the wealthiest part of Ispahan, Persians standing atop the wall of the city, the plain beyond, and the Ghazna encampment that stretched into the hills.

He waited for a long time with the wind whipping his hair and beard, and Alā did not appear.

As more time elapsed he began to blame himself for not having killed the Shah, certain Alā had gulled him and then made good an escape.

But presently he saw.

The western gate was hidden from his sight but there on the flat plain beyond the wall the Shah emerged from the city, astride a familiar mount, the savagely beautiful white Arabian stallion, which was tossing its head and prancing smartly.

Rob watched Alā ride straight for the enemy camp. When he was close, he reined up the horse and stood in the stirrups as he shouted his challenge. Rob couldn't hear the words, only a thin, unintelligible shouting. But some of the king's people could hear. They had been raised on the legend of Ardewan and Ardeshir and the first duel to choose a *Shahanshah,* and from the top of the wall rose the sound of cheering. In the Ghazna camp, a small group of horsemen rode down from the area of officers' tents. The man in the lead wore a white turban but Rob couldn't tell if it was Masūd. Wherever Masūd was, if he had heard of Ardewan and Ardeshir and the ancient battle for the right to be King of Kings, he cared nothing for legends.

A troop of archers on fast horses burst from the Afghan ranks.

The white stallion was the fastest horse Rob had ever seen, but Alā didn't try to outrun them. He stood in the stirrups again. This time, Rob was certain, he shouted taunts and insults at the young Sultan who would not fight.

When the soldiers were almost on him, Alā readied his bow and began to flee on the white horse, but there was no place to run. Riding hard, he turned in the saddle and loosed a bolt that felled the leading Afghan, a perfect Parthian shot that drew cheers from those watching on the wall. But an answering hail of arrows found him.

Four arrows found his horse as well. A red gush appeared at the stallion's mouth. The white beast slowed and then stopped and stood, swaying, before it crashed to the ground with its dead rider.

Rob was taken unawares by his sadness.

He watched them tie a rope to Alā's ankles and then pull him to the Ghazna camp, raising a trail of gray dust. For a reason Rob didn't understand, he was especially bothered by the fact that they dragged the king over the ground face down.

He took the brown horse to the paddock behind the royal stables and removed the saddle. It was a task to open the massive gate alone but the place was as unattended as the rest of the House of Paradise, and he manhandled it himself.

"Goodbye, friend," he said.

He slapped the horse on the rump and when it joined the herd he shut the gate carefully. Only God knew who would own the brown horse by morning.

At the camel paddock he collected a pair of halters from the impedimenta hanging in an open shed and chose the two young, strong females he wanted. They knelt in the dust chewing their cuds, watching his approach.

The first tried to bite off his arm when he drew near with the bridle; but Mirdin, that most gentle of men, had shown him how to reason with camels, and he punched the animal so hard in the ribs that the breath whistled from between the square yellow teeth. After that the camel was tractable and the other animal gave no trouble, as though it learned by observation. He rode the larger and led the second beast on a rope.

At the Gates of Paradise the young sentry was gone, and as Rob traveled into the city it appeared Ispahan had gone mad. People were rushing everywhere, bearing bundles and leading animals laden with their belongings. The Avenue of Ali and Fatima was in an uproar; a runaway horse careered past Rob, causing the camels to shy. In the marketplaces, some of the merchants had abandoned their goods. He saw covetous glances directed at the camels, and he took his sword from its sheath and held it across his lap as he rode. He had to make a wide berth around the eastern part of the city in order to reach Yehuddiyyeh; people and animals already were backed up for a quarter of a mile as they tried to flee Ispahan through the eastern gate to evade the enemy camped beyond the western wall.

When he reached the house, Mary opened the door at his call, her face ashen and her father's sword still in her hand.

"We are going home."

She was terrified but he saw her lips moving in thanksgiving.

He took off the turban and Persian clothing and put on his black caftan and the leather Jew's hat.

They assembled his copy of Ibn Sina's *Canon of Medicine,* the anatomical drawings rolled and inserted into a length of bamboo, his casebook, his kit of medical tools, Mirdin's game, foodstuffs and a few drugs, her father's sword and a small box containing their money. All this was packed on the smaller camel.

From one side of the larger camel he hung a reed basket and from the other, a loosely woven sack. He had a tiny amount of *buing* in a small vial, just enough to allow him to wet the end of his little finger and let Rob J. suckle the fingertip, and then do the same for Tam. When they were sleeping he placed the older boy in the basket and the baby in the sack, and their mother mounted the camel to ride between them.

It wasn't quite dark when they left the little house in Yehuddiyyeh for the last time, but they didn't dare delay, since the Afghans could fall upon the city at any moment.

Darkness was complete by the time he led the two camels through the deserted western gate. The hunting trail they followed through the hills passed so close to the Ghazna campfires that they could hear singing and shouting, and the shrill cries of the Afghans working themselves into a frenzy for the pillaging.

Once a horseman seemed to be galloping straight at them, yipping as he rode, but the hoofbeats veered away.

The *buing* began to wear off and Rob J. started to whimper and then to cry. Rob thought the sound doomingly loud, but Mary took the boy from the basket and silenced him with her teat.

There was no pursuit. Soon they left the campfires behind, but when Rob looked back whence they had come a roseate nimbus had appeared low in the sky and he knew Ispahan was burning.

They traveled all night and when the first thin light of morning came, he saw he had led them out of the hills and no soldiers were in sight. His body was numb, and his feet . . . he knew that when he stopped walking pain would be another enemy. By this time both children were wailing and his gray-faced wife rode with closed eyes, but Rob didn't stop. He forced his tired legs to continue to plod, leading the camels west, toward the first of the Jewish villages.

PART SEVEN

The Returned

Chapter 75

LONDON

They crossed the great channel on March 24, Anno Domini 1043, and touched land late in the afternoon at Queen's Hythe. Perhaps if they had come to the city of London on a warm summer's day the rest of their lives might have been different, but Mary landed in a sleety spring rain carrying her younger son, who, like his father, had retched and vomited from France till journey's end, and she disliked and mistrusted London from the damp bleakness of the first moment.

There was scarcely room to disembark; of fearsome black naval ships alone, Rob counted more than a score riding the swells at anchor, and merchant craft were everywhere. They were, all four, exhausted by travel. They made their way to one of the market inns Rob remembered at Southwark but it proved a sorry haven, crawling with vermin that added to their misery.

At earliest light next morning he set out alone to find them a better place, walking down the causeway and over London Bridge, which was in good repair, the least changed detail of the city. London had grown; where there had been meadows and orchards he saw unfamiliar structures and streets that meandered as crazily as those in Yehuddiyyeh. The northern quarter of the town made a complete stranger of him, for when he was a boy it had been a neighborhood of manor houses set off by fields and gardens, the properties of old families. Now some of these had been sold and the land converted to use by the dirtier trades. There was an iron works, and the goldsmiths had their own cluster of houses and shops, as did the silversmiths and the copper workers. It was not a place he chose to live, with its pall of misty wood smoke, the stink of the tanneries, the constant clang of hammers on anvils, the roaring of the furnaces, and the tapping, beating, and banging of work and industry.

Every neighborhood came up lacking something in his eyes. Cripplegate was hard by the undrained moor, Halborn and Fleet Street remote from the center of London, Cheapside too crowded with retail business. The lower part of the city was even more congested but it had been a heroic part of his childhood and he found himself drawn back to the waterfront.

Thames Street was the most important street in London. In the squalor of the narrow lanes that ran from Puddle Dock on one end of it and Tower Hill on the other lived porters, stevedores, servants, and other unprivileged folk, but the long stretch of Thames Street itself and its wharves were the prosperous center of the export, import, and wholesale trades. On the south side of the street, the river wall and the quays compelled a certain amount of alignment, but the north side ran crazily, sometimes narrow, sometimes broad. In places, great houses pushed gabled fronts out as pregnant over-hangs. Sometimes a small fenced garden poked out or a warehouse stood back, and most of the time the street was filled with humanity and animals whose vital effluvia and sounds he remembered well.

In a tavern he inquired about empty housing and was told of a place not far from the Walbrook. It proved to be next to the small Church of St. Asaph, and he told himself Mary would like that. On the ground floor lived the landlord, Peter Lound. The second floor was to let, being one small room and one large room for general living, connected to the busy street below by the steep stairway.

There was no sign of bugs and the price seemed fair. And it was a good location, for along the better side streets on the rising land to the north, wealthy merchants lived and kept their shops.

Rob lost no time in going to Southwark to fetch his family.

"Not yet a fine home. But it will do, will it not?" he asked his wife.

Mary's eyes were timid and her reply was lost in the sudden ringing of the bells of St. Asaph's, which proved to be very loud.

As soon as they were settled he hurried to a sign-maker's and ordered the man to carve an oak board and blacken the letters. When the sign was done, it was fastened next to the doorway of the house on Thames Street, so all might see it was the home of Robert Jeremy Cole, Physician.

At first it was pleasant for Mary to be among Britons and speak English, although she continued to address her sons in Erse, wanting them to have the language of the Scots. The chance to obtain things in London was heady fare. She found a seamstress and ordered a dress of decent brown stuff. She would have wished a blue such as the dye her father once had given her, a blue like summer sky, but of course that was impossible.

Nevertheless, this dress was comely—long, girdled, with a high round neck and sleeves so loose they fell away from her wrists in luxurious folds.

For Rob they ordered good gray trousers and a kirtle. Though he protested the extravagance, she bought him two black physician's robes, one of light unlined stuff for summer and the other heavier and with a hood trimmed in fox. New garments were overdue him, since he still wore the clothing bought in Constantinople after they had completed the trail of Jewish safe places like following a chain, link by link. He had trimmed the bushy beard to a goatee and traded for Western dress, and by the time they joined a caravan, Jesse ben Benjamin had disappeared. In his place was Robert Jeremy Cole, an Englishman taking his family home.

Ever frugal, Mary had kept the caftan and used the material to make garments for her sons. She saved Rob J.'s clothing for Tam, though this was made difficult by the fact that Rob J. was large for his age and Tam slightly smaller than most boys because he had experienced grave illness on their journey west. In the Frankish town of Freising both children had been taken by quinsy throats and watery eyes, and then racked by hot fevers that terrified her with the thought of losing her sons. The children had been febrile for days; Rob J. was left with no visible defect but the illness had settled in Tam's left leg, which became pallid and appeared to be lifeless.

The Cole family had come to Freising with a caravan that was soon scheduled to depart, and the caravan master said he wouldn't wait for illness.

"Go and be damned," Rob had told him, because the child required treatment and would receive it. He had kept hot moist bandages on Tam's limb, going without sleep in order to change them constantly and to engulf the small leg in his large hands and bend the knee and work the muscles again and again, and to pinch and squeeze and knead the leg with bear fat.

Tam recovered, but slowly. He had been walking less than a year when stricken; he had had to learn again to creep and to crawl, and this time when he took his first steps he was off balance, the left leg being slightly shorter than the other.

They were in Freising not quite twelve months waiting for Tam's recovery and then for a suitable caravan. Although he never learned to love the Franks, Rob came to mellow somewhat regarding Frankish ways. People had come to him there for doctoring despite his ignorance of their language, having seen the care and tenderness with which he treated his own child. He had never stopped working on Tam's leg, and although the boy sometimes dragged his left foot a bit when he walked, he was among the most active children in London.

Indeed, both her children were more at ease in London than their mother, for she couldn't reconcile herself. She found the weather damp and the English cold. When she went to the marketplace she had to steel herself against slipping into the spirited Eastern haggling to which she had grown affectionately accustomed. The people were generally less amiable here than she had expected. Even Rob said he missed the effusive flow of Persian conversation. "Though the flattery was seldom more than sheep jakes, it was pleasant," he told her wistfully.

She felt herself in turmoil concerning him. Something was amiss in their marriage bed, a joylessness she couldn't define. She bought a looking-glass and studied her reflection, noting that her skin had lost luster under the cruel sun of travel. Her face was thinner than once it had been, and her cheekbones more pronounced. She knew her breasts had been altered by nursing. Everywhere in the city, hard-eyed tarts walked the street and some of them were beautiful. Would he turn to them, sooner or later? She imagined him telling a whore what he had learned of love in Persia and drew pain from the thought of them rolling about in laughter as once she and Rob had done.

To her, London was a black quagmire in which they already stood ankle deep. The comparison was not accidental, for the city smelled more foul than any swamp she had encountered in her travels. The open sewers and dirt were no worse than the open sewers and dirt of Ispahan, but here there were many times the number of people and in some neighborhoods they lived crammed together, so the accumulated stench of their bodily wastes and garbage was an abomination.

When they had reached Constantinople and she found herself once again among a Christian majority she had indulged in an orgy of churchgoing, but now that had palled, for she found London's churches overpowering. There were far more churches in London than there had been mosques in Ispahan, more than a hundred churches. They towered over every other sort of building—it was a city built between churches—and they spoke with a constant booming voice that made her tremble. Sometimes she felt she was about to be lifted and carried away by a great churchly wind stirred up by the bells. Though the Church of St. Asaph was small, its bells were large and reverberated in the house on Thames Street, and they rang in dizzying concert with all the others, communicating more effectively than an army of *muezzins*. The bells called worshipers to prayer, the bells witnessed to the consecration of the Mass, the bells warned laggards about the curfew; the bells rocked the steeples for christenings and weddings and sounded a grim and solemn knell for every soul passing on; the bells clanged the alert for fire and riot, welcomed distinguished visitors, pealed to announce each holy day, and tolled with muffled tones to mark disasters. To Mary, the bells were the city.

And she hated the damned bells.

The first person brought to their door by the new sign was not a patient. He was a slight, stooped man who peered and blinked through narrowed eyes.

"Nicholas Hunne, physician," he said, and cocked his balding head like a sparrow, awaiting a reaction. "Of Thames Street," he added meaningfully.

"I've seen your sign," Rob said. He smiled. "You're at one end of Thames Street, Master Hunne, and I now establish myself on the other end. Between us there are enough ailing Londoners for the distraction of a dozen busy physicians."

Hunne sniffed. "Not so many ailing folk as you may think. And not such busy physicians. London is already too crowded with medical men, and in my opinion an outlying town would make a better choice for a physician just starting out."

When he asked where Master Cole had trained, Rob lied like a rug dealer and said he had apprenticed for six years in the East Frankish Kingdom.

"And what shall you charge?"

"Charge?"

"Yes. Your fees, man, your schedule of fees!"

"I haven't given it sufficient thought."

"Do so at once. I'll tell you what is the custom here, for it wouldn't do for a newcomer to undercut the rest. Fees vary depending upon the patient's wealth—heaven's the limit, of course. Yet you must never go beneath forty pence for phlebotomy, since bloodletting is the staple of our trade, nor less than thirty-six pence for the examination of urine."

Rob stared thoughtfully, for the quoted fees were ruthlessly high.

"You shan't bother with the rabble who cluster at the far ends of Thames Street. They have their barber-surgeons. Nor will it be fruitful to yearn after the nobility, since these are tended by only a few physicians—Dryfield, Hudson, Simpson, and that lot. But Thames Street is a ripe enough garden of rich merchants, even if I have learned to get payment before treatment is begun, when the patient's anxiety is highest." He cast Rob a shrewd glance. "Our competition need not be all disadvantage, for I've found it impressive to call in a consultant when the afflicted is prosperous, and we shall be able to employ one another with profitable frequency, eh?"

Rob took several steps toward the door, ushering him out. "I prefer to work largely alone," he said coolly.

The other colored, for there was no mistaking the rejection.

"Then you will be content, Master Cole, for I shall spread the word and no other physician will come within hailing distance of you." He nodded curtly and was gone.

Patients came, but not often.

It was to be expected, Rob told himself; he was a new herring in a strange sea, and it would take time for his presence to be realized. Better to sit and wait than to play dirty, prosperous games with such as Hunne.

Meantime, he settled in. He took his wife and children to visit his family graves and the little boys played among the markers in the churchyard at St. Botolph's. By now he acknowledged, deep in the most secret part of himself, that he would never find his sister or his brothers, but he took comfort and pride in this new family he had made, and he hoped that somehow his brother Samuel and Mam and Da could know about them.

He found a tavern he liked on Cornhill. It was called The Fox, a workingmen's public house of the kind in which his father had sought refuge when Rob was a boy. Here he avoided metheglin again and drank brown ale, and he discovered a contractor-builder named George Markham who had been in the carpenters' guild at the same time as Rob's father. Markham was a stout, red-faced man with black hair gone snowy at the temples and at the bottom of his beard. He had been in a different Hundred than Nathanael Cole but remembered him, and it turned out he was nephew to Richard Bukerel, who had been Chief Carpenter then. He had been a friend of Turner Horne, the Master Carpenter with whom Samuel had lived before he had been run over on the docks. "Turner and his woman were killed by marsh fever five years ago, along with their youngest child. That was a terrible winter," Markham said.

Rob told the men in The Fox that he had been abroad for years, learning to be a physician in the East Frankish Kingdom. "Do you know an Apprentice Carpenter named Anthony Tite?" he asked Markham.

"He was a Companion Joiner when he died last year of the chest disease."

Rob nodded, and they drank in silence for a time.

From Markham and others at The Fox, Rob caught up on what had been happening to England's throne. Some of the story he'd learned from

Bostock in Ispahan. Now he discovered that after succeeding Canute, Harold Harefoot proved a weak king but with a strong guardian in Godwin, Earl of the West Saxons. His half-brother Alfred, who called himself the Atheling or Crown Prince, came from Normandy, and Harold's forces butchered his men, put out Alfred's eyes, and kept him in a cell until he died horribly from the festering of his tortured eye sockets.

Harold quickly ate and drank himself to death and Harthacnut, another of his half-brothers, returned from fighting a war in Denmark and succeeded him.

"Harthacnut ordered Harold's body dug up from Westminster and thrown into a fenny marsh near the Isle of Thorney," said George Markham, his tongue loosened by too much drink. "His own half-brother's body! As if it were a sack of shit or a dead dog."

Markham told how the corpse that had been King of England lay in the reeds while tides ebbed and flowed over it.

"Finally, a few of us sneaked down there in secret. Cold it was, that night, with a heavy fog that mostly hid the moon. We placed the body in a boat and guided it down the Thames. We buried the remains decently in the tiny churchyard of St. Clement's. It was the least Christian men could do." He crossed himself and took a deep draught from his cup.

Harthacnut had lasted only two years as king, dropping dead one day at a wedding feast, and at last it was Edward's turn. By then Edward had married Godwin's daughter and he too was firmly dominated by the Saxon earl, but the people liked him. "Edward's a good king," Markham told Rob. "He's built a proper fleet of black ships."

Rob nodded. "I've noted them. Are they fast?"

"Fast enough to keep the sea lanes free of pirates."

All this royal history, embellished with tavern anecdotes and recollections, created thirsty throats that demanded to be whetted, and it required many a toast to the dead brothers and certainly to the living Edward, monarch of the realm. So several evenings Rob forgot his inability to manage spirits and reeled from The Fox to the house on Thames Street, and Mary was faced with the task of undressing a surly sot and putting him to bed.

The sadness in her face deepened.

"Love, let us go away from here," she said to him one day.

"Why, where should we go?"

"We could live in Kilmarnock. There is my holding there, and a circle of kinsmen who would be warmed to see my husband and sons."

"We must give London more chance than that," he said gently.

He was no fool, and he vowed to be more careful when he went to The Fox, and to go there less often. What he didn't tell her was that London had become a vision for him, more than just an opportunity for a living as a leech. He had absorbed things in Persia that were now a part of him, things they didn't know here. He yearned for the open exchange of medical ideas that had existed in Ispahan. That required a hospital, and London would be an excellent location for an institution like the *maristan*.

That year the long wintry spring turned into a wet summer. Each morning thick fog hid the waterfront. By midmorning, on days when it didn't rain, the sun cut through the gray gloom and the city was coaxed into instant life. This moment of rebirth was Rob's favorite time for walking, and on a particularly lovely day the dissolution of the fog came when he was passing a commercial wharf on which a large party of slaves was stacking iron pigs for shipment.

There were a dozen piles of the heavy metal bars. They had been stacked too high, or perhaps there was an irregularity in one of the rows. Rob was enjoying the gleam of the sun on the wet metal when the driver of a dray, with loud commands and a cracking of his whip and tugging on his reins, backed his dirty white horses too far and too fast, so that the rear of the heavy wagon hit the pile with a thud.

Rob long had vowed that his boys would not play on the docks. He hated drays. Never did he see one but that he thought of his brother Samuel being crushed to death under the wheels of a freight wagon. Now he watched in horror as another accident occurred.

The iron bar at the top was jarred forward, so that it teetered at the edge and then began to slide over the lip of the pile, followed by two more.

There was a shouted cry of warning and a desperate human scattering, but two of the slaves had others in front of them. They fell as they scrabbled, so that the full weight of one of the pigs of iron came down on one of them, crushing life from him in an instant.

One end of another pig slammed down on the other man's lower right leg, and his screaming incited Rob to action.

"Here, get it off them. Quickly and carefully, now!" he said, and half a dozen slaves lifted the iron bars from the two men.

He had them moved well away from the pile of iron. A single glance was all that was necessary to ascertain that the man who had taken the full brunt was dead. His chest was crushed and he had been throttled by a broken windpipe, so that his face already was dark and engorged.

The other slave no longer was screaming, having fainted when he was moved. It was just as well; his foot and ankle were fearsomely mangled and Rob could do nothing to restore them. He dispatched a slave to his house to fetch his surgical kit from Mary, and while the wounded man was unconscious he incised the healthy skin above the injury and began to flay it back to make a flap, and then to slice through meat and muscle.

From the man arose a personal stink that made Rob nervous and afraid, the stench of a human animal who had sweated in toil again and again until his unwashed rags had absorbed his rotten smell and compounded it and made it almost a tangible part of him like his shaven slave's head or the foot Rob was in the process of removing. It caused Rob to remember the two similarly stinking stevedore slaves who had carried Da home from his job on the docks, home to die.

"What in hell do you believe you're doing?"

He looked up and struggled to control his expression, for standing next to him was a person he had last seen in the home of Jesse ben Benjamin in Persia.

"I am tending a man."

"But they say you're a physician."

"They are right."

"I am Charles Bostock, merchant and importer, owner of this ware-house and this dock. And I'm not so foolish, God's arse, as to hire a physician for a slave."

Rob shrugged. The kit arrived and he was ready for it; he took up his bone saw and cut off the ruined foot and sewed the flap over the blood-oozing stump as neatly as al-Juzjani would have demanded.

Bostock was still there. "I meant my words precisely," he was saying. "I ain't to pay you. Not a ha'-penny shall you get from me."

Rob nodded. He gently tapped the slave's face with two fingers and the man groaned.

"Who are you?"

"Robert Cole, physician of Thames Street."

"Are we acquainted, master?"

"Not to my knowledge, master merchant."

He collected his belongings, nodded, and went away. At the end of the dock he risked a glance back, and he saw Bostock standing as one trans-fixed, or deeply puzzled, and continuing to stare after him as he made his escape.

He told himself Bostock had seen a turbaned Jew in Ispahan, with a bushy beard and Persian clothing, the exotic Hebrew Jesse ben Benjamin.

And on the dock the merchant had spoken with Robert Jeremy Cole, a free Londoner in plain English garb, his face . . . transformed? . . . by a close-trimmed beard.

It was possible Bostock wouldn't remember him at all. And equally possible that he would.

Rob worried the question like a dog with a bone. It was not so much that he was frightened for himself (although he *was* frightened) as that he was concerned over what would happen to his wife and sons in the event that trouble should claim him.

And so when Mary chose to talk about Kilmarnock that evening he listened with a dawning realization of what had to be done.

"How I wish we could go there," she said. "I've a yearning to walk the ground I own and to be again among kinsfolk and Scots."

"There are things I must do here," he said slowly. He took her hands. "But I think that you and the young ones should go to Kilmarnock without me."

"Without you?"

"Yes."

She sat perfectly still. The pallor seemed to heighten her high cheekbones and cast interesting new shadows in her slender face, making her eyes appear larger as she examined him. The corners of her mouth, those sensitive corners that always betrayed her emotions, told him how unwelcome was the suggestion.

"If that is what you want, we shall go," she said quietly.

In the next few days he changed his mind a dozen times. There was no outcry or alarm. No armed men came to arrest him. It was obvious that though he had seemed familiar to Bostock, the merchant hadn't identified him as Jesse ben Benjamin.

Don't go, he wanted to tell her.

Several times he almost said it, but always something kept him from uttering the words; within him he carried a heavy burden of fear, and it could do no harm if she and the boys were safely elsewhere for a time.

So they spoke of it again. "If you can get us to the port of Dunbar," she said.

"What is in Dunbar?"

"MacPhees. Kinsmen to Cullens. They will see to our safe arrival in Kilmarnock."

Dunbar proved no problem. It was by then almost the end of summer, and there was a flurry of sailings as owners of ships attempted to crowd in last short voyages before storms closed off the North Sea for another winter. In The Fox, Rob heard of a packet boat that stopped at Dunbar. It was called the *Aelfgifu* after Harold Harefoot's mother, and its captain was a grizzled Dane who was happy to be paid for three passengers who would not eat much.

The *Aelfgifu* would leave in less than two weeks, and it demanded hurried preparation, mending of clothing, decisions about what she would take and what she would not.

Suddenly, their leavetaking was a few days away.

"I'll come for you in Kilmarnock when I'm able."

"Will you?" she said.

"Of course."

On the night before departure she said, "If you cannot come . . ."

"I *shall.*"

"But . . . if you do not. If the world should keep us apart in some way, know that my kinsmen will raise the boys to manhood."

That served to annoy him more than it reassured, and it so fueled his fears that he was sorry he had suggested that they part from him.

They touched each other carefully, all the familiar places, like two sightless people wishing to store the memory in their hands. It was a sad lovemaking, as though they knew it was for the last time. When they were done, she wept soundlessly and he held her without words. There were things he desired to say but could not.

In the morning he put them aboard the *Aelfgifu* in gray light. She was built along the lines of a stable Viking ship but only sixty feet long, with an open deck. There was one mast, thirty feet high, and a large square sail, and the hull was built of thick overlapping planks of oak. The king's black ships would keep pirates far out to sea and the *Aelfgifu* would hug the coast, putting in to deliver and take on cargo and at first sign of a storm. It was the safest sort of boat.

Rob stood on the dock. Mary was wearing her invincible face, the armor she wore when she had girded herself against the threatening world.

Though the boat was only rocking in the swells, poor Tam already looked greenish and distressed. "You must continue to work his leg," Rob called, and made massaging motions. She nodded to show she understood. A crewman lifted the hawser away from the mooring and the boat swung free. Twenty oarsmen pulled once and it was sucked into the strong outgoing tide. A good mother, Mary had placed her boys on cargo in the boat's very heart, where they couldn't fall overboard.

She leaned down and said something to Rob J. as the sail was raised.

"Fare thee well, Da!" the thin, obedient voice shouted clearly.

"Go with God!" Rob called.

Too soon they were indeed gone, though he stayed where he was and strained his eyes peering after them. He didn't wish to leave the dock, for it struck him that he had come again to a place he had been when he was nine years old, without family or friends in the city of London.

Chapter 76

THE LONDON LYCEUM

That year on the ninth of November a woman named Julia Swane became the chief topic of conversation in the city when she was arrested as a witch. It was charged she had transformed her daughter Glynna, age sixteen, into a flying horse and then had ridden her so brutally the girl was permanently maimed. "If true, it is heinous and wicked, to do that to one's child," his landlord told Rob.

He missed his own children grievously, and their mother. The first ocean storm had come more than four weeks after they had left him. By that time they must long since have landed at Dunbar, and he prayed that wherever they were, they would wait out storms in safe places.

Again he became a solitary wanderer, revisiting all the parts of London he had known and the new sights that had emerged since his boyhood. When he stood before King's House, which once had seemed to him the perfect picture of royal magnificence, he marveled at the difference between its English simplicity and the soaring lushness of the House of Paradise. King Edward spent most of the time in his castle at Winchester, but one morning outside King's House Rob witnessed him walking in silence among his housecarls and henchmen, pensive and introspective. Edward looked older than his forty-one years. It was said his hair had gone white when he was very young, on hearing what Harold Harefoot had done to their brother Alfred. Rob didn't think Edward nearly so kingly a figure as Alā had been, but he minded himself that Alā Shah was gone and King Edward was alive.

From Michaelmas onward that autumn was cold and scourged by winds. Early winter came warm and rainy. He thought of them often, wishing he knew exactly when they had arrived in Kilmarnock. Out of loneliness he spent many an evening at The Fox but tried to keep his thirst in check, not wishing to fall into brawling as he had done in his youth. Yet the drink brought him more melancholy than ease, for he felt himself turning into his father, a man of the public houses. It caused him to resist the drabs and the available females made more attractive by a troubling horniness; he told himself bitterly that despite the drink he must not become entirely transformed into Nathanael Cole the married whoremaster.

The advent of Christmas was difficult, a holiday that begged to be spent with family. Christmas Day he ate a purchased meal at The Fox: the head-cheese called brawn and a mutton pie, washed down by a prodigious amount of mead. Making his way home he came upon two sailors beating a man whose leather cap was in the mud, and Rob saw that he wore a black caftan. One of them held the Jew's arms behind his back while the other delivered punches that thudded sickeningly each time they landed.

"Cease, damn you."

The puncher paused in his work. "Shove away, master, while it's yet safe."

"What has he done?"

"A crime committed a thousand years ago, and now we'll send the stinking Frenchy Hebrew back to Normandy dead."

"Leave him be."

"You like him so, we'll watch you suck his cock."

Alcohol always built an aggressive fury in him and he was ready. His fist smashed into the tough and ugly face. The accomplice released the Jew and sprang away as the sailor he had knocked down climbed to his feet. "Bastard! You'll drink the Saviour's blood from this fucking Jew's cup!"

Rob didn't chase them when they ran. The Jew, a tall man of middle age, stood with heaving shoulders. His nose was bloody and his lips smashed but he seemed to weep more from humiliation than from hurt.

"Halloa, what is happening?" asked a newcomer, a man with frizzy red hair and beard and a large vein-purpled nose.

"It isn't much. This man was waylaid."

"Hmmm. You're certain he was not the instigator?"

"Yes."

The Jew had won control of himself and found his voice. It was clear he was expressing gratitude, but he spoke in voluble French.

"Do you understand that language?" Rob asked the red-haired man, who shook his head scornfully. Rob wanted to speak to the Jew in the Tongue and wish him a more peaceful Festival of Lights, but in the presence of the witness he didn't dare. Presently the Jew picked up his hat and went away, and so did the bystander.

On the riverfront Rob found a small public house and rewarded himself with red wine. The place was dark and airless and he carried the flask of wine onto a dock to drink, sitting on a piling his father might have set, with the rain soaking and the wind buffeting him and the dangerous-looking gray waves curling through the waters below.

He was satisfied. What better day to have prevented a crucifixion?

The wine wasn't a regal vintage and it stung when swallowed, but nonetheless it pleased him.

He was his father's son and could enjoy drink if he allowed himself.

No, the transformation already had taken place; he *was* Nathanael Cole. He was Da. And in some strange way he knew he was also Mirdin and Karim. And Alā and Dhan Vangalil. And Abu Ali at-Husain ibn Abdullah ibn Sina (oh, yes, *especially* he was Ibn Sina!) . . . But he was also the fat highwayman he had killed years ago, and that pious old shit, the *hadji* Davout Hosein . . .

With a clarity that numbed him more than the wine, he knew he was all men and all men were part of him, and that whenever he fought the fucking Black Knight he was simply fighting for his own survival. Alone and drunk, he perceived that for the first time.

When he had finished the wine he slid from the piling. Carrying the empty flask, which soon would contain medicine or perhaps somebody's piss to be analyzed for a fair fee, he and all the rest of them walked carefully and unsteadily from the dock toward the safety of the house on Thames Street.

He hadn't remained behind without wife and children to turn into a sot, he told himself severely on the following day, when his head had cleared.

Determined to tend to the details of healing, he went to an herb seller's shop on lower Thames Street to renew his supply of medicinals, for in London it was easier to buy certain herbs than to try to find them in nature. He had already met the proprietor, a small, fussy man named Rolf Pollard who appeared to be a capable pharmacist.

"Where shall I go to find the company of other physicians?" Rob asked him.

"Why, I should say the Lyceum, Master Cole. It's a meeting held regularly by the physicians of this city. I don't have details, but doubtless Master Rufus does," he said, indicating a man at the other end of the room who was sniffing a branch of dried purslane to test its volatility.

Pollard led Rob across the shop and introduced him to Aubrey Rufus, physician of Fenchurch Street. "I've told Master Cole of the Physicians' Lyceum," he said, "but couldn't recall the particulars."

Rufus, a sober fellow about ten years older than Rob, ran a hand over his thinning sandy hair and nodded pleasantly enough. "It's held first

Monday eve of each month, dinner hour in the room above Illingsworth's Tavern on Cornhill. Mostly it's an excuse to make gluttons of ourselves. Each man buys his own food and drink."

"Must one be invited?"

"Not at all. It is open to London physicians. But if an invitation is more pleasing, why I invite you now," Rufus said affably, and Rob smiled and thanked him and took his leave.

So it happened that on the first Monday of the slushy new year he went to Illingsworth's Tavern and found himself in the company of a score of medical men. They sat around tables talking and laughing over drink, and when he came in they inspected him with the furtive curiosity a group always directs at a newcomer.

The first man he recognized was Hunne, who scowled when he saw Rob and muttered something to his companions. But Aubrey Rufus was at another table and motioned for Rob to join him. He introduced the four others at the table, mentioning that Rob was recently arrived in the city and set up in practice on Thames Street.

Their eyes contained varying amounts of the grim wariness with which Hunne had regarded him.

"Under whom did you prentice?" asked a man named Brace.

"I clerked with a physician named Heppmann, in the East Frankish town of Freising." During the time they had spent in Freising while Tam was ill, Heppmann had been their landlord's name.

"Hmmph," Brace said, doubtless an opinion of foreign-trained physicians. "How long an apprenticeship?"

"Six years."

His questioning was diverted by the arrival of the victuals, overdone roast fowl with baked turnips, and ale that Rob drank sparingly, not wanting to make a fool of himself. After the meal it turned out that Brace was the lecturer of the evening. He spoke on cupping, warning his fellow physicians to heat the cupping glass sufficiently, since it was the warmth in the glass that drew the blood's ugliness to the surface of the skin, where it might be eliminated by bleeding.

"You must demonstrate to the patients your confidence that repeated cupping and bleeding will bring cures, so they may share your optimism," Brace said.

The talk was ill prepared, and from the conversation Rob knew that by the time he was eleven Barber had taught him more about bleeding and cupping, and when to use them and when not to use them, than most of these physicians knew.

So the Lyceum was quickly a disappointment.

They seemed obsessed with fees and income. Rufus even envyingly joshed the chairman, a royal physician named Dryfield, because each year he was furnished with a stipend and robes.

"It's possible to heal for a stipend without serving the king," Rob said.

Now he gained their attention. "How might this happen?" Dryfield asked.

"A physician might work for a hospital, a healing center devoted to patients and the understanding of illness."

Some looked at him blankly but Dryfield nodded. "An Eastern idea that is spreading. One hears of a hospital newly established in Salerno, and the Hôtel Dieu has long been in Paris. But let me warn you, folk are sent to die in the Hôtel Dieu and then forgotten, and it is a hellish place."

"Hospitals needn't be like the Hôtel Dieu," Rob said, troubled that he couldn't tell them of the *maristan*.

But Hunne cut in. "Perhaps such a system works well for the greasier races, but English physicians are more independent of spirit and must be free to conduct their own businesses."

"Surely medicine is more than a business," Rob objected mildly.

"It is less than a business," Hunne said, "fees being what they are and new shitty-legged come-latelys arriving in London all the time. How do you count it as more than a business?"

"It is a calling, Master Hunne," he said, "as men are said to be divinely called to the Church."

Brace hooted. But the chairman coughed, having had enough of wrangling. "Who will offer the discourse next month?" he asked.

There was a silence.

"Come now, each must do his share," Dryfield said impatiently.

It was a mistake to offer at his first meeting, Rob knew. But nobody else said a word and finally he spoke. "I'll lecture, if it's your desire."

Dryfield's eyebrows went up. "And on what subject, master?"

"I'll speak on the subject of abdominal distemper."

"On abdominal distemper? Master . . . ah, Crowe, was it?"

"Cole."

"Master Cole. Why, a talk on abdominal distemper would be splendid," the chairman said, and beamed.

Julia Swane, accused witch, had confessed. The witch's spot had been found in the soft white flesh of her inner arm, just beneath the left shoulder. Her daughter Glynna testified that Julia had held her down and laughed while she was used sexually by someone she took to be the Fiend. Several of her victims accused her of casting spells. It was while the witch was being tied into the dunking stool before immersion in the icy Thames that she decided to tell all, and now she was cooperating with the evil-rooters of the Church, who were said to be interviewing her at length regarding all manner of subjects relating to witchcraft. Rob tried not to think of her.

He bought a somewhat fat gray mare and arranged to board her at what had been Egglestan's stables, now owned by a man named Thorne. She was aging and undistinguished but, he told himself, he wouldn't be playing ball-and-stick on her. He rode to patients when summoned, and others found their way to his door. It was the season for croup and though he'd have liked Persian medicinals such as tamarind, pomegranate, and powdered fig, he made up potions with what was at hand: purslane steeped in rose water to produce a gargle for angry throat, an infusion of dried violet to treat headache and fever, pine resin mixed with honey to be eaten against phlegm and cough.

One who came to him said his name was Thomas Hood. He had carroty hair and beard and a discolored nose; he seemed familiar and presently Rob realized the man had been the bystander at the incident between the Jew and the two sailors. Hood complained of thrushlike symptoms but there were no pustules in his mouth, no fever, no redness in the throat, and he was far too lively to be afflicted. In fact, he was a constant source of personal questions. With whom had Rob apprenticed? Did he reside alone? What, no wife, no child? How long had he been in London? Whence had he come?

A blind man would clearly see this was no patient but a snoop. Rob told him nothing, prescribed a strong purgative he knew Hood wouldn't take, and ushered him out amid more questions he ignored.

But the visit bothered him inordinately. Who had sent Hood? For whom was he inquiring? And was it only coincidence that he had observed Rob's routing of the two sailors?

On the following day he learned some possible answers when he went to the herb seller's to buy ingredients for remedies, and again found Aubrey Rufus there on the same errand.

"Hunne is speaking against you when he can," Rufus told him. "He says you are too forward. That you have the appearance of a ruffian and blackguard and he doubts you are a physician. He seeks to close membership in the Lyceum to any who haven't prenticed to English physicians."

"What is your advice?"

"Oh, do nothing," Rufus said. "It's apparent he cannot reconcile himself to sharing Thames Street with you. We all know Hunne would rip away his grandfather's ballocks for a coin. No one will pay him heed."

Comforted, Rob returned to the Thames Street house.

He would overcome their doubts with scholarship, he decided, and fell to work preparing the discourse on abdominal distemper as though he would be giving it in the *madrassa*. The original Lyceum near ancient Athens was where Aristotle had lectured; he wasn't Aristotle, but he had been trained by Ibn Sina and would show these London physicians what a medical lecture could be like.

There was interest, certainly, because every man attending the Lyceum had lost patients who had suffered agony in the lower right portion of the abdomen. But there was also general scorn.

"A little worm?" drawled a wall-eyed physician named Sargent. "A little pink worm in the belly?"

"A wormlike appendage, master," Rob said stiffly. "Attached to the cecum. And suppurating."

"Galen's drawings show no wormlike appendage on the cecum," Dryfield said. "Celsus, Rhazes, Aristotle, Diascorides—who among these has written of this appendage?"

"No one. Which does not mean it isn't there."

"Have you dissected a pig, Master Cole?" Hunne asked.

"Yes."

"Well, then you know that a pig's innards are same as a man's. Have you ever noted a pink appendage on the cecum of a pig?"

"It was a small pork sausage, master!" a wit cried, and there was general laughter.

"Internally, a pig appears to be same as a man," Rob said patiently, "but there are subtle differences. One of these is the small appendage on the human cecum." He unrolled the Transparent Man and fixed the illustration to the wall with iron pins. "This is what I am talking about. The appendage is depicted here in the early stages of irritation."

"Suppose the abdominal illness is caused precisely in the way you have described," said a physician with a thick Danish accent. "Do you then suggest a cure?"

"I know of no cure."

There were groans.

"Then why does it matter a whitebait whether or not we understand the origin of the disease?" Others voiced agreement, forgetting how much they loathed Danes in their unified eagerness to oppose the newcomer.

"Medicine is like the slow raising of masonry," Rob said. "We are fortunate, in a lifetime, to be able to lay a single brick. If we can explain the disease, someone yet unborn may devise a cure."

More groans.

They crowded about and studied the Transparent Man.

"Your drawing, Master Cole?" Dryfield asked, noting the signature.

"Yes."

"It is an excellent work," the chairman said. "What served as your model?"

"A man whose belly was torn."

"Then you've seen only one such appendage," Hunne said. "And no doubt the omnipotent voice that summoned you to our *calling* also told you the little pink worm in the bowel is universal?"

It drew more laughter and Rob allowed himself to be stung. "I believe the appendage on the cecum *is* universal. I have seen it in more than one person."

"In as many as . . . say, four?"

"In as many as half a dozen."

They were staring at him instead of at the drawing.

"Half a dozen, Master Cole? How did you come to see inside the bodies of six human folk?" Dryfield said.

"Some of the bellies were slit in the course of accidents. Others were laid open during fighting. They were not all my patients, and the incidents occurred over a period of time." It sounded unlikely even to his own ears.

"Females as well as men?" Dryfield asked.

"Several were females," he said reluctantly.

"Hmmmph," the chairman said, making it clear he thought Rob a liar.

"Had the women been dueling, then?" Hunne said silkily, and this time even Rufus laughed. "I call it coincidence indeed that you have been able to look inside so many bodies in this manner," Hunne said, and seeing the fierce glad light in his eyes, Rob was aware that volunteering to give a lecture at the Lyceum had been a mistake from the start.

Julia Swane didn't escape the Thames. On the last day of February more than two thousand people gathered at daybreak to watch and cheer as she was sewn into a sack, along with a cock, a snake, and a rock, and cast into the deep pool at St. Giles.

Rob didn't attend the drowning. Instead he went to Bostock's wharf in search of the thrall whose foot he had removed. But the man wasn't to be found and a curt overseer would say only that the slave had been taken from

London to another place. Rob feared for him, knowing that a slave's existence depended on his ability to work. At the dock he saw another slave whose back was crisscrossed with whipping sores that seemed to gnaw into his body. Rob went to his house and made up a salve of goat grease, swine grease, oil, frankincense, and copper oxide, then he returned to the wharf and spread it on the thrall's angry flesh.

"Here, now. What in the bloody hell is this?"

An overseer was bearing down on them, and although Rob hadn't quite finished spreading the salve, the slave fled.

"This is Master Bostock's wharf. Does he know you're here?"

"It doesn't matter."

The overseer glared but didn't follow, and Rob was glad to leave Bostock's wharf without further trouble.

Paying patients came to him. He cured a pale and weepy woman of the flux by dosing her with boiled cow's milk. A prosperous shipwright came in with his kirtle soaked in blood from a wrist so deeply cut that his hand seemed partially severed. The man readily admitted he had done it with his own knife, seeking to end his life while despondent with drink.

He had almost reached the mortal depth, stopping just short of the bone. Rob knew from the cutting he had done in the *maristan*'s charnel house that the artery in the wrist rested close to the bone; if the man had sliced a hair deeper he would have achieved his drunken desire for death. As it was, he had severed the tough cords that governed movement and control of the thumb and first finger of his hand. When Rob had sewn and dressed the wrist, those fingers were stiff and numb.

"Will they regain movement and feeling?"

"It's up to God. You did a workmanlike job. Should you try again, I think you'll kill yourself. Therefore, if you desire to live, you must shun strong drink."

Rob feared the man would try again. It was the time of year when cathartics were needed because there had been no greens all winter, and he made up a tincture of rhubarb and within a week dispensed it all. He treated a man bitten in the neck by a donkey, lanced a brace of boils, wrapped a sprained wrist, and set a broken finger. One midnight a frightened woman summoned him well down Thames Street—into what he had come to regard as no-man's land, the area midway between his house and Hunne's. He would have been fortunate had she summoned Hunne, for her husband was grievously taken. He was a groom at Thorne's stables who had cut his thumb three days before, and that evening he had gone to bed with pains in his loins. Now his jaws were locked, his spittle became frothy and could scarcely pass through his clenched teeth, and his body assumed the shape of a bent bow as he raised his stomach and supported himself on his heels and the top of his head. Rob never had seen the disease before but recognized it from Ibn Sina's written description; it was episthotonos, "the backward spasm." There was no known cure, and the man died before morning.

The experience at the Lyceum had left the taste of ashes in Rob's mouth. That Monday he forced himself to attend the March meeting as a spectator who held his tongue, but the damage already was done and he saw that they regarded him as a foolish braggart who had allowed his imagination to rule. Some smiled at him in derision while others regarded him coldly. Aubrey Rufus didn't invite his company but glanced away when their eyes met, and he sat at a table with strangers who didn't address him.

The lecture concerned fractures of the arm, forearm, and ribs, and dislocations of the jaw, shoulder, and elbow. Given by a short, round man named Tyler, it was the poorest kind of lesson, containing so many errors in method and fact that it would have sent Jalal the bonesetter into a rage. Rob sat and kept his silence.

As soon as the speaker was done, they turned their conversation to the witch's drowning.

"Others will be caught, mark my word," said Sargent, "for witches practice their foul art in groups. In examining folks' bodies, we must seek to detect and report the devil's spot."

"We must take care to appear above reproach," Dryfield said thoughtfully, "for many think physicians are close to witchcraft. I've heard it said that a physician-witch can cause patients to foam at the mouth and stiffen as though dead."

Rob thought uneasily of the stable groom who had been taken by episthotonos, but no one accosted or accused him.

"How else is a male witch recognized?" Hunne asked.

"They appear much as any other men," Dryfield said. "Though some say they cut their pricks like heathens."

Rob's own scrotum tightened with fear. As soon as possible he took his leave and knew he wouldn't return, for it wasn't safe to attend a place where life could be forfeit if a colleague should witness him passing water.

If his experience at the Lyceum had resulted only in disappointment and tarnished reputation, at least he had hope in his work, and rude health, he told himself.

But the following morning Thomas Hood, the red-haired snoop, appeared at the house on Thames Street with two armed companions.

"What can I do for you?" Rob asked coldly.

Hood smiled. "We are all three summoners for the Bishop's Court."

"Yes?" Rob asked, but he already knew.

It pleased Hood to hawk and spit onto the physician's clean floor. "We are come to place you in arrest, Robert Jeremy Cole, and bring you to God's justice," he said.

Chapter 77

THE GRAY MONK

"Where are you taking me?" he asked when they were on their way.

"Court will be held on the South Porch at St. Paul's."

"What is the charge?"

Hood shrugged and shook his head.

When they arrived at St. Paul's he was ushered into a small room filled with waiting folk. There were guards at the door.

He had a sense that he had lived through this experience before. In limbo all morning on a hard bench, listening to the gabble of a flock of men in religious habit, he might have been back in the realm of the Imam Qandrasseh, but this time he wasn't there as physician to the court. He felt he was a sounder man than he had ever been, yet he knew that by churchly reckoning he was as guilty as anyone hailed to judgment that day.

But he was not a witch.

He thanked God that Mary and their sons weren't with him. He wanted to request permission to go to the chapel to pray but knew it wouldn't be granted, so he silently prayed where he was, asking God to keep him from being sewn into a sack with a cock, a snake, and a stone and cast into the deep.

He worried about the witnesses they might have summoned: whether they had called the physicians who had heard him tell of poking about within human bodies, or the woman that had watched him treat her husband who had stiffened and foamed at the mouth before dying. Or Hunne, the dirty bastard, who would invent any sort of lie to make him out a witch and be rid of him.

But he knew that if they had made up their minds, witnesses wouldn't matter. They would strip him and see his circumcision as proof, and they would search his body until they decided they had found the witch's spot.

Doubtless they had as many methods as the Imam for gaining a confession.

Dear God . . .

He had more than enough time for his fear to mount. It was early afternoon before he was called into the clerics' presence. Seated on an oak throne was a squinting elderly bishop in faded brown wool alb, stole, and chasuble; from listening to others outside Rob knew he was Aelfsige, ordinary of St. Paul's and a hard punisher. To the bishop's right were two middle-aged priests in black, and to his left, a young Benedictine in severe dark gray.

A clerk produced Holy Writ, which Rob was bade to kiss and swear solemn oath that his testimony would be true. It began matter-of-factly.

Aelfsige peered at him. "What is your name?"

"Robert Jeremy Cole, Excellency."

"Residence and occupation?"

"Physician of Thames Street."

The bishop nodded to the priest on his right.

"Did you, on the twenty-fifth day of December last, join with a foreign Hebrew in unprovoked attack on Master Edgar Burstan and Master William Symesson, freeborn London Christians of the Parish of St. Olave?"

For a moment Rob was puzzled and then he felt tremendous relief as he realized they weren't stalking him for sorcery. The sailors had reported him for coming to the aid of the Jew! A minor charge, even if he were to be convicted.

"A Norman Jew named David ben Aharon," the bishop said, blinking rapidly. His vision appeared to be very bad.

"I have never before heard the Jew's name nor those of the complainants. But the seamen have reported it untruly. It was they who had been unfairly ganging on the Jew. That was why I intervened."

"Are you a Christian?"

"I am baptized."

"You attend regular service?"

"No, Excellency."

The bishop sniffed and nodded gravely. "Fetch the deponent," he told the gray monk.

Rob's sense of relief dissipated at once when he saw the witness.

Charles Bostock was richly clothed and wore a heavy gold neck chain and a large seal ring. During his identification he told the court he had been elevated to the rank of thane by King Harthacnut in reward for three voyages as a merchant-adventurer, and that he was an honorary canon of St. Peter's. The churchmen treated him with deference.

"Now then, Master Bostock. Do you know this man?"

"He is Jesse ben Benjamin, a Jew and a physician," Bostock said flatly.

The nearsighted eyes fixed on the merchant. "You are certain of the Jew portion?"

"Excellency, four or five years ago I was traveling the Byzantine Patriarchate, buying goods and serving as envoy from His Blessed Holiness in Rome. In the city of Ispahan I learned of a Christian woman who had been left alone and bereft in Persia by the death of her Scottish father, and had married a Jew. Upon receiving invitation, I could not resist going to her home to investigate the whisperings. There, to my dismay and disgust, I saw that the stories were true. She was wife to this man."

The monk spoke for the first time. "You're certain this is he, good thane, the same man?"

"I am sure, holy brother. He appeared some weeks ago on my wharf and tried to charge me dear for butchering up one of my thralls, for which of course I would not pay. When I saw his face I understood that I knew it from somewhere, and I studied on the matter until I recalled. He is the Jew physician of Ispahan, of that there is no doubt. A despoiler of Christian females. In Persia, the Christian woman already had one child by this Jew and he had bred her a second time."

The bishop leaned forward. "On solemn oath, what *is* your name, master?"

"Robert Jeremy Cole."

"The Jew lies," Bostock said.

"Master merchant," the monk said. "Was it only a single time that you saw him in Persia?"

"Yes, one occasion," Bostock said grudgingly.

"And you did not see him again for almost five years?"

"Closer to four years than five. But that is true."

"Yet you are certain?"

"Yes. I tell you, I have no doubt."

The bishop nodded. "Very well, Thane Bostock. You have our thanks," he said.

While the merchant was escorted away, the clerics looked at Rob and he struggled to remain calm.

"If you are a freeborn Christian, does it not seem strange," the bishop said thinly, "that you are brought before us on two separate charges, and the one states that you aided a Jew and the other states that you are a Jew yourself?"

"I am Robert Jeremy Cole. I was baptized half a mile from here, in St. Botolph's. The parish book will bear me out. My father was Nathanael, a journeyman joiner in the Corporation of Carpenters. He lies buried in St.

Botolph's churchyard, as does my mother, Agnes, who in life was a seamstress and an embroiderer."

The monk addressed him coldly. "Did you attend the church school at St. Botolph's?"

"Two years only."

"Who taught the Scriptures there?"

Rob closed his eyes and wrinkled his brow. "That was Father . . . Philibert. Yes, Father Philibert."

The monk glanced inquiringly at the bishop, who shrugged and shook his head. "The name Philibert isn't familiar."

"Then Latin? Who taught you Latin?"

"Brother Hugolin."

"Yes," the bishop said. "Brother Hugolin taught Latin at the St. Botolph's school. I recall him well. He has been dead these many years." He pulled his nose and regarded Rob nearsightedly. Finally he sighed. "We shall check the parish book, of course."

"You will find it as I have said, Excellency," Rob told him.

"Well, I shall allow you to purge yourself by oath that you are the person you claim to be. You are instructed to appear again before this court in three weeks' time. With you must come twelve free men as compurgators, each willing to swear that you are Robert Jeremy Cole, Christian and freeborn. Do you understand?"

He nodded and was dismissed.

Minutes later he stood outside St. Paul's scarcely crediting that he was no longer exposed to their sharp and pecking words.

"Master Cole!" someone called, and he turned and saw the Benedictine hastening after him.

"Will you join me in the public house, master? I would like to speak with you."

Now what? he thought.

But he followed the man across the muddy street and into the tavern, where they took a quiet corner. The monk said he was Brother Paulinus, and both of them ordered ale.

"I thought that in the end the proceedings went well for you."

Rob said nothing, and his silence raised the monk's eyebrows. "Come, an honest man can find twelve other honest men."

"I *was* born in St. Botolph's Parish. Which I left as a young boy," Rob said gloomily, "to wander England as a barber-surgeon's helper. I will have damn-all of a time finding twelve men, honest or otherwise, who remember me and will be willing to travel to London to say so."

Brother Paulinus sipped his ale. "If you do not find all twelve, the issue is thrown into doubt. You will then be given an opportunity to prove your innocence by ordeal."

The ale tasted of despair. "What are the ordeals?"

"The Church uses four ordeals—cold water, hot water, hot iron, and consecrated bread. I can tell you that Bishop Aelfsige favors hot iron. You will be given holy water to drink and holy water will be sprinkled on the hand to be used for the ordeal. Your choice of hand. You will pick a white-hot iron from the fire and carry it nine feet in three steps, then you will drop it and hasten to the altar, where the hand will be wrapped and sealed. In three days the wrapping will be removed. If your hand is white and pure within the wrapping, you will be declared innocent. If the hand is not clean, you will be excommunicated and given over to civil authority."

Rob tried to conceal his emotions, but he had no doubt that his face had lost color.

"Unless your conscience is better than those of most men born of women, I think you must leave London," Paulinus said drily.

"Why are you telling me these things? And why do you offer me advice?"

They studied one another. The man had a tight-curled beard and tonsure the light brown of old straw, eyes color of slate and just as hard . . . but secretive, the eyes of a man who lives within himself. A slash of righteous mouth. Rob was certain he had never seen this man before he had entered St. Paul's that morning.

"I know you are Robert Jeremy Cole."

"How do you know it?"

"Before I became Paulinus in the Community of Benedict I was named Cole. Almost certainly I am your brother."

Rob accepted it at once. He had been ready to accept it for twenty-two years and now he felt a rising jubilation that was cut short by a quick and guilty caution, a sense of something amiss. He had started to rise, but the other man was still seated, watching him with an alert calculation that caused Rob to sit back into his chair.

He heard his own breathing.

"You are older than the baby, Roger, would be," he said. "Samuel is dead. Did you know that?"

"Yes."

"Therefore, you are . . . Jonathan or . . ."

"No, I was William."

"William."

The monk continued to watch him.

"After Da died you were taken by a priest named Lovell."

"Father Ranald Lovell. He brought me to the Monastery of St. Benedict in Jarrow. He lived only four more years himself, and then it was decided I should become an oblate."

Paulinus told his story sparely. "The abbot at Jarrow was Edmund, who was the loving guardian of my youth. He challenged and molded me, with the result that I was novice, monk, and provost, all at an early age. I was more than his strong right arm. He was *abbas et presbyter,* devoting himself wholly and continuously to reciting the *opus dei* and learning, teaching, and writing. I was the stern administrator, Edmund's reeve. As provost I was not popular." He smiled tightly. "When he died two years ago I was not elected to replace him, but the archbishop had been watching Jarrow and asked me to leave the community that had been my family. I am to take ordination and serve as auxiliary bishop of Worcester."

A curious and loveless reunion speech, Rob thought, this flat recital of career with its implicit admission of expectation and ambition. "Great responsibilities must lie in store for you," he said bleakly.

Paulinus shrugged. "It is with Him."

"At least," Rob said, "now I need find only eleven other compurgators. Perhaps the bishop will allow my brother's testimony to count for several others."

Paulinus didn't smile. "When I saw your name in the complaint, I made an inquiry. Given encouragement, the merchant Bostock could testify in interesting detail. What if you are asked whether you have pretended to be a Jew in order to attend a heathen academy in defiance of the Church?"

The tavern girl came to them and Rob waved her away. "Then I would reply that in His wisdom God has allowed me to become a healer because He did not create men and women solely for suffering and dying."

"God has an anointed army which interprets what He intends for man's body and his soul. Neither barber-surgeons nor heathen-trained physicians are anointed, and we have enacted churchly laws to stop such as you."

"You have made it difficult for us. At times you have slowed us. I think, Willum, that you have not stopped us."

"You will leave London."

"And is your concern because of brotherly love, or fear that the next auxiliary bishop of Worcester will be embarrassed by an excommunicated brother who has been executed for heathenism?"

Neither spoke for an endless moment.

"I have searched for you all my life. I always dreamed of finding the children," he said bitterly.

"We are no longer children. And dreams are not reality," Paulinus said.

Rob nodded. He pushed back his chair. "Do you know of any of the others?"

"Only the girl."

"Where is she?"

"She is dead these last six years."

"Oh." Now he stood heavily. "Where shall I find her grave?"

"There is no grave. It was a great fire."

Rob nodded, then he walked away from the public house without looking back at the gray monk.

Now he was less afraid of arrest than of killers hired by a powerful man to get rid of an embarrassment. He hurried to Thorne's stables and paid his bill and took his horse. At the house on Thames Street, he paused only long enough to collect the things that had become essential parts of his life. He was weary of leaving places in a desperate hurry and then of traveling vast distances, but he had become swift and expert at it.

When Brother Paulinus was seated at his evening meal in the refectory at St. Paul's, his blood brother was departing the city of London. Rob rode the plodding horse over the muddy Lincoln road leading to the north country, chased by furies but never escaping them because some of them were carried within himself.

Chapter 78

THE FAMILIAR JOURNEY

The first night he slept soft on a hay pile by the side of the road. It was last fall's hay, ripe and rotten below the surface, so he didn't burrow into it, but it still gave off a little heat and the air was mild. When he awoke in the dawning his first thought was the bitter realization that he had left behind in the house on Thames Street the Shah's Game that had been Mirdin's. It was so precious to him that he had carried it across the world from Persia, and the reality that it was lost to him forever was a stab.

He was hungry but didn't want to try for a meal at a farmhouse, where he would be well remembered to anyone who might be seeking after him. Instead, he rode half the morning with an empty belly until he came to a village with a marketplace, where he bought bread and cheese to satisfy his hunger and extra to carry with him.

He brooded as he rode. Finding such a brother was worse than never finding him, and he felt cheated and denied.

But he told himself he had mourned Willum after they had lost each other as boys, and he would be happy not to set eyes upon the cold-eyed Paulinus again.

"Go to hell, auxiliary bishop of Worcester!" he shouted.

The yell sent the birds fluttering out of the trees and caused his horse to prick up its ears and shy. Lest it lead anyone to think the countryside was under attack, he sounded the Saxon horn, and the familiar moan drew him back into his childhood and youth and was a comfort to him.

If there were pursuers they would search along the main routes, so he turned off the Lincoln road and followed the coastal roads linking the seaside villages. It was a trip he had made a number of times with Barber. Now he sounded no drum and gave no entertainment, nor did he seek out patients for fear a search was under way for a fugitive physician. In none of the villages did anyone recognize the young barber-surgeon of long ago; it would have been impossible to find compurgators in these places. He would have been doomed. He knew he was blessed to have escaped, and the bleakness left him as he realized that life was still full of infinite possibilities.

He half-recognized some places, noting that here a landmark house or church had burned to the ground, or that there, where a new dwelling had been raised, forest had been cleared. He made painfully slow progress, for in places the tracks were deep muck and soon the horse was in very bad shape. The horse had been perfect for carrying him to midnight medical calls at a dignified pace, but it was unsuitable for traveling open country or muddy roads—elderly, broken-down, and dispirited. He did his best by the beast, stopping frequently to lie on his back by a riverside while the animal cropped the new green grass of spring and rested. But nothing would make the horse young again, or fit to ride.

Rob husbanded his money. Whenever permission was given or sold he slept in warm barns on straw, avoiding people, but when it was unavoidable he sheltered in inns. One night in a public house in the harbor town of Middlesbrough, he watched two seamen putting away a fearsome amount of ale.

One of them, squat and broad, with black hair half hidden by a stocking cap, pounded the table. "We need a crewman. Bound down the coast to port of Eyemouth, Scotland. Fish for herring all the way. Is there a man in this place?"

The tavern was half full, but there was a silence and a few chuckles, and no one stirred.

Dare I? Rob wondered. It would be so much faster.

Even the ocean was better than floundering the horse through the mud, he decided, and he rose and went to them.

"Is it your boat?"

"Yes, I am the captain. I am Nee. He is Aldus."

"I am Jonsson," Rob said. It was as good a name as any other.

Nee peered up at him. "A big fucker." He took Rob's hand and turned it over, prodding at the soft palm contemptuously.

"I can work."

"We'll see," Nee said.

Rob gave the horse away that night to a stranger in the tavern, for there would be no time to sell it in the morning and the animal would have brought little. When he saw the weathered herring boat he thought it was as old and as poor as the horse, but Nee and Aldus had spent their winter well. The boat's seams were caulked tightly with oakum and pitched, and it rode the swells lightly.

He was in trouble a short time after they were under way, leaning overboard and vomiting while the two fishermen cursed and threatened to throw him into the sea. Despite the nausea and vomiting he forced himself to work. Within an hour they let out the net, dragging it behind them as they sailed and then all three of them hauling together to bring it in, empty and dripping. They let it out and pulled it back again and again, but they brought in few fish, and Nee became short-tempered and ugly. Rob was convinced that only his size kept them from treating him badly.

The evening meal was hard bread, bony smoked fish, and water that tasted of herring. Rob tried choking down a few bites but cast it up. To make matters worse, Aldus had a loose stomach and soon made the slop bucket an offense to the eyes and nostrils. It was nothing to faze one who had worked in a hospital, and Rob emptied the bucket and rinsed it in sea water until it was clean. Perhaps the accomplishment of the homely chore took the other two men by surprise, for after that they didn't curse him.

That night, lying cold and desperate as the boat heaved and yawed in the darkness, Rob crawled again and again to the side, until he had nothing left in him to vomit. In the morning the routine began again, but on the sixth dragging of the net, something changed. When they tugged on it, it seemed anchored. Slowly, laboriously, they gathered it in, and finally it brought them a silvery, wriggling stream.

"Now we catch herring!" Nee exulted.

Three times the net came in full, and then with lesser amounts, and when there was no more room to store fish they steered before the wind for land.

Next morning the catch was taken by merchants who would sell it fresh and sun-dried and smoked, and as soon as Nee's boat had been unloaded, they put out to sea again.

Rob's hands blistered and smarted and toughened. The net tore and he learned how to tie the knots needed to make repairs. On the fourth day, without his notice, the queasy illness disappeared. It didn't come back. I must tell Tam, he thought gratefully when he realized.

Each day they inched farther up the coast, always putting into a new harbor to sell the latest catch before it could spoil. Sometimes on moonlit nights Nee would see a spray of fish tiny as raindrops, breaking water to escape a feeding school, and they would drop the net and drag it along a path of moonshine, pulling in the gift of the sea.

Nee began to smile a lot and Rob heard him tell Aldus that Jonsson had brought good fortune. Now when they put into port of an evening, Nee bought his crew ale and a hot meal and the three of them sat up late and sang. Among the things Rob learned as a crewman was a number of filthy songs.

"You would make a fisherman," Nee said. "We'll be in Eyemouth five, six days, repairing nets. Then we go back toward Middlesbrough because that is what we do, drift for herring between Middlesbrough and Eyemouth, back and forth. You want to stay?"

Rob thanked him, pleased the offer was made, but said he would leave them in Eyemouth.

They arrived a few days later, sailing into a crowded, pretty harbor, and Nee paid him off with a few coins and a clap on the back. When Rob mentioned his need for a mount, Nee led him through the town to an honest dealer who said he could recommend two of his horses, either a mare or a gelding.

The mare was a prettier animal by far. "I once had good luck with a gelding," Rob said, and chose to try a gelding again. This one was no Arabian horse but a scrubby-looking English native with short, hairy legs and a tangled mane. It was two years old and strong and alert.

He arranged his pack behind the saddle and swung up onto the animal, and he and Nee saluted one another.

"May you find good fishing."

"Go with God, Jonsson," Nee said.

The wiry gelding gave him pleasure. It was better than its appearance and he decided to call it Al Borak, after the horse Muslims believed carried Mohammed from earth to the seventh heaven.

During the warmest part of each afternoon he tried to pause at a lake or a stream to give Al Borak a bath, and he worked at the tangled mane with his fingers, wishing he had a strong wooden comb. The horse seemed tireless and the roads were drying, so he traveled faster. The herring boat had taken him beyond the land with which he was familiar and now everything was more interesting because it was new. He followed a bank of the River Tweed for five days, until it turned south and he turned north, entering the uplands and riding between ridges that were too low to be called mountains. The rolling moors were broken in places by rocky cliffs. This time of year snowmelt still rushed down the hillsides and each stream crossing was a feat.

Farms were few and widespread. Some were large holdings, others were modest crofts; he noted that most were well kept and had the beauty of order that could be achieved only through hard work. He sounded the Saxon horn often. The crofters were watchful and guarded but no one tried to harm him. Observing the country and its people, for the first time he comprehended certain things about Mary.

He hadn't seen her in many long months. Was he on a fool's errand? Maybe by now she had another man, perhaps the damn cousin.

It was terrain pleasing to men but designed for sheep and cows. The tops of the hills were largely barren but most of the lower slopes consisted of rich pastureland. All the shepherds used dogs and he learned to fear them.

Half a day beyond Cumnock he stopped at a farm to ask permission to sleep that night on their hay, and he found that the day before, the woman of the place had had a breast ripped off by one of the dogs.

"Praise Jesus!" her husband whispered when Rob said he was a physician.

She was a stout female with grown children, and now she was out of her mind with pain. It had been a savage attack, as if she had been bitten by a lion. "Where is the dog?"

"The dog is no more," the man said grimly.

They forced grain liquor into her. It made her choke, but it helped her while Rob trimmed ragged flesh and sewed. He thought she'd have lived anyway, but there was no doubt she was better off because of him. He should have watched over her a day or two, but he stayed a week, until one morning he realized he was still there because he wasn't far from Kilmarnock and he was afraid to finish his journey.

He told her husband where he wanted to go and the man showed him the best way.

Her wounds were still on his mind two days later when he was accosted by a great growling cur that blocked the horse's way. His sword was half drawn when the animal was called off. The shepherd said something crisp to Rob in the Erse.

"I haven't your language."

"Ye be on Cullen land."

"That's where I want to be."

"Eh? Why is that?"

"I'll tell that to Mary Cullen." Rob appraised him and saw a man who was still young, but weathered and grizzled and as watchful as the dog. "Who are you?"

The Scot stared back at him, seeming undecided about whether he wanted to answer. "Craig Cullen," he said finally.

"My name is Cole. Robert Cole."

The shepherd nodded, appearing neither surprised nor welcoming. "Best follow," he said, and started off afoot. Rob hadn't seen him signal the dog but the beast held back and trailed close behind the horse, so that he came in between the man and the dog, delivered like a stray thing they had found in the hills.

The house and barn were of stone, well-laid long ago. Children stared and whispered as he rode in, and it took him a moment to realize his sons were among them. Tam spoke quietly to his brother in the Erse.

"What did he say?"

"He said, 'Is that our Da?' I said you was."

Rob smiled and wanted to gather them up, but they shrieked and scattered with the rest of the children when he swung from the saddle. Tam still hobbled but was able to run with ease, Rob noted gladly.

"They're just shy. They'll be back," she said from the doorway. She kept her face averted and wouldn't meet his eyes; he thought she wasn't glad to see him. Then she was in his arms, where she felt so fine! If she had another man, right there in the barnyard they gave him something to think about.

Kissing her, he discovered she was missing a tooth, to the right of the middle of her upper jaw.

"I was struggling to get a cow into the pen and fell against her horns." She was crying. "I am old and ugly."

"I didn't take a damned tooth to wife." His tone was rough but he touched the gap with a gentle fingertip, feeling the wet, warm springiness of her mouth as she sucked his finger. "It wasn't a damned tooth I took to my bed," he said, and though her eyes still glittered, she smiled.

"To your wheat field," she said. "Right down in the dirt next to mice and crawling things, like a ram doing a ewe." She wiped her eyes. "You'll be worn and hungry," she said, and took his hand and led him into a kitchen house. It was strange for him to see her so at home here. She gave him oat cakes and milk and he told her of the brother he had found and lost, and about fleeing London.

"How strange and sad for you . . . If it hadn't happened, would you have come to me?"

"Sooner or later." They kept smiling at one another. "This is a beautiful country," he said. "But hard."

"Easier with warmer weather. Before we know, it will be plowing time."

He could no longer swallow the oat cakes. "It is plowing time now."

She still colored easily. It was a thing that would never change, he noted with satisfaction. As she led him to the main house they tried to keep hold of one another but it led to tangled legs and bumped hips, so that soon they were laughing so hard he feared it would interfere with the lovemaking, but that didn't prove to be a problem.

Chapter 79

LAMBING

Next morning, both with a child before them in the saddle, she led him through the enormous, hilly holding. Sheep were everywhere, lifting black faces, white faces, and brown faces from the new grass when the horses passed. She took him a distance, showing everything proudly. There were twenty-seven small crofts on the outskirts of the large farm. "All the crofts-men are my kin."

"How many men are there?"

"Forty-one."

"Your entire family is gathered here?"

"The Cullens are here. The Tedders and the MacPhees are our kinsmen too. The MacPhees live a morning's ride away, through the low hills to the east. The Tedders live a day's ride to the north, through the clough and across the big river."

"With the three families, how many men do you have?"

"Perhaps a hundred and a half."

He pursed his lips. "Your own army."

"Yes. It is a comfort."

There seemed to him to be unending rivers of sheep.

"Fleeces and hides are why we keep the flocks. The meat spoils quickly, so we all eat it. You will grow weary of mutton."

He was pulled into the family business that morning. "Spring birthings already have begun," Mary said, "and night and day everyone must help the ewes. Some of the lambs have to be killed in the third to tenth day of life, when the pelts are finest." She turned him over to Craig and left him. By midmorning the shepherds had accepted him, observing that he was cool during problem births and knew how to whet and use knives.

He was dismayed by their method of altering newborn male lambs. They bit off the tender gonads and spat them into a bucket.

"Why do you do that?" he asked.

Craig grinned at him with a bloody mouth. "Gotta take the balls. Can't have too many rams, can ye?"

"Why not use a knife?"

"This is the way 'twas always done. Fastest way, and causes the lambs t'least pain."

Rob went to his pack and took out the scalpel of patterned steel, and soon Craig and the other shepherds grudgingly acknowledged that his way also was efficient. He didn't tell them he had learned to be fast and skillful in order to spare pain to men in the process of turning them into eunuchs.

He saw that the shepherds were independent men, and with indispensable skills.

"No wonder you wanted me," he told her, later. "Everyone else in this bloody country is kin."

She flashed a tired smile, for they had been skinning all day. The room stank of sheep but also of blood and flesh, not uncomfortable smells for him because they were reminders of the *maristan* and the hospital tents in India.

"Now that I'm here, you'll need one less shepherd," he said to her, and her smile faded.

"*Whisht,*" she said sharply. "Are you crazy?"

She took his hand and led him out of the skinning room to another stone outbuilding. Inside were three whitewashed rooms. One was a study. One clearly had been set up as an examining room, with tables and cabinets duplicating the room he had used in Ispahan. In the third room there were wooden benches on which patients would sit while waiting to see the physician.

He began to learn about the people as individuals. A man named Ostric was the musician. A skinning knife slipped and sliced into an artery in Ostric's forearm, and Rob halted the bleeding and closed the wound.

"Shall I be able to play?" Ostric said anxiously. "It's the arm that bears the weight of the pipes."

"A few days will make all the difference," Rob assured him.

Several days later, walking through the tanning shed where the pelts were cured, he saw Craig Cullen's old father Malcolm, cousin to Mary. He stopped and studied the man's clubbed and swollen fingertips and saw how his fingernails had curved strangely as they grew.

"For a long time you've had a bad cough. And frequent fevers," he told the old man quietly.

"Who has been telling you?" Malcolm Cullen said.

It was a condition Ibn Sina had called "Hippocratic fingers," and it always meant lung disease. "I can see it in your hands. Your toes are the same way, are they not?"

The old man nodded. "Can you do ought for me?"

"I don't know." He placed his ear against the chest and heard a crackling sound such as made by boiling vinegar.

"You're full of fluid. Come to the dispensary some morning. I'll drill a small hole between two ribs and tap that water, a little at a time. Meanwhile, I'll study your urine and watch the progress of the disease, and I'll give you fumigations and a diet to dry up your body."

That night Mary smiled at him. "How have you bewitched old Malcolm? He is telling everyone you have magical powers of healing."

"I've done nothing for him yet."

Next morning he was the only one in the dispensary; there was no Malcolm or any other living soul. Nor the morning after that.

When he complained, Mary shook her head. "They won't come until after lambing is done, it's their way."

It was true. No one came to him for ten days more. Then it was the quieter time between the lambing and the labor of shearing, and one morning he opened the dispensary door and the benches were filled with people and old Malcolm wished him a fine day.

After that they came readily each morning, for word spread in the cloughs and vales among the hills that Mary Cullen's man was a true healer. There never had been a physician in Kilmarnock and he recognized that he would spend years trying to undo some of the self-doctoring. In addition, they led their ailing animals or, if they could not, they weren't bashful about summoning him to their barns. He became well acquainted with foot rot and sore mouth. When opportunity arose, he dissected a cow and some sheep so he could know what he was doing. He found them nothing like a pig or a man.

In the darkness of their bedchamber, where these nights they were willingly employed in the task of starting another child, he tried to thank her for the dispensary, which, he'd been told, was the first thing she had done on returning to Kilmarnock.

She leaned over him. "How long would you stay with me without your work, *Hakim?*"

There was no sting in the words, and she kissed him as soon as she said them.

Chapter 80

A KEPT PROMISE

Rob took his boys into the forest and the hills and searched out the plants and herbs he wanted, and the three of them gathered the medicinals and brought them back, drying some and powdering others. He sat with his sons and taught them carefully, showing them each leaf and each flower. He told them about the herbs—which was used to cure the headache and which for cramp, which for fever and which for catarrh, which for bleeding nose and which for chilblains, which for quinsy and which for aching bones.

Craig Cullen was a spoonmaker and turned his craft toward the fashioning of covered wooden boxes in which the pharmacy herbs could be kept safe and dry. The boxes, like Craig's spoons, were decorated with carved nymphs and sprites and wild creatures of every sort. Seeing them, Rob was inspired to draw some of the pieces that made up the Shah's Game.

"Could you make something like these?"

Craig looked at him quizzically. "Why not?"

Rob drew likenesses of each piece and the checkered board. With very little guidance Craig carved everything, so that presently Rob and Mary once again spent some of their hours at a pastime taught him by a dead king.

Rob was determined to learn Gaelic. Mary owned no books but set out to teach him, beginning with the eighteen-letter alphabet. By now he knew what must be done to learn a strange language and all through the summer and autumn he labored, so that by early winter he was writing short sentences in the Erse and trying to speak it, to the amusement of the shepherds and his sons.

As he had supposed, winter there proved hard. The bitterest cold came just before Candlemas. After that was the time of the huntsmen, for snowy ground helped them track venison and fowl and hunt down catamounts and wolves that harried the flocks. In the evenings there were always people

593

gathered in the hall in front of a great fire. Craig might be there whittling, others would sit and repair harness or accomplish whatever homely tasks could be done in warmth and company. Sometimes Ostric played his pipes. They made a famous woollen cloth at Kilmarnock, dying their best fleeces the colors of heather by steeping them with lichens picked from the rocks. They wove in privacy but congregated in the hall for waulking, the shrinking of the fabric. The wet cloth, which had been soaked in soapy water, was passed around the table while each woman pounded and rubbed it. All the while they sang waulking songs, and Rob thought that their voices and Ostric's pipes made a singular sound.

The nearest chapel was a three-hour ride and Rob had believed it wouldn't be difficult to avoid priests, but one day in his second spring in Kilmarnock there appeared a small, plump man with a tired smile.

"Father Domhnall! It is Father Domhnall!" Mary cried, and hastened to bid him welcome.

They clustered about him and greeted him warmly. He spent a moment with each, asking a question with a smile, patting an arm, dropping a word of encouragement—like a good earl walking among his churls, Rob thought sourly.

He came to Rob and looked him over. "So. You are Mary Cullen's man."

"Yes."

"Are you a fisher?"

The question disconcerted him. "I fish for trouts."

"I'd have wagered so. I would take you after salmon tomorrow in the morning," he said, and Rob said he would go.

Next day they walked in gray light to a small, rushing river. Domhnall had brought two massive poles that were surely too heavy, and stout line and long-shanked feathered lures with barbs hidden treacherously in their handsome centers. "Like men I know," Rob observed to the priest, and Domhnall nodded, regarding him curiously.

Domhnall showed him how to fling the lure and bring it back through the water in little surges that resembled the darting of a small fish. They did it again and again with no result, but Rob didn't care, for he was lost in the rush of the water. Now the sun was up. High overhead he watched an eagle floating on nothing, and somewhere nearby he heard the cry of a grouse.

The big fish took his lure at the surface with a slash that sent a spout of water into the air.

It began to run upstream at once.

"You must go toward him or he'll break the line or tear out the hook!" Domhnall shouted.

Rob was already splashing into the river, clattering after the salmon. Expending its first surge of strength the fish almost did him in, for he fell several times in the frigid water, following over the stony bottom and floundering in and out of deep pools.

The fish ran again and again, taking him up and down the river. Domhnall had been shouting instructions, but once Rob looked up at the sound of a splash and saw that Domhnall now had troubles of his own. He had hooked a fish and was in the river too.

Rob fought to keep the fish in the middle of the stream. Eventually the salmon seemed under his control, though it felt dangerously heavy at the end of his line.

Soon he was able to skid the feebly struggling fish—so big!—into shingled shallows. As he grasped the shank of the lure, the salmon gave one last convulsive leap and the hook tore free, bringing with it a strip of bloody tissue from within the fish's throat. For a moment the salmon lay motionless on its side and then, as Rob saw a thick haze of blood rise darkly from its gills, it flipped into deep water and was gone.

He stood trembling and disgusted, for the blood cloud told him he had killed the fish, and now it had been wasted.

Moving more by instinct than out of hope, he walked downstream, but before he had taken half a dozen steps he saw a silvery patch in the water ahead and splashed toward it. He lost the pale reflection twice as the fish swam or was moved by the river. Then he saw he was right on top of it. The salmon was dying but not quite dead, pressed against the upstream side of a boulder by the strong current.

He had to immerse himself in the numbing water to take it in both arms and carry it to the bank, where he ended its pain with a rock. It weighed at least two stone.

Domhnall was just landing his fish, which wasn't nearly as large.

"Yours is enough flesh for us all, eh?" he said. When Rob nodded, Domhnall returned his salmon to the river. He held it carefully to let the water do its work. The fins moved and waved as languorously as if the fish were not struggling to maintain its existence, and the gills began to pump. Rob saw the quiver of life run through the fish, and as he watched it move away from them and disappear into the current, he knew that this priest would be his friend.

* * *

They took off their sodden garments and spread them to dry, then lay near them on a huge sun-warmed rock.

Domhnall sighed. "Not like catching trouts," he said.

"The difference between picking a flower and felling a tree." Rob had half a dozen bleeding cuts on his legs from falling in the river, and innumerable bruises.

They grinned at one another.

Domhnall scratched his round little belly, white as any fish's, and lapsed into silence. Rob had expected questions, but he perceived it was this priest's style to listen intently and wait, a valuable patience that would make him a deadly opponent if Rob should teach him the Shah's Game.

"Mary and I are not married in the Church. Do you know that?"

"I had heard something."

"Well. We have been truly wed, these years. But it was a hand-held union."

Domhnall grunted.

He told the cleric their story. He didn't omit or make light of his troubles in London. "I would like you to marry us, but I must warn that perhaps I've been excommunicated."

They dried lazily in the sun, considering the problem.

"If this auxiliary bishop of Worcester could have done, he would gloss it over," Domhnall said. "Such an ambitious man would rather have a missing and forgotten brother than close kin scandalously driven from the Church."

Rob nodded. "Suppose he could not cover it over?"

The priest frowned. "You have no sure proof of excommunication?"

Rob shook his head. "But it is possible."

"Possible? I cannot run my ministry according to your fears. Man, man, what do your fears have to do with Christ? I was born in Prestwick. Since ordination I have never left this mountain parish and I expect I will be pastor here when I die. Other than yourself, never in all my life have I encountered anyone from London or from Worcester. I have never received a message from an archbishop or from His Holiness, but only from Jesus. Can you believe it is the will of the Lord that I not make a Christian family of the four of you?"

Rob smiled at him and shook his head.

All their lives the two sons would remember the wedding of their parents, and describe it to their own grandchildren. The Nuptial Mass in the Cullen hall was small and quiet. Mary had a dress of light gray stuff and wore a silver brooch and a roeskin belt studded with silver. She was a composed bride, but her eyes shone as Father Domhnall declared that ever more and in sanctified protection she and her children were irreversibly joined to Robert Jeremy Cole.

Thereafter Mary sent invitations for all her kinfolk to meet her husband. On the appointed day the MacPhees came west through the low hills and the Tedders crossed the big river and came through the clough to Kilmarnock. They came bearing wedding gifts and fruit cakes and game pies and casks of strong drink and the great meat-and-oats puddings they loved. At the holding, an ox and a bull were slowly turning on spits over open fires, and eight sheep and a dozen lambs, and numerous fowl. There was the music of harp, pipe, viol, and trump, and Mary joined in when the women sang.

All afternoon, during the athletic contests, Rob met Cullens and Tedders and MacPhees. Some he admired at once and others he did not. He tried not to study the male cousins, who were legion. Everywhere, men began to become drunk, and some tried to force the groom to join them. But he toasted his bride and his sons and their clan, and for the rest he put them off with an easy word and a smile.

That evening, while the roistering was still in high progress, he walked from the buildings, past the pens and away. It was a good night, starry but still not warm. He could smell the spice of the gorse, and as the sounds of the celebration faded behind him he heard the sheep and the nickering of a horse and the wind in the hills and the rushing of streams, and he fancied he could feel taproots emerging from the soles of his feet and pushing deep into the thin, flinty soil.

Chapter 81

THE CIRCLE COMPLETED

Why a woman should quicken with new life, or not, was the perfect mystery. After bearing two sons and then passing five years in barrenness, Mary ripened with child following their wedding. She was careful at her work, quicker now to ask one of the men to help her with a task. The two sons trailed after her and did light chores. It was easy to see which child would be the sheepman; at times Rob J. seemed to enjoy the work, but Tam was always eager to feed the lambs and begged for a chance to shear. There was something else about him, seen first in the crude outlines he scraped into the earth with a stick, until his father gave him charcoal and a pine board and showed him how things and people might be pictured. Rob didn't have to tell the boy not to leave out the flaws.

On the wall above Tam's bed hung the rug of the Samanid kings, and it was understood by everyone that it was his, the gift of a family friend in Persia. Only once did Mary and Rob face the thing they had compressed and pushed into the recesses of their minds. Watching him run after a straying ewe, Rob knew it would be no blessing for the boy to learn he had an army of foreign stranger-brothers he would never see. "We will never tell him."

"He *is* yours," she said. She turned and held him in her arms, and between them was the thickening bulge that was to be Jura Agnes, the only daughter.

Rob learned the new language, for it was spoken all about him and he applied himself. Father Domhnall loaned him a Bible written in the Erse by monks in Ireland, and as he had mastered Persian from the Qu'ran, he learned the Gaelic from Holy Scripture.

In his study he hung the Transparent Man and the Pregnant Woman and began to teach his sons the anatomical charts and answer their questions. Often when he was summoned to tend a sick person or an animal, one or both of them went with him. On such a day Rob J. rode behind his

598

father on Al Borak's back, to a hill-croft house that stank of the dying of Ostric's wife, Ardis.

The boy watched as he measured out and gave her an infusion, and Rob poured water on a cloth and handed it to his son.

"You may bathe her face."

Rob J. did it gently, taking great care with her cracked lips. When he was finished Ardis fumbled, taking the young hands in hers.

Rob saw the tender smile change into something else. He witnessed the confusion of first awareness, the pallor. The starkness with which the boy thrust away her hands.

"It's all right," he said. He put his arms around the thin shoulders and held Rob J. tight. *"It is all right."* Only seven years old. Two years younger than he had been himself. He knew, wonderingly, that his life had completed a great circle.

He comforted and tended Ardis. When they were outside the house, he took his son's hands so Rob J. could feel his father's living strength and be reassured. He looked into Rob J.'s eyes.

"What you felt in Ardis, and the life you detect in me now . . . to sense these things is a gift from the Almighty. A good gift. It isn't evil, don't fear it. Don't try to understand it now. There will be time for you to understand it. Don't be afraid."

The color was returning to his son's face. "Yes, Da."

He mounted and swung the boy up behind his saddle, and took him home.

Ardis died eight days later. For months after that, Rob J. didn't come to the dispensary or ask to accompany his father when he went to tend the sick. Rob didn't urge him. Even for a child, he felt, involving oneself with the world's suffering had to be a voluntary act.

Rob J. tried to interest himself in herding the sheep with Tam. When that palled, he went off alone and picked herbs, hour after long hour. He was a puzzled boy.

But he had complete trust in his father, and the day came when Rob J. ran after Rob as he was riding out of the farmyard. "Da! May I go with you? To tend the horse and such?"

Rob nodded and pulled him up behind the saddle.

Soon Rob J. began coming to the dispensary sporadically and his instruction resumed; and when he was nine years old, at his own request he began to assist his father every day as apprentice.

The year after Jura Agnes was born, Mary gave birth to a third male child, Nathanael Robertsson. A year later there was the stillbirth of a boy who was christened Carrik Lyon Cole before burial, and then two difficult miscarriages in succession. Though she was still of childbearing age, Mary didn't become pregnant again. It grieved her, he knew, for she had wanted to give him many children, but Rob was content to see her gradually regain her strength and spirit.

One day when his youngest child was in his fifth year, a man in a dusty black caftan and bell-shaped leather cap rode into Kilmarnock, leading a laden ass.

"Peace unto you," Rob said in the Tongue, and the Jew gaped at the language and answered, "Unto you, peace."

A muscular man with a great, unkempt brown beard, skin burnt by travel, and exhaustion pulling at his mouth and making lines in the corners of his eyes. He was Dan ben Gamliel of Rouen, and a long way from home.

Rob saw to his beasts and gave him water in which to wash and then set before him unforbidden foods. He found his own grasp of the Tongue was poor, for a surprising amount had slipped away from him, but he made the blessings over the bread and the wine.

"Are you then Jews?" Dan ben Gamliel said, staring.

"No, we are Christians."

"Why do you do this?"

"We owe a great debt," Rob said.

His children sat at the table and stared at a man who looked like no one they had ever seen, listening in wonder as their father joined him in uttering strange blessings before they ate their food.

"After we have eaten, you may care to study with me." Rob felt the rise of an almost-forgotten excitement. "Perhaps we may sit together and study the commandments," he said.

The stranger peered at him. "I regret— No, I cannot!" Dan ben Gamliel's face was pallid. "I am not a scholar," he muttered.

Masking his disappointment, Rob took the traveler to a good place to sleep, as it would have been done in a Jewish village.

Next day he rose early. Among the things he had taken from Persia he found the Jew's cap and prayer shawl and phylacteries and went to join Dan ben Gamliel at morning devotions.

Dan ben Gamliel stared as he bound the little black box to his forehead and wound the leather around his arm to form the letters in the name of the Unutterable. The Jew watched him sway and listened to his prayers.

"I know what you are," he said thickly. "You were a Jew and you became an apostate. A man who has turned his back on our people and our God and given his soul to the other nation."

"No, it isn't so," Rob said, and saw with regret that he had disrupted the other's praying. "I will explain when you have finished," he said, and withdrew.

But when he returned to summon the man to the morning meal, Dan ben Gamliel wasn't there. The horse was gone. The ass was gone. The heavy load had been picked up and carried away, and his guest had fled rather than expose himself to the dread contagion of apostasy.

It was Rob's last Jew; he never saw another nor spoke the Tongue again.

He felt his memory of Persian slipping from him too, and one day determined that before it abandoned him, he must translate the *Qānūn* into English so he might continue to consult the Master Physician. It took him a dreadfully long time. Again and again he told himself that Ibn Sina had written *The Canon of Medicine* in less time than it took Robert Cole to translate it!

Sometimes he regretted wistfully that he hadn't studied all the commandments at least once. Often he thought of Jesse ben Benjamin but increasingly made peace with his passing—it *was* hard to be a Jew!—and he came almost never to speak of other times and places. Once when Tam and Rob J. were entered in the running contest that each year celebrated the feast day of St. Kolumb in the hills, he told them of a runner named Karim who had won a long and wonderful race called the *chatir*. And rarely —usually when engaged in one of the mundane tasks that marked the even rhythm of a Scot's days, mucking the pens or moving drifted snow or hewing firewood—he would smell the cooling heat of the desert at night, or remember the sight of Fara Askari kindling Sabbath tapers, or the enraged trumpet call of an elephant charging into battle, or the breathless sensation of flying perched atop the long-legged stagger of a racing camel. But it came to seem that Kilmarnock had always been his life, and that what had happened before was a tale he had heard told around the fire when the wind blew cold.

His children throve and changed, his wife turned finer with age. As the seasons slipped by, only one thing was constant. The extra sense, the healer's sensitivity, never abandoned him. Whether he was called lonely in the night to a bedside or hurried of a morning into the crowded dispensary, he could always feel their pain. Hastening to struggle with it, he never failed to know—as he had known from the first day in the *maristan*—a rush of wondering gratitude that he was chosen, that it was he whom God's hand had reached out and touched, and that such an opportunity to minister and serve should have been given to Barber's boy.

ACKNOWLEDGMENTS

The Physician is a story in which only two characters, Ibn Sina and al-Juzjani, are taken from life. There was a shah named Alā-al-Dawla, but so little information survives that the character of that name is based on an amalgam of shahs.

The *maristan* was depicted from descriptions of the medieval Azudi hospital of Baghdad.

Much of the flavor and fact of the eleventh century is forever lost. Where the record was nonexistent or obscured, I did not hesitate to fictionalize; thus, it should be understood that this is a work of the imagination and not a slice of history. Any errors, large or small, made in my striving to faithfully recreate a sense of time and place, are my own. Yet this novel could not have been written without the help of a number of libraries and individuals.

I am grateful to the University of Massachusetts at Amherst for granting me faculty privileges to all of its libraries, and to Edla Holm of the Interlibrary Loans Office at that university.

The Lamar Soutter Library at the University of Massachusetts Medical Center in Worcester was a valuable resource for books about medicine and medical history.

Smith College was kind enough to classify me as an "area scholar" so I might use the William Allan Neilson Library, and I found the Werner Josten Library at Smith's Center for the Performing Arts to be an excellent source of details about clothing and costumes.

Barbara Zalenski, Librarian of the Belding Memorial Library of Ashfield, Massachusetts, never failed me, no matter how much searching she faced in fulfilling a request for a book.

Kathleen M. Johnson, Reference Librarian at the Baker Library of Harvard's Graduate School of Business Administration, sent me materials on the history of money in the Middle Ages.

I should also like to thank the librarians and libraries of Amherst College, Mount Holyoke College, Brandeis University, Clark University, the Countway Library of Medicine at Harvard Medical School, the Boston Public Library, and the Boston Library Consortium.

Richard M. Jakowski, V.M.D., Animal Pathologist at the Tufts-New England Veterinary Medical Center, in North Grafton, Massachusetts, compared the internal anatomy of pigs and humans for me, as did Susan L. Carpenter, Ph.D., post-doctoral fellow at the Rocky Mountain Laboratories of the National Institute of Health, in Hamilton, Montana.

Over a period of several years, Rabbi Louis A. Rieser of Temple Israel of Greenfield, Massachusetts, answered question after question about Judaism.

Rabbi Philip Kaplan of the Associated Synagogues of Boston explained the details of kosher slaughtering to me.

The Graduate School of Geography at Clark University furnished me with maps and information about the geography of the eleventh-century world.

The faculty of the Classics Department at the College of the Holy Cross, Worcester, Massachusetts, helped me with several Latin translations.

Robert Ruhloff, blacksmith of Ashfield, Massachusetts, informed me about the blue patterned steel of India and introduced me to the blacksmiths' journal, *The Anvil's Ring*.

Gouveneur Phelps of Ashfield told me about salmon fishing in Scotland.

Patricia Schartle Myrer, my former literary agent (now retired), provided encouragement, as did my present agent, Eugene H. Winick of McIntosh and Otis, Inc. It was Pat Myrer's suggestion that I write about the medical dynasty of a single family over many generations, a suggestion that has led me to the sequel to *The Physician*, now in progress.

Herman Gollob of Simon & Schuster has been the ideal editor—tough and demanding, warm and helpful—and he has made publication of this book a meaningful experience.

Lise Gordon helped copy-edit the manuscript and, along with Jamie Gordon, Vincent Rico, Michael Gordon and Wendi Gordon, gave me love and moral support.

And, as always, Lorraine Gordon provided criticism, sweet reason, steadiness and the love for which I have long been very grateful.

Ashfield, Massachusetts
December 26, 1985

ABOUT THE AUTHOR

Noah Gordon has been a reporter and science editor, a publisher of medical journals, and a best-selling novelist whose works include *The Rabbi*, *The Death Committee*, and *The Jerusalem Diamond*. He and his wife, Lorraine, live on a tree farm in the Berkshire Hills of western Massachusetts, where she is editor of the local newspaper and he is an Emergency Medical Technician in their little town's volunteer ambulance service. They have three grown children, Lise, Jamie, and Michael. Noah Gordon is now writing the second of a projected series of novels about the Cole medical dynasty.

1 Wk.

F   Gordon, Noah.

c.1   The physician

DATE			

August 1986